MONUMENTS OF GRASS

~

BOOK THREE – THE CLAIM

MONUMENTS OF GRASS

An American Romance

BOOK THREE – THE CLAIM

1863

* * *

BRENDAN FRAIN

Monuments of Grass: The Claim

2nd (revised) edition © Brendan Frain 2025

Originally published in 2022

ISBN: 978-1-7640051-2-8 (paperback)
ISBN: 978-1-7640051-9-7 (ebook)

Book design and typesetting by Typography Studio

Published by Brendan Frain

A catalogue record for this
book is available from the
National Library of Australia

For Sat,
My homestead

Introduction

IN THE SEVEN DECADES following the 1783 Treaty of Paris the United States doubled and tripled in size to span the entire continent from the Atlantic to the Pacific Ocean. The first major acquisition was the Louisiana Purchase from the French Government in 1803. (See map 1, following.) This added almost a million square miles of territory stretching from the Mississippi River to the Rocky Mountains. Other major acquisitions included Texas (1845) and Oregon Country (1846) and a vast tract of land in the Western United States surrendered by Mexico in 1848. By the outbreak of the Civil War in 1861 the United States had grown from sixteen states (in 1800) to thirty-four.

The rapid expansion brought problems, not least the troubling question of whether the new states were to be admitted to the union as free states or 'slave states'. A constitutional balancing act began with the admission of Missouri as a slave state in 1821 and the counterbalancing admission of Maine as a free state. In the following decades the rift between free and slave states grew wider, exacerbated by political tensions arising from economic and cultural differences between the agrarian southern states and the industrial northern states. A popular abolitionist movement further contributed to the resentment growing on both sides of the divide.

Matters came to a head with the election of the anti-slavery Abraham Lincoln to the presidency in 1860. Before his inauguration, seven southern states seceded from the Union. Within weeks of Lincoln's swearing-in, the first shots were fired at Fort Sumter, South Carolina, in 1861 and the Civil War had begun. By the time Book Three: The Claim opens, the bloody and defining battle of Gettysburg (1863) is underway.

The Post-Civil War United States was characterised by Reconstruction: the effort to reintegrate the defeated Southern States and their populations back into the Union. The country underwent profound change as it struggled to redress the political and economic legacy of the war and the inequities of slavery.

The dramatic expansion of the railway network and the invention of the telegraph revolutionised transportation and communication. Just six years after the war the Transcontinental Railway was completed, linking America from coast to coast. A journey that once took months now took days. Trade boomed and new towns sprang up along the railroad lines.

The war prompted significant changes in firearms as the rifle, and later the repeating rifle, replaced the musket. Photography also underwent a transformation as the Civil War era daguerreotype camera was replaced by the Kodak roll film camera in 1888.

In 1862 Congress passed the Homestead Act granting families 160 acres of land upon payment of a small registration fee. The Act lured tens of thousands of settlers westwards into Minnesota, Nebraska and Kansas. By the turn of the century more than 80 million acres had been claimed by a total of 600,000 homestead farmers.[1]

Despite its distant location in the Upper Midwest, the Dakota Territory proved attractive to homesteaders as the railway companies campaigned to entice settlers. The Missouri River formed an artery for transporting settlers to the high grass plains of the Territory where they took possession of land formerly claimed by the Sioux and other tribes.

"The Territory's population grew significantly, from 4,837 in 1860 to 158,724 by 1880, driven by immigration and the promise of land and opportunity. This population boom was critical for the territory's path to statehood as it demonstrated the region's viability and potential for development."[2] North Dakota was admitted to the Union simultaneously with South Dakota in 1889 as the 39th and 40th states.

The combined effects of the railway and the mass influx of homesteaders had devastating consequences for Native American tribes and the vast herds of buffalo that grazed the Northern and Central Great Plains. Hunters armed with new, large-calibre rifles flocked to take advantage of the booming demand for buffalo robes transported by the railways to eastern markets. It is estimated that up to 200,000 buffalo a year were slaughtered for their robes, the carcasses left to rot in the prairie grass. The railways encouraged a lucrative sports market whereby hunters crammed into railway cars shot from moving trains that kept pace with the buffalo as they ran alongside the tracks.

From a population estimated at 20-30 million at the turn of the century, the enormous buffalo herds were reduced to approximately 300 survivors by 1883, perhaps the greatest mass slaughter of a species in human history. A contemporary newspaper account gives a glimpse of the unfolding apocalypse:

With reference to the wholesale slaughter of buffalo on the plains, a Western paper says: Mr. Lessing estimates that there are at least two thousand hunters in camp along there waiting for buffalo. He came across one party of sixteen, who stated that they killed twenty-eight thousand buffaloes during the past summer, the hides of which only were utilized. If sixteen hunters can kill this many animals, how great must be the slaughter upon the broad extent of the bison range?[3]

After a long and bitter struggle against the US Army and deprived of their major food source, the remaining Native American tribes were forced onto reservations. Thus, a subsistence lifestyle that had endured for a thousand years was all but wiped out in little more than the span of a single lifetime.

1. www.britannica.com/event/Homestead-Movement
2. The Birth of Dakota Territory: A Landmark in American Expansion – Keep It America
3. Nashville Union, January 6, 1874. Quoted in All About Bison: Last of the Bison (allaboutbison.com)

Maps

Map 1 that follows shows the territorial growth of the United States from its founding up to 1853, eight years before the Civil War.

Map 2 shows the United States at the commencement of the Civil War. Note the number of Territories, including Dakota, yet to be admitted as states.

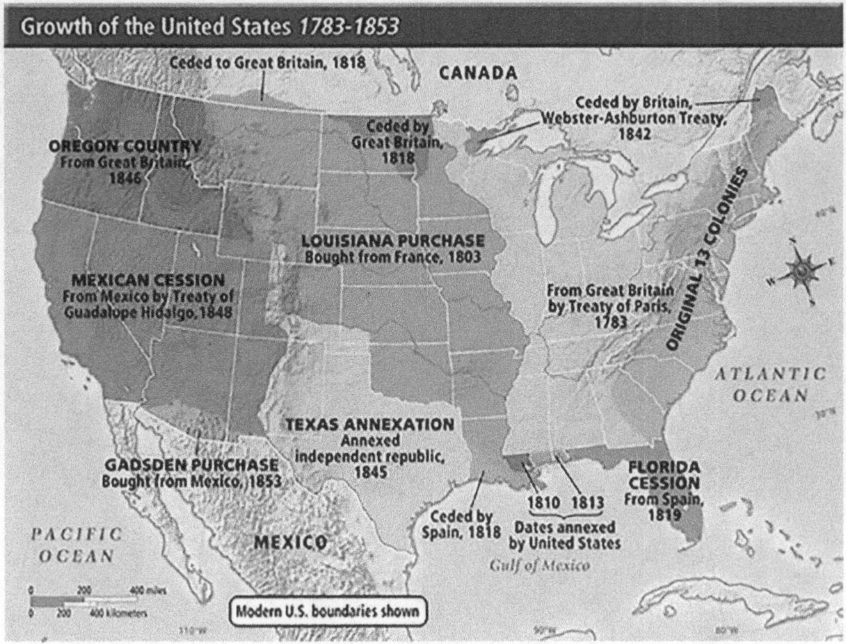

Map 1: Territorial growth of the United States up to 1853

Map 2: America in 1861

Contents

T H E   C L A I M

THE CLAIM

This land is rich and wonderful. Bounty is at hand.
—JOHN BLAIR SMITH TODD, first delegate to
Congress from Dakota Territory

Gettysburg

Goodness! The noise of the bursting shells was so loud I feared my ears would crack! And after, the fields were that congested with the dead and wounded you could hardly see the grass. But the truth is that hardly a soul expected the war would come to our quiet little town! Two weeks before the battle we heard that General Lee and his army had crossed the Potomac and was headed north. But Mr Shorely down at the telegraph office assured us that the Rebels were marching on Baltimore, and then Washington. So, we had a great fright when the Confederates suddenly turned up in Chambersburg! We heard terrible rumours about the Rebels murdering folk and seizing food and provisions to feed the army. Some people fled, taking the railroad to Hanover, or sent their valuables to Philadelphia for safety. Many drove their horses and livestock out of town, hoping to keep them from the Rebels. My housemaid, Libby, was greatly alarmed that she and the other Negroes would be captured and sent back south to be sold back into slavery. Indeed, when we heard that the Confederates were advancing towards Gettysburg, many of the Negroes fled into the woods to hide. And then, in late June, a rag-tag band of Confederate cavalry and infantry showed up, demanding food and supplies. They ransacked the stores and houses and scared the townsfolk half to death before leaving. Then on June 30 Union cavalry arrived and took up position in the town. Oh, but we were glad to see them! People flocked to the streets and dished out food and milk to the soldiers. Word came that the Confederates had retreated to Cashtown. We thought we were saved! I remember that the morning of the battle was hot and cloudy. About nine o'clock I called for Libby and said to her that I heard firing to the northwest of town. She listened and heard it, too. A short time later we heard the boom of cannon fire, and then shells started to burst over the town. We heard screams from the street and saw people hurrying for shelter. Some children stood on a fence to try and see the fighting. I hurried out to scold and despatch them back to their homes. We heard musket fire, and I sent Libby down to the cellar to take refuge. Before joining her, I went upstairs to peek out the window. I saw Union infantry advancing up the Emmitsburg Road together with lots of wagons. There were officers dashing about the street yelling at everyone to stay inside and take cover. I took fright and ran down to the cellar to join Libby.

—THE WIDOW MERRITT. *The Star and Sentinel, May 1873*

'ROUSE UP! ROUSE UP!' The blue-uniformed corporal passed from tent to tent, repeating the words. He bent down to peer inside one tent. 'Sutter! On your feet! You, too, McLennan!' He advanced to the next tent in the dawn light, continuing his reveille.

'Rouse up! Rouse up!'

A bushy-haired youth stuck his head out from under the canvas sheet. 'God Almighty if it ain't still dark!' He turned to address his companion inside the tent. 'What in tar's the hurry? I wager there ain't a Reb within a hundred mile of Emmitsburg!'

A prolonged yawn sounded from within. 'Did the corporal bring coffee?'

The youth laughed. 'Goldurn, Purchase. I swear you'd drink coffee in your sleep!'

Another youth poked his head out of the adjoining tent, his face still groggy with sleep. 'Abe, was that you cutting farts last night?'

'Shucks. That weren't nothing but thunder. Where's Elias?'

'Still sawing logs!' The sleepy youth turned his head. 'Elias! Git yourself up! The Rebs have stopped by for breakfast.'

A LITTLE LATER, ALL four companions were crouched in the cool, dewy grass drinking black coffee and eating hardtack. The sun was rising, and thick mist blanketed the surrounding fields. A sergeant came along the campfires, issuing instructions.

'Each man sixty rounds and a day's rations,' he said before passing on to the next fire.

The bushy-haired youth grimaced and spat a mouthful of coffee into the grass. 'I sure am sick of eating meals that ain't fit for a hog!'

'Why, Abe, this food is fit for a hog,' argued one of his companions, a thin, jug-eared fellow who, like his comrades, seemed barely on the cusp of manhood.

Abe cut a sour face. 'I say we sneak into town and buy us a beefsteak. What say you, Purchase?'

'A beefsteak and a keg of beer!'

'The colonel would shoot you!'

'I reckon you would point me out, too, Elias!' Abe fixed the speaker a scornful glance.

'Hell no.' Elias cast a sly look at the smooth-cheeked youth who sat opposite. 'But I reckon Winslow here might.'

The named youth laughed, spitting out crumbs of hardtack. 'Aye. And gladly volunteer to shoot you myself, Abe, in revenge for all those farts you thundered last night. I swear I thought Johnny Reb had fixed us with his cannon!'

'Go to, yerself!'

Winslow grimaced as he chewed the hard tack. 'By Molly if it don't get harder by the mouthful!'

'You were a baker, Winslow. Why don't you bake us a cake?'

'And fill it with whisky!'

Winslow tossed aside the remaining hardtack. 'I told you, I bake bread, not cake.' He spat out a mouthful of coffee, a look of disgust on his face.

'Will you go back to it—after the war?'

The question brought a temporary lull to the banter. Eyes turned to Winslow as he shook the coffee grounds from his cup.

'I have hopes to open my own bakery,' he admitted.

'In Philly?'

Winslow nodded, his face solemn in the morning light.

'Why then, I shall be your first customer.' Elias took out a pipe. 'I reckon you owe me a loaf anyway, for saving your dumb neck back at Fredericksburg.'

Winslow laughed. 'You did, too!'

'Heck. That Reb was already half-dead,' argued Purchase. 'I shot him myself.'

'But still of a mind to run me through—no matter! If Elias hadn't shoved me aside, I would be skewered like hog on a spit.'

'And what about you, Elias?' asked Abe.

Elias spat tobacco juice into the fire. 'I reckon I'll find work on the railroads.'

'I supposed you were going out west to shoot Indians!'

'And where do you suppose the durn railroads are?'

'And you, Purchase?' Abe turned to his tent mate.

'I'll go back home to St Charles.'

'And then?'

'I guess I'll farm, maybe.'

'Come out west with me,' said Elias. 'We can pal together.'

'No, I reckon the railroad is not for me.'

'It would be something, though, to ride that fast! *Whoo! Whoo!*' Elias hooted through his hands.

'Have you ever rode it?' goaded Abe.

'Rode what?'

'The railroad, dunce!'

'You ride a train, knucklehead. Not a railroad. Ha! Now who's the dunce?'

Abe tugged on a shoe. 'Durn old railroad, anyhow!'

'Why farm?' Elias cocked an eyebrow at Purchase. 'Ain't you up for some adventuring after all this kerfuffle?'

'I've had enough 'venturing with Johnny Reb trying to blow my head off.'

'They say they are giving away land out west,' said Abe.' Maybe I'll grab me some.'

'And do what?' Winslow fixed Abe a sceptical glance.

'I'll farm, like Purchase said.'

'Ha! Purchase was born on a farm. You can't even grow a beard!'

'The only thing he can grow is the dirt under his toenails,' mocked Elias. 'And farts!'

The companions burst into laughter. Abe flushed angrily. 'I guess I can learn—' He was interrupted by shouts and the blast of a bugle from farther down the line of tents. Around them, men began to put out the campfires.

Purchase shook out his tin cup. 'Rouse up, boys, time to go find Johnny Reb.'

SHORTLY BEFORE 8 AM, Purchase and his companions stood in column awaiting the word to march. The sun was already warm, and thick mist rose from the fields on either side of the road. Purchase tugged the collar of his grey linen shirt, already sweating inside the wool-lined fatigue blouse. An officer rode down the line on a dun mare. 'Get ready, the Fifty-Sixth,' he called. 'We follow the Seventy-Sixth, New York.'

Elias groaned. 'And guzzle their dirt all the way!'

Minutes later, the long column set off, the thousands of tramping feet raising clouds of dust from the road. Marching out of Emmitsburg, they passed several small hamlets, the occupants coming out to stare or offer treats while children ran alongside. As they crossed the line north into Pennsylvania, the loudest cheers were reserved for the Fifty-Sixth Regiment. 'Go shoot them Rebs!' a man hollered, raising hurrahs from those alongside him.

'Where are they?' asked Purchase as he passed the man.

'Where?' The man looked bewildered. 'The devil if I know!' he said, to laughter.

A woman, holding a mess of ripe cherries in her apron, thrust a handful at Purchase as he passed. 'God bless, boys!'

'Thank you, Ma'am!' He gulped the cherries. Beside him, Winslow did the same, smearing his mouth with juice.

Two miles outside Gettysburg, the long column came to a halt. Purchase and his company waited beside a farmhouse as staff officers conferred over a map. Across the dusty thoroughfare, Purchase listened in, cocking his head to hear.

'They say Buford's getting whipped,' he relayed to his comrades.

'Dash!' Abe scoffed at the notion. 'Then where are the Rebs?'

'There's your answer!' Winslow pointed to the trees in the distance. Wreaths of grey smoke showed where artillery shells were bursting. The faint boom of cannon fire came to their ears. The staff officers stopped conferring to watch. A ripple of excitement ran through the column.

'Jessy! I hope they don't tar and feather Johnny Reb afore we arrive!'

'Why, you figure to bake a Johnnycake!'

'Here comes the colonel!'

A horseman dressed in a dusty blue sack coat and battered Hardee hat rode down the line, flanked by two aides. 'That way, boys!' He pointed with his drawn sabre to the fields lining the road. 'Across the fields, double-quick!'

The column broke from the road and headed west across the fields, their progress encumbered by the Springfield muskets and heavy knapsacks. They climbed over fences or knocked them down to ease the passage of those following. As they marched, the sound of cannon fire and exploding shells grew louder. Purchase looked ahead but could see nothing beyond the wooded bluffs in the distance and the smoke of the shells.

'Where in fishhooks are they?' yelled Winslow beside him.

'We'll find out!'

'Durn!' Purchase flinched as a shell burst overhead and iron fragments rained down. Glancing at a ridge in the distance, he saw flashes and smoke balls as cannons erupted. The men instinctively ducked as the artillery found the range and more shells burst in the air above their heads.

'Load at will!' A staff officer rode down the line, shouting out the order as the men broke into a run. Purchase reached for his ramrod and began loading as he rushed forward, the rattle of ramrods filling the air. As the artillery fire grew heavier, they hurried toward a ridge on which stood a brick building crowned by a cupola.

Panting heavily, Purchase ascended the ridge, encumbered by the weight of the equipment. Beyond the brick building could be seen a group of Union cavalry falling back along the Mummasburg Road. Every now and then they stopped to exchange fire with a pursuing group of Confederates.

'Keep going! Across the pike!' Two officers galloped back and forth alongside the column, urging it toward the Chambersburg Pike directly ahead. The sound of cannon fire was now much louder. They heard the rattle of small-arms fire as they reached the pike. Here they stopped for a few minutes to regroup.

An aide galloped down the line bringing fresh orders. 'Forward to the cut! Double-quick!'

THE UNFINISHED RAILROAD CUT ran parallel to the road and they crossed it and headed toward a rise some two-hundred-fifty yards distant. As they breasted the rise, they came under intense small-arms fire. The regiment formed a defensive line with the Seventy-Sixth to their right.

Ahead of them lay a wheat field. A double line of grey-clad troops advanced through the unharvested wheat, stopping to reload and fire. Purchase instinctively ducked as Minié balls whipped through the air. One struck a soldier not five feet away. The man gave a sharp cry and fell to the grass.

'Hold fire!' The order rang out even as he aimed the musket.

'Why aren't we shooting back?' Confused and alarmed, Purchase turned to look for the colonel. Another volley erupted from the advancing line, and he heard cries of pain as men crumpled where they stood. 'Hold fire!' came the repeated command.

'Who the devil are they?' He heard one officer exclaim to another as smoke drifted across the pastures.

'They are shooting at us ain't they?' a voice shouted. 'That's good enough for me!'

The colonel himself rode up, leaning forward on the horse to peer through the smoke. Another volley rang out amid cries of frustration and alarm from those around Purchase. Straightening up, the colonel raised an arm and shouted at the top of his voice. 'Ready, right oblique, aim, fire!'

Flashes of fire and puffs of white smoke erupted all along the line. Through the smoke, Purchase saw the Confederates advancing steadily toward them, flags flying and drums beating. Officers rode just behind the infantry, sabres gleaming in the sunlight.

Abe shouted in his ear. 'It's the whole Rebel army!'

At that moment, the Confederates unleashed another volley, the fire raking the Union lines.

'To the front, fire!'

Purchase discharged his musket as the entire regiment again opened up on the Rebels. He glimpsed dozens of Confederates fall beneath the withering fire before gunpowder smoke again blocked his vision. The order to fire came again and he shot blindly through the thick smoke. This continued for some minutes, the men both receiving and returning fire until a voice cried out an urgent warning.

'They've flanked us!'

'Change front to the rear!'

Purchase sensed rather than saw his comrades change position as another volley ripped through the smoke, enfilading their right flank.

'Fire to the front!'

The musket fire was now so intense that Purchase was unable to tell whether it came from the front or rear or, indeed, from all sides. Clouds of smoke prevented him from seeing the enemy while bursting shells added to the noise and confusion. Standing at his shoulder, Winslow uttered a strangled cry and collapsed to the ground.

'Harry!' He bent over his companion.

Winslow lay deathly still. A ball had smashed into his mouth, ripping open the jaw and passing out through the back of the head.

'Elias? It's Harry! He's been killed!' His despairing cry went unheeded as Elias reloaded and fired, deaf to his pleas amid the tremendous rattle of musket fire.

'Elias!' He stood again, flinching in the hailstorm of lead. He tugged his companion's shoulder, but Elias seemed as if possessed, firing and reloading with a dazed look on his face.

The Confederate line was now no more than twenty yards distant, the two lines firing at point-blank range through the dense white fog.

Purchase fired blindly, shooting and reloading, at times uncertain where the enemy was or whether it was indeed the enemy or the New York regiment to their right that they had unwittingly engaged. Bodies were toppling all around him as the unrelenting Confederate fire raked the line. Through the smoke, he glimpsed masses of Confederate infantry within yards of their position. A grey-clad figure loomed out of the mist, and he fired, forgetting to remove the ramrod in his haste. The man gave a strangled shout and fell backward, the ramrod pierced through his chest.

Next moment, Purchase was immersed in the very press of battle as all around him Union and Confederate fought hand-to-hand. Bloodcurdling Rebel yells rose above the noise of the guns, the Confederates pressing their advantage as the Union line sagged and threatened to collapse. Through the confusion, Purchase heard a bugle call and the order to retreat. An officer, now unhorsed, moved along the line, sabre drawn, shouting orders. The officer reeled suddenly and stumbled about as though in a pantomime before falling forward, flat on his face. He tried to get to his feet but was immediately run through by a Rebel bayonet.

'Fall back the 56th!' came a shouted command.

Still facing the oncoming enemy, the regiment fired and retreated, stopping to discharge volleys at intervals. Disoriented by the exploding shells and the deafening rattle of musket fire, Purchase fell over a body, discharging his musket into the air. Scrambling to his feet, he felt a rush of panic as he found himself lost amid the smoke and noise. Forms loomed about him and he froze, unable to tell friend from foe. A ball whipped through his forage cap, almost lifting it off his head. Terrifying Rebel yells—loud, ululating *woo-yips!*—sounded on all sides, the triumphant cries piercing through the noise and smoke. Musket balls whizzed through the air and he spun around in confusion, uncertain of the whereabouts of his comrades.

He heard a bugle call and ran toward the Union lines—halting in shock as he found himself amid a throng of grey-clad troops. The Confederates seemed as startled as himself, staring at him in open-mouthed astonishment. Recovering, a bearded Confederate lunged toward him with a bayonet. His heart pounding fit to burst, he turned and fled back the way he had come, ducking and weaving as slugs hissed through the air in pursuit.

He caught up with his own retreating troops, screaming at them not to fire as muskets swung in his direction. 'Union!' he hollered. 'Union!'

Safely back within his own lines, he bent over, heaving in shock at the narrowness of his escape.

'Purchase! I feared you were dead!' Abe gripped him by the shoulder, a relieved look on his face. An officer shouted a command and the men started moving again. 'Hurry!' Abe tugged him along. 'We are in retreat!'

They joined hundreds of other Union troops in streaming toward a ridge where the brigade had redeployed in a defensive position. Behind them, the sound of firing lessened.

'Abe! Purchase!'

Elias hurried to join them as they headed to where the regimental colour flag had been stuck into the grass. 'Thank God! I feared you both were lost.' Elias looked past them at where men were still falling back in retreat. 'Did you see Winslow? I can't find him.'

'He got kilt!,' Purchase burst out. 'Right next to me.'

Elias' mouth dropped open. 'Winslow? You are certain?'

'Shot through the head. He was stone dead.' Purchase's voice was hoarse and he longed, desperately, for water.

His comrades gaped at him, shocked into silence.

'We joined together. On the same day!' Elias stared beseechingly as if the news might yet prove untrue. After a moment, he sank to the ground, tears falling down his cheeks. 'Poor Harry!'

'He was talking and laughing just this morning.' Abe looked from one comrade to the other, a distraught look on his face.

'Did you take anything from him? His ma would want it.' Elias looked up at Purchase, his face wet with tears.

'I forgot to,' mumbled Purchase. 'He was dead as anything.'

A lieutenant approached, his blue tunic grey with dust. 'Drink some water, boys. And see to your rifles.'

The companions slumped to the grass, each man alone with his thoughts. A boy came by, pushing a keg of water on a handcart. Purchase filled his bottle and drank thirstily, trying to blank the image of Winslow's smashed and bloodied face from his mind. The noise of battle continued to their rear, the dull rumble of cannon fire interspersed with the noise of exploding shells. He took off his forage cap and examined the spot where the ball had flown through. 'An inch lower and my brains would be splattered all over the grass,' he said, showing the cap to his companions.

'Along with poor Harry,' lamented Elias.

Still unnerved by the close call, Purchase got to his feet.

'Where are you going?' Abe made as if to stand with him.

'Nowhere. Sit tight, I'll be back.'

He trudged up the rise toward the ridge, making his way past tired and dispirited soldiers from both his own regiment and the Seventy-Sixth New York. Reaching the top, he turned to look out over the battlefield.

'Best keep your head down,' warned a reclining soldier. 'There are Reb sharpshooters about.'

Ignoring the advice, he shaded his eyes. In the distance, columns of grey-clad Confederate troops wheeled and marched as though practising a drill, bugles sounding and colours flying. A thin blue line of Union troops, stretched to right and left in front of the advancing Rebels poured volley after volley into the enemy ranks. The scene struck him as unreal, as if the various troops were lead soldiers from a child's playbox. Cannon—whether from Union or Confederate batteries, he could not tell—boomed with a sound like growling thunder, the noise reverberating through the air. Puffs of white smoke drifted across the battlefield. His gaze lingered on the sight of a half dozen horses, still wearing saddles and bridles, as they grazed amid the mayhem. He was still gazing at the horses when a shell burst low overhead.

Scrambling back down the ridge, he rejoined his companions.

'What in tar is happening?' demanded Elias. 'Are we in retreat?'

'How in blazes should I know?' answered Purchase. 'There are Rebs everywhere.'

ALTHOUGH THE SKY WAS overladen with cloud, the day grew hotter, the humidity further taxing the exhausted men. The wool uniform felt prickly and uncomfortable against his skin, and he scratched vigorously at an itch on his forearm. He drained his canteen as a cry went up for more water. To shouts of relief, a dozen resupply wagons were seen lumbering up the Chambersburg Pike. As the men waited for replenishment, the officers went around assessing their losses. Purchase saw Colonel Hoffmann in conversation with another officer, both men grim-faced.

'Do we stay here all day?' asked Abe, his voice agitated. 'I don't see Foley or Wasserman or anyone from A Company. Where are they?' He looked around as if expecting the named men to pop up and surprise him.

'What are you thinking?' Elias was looking at Purchase, his face distressed. 'Is it about Harry? I can't bear to think about him.'

'Me, either.'

'How did he die? Tell me again!'

Grimacing, Purchase rubbed his face between his hands. 'I saw him fall. He was already dead when he hit the ground.'

'We were friends since boyhood.' Elias choked back tears. 'Now I'll never get to taste his bread again.' He wiped his eyes with his sleeve. 'His ma will miss him awful.'

AT 1 PM, THE order came through to move forward again. As the men formed up, Purchase tugged Abe by the arm to draw his attention to the diminished ranks.

'God Almighty!' Abe cursed in disbelief. 'We must be down by half!'

Advancing in column and flanked by the two equally depleted New York regiments, they headed for a wood. Beyond the trees came the sound of heavy musket fire. They passed the bodies of dozens of Union soldiers killed in the retreat. With a horrified oath, Purchase sidestepped the body of the corporal who had roused them that morning. 'Did you see?' He turned to Abe, who gave no indication of having heard, his face grim as he stared ahead.

The gunfire grew louder as they passed through the trees, the constant boom of cannon ringing in their ears. A man in front stumbled and struck his head on an overhanging branch, the resulting stream of profanity drawing strained laughter.

The crack of small-arms fire was now loud in the air. *Someone is taking hell. I hope it's not us.* Purchase glanced at his companions, their faces betraying the same thought. Shells burst above them and stray musket balls hissed through the trees. Clearing the woods, they deployed in a defensive position behind a fence. He gripped his musket, his heart pounding. Elias and Abe were on either side.

'Get ready, boys!'

A long line of Confederates approached their position. Heavy fire came from their right flank where the Second Brigade was already engaged. The cloud cover cleared overhead, and the Rebels advanced in glorious sunshine, bugles sounding and flags held aloft. Purchase turned to Abe and Elias. 'Whatever happens, we stick together!'

'Those are the Twenty-Third North Carolina.' A man to their right shielded his eyes to observe. 'We fought them before, at Chancellorsville.'

'You recognise the colours?'

The man, a veteran in his twenties, nodded. 'My brother fights with them.'

The advancing Rebels were spread out in a long, double line, advancing as if on parade, colours gaily flying, drums tapping, and muskets shouldered. Purchase took off his cap to wipe his forehead. He stank to himself of sweat and dirt, the wool jacket stifling in the humid heat.

The Confederates came closer, marching across the open ground with a bold, confident air. The ground was mostly flat, no trees or bluffs concealing their advance. They formed an oblique line, as if uncertain of the position of the Union troops, who were stationed just behind the ridge. A fierce thirst for revenge—for Winslow, for their previous retreat—gripped Purchase as he stared at the approaching ranks. He glanced at his companions, sensing that they, too, felt it.

A sergeant crept up behind them. 'Steady, boys; steady,' he said. 'Wait for the order.' He squinted at the approaching lines. 'A turkey shoot!' he predicted.

The Rebels had now closed to within one hundred yards, their muskets still shouldered, colours fluttering on the staffs. It seemed to Purchase as if the men were indifferent to, or unaware of, the troops awaiting them despite heavy fire coming from the Union right flank. He licked his dry lips, able to pick out individual faces among the approaching ranks. A stillness ran along the line and he tensed.

'Fire!'

A hailstorm of lead poured forth from over five hundred muskets, the noise deafening, the smoke instantly blotting out the battlefield. The men continued to fire, pouring shot after shot into the Confederate ranks. After some minutes of sustained fire, they halted, although unbidden, as if sensing the great calamity they had inflicted upon the enemy. As the smoke slowly cleared, Purchase sucked his breath in horror. The open field before them was as if scythed clean of Rebels. The proud, advancing ranks had been decimated, the grass strewn with hundreds of dead or dying Confederates. Across the broad swale, he saw wounded Rebels wave hats or patches of cloth in surrender. Hardly had he begun to take in the enormity of the devastation wrought upon the enemy troops than the air was rent by yells and shouts as the Union troops to their right charged the ragged remnants of the Confederate line.

'Hold fire! Hold fire!' an officer shouted, afraid that any further shooting would inflict casualties on their own troops.

Using bayonets and clubbed muskets, the victorious Federals herded the shocked and dazed survivors together as captives. The Confederates came quietly, shoulders slumped, faces ashen. One or two of the wounded called out piteously, beseeching their captors for water. An elderly, grey-haired man limped past, blood running down his neck and collar from a wound in his scalp. An officer, tall and of impressive bearing, halted as the line briefly stopped. With a shock, Purchase saw that the man's right arm was a bloody stump at the elbow. The man felt his gaze and returned it, a look of furious anger in his eyes.

'By shucks but we showed 'em!' Abe crowed with victory, a gloating look on his face.

'Where's your durn Dixie now!' another man taunted.

As the line of Rebel prisoners passed, Purchase sat down, his back against the fence. He was about to take a swallow of water when the man sitting next to him jumped suddenly to his feet and hurried toward the stricken field.

'Anderson!' A sergeant bellowed after the man. 'Where in hellfire is he off to?'

Before Purchase could say something, the sergeant hauled him to his feet. 'Get after him! Fetch him back or by God he'll be shot for desertion!'

Purchase scrambled over the fence, hastening after the other man. 'Anderson, wait!' he shouted. In response, the other man broke into a run. 'Hold up, consarn it!' Purchase made himself smaller as he ran, fearful of being shot by a wounded Reb. Ahead of him, Anderson had suddenly stopped. Purchase caught up, panting and out of breath.

'Sweet Jesus, they are still in line!' Anderson moaned with horror.

And it was true, Purchase saw at once. The line of dead Confederates lay in perfect alignment, as if settled down to sleep in their parade position. Most still clutched muskets to their breasts. Many had five or six fatal wounds inflicted by the Union volleys. The pastures shimmered in the hot sunlight: the grass soaked with blood. A slight depression—the only cover available, and where a few desperate survivors had taken refuge— was stained crimson from the carnage. Purchase swallowed, hardly able to comprehend the rows of dead and mangled bodies.

'He was the youngest.' Anderson stared wide-eyed at the bloody field, his face wretched with grief. 'The fool insisted on joining up with the Rebs.' Distraught, Anderson moved among the corpses, searching the dead faces and turning over bodies. 'Mort! Are you there? It's Frank! Can you hear me?'

'We must go back!' urged Purchase. 'The colonel will have you shot!' Across the fields, less than a quarter mile distant, a double column of Confederate troops were advancing at the quick. Purchase glanced toward his own line. The regiment was withdrawing in the face of this new threat. He saw Elias stand up and wave his cap while hollering at him.

'Leave it now!' He remonstrated, turning back to Anderson. 'You'll get us both shot!' He took the other man by the shoulder.

'Mort!' Anderson tore free from Purchase's grip, a wild look on his face. 'Mort! It's Frank. I've come to take you home.' He wandered off among the rows of dead and dying, calling out across the sprawled bodies. 'Answer me, Mort! I've come to save you!'

Purchase watched hopelessly for a few moments before hurrying back to his regiment.

'What happened? Where's Anderson?' Elias and Abe helped him back over the fence.

'He's out of his wits looking for his brother.' Purchase shook his head, eyes full of horror at what he had seen. 'The slaughter is awful. The entire brigade is cut down.'

'Serves them right!' Elias stared angrily at the bloody fields. 'They shot Winslow.'

'Where's the sergeant? I must report.'

My relief party was one of the first on the scene after the smoke had cleared and the Yankees chased from the field. My cousin, Fergus, was a private in the 5th South Carolina regiment, having been posted to the regiment only two weeks before Gettysburg. His uncle, Isaiah, had joined up with the Federals as soon as the war broke out. I enlisted with the 20th North Carolina, part of General Iverson's brigade. On that day I was part of a foraging unit ordered to search Yankee farmhouses for any supplies we might use. We had confiscated some saddles and muskets when an officer galloped up and ordered us back to the field right away. 'Your comrades have great need of you!' he said. By the time we arrived at the fighting, the Federals had been driven from the hill, but at an insupportable cost to our gallant boys. I saw at once that a great slaughter had taken place, with our dead and dying comrades lying everywhere you looked. A few stragglers wandered about in a daze. I recognized one of them, Pvt Fitzsimmons, and grabbed him. 'What in thunder happened?' I asked. He could not seem to recognize me, even though we had bivouacked together many times. I shook him and asked again, but he was like a man walking in his sleep. His eyes were wild and he kept mumbling over and over like a lunatic. All around were the bodies of my slain companions. Many had been shot three or four times, their heads blown apart by musket balls. I learned later that the Yankees had kept firing even when our brave boys waved hats and begged to surrender. I walked up and down the ranks of the fallen, scarcely able to speak. The cries of the wounded were pitiful to hear. The sun was fierce, and they begged me for water, their tongues so swollen they could hardly do anything but moan. I saw many comrades I had soldiered with ever since Williamsburg. They were lying in rank, stretched out in perfect lines like a drill exercise. I remember the grass was so sodden with blood that it leaked into my boots. My companions were ashen-faced and weeping from the agony of seeing so many splendid comrades taken to eternity. I could barely refrain from bursting into tears. It was the god-awfulest thing you ever did see.

—SGT REBUS HANLON, 20th North Carolina Regiment. Undated letter, circa 1876, Richmond Public Archives

2

Libby

My family owned an orchard up on Oak Ridge. We stayed with relatives in the town until the fighting was over. When we returned, everything was stolen or ransacked. Pa had taken the precaution of moving most of the livestock before the battle. But the grain and flour barrels were emptied, and the smoked hams left hanging in the barn were gone. We found scraps of meat on the ground and supposed the Rebs had eaten them then and there. The scenes after the battle were ghastly to behold. There were dead horses everywhere, as well as lots of ordnance including a broke-down cannon and, of course, the corpses. I remember it was hotter than Hades and the stench from all the bodies was enough to drive a person clear out of his wits. The dead soldiers were scattered for miles across the fields and orchards. So many you couldn't count. For years afterward, the plough turned up bits of uniforms, musket balls, buckles, and leather slings. In the year after the war, we had the best harvest ever. My father said it was downright tragic that so many young men had given their blood just to water the crops. He took the battle hard—his younger brother, Joshua, had perished in the Union army at Chancellorsville. Ten years after the battle, he finally sold the orchard. He couldn't stand seeing one more bone or patch of uniform turn up. The place was all run-down anyway when he sold it. He just let it slowly fall apart. There were others, too. Farmers who abandoned their fields and coloureds who refused to work once the sun began to set. 'There be ghosts, massa,' one of them said to me. And who knows but he was right? The worst part was the children—who could not be deterred from wandering the fields and picking up pieces of unex-ploded ordnance. They didn't realise the danger although we repeatedly warned them. Several were killed or had their limbs blown off even years after the fighting had stopped. I guess you could say the battle continued for us in Gettysburg for years afterwards. The town was never the same. After pa died, I moved away—to New York, first, and then, Washington and then Philly. I married twice, but neither lasted. I could never forget all that had happened.

—JONATHAN BOOTHBY, *The New York Times*, August 1893

PURCHASE SAT BACK AGAINST a tree, his mouth dry, his entire body consumed with the fierce heat. 'When will they relieve us?' he asked the equally exhausted Abe on his right.

'When we are dead!' Abe drained the last of his water bottle. 'I swear, I'm sick to death of this durn war. It's nothing but march, shoot! March, shoot!'

'At least you are shooting Rebs,' said Elias, sitting to Purchase's left. 'Grass-bellied snakes!' he added, his voice bitter.

Almost out of ammunition, the brigade had abandoned the field in the face of the Confederate reinforcements. They had stopped briefly to resupply, taking shelter behind a rise. Enemy cannon opened up as they waited, the depleted regiment taking several more casualties from shell bursts.

A soldier straggled in, his head bare and his coat ripped at the shoulder. 'I played possum!' he crowed. 'The Rebs passed right by me!' He looked around, a frantic look on his face 'Where in 'nation is my company? I lost my durn company!' Dragging his musket on the ground, he continued on, calling out for his lost comrades.

After a half hour's respite, the order came to retreat along the railroad tracks leading into the town. The exhausted brigade had been in battle for almost six hours, the men fatigued and hungry. 'Beer and beefsteak await,' came the grim jest as they set off. They had barely reached the tracks when shots rang out from Confederate sharpshooters concealed in a grove of trees.

'The Rebs are on our heels!' a panicked voice shouted, and the column broke into a run. Abe gave a hoarse cry and pitched forward onto the tracks. Purchase turned back, yelling for Elias to stop as he knelt to examine their wounded companion.

'Don't leave me!' Abe pleaded, clutching Purchase's wrist. He had been struck by a bullet just above the hip.

Purchase looked at Elias. 'Help me carry him.'

Hauling the wounded and groaning Abe to his feet, they each folded an arm around his waist and half-dragged, half-carried their companion behind their fleeing comrades. Elias glanced back. 'I can see a Reb!' he shouted.

'Hurry!'

Walking as fast as they were able, they supported the hobbling Abe as he groaned and cried out in pain. 'I'm done for!' he gasped, his face bloodless.

'Hang on, Abe! In the town, we'll find you a doctor.'

Musket balls whizzed past as they came upon the bodies of several of their fellow soldiers who had fallen victim to the sharpshooters. Burdened by their wounded companion, they had fallen farther behind the retreating brigade and were in dire peril of being killed or captured. Purchase was wondering whether to abandon the tracks and take refuge in the long grass when he felt something splatter his face and Abe slumped suddenly, a dead weight in his grasp.

'Suffering Jesus!' Elias almost dropped his mortally wounded comrade in fright. 'His head's blown off!' Elias's face, too, was splattered with blood.

'Set him down!'

They lay their dead comrade on the ground, flinching as more bullets tore through the air. 'Leave him!' Elias shouted. 'Run like the very devil!'

Together, they fled after the retreating regiment, barely ahead of the pursuing Confederates.

REACHING THE TOWN, THEY found scenes of chaos, the streets crowded with wagons, ambulances and retreating infantry. Yells and curses sounded in the air as the desperate troops attempted to navigate the congested streets ahead of the rapidly-advancing Rebels.

'Stay close!' Purchase shouted, as he and Elias threatened to become separated in the crush. Spying a soldier from the Seventy-Sixth New York, he grasped the man by the shoulder. 'Where's the brigade? Where are we headed?'

The man started, a wild look on his face. 'The Baltimore Pike! Head for the Pike!' Next moment, he had plunged back into the crowd and was gone. Purchase looked around for Elias to relay the news but could see nothing of his companion.

'Elias! Elias!' Shouting above the turmoil, he found himself pressed up against a house as a wagon forced its way through the crowd, the driver yelling out oaths as he fought to control the frightened horses. An artillery shell burst overhead, and everything went black.

Late in the morning of July 1, the sounds of battle grew louder. And soon the artillery shells, which we had seen bursting in the distance, began to rain down much nearer the houses. 'Gracious!' I said to Libby, my housemaid. 'The Rebels are shelling the town!' We had crept up from the cellar to observe what was going on. The scene that met our eyes was beyond telling. The streets were filled with Federal troops and wagons of every description. The noise and confusion was that loud! A body could hardly move for all the crowding. Soldiers were shouting and cussing and trying to find their way through the streets. We heard a rumour that the Confederates had seized the Baltimore Pike, which runs into the town, and were closing in from that direction. But it turned out that was not true. Shells were exploding and men and livestock were panicking as the Rebels swept in from the north end of town, hard on the heels of the Federals. Bullets buzzed through the air like angry hornets. One struck the corner of the house. You can still see where it knocked the plaster. The Federals were running down alleys and dead-end streets in their rush to escape the pursuing Rebels. We heard later, from Mr Foley, who runs the general store, that soldiers ran through the doorway and out the back—stopping only to scoop handfuls of sugar from the barrels! Just as Libby and I prepared to flee back to the cellar, there was an almighty bang and a shell crashed just over the roof! 'Mercy!' I cried. Libby fell to her knees, praying the Lord for salvation. A window in the upper room, where we were, had broken to bits—glass everywhere! I peeked out. All was bedlam below. Three or four people were crying and carrying on and wailing that they were mortally wounded. I saw a federal soldier lying flat on his back and people stamping all around him in a panic to get away from the shelling. I called Libby to see and said we have to check if the man is dead or alive, else he would get stomped by the horses. We opened the door and inspected the soldier to see if he was breathing. And all the while, people were scrambling past and bullets flying and horses snorting and whinnying! I feared we might get swept away in the mad rush. The soldier was alive, we judged, although unconscious and bleeding heavily from a wound to his scalp. 'Help me!' I said to Libby. 'Get him inside before the Rebels come along and shoot him!' Together we dragged the poor soul through the doorway and into the house. Libby was greatly concerned lest the Rebels come and shoot us for harbouring a fugitive. But I calmed her down and we set to doing what we could for the wounded youth—for he was no more than that. I cleaned and sewed the wound—removing a small piece of shrapnel, and Libby wrapped his head with a bandage. While we were doing this, the soldier came to and jumped up in fright! We had to hold him down while we explained that we meant no harm and were trying to help. This settled him a bit, although he asked after someone—a comrade, I suppose. I assured him no other soldiers had been injured by the shell. He shortly became feverish and I was afraid he would die during the night. But next morning, he seemed better and asked for water. He begged for news of his company and mentioned the Baltimore Pike where, he said, they were headed. All of a sudden, he became agitated and insisted he must leave to rejoin his regiment. I hushed him and told him he was in no fit manner to travel. Besides, I told him, the Confederates were now occupying the town, and he would be fortunate not to be captured or shot. At this, he became alarmed, and I assured him we would hide him from the Rebels. I left him then, for a moment, to peep through the window. The streets that had previously been packed with fleeing Federal troops were now crowded with Rebs. They were an unruly bunch—seemingly without officers and going from house to house in search of Federals or, more likely, whatever they could steal! I saw a half-dozen crash through the door of Mrs. Winfield's opposite. She confessed to me later she near had heart failure as these wild, bearded men pushed into her parlour screaming and yelling for Federals! They ransacked her pantry before leaving and laughed when she threatened to complain to General Lee himself. I was mortal afraid that they would cross the street and come to my house next. But there was a commotion down the block, and they ran to see. Nevertheless, we were in grave danger that they would return. Libby was beside herself as we had heard rumours that the Rebs were seizing Negroes as well as Federals and shipping them back South to be sold. The Negroes, I mean. Meanwhile, the wounded soldier was moaning and asking for water. I gave him some and told him that my own dear Walt had enrolled with the Union the year war broke out and had perished at Bull Run. He expressed his sorrow at this, for which I thanked him. Things quieted down for a bit, and we heard that the Federals had retreated to the heights south of town and were dug in, awaiting the Confederate attack. The Rebels occupied our town for the next two days, commandeering many of the houses as hospitals to treat their wounded. They used others as sniping posts to fire upon the Union troops gathered on the heights. On the morning of the second day, we were warned by a neighbour that the Confederates were engaged in a house-to-house search for hidden Union troops. Fearing they would arrive at any moment, I hid Libby and the soldier—I forget his name—in a small alcove just beneath the attic. My husband had prepared it as soon as the war broke out. 'You never know, Sarah,' he said. And he was right! They had barely concealed themselves there when there came a frightful pounding at the door. I opened it to find myself confronted by a burly man in a dusty grey coat who demanded entrance. 'Do you harbour any Federals?' he roared. Lord, but he gave me a scare! 'No, sir,' I lied. 'I am a widow living on my own.' 'What happened to your husband?' he asked. 'He was killed,' I answered truthfully. 'At Bull Run.' At that he seemed to soften.

'That was a hard battle,' he said. 'I am sure your husband fought valiantly.' He then asked me to stand aside while he ordered two or three soldiers to search the parlour, pantry, and cellar. When they returned—clutching some apples and a sack of flour! —he ordered them upstairs to check the attic. My heart was in my mouth as I heard them tramping around! The Rebel looked me in the eye and asked again was I harbouring someone. 'It will go hard, with you, Ma'am,' he said, 'should you be lying to me.' I assured him again that I was alone and asked how I, a frail widow on her own, could offer refuge to a soldier—Union or Confederate? Lord, but I almost said 'Rebel' in my fright! At that moment, the soldiers returned down the stairs and said that there was no one else in the house. The man apologized and ordered the soldiers to move on to the next house. He thrust some Confederate notes into my hand. 'For the provisions,' he said. Before leaving, he tacked a notice to the door that the house had been searched. 'Occupant not to be disturbed further,' he wrote beneath it, for which kindness I thanked him. The Rebels finally left on the third of July, having been defeated in the battles that followed on the outskirts of town. On the morning of the fourth, we heard another commotion and saw Union troops march back into the street. The young soldier bid me profuse thanks and, although still weak from his wound, insisted on leaving to find his regiment. I often wonder what became of that young man, and whether he survived the dreadful battles that followed.
—THE WIDOW MERRITT, *The Star and Sentinel*, p. 3, May 1873

He took his leave of the widow as soon as his health allowed, giving grateful thanks for her kindness and bravery in hiding him from the Rebels. The streets were full of townsfolk and Union troops milling together in the bright sunlight. Bareheaded and sans musket, he headed along the crowded thoroughfare, grimacing at the noise and recoiling from the passing wagons. An officer on horseback approached and he hailed the man. 'Sir, I am looking for my regiment, the Fifty-Sixth Penn, First Corps.'

The officer pulled rein and looked around distractedly at the munitions and supply wagons trundling down the street. 'The Fifty-Sixth? I have no idea.' He cursed as he observed a collision between two wagons before turning his attention back to Purchase, noting the bandage around his head. 'You hardly seem fit to travel.'

'I'm all right. I just need to find my regiment.'

An ambulance wagon approached and the officer held up a hand, bidding it stop.

'I'm in a hurry, major,' the driver protested. 'I have wounded here.' The wagon was open at the sides, the box occupied by four men lying on stretchers.

'Where are you headed?'

'The McPherson Farm, up on the Chambersburg Pike.'

Taking out a notebook from his pocket, the major scribbled a note and tore out the page, handing it to Purchase. 'You are seconded to the Ambulance Corps. Report to Captain Miller at the McPherson Farm. That's where the First Corps wounded are being treated. This man will take you there.'

'But I must find my regiment!'

The officer frowned. 'The regiment can wait. You are needed here. Do you not wish to help your wounded comrades?'

'Major, I must get on,' insisted the driver.

'Then take him with you.' The officer gestured to Purchase. 'Climb on!'

Still protesting, Purchase climbed onto the wagon seat.

'Har!' The driver shook the reins and the conveyance lurched forward. From the back came cries and groans as the wagon bounced over a rut. Purchase winced, the ache in his head exacerbated by the pitching motion.

The driver glanced at him. 'What happened to you?'

'I was wounded. I must get back to my regiment.' He glanced behind. 'Stop! I must get down.'

'The hell you will!' The driver flicked the whip. 'We are working night and day here. We need all the spare hands we can get. Don't you fret about your regiment; we have dozens of lost soldiers working with us. Hell, you might even find some of your own boys hiding up there.' He shook the reins. 'Har!'

Miserable, and weak from the barely healed wound, Purchase gripped the seat as the wagon rocked and bounced along the pike. A wave of nausea swept over him, and he feared he might faint or vomit.

The wagon shared the congested road with columns of marching men and scores of other conveyances and supply wagons. Troopers on horseback cursed the marching men forcing them to make room for the wagons. Purchase scanned the wounded as an ambulance wagon jostled past, hoping to pick out a face he recognised.

'Don't you jump, now!' the driver warned. 'You have your orders.'

'I recognise this spot!' Purchase exclaimed as they approached a farmhouse set back from the fenced road. 'There's a railway cut over there.' He pointed beyond the barn. 'That's where we fought the Rebs.'

'Is that where you got hit?'

'No, that was later. In the town.'

'Yip!' The driver shook the reins as they turned off at a section where the log fence had been knocked down. The wheels bounced as the wagon jolted over the grass toward the farmhouse, the lurching progress drawing further agonised cries from those in the back.

'Nearly there, boys!'

'WHOA!' THEY PULLED UP in front of the barn behind a line of departing ambulances. Soldiers and orderlies flocked around each arriving wagon, ferrying the wounded inside the barn. As their turn came, a half dozen men ran to meet them. 'Stand clear!' a voice shouted as yet another wagon arrived hard on their heels.

Climbing down, Purchase assisted as the stretchers were pulled, one by one, from the wagon. They were laid in a row alongside dozens more as a surgeon carried out a quick inspection and issued orders. Orderlies approached, carrying fresh stretchers, which they placed in the back of the ambulance.

'You make sure you report to the captain,' said the driver before turning around the empty conveyance. 'You'll find him in the barn, most like.'

Purchase was profoundly shocked to come upon a pile of discarded limbs—arms and legs, the latter still wearing shoes or boots—stacked against the barn wall like so much cordwood. 'You harden to it,' called out a passing stretcher bearer, seeing his grimace.

As he passed from the bright sunlight into the dim interior of the barn, his gorge rose at the overpowering stench of blood and death. The sickly smell of morphine sulfate and chloroform hung heavily in the air. Wounded soldiers were organised in rows three lines deep along the walls. Some lay on stretchers, their faces listless and ashen-coloured. Others sat up, their backs propped against the barn wall, their eyes dull as they awaited their turn on the operating tables. Many were horribly disfigured by musket or grapeshot, the gaping wounds looking gangrenous and weeping pus.

In the middle of the barn, harried surgeons operated on men stretched out on a dozen makeshift tables constructed from ties from the nearby railroad. Those being operated on drifted in and out of consciousness as the surgeons swiftly and efficiently amputated arms and legs. He saw one man cry out in protest as a rag soaked in chloroform was pressed to his face. The man struggled for a bit and then lay quiet.

'Is he under?' A waiting surgeon asked, his tunic splattered with blood, his face etched with fatigue. He held a bloody saw in his hand. Another surgeon yelled for assistance as one soldier was lowered from a table to be immediately replaced by another. Orderlies mopped up blood and vomit as the exhausted surgeons worked nonstop. From all around came a chorus of unearthly shrieks and groans.

The nauseating stench of death and butchery was so overpowering that Purchase reeled on his feet, almost overcome with horror. His nose, eyes, mouth and skin felt as if indelibly dyed with the heavy, drenching odours of blood, piss, shit and ether—a stench so oppressively foul that it lingered in his nostrils for years afterwards.

He was unable to tear his gaze from the rows of dead and dying, some of whom reached out piteously, eyes bright with fever or imminent death. Civilians moved along the rows, offering water to parched throats or a word of comfort to those too injured to respond. A half-dozen women handed out biscuits and fruit or knelt next to the stretchers, ministering to the frightened men in soothing voices. A clergyman clasped the hand of a weeping youth missing both his lower limbs. Many of the wounded lay motionless—whether alive or dead, Purchase could not tell, their limbs blackened and festering with untreated wounds. Flies buzzed the sick and dying as shouts came from outside and more casualties were carried in.

'Mind!' An orderly hurried past, his arms full of freshly amputated limbs to add to the pile outside the door. The sound of a saw grinding into bone came from a nearby table, the surgeon grunting with the effort. Faint with dizziness and revulsion, Purchase sagged against a post. A hand steadied him, and he looked up to see the same stretcher-bearer, a sympathetic look on his face.

'Go outside for a while. Get some fresh air before you come back in again.'

Trying to hold down his nausea, Purchase exited the barn. Outside, the sun blazed down, the brightness contrasting with the hellish suffering within. Leaning one hand against the barn wall, he promptly retched into the grass.

'Tarnation!' A passing orderly shot him an angry look. 'We have sufficient of that inside the barn!'

He retched again, gasping for air while drooling spit and vomit into the grass. A fresh pile of discarded limbs lay nearby, and he looked away, wiping his mouth. Walking to the shade of a tree, he surveyed his surroundings. On the pike, a long column of soldiers trudged past. He stared, suddenly envying the hot-blooded innocence of the battlefield.

'Hurry up and clear the wagons!' An officer shouted orders as a group of soldiers scrambled to unload yet another ambulance. The officer turned around to look for more hands, and Purchase shrank back behind the tree. Someone yelled, and the officer hurried inside behind the stretcher-bearers. Purchase headed for the pike, unnoticed amid the confusion. Reaching the road, he slipped in among the weary column, profoundly thankful to leave the barn and its stink and misery behind him.

My name is Libby—just Libby, if you please, and back in '63 I was employed in Gettysburg as a housemaid to the widow Merritt. Early on the morning of July 1, we heard cannon fire and saw Federals march through the streets. I remember people flocking outside to cheer and offer treats. Of course, I was happy to see them. I had escaped from slavery in 'Ginny but two years before and was scared to distraction that I would be sent back. But later that same day, the Union troops came fleeing back into town with the Rebels hot on their heels! Mrs Merritt wanted me to hide in the cellar, but then we heard an explosion just outside the house. Sweet Jesus, but I can still hear it in my ears to this day! A federal had been wounded and was lying outside in the street, in danger of being trampled by all the wagons that were trying to escape the town. Mrs Merritt—she was a kindly woman, and good to me—went outside to see and I helped her drag the soldier indoors. We gave him what help we could. He was a young man—no more than a boy, really. No sooner had the Federals escaped than the Rebels entered, yelling and screeching to beat the band! They started raiding the houses and shops, looking for things to steal and Union troops to capture. I hid along with the soldier in a small hidey-hole up near the attic. We heard soldiers come looking for us and held our breath. Lord have mercy but I was fearful of being discovered! One soldier banged the wall with his musket, and I thought we were cooked like a goose! But shortly after they left, and we were able to crawl out again. I remember best after the battle. The Union troops came back again, and it was safe to go outside and look around. To my dying day I shall never forget the sight that met my eyes. Dead soldiers! As far as a body could see! The sun was terrible hot and the bodies were festering with flies and maggots. Most of them were black and terrible to behold. I saw arms and legs and bits of brain lying everywhere. Dead horses and mules lay along with the men, their flesh roasting and putrefying in the sun. It was enough to make a body die of fright. The stench hung all over the town for weeks afterward. Amos, a field hand I knew, said that up on Oak Hill the sights were even more terrible—so terrible he could hardly stand to walk up there, even years after the battle. He swore certain that ghosts could be heard wailing and crying out to give a soul the jeepers! Folk talk now of a glorious victory. But they did not see what I did. I shall not sleep tonight for remembering. Not far from the town, I saw forty or fifty bodies, Rebels and Federals alike, all jumbled together in one awful pile. Some had their heads blown off by cannon or were run through with a bayonet. Albert Watson, the gentlemen who owned the horse barn on Wigmore Street, said a few had probably survived for a day or two and died of thirst in the terrible heat. I felt great sorrow for their mamas—not to know how or where their sons had perished. I am old now—older than Mrs Merritt was when she died ten years after the battle. Her husband perished fighting for the Union, but two of her uncles had joined up with the Rebels. What happened to them, I do not know. She refused to speak of them ever after. The graves? Shallow, Amos told me. More like trenches. At first, every corpse was buried where it lay—Federal and Confederate together. They had to—the stink was petrifying! And then, just when they were buried, the rains came and washed them up again! The last thing I remember was a bunch of coloured field hands burying some Confederates late into the night, working by moonlight to cover the bodies.

—LIBBY, coloured housemaid,
Philadelphia Tribune, March 1905.

3

Kansas City

BOVE THE NONDESCRIPT BUILDING, a sign read *Upper Missouri Fur Company*. The young man walked up the steps to the porch to where an unshaven, middle-aged man sat idly rocking in a chair. The man looked the youth up and down. 'Yes?' he said.

'I heard you were hiring. I'm looking for work—as a buffalo hunter.'

'What's your name, son?'

'Purchase McLennan.'

The man chewed slowly on a plug of tobacco as he considered this. 'You from 'round here, Purchase?'

'Missouri.'

'Big state, Missouri.'

'St Charles, outside of St Louis.'

'St Charles,' the man repeated. 'Outside of St Louis.' He studied Purchase's wide-brimmed hat. 'You were in the war?'

'I was.'

'Union or Reb?'

'Union.'

'You shoot many Rebs?'

'A few.'

The man leaned over and spat out a mouthful of tobacco juice. 'How was it?'

'How was it?'

'I heard things.' The man gazed out over the street, his jaws slowly and deliberately masticating the tobacco. He motioned to the rifle Purchase had set down against the wall. 'That a Sharps?'

'It is.'

'I guess you can use it?'

'I can.'

'You ever shoot a buffalo?'

'No.'

'Flies!' The man spat and swiped his mouth. 'Lucifer's spawn!' Grimacing with distaste, he settled back in the rocker. 'Simkins is my name,' he said. 'Esmus Simkins.'

'I'm pleased to meet you, Mr Simkins.' Purchase wondered if he should extend a hand at this late introduction and decided not to.

'How did you get here—from St Louie?'

'By train. I arrived last night. Someone said you were hiring?'

'Who?' Simkins squinted with the question.

'Someone. A man at the station.'

'A man at the station?' Simkins mulled on this. 'The camp is a long ways,' he said. 'Up in the Dakota Territory. Did your man mention that?'

'He did.'

'A mighty informed fellow! And you never shot buff?'

'No. But I'm a handy shot.'

Simkins rolled the plug from one side of his mouth to the other. 'Buff are mostly stupid, anyways.' He ruminated on this truth, chewing the plug.

'So, are you hiring?'

'Am I hiring?' Simkins considered the question as if reluctant to quit the comfortable chair. 'Why go all the way up north to shoot buff? The Union Pacific is hiring right here in town and paying sixty cents a critter. All you have to do is hop the train and you'll be up to your neck in buff.'

'I have my reasons.'

Simkins chewed on this for a minute or so. 'Well, hell!' he said, and squirted a stream of yellow tobacco juice over the porch rail. He rose to his feet, issuing a long groan with the effort. 'I guess we'd better not disappoint your man at the station.'

Opening the door to the office, he motioned for Purchase to step inside. The room was sparsely furnished with a small desk and a single chair. 'How much did you pay for your ticket from St Louis?'

'Seven dollars, forty-four cents.'

'Seven dollars, forty-four cents.' Simkins took a sheet of paper from the desk drawer. 'Pay is fifty cents a buff, tongue included. Wages paid twice a month—less room and board. You are bound for one year. The company pays your passage—from here, not St Louis, and draws it from your wages.' He took a steel pen and bottle of ink from the drawer. 'Sign there if you're still interested.' He looked on as Purchase signed. Taking back the paper, he added his signature and blew on the ink.

'I'm waiting on some supplies for the camp,' he said, peering at the ink as it dried. 'They should be here in two or three days. Report back here on Thursday. There's a packet steamer leaving for Fort Benton at six o'clock in the morning. Be here, in this office, by five o'clock and I'll see you on board. Oh, and unless you're figuring on sleeping with your man down at the railway station, you'll find a bed at Mrs. Lewis', thirty-four Poplar Street.'

He accompanied Purchase out the door. 'There are two others,' he said. 'Young fellows, like yourself.'

'Others?'

'Signed up, along with you. 'You'll meet them on Thursday, I expect. Unless they've run home to mammy.' Simkins sank back in the rocker and put his feet up on the rail. 'That's it,' he said, and closed his eyes.

'My great-grandpappy was there,' Purchase could not resist saying.

'Who and where?' Frowning, Simkins opened his eyes.

'Up in the territory—shooting buffalo.'

'Is that so?' Simkins closed his eyes again.

'Is there a … rock buffalo up there?'

'Rock buffalo?' Simkins regarded Purchase with baffled amazement. 'Why in the name of Gertrude Frockenback would there be a *rock* buffalo?'

'It's just that—' Purchase halted, unsure what to say. 'Something I heard,' he said.

'From your man at the station?'

'No. ''Taint nothing.' Purchase turned and stepped back onto the street.

'We don't pay for shooting no rock buff!' Simkins called after him. 'Only the regular, hairy kind.' Settling back in the chair he closed his eyes. 'Why in tar would you shoot a rock buff?' he grumbled to the air.

Purchase made his way to the Poplar Street address, glad to find it near to the riverfront. Having secured a shared room for the night, he left his rifle and rucksack in the custody of Mrs. Lewis and ventured out to explore the city.

THE DAY WAS WARM and humid, and still shy of noon. The Kansas City streets were bustling with construction activity. Carts ferried bricks from one site to another as men dug trenches or put-up wood frames. He nodded to passers-by, excited and curious to be in such a grand metropolis. The traffic increased as he neared Main Street, and he quickened his step. Turning the corner, he was confronted by a busy thoroughfare congested with conveyances of every sort. Slow-moving ox-drawn wagons contested for space with drays, farm carts, buggies, carriages and coaches, the drivers rudely shouting for passage.

'Clear the way!' A driver shook the reins as a large, cumbersome wagon made its way along the crowded street. 'Watch out! Durn it!' Curses flew from his tongue as a man darted in front of the lumbering conveyance.

Purchase lingered to observe, enjoying the hurly-burly. Pedestrians thronged the paved sidewalks, each one in a hurry to be somewhere. Dogs leapt and barked amid the creaking wheels and bellowing oxen. Vendors shouted their wares in front of the stores lining the street, the chaotic hustle and bustle reminding Purchase of carnival sideshows. A crowd had gathered on the sidewalk, staring down the street in anticipation. Men held small children on their shoulders, others waved the Stars and Stripes. Curious to observe why, he found a place among the spectators. 'What are you waiting for?' he asked the man next to him.

'Listen!'

From farther down the street came the noise of a brass band—the sound reinforcing his earlier impression of a carnival. Applause broke out around him as a military band marched up the street between the lines of cheering spectators. Small boys strutted alongside, sticks held against their shoulders. A troop of soldiers marched behind the band. An officer with a drawn sword led the way, directing voluble oaths at any and all who dared obstruct his path. The band came nearer, the blare of French horns vying with the sound of bassoons, trombones, flutes, and clarinets—the ensemble marshalled by the thumping beat of a pair of bass drums.

The parade filed past, the crowd calling out loud *huzzahs!* as the band ended one tune and abruptly launched into 'Yankee Doodle.' Among the cheers were several scattered boos. He saw one man glower at the passing troops while another spat in the road in advance of the band, making no effort to disguise the hatred on his face. The gestures of dissent, however, were drowned out amid the festive air. He scanned the faces of the soldiers as they filed past, their uniforms coated with dust.

As the noisy parade receded, he continued along the sidewalk, giving way to men stepping out from the stores, arms loaded with provisions. Several large Conestoga wagons sat in the street, their beds overflowing with spare yokes, wheel bands, bridles, tools, and pots and pans. Women tending babes sat amid the jumble as the men stuffed yet more parts or supplies on top of those already piled in the back.

'Where you headed, friend?' he asked of an elderly man leaning against the wheel of an open schooner.

'California, along the Santa Fe Trail.' The man gestured. 'Soon as the scout arrives.'

'California?' Purchase shook his head. 'A long way,' he said.

'It be that.' The speaker looked up as a burly man emerged from a nearby store carrying sacks of animal feed across his shoulders. 'It be that,' he repeated, straightening up to receive the sacks.

A long line of covered wagons, each drawn by a team of oxen, made its way up the street, wheels rattling and leather harnesses creaking. Men and women trudged alongside the slow-moving conveyances. Not far behind, a man accompanied by two panting dogs drove a herd of hogs. A woman walked alongside one wagon, holding the hand of a small child. She glanced at Purchase as she passed, and he tipped the brim of his hat. The driver, a rough looking fellow, gave a hard stare in his direction. Leaning to one side, the man spat a stream of tobacco juice into the street. 'Har!' He roared, his eyes still on Purchase as he shook the reins.

The wagons creaked past, their beds packed to the canvas bonnets with spare parts, furniture, shovels, and pickaxes. Young children perched precariously atop the piled goods, looking out with grimy faces as they passed. 'Emigrants!' a man beside him spat. The man coughed and waved his hand at the clouds of dust driven up by the wheels. 'They sure do raise a stink!'

Purchase waited for the line of conveyances to pass before crossing the street.

'We're off to old Oregon!' a boy chirped from the back of the rearmost wagon as Purchase crossed behind the conveyance. The remark drew laughter from a curly-headed sibling.

No sooner had Purchase stepped foot on the opposite sidewalk than he was accosted by a lean, bowler-hatted man in a gaudy yellow waistcoat and green wool trousers. 'Howee, young fella! Free land—or as good as!' The man pointed a stick up at the storefront behind him. A large, hand-painted sign proclaimed it the home of the *Nebraska Territory Land Office*. The huckster beamed. 'You look like a man who would be proud to own a few acres of God's finest land. Up in the territories. Finest Nebraska homesteads—all for cents an acre! What say you, young fella? A golden opportunity to start yourself out in life!'

The man extended an arm as Purchase made to pass, blocking his path and attempting to steer him into the storefront where another man waited inside beside a table strewn with maps and papers. 'Special offer today—just for you! Forty acres for less than a dollar per acre!'

'Not for me.' Purchase shook his head and again attempted to pass.

'And why not?' The huckster looked indignant. 'Hell, I'm practically giving away the land—God's finest acres. Ripe for the plough!'

'Not for me!' He repeated, frowning at the man's bellicosity.

'You afraid of a little hard work? Why, I never took you for such—with your hat and all!' The man glared, his manner alternating between cajoling and bullying. 'Less than a dollar an acre! Railway land if you like—for when the trains come through!'

'I said no!' Purchase pushed past.

'I never saw the such!' The indignant huckster stabbed the air with the stick. 'Looky here! A fellow turning up his nose at riches! Afraid of a little honest work! Come, friends!' The man's tone abruptly altered as a group of emigrants—the women clad in sunbonnets and calico dresses, the men in farm hats and homespun shirts—caught his attention. 'This way, folks! Land for the giving! Christian land for God-fearing pilgrims!'

As Purchase made his way along the street, the baiters employed by the stores importuned him to buy gold pans, axes, rope, buckskin shirts, overalls, hats, canteens, or muskets. 'To keep the bloodthirsty Injuns at bay!' one proprietor insisted, thrusting a carbine at him.

'Shovels to dig for gold!' the proprietor of a mining store called out as he passed by. The man held up a long-handled shovel. 'Jest beneath the surface. Gold lying everywhere! Why pay ten times the price in Californee? You, sir!' The man beamed as a youth in a cotton shirt and leather boots stopped to examine the shovel. 'Why, dig with this and you'll be rich as anything by suppertime!'

HE ATE A STEAK with gravied potatoes at a small, inexpensive restaurant, lingering over a cup of coffee to observe the constant bustle of the sidewalk through the window. He listened in on the conversations around him, the topics being all about land, emigrants, or the latest rumoured gold discoveries.

'I declare!' a florid-faced man in an embroidered waistcoat turned to include the other patrons in his pronouncement. 'It looks like someone flapped a blanket and the entire nation shook west!' He gazed around, seeking approbation for the remark. With nonforthcoming, he continued. 'Oregon! Santa Fe! California! The Great Salt Flats! Where in jiminy does it end? And up the Missouri by steamboat—to the Nebraska and Dakota Territories! All the way up to Montana!' The speaker stared around the busy room as if daring anyone to gainsay him. 'Why, the good ole USA tilts to one side as we speak!' He attempted to catch Purchase's eye. 'Soon there'll be none left but Injuns and niggers to run the country!' He noisily gurgled his coffee. 'Injuns and niggers!' he repeated, looking around in the hope that someone would take him up.

EXHAUSTED BY THE FRANTIC metropolis, Purchase returned to his room where he sat down on the bed and wrote a letter to his parents back in St Charles.

Dear Pap,

It was just like you said. I got signed up as soon as I arrived. I leave in a few days on a steamboat. The cost of the passage is deducted from my pay. I guess I might get to lay eyes on great-grand pappy's supposed buffalo after all! I only say supposed because I mentioned it to the man that did the hiring and he had no knowledge of it. But then he was an ornery fellow and mightn't have said, even if he did. The train ride was special. I left St Louis at 6 am and arrived in Kansas at nine o'clock that same night! Imagine that! Just outside of Independence we passed by the longest wagon train you ever did see. The conductor swore it was two hundred wagons or more—and all headed for the new territories in the West. It was too late to find a room, so I slept at the station along with half a dozen other men, all ex-army, like me. Kansas City sure is busy! The town is jack-full of people intent on moving out West to homestead or mine for gold. The streets are crowded with wagons, with more arriving by the minute. I never saw so many shops or fancy build-ings. But the town is swarming with bandits, pickpockets, hucksters and flimflammers. One fellow was shamelessly hawking free govt. land—at $1 per acre! I overheard a businessman on the train complain that the land grants were snatched up by speculators and profiteers who 'lease' it to gullible families and defend the charges as arising from improvements to the soil! Another fellow—on his way to California—bragged that large nuggets were lying on the ground just waiting to be picked up. He tried to persuade me to go in with him as a 'partner,' provided I hand over $100 dollars for equipment and general expenses! I brushed him off. 'I'm after gold of a different sort,' I told him. 'Buffalo gold!' He stared like I was a lunatic! There are two other men hired with me. As soon as I lay eyes on great-grandpap's buffalo, I will write and let you know. I hope I find it. Give all my love to mother, and my fond wishes to Sam and Lilly. Tell them their brother is off to the wild frontier to shoot buffaloes. I will try not to get scalped!

Your loving son,
Purchase

HE ATE AN APPLE for supper and then lay down on the narrow bed, closing his eyes even though the June sun had still not set. *I got to ride a train after all, Wins. I am sorry you couldn't come with me. Or you, Abe, or you, Elias. I will shoot a buff for you.*

He turned on his side, too wound up to sleep. '*It's been three years now, son, and you can't seem to stick a job for hardly more than a month. Your mother worries.*' He opened his eyes, hearing footsteps on the stairs. *I'm sorry, Pa. I can't seem to get going again, like I used to.* The footsteps passed along to another room, and he closed his eyes again. His father sighed. '*I guess my Pa was the same—and his before him. At least old man McLennan had that buffalo to occupy his mind.*' He regarded Purchase, a sober look on his face. '*I reckon, son, it's time you found your own buffalo.*'

With two more days to kill, he wandered back to the railroad station the following morning, idly contemplating a ride to the next stop along the line. He found the station full of men carrying rifles, a buzz of excitement in the air. 'What's all the to-do?' he asked one of the men waiting to climb on board.

'This is a sports train,' the man said, his face alive with anticipation. 'All the buff you can shoot!' He climbed the steps to the carriage, stopping to glance back. 'Join us! Buy a ticket!'

A porter approached, carrying a large case. 'How far is the train going?' asked Purchase.

'To the end of the line: Sheridan.'

'How far is that?'

'Sheridan? Four hundred and five miles.'

'Can I make it there and back by tomorrow?'

'Sheridan? Not a chance. But there's a Kansas City express that leaves Hays City every day at seven o'clock sharp. That will have you back here by nightfall.' He shook his head as Purchase made to ask another question. 'I got to put this on board! Tickets over there,' he said, nodding toward a wicket.

Making his way to the office, Purchase stopped before a large, colourful poster. *Grand Sport! Take the Union Pacific and Shoot All the Buffalo You Please! Guaranteed Herds to Shoot!*

Ten minutes later, ticket in hand, he boarded the train. The carriage was crowded, but he found a spare seat alongside a man balancing a rifle between his knees.

'Name's Smith, Rebus Smith,' said the man, offering his hand.

'Pleased to meet you, Mr Smith. McLennan. Purchase McLennan.'

'Call me Rebus. Is this your first shoot, Mr McLennan?'

'Please, Purchase. Shoot?'

'Buffalo shoot. The Kansas plains are pure buffalo range all the way to the Rocky Mountains. Better than six hundred miles of nothing but buff far as the eye can see.'

Purchase made a rueful face. 'Wish I had time to go fetch my rifle.'

'Why, never mind. The porter will hand out guns as soon as we sight the herds.' Noting Purchase's look of surprise, Smith chuckled. 'The railroad keeps guns for shooting—buff or Indians, no difference.'

'You've done this before?'

'Three times.' Smith patted his rifle. 'It's powerful fun.'

'That looks a fine weapon.'

'It is!' Beaming, Smith held up the rifle for Purchase to observe. 'Henry repeater. Sixteen shots.' Patting the stock, he put the rifle back between his knees.

'Are the Indians likely to cause trouble?'

Smith blew his nose into a large handkerchief. 'Ever since Sand Creek, the Cheyenne have been het up. They hate the railroad worse than the devil himself.'

'Sand Creek?'

'Some soldier boys shot up a Cheyenne camp.'

A man on the seat in front turned to join in. 'The savages have been scalping and murdering all across the plains. It's high time the government dealt with the vermin once and for all.'

'High time,' the man's seatmate agreed.

The whistle blew and the train slowly chugged forward to cheers from the packed carriage.

Smith pulled a flask from out of his pocket and took a slug before offering it to Purchase. 'Whisky?'

He took a drink to be polite. The other man put the flask back in his pocket and pulled his hat over his eyes. 'Nothing to see for a while,' he said. 'Wake me up if we run into Injuns.'

WITHIN THE QUARTER HOUR, they had left the city buildings behind. The Kansas landscape was flat and dotted with farms and homesteads. After another hour, they left these behind, also, as the cultivated pastures gave way to mile after mile of treeless, featureless plain. The day was hot and the air inside the carriage stifling in spite of the open windows.

Fifty miles outside Kansas City, his eye was caught by what appeared to be piles of snow gleaming on the arid, short-grass plain. Screwing up his eyes he strained to make out the nature of the mounds.

'Bones,' said Smith, opening his eyes and following his gaze. 'From buff taken in winter and stripped for hides.'

The stripped bones were scattered over the prairie in such plentiful abundance they resembled a snowfield. 'That's a lot of buffalo.'

Smith laughed. 'Buff are like gnats—there's no end of them!'

Closing his eyes, Purchase dozed off, doing his best to ignore the hard seat. He awoke to find passengers getting up to close the train windows. At the same time a powerful, odorous stench hit his nostrils. 'Petrify!' He put a hand over his nose. Through the window, he saw piles of decayed carcasses lining the trackside. Most had been stripped of flesh and fur, but enough rotted meat remained to send up a putrid, overpowering stink that, even inside the carriage, made his eyes water.

Sitting up, Smith took a snuff box from his pocket and put a pinch in his nose. 'It blocks the stench,' he said, offering the box.

'I'll pass, thank you.'

'Suit yourself. But the stench does get mighty tiresome.'

Purchase heard exclamations of disgust from the rest of the carriage as men pulled out neckerchiefs to cover their noses or drank whisky to drown the stink. He saw two women clasp perfumed handkerchiefs to their faces as the train rolled on past the rotted carcasses.

'What happened to them?' he asked.

'Shot from the train most likely—or by hunters to feed the graders. They take the best bits and leave the rest to the buzzards.'

Lulled by the drowsy heat, the creaking sway of the carriage, and motion of the wheels, Purchase dozed off again, in spite of the putrid stench.

HE AWOKE TO A bustle of excitement in the carriage. Men were standing at the windows, peering out. There was a chorus of eager voices and the snap of hammers as rifles were cocked. The conductor passed through the carriage carrying an armful of rifles. 'Carbines for use!' he called out, swaying with the motion of the train. 'Courtesy of the Union Pacific!'

'Here!' Smith beckoned the man. 'Help yourself, partner,' he said to Purchase.

The conductor leaned forward and allowed Purchase to take a Sharps carbine from the pile. 'Cartridges in my pocket!' he said.

Smith obligingly retrieved a box and handed it to him.

Getting to his feet, Smith claimed the window space next to their seat. 'There they are!'

Joining his companion, Purchase caught sight of a buffalo herd about a half-mile distant. An overeager shooter fired at the animals, drawing a scornful glance from Smith. 'Durn copperhead!'

The train whistle blasted as they passed more and more buffalo. Soon, they were immersed in a great mass of the teeming beasts. Above the clatter of the iron wheels and the rhythmic clank of the pistons came a tremendous rumbling bellow that rolled and shook like the noise of distant thunder. Purchase gazed out the window, astounded at their number. It seemed to him that the abundance was so great that it dimmed the light within the carriage.

'They're like pigeons!' a man whooped.

'More like locusts!' claimed another. 'I never saw so much of anything!'

A rattle of gunfire sounded from inside the carriage as the eager passengers crowded the windows, firing indiscriminately into the bellowing, grunting herd who stood, as if stupefied, watching this strange, noisy creature in their midst. He felt the train slow as the driver obligingly cut power for the benefit of the shooters. Rifle barrels poked through the windows almost within touching distance of the buffalo. He saw the two women aiming rifles, their faces bright with excitement as they shot into the prodigious tide. Spooked by the train, the nearer buffalo broke into a run, their great, woolly heads bobbing and dipping above the pounding hooves as they galloped alongside the tracks.

'Hell and damnation!' A man standing at the next window swore, ducking as he did so. A hapless shooter had discharged his gun inside the carriage, the shot ricocheting off the woodwork. The shooter, red-faced, mumbled apologies as glares and curses were directed his way.

'Come with me!' Smith tugged him by the arm. 'If we stay here, we are in danger of getting shot!'

Purchase followed his new companion through the carriage to the connecting platform. That, too, was crowded with shooters, the men boasting and arguing over kills. The train had now slowed to less than ten miles per hour as the great torrent of buffalo surged alongside.

Smith climbed up on the platform rail to reach the roof. Purchase followed, surprised to find the top crowded with men lying down to shoot. The other carriage roofs were similarly occupied, dozens of men firing from atop each carriage. Loading the Sharps, he found space between Smith and another man.

Eager for his first kill, he sighted on the animals. It took him a moment to pick a target from the jostling multitude, the heaving bodies so closely crowded together as to defy choice. Targeting a large, thundering bull, he fired. The shot struck home, along with a dozen other shots from those around him. The animal continued running as blood issued from its nostrils. A moment later, it stumbled and disappeared beneath the frantic hooves of its companions. He switched to another animal, striking it on the hump.

He felt the carriage bounce as a buffalo slipped and was crushed beneath the wheels. The driver gave several furious blasts of the steam whistle as the brakemen rushed to apply the brakes. The train shuddered to a halt to avoid a collision with a solid mass of buffalo that swarmed across the tracks just ahead. The air was full of dust through which sounded the rumbling thunder of the herd—the noise punctuated by the sharp crack of rifles. He felt the carriage beneath him sway dangerously as the brown tide washed up against it. Smith shouted an explanation while reloading. 'The driver won't go—he won't risk overturning the train!'

The day wore on as the stupendous herd engulfed the train on all sides, rocking the carriages with the weight of their number and blocking the tracks for a mile ahead. The rifle barrel was red-hot from firing. He got up and walked along the top of the carriages to allow it to cool down. He made his way past the recumbent, shooting men, marvelling at the number of buffalo browning the plain as far as the eye could see. The gunfire that poured into the herd from all along the six-carriage train seemed no more than a minor irritant to the swarming multitudes. Hundreds of cows, bulls, and calves lay dead or fatally wounded alongside the tracks—their companions steering around or jumping across the bodies with no more notice than if they were a shrub or some other natural obstacle.

THE EARLIER WHOOPS OF excitement had stopped as the slaughter continued, and boredom set in. The passengers mechanically reloaded and fired, stopping only to take food or drink or to allow their guns to cool. Walking back along the carriage roof he rejoined Smith, where the latter had taken a moment to rest and drink whisky. 'I got forty, at least!' said Smith, his face red from the sun and the exertion of shooting. 'Although,' he conceded, 'it's hard to know if I or the next man got in the killing shot.' Taking off his hat, he brushed an arm across his brow. ''Tis thirsty work!'

'When will the train get moving again?'

'Whenever the herd permits. We can't be more than ten miles from Hays. Are you stopping there?'

'Yes. I have to catch the express back tomorrow.'

'Then sleep on the platform to save money. Half these knuckleheads will be going back with you now that they've had their fill of buffalo.'

'I've used up all my bullets.'

'Ask the conductor for more. And don't let him charge you. If he tries, remind him it's included in the price of the ticket.'

The sun was starting to set as he fired through the second box of bullets, reckoning up his tally at fifty hits, although how many buffalo were actually brought down as a result of the shots he could not say. Eventually, after being stranded for several hours, the train put on steam and slowly got underway again. The shooters now crowded to the far side of the carriage, firing continuously as the last of the buffalo streamed off into the distance.

Before climbing down, he looked back at the buffalo carcasses dotting the plain alongside the tracks. 'Will they use any for meat—or their hides?' he asked.

'Summer hides ain't worth a spit. And the meat is too much trouble. Besides, you can buy a fine buffalo steak for a few cents at any stop along the line.'

'We sure killed us a few.'

'Now you see where the stink comes from! And think—you may well get to do the same again on the way back!'

4

The Annabelle

SHORTLY BEFORE DAWN, HE made his way through the spring darkness to the fur company office. A lamp burned through the window. He opened the door to find Simkins leaned back in a chair drinking a cup of coffee. Two other men—both wearing forage caps—sat on the bare floor, their backs against the wall. They appeared to have been bickering but fell silent as he stepped inside.

'Well-a-day! The third of our party arrives!' Simkins swilled a mouthful of coffee. 'I guessed you might scamper on back to St Louis—with your railroad man.' He picked at a tooth and examined his fingernail. 'Purchase McLennan, meet Mr Hester. Mr Hester, and …' Frowning, he reinserted the finger into his mouth, studying the second man. 'Mr Huckstep, Esquire!'

The men, about the same age as himself, stood up to offer handshakes. 'Jubal Hester,' said the first. 'Missouri.' He was dressed in a faded army jacket and canvas trousers. He had taken off his cap and his long hair fell about his shoulders. He had a devil-may-care look about him and shook Purchase's hand with a strong and confident grip.

'Cory Huckstep,' said the second. 'Kansas.' He was dressed in a wool jacket and fustian trousers. He was unshaven and looked to one side as he shook hands.

'Purchase McLennan. Missouri,' Purchase said, introducing himself. 'St Charles,' he added as Jubal made to open his mouth.

'Which regiment?'

'The Fifty-Sixth Penn. I joined up in Philly,' he said in response to Jubal's questioning look.

Jubal nodded. 'Fourth Missouri.' He directed a scornful look at his companion. 'And don't stand for his guff. A dodger—in spite of the cap.'

Huckstep bristled. ''Tweren't my war!'

'Then whose war was it?'

'Now then, boys.' Simkins, who had observed the introductions with a jaundiced eye, set down the coffee cup. 'Save your sass for the buffalo—or the Injuns.' He leaned the chair back against the wall. 'Mr Hester here is a riverboat man,' he said.

'Was,' corrected the other. 'I had hoped to be a pilot—afore the war,' he explained to Purchase. 'I made a few dozen trips up and down the river as a rooster.'

'That be "deckhand" in polite parlance,' said Simkins. He took out a pocket watch which he consulted. 'Cometh the hour!' Standing up he placed a crumpled felt hat on his head. 'All right, gentlemen. Let's find that steamer.'

Purchase's new companions resumed their bickering as they made their way through the streets to the riverfront. 'I ain't to be blasted for refusing to be shot at on behalf of some nap-head I ain't even met!' Huckstep protested.

'Then join the Rebs, why didn't you!'

'Same thing!'

Despite the early hour, the riverfront was crowded with people and livestock. A half-dozen stern-wheelers sat sideways to the levee, each one bustling with activity. Shouts and whistles filled the air as trunks and crates were carried on board amid a throng of embarking or disembarking passengers. Thousands of kegs and staved barrels stood in large squares along the landing. Drays and carts loaded with baggage and freight lumbered up and down the levee, the drivers shouting out, 'Way!' Mates supervised the loading, standing at the top of the long gangways, their profanity-laced voices bellowing above the noise. Sweating Black roustabouts, stripped to the waist, carried boxes and trunks up the gangways while being subjected to a constant stream of abuse from the bullying mates.

'Shoulder the crate you crab-faced, shovel-necked, nap-headed spawn of Lucifer!' a mate bawled furiously from the deck of a steamer as a line of roustabouts carried freight up the gangway.

The roustabout thus addressed stopped to shift the crate from his arms to his back, holding up the line as he did so. The mate, a gimlet-eyed tyrant in a sweat-stained waistcoat, threw up his arms in despair. 'Help me, Mother!' he implored, looking upward with a tragic expression on his face. 'Have pity on me that is burdened—nay, inflicted, with the doltish sons of Africa, the sea-scum boil, the shamb—' He broke off, a look of incredulity on his face as another man put down his load and helped his companion transfer the crate to his back. 'By the seven gates of Hell! Did I give leave for a tea party?' His tirade was halted by the approach along the deck of a tall figure wearing a black, peaked cap on his head. 'Make way for the captain! Stand aside, you jabbering apes! Aside, I say!'

They continued past two more boats, Simkins forging a path through the crowded levee. 'Here's your boat, boys. The *Annabelle*.' He stopped in front of a stern-wheel packet that sat between two other steamers.

The *Annabelle* loomed larger than its berth companions—being one hundred seventy feet long and thirty feet wide. Two tall, cylindrical chimneys protruded from its upper deck, smoke wisping up from the funnels. It was drawn up, bow-first, to the levee. Loading stages were extended either side of its spoonbill bow. A queue of passengers—men, women, and children, the men burdened with trunks, boxes, and pieces of furniture—stood in line, awaiting the signal to board. The open main deck was already jam-packed with crates, kegs, hundreds of barrels of crop seed, and bundles of cordwood. Cows, goats, and hogs were penned in small enclosures between the piles of freight. A team of mules was driven up one of the stages, the passengers secondary to the freight and livestock. Up on the boiler deck, several well-heeled passengers leaned against the rails to gaze down at the lively scenes below.

'You'd best buy food if you plan on eating.' Simkins pointed to where people clustered around a small shack on the edge of the landing. 'Go ahead,' he said, 'while I purchase the tickets.' With that, he disappeared into the busy throng in search of a clerk.

'How in blazes are we supposed to squeeze in?' Huckstep stared, open-mouthed, at the line of emigrants. Two dozen blue-clad soldiers lounged in a separate line.

'They're headed west to start new lives,' put in a man standing nearby. 'They'll be getting off at points along the way.'

They purchased food from the stall—Purchase buying bologna sausage, dried herring, and crackers, which he stowed in his rucksack. On returning to the line, they found Simkins waiting, tickets in hand. 'You each owe the company nine dollars,' he said, distributing the tickets.

They took their place in line behind a large family of Russian émigrés, the men and boys dressed in neat brown shirts and jackets, the women and girls in woollen smocks and aprons. The grandmother sat on a trunk peeling slices from an apple and handing the pieces out to the children while gossiping nonstop in her native Russian.

Huckstep groaned in frustration. 'By the time we board, the only space will be with the hogs!'

'Best not to stand by the guards,' advised Simkins. 'Any knock will send you over the side. Hang on to your money,' he said, his jaws working around a plug of tobacco. 'There'll be thieves, pickpockets, cutthroats, card sharps and God knows what other specimens on board.'

'How long will it take?' asked Purchase.

'Depends. One month, maybe two if the boat gets stuck on a sandbar or strikes a snag, or Indians attack or the boilers blow.'

'Is that all?' Huckstep grimaced.

'Hell no!' Simkins spat a gob of tobacco juice. 'There's cholera, pox, lice, brawls, drownings, storms, collisions, breakdowns, frisky livestock, fits, and general sinkage. And that's just the boat. The camp is less pleasant.' He chawed the tobacco, savouring the recitation. 'Bon voyage!' With that, he turned on his heels and left.

'He might have told us all that afore we signed up!' Huckstep glared after the agent.

'Is he right?' Purchase looked to Jubal for confirmation.

'Yes and no. Heck, we could hit another boat and sink or just as well go smooth as icing all the way up to Fort Buffalo.'

'Fort Buffalo?'

Jubal looked surprised. 'The name of the camp. Simkins didn't tell you?'

'I don't think he mentioned it.'

'The army built a fort there to scare off the Indians.'

'Are they peaceful?'

'The army? Heck no!' retorted Jubal, drawing a grin from Purchase.

Huckstep eyed Jubal, a worried frown on his face. 'I was told the Injuns were friendly.'

'Who by—Simkins?' Jubal sighed in mock exasperation. 'He didn't want to scare you off clear back to Wichita.'

'I ain't from Wichita!'

'Never said you were!'

A WHISTLE BLEW AND slowly the line of passengers began to move forward. When it came their turn to board, they found themselves engulfed in a mob of jostling men and women, each one pushing to find space on the crowded deck.

'Over here!' Making liberal use of his elbows, Jubal led the way to a space beside a stack of crates and boxes standing higher than a man. 'These are marked for Fort Benton, at the top of the river. They'll shelter us from wind and rain.' He set down his rucksack and claimed the space.

Purchase squeezed into the space, as did Huckstep, the latter still complaining at the crowded deck. 'Blamed if we don't sink afore we set off!'

Moving a large trunk, they sealed off the space as best they could. 'Hey!' Purchase pointed to the tags on a nearby pile of crates. 'Fort Buffalo,' was inked on each of the tags. 'These must be the supplies Mr Simkins was waiting on.'

'A good omen!' declared Jubal, pleased at the coincidence.

Thus settled, they took the time to observe their fellow passengers. Men and women, many of the latter with small children in their arms, pushed through the congested deck, struggling to find a free space amid the cargo. Those who had boarded earlier had set up small refuges which, like Purchase and his companions, they attempted to protect using whatever baggage or possessions they had taken on board. Women nursed infants or sat alongside crying children as their husbands attempted to secure their trunks and boxes. Several roustabouts shoved through, shouting to make room for the passage of yet more cargo.

'Purchase! Did you hear me?' Jubal was trying to get his attention.

'What is it?'

'The rooster said we were carrying better than two hundred tons of freight. God knows how much extra in passengers and baggage.'

'Did you mean it—about the Indians?' he asked, Huckstep being out of earshot.

Jubal shrugged. 'Blazes if I know. Sometimes they are sociable, other times standoffish. Ever since that Fetterman business they've been ornery.'

Purchase eyed his companion curiously. 'Why are you headed upriver to shoot buff—if you don't mind me asking? The railway is paying good wages right here in Kansas.'

'I might ask you the same.'

'I have reason.'

'So do I—two of 'em. One with a busted jaw.'

'And Huckstep?' Purchase nodded toward their companion, who was gawking at a party of men dressed in stove hats, who were loudly haranguing the boat's clerk.

Jubal cast a contemptuous glance at the other man. 'I don't doubt but that he is one step ahead of the law. He probably figures to hide out until whatever trouble he's in is forgotten about.'

'You think so?'

'I'd bet a dollar on it. The blowhard has lied about the war and everything else. Hell, it wouldn't surprise me if he was a bushwhacker.'

As the lingering dawn gave way to full light, the landing stages were swung on board and the pilot gave a long blast on the steam whistle. Purchase felt the deck tremble as the engines thrummed. A bell clanged and the paddle wheels thrashed into motion, backpaddling them away from the landing. The whistle sounded several, drawn out *whooos*. The paddles reversed direction and they slowly started upriver, thick black smoke belching from the stacks.

THE NOVELTY OF HIS first ride aboard a steamboat quickly wore off as the *Annabelle* proceeded, the boat reaching five miles per hour at times. Barely able to stretch out due to the lack of space, he mostly sat with his knees drawn up, getting to know his new companions as the deck hummed beneath him. The noise of the boilers and the smell of smoke added to the stink of sweat and odorous fragrances emitted from the crowded men and women. Innately distrustful of Huckstep—who intimated, *sotto voce* when Jubal dozed off, that he had in fact been an 'agent for Union intelligence'—he deliberately struck up a conversation with a heavily-bearded farmer headed for the frontier. 'Where to?' he asked.

'Where the soil is good, and the land is free,' the farmer answered. 'The Nebraska Territory.'

'Just you and your family?' He asked, glancing at a careworn woman and three young children seated behind the man.

'My family and a dozen others!' The man gestured proudly toward the mountains of freight. 'We got timber, nails, axes, sledges, and saws to beat the band. Hogs, too, and three cows—which we share. Plenty of crop seed, too. By winter, we aim to be set up with houses and a barn.'

'Good luck to you,' said Purchase, and pulled his hat down over his eyes as a signal he was about to doze off. Despite this signalling, Huckstep nudged his foot to indicate a comely young woman as she struggled to navigate the deck in search of someone.

'You lost, miss?' Huckstep called out. 'Mebbe I can help?' He winked at Purchase, a leer on his thin, stubbled face.

When he woke again, they were in the middle of a broad stretch of river. A relative hush had fallen over the deck as the men and women settled into the voyage, eating or chatting as the children slept and the steamer ploughed ahead against the current. At one point, he heard a murmur from those around him and glanced toward a clearing on the shore. A number of tiny wooden crosses decorated the grass.

'Cholera,' a man beside him said, and shuddered.

Toward noon, a commotion arose, and three or four angry men pushed through the deck toward the rails, a struggling man held firmly in their grasp. 'He interfered with a woman!' one of the abductors said out loud. Reaching the rails, they unceremoniously tossed the shouting, cursing fellow overboard.

'Good riddance!' they jeered as he flailed frantically in the river.

'He can't swim!'

'Now would be a good time to learn!'

Purchase watched as the man gasped and struggled to keep afloat. An arm was raised despairingly as the fellow sank beneath the murky flow, failing to come up again.

'Serves him right,' said Jubal beside him.

The sun was hot and the river choppy—the shore a half mile distant on either side. Sandbars dotted the broad channel as branches, logs—and a dead cow—floated past. A few miles from Atchison, they passed a half-sunken steamer lying abandoned against the shore.

'Her boilers blew,' a voice said. 'Durn killed half the passengers!'

They put in at a dozen towns, small and large, along the way. At each one, the *Annabelle* beached, bow-first, onto the levees to take on or discharge passengers and transfer volumes of cargo and freight. Each landing was advertised by long blasts on the three-toned steam whistle. 'Every pilot has his own tune,' said Jubal. 'You can shut your eyes and know the boat by the sound.'

The boiler deck passengers kept mainly to themselves, gazing down at the crowded main deck or standing at the rail to observe the scenery. At one stop, a politician came on board, holding office on the upper deck until disembarking at the next town. He shook hands effusively before making his way down the gangway, greeting and backslapping all and sundry. 'Remember to vote Sherman, boys!'

THEY ENTERED UPON A stretch of open country, the passing shoreline mostly undistinguished save for mile upon mile of cut tree trunks. Purchase remarked upon the fact to Jubal.

'They've all been chopped down for fuel. You won't see any trees again until we are far upriver. The boats gobble up trees everywhere they go.'

'Then where will we get more fuel? Unless,' Purchase motioned to the stacks of cordwood, 'These are intended to last us all the way?'

Jubal laughed. 'They won't take us as far as St Joseph! She'll easily burn through fifty cords a day.'

'How many trees is that?'

Jubal shrugged. 'I guess mebbe eighty or a hundred trees a day?'

Purchase whistled. 'Just for one boat? No wonder the banks are bare. Where does the wood come from?'

'Woodlots. You'll soon see.'

And see he did, as they put in to shore every ten or twelve miles to collect cordwood at the many woodlots along the river. Following Jubal's lead, he went ashore with the wooders, helping to carry as many as thirty cords at a time back on board. 'This will earn us some scraps from the cook,' panted Jubal. He flashed a contemptuous look at where Huckstep remained resolutely on board. 'Durn two-bit shirker!'

Four days out from Kansas City, they put in at Council Bluffs, on the east side of the river. The levee and nearby flats were crowded with hundreds of ox-drawn wagons. He watched as a large party disembarked. The women wore long, pastel dresses, their hair combed up on their heads. The men wore broad-brimmed straw hats and white shirts under sober black homespun.

'Mormons,' said Jubal, coming to join him. 'Bound for the Salt Lakes.'

'What will they do there?' he asked, gazing at a young woman who was assisted by her husband as she stepped across a wagon tongue.

'Worship. It's said they are congregating there to build a great temple.'

'All of them?' Purchase nodded to indicate the abundance of wagons gathered on the flats.

'Not all, friend.'

They turned to see one of the boiler deck passengers standing behind them, a cigar in his mouth as he regarded the activity on the landing. He blew out a stream of smoke. 'Pardon the interruption, gentlemen, but I happen to know the area well. There are trails here that run to Santa Fe, California, and Oregon, as well as to Salt Lake. The wagons will take the Platte River Road, along with a hundred other trains. My, but she is winsome,' he said, his gaze shifting to the young woman. Just then a female voice hollered down from the boiler deck and the man coughed. 'Mother calls!' he said, hastening away in response.

'What are you two gawking at?' Huckstep joined them at the rail. 'Whoo-ee!' he exclaimed as his eye fell on the same Mormon girl—now in animated conversation with a group of women.

'She's not for the likes of you, Cory. She's a pious believer.'

'Ha! As if I care a bent nickel for a fish-eyed Mormon. They say they do blood sacrifices and worship idols.'

'Why then, I take it back. She may be of your sort after all.'

As more passengers and freight were taken aboard, they were given leave to go ashore to purchase food from shops in the town. They stocked up on apples, sausages, bread, and dried fish before making their way back through the busy streets. To Purchase's annoyance, they were bailed up on every corner by hucksters, each one hawking 'prized' land claims, 'guaranteed' gold options, or cheap passage out west—the vendors invariably expressing outrage as their 'one-in-a-million bargains' were rebuffed.

'Some folk—why you cain't beat opportunity into them!' A whiskery-cheeked man snorted in disgust as Jubal rudely brushed off his insistent overtures. 'Why, I guess I'll jest sip on champagne and smoke cigars while you chowderheads dig for turnips!'

Angered at the man's tone, Jubal made to turn back, 'Why, and I guess I'll jest fix it so you don't sip nothing 'cepting your own bile!'

'Give him what for! Shut his yap!' Huckstep hooted with glee, egging on his irate companion.

Purchase grabbed his arm. 'Leave it be, Jubal. We have a boat to catch.'

They continued along the busy street as the indignant huckster vented his spleen. 'Pinheads! Shit lickers! Banjo-faced claim-jumps!'

BORED BY THE INCESSANT talk of land grants and mining digs, Purchase rarely indulged in conversation with his fellow deck passengers, preferring to observe the crew as they operated the boat. The Negro roustabouts sang out and hollered to one another as they went about their duties—rolling their eyes or laughing at the profane tongue-lashings unleashed by the hectoring mates. The careless ways and strutting bravado displayed by the roustabouts frequently resulted in an exchange of insults as they worked alongside each other, one man belittling the other in a series of taunts and rolling invectives that finely categorised his companion in terms of parentage, ancestry, social standing, or lack of success with the fairer sex. These contests, for such they were, invariably ended with one or other of the combatants bursting into laughter at some unanswerable volley. The quick-fire exchanges entertained Purchase as he laughed at the dexterous wit and verbal artillery employed on either side.

He was lounging by the guardrails when a bellicose passenger took exception to the 'insolent' manner of a deckhand.

'For pity's sake, shut that tuneless, spine-curdling, wit-befouling screech!' The man objected as a Black rooster, known for his singsong chants and hollers, warbled his way down the deck.

Next moment, the Negro lay stretched out on the deck, felled by a tremendous blow from the outraged passenger. A mate had witnessed the event and taking umbrage at this high-handed infringement upon his prerogative, promptly launched himself at the assailant. The two rolled about the deck, kicking and punching, as the onlookers hastily scrambled to give space. The melee ended with the Negro being unceremoniously kicked off the boat at the next stop.

In contrast to the cheerful wit of the roustabouts, the three dozen army recruits on board proved a constant and never-ending source of irritation. An undisciplined, rowdy bunch, hardly yet able to grow a whisker between them, they were governed by men scarcely older and more experienced than themselves. Whenever the opportunity arose, the soldiers indulged in whisky, becoming at times so drunk they were unable to stand. The loutish behaviour incensed their commanding officer, a gruff veteran of Bull Run where he had been shot through the arm so badly he almost lost the appendage.

'I was posted to command this godforsaken rabble for my sins,' he said, having spotted Purchase as ex-Union.

The major had come down from the upper deck to denounce some offensively uncouth behaviour on the part of his charges. Having offered profuse apologies to the offended passengers and after roundly and publicly chastising the culprits, he paused at the foot of the boiler stairs to reminisce about the war in between puffs of a cigar.

'Which regiment were you with, son?' The major regarded Purchase through a cloud of smoke.

'The Fifty-Sixth Penn.'

'Which division?'

'First, Second Brigade.'

The major's eyes widened. 'Cutler's brigade!'

'Did you know him?'

'By reputation only. You boys have a hard time of it?'

'We gave as good as we got.'

The major nodded, his face grave. 'No doubt,' he said. 'No doubt.' He made to ascend the stairs. 'Pity those sons of bitches escaped the war,' he said, frowning and shaking his head as howls of laughter greeted some fresh tomfoolery farther along the deck.

The recruits were inveterate and profane gamblers, their loud whoops and caws frequently disturbing the peace of the deck. When tired of spinning coins or turning cards, they loved to wager on arm wrestling—the contests frequently erupting into quarrels. One humid evening, the boat captain himself had to intervene when an arm-wrestling contest between the troopers and some passengers erupted into a mass brawl.

Huckstep snickered as he watched the latest incident from a safe distance. 'A silver dollar that big farmer lays out the sergeant!'

'Stand down, dammit!' The major roared down from the boiler deck as more combatants rushed to join the fray.

The warring parties withdrew, threatening and insulting one another as the cursing mates and a furious lieutenant forcibly separated them. 'Save your darn pep for the Injuns!'

THEIR STEADY PROGRESS UPRIVER was continuously tested by the notoriously fickle Missouri and its thousand and one dangers. It seemed as though they passed a wrecked steamboat every mile or so, Purchase losing count at over thirty. 'Blown boilers most of them, snags and rocks the others,' explained Jubal. 'Lots of drownings and scaldings.'

One morning, they had barely got underway in the dawn darkness when the boat hit a snag, the collision jarring enough to make Purchase grab for a rail. The whistle blew and bells jangled as deckhands ran forward to examine the damage. The pilot was called down for consultation as the passengers waited anxiously for news. After a quarter-hour, the whistle blasted, and they got underway again to a collective sigh of relief.

'It ain't a proper voyage unless we hit a snag,' assured Jubal. 'It's half the fun of running the river.'

The ever-shifting channels and varying water levels posed additional hazards as the boat entered a series of long, looping bends. A crewman was posted at the bow to call out the depth as the pilot searched for a channel that had been in one spot on the previous voyage but had now shifted to another. At times, the wheel barely turned as the pilot sent men out in a small boat to scout the water for snags or sawyers. Twice the passengers were disembarked to lighten the boat as it attempted to crawl or 'grasshopper' over sandbars.

Standing on the shore, Purchase watched as the two long spars at the bow of the boat were lowered into the mud. A wire cable ran back to the steam-powered capstan. As the cable was winched tight, the angled spars would rise up erect, the cable inching the boat forward a few feet at a time. Meanwhile, the paddle wheel churned furiously to suck sand and water under the boat and thus create a shallow draught for the hull.

As the boat cleared the bar, Purchase overheard a man remark to his companion to be sure to board quickly once the stages were lowered. 'Else the captain may leave us behind.'

'You jest?' said his companion.

'Not a bit! Two years ago we passed a bunch of people hollering and waving on shore. The previous boat had abandoned them there. The pilot was afraid to stop once he had gained deeper water.'

'And what happened—did you pick them up?'

'Do you think the pilot would risk getting stuck himself?'

He repeated the anecdote to Jubal, who nodded soberly. 'I have heard the same story.'

One afternoon, they put into shore as a tremendous thunderstorm shook the boat and roiled the murky waters. The rain lashed down for an hour, soaking the deck and cooling the air to such a degree Purchase put on his canvas duster to keep warm. He sat in the lee of the boiler deck, his arms wrapped around his body as he stared at the sheeting rain. And through the rain and gloom, he fancied he glimpsed, waiting for him somewhere out on the northern plains, the looming figure of the fabled rock buffalo.

5

The Missouri

OUR DAYS AFTER LEAVING Council Bluffs, a series of repeated whistle blasts drew cheers from the crew.

'What's the commotion?' he asked Jubal, who had joined in the cheers.

Jubal pointed ahead to where a stretch of lighter-coloured water showed where yet another river branched into the Missouri. 'That's the Big Sioux. It marks the beginning of the upper river. From here on in is just grass, buffalo, and Indians.'

'You have been here before?'

'Only to this point, never beyond.'

'And where is this point, exactly?'

'We are now in the Dakota Territory.'

'Then we must be near the camp?'

Jubal chuckled. 'Not halfway!'

They remained companionably silent for a few minutes, gazing at the churning flood as it flowed beneath the boat. He glanced at Jubal, liking the man's open, affable air. 'Do you know much about the buffalo camp?'

'Only what I heard from the skinners and such coming back down the river.'

'Did they happen to mention a rock buffalo?'

'A what?' Jubal frowned as if he had misheard the question.

'A rock—stone—figure of a buffalo, I guess you'd say.'

'Where?' Jubal looked mystified at the notion.

'I don't know, exactly,' Purchase admitted. 'But it's somewhere to the northwest of a river called the Heart. Have you heard of such a stream?'

Jubal eyed him to make sure he wasn't joking. 'No, but there are more rivers up ahead than you can shake a stick at. You could ask the pilot, he would know for sure. But how do you know of it—since you've never been to the territories?'

'My great-grandpappy was one of the first white men in this country, a long time ago. It was passed down that he carved a giant stone buffalo somewhere out on the open prairie.'

'So that's what fetches you here!' Jubal regarded him for a moment, a look of intense curiosity on his face. 'Why?' he asked.

'Why what?'

'Why did your great-grandpa carve himself a buffalo?'

'No one knows.' A little embarrassed under his companion's gaze, Purchase shrugged. 'It's a family legend,' he added, 'passed down. But my pap swears it's true.'

'He has seen it?'

'No. His pa told him.'

'Then he had seen it?'

'Yes. He helped carve it in his youth.'

To his considerable relief, Jubal did not scoff at the account, as he had feared, but simply looked out over the river. 'Well,' he said, after a pause. 'I sure would like to see such a thing.'

THE PASSING COUNTRY WAS now exceedingly wild. Occasionally they passed a small hamlet or trading post, the occupants coming outside to wave at the pilot's ostentatious blast on the whistle. Purchase kept a close eye on the miles of grassy bluffs, surprised not to see any buffalo. Where are they? he wondered.

Most of the emigrant families had disembarked downstream, although a few stayed on board, willing to risk everything to farm in wild Indian country farther upriver. The other passengers consisted of the soldiers or miners en route to Fort Benton. They seemed familiar with the passage and passed the time by congregating on the hurricane deck to shoot at any wildlife spotted along the bank.

After traversing a relatively straight and flat portion of the river, they embarked on a series of horseshoe bends that snaked in great loops through the grasslands. 'My, but he can read,' praised Jubal, professing admiration for the skill of the pilot in finding slack water when rounding the bends or in searching out the shifting, deep-water channels. 'The levels ain't nothing, though,' he said. 'What he worries about day and night are sawyers. They will hole a boat quicker than a fart.'

The occasional sunken vessel they encountered, the decks shimmering through the water, was a grim reminder of the dangers of overconfidence or incautious haste in the face of such hazards.

High winds were yet another threat. Despite the pilot's skill at negotiating such gales, they beached twice within the span of three days. The experienced deckhands accepted such incidents with resigned shakes of the head. 'We done run aground same place last year,' said one. 'The devil hisself must lure boats up onto the bank.'

He had just awoken from a nap when the bells began to clang furiously as the boat turned sharply for shore. 'What is it?' he asked.

For answer, Jubal—who had jumped to his feet—pointed to a dark cloud rapidly approaching from the northwest. 'Sandstorm! The pilot is taking us to shelter.' They had barely gained the protection of a high bank when they were engulfed by the blinding sand. The sky darkened and the boat shook as if from a storm of hail. In spite of taking shelter and binding a neckerchief around his face, Purchase tasted the stinging grit on his tongue as the wind-whipped sand covered the deck in a fine layer.

They lay to for the night as the storm blew itself out. They resumed at 4 am in the morning, the pilot anxious to make up time. 'I got sand every-where!' complained Huckstep, scratching at his body through his shirt. 'When will we get to the consarned camp? Tell me, when?'

YELLS AND GUNSHOTS ERUPTED from the port side. Hurrying to investigate, he saw four buffalo swimming alongside the boat. The miners poured shot after shot into the creatures before dropping ropes and hauling two on board. That night and for the next two nights all were invited to partake freely in a sumptuous roast as the cook butchered and cooked the flavoursome meat. Purchase ate hungrily, heartily sick of the usual fare of salt pork and navy biscuits—purchased from the same cook ever since they left the settlements behind.

Twenty miles south of the Niobara River, they hit upon a stretch of water full of shallows, rapids, sandbars, and snags. Coming to a halt, the boat was forced to 'walk' over a long sandbar to find sufficient water. The tiresome process aggravated the irascible major to such an extent that he took out his pistol and fired wildly at every passing bird. Finally, after a slow, tortuous navigation, they encountered deeper water and picked up speed again, the stacks belching out thick black smoke.

The following day, the whistle blew as the pilot alerted passengers and crew to thousands of buffalo streaming over the grassy bluffs. Beside Purchase, Huckstep whooped and aimed an imaginary rifle. 'There goes our meal ticket!'

The officers and a few upper deck passengers gathered on the hurricane deck, rifles in hand, to take advantage of the bounty. Purchase joined them at the invitation of the major. The pilot obligingly steered closer to shore to enable them to blast away at the herd. He emptied the Sharps, uncertain whether he struck any of the swarming beasts. The shooters fired dozens of rounds as the buffalo fled across the low hills, their roars and bellows sounding above the churn of the paddle wheel. The shooting gallery continued throughout the day as buffalo, ducks, geese, deer, coyotes, and even fish fell to the repeated volleys.

Thirty miles above the Niobara, they put in at Fort Randall, where the unruly soldiers disembarked under the baleful eye of the major. Another three dozen soldiers boarded in their place, headed for forts near the head of the river. 'Let's hope they are less ornery than the last bunch,' said Jubal as the soldiers filed up the gangplank, heavy knapsacks on their backs.

ONE MORNING, PURCHASE HEARD warning shouts. 'What is it?' he called out, hurrying to the side.

For answer, Jubal pointed to three mounted Indians sitting motionless on the shore to watch their passage. The Indians were stripped bare to the waist, their naked legs dangling from the sides of their ponies.

A soldier propped his gun on a stack of cordwood but was prevented from shooting by a sergeant who tugged his arm. 'Why stir up mischief?' he said.

'Who are they?' he asked the sergeant.

'Sioux, like as not.'

He stared at the Indians, his mind registering all the tales he had heard of their savagery and warlike demeanour. 'They seem peaceful enough,' he said.

'They don't mind the boats so much, it's the buffalo hunters who stick in their craw.'

They were nearing the Cheyenne River when the whistle blasted and the wheel spun furiously in reverse. Hurrying to the foredeck, Purchase witnessed several hundred buffalo swimming across the river ahead of the boat. Thousands more waited on shore for their turn to enter the water. Fetching their weapons, the miners and officers poured round after round into the swimmers. Before long, dozens of carcasses floated downriver past the boat. But the repeated volleys seemed to make not the least impression on the swimming herd, their numbers so great Purchase fancied he could walk across their backs like a great, woolly raft. As the vanguard gained the opposite shore, more splashed into the water from the host still on dry land. The shooters kept up the firing for the next two hours, halting only to preserve their munitions supply.

A small cannon was mounted on the foredeck to deter Indians. The pilot came down to commandeer the weapon, ordering it be filled with boiler rivets, no shot being available. As soon as this was done, he sighted the cannon and, lighting a cigar, applied it to the fuse. There came a loud bang as dozens of projectiles flew out of the mouth of the cannon and directly into the massed ranks of swimming buffalo. Loud cheers greeted the successful shot as two or three buffalo stopped swimming and floated in the bloody water, their sides shredded by the ironware.

'Again!'

The cannon was discharged twice more, ceasing only when the supply of rivets was in danger of being exhausted. Purchase counted a dozen buffalo as they floated past the boat, some still kicking vainly in an attempt to stay above water as their blood pumped into the river.

'Hullaballoo!' Huckstep laughed in admiration. 'It's like mowing down a field of Yan—Rebs!'

Purchase gave him a sharp look but held his tongue.

It was late afternoon before the buffalo armada had finished crossing and the boat was free to continue.

The following day, a party of deckhands were put ashore to find wood, Purchase and Jubal joining the expedition. Pulling two carts by hand and protected by a dozen soldiers, they ventured inland for more than a mile before coming across a grove of cottonwoods. Many of the trees had already been felled, ruts in the grass showing where the cut lumber had been hauled back to shore.

They felled and cut up a dozen trees, anxious to finish before nightfall. As dusk fell, they worked by the light of lamps and fires, the mate urging them on. Exhausted, Purchase leaned on the axe as the mate and the sergeant in charge of the protection detail held a conversation. 'Surely they don't intend us to walk back to the boat in the dark?' groaned Jubal beside him.

The mate approached. 'We sleep here for the night, boys. The army will stand guard. Get your heads down. What?' he barked as a voice protested. 'You'll eat back on the boat—if you do your job!'

The morning dawned fresh and clear. Purchase helped load the carts with wood. Four men then pulled each cart by its short yoke while the others pushed, heaving and straining over the rough ground. The going was slow and laborious—the soldiers taking turns to push and relieve the exhausted wooders. They had covered but half the distance back to the boat when a cry of alarm rang out. Purchase glanced up to see, mounted on a bluff not five hundred yards distant, forty or fifty Indians armed with lances and bows.

He and Jubal exchanged startled glances before dashing to the cart to retrieve their rifles. The soldiers had drawn up in a defensive line facing the Indians, who watched impassively, making no move to either attack or withdraw.

A nerve-racking quarter-hour passed as the Indians sat in silence, giving no sign as to their intention.

'What the devil are they waiting for?' someone asked.

The mate spat into the grass. 'It could be one thing, it could be another. You never know with Injuns. Mebbe they don't like the odds. The soldiers will drop a dozen if they charge. Or mebbe they want to force a trade.'

The tense stalemate ended only when another party—sent from the boat to investigate the delay—arrived on the scene, well-armed with carbines and pistols. The boat's clerk, in charge of the rescue party, boldly advanced to parley with the Indians. They watched from behind the cart as he handed some supplies to the chieftains before sitting down in the grass, chatting amiably with the chiefs. A short time later, he got to his feet and waved his hat, signalling the men back to the boat.

'What is going on?' Purchase asked the mate as the Indians followed closely behind, while another bunch rode on ahead to where the *Annabelle* was anchored.

'The same thing as always, I expect.' The mate cleared his throat and spat. 'They claim that this is their land and, as such, their wood. They will demand payment.'

The assessment proved correct as the Indians and the boat captain negotiated onshore, the Indians demanding coffee, sugar, beans, and whisky before allowing the steamer to continue on its way.

'Were they truly hostile?' Purchase heard a man ask a lieutenant from the rescue party.

'Generally, you'd be wise to consider any Indian hostile until he is no longer breathing,' the lieutenant answered.

THEY HAD BEEN ON the river for twenty-five days and covered almost a thousand miles when, late on a humid afternoon, he heard a deckhand sing out, 'Heart River, ahead!'

It's true! Purchase's heart leapt at this first tangible evidence of the veracity of the oft-repeated family tale. He caught the eye of Jubal, who stared back, an amazed look on his face. He leaned on the rail as they passed the river mouth, wishing his pa were here to share in the moment. A large, treeless bluff stood above the junction where the two rivers joined. *Somewhere northwest of the Heart.* His mind racing with anticipation, he scanned the shore as if the half-mythical rock were somewhere to be seen.

Jubal came forward to compliment. 'Maybe that family yarn has legs after all.'

'I'm certain of it. However, I will not be entirely satisfied until I lay eyes on it.'

'It sure would be something to see, a rock buffalo.' Jubal shook his head in wonder.

That night, he dreamed of the fantastical beast, seeing in his mind a sketch his grandfather had once made to illustrate the truth of his patrimony. 'I can't recollect how big, exactly, he said it was,' his pa said, laying out the drawing for Purchase to see. 'Only that it was big—far bigger than a man. But one day, mayhap, you will see for yourself.'

'Why don't you go see for yourself, pa? And take me with you!'

'I can't. It's too far. Besides, I have things to keep me here. But maybe you will—and return and tell me all about it.' Horizon McLennan mussed his son's hair. 'Who knows?' he said.

'Soon, now pa,' he murmured. 'Soon.'

THE FOLLOWING MORNING THE whistle blasted and a deckhand stationed in the bow sang out, 'Fort Buffalo!'

'God Almighty, but we're here!' Jubal and Huckstep began to gather their things, their faces alight with anticipation and relief that the long journey was done. Purchase followed suit, hoisting the rucksack onto his back as the wheel stopped turning and then put into reverse. On the shore, a few hundred yards ahead, stood a fort flying the Stars and Stripes. A bunch of soldiers were gathered outside the stockade, lounging against the log palisade as they watched the boat.

Purchase stood with Jubal and Huckstep, impatient to be off the boat, as the bow shuddered up onto the levee.

'Howdy, boys!' An officer called out from the shore as a landing stage was swung down. A wagon was brought forward, and the deckhands began to transfer supplies, hand over hand, to the waiting soldiers. Purchase made his way past the work party and onto the grass, thankful to be on solid ground once more.

'Over here!' Two men sat on a wagon set back in the long grass. The driver waved his hat, calling them over. 'You the new runners? We been going back and forth for three days. We feared mebbe you had sunk or been scalped by Indians.'

'We nearly were,' said Huckstep.

'Name's Stringer,' said the driver. 'This here is Bose,' he motioned to his companion, a short, stocky man who yawned in reply. Both men were clad in bloodstained buckskins and moccasins. A peculiar stink came from both, which Purchase imagined to be buffalo grease.

'Hope you brought the freight,' said Stringer. 'Otherwise, the boss will crack on something fierce.'

'There are crates on board,' said Purchase.

Stringer nodded. 'Then we wait our turn.'

After the troopers had finished unloading the military supplies, Stringer drove the wagon up to the boat. 'Blackie! Stove-pot!' he called out, hailing two of the deckhands.

'Jump to it! Get these crates off-loaded!' The mate clapped his hands and glanced up at the hurricane deck where the pilot stood smoking a pipe as he looked down at proceedings.

A line was formed, and the camp supplies passed down to the wagon and loaded onto the backboard. Stringer and his companion took down a half-dozen tied sacks, which they handed to the roustabouts. 'Some salt tongue to chaw on,' said Stringer, 'compliments of Mr Ludlow.'

The whistle sounded and the landing stage was swung back aboard. They watched the steamer backpaddle in the water. A mere twenty yards out from shore, the whistle blasted a second time and the wheel reversed. A bell clanged and the boat slowly resumed its journey upstream, smoke pouring from the stacks.

Stringer climbed up onto the seat. 'Let's head back to camp. Mr Ludlow will be waiting on these supplies.'

'How far is it?' asked Jubal.

'Not so far.' The driver motioned to the distance. 'Over that ridge, and the next one and then some. Throw your packs in the back.' With a flick of the reins, he set off as the three companions walked alongside. The day was hot and the ground uneven, but Purchase welcomed the exercise after the confines of the boat.

They followed a dusty track past the fort. The gates were open and the flat, dusty parade ground visible. A few bored troopers stood outside the gates to watch them pass. 'Welcome to Fort Buffalo,' said Stringer. His companion gave a chuckle.

'Are you going to ask?' hissed Jubal beside him.

'Ask what?' demanded Huckstep, overhearing.

'Nothing. About the camp, that's all.' Purchase frowned at Jubal, warning him to drop the subject.

They soon left the fort behind, entering a realm of blowing grass and rolling bluffs that stretched away on all sides. 'It looks awful lonesome,' said Jubal.

Purchase tugged at his collar, struck by the encompassing solitude. The only sounds were the creak of the wagon wheels, the snuffling of the mules, and the omnipresent wind gusting through the dry grass. It's somewhere out there, he told himself. It has to be.

'Consarn it!' Huckstep, walking ahead of the wagon, gave a startled shout and hopped on one foot. The other was covered with a soft, brown sludge. Cursing, he furiously scraped his boot in the grass.

Stringer gave a guffaw. 'That's pure, high-grade buffalo shit! Soon you won't give a mind when you swallow it, bathe in it, or fry it up for supper!'

After walking for just under a half-hour, they crested a small rise. Stringer pointed the whip to where a cluster of tents and wagons occupied a plot of land amid the swelling bluffs. 'Gentlemen! Your grand hotel awaits!'

6

The Buffalo Camp

T HE CAMP WAS A ramshackle collection of tents, tipis, mud dugouts, a sod house, and three wood-frame buildings. A dozen wagons and a large, penned enclosure containing a remuda of horses, mules and Indian ponies completed the camp. A work gang laboured on a half-completed log building. Six or seven Indian women cut up meat or cooked over open fires. A number of fresh hides, thick with buzzing flies, were staked out in the grass, the stench of tanning and butchery pervading the air.

'Phooey!' Huckstep pinched his nose in disgust. 'I never smelt such a stink!'

'It makes your eyes water,' agreed Purchase, the stench reminding him of the buffalo carcasses strewn along the railroad track.

Stringer climbed down from the wagon as a short man in rolled up shirt sleeves and brown linen trousers advanced to meet them. 'That's Mr Ludlow, boss of this outfit,' said Stringer. 'Hey boss! We found 'em.'

'Howdy, boys. Welcome.' Ludlow stuck out his hand. He stood barely five and a half feet tall, his lips framed by a huge moustache that hung down both sides of his chin. He wore a Stetson with an incongruously tall crown, no doubt, thought Purchase, to add inches to his height. His freckled skin was burned by the sun. He had a busy, impatient air about him, his eyes constantly glancing from one thing to another.

'Spend today settling in and finding your feet. The foreman, Mr Baumann here—' he indicated a stout fellow in a striped flannel shirt and suspenders who stood behind him—'will see you squared away and show you the ropes.' Without more ado, he turned to Stringer. 'The supplies arrive safely?'

They followed Baumann to a row of canvas tents. 'Three to a tent,' he said. 'The nights are warm, and you'll have plenty of robes to snuggle under when they get colder. If it gets really cold—and it can freeze the balls off a buff come—'

Baumann broke off as a thin, morose-looking individual with a pitted face, approached. 'These the new runners?' The man spoke to Baumann with a cursory glance at the companions.

'Fresh from the boat.'

'Showing them the ropes?'

'I am.'

'Hope they are better than the last lot.' the other man made a chewing motion and frowned at something in his mouth before walking off.

'Who in Sam Hill was that cheerful puss?' asked Jubal.

'That's Mr Jesper, second-in-command to the boss. Don't mind him— though he's an awkward cuss on his best day. Now, where was I?'

'You were talking about—'

'Right. The tents. If it gets sharp cold you can move into one of the tipis until the bunkhouse is finished. They are big enough to hold a firepit.'

'When will that be?' asked Huckstep. 'The bunkhouse, I mean?'

Baumann studied him for a moment. 'With luck by the time the snow comes,' he said. 'You other boys all right with the tent?'

'Fine by me,' said Purchase.

Jubal nodded. 'Minds me of the army.'

'Nothing much happens until winter,' continued Baumann. 'Most of the boys have left for Leavenworth or Omaha. They'll be back, skint as a flint, afore winter. If you plan on sticking around, you can earn a few dollars by working around the camp, hauling supplies, and shooting a few buff for our-selves, the soldiers, and the boats. If that don't appeal, go visit Fort Benton or any other place that takes your fancy. Just be sure to be back here before the ice closes off the river.'

'What about Injuns?' asked Huckstep.

'The Sioux will leave you alone, mostly. We pay them coffee, sugar, and beans once a month for the privilege. But they are drawn from different bands, and not all of them are friendly. So be sharp. Don't get caught out on the grass alone. You're likely to get pricked full of arrows. Ever since that Fetterman shindig they are spoiling for a fight.'

Purchase caught a glance from Jubal that said, '*Told you so!*'

'How many buffalo are we expected to take?' Purchase asked.

'You have a daily quota of twenty-five each.'

The companions exchanged glances at the figure.

'What? Twenty-five!' Baumann gave a derisive snort at their doubtful expressions. 'An experienced runner would take that many afore he had drunk his first coffee.'

'What about cartridges?'

'The shot men will cast the lead and keep you supplied. That comes out of your pay. What else?' Baumann asked the question of himself, tugging at his chin as he looked around the tent.

'Is there a buffalo—a rock buffalo—somewheres around here?' asked Jubal. He shrugged off Purchase's annoyed glance.

Baumann gave Jubal a curious look. 'Matter of fact there is. How in tar did you know?'

'Heard about it on the boat. Whereabouts is it? I'd like to set eyes on it.'

'About six or seven miles thataways.' Baumann flapped his hand at the horizon. 'The queerest thing you ever did see.'

In spite of his irritation with Jubal, Purchase's heart raced at the confirmation. 'Was there a fur post here—from before?' he asked.

'Hell if I know. Where, and how long ago?'

'I don't exactly know. A hundred years, maybe more?'

'A hundred years! God Almighty.' Baumann fixed Purchase an incredulous look. 'There were no white men here that long ago. Why in blazes would there be a post?'

'Something I heard.'

'On the boat?' Baumann gave a sceptical look.

Purchase nodded. 'Just talk.'

'Well, if there was a post here—which I highly doubt—and if it was built close to the river, which it probably was, then it's likely buried under a foot of mud by now. The river changes course like a snake wriggles in the grass. Anything else?' He raised an inviting eyebrow. 'No questions on Indian rain dances, the number of mule farts, the length of the grass? No? Then I reckon you scholars ought to stow your gear and wander around the camp and introduce yourselves. The boys can be ornery at times, but mostly they are friendly. Oh, and no liquor except when permitted.'

'When is that?' asked Huckstep.

The question drew a considered glance. 'When would you like? I'll see if I can make arrangements.'

'After supper would be good. Maybe a drop with it.'

'Sure. Would you prefer it served up in a glass or a silver tumbler?'

Before the confused Huckstep could respond, Jubal punched him on the shoulder. 'Don't mind him! He's as dry as a church mouse.'

'For hours at a time,' added Purchase.

Baumann stared a moment and then gave out a loud guffaw.

'So be it!' he said. 'So be it!'

'What in cornswill was that about?' demanded Huckstep as Baumann departed, still chuckling.

'Your durn mouth!' Jubal swiped the other man across the top of the head.

THEY WANDERED AROUND THE camp, introducing themselves while taking in the scale of the operation. A cook named Sánchez was roped in to act as guide by a passing Jesper. An affable, if sombre faced individual wearing a dirty wool cap, he led them to where a half dozen of the thin, mangy, summer hides were pegged in the grass and covered in flies. Entrails and bits of flesh splattered the ground, and a stench of blood and grease filled the air.

Jubal waved a hand under his nose. 'Hoodee! What a stench!'

Sánchez looked at him in surprise. 'I don't smell nothing,' he said.

'Who are the squaws?' Huckstep shot a look of disgust at the sweating, grease-covered women sitting cross-legged around a nearby fire.

'Ricks and Chippewa, mostly. A few Mandan. Slave women owned by the Sioux.'

'They sure look ugly.'

'The Sioux allow them to scrape and butcher in return for whisky, coffee, and flour. We keep them sweet and in return they allow us to hunt and use the squaws.'

'Use?' asked Huckstep, his face showing interest.

'How many robes does the company take—in season?' Purchase asked before Sánchez could respond.

'In winter? Around twenty-five to thirty thousand, I guess.'

Purchase whistled at the figure, swapping glances with Jubal. 'And how many runners? In winter, when they are all here?'

'Lots. Maybe twenty or thirty, including you boys.'

'How many altogether—in the camp?' asked Jubal.

'Now?'

'In winter.'

Sánchez ran a finger over his lip to think. 'Around fifty to sixty, maybe. There's the runners and skinners, three cooks, two wranglers, six—no, seven—teamsters, the bosses, the general hands. That's it, I think.' He scratched his head.

They continued their tour of the camp, stopping before the log bunkhouse under construction. Half a dozen men sawed or banged away in the heat. Four were Negro and two Chinese.

'The new bunkhouse,' explained Sánchez. 'Come winter it gets colder than a whore's teat. Come.' He led them past the buildings and the row of tents to point to a line of latrines dug in the earth. 'Do your business there,' he said. The pungent odour caused them to step back.

'Tarnation! If that ain't the god-awfullest stink in all creation!' Huckstep buried his nose in his sleeve.

'Jest make sure you don't fall in,' said Sánchez, his voice serious.

The next stop was the large smokehouse. Sánchez pulled open the door to reveal a number of barrels. 'Buffalo tongues,' he said. 'We pickle 'em first and then ship them downriver to Leavenworth and Kansas City.'

The tour concluded before a large freight shed which contained a huge quantity of stiff buffalo hides. The robes were piled in stacks that reached to the height of the roof. Sánchez looked pleased at Purchase's surprised exclamation. 'Winter robes. There were too many to ship all at once. They are waiting for the next steamer.'

'Where will they go?'

Sánchez shrugged. 'Leavenworth is all I know. After that, I hear they get shipped east to New York or Baltimore.' He shut the door. 'That's it. Chow is in an hour or so. You'll hear the bell ring. We eat over there, by the chuck wagon.' He pointed to where four long plank tables stood in the grass. With that, he walked off.

'Hold up!' A bulky man approached, patting his bald head with a strip of cloth. 'The hell with this stinking heat anyway!'

He stopped before them, mopping his neck. 'Jeb Halverson,' he said, 'boss teamster,' and stuck out a large hand. You boys the new runners?' At their nods, he continued. 'Do you aim to stick around for the rest of the summer?'

'I'd like to see Fort Benton,' said Jubal. 'I always wanted to run the length of the river,' he said to Purchase.

'That's better than a thousand miles upriver,' said Halverson. 'If you go, make sure you get back in time. What about you?' he asked Huckstep.

'There must be some decent saloons somewhere?'

Halverson chuckled. 'Fort Langlois, fifty miles upriver, has all the saloons you can handle. Aye, with gambling dens and dancehall gals included. It's a rough place—full of soldiers, miners, traders, Indians, slaves, Chinese, brawlers, ne'er-do-wells, and all-around desperadoes. If you go there, look out you don't fetch yourself a bullet.' 'And you?' Halverson turned to Purchase.

'I guess I'll stick around, get to know the country. Is there a horse I can use?'

'You can take one from there.' Halverson raised an arm to indicate the corral. 'Mace, the wrangler, will set you up with a saddle and mount. But be careful. The Sioux will take advantage of a man alone, 'specially if they suspect he's a runner.'

'Just how bad are they?' asked Huckstep, a note of alarm in his voice.

Halverson made a rumbling sound and hawked a gob of spit into the grass. 'They can be terrible bad. They kilt a few boys some months back. They get antsy as more hunters and miners come into the territory. The dead buff drive them crazy. If they give you any trouble, back off and let them take the meat. You can always shoot more.'

'Have you been here long?' asked Purchase.

'Four years. Every two years or so I go downriver and whoop it up.'

'This is a permanent camp?'

'It is. There are a few pesky independents about, but this is the only permanent camp for …' the other man rubbed his jaw '… well, forever, I guess. The boss figured it made no sense to start up new again each winter.'

'By "boss" you mean owner?' asked Purchase Halverson laughed. 'I don't—even if he thinks so! The owners are down in Kansas City.'

'When is the next boat—upriver?' asked Jubal.

Halverson scratched his chest. 'Two or three pass by every day. Anyone of them will fetch you up to Benton, or to Fort Langlois,' he added, looking at Huckstep.

'What do you think?' asked Purchase as the three made their way back to the tent.

Huckstep grimaced. 'I didn't come here to fight no Injuns.'

'With luck, you won't have to.'

'It seems on the square,' said Jubal. 'I guess we'll find out.'

'Thirty buff a day?'

'I reckon we'll get used to it. At least we don't have to skin 'em.'

'Do those squaws wax the candle, do you reckon?' asked Huckstep, looking over at the Indian women.

As his companions dozed in the warm tent, Purchase walked away from the camp and up into the surrounding bluffs, taking the Sharps for security. The day was hot and humid, a warm breeze not quite keeping the flies at bay. Standing on a rise, he surveyed the endless, rolling swathes of grass that stretched to the sky whichever way he looked. Nothing moved except the long stalks rustling in the wind. *He maybe hunted here or nearby.* He marvelled at the notion as he pictured the family patriarch scouting these same hills. An image of an old, grey-bearded man sprang to mind—one he instantly dismissed. *He was no older than myself, when he first came here.*

Younger, even, perhaps. The sound of the dinner bell reached his ears and he set off down the rise, bound and determined to set eyes on the fabled rock before the week was out.

7

Buffalo Rock

'COME WITH US!' URGED Jubal as he and Huckstep boarded a steamboat back at the levee the following day. 'There's nothing here but grass and flies!'

'And buffalo shit!' added Huckstep.

Purchase shook his head. 'I'll see you when you get back. Don't lose all your money—or your hair!'

He watched the boat leave and then returned to the camp to ask the wrangler for a horse.

'They are Indian ponies, but broke to the bridle,' said Mace, cutting out a blue roan stallion. 'This one has the best wind.'

The horse was small—standing no higher than fourteen hands, but sturdy-looking with prominent withers and a pronounced, sloping croup. 'Same size as the boss!' joked Mace 'You'll find saddle and harness over there.' He pointed to a shed.

'What's his name?' asked Purchase, stroking the horse on the muzzle.

'He don't have one. Call him what you want. Don't spare his feelings.'

Purchase thought for a moment. 'I'll call him Pike,' he said.

'Pike? Ain't that a fish?'

'It's a road, also. Like the Baltimore Pike.'

'It's just a durn horse.' Mace walked off, shaking his head.

Twenty minutes later, Purchase rode out of the camp armed with Baumann's directions to locate the rock. As the camp disappeared behind him the other man's warning rang in his ears. 'If you see Injuns, don't stop to say hello!'

The day was hot and sticky, flies and gnats a constant, irritating presence in between gusts of wind. The green sward rolled away on all sides, the uplands a giant patchwork of sunlight and shadow. The horse felt eager and sure-footed beneath him and he arched his back, wondering how long it had been since he rode for any considerable length of time. He spotted thousands of buffalo resting or wallowing in small groups along with hundreds of deer and antelope. He kept an alert eye out for Indians, the grisly tales he had heard at camp ensuring his vigilance. In spite of the danger, he found it hard to contain his excitement at the prospect of setting eyes on the giant rock—an enticing vision from as long ago as he could remember.

'How big is it, Pa? As big as an elephant?'
'Bigger than ten elephants!'
'And Grandpa built it?'
'My great-grandpa. Your great-great-grandpa.'
'And it belongs to us?'
'I suppose you might say it belongs to every—well, kinda.'

After walking the horse for over an hour, he stopped atop a ridge to rest the animal. Taking off his hat, he scanned the surrounding hummocks while mopping the sweat from his face and neck. *I should have brought a glass.* He had ridden, he figured, around five miles from the camp. He turned and stared at the way he had come, berating himself for failing to keep better track of his whereabouts. The thought of being lost in the vast, sprawling grasslands caused a prickle of alarm before he oriented himself, his eye picking out a remembered contour that signalled the way back.

He patted the neck of the roan as it cropped the grass. 'I'll wager that you know the way better than I do.' Shading his eyes, he scanned the horizon again, squinting in the bright sunlight. *I've never known such emptiness,* he though. His eye alighted on something—a hill or mound rising from the plain, he couldn't say which. He screwed up his eyes, staring hard at the feature. *What in creation?* He sucked in his breath, his eyes fixed on the object as its true nature dawned upon him. *Surely, that's a head? And could that be a hump?* He raised himself in the stirrups, eyes narrowed against the glare. *By God, but it is!* He whooped with excitement. 'It's the buffalo!'

'Skit!' He kicked the horse into a trot, ignoring the warning he had received from Mace. 'Greenhorns always think they can get where they are going faster by tiring the horse,' the wrangler had cautioned. 'But this country is too big to rush. Save the steam for when you need it.'

He rode through an extensive patch of pale, mauve-coloured flowers, his gaze fixed on the solitary object—its distinctive shape becoming clearer with each passing yard. A band of antelope took flight as he approached. Sparrows flew up from the grass, and drifting clouds briefly threw the grasslands into checkered shade. He was much closer now, his eyes scarcely believing that they at last beheld the fabled creature that had haunted his dreams ever since childhood. *You were right, pa! Everything you said.*

RIDING INTO THE NARROW band of shade cast by the great monolith, he drew rein and sat spellbound by the sheer size of the granite colossus. He walked the pony around the rock, his eyes never straying from the immense figure as it towered above him like a beast from myth or legend. Abandoning the horse, he walked up to the object and ran his hands over the stone frontispiece, hardly able to credit the evidence of his senses. *It's just as you described, Pa—only bigger!* Standing back in the grass, he gazed up at the blunt, gigantic head. 'How in creation did he do it?' he asked out loud, the question echoing in the noon stillness. A thrill of pride coursed through him at his umbilical connection to the wondrous beast. *He carved this. Boundless McLennan, my ancestor.*

The horse nickered and he spun around, instantly alert. He could see nothing except the tidal waves of grass. Berating himself for carelessness, he hurried to the pony and took the Sharps from its sleeve. *Indians could come around that rock and be on me before I could think.* After a period of suspenseful vigilance, he breathed more easily, the tension seeping from his limbs.

Opening the saddlebag, he took out a hammer borrowed from the camp, and a chisel he had brought with him for the purpose. *He must have used one, just like this, to cut the stone.* Flexing his fingers around the iron haft, he walked to the front of the rock. After another, searching sweep of his surrounds, he knelt at the base. Laying the edge of the chisel against the rock he struck a tentative blow, shocked at the hardness of the granite. He struck again, harder, and yet again, chipping off a flake of rock, which he tucked into his shirt pocket. *For you, pa.* He struck again, several blows. *And one for me.*

Climbing back into the saddle, he surveyed the huge sculpture for several more minutes before turning the horse for camp. Several times as he rode away he turned in the saddle to glance back, his senses confounded at each instance.

'How did he do it, Pa—make the buffalo?'
'I don't know, son. It's a mystery.'
'Why did he do it?'
'I guess he wanted to leave a mark. Something to be remembered by.'

He glanced behind one last time. The granite bison towered above the grass in striking, solitary splendour. *I should put up a marker. Claim it as a McLennan. Let the world know who made* it. With this thought in mind, he continued homeward, his mind fixated on the enormous figure, its wind-burnished contours irrevocably impressed upon his soul.

A MILE FROM THE camp he was jumped by a party of Indians. He had just crossed a dry creek bed when some instinct made him glance up at a ridge several hundred yards to his right. Halted on the rise, watching him, were six or seven Indians. They held long lances, feathers fluttering in the wind. He licked his dry lips and reined the horse, uncertain whether to run or attempt to parley. For a long moment the two parties regarded each other, as if waiting for the other to make the first move. He had just decided to make a run for it when one of the Indians raised his lance and pointed the tip at where he sat. With loud whoops the Indians charged down the slope toward him. He was already in motion, hollering at the roan as he lashed it into a gallop.

Bending low in the saddle, he whipped the horse into a lather as fierce cries rose in his wake. He flew across the grass, the Indians in close pursuit. They were no more than three or four hundred yards behind, urging the ponies to run faster, intent on their prey. The roan was snorting and blowing as it thundered through the long grass. The shrill cries seemed closer, and he lashed the horse while praying for sight of the camp. He bent lower, his heart pounding madly as he clung to the fleeing horse. Just ahead, the camp came into view. He glimpsed figures running in alarm, rifles in hand, to take up position beside a wagon. The cries behind him abruptly faded and he risked a look back—vastly relieved to see that the Indians had pulled up their horses and abandoned the pursuit.

'Whoa!' Skidding to a halt, he leapt down from the sweating horse. Ludlow, Baumann, Halverson, Mace, Stringer, and half a dozen others surrounded him, rifles in hand. 'You brought back guests!' said Halverson.

Heaving for breath, he stared back at the Indians, who had turned their ponies and were departing at a walk through the grass.

'What happened?' Ludlow's face was creased with concern.

'They jumped me a mile back! Were they Sioux?'

'Hell, yes.' Baumann placed the rifle stock on the ground. 'Shucks, they were just saying hello.'

Purchase grimaced, his heart racing, too spent to join in the relieved laughter.

'Keep a sharp eye in case they come back.' An exasperated look on his face, Ludlow stalked off.

'Fergit that raise!' Halverson slapped him on the back, provoking more laughter with the jest.

Retiring to the tent, he sat down on the cot, still panting for breath. *If I hadn't looked up when I did.* He sat in the stuffy tent, listening to voices outside, his thoughts revolving between the Indians, the rock, and the pounding of his heart. It was not until two hours later, and a walk around the camp—where he was greeted with amused looks—that he felt calm enough to sit down and compose the letter that had been on his thoughts all the way back from the rock.

Dear Pa,

Today I saw the buffalo! It was just as you described—only bigger! It must stand seventy feet high or even higher. I never saw anything like it. It's hard to describe. The detail is real fine. You could swear it was looking at something in the distance. I hate to think how hard it was to carve. I hammered off a small piece, which I will bring back to St Charles to show you—solid proof of everything you said! I can still hardly believe it—after all these years of trying to picture it in my mind. Tell Sam it would make his hair stand on end. I haven't mentioned to anyone that Great-grandpappy built it. They'd think me bragging, or a lunatic most likely! I wish I could draw you a picture, but my fingers are thicker than a New Orleans cigar. But imagine the tallest buffalo you ever did see, standing stock-still and surrounded by nothing but grass. Heck. That doesn't do it justice. Not even close. You just have to see it for yourself. I am sending this downriver by the next steamboat. The fellows at the camp tell me you should receive it about five or six weeks from the date of despatch. I hope so.

Before finishing the letter, he deliberated whether to tell of his narrow escape from the Indians but decided against it. Ma would just fret, he told himself. He was still staring at the letter, his head full of thoughts, when the dinner bell sounded. Carefully folding the letter, he placed it in his shirt pocket.

THE NEXT MORNING, HALVERSON approached. 'If you ain't too frazzled about them Injuns jumping you, we need a buff for the smokehouse. Are you game?'

'Sure.' He hesitated.

'You have shot buff before?'

'From a train.'

'From a—?' Halverson stared, his mouth open. 'Didn't that fellow—the agent, down in Kansas City—ask you?'

'He didn't seem to mind.'

'I guess he didn't!' Halverson deliberated a moment, idly brushing away a fly as he stared at the ranges. 'I guess I could show you. I've nothing better to do.' Making up his mind he turned away. 'Get some chow and be ready to leave within the hour.'

After grabbing some breakfast he waited as Halverson came up, driving a wagon drawn by two mules. 'Climb in.' Halverson patted the bench seat.

'We are not taking horses?'

'No need.'

'What if we run into Indians again?'

'Then we stand them off.'

Purchases clung to the seat as the wagon bounced and jarred over the grass. Halverson half turned to him. 'I guess you can shoot at least?'

'I was in the war.'

Halverson made a rumbling sound but said nothing for a few moments. The wagon hit a fold and pitched to one side. 'Whoa, boys! Yankee or Reb?'

'Yankee.'

'And that fellow Huckstep, what was he?'

'I don't know what he was—or whether he was even in the war. Jubal reckons he was a bushwhacker.'

Halverson nodded, his expression sober. 'It wouldn't surprise. What made you decide to become a runner? 'Specially as you hadn't shot a buffalo—'cepting from a train.'

'I wanted to earn a stake.'

'Then you are in the right business. Buffalo are the wealth of these plains. Hides are running at better than two dollars eighty apiece. Shoot enough buff and you can earn yourself a tidy sum over the winter.' The teamster was bluff but genial and seemed genuine in his desire to show Purchase the ropes.

'Were you a runner, yourself?'

'I was. Skit now!' Halverson flicked the reins. 'I used to trap beaver—in the mountains—but they're all tapped out, so I turned to buffalo. They ain't never getting tapped out! But hell, a man gets old and tired of crawling on his belly and scratching for lice.'

Purchase hung on as the wagon lurched sideways over a rut.

'Har!'

They had left the camp behind and were deep in the rolling grasslands. The morning was hot and sticky with a warm southwester driving away the flies. 'Your first job is to find the buff,' said Halverson 'They can be anywhere. There's lots of 'em, but then there's lots of country, too. Usually they'll be in small groups—anywhere from a dozen to sixty or more. The best time is afore first light. They'll be chewing or wandering around and generally minding their own business. Whoa!' Hauling back on the reins, Halverson halted the wagon. Climbing down, he leaned in to fetch his rifle. Purchase followed suit.

'That's a good spot.' Halverson nodded toward some bluffs about a quarter mile distant. 'When I was still a runner, I often found buff feeding there.' No sooner were the words out of his mouth than a solitary buffalo appeared over the rise, followed by at least a dozen more. 'See if I ain't telling the truth!'

They set off toward the feeding buffalo, careful to keep downwind of the creatures. 'Get close—to under three hundred yards. Stay downwind. They get spooked quicker than a cat.'

Dropping to their bellies, they squirmed through a patch of sagebrush. Halverson raised his head to scout the ground. 'Over there!' He squirrelled toward a gulley, Purchase close behind. They rested there, slaking their thirst with the canteens. The buffalo remained in place a short distance away, engrossed in feeding.

'Mind if I see your gun?' asked Halverson.

Purchase handed over the Sharps. Halverson peered at the breech. 'A forty-ninety,' he said, hefting the weapon. He peered along the barrel. 'What grain do you use?'

'Three fifty.'

'I recommend four hundred or better. The shot boys will recast cartridges to suit. But I prefer to cast my own. I don't trust a cartridge unless I make it.'

'That a Remington?' asked Purchase, indicating Halverson's own gun.

'It is.' Halverson handed him the rifle. 'I used a Springfield for years afore picking up this one. That's what they call a rolling block,' he said as Purchase examined the breech. 'It shoots straight. Truest gun I ever owned.'

'I heard that—about the reliable shot.' He handed back the rifle. 'But I'll stick to the Sharps.'

'Can't blame you. Fine gun. Most of the boys use it—'cepting those, like me, who prefer the rolling block. You ready to shoot some buff?'

Halverson pulled two lengths of brass tubing from the rifle sleeve. 'First you make a stand.' He drove the tubes into the earth, forming a crotch. 'Make it high,' he said. 'Killing is hard work. I like to sit. Others prefer to kneel. Jest don't lie on your belly like most greenhorns. One, you can't see clearly; and two … ' He scratched his head. 'Hell if I remember two!'

'You'll have to make your own—and bring it along,' said Halverson as he saw Purchase look around for some sticks. 'For now, jest kneel and fire. Two!' he said, remembering. 'You'll blow your ear drum from laying your ear against the stock.' He spread a patch of cloth in the grass and, with one eye on the herd, took a number of metallic cartridges from his belt and laid them carefully on the cloth. 'I count thirty two buff. Fifteen apiece, and two spares.'

'We are going to take them all? I thought you said just one—for the smokehouse?'

'You need the practice, don't you? Or just how many did you shoot from that train?' Halverson glanced at the paper-wrapped cartridges Purchase had laid out. 'Always save a half dozen,' he said, 'in your belt. And one extra, in your pocket.'

At Purchase's raised eyebrow Halverson elaborated. 'Many greenhorns get carried away and shoot their entire belt. Then if they run into Injuns …' He didn't finish.

'And the one in the pocket?'

'That's for you—if you finish the other six.' He made a wry face at Purchase's expression. 'Don't fret too much. Injuns are chickenshit scared of buffalo guns. Unless they can rush or bushwhack you, they won't take a chance on getting shot.'

'And what happens if they take you?'

Halverson spat. 'Jest make sure they don't. Now look at the buff. What do you see?'

'There's a big bull and—'

'Forget the bull. He don't count. Look at the cows.'

Purchase squinted at the grazing herd. 'Most of them look like cows.'

'But where's the boss cow?'

'I don't—'

'See that one—over there, to the left of that calf?'

At his nod Halverson continued. 'She's the boss. She's older and bigger than the other cows. They'll follow her, not the bull. The thing to remember,' Halverson put a stalk of grass in his mouth, 'is that buff are the stupidest critters on God's earth. If you understand that—and can pick out the boss cow—then you can take your time and shoot 'em one by one until you've dropped them all.'

'They won't run off—after the first shot?'

'Not if that first shot drops the boss. They'll bawl and whine and mill around and act like they don't know grass from shit. But they won't leave without her to lead them. Some runners deliberately aim to wound the boss rather than kill it. That confuses 'em even more.'

'What if another cow steps up?'

'If it happens, then shoot her, too. Then take your time and kill all the rest. The mistake most greenhorns make is to lose their heads and blaze away. That causes the herd to gallop off in a panic. Take your time. One shot a minute is plenty. They won't go anywhere without the cow.'

'They won't charge?'

'Mebbe they would—if they knew where. But in addition to being stupid, buff are half-blind, and can't smell you if you're downwind. So, take it easy and figure on killing them all.' Seeing Purchase hesitate, Halverson frowned. 'Son. Running ain't sport or target practice. It's business. Think of each buff as a half dollar in your pocket.' He squinted up at the sun. 'You ready? Go ahead, take the cow.'

He watched as Purchase loaded and cocked the Sharps. 'What shot are you going for?'

'The lungs?'

'I prefer the neck. But whatever suits.'

Raising the laddered sight, Purchase sighted on the cow as it munched the grass. He shifted the sight from the neck to the lungs. Holding his breath, he pulled the trigger. Flame spurted from the barrel. Through the smoke, he saw the cow jerk and then drop to the grass. Proud of the shot, he turned to Halverson for approval even as he heard the crack of the other man's rifle as another buffalo dropped in its tracks.

The shots caused consternation among the herd. Bellowing and grunting, they surrounded the fallen cow, pawing her with their hooves or digging her flanks with their horns. The big bull gave out a roar and turned in a circle, ferociously eyeing the grass for the source of the danger. Moments later, Halverson's gun fired again and the bull staggered, venting jets of crimson blood through his nostrils. He made to trot off through the grass but swayed to one side as if drunk and then collapsed to his knees. A second shot put him on his side. 'That's a wasted bullet,' Halverson muttered.

Purchase fired again, cursing as he struck a cow on the flanks.

'Take your time!' Halverson fired again, dropping another buff.

Taking a deep breath to steady himself, Purchase cocked the Sharps. 'Tarn!' he muttered as the gun misfired. Levering open the breech, he removed the cartridge and blew down the barrel. He inserted another cartridge and closed the breech. Peering through the smoke, he sighted on a buffalo and fired.

Within fifteen minutes, the entire herd of thirty-two animals lay slaughtered. Just as Halverson had predicted, the buffalo had milled around in confusion, bellowing in panic as each new shot rang out and another of the group dropped to the grass. When the herd was reduced to three—two spike bulls and a reddish calf—the survivors at last attempted to bolt only to be shot within yards of their dead companions. Purchase had shot 10 of the bunch—and missed as many—using all seventeen cartridges in the process, while his companion had accounted for the remainder.

'Don't overheat the gun,' Halverson cautioned. 'In winter, lay it in the snow awhile until it cools off.' He drank thirstily from the canteen. 'That's it.' He gave a loud belch and wiped his mouth. 'That's how you shoot buff.'

8

A Theft and a Killing

THROUGHOUT AUTUMN, THE CAMP swelled in size as runners, hide men, teamsters, shot men, cooks, and assorted others returned from their summer sojourns in Leavenworth, Omaha, Kansas City, or other points along the Missouri. Jubal and Huckstep had returned from Fort Benton and Fort Langlois on one of the last downriver steamers before the ice closed in. Both admitted to being 'flat busted' and eager to earn back a stake by bringing in hides. Huckstep in particular was disgruntled, walking about with a long face.

'He told me he was so broke he had to trade his knife for a ticket back,' Jubal told Purchase. 'Not that I fared much better myself,' he added ruefully. 'How did you pass the time?'

Upon learning of Purchase's discovery of the rock, Jubal pestered him for information, listening avidly as he attempted to describe the massive object.

'Consarn! I wish I had seen it with you.'

'You will see it soon enough. It's not that far.'

'Still and all! And the Sioux almost took your hair.'

Huckstep badgered him for details about the incident, wanting to know how close the Indians had got, their number, and the weapons they carried.

'I didn't get a proper description. I was bent over the neck of my horse and clinging on for dear life.'

Huckstep licked his lips. 'I jest hope I don't run into the same bunch.'

THE AIR TURNED COLD and frost was on the ground as the camp prepared for the great winter hunt. Assured in his shooting skills and bolstered by the lessons imparted by Halverson, Purchase was confident of meeting whatever numbers Ludlow might set him. In between getting to know the best hunting grounds, he had made several more visits to the rock in spite of the danger posed by Indians. Something about the stone beast—whether his umbilical relation to it, or its stark, brooding presence, or both—preoccupied his waking thoughts. He cast frequent, ruminative glances in its direction as he hunted the bluffs. And always the unspoken question haunted him: What possessed him to do it?

He tried his hand at making a sketch to send to his father, grumbling in frustration at the result. 'It looks like a durned cow!' After several unsuccessful renderings he gave up and stretched out on the narrow cot, hands folded beneath his head as he pictured himself astride the rock, hammer in hand, while painstakingly chipping away the ironlike granite. How in blazes did he do it? How long did it take, and who, if anyone, helped beside his two sons? The questions coalesced to form a mystery that picked away at him, still niggling his thoughts as final preparations were made for the hunt.

Standing outside the tent in the cold darkness of dawn, he ran his eye over some latecomers. 'Who's that?' he asked, indicating a man with a monstrously fat belly who sat on a chair next to a fire to pull his boots on, wheezing heavily all the while.

'That's Pickler, one of the skinners.'

'And him?' He motioned to a rough-looking fellow in a forage cap bent over a rifle he was cleaning.

'Jake something or other. He was at Sand Creek—so he never tires of telling everyone within earshot. He brags he took a dozen scalps.'

'That's what we need around here,' said Huckstep, interrupting. 'Another Sand Creek. Hell, a dozen more!'

Baumann came up. 'Time to go,' he said, 'while the buff are still breathing.'

Purchase was introduced to his assigned skinners. To his surprise, the first of the two turned out to be the same grossly fat man he had observed earlier. Purchase found him chewing tobacco and leaning against a wagon. The fellow looked dirty and slovenly and stank to high heaven. He wore a leather apron heavily stained with years of blood and grease. Chewing a plug of tobacco, he regarded Purchase through narrow, pig eyes set in a face jowly with fat. 'You ever shoot buff before?' he demanded, dispensing with formalities. As he talked he scratched and itched continuously over all parts of his body as if afflicted with the mange.

'I've been shooting them all summer.'

Making an obscene gurgling noise in his throat, Pickler hawked in the grass. 'I sure hope so. I don't aim to be out of pocket 'cos you can't shoot.'

His eyes narrowed at the skinner's tone. 'I'll shoot as many as you can skin.'

'We'll see if your musket ain't as reliable as your mouth!' Pickler shifted the plug from one side of his mouth to the other, and hitched his trousers at the crotch, a derisive look on his face.

Purchase left the fellow to attend to the wagon and supplies while he went to fetch a horse. He found Jubal waiting at the pen as the wrangler cut him out a mount. 'Did you meet your skinners?' he asked.

'I did. The fellows stank to peel wood!'

'So, mine is not the only ape?'

Jubal laughed. 'You got to be part ape to get the job!'

When he returned, he found Pickler sitting against the wagon wheel sharpening a knife. Just then, the second skinner approached—a slight fellow with a tetchy expression on his face. He nodded at Purchase but didn't offer to shake hands. 'Tully,' he muttered when asked his name.

'Stink!' Pickler corrected. 'Go fetch the jerky.'

Without a word, the other man turned and headed back to the chuck wagon. Pickler watched him go. 'Durn grease spot!'

'Are you ready?' asked Purchase as Tully returned with the jerky.

Pickler spat out a stream of juice. 'Don't I look ready?' Shifting on the bench seat, he let loose a long, grumbling fart.

A SHORT TIME LATER, they set off into the grassy wilds, Purchase riding alongside as the wagon creaked and trundled over ruts and hollows. After travelling a mile, he left Pickler and the wagon behind while he spurred ahead in search of buffalo. The morning greyness had lifted, giving way to a blustery, cloudy day. A light dusting of snow whitened the prairie grass. He covered another mile before he spotted a group of twenty buffalo feeding in the grass. They looked fat and healthy, their thick, glossy pelage a stark contrast to the thin, patchy coats of summer. Glancing behind, he saw the wagon following in the distance.

He turned the horse loose to graze while he continued on foot. As he neared the herd, he dropped to his belly and squirmed through the cold switchgrass. The animals kept feeding, oblivious to his presence. Closing to within two hundred yards, he crawled into a dry wallow. Copying Halverson, he had obtained some brass tubing to use as rest sticks. He dug these into the hard ground, pushing them firmly into place to form a crotch about three feet high.

Dipping his hand into the cartridge box—a souvenir of the war—he took out a handful of recast bullets sealed in their paper cartridges. He had taken Halverson's advice and switched to a 420-grain bullet, finding the heavier projectile killed more efficiently. He had also developed a preference for the neck shot as opposed to the lungs. But, for variety, he experimented with both when killing.

Next to the cartridges he placed a tin of percussion caps and removed the lid. The herd gave a series of loud bellows, and he looked up, concerned that they had spooked. But after a few moments spent milling and sniffing the air, they resumed feeding. Jerking down the lever, he inserted a paper cartridge into the chamber. He made himself comfortable behind the rest, sitting cross-legged in the dirt while resting the Sharps on the stand. Setting the rifle at half-cock, he put a percussion cap on the nipple and raised the rear sight. Bending forward, he searched out the boss cow, deciding on a mature female that chewed placidly in the grass. He set the weapon at full cock, the audible click drawing a suspicious grunt from a bull. Raising its massive head, it peered around, its small eyes barely able to see through the thick mass of wool covering its face.

The Sharps gave a familiar kick as flame spurted out of the muzzle. The cow bellowed and dropped to her knees. After a moment, she toppled to her side where she kicked and grunted in the grass. The herd crowded around in confusion, standing over the stricken cow. He fired again, dropping a second animal. And then another. The herd began to panic, falling in behind a cow as it attempted to lead the others off into the grass. Slightly adjusting his position, he shot her in the side, missing the heart. Tossing her head, she wheeled off in a different direction, gaining a few yards before a second shot collapsed her lung.

He dropped the surviving buffalo as they returned to the boss cow, poking her with their horns or striking with their feet while grunting and snorting. He left them for the skinners to find, the humped, bloody carcasses dotting the whitened grass.

Proceeding on foot, he crossed over a bluff in search of another herd. Spotting a group of a dozen, he proceeded down the rise, keeping to downwind as he stalked the herd. He crept up to within 150 yards before opening fire. Soon, all twelve lay dead in the grass. *Let the fat son of a bitch skin that lot.*

AS THE AFTERNOON WANED, he found himself miles from camp, on foot, and the wagon nowhere in sight. Satisfied with the tally, he made his way back toward where the wagon should be. He heard a trampling noise as a herd of several hundred buffalo streamed over a nearby rise in a cloud of snow and frosted breath. He heard whoops and threw himself down on his belly. A party of Indians pursued the herd, steering their ponies alongside the beasts and jabbing them with long lances. Concealed in a gully, he watched the Indians chase the fleeing animals into the distance. Dozens of women and children followed the hunting party, small groups clustering around each carcass as they followed the trail of dead buffalo.

He found Pickler standing astride one of the kills, slicing it up the belly as he prepared to take the robe. Tully was bent over another, cutting out the tongue. A wood tub containing meat packed in salt sat in the back of the wagon. He walked up to the small fire the skinners had started with dried buffalo chips to heat up coffee. Pickler paid him no attention as he methodically stripped the warm pelt and pulled it onto the grass. The late afternoon shadows lengthened and the skinners returned to the wagon, Pickler perspiring heavily in spite of the cold air. 'That's all,' he said, humping a last bloody hide into the back of the wagon. 'The others can feed the crows.'

'Did you at least get all the tongues?' he asked, riled at leaving the other carcasses.

Pickler snarled. 'What in hellfire do you think?'

Purchase gave the other man a hard stare, half-tempted to call him on his insolence. Pickler let loose another fart. 'We ain't got all day!' he said, hauling his fleshy bulk up onto the wagon. 'Stink, kick the fire out.'

Back at the camp the hides were unloaded and staked out in the grass to dry, the robes already starting to stiffen in the cold air. 'Beat twenty-three!' Jubal walked up, an elated look on his face.

'I can and do. Thirty-two.'

'Mother McGee!' Jubal shook his head in admiration.

Huckstep approached, a sour look on his face. 'How many?' asked Jubal.

'No more than twelve. But another dozen ran off that are probably dropped somewhere close by.'

Jubal opened his mouth to say something when Baumann walked up, having overhead the conversation. 'Do I believe my ears? You only fetched down twelve?' He stared at Huckstep, an incredulous expression on his face.

'There were Injuns everywhere! I had to take cover.'

'Your hide man says different.'

'He was a mile back! What in blazes does he know?'

'You'd best double that number tomorrow, at least.' Baumann turned to Purchase and Jubal. 'Well done, you two.' He cast a dire glance at Huckstep. 'There are some that are runners, and others that oughta be skinners.' With that warning, he walked away.

Huckstep glowered after the departing figure. 'Durn him, anyway! He has it in for me, plain and simple. Jug-eared old coot!'

Jubal snorted. 'If you stayed off the whisky, your hand wouldn't shake so you could hardly point a gun.'

'Ain't nothing wrong with my hand!'

'You'd better watch out, Cory,' taunted Jubal. 'Else you'll be riding the wagon with the skinners—and stinking to high heaven! Shucks, you'll have to find yourself another tent!'

'I ain't skinning for beans! He's jest trying to rile me.'

'Maybe you should spend less time in the saloon and more time in the field,' chided Purchase.

'A fellow has to take a break, don't he? Who can shoot buff twelve months of the year?'

'Purchase does.' Jubal grinned at his companion. 'What do you reckon?'

'I reckon it makes no sense to spend the winter making hard dollars and then blowing your stash in three days whoring and gambling.'

'See, Cory? You ought to follow Purchase's example.'

'I ain't skinnin'!' Huckstep strode off, his face like thunder.

'There goes an unhappy man, Purchase.'

'The marvel is Baumann ain't fired him already.'

'I reckon he takes a grim pleasure in watching the lazybones sink deeper into his own shit. Does it strike you he's getting antsier by the day?'

'He's missing his saloon.'

'So am I!'

THE KILLING CONTINUED THROUGH the winter, the runners stalking the buffalo through deep snow that hampered the animals' ability to escape. By late February, Purchase had tallied up over twenty-five hundred robes, the thick, prime fleeces stacked in piles ready for the first steamer after breakup. Jubal had secured a lesser hoard but nevertheless chortled with glee as he estimated his return on the bounty. 'I figure on clearing eight hundred dollars,' he said. 'How about you?'

'Just over twelve hundred, by my count.'

Jubal whistled. 'What will you do with it?'

'I sure as blazes won't spend it on cards or whisky.'

They were sitting in the newly built bunkhouse before supper, gathered around the woodstove for warmth. He had the Sharps in his hands and was polishing the breech with a greased rag. Huckstep was seated at the table, engaged in a card game. Their companion had continued to struggle, barely reaching his quota most days, and arguing with a succession of hide men before taking refuge in whisky at night.

'We could quit this camp and go panning for gold in Montana Territory. What do you say, Purchase?' asked Jubal. 'We could have some fun. Why, they say there are nuggets jest lying—'

'Durn my luck!' Jumping to his feet, Huckstep threw down a hand. Muttering to himself, he positioned himself in front of the stove, holding out his hands for warmth. 'If'n I had any, it would be pure bad!'

'How much you lost already?' asked Jubal.

'It don't matter. I'll double it when I get to Kansas City. And I won't have to freeze my pecker, neither!'

'Shucks! Such a tiny pizzle ain't worth freezing!'

Purchase watched the disgruntled Huckstep walk off. 'Is it true that he lost his earned credit—such as it is—to the cooks?'

'Down to the grease on his boot heels. He's about as useful a card player as he is a runner.'

'A cautionary tale, Jubal.'

'What? No use preaching on me. At least I got the sense to leave the table afore I go flat bust.'

'Truth is, I never did take to the fellow. Ever since Kansas.'

'He's a hard one to fetch to.'

The dinner bell sounded. 'Come on. Let's eat.'

WITH THE WINTER HUNT finished, the camp busied itself with drying and sorting the hides while awaiting the arrival of the first steamer. Purchase joined the teamsters in freighting stacks of hides and crates of salted tongues to the landing, where they were locked in a warehouse to await shipment. The prairie grass was heavy with water, and he returned splattered with mud from the wagon wheels. Jubal laughed when he saw him. 'You take a dirt bath on the way back?'

'Laugh as you like. It's your turn next!'

The weather grew warmer, and the groundwater melted. An air of festive cheer ran through the camp as the runners and skinners looked forward to spending the summer in Yankton, Sioux City, or Omaha. 'Where in perdition are the durn boats?' was the question on everybody's lips as the days continued mild and dry.

Returning one afternoon from a trip to the fort, Purchase noticed an air of disquiet in the camp. Puzzled as to the cause, he went to look for Jubal. He found his companion in a towering rage, muttering and cursing as he strode up and down in front of the tent.

'What is it?' he asked, climbing down from the horse. 'Is it the Sioux?'

'Huckstep!' Jubal spat the name.

'What about him?'

'He finally got himself fired, that's all. For drunkenness. At breakfast, would you credit?'

'Where is he?'

'That's jest it!' Jubal punched his palm in angry frustration. 'He's high-tailed it and taken my stash with him! Heck, it was only twelve dollars!'

Purchase stared for a moment and then rushed inside to check on his own stash of reserve dollars, secreted inside a boot. Jubal heard him shout from inside the tent. 'That no-good sidewinder!'

'Yours, too?' he asked as Purchase emerged.

Purchase nodded, his blood boiling. 'Where would he head for?'

'He stole a horse, so Fort Rice is my guess. He'll lay up there until it's safe to take a boat downriver. He probably figures we won't bother chasing him that far.'

'He don't know Ludlow.'

At that moment, Halverson rode up, accompanied by half a dozen heavily armed men. 'Come on!' he said, 'if you're coming!'

'All this for a stolen horse?' Purchase asked, minutes later as they rode out of camp in pursuit of the fugitive.

'The boss is making a point. Besides, he's got our stash!'

Fifteen miles south of the camp, Halverson raised a hand. 'Hold up!' The sweating, blowing horses were reined to a halt. A half mile ahead, buzzards circled above the grass. Halverson reached into his saddle bag for a pair of field glasses. He peered through them at what it was that lay obscured in the reeds. 'Take a look.' He handed Purchase the glasses.

Purchase spotted what appeared to be a body lying amid the bluestem. He nodded at Halverson, who took back the glasses and swept the range. 'Be sharp, boys. The devils could be lurking in a draw.'

They set off toward the spot at a walk, the men cradling their rifles while vigilantly scanning the surrounding bluffs.

'Whoa, fella!' Halverson drew rein. He looked down at what lay in the grass. 'Guess he won't be catching that boat,' he said.

A barely recognisable Huckstep was staked out in the flattened grass, his white, shocked face a gruesome mask of blood and terror. He had been scalped, stripped of his clothes, and tortured. The naked torso was blackened and burned and marred by ugly cuts and stab wounds.

'They did for him, all right.' Halverson stood over the body. Splinters of wood had been forced into the flesh and then set alight. The privies had been hacked off and jammed into the mouth—a length of sinew tying shut the jaws to keep them in place. The toes and fingers had been sawed off—sport, Purchase guessed—before the kill. Halverson removed his hat. 'Poor devil. I guess he won't be losing no more at cards.'

'Or missing his quotas,' another man said.

The horse was missing, a fact which caused Jubal to rumble in disgust. 'I guess the blamed Sioux got our stash!'

'Wait a minute!' A man crouched down in the grass, rifling through the clothes stripped from Huckstep and cast aside. 'This yours?' He held up a thin wad of dollars.

'Thunderation!' Whooping at his good fortune, Jubal snatched the cash. 'Yours is here, too, Purchase,' he said, counting the notes.

The buzzards made whistling calls overhead, the noise alarmingly loud in the bright air. Halverson pushed the hat back on his head. 'Let's get the blazes out of here,' he said.

'Ain't we at least going to bury him?' someone objected.

'Did you happen to bring along a spade? No? In any case, stick around if you want. I'm sure the Sioux would be obliging.'

'He was a no 'count, anyway. Not worth getting scalped for,' said one.

'Let the coyotes finish him,' agreed another.

They rode back to camp in silence, each man preoccupied with his own thoughts. Behind them, the buzzards descended.

'He didn't deserve that—in spite of his cussedness,' Purchase conceded to Jubal.

'No. I guess he didn't. Hell, I'd let him keep the durn money if it would change things.' Jubal shuddered. 'I sure hope the Sioux never take me alive!'

Purchase patted his pocket, feeling the hard bullet through the wool. 'Jest make certain you save that last cartridge.'

9

A Quarrel and a Liaison

H E WAS SEATED AT the chuck wagon, eating supper along with the rest of the company. The men were in a cheerful mood, news having spread of the arrival of the first steamer earlier that day. Many of the runners and skinners were happily making plans to leave on the morrow. Jubal had been away since morning, leaving without saying where he was going. He returned with a big grin on his face. 'I saw it!' He squeezed in alongside Purchase.

'You saw what?'

'The buff!' His face beaming, Jubal tucked into a plate of ribs and beans.

A man looked up, grease glistening on his mouth. 'What in flim-flam are you talking about? It don't take no brains to see a buff. The durn things are everywhere, thick as flies!'

'Not *a* buff. *The* buff! It was just like you said.' Jubal grinned at Purchase, his eyes shining. 'Bigger than all get out and standing there like it owned the grass.'

'You're talking about the Indian rock?' A hunter named Comstock looked up from his plate.

'I am. But it weren't Indians that carved it. It was none other than Purchase's granddaddy.'

The claim brought a surprised stare from Comstock.

'Repeat that!' Pickler roared from farther up the table as the rest of the table fell silent.

'I said,' Jubal answered, his voice testy. 'That Purchase here—his granddaddy carved it.' Astonished eyes turned to Purchase. Torn between pride and alarm at Jubal's revelation, he nevertheless nodded to affirm the claim.

'That's a damn lie!' Pickler spat food from his mouth. 'Even a flint-sided numbskull knows it was the Injuns that built it—hundreds of years ago and more.'

'No, they didn't,' said Purchase. 'It was my great-grandpa that carved it. And not much more than a hundred years ago.'

Gasps of amazement greeted the claim. 'Everyone knows it was Indians,' demurred Comstock.

'Purchase here knew all about it—even down in Kansas City,' argued Jubal. 'How the deuce would he know such a thing existed if he hadn't even travelled here?'

'Turdshit!' snorted Pickler. 'He could have heard of it. That rock was carved out by the heathen long afore this country was even heard of.' Heads nodded in agreement. Then suddenly everybody started talking at once, most taking Pickler's side, a few intrigued doubters wishing to hear more from Purchase.

'What proof do you have?' demanded one.

'My father told me about it since I was a boy. And his father before him.'

'You call that proof?' Pickler pounded the table, causing plates to jump. 'Hell, my pa told me my ma was a princess!' The riposte brought howls of laughter.

'I believe Purchase,' insisted Jubal.

'And I believed my pa!' The gloating rejoinder brought more laughter.

Purchase laid a hand on Jubal's arm as his companion stiffened.

'Let it lie. He ain't worth it.'

'Ha! I reckon your mother was no princess. Look at you!'

The remark brought instant quiet, the table looking from Jubal to Pickler. The latter clenched his ham-like fists, an air of menace about him that betokened imminent danger. 'You insulting my mother—you gawk-eyed toothpick?'

'I reckon I'm insulting you—except you're too darn stupid to know it.'

With a roar, Pickler jumped to his feet, sending plates flying from the table. 'You knock-sided, bucket-faced puke shit! I'll snap your neck and skin your hide!'

'Try it! You tub of mule grease.'

'Hold it right there!' Ludlow's voice rang out in the semidarkness. He strode up to the table, flanked by Baumann and Halverson. 'What the blazes is going on?' He confronted the belligerent Pickler who pointed an accusing finger at Purchase.

'That pecker-head is stirring up trouble by telling lies!'

'He didn't say nothing! I did.'

Ludlow cast a stern look at both would-be combatants. 'Finish your supper. And no more palaver—if you still want a job!'

The remainder of the supper finished in subdued silence, the aggrieved Pickler muttering to himself in between throwing dire glances at Purchase and Jubal.

Back at the bunkhouse Jubal threw some more wood into the stove, still seething over the incident. 'I should have pounded his pig head into the dirt.'

'He's plenty big.'

'Fat ain't big!'

Just then the door opened and Stringer stuck his head in. 'The boss wants to see you.' He looked at Purchase.

'I asked you not to say anything!' Shooting a cross look at Jubal, Purchase followed Stringer out the door.

LUDLOW'S CABIN WAS SNUG and warm. A fire blazed in the hearth. 'Sit down.' Ludlow's voice was abrupt. His deputy, the taciturn Jesper sat to one side, eyeing Purchase.

'What's this guff about your grandpa and that Indian rock?' Ludlow sat in a rocker, his foot tapping in agitation as he waited for an answer.

'It's not guff, it's true. My great-grandpa built that rock.'

'Built it?'

'Carved it, I mean. Shaped it into a buffalo.'

Ludlow pinched his nose and shot a pained look at Purchase. 'Why would you claim such a thing? Everyone knows the Indians carved it.'

'They worship it,' added Jesper, his eyes fixed on Purchase. 'They reckon the buffalo is some type of heathen totem.'

'Well?' Ludlow waited for a reply.

'How would Indians carve it? Did they have hammers and chisels a hundred years ago?'

Ludlow stopped short and looked at Jesper, who raised an eyebrow. 'Weather did most of it,' the latter opined. 'It was already half a buffalo— through natural forces.'

'Natural forces,' said Ludlow, nodding. 'Jest like that—what do you call it—Stonehinge. The Indians just finished it.'

'Smoothed it,' agreed Jesper.

'Smoothed it, using rocks.'

'And how did they get up there, on top?'

'Hell, they climbed! How else?'

'Climbed,' affirmed the deputy.

'There are bolts in the rock. I saw them.'

Ludlow scratched his face. Jesper rubbed his nose. 'Put there later,' the latter ventured.

'Why would someone come along and stick bolts in the rock? For what purpose?'

'Durned if I know, or care.' Ludlow gestured toward the door. 'I want no more of this nonsense, granddaddy or not. Your job is to hunt buffalo, not to—'

'Cook up tall tales.'

'Cook up tales! You hear me?'

'I didn't cook up anything—or start anything.' Purchase stood up.

'Well, don't. Hell, you are a good runner. One of my best. But put a cork in all this … buffalo rigmarole. Understand?'

'Fine by me.' He paused, hand on the door. 'It's true, anyway,' he said.

THAT SUMMER, HE TOOK to bed a willing Mandan woman from a small village less than seven miles from the camp. He had met her on the boat back from Fort Benton, having visited the fort on Jubal's recommendation to see more of the territory. Half Moon, the name she called herself in English, was accompanying her father, who made it a practice to travel in a steamboat at least twice a summer for the sheer novelty of it. The father—a genial, expansive fellow—spoke a smattering of English and insisted on dressing in wool jacket and trousers like the fur agents he admired.

Through him, Purchase learned that the Mandan were allowed to maintain their settlement at the behest of the Sioux—who valued the crops and artefacts the tribe provided, as well as their known skills at trading.

'The Sioux permit them to occupy Lakota land because it suits them,' an army officer familiar with the situation advised on the same boat passage. 'As soon as their usefulness ends …' he drew a finger across his throat.

He had entertained no thought of bedding a woman, let alone an Indian one, prior to setting eyes on Half Moon—who was slender and fine-featured. Her father had not been indifferent to the glances that passed between them as the boat made its way back downriver, and, indeed, encouraged the liaison.

'He figures she's safer with you than with some Sioux buck who might lay eyes on her,' the same officer advised. 'I recommend you pursue your interest, Mr McLennan. I myself have taken no less than three Indian consorts and find them—contrary to popular opinion—to be fine and accommodating bed mates. It's a common thing, here in the territories. No one will think the less of you for it, I assure you.' He shrugged. 'After all, there are no white women north of the Big Sioux. One must take where one can, do you not think?'

Intrigued by the notion, he no longer disguised his interest in the young woman, eyeing her boldly and frankly as she flashed unreadable glances at him in return.

'Offer the father something—a gun or a decorated belt buckle or some such knickknack,' advised the officer, who regarded the affair with an amused and benevolent eye—a diversion to make the passage less boring.

Thus it was that, in imitation of several of the 'permanent men', he took Half Moon as his consort, moving into a vacant tipi on the edge of camp. 'Your business is your business,' was the only comment offered by Ludlow when he returned with the girl in tow. 'As long as you keep quiet about that durned rock.'

Half Moon was, she revealed, 'seventeen summers' and, surprisingly, a virgin. 'Most eligible Mandan bucks are dead or banished for their own protection,' explained Baumann who had previously taken a Mandan wife for a summer. 'Heck, they used to own this land—afore the Sioux came by a-slaughtering!'

The liaison lasted barely eight months. The following spring Half Moon returned to her father's tipi, expressing homesickness and disgust at conditions in the camp. 'Stink like dogs!' she complained, holding her nose. He tried, unsuccessfully, to woo her back, showering both her and her father with gifts, but to no avail.

'She stay here,' her father, Eats Much Corn, said, shrugging off yet another refusal by his daughter to accompany Purchase back to the camp.

'You are not worried that some Sioux buck might come and claim her?'

The father sat forward, his face grim. 'Sioux!' He spat the word.

Purchase omitted all mention of the liaison in letters to his parents, announcing instead that he liked the Indian territory and wished to stay there once he had added to his already considerable stake. *It's fine farming country*, he wrote, withholding the fact that the rock had long since laid such powerful hold on his affections that he could no longer bear to contemplate living away from its aloof, inscrutable presence.

10

The Great Harvest

F IVE YEARS OF BUFFALO running had netted him a considerable stake, which was carefully enumerated in an account book kept by Ludlow and a copy countersigned by both men. Anxiety over the security of the credit was allayed by occasional reports rendered by buffalo runners returning from sojourns in Kansas or St Louis who testified to the honesty of the company's offices in both cities in acknowledging and paying out on the credit. 'They are a regular business,' assured Jubal, returning, flat broke, from two months in Kansas City.

The company's credit was also acknowledged in the stores that had established themselves among the motley collection of timber buildings, tents, and sod houses that flourished in the protective shade of the fort. Using lumber brought in by steamboat, the nascent settlement now boasted two saloons as well as a hardware store and trading post—all four enter-prises having sprung up to meet the growing influx of miners, prospectors and hunters, the latter lured to the territories by the great bonanza prom-ised by the inexhaustible herds of buffalo.

'Another outfit!' Jubal muttered as they watched the deckhands unload yet another wagon, its eager owners already disembarked and waiting on the levee. The two companions had accompanied Stringer to the landing, transporting a large stash of hides and salted tongues. As Stringer haggled with the boat clerk, they watched the owners hitch the waiting mule team to the wagon, looking busy and impressive as they fastened the traces. Climbing aboard, they set off, clutching their rifles, pleased and proud as they swayed on the seat. 'Greenhorns!' spat Jubal.

'That's the last bunch.' Stringer handed several bills of lading to the boat's clerk.

They got Stringer to drop them off at Doyle's saloon, promising to be back in camp by supper. 'Don't go walking into any Injuns!' the teamster called out as they jumped down from the backboard.

THE SALOON WAS A frame-built single room with a dirt floor, a bar, and six small tables. The only decoration was a yellowing poster stuck on the wall proclaiming free land in Nebraska, 'The Garden of the West!' To Purchase's surprise, a much-thumbed newspaper lay on the counter. 'It's only a month old,' he said, picking it up. Ordering whiskies, they sat at a table.

'There goes another,' said Jubal as a wagon rumbled past. 'Durn tin-horns! They spook the herds and annoy the piss out of the Indians.'

'I can see why,' muttered Purchase, peering at the front page.

'See why what?'

'Why they come. Listen.' Smoothing the newspaper with one hand, Purchase peered at the tiny print.

A booming market has developed in "flint" buffalo hides. The buffalo is now a valuable source of leather thanks to new tanning methods designed to make its hide as useable as its bovine counterpart. Whereas—

'Bovine! What in tar—'

'Cow.'

'Then why in thunder don't it say so?'

… Whereas previously, cows were treasured for their winter coats and tender meat, now bulls and calves are equally valued for their hairless hides, which are turned into shoes and belts. Whole armies are said to march on buffalo leather. And factories could not operate without leather for belts to drive their machines. Since the thrust of the railroads through Colorado and Kansas split the teeming swarms into southern and northern herds, the great buffalo harvest continues, unabated by season or regulation.

Purchase looked up. 'Southern and northern? I didn't know that.' He continued reading:

With fierce competition for the southern herd, attention is now switching to the herds concentrated along the upper Missouri. Last year, alone, over one hundred thousand hides were shipped south to Leavenworth and St Louis by steamboat. It is said that the railroads shipped a half a million more. Hundreds of jobless young men from the cities flock to the territories to claim a share of the bonanza.

He set down the newspaper. 'That explains your wagons,' he said. 'At three dollars a hide, that's a powerful lot of money.'

'Three dollars! Then how come we only make fifty cents a buff? Mebbe it's time you and I started up our own outfit.'

'Great snakes! I asked you that at least six times in the last two years! Are you ready to start?'

Jubal grinned and waved a hand. 'Nah. Too lazy.'

The door opened and a man dressed in a sack coat, waistcoat, and woollen trousers entered. He carried a large valise and wore a bowler hat, which he now removed to mop his face with a neckerchief. 'A libation—of whatever sort!' he demanded of the barkeep, a slovenly individual who studiously picked his nose as he regarded the newcomer. 'Of whatever sort so long as its whisky!'

Served a whisky, the man downed it in a gulp. 'God's blood but I am sick of steamers! Another!' Downing the second glass with a similar gulp, he vented an exasperated sigh. 'We lost a flue north of Omaha and hit a log south of Fort Pierre that almost sent us to the bottom! Goodly physician, another!' Eying Purchase and Jubal, the only other patrons, he slapped dust from his clothes.

'Gentlemen, may I join you?'

'Help yourself.' Jubal kicked out a chair.

Breathing heavily, the man sat down. 'Greatly obliged.' He stuck out a hand. 'Morgan Blainey, hide agent.'

'Sounds like you had a rough trip,' said Purchase, introducing himself and Jubal.

'Rough?' Blainey shuddered. ''Tis a miracle I sit before you, gentlemen. A gilt-edged miracle!'

They looked up as another wagon drove up from the landing. Jubal frowned as the noisy equipage creaked and rumbled along the street. 'That's the third in as many minutes!'

'Another, gentlemen, on me?' At their nods, Blainey held up three fingers to the barkeep. 'The wagons? Better get used to them, friend. There are plenty more on the way. When we left Omaha, there must have been two dozen more stranded on the landing, awaiting the next boat. And why not? The whole country's bat crazy for buff hides. The tanneries will take them all—cows, bulls, calves, whatever the time of year. I heard of a tannery in England that placed a contract for ten thousand hides just last month.'

'Not to mention the tongues,' Purchase inserted, mindful of the cargo they had just delivered to the steamer.

'Correct, friend. To my certain knowledge, Dodge City alone sold forty-eight thousand salted tongues in a single year. Mind, I detest the taste myself. But as they say, each man to his own poison.'

Jubal gave a snort. 'Do they figure all they have to do is turn up with a pea shooter and buff will race up jest begging to be shot?'

The agent stared at his empty glass. Purchase signalled the barkeep.

Blainey gave a gratified sigh as the man approached with a bottle. 'And who can blame them? There are no jobs in the cities. They must feed themselves somehow.' He eyed Purchase with sudden interest. 'Say, do you fellas have a dealer to handle your hides?'

'We work for the Missouri Company. They have a contract with a fellow down in Leavenworth.'

'Oh.' The agent looked disappointed. 'That would be Lobenstein, I hazard?' He looked to Purchase for confirmation. 'No matter!' he said, brightening at the latter's shrug. 'I've signed up half these fish already—on the boat. Although, God knows if they can tell one end of a buff from the other!'

The door opened and one of the 'fish' stepped through, a pleasant-faced youth carrying a rifle. 'Howdy!' he said, recognising the agent.

'Come, Henry. Join us.' Blainey looked around for another chair, but there wasn't one. The youth walked over, resting the rifle stock on the dirt floor. 'Gentlemen, may I present Mr Henry Clarke. Come all the way from New York to make his fortune—a bona fide buffalo hunter!'

'Runner,' the youth corrected, causing Jubal to raise an eyebrow.

'That's a fine-looking gun.' Purchase eyed the rifle.

'The new Sharps!' The youth proudly held up the rifle. 'Fifty calibre. It will drop a buff at a thousand yards.' To Purchase's surprise, he handed the weapon over for inspection. 'Finest gun there is.'

Purchase examined the rifle, curious at the octagonal barrel, double trigger, and slim lock plate.

'Twelve pounds,' bragged the youth. And hardly any kick!'

Purchase handed back the gun. 'Have you shot buffalo before?'

Clarke hesitated and looked mildly uncomfortable. 'We kilt a few dozen from the boat on the way up. But heck, I can hit a tin can at five hundred yards. I reckon I can hardly miss a big old buff at three hundred.'

'You work for a company?' asked Purchase.

The young man shook his head. 'I got my own outfit—wagon, skinners, cook, powder and lead. The works!' He beamed at Purchase. 'What do you make of that?'

'Be careful. The Sioux, Cheyenne, and Arapahoe have teamed up to murder white folk. They especially don't care for hunters.'

'Runner, if you please. Besides, any Injun that figures to bother me had better watch out for Lucy.' He patted the gun.

The door opened and a man stuck his face in. 'Henry?' he called, his voice impatient.

'A pleasure, gentlemen.' The youth tipped his hat. 'See you on the range.'

They watched him leave. 'And that's the boss!' The agent shook his head.

'Your client is likely to get himself kilt or scalped,' said Jubal. 'We found two greenhorns but a month ago, stuck full of arrows. The Sioux are on the warpath as far as runners are concerned.'

'He'll learn. And if not, there's plenty more where he came from.' The agent scratched his neck and stared at the bulky valise, as if trying to remember something.

'Well, if he's anyway near as good with that Sharps as he reckons, there's plenty of buff to choose from.'

'Plenty. But not as big as the southern herd, in my estimation.'

'Southern? You mean down in Kansas?'

'Kansas, Nebraska, Oklahoma, Texas …' The agent patted his belly, expansive in his knowledge. 'The railroad's split the buffalo up into two main herds: northern—' he made a small circle with his finger, 'and southern.'

'Heck, everyone knows that.' Jubal winked at Purchase.

'And you reckon the southern herd is bigger?'

'Reckon? I know. Jimminy crack! If you could see the Kansas plains … Why they're black with buff.'

'I've seen them.'

'Then you know. Dollars on legs, gentlemen. Dollars on legs.'

'THAT AGENT WAS A card,' said Jubal as they walked back to camp.

'Sure was. Although he didn't seem too impressed by his clients.'

'He likely reckons on half of them getting lost or kilt afore they hand over any hides.'

Just before the camp, they encountered Henry Clarke again. He was standing by the wagon where it stood propped up in the grass as three men sweated to remove a wheel.

'Howdy!' The youth called out as they approached. 'That your camp?' He nodded to the huts and tents in the distance.

'It's the durn axle!'

Clarke bent to see as one of the men crawled out from underneath the wagon. 'Can you fix it?' He asked, an anxious look on his face.

'Not this side of Hades.' The man shook his head at his companions.

'We have a blacksmith in camp,' said Purchase. 'He might be able to help.'

'Thank God!' Clarke wiped an arm across his brow.

'Come with us,' offered Jubal. 'We'll introduce you.'

The youth nodded, looking greatly relieved. 'Stay here,' he said to the men, who glanced at each other. 'We haven't even started!' he said, his voice agitated as they set off for the camp.

'Better get used to it. And keep a close eye on those mules. The Indians will steal them if they can.'

Clarke looked horrified. 'You say! I borrowed the money to outfit the wagon.'

Purchase laid a hand on the youth's shoulder. 'Things will look up once you start bringing in buff.'

Clarke nodded, his face downcast. 'Phew!' His face suddenly wrinkled in disgust. 'What in perdition is that stink?'

Jubal laughed. 'That would be buffalo perfume, friend. Get used to it!'

OVER THE YEARS, HE had grown into an experienced and deadly marksman—the best in the camp, according to no less an authority than Halverson himself. On successive days the previous week he had dropped 80, 93, and 112 buffalo from a single stand using two rifles, the second borrowed from Halverson. The tally was a camp record, which drew a public handshake from Ludlow. 'Wish everyone was as sure-fire reliable,' he said, with a pointed glance at Jubal.

'Leave some for me!' grumbled the latter after Ludlow had left. 'I'm on thin ice with the blamed sorehead ever since that short count last week.'

'You'll make it up. I never saw so much buffalo.'

Jubal pondered this. 'True. The more we hunt, the more they seem to spring up.' He took a scrap of jerky from his pocket and chewed on it, still mulling the fact. 'Ever since we started hunting year-round there seem to be more of the critters, not less. How do you account for that?'

'It's their nature, I guess.'

'What in sand creek does that mean?'

'It means that the more we kill, the more they … multiply, to make up for the fact.'

Jubal frowned. 'You think so?'

'How else to explain it?'

'Mebbe they are coming in from elsewhere—fresh herds. From up in Montana or Canada way.'

'I doubt it.'

'Makes more sense than multiplying. Heck, you're shooting whole herds by yourself.'

'As long as there are plenty to go around—for both us and the Sioux—I could care less whether they emigrate or procreate.'

Jubal chewed on another bite of jerky. 'The durn range is overrun with greenhorns. Last week I must have seen a dozen outfits.'

'They are a strife.'

'They are riling up the Sioux. Comstock said he came across a big party jest two days ago. Reckoned they had murder on their mind. He hightailed it out of there.'

Purchase got up, suddenly hungry. 'Where did you find that jerky?'

The next afternoon, he had returned from the hunt and was sitting outside the bunkhouse cleaning the Sharps. Jubal sat alongside, wrapping some cartridges, both men enjoying the warm spring sunshine.

'Hey, Purchase!' Jesper approached. 'You keep going the way you are and you'll earn yourself an extra skinner.'

'Thunderation, Purchase! You must be working that tub of guts Pickler to the frizzle!' said Jubal as Jesper departed.

'It ain't me. It's Ludlow. He'd work us night and day if he could.'

The booming trade in flint hides ensured the camp was now a year-round concern as more and more hunters flocked to the territory to claim a share of the wealth. So great was the flow of hides from the camp to the steamboat landing that Ludlow was forced to purchase additional wagons. The previous year, the company had shipped seventy-five thousand hides—intended for both leather and fur—south to Leavenworth.

'And that ain't scratch, compared to what's going on in the southern plains and elsewhere,' Ludlow had announced, professing, for the first time, a concern that even the inexhaustible buffalo herds could not long sustain such a murderous harvest. 'Every tinhorn factory worker, farmer, whore, and card sharp fancies themselves a hunter,' he complained to Jesper, within earshot of Purchase and Jubal. 'The damn fools are shooting calves, cows, spike bulls—anything with a pair of horns.' The recitation caused Ludlow to scratch furiously at his neck, his ire aroused at the newcomers, who were known to blaze away at unweaned calves and pregnant cows in the mad rush to cash in on the great hide bonanza. 'And another thing,' he grumbled, 'the damn Indians are mad as hellfire.'

'The Sioux are boiling,' agreed Jesper.

'Boiling! And likely to bubble over and scald the hell out of everyone!'

Purchase watched them go, still cussing at the greenhorn hunters and fretting about the Sioux. 'What do you think?' he asked Jubal.

'I reckon it's his pocket, not our scalps, that he's worried about.'

'He's right, though.'

'About what?'

'The Sioux.'

He set out at dawn the next day, leaving Pickler and Tully to follow on. By daylight, he had spotted a group of twenty buffaloes and set up his stand. Working quickly, he dispatched the group and set off in search of another, leaving the carcasses for Pickler to find. By noon, he was done, having almost doubled his quota.

On his way back to the camp, he passed two separate runners scouting for buffalo—both men part of the recent influx of greenhorn outfits. One of them called out a cheery 'Hello!' cupping his hands to yell.

'Lord Almighty!' He shook his head.

The increasing prevalence of the inexperienced and hastily put-together hunting outfits—made up of jobless labourers, ex-railroaders, freighters, and unskilled hands from the cities, was a source of much grumbling among the established runners in the camp. The competition for 'ownership rights' of nearby herds forced the company men to scout farther afield in search of buffalo, thus putting them at greater risk of Indian attack. The sight of abandoned buffalo carcasses—stripped of their thin summer hides, the tongues removed, the bodies left to rot on the baking plain—had aroused the Indians to madness. In revenge, they exacted a grim and terrible retribution on any runner or skinner unfortunate enough to be caught out alone on the plains. Tales of narrow escapes were increasingly frequent around the supper table, as were rumours of the dreadful tortures inflicted on anyone foolish enough to let themself be captured alive.

Mindful of the risk, Purchase kept a sharp eye out as he scouted the bluffs. On several occasions, he had avoided detection only by throwing himself into a wallow or gulch and concealing himself there until the danger had passed. Once, an Indian had ridden up to within yards of where he lay hidden, the warrior stopping to scout the waving grasslands as Purchase kept tight hold of the Sharps. Others, especially the unwary tenderfeet lured from the cities by the prospect of enriching themselves from the great buffalo harvest, were not so fortunate.

One morning in midsummer, drawn by circling buzzards, he came upon four bodies lying in the grass. All four had been scalped and mutilated. He searched the surrounding hummocks, holding the Sharps at the ready. Satisfied that no hostiles lurked in ambush, he examined the corpses, grimacing at the grisly spectacle. The bodies had been mutilated and then burned. He found a fifty calibre Sharps lying alongside one of the bodies and uttered an exclamation as he studied the barely recognisable remains. 'You never did have much luck,' he muttered, stifling his revulsion at the gouged eye sockets. The nose and ears were missing from all four bodies, and he presumed them taken as trophies. He stood for a while contemplating the burned-out wagon, the cold, charred timbers suggesting the massacre was at least a day old. He turned away and headed for the wagon to warn the skinners.

He found them a half mile away, preparing to divest the hides from his earlier kills. Tully turned white when told of the slaughter, his lips trembling as though he were about to burst into tears. Pickler was more truculent but nevertheless eager to head back to camp. 'Consarned Injuns!' The skinner hauled his fleshy bulk up onto the wagon. 'Push over!' Using his bulk to squeeze Tully to one side, he took up the reins. 'Har! Git, you mangy wolf bait!'

The news caused consternation back at the camp, the men already rattled by a close encounter the day before when a party of Sioux had threatened a wagon—the Indians prevented from an outright assault only by the timely arrival of another runner. Unwilling to face two buffalo guns, they had retreated with taunts and threats. A concerned Ludlow immediately sent riders to alert those wagons still out on the range. 'Tell them head back, pronto!' he shouted after the riders.

Told by Purchase of the massacre and the fate of Clarke, Jubal muttered and scratched his throat. 'I'm powerful sorry to hear it. But he had no business being out here. What did he know of the territories, or Injuns, or buff come to that?' He nodded at the weapon Purchase carried. 'That his Sharps?'

'It is. I figured I'd use it as a spare.'

'Might as well. It sure won't do him any good. But how come the Sioux didn't take it?'

'Maybe in the excitement—or maybe because it was out of ammo and they don't have any.'

News of the massacre spread quickly, the accounts gaining in gruesome detail with each telling. The lurid reports drove the small hunting outfits back to the fort for safety—the frightened greenhorns too jittery to venture forth with so many Indians after their blood. 'It ain't all bad,' Jesper was reported as saying on hearing this. 'Leastways we get the range to ourselves.'

THE FRAUGHT SITUATION WITH the Indians meant he was unable to visit the rock—a solo journey across the plains being out of the question. Instead, he tried to supplement his meagre information about the object by questioning a few of the older officers when next he visited the fort. 'What do you know of it?' he asked a veteran of Antietam, who had been stationed at various forts in the territories the past several years.

'The Injuns built it—that's all I know. Not the present lot, but others, hundreds of years ago. Maybe more.'

'How did they manage it—without tools?'

'They had tools. Flints, stones, and such.'

'Would that be sufficient to carve granite?'

'Sure. Given enough time—and Injuns.'

He received no further enlightenment when directed to a grizzled trooper, the oldest man at the post and the longest serving.

'Yeah, I seed it. Durndest thing I ever saw!'

'Do you have any information on who—or how, it was built?'

'Injuns! Who else?'

'I found an old bolt hammered into the rock.'

The trooper considered this. 'Probably some nosy easterner.'

'Why?'

'Why what?'

'Why would he bother sinking a bolt into the rock?'

'Hell if I know! Why don't you ask him?'

That the great rock was an object of so little curiosity amazed and confounded him—everyone he questioned on the matter dismissing it as part of the landscape—of no more significance than the bluffs or endless acres of grass. When, in exasperation, he floated the idea of one day climbing it, the suggestion was met with looks of pure astonishment.

'Why in Joseph H. Smith would anyone want to risk their neck doing such a fool thing?' Baumann, to whom he had vouchsafed the suggestion, stared in bewilderment.

'No reason. I just thought it might be fun to see out over the grass from up there. That's all.'

'Fun? If you want fun, get drunk and save your neck!'

After a series of such rebuffs, he dropped the matter entirely, aware he was gaining a reputation for an unhealthy preoccupation with the object. 'Still think your granddaddy raised it up?' Pickler mocked on the rare occasion the hunt brought them within distant sight of the monument.

'Go tend to your business!' He jabbed a thumb at the buffalo carcasses lying in the grass.

Pickler laughed, a harsh, mocking sound. 'I'll do that while you go climb that fool rock!'

That does it! He sat down to eat some buffalo jerky, swearing to himself never to say another word on the subject.

But even though he maintained his silence—ignoring the occasional barb—he was unable to keep his thoughts from straying back to the giant rock. *How did he climb it? Where did he get the tools to shape it? Who helped him? Surely, he could not have managed it alone—or with just his two sons? Did the Indians help?* Finally, tired of his own incessant pondering, he thrust the object from his mind, fearing he would go mad with unanswerable questions.

'How long do you figure to stay here?' Jubal asked one evening after supper. The air had turned cooler, and they were lying around a fire, idly passing the time by swapping a bottle of whisky back and forth.

'Not much longer. That's for sure. I'm tired of running. Hell, it's no fun. The buff just stand there waiting their turn.'

'I heard a fellow the other day—in town—say that buff are no longer killed, they are harvested, like wheat or corn,' said Jubal.

'In town?' Purchase pondered the description.

'Well, what passes for the sorriest town you ever did see.' Jubal passed back the bottle. 'Anyway, what will you do if you don't shoot buff?'

'I'd like to farm—get hold of some land.'

'Where?'

'Maybe around here.'

'Around here! The Indians would scalp you for sure. This ain't no land for a white man—not unless he's running buff.'

'Who knows? Someday, maybe.'

'That day would have to be after they wiped out all the cuss-darned Injuns.'

'What about you? What will you do—after?'

'I'd like to travel some—to New York and Boston.'

'And what would you do for work?'

'Thunder if I know!'

In the silence that followed, Jubal gazed up at where pale stars glimmered through the dusk. Raising himself on one elbow, he looked over at Purchase. 'Why don't we go together?'

'Where?'

'New York, Baltimore, shucks, maybe even Californy. We could pan for gold. What do you say, Purchase? You and me.'

He thought about it, taking a pull of the whisky before handing the bottle back. 'I guess I could put off farming, for a while.'

Jubal's face lit up. 'It would be a grand adventure. Heck, we could even scout for the wagon trains headed west. Or mebbe open up a saloon in San Francisco.'

Purchase laughed. 'Strike the saloon. You'd be our best customer.'

'But you mean it—about palling up and mebbe heading west?'

'Sure, why not? I could come back here when the Indians have quit scalping and murdering.'

'You may not want to come back. You might get snapped up by a purty little California gal!'

'Maybe.' He was already back to thinking of the rock, planning to one day live near it.

'They sure look pretty, don't they?' Jubal gazed up at the stars.

'They do that.'

'Do you reckon anyone's up there?'

'In the stars?'

'On the moon.'

'It would be a thing.'

Jubal sighed. 'It sure would,' he agreed. 'It sure would.'

11

A Desperate Struggle

H E HAD BEEN OUT for less than an hour, settling down to draw aim on a stand of buffalo, when he heard a gunshot in the distance. He cocked his head, listening intently. Another gunshot sounded. He got to his feet, certain the sound came from where he had left the wagon a mile or so back. *Probably just another runner*. After listening a while longer, he returned to the stand, but a growing unease caused him to abandon it without firing a shot. He stood up. The hillsides were bare, the empty, rustling grass the only motion. Then he spotted a thin column of black smoke rising into the air.

He was making his way back, every sense alert, when he heard a horse grunt. He threw himself headlong to the grass. Moments later, a party of mounted Sioux appeared over a ridge a short distance ahead.

Breathing heavily, he peered through the reeds. The Indians were spread out in a line and appeared to be searching as they moved slowly through the grass. The smoke trail behind them had thickened and he knew with ominous certainty what had taken place. They have slaughtered the skinners and now they are hunting the runner—me! His mind flashed to Pickler and Tully. He saw them lying in the grass, butchered and scalped, the wagon on fire. He blinked the images from his mind as the line of Indians drew closer. They appeared to be in no hurry, stopping every now and then to signal one another or to scour the windswept grass. Long familiar with the habits of runners, they counted on finding their prey within a mile or so of the wagon, probably concealed, as indeed he was, and watching them. So confident were they of his proximity that one of the Indians half-raised himself from his pony to call out in a taunting, mocking voice, 'We find you, John-ee! We find you!'

Squirrelling on his elbows, he moved back through the grass, searching for some cover. He chanced upon an old wolf den and concealed himself there while racking his brains for a way out of the predicament. Peering at the line of slowly advancing Sioux, he counted eleven warriors, each bedecked in war paint and carrying hide shields and lances. Three or four carried rifles. The nearest Indian was now less than four hundred yards away. He could hear clearly the snorts of the ponies and the voices of the riders as they called out to one another. One leaned down and jabbed at a hollow with his lance. His companions were equally vigilant, their painted faces arrogantly confident of finding their prey.

I can't let them get on top of me. Propping himself on his elbows, he sighted the Sharps. The slight movement drew attention and one of the Indians glanced his way. The gun gave a sharp *crack!* and the Indian toppled sideways as the pony whinnied in fright. He jerked the lever and fed another shell into the chamber. One of the riders gave a bloodcurdling whoop and lashed the pony directly toward him. The shot blew the Indian clean from the horse. Seeing this, his companions whipped their mounts into a retreat. Sliding down from the ponies, they threw themselves into the thick bluestem.

Silence followed as he surveyed the blowing grass. The Sioux were concealed several hundred yards from where he lay. Raising the rear sight, he drew bead on a pony which had wandered a few yards in advance of the others. Carefully sighting on the chest, he dropped it with a single round.

The shot caused consternation. The concealed Indians leapt to their feet and hurriedly retreated a farther distance, shooing their mounts before them. He fired again as they retreated, striking another pony on the flanks. The horse stumbled, fell, and picked itself up, staggering in shock. Its owner pulled it to a safer distance while answering puffs of smoke rose up from the rest of the party. He squinted through the stalks, confident the shots would not reach him. He rose a little higher to try to spot the Indians, who seemed undecided what to do next. They won't rush me, he thought. They have too much sense for that.

He glanced up at the sky. Clouds were gathering and a cold wind ruffled the grass. A silence had fallen, and he risked getting up on his knees to see over the tall stalks. The concealed Indians called out threats and taunts. 'We take hair, John-ee! Like fat man!' A lance poked up and waved in the air. He saw a dark strip atop the point and his mouth tightened. 'See John-ee! He long time to die!'

Ignoring the taunts, he focused on the stiff reeds, straining for any movement. The only sound was that of the wind gusting through the grass. Glancing behind him, he studied the lush slopes. I could steal back, and around. With luck, run into another wagon. He had no sooner decided on this course of action than he glimpsed a movement in the long grass about four hundred yards ahead and to his right. Raising the Sharps, he fired. An agonised shriek rang out. He scanned the grass to his left, detecting a scurrying motion as the Indian hidden there squirrelled backward out of range. He let the man go, figuring not to enrage them so much that they would throw caution to the wind and risk a frontal charge. Opening the canteen, he took a small swig, decided now to wait before attempting to make an escape. *The boys will have seen the smoke and come looking for me*, he consoled himself. He settled down to wait, feeling for the reserve cartridge in his pocket, grimly comforted by the feel.

The standoff lasted less than an hour. The cloud cover had thickened, and a moist wind blew into his face. Soon enough, rain sheeted down as the storm broke, drenching the bluffs. He saw the Indians break cover and dash toward the ponies. Jumping onto their backs, they raced off into the grass, evidently figuring he wasn't worth enduring a prairie downpour. He watched them go, water rising up like smoke from the flashing hooves. He waited another quarter-hour, getting soaked to the skin, before cautiously emerging from the den. He set off through the wet grass, a protective leather sleeve over the Sharps. A short distance from the den, he came across the body of the shot Indian. The dead man lay face down, a bloody gash on his shoulder showing where the slug had torn down through the lungs.

The rain lashed down and he shivered, his buckskins heavy with moisture. Unable to see more than a few yards ahead, he continued on, senses vigilant for danger. A little farther on, he came across the carcass of the horse he had wounded on the flank. Its throat had been cut and the rope bridle and wool blanket stripped from the body.

The rain stopped and the clouds parted, allowing rays of sunlight to illuminate the drenched prairie grass. A short time later, he reached the camp. The downpour had put out the fire, the charred wagon embers still smoking. He found Pickler first. The skinner was on his back, his fat belly slashed open, the guts pulled out and wrapped around his neck like a crimson neckerchief. The skin had been peeled from his thighs and arms—a mocking reference to the dead man's trade. Unusually, the eyes had been left in his head, as well as the tongue. *They wanted him to see what they were doing—and to hear him scream.* And indeed, the skinner's mouth was open, the lips drawn back in a snarl. *He no doubt cursed them as they worked on him.* He found Tully a few yards away, the broken body dreadfully mutilated. He stood up, averting his eyes from the wanton slaughter. *They killed the mules as well. And took the hides. He'd have hated that.*

'PURCHASE!' JUBAL RUSHED UP to meet him as he approached the tents. 'We thought you had been kilt!' Wagons had been drawn up in a line and armed men stood in the grass behind the conveyances.

He glanced around the camp. 'What's happening?'

'We got word the Sioux are planning to attack. The boss has sent to the fort for soldiers. But what happened to you?' Jubal's face was concerned. 'The boss will want to speak with you.'

'In a moment. I must change my shirt. I'm soaked to the bone.'

While changing the shirt, he briefly recounted the story of what had happened to the skinners. He repeated the account to Ludlow as the latter listened along with Halverson, Baumann, and Jesper. 'We figured you were in trouble,' said the latter. 'One of the boys came back and said he saw smoke and heard firing from where you were.'

'And you didn't think to send help?'

'Hell, we were told the devils were about to fall upon the camp,' interrupted Ludlow. 'I had every man jack stand to arms.'

'They still might,' said Halverson. 'They are fired up like all-perdition.'

'I doubt they will try a frontal assault. I killed three and it put the wind up them.'

'There are reputed to be three hundred Sioux, with another hundred Arapahoe,' said Jesper. 'Doubt that!'

'That many?' Shocked, he glanced at Halverson for confirmation.

The other man nodded, his face sombre. 'If Stinks Like a Bear is to be believed.'

'I don't doubt him,' said Ludlow. 'The fellow has been right enough in the past.'

'Them soldiers can't come quick enough,' said Jesper.

After visiting the chuck wagon and swallowing a few mouthfuls of hot food, he made his way back to Jubal. 'I can't believe the Indians would be so foolish as to attack an armed camp,' he said.

'They might. According to Stinks, they are being whipped up by a medicine man. He says that he has put a spell on our guns and that our bullets can't harm them.'

'When will the soldiers get here?'

'Soon. Two hours or so, I expect.'

Purchase peered at the rolling uplands. The sky was blue again and the wet pastures gleamed in the sunlight. 'Let's hope so. Four hundred is a powerful lot of Injuns.'

'I'm sorry I couldn't go in search of you. The boss locked down the camp and had us all stand to arms like we were durn soldiers again.'

'It's all right. I'm just glad I escaped with my hair.'

'Me, too, Purchase. Me, too.' Jubal's voice was sombre with relief.

They heard a yell and saw a rider spur through the grass toward them. 'Don't shoot!' voices shouted.

'It's Miller,' said Jubal. 'The boss posted him up on the ridge.'

The rider jumped down from his panting horse as men clustered anxiously around him. 'They're coming, boys! The whole Sioux nation!'

IT WAS DARK AND the men were on edge. A detachment of forty soldiers had arrived from the fort armed with breech-loading Springfields. The reinforcements helped calm nerves frayed by signs of constant Indian activity in the surrounding hummocks. Throughout the night, the men kept vigilant watch as hoots and cries from the long grass signalled a considerable Indian presence.

'They won't attack until dawn. And if they try a full-frontal assault we'll consign them all to Injun hell!' Ludlow walked along the defensive line, displaying surprising grit as he reassured the sleepless men. 'Get your heads down, boys. We have the army to back us up. Why, I almost pity the red devils!'

Purchase lay down in the grass behind a wagon wheel and tried to follow Ludlow's advice while urging Jubal to do the same. 'Get some sleep. You heard the boss. They won't attack at night.'

Jubal peered out over the dark prairie, his rifle propped against the backboard. 'I can't sleep. It 'minds me of something.'

'What?'

'Gettysburg. Remember?'

'Sure. What about it?'

'I was up on Culp's Hill.'

'What in blazes were you doing up there?'

'I was a messenger—a runner.' Jubal laughed softly in the darkness. 'Same as now. 'Cept I was running Graybacks then. Anyhow. This 'minds me of the night before the battle. The Rebs were somewhere below, and we knew they would attack at first light. We could hear their yells in the darkness as they tried to shake us. Listen!'

Purchase listened as a series of hoots floated on the darkness.

'See what I mean? Same thing.'

'Well, we whipped the Rebs and we sure as heck are going to whip the Sioux. Now good night. I want to get some shut eye. And I advise you to do the same.'

When he opened his eyes again, Jubal was lying on the grass, fast asleep. It was past sun-up and men were moving about the camp as fires were lit and coffee put to boil. The morning was fresh and clear with a steady nor'-wester blowing toward the camp. He stood up, shivering, and slapped his arms to restore the blood. Jubal gave a loud snore and muttered in his sleep. *He's right. It's like Gettysburg—the morning we marched on the town.* A strange feeling of repeatability haunted him for a moment as he recalled Winslow, Abe, and Elias, sticking their sleepy heads out the tent flaps.

'Rouse up!' He shook his sleeping companion. 'Let's get some coffee.'

The tension of the previous night had eased, and the men looked in confident spirits as they drank coffee and chewed on beans and buffalo jerky while waiting for whatever the morning might bring. The breeze had gotten warmer and stronger, and he loosened his jacket. *Maybe they have seen the troopers,* he told himself, *and gone off in search of easier targets.*

There was a brief commotion over where the troop commander had set up his command post and he went over to listen. One of the scouts had returned, his face ruddy in the morning sunshine. 'More Sioux have joined up,' he was saying. 'I reckon there must be four to five hundred hostiles out there.'

The news sent waves of apprehension through the surrounding listeners, which the officer in charge, a lieutenant, did his best to quell. 'There ain't no redskin alive that would dare rush a bunch of breech-loaders. You hear? We have better than eighty guns to bring to bear. Get back to your posts and keep sharp watch. Hell, I expect the savages have gone to take breakfast at Doyles!'

The remark brought laughter and some reassurance as the men took up position behind the line of wagons.

'I wish they'd shit or get off the durned pot.' Jubal, his stubbled face tense, leaned against the wagon. 'What do you reckon?'

'I reckon I've had enough of running,' said Purchase, his mind suddenly made up. 'Are you still keen to head out west?'

'Hell, yeah!'

'Then let's quit—this summer. Take a steamer down to Kansas City. From there we can buy horses or take the train to wherever we want.'

'New York first!'

'New York first, if you like.' Purchase tugged at his jaw. 'Anywhere's so long as it ain't this damn buffalo camp.'

Jubal grinned. 'Tarn, Purchase. We are going to have the adventure of all creation! I know it.'

They talked over their plans for a few minutes, each proposing more outlandish schemes until they broke into laughter. 'I can hardly wait!'

'To see New York?'

'To see the look on Jesper's face when we quit!'

The talk died away as the morning continued warm and gusty and they waited for some sound or incident to disturb the silence. Purchase took off his jacket and sipped water, sweating in the sun. All around, men were checking their weapons or looking out over the grass, an air of nervous expectancy permeating the camp. The lieutenant walked along the line of wagons, reassuring the men by his presence as he gave last-minute orders to strengthen the defences.

HE WAS SEATED ON the wagon tongue gazing out over the rolling bluffs when a cry broke the fraught silence.

'Looky there!' A teamster leapt up onto a wagon and pointed to where a broad curtain of smoke hung in the distance. As they watched, it became clear that the smoke was advancing toward them. 'The devils have fired the grass!' yelled the teamster.

Purchase saw flashes of fire where the grass burned beneath the smoke. Around him, men were rushing to find containers of water. 'We gotta retreat or get burned alive!' A man yelled.

'No! We stand here. We'd get cut to pieces in the open.' The lieutenant, a veteran of several Indian campaigns, peered through his field glasses. 'Get ready! They will come in after the smoke. He held up a licked finger. 'The wind is changing, boys!'

'It's true!' Jubal stuck out his tongue. 'It's shifting in our favour, by God!' The news brought cheers.

But the smoke was now no more than three hundred yards from the wagons. The acrid smell stung Purchase's nose as the dry grass crackled and burned. He heard whoops and the thunder of hooves.

He tensed, sighting along the muzzle.

'Brace yourselves!'

The Indians rode out of the smoke, whooping and shrieking and seeming like demons from hell as they charged pell-mell at the defenders. A rattle of gunfire rang out as the men opened fire. He glanced to where the blue-coated troopers knelt in a line, the lieutenant standing behind, sword raised. Again, he had a brief flash of having witnessed the same scene before—whether illustrated in a book or seen in life, he could not tell. A sharp, disciplined volley sounded at the lieutenant's command. Beside him, Jubal's gun barked out flame and smoke. He sighted the .50 calibre Sharps on the mass of dark, shrieking forms charging toward him and fired, unable to tell whether he had hit anyone or not. Jerking open the breech, he inserted a cartridge into the chamber as the Sioux, uttering wild cries, fell upon the camp.

The momentum of the Indian charge took them through the line of wagons. Wheeling and regrouping, they rushed back, discharging arrows and uttering hideous shrieks. Gunpowder, smoke from the grass fire, and dust kicked up by the racing ponies made it difficult to distinguish targets. He stood side by side with Jubal, firing at phantoms as the Sioux raced up and down like banshees, appearing and vanishing in the smoke. Gunfire rattled with a noise like firecrackers, the noise cutting through the frenzied yells and the thunder of pounding hooves.

He glimpsed one Indian charge boldly into the midst of six or seven defenders and fling himself onto the men. Jubal yelled out a warning and he spun around as two mounted Indians rushed toward them. Jubal shot the first, the slug blowing off the top of the warrior's head. The second Indian continued toward Purchase, his face wild as he leaned from the saddle, a raised tomahawk in his grasp. The Sharps misfired and he leapt sideways to avoid the wild, swinging blow. He tripped, falling heavily in the grass. By the time he scrambled back to his feet, the Indian had vanished in the smoke.

'Hold fire!' The lieutenant's voice rang out as the Indians disappeared back into the smouldering grass, their wild yells receding on the air. 'Ready your arms! They'll try again!'

A pause followed as the harried defenders regrouped. Several shots rang out as they despatched wounded Indians lying in the grass. He saw wounded or dying men being carried into the bunkhouse and the door barred behind them.

'Hellfire, but we might not survive a second charge like that!' Jubal breathed heavily. He had a cut above his scalp where an arrow had grazed him. 'Another fraction and I'd be stretched in the grass like a flint hide,' he said, attempting levity as he fingered the cut.

A skinner came up to them lugging a box of cartridges. 'Help yourselves,' he said. 'The boss said to hoard your shots. But heck, what would he know?' He spat in the grass. 'Thank God for the army boys, is all.'

The sun beat down relentlessly. Purchase wiped down both Sharps, opening the breech to look for fouling in the one that had misfired. Around him, the men looked on edge as they braced for the next assault.

'Drag those wagons closer!' The lieutenant walked up and down, issuing orders and doling out what reassurance he could. 'A few more volleys like the last and they'll lose all stomach for the fight. Hold your nerve, boys! Hold your nerve.'

A long, ululating cry sounded from the smoking grass and the men braced. The Sioux had regrouped and were preparing for a second assault. Through the drifting smoke, Purchase glimpsed hundreds of riders milling around, waiting for a command. 'Did you say New York, and then Californy?'

'Sure. Want to leave right now?'

'I would, but I have some small business to take care of first.'

'I reckon New York will still be there in a month or so.'

'Here they come, boys!'

The Indians launched the second attack by splitting into three columns—two directed to strike at the flanks, while a third struck the front. The lieutenant had anticipated the tactic, drawing on his experience to set the defenders accordingly. As a result, the Indians charged into withering fire on all three fronts. But in spite of heavy losses, their momentum allowed them to breach the line of defences a second time. Turning on the fly, they let loose a hail of arrows that hissed through the air with lethal effect.

Near Purchase, one of the skinners uttered an agonised cry and slumped to the ground, his chest pierced by a feathered shaft. The Sioux were now everywhere at once, whooping and shrieking as they fell upon the defenders with hatchets and clubs. The desperate men resorted to pistols and knives as they fought for their lives.

Panic started to spread as the battle raged. Purchase saw one of the cooks dash beneath a wagon and cower there, arms over his head. A mounted Indian loomed up out of the smoke and he shouted hoarsely to Jubal. Drawing back his arm, the Indian made to hurl a lance. The Sharps erupted in flame and sent the Indian sprawling backward over the flanks of the pony as it raced off in fright. Through the dense, drifting smoke, men grappled hand to hand as the Indians leapt from their horses—flinging themselves on the defenders with reckless fury. Cries of triumph rent the air, the Sioux sensing victory as they pressed home the attack. The Sharps was red-hot in his hands as he fired again and again. He glimpsed Jubal despatch an Indian at point-blank range, a wild look on his face as he stood over the stricken buck and fired.

An Indian rushed up out of the smoke and thrust at him with a lance. Dropping the empty Sharps, he seized the shaft, wrestling for possession. The Indian snarled in rage, his painted face grotesque and hateful as he attempted to grab back the lance and spear Purchase. Suddenly, a volley of rifle fire erupted from the smoke and the Indian shrieked and collapsed to the ground. As he groaned and tried to get back to his feet, Purchase reversed the lance and ran him through the belly. He stabbed him again as a second volley rang out.

Blue-coated troopers loomed through the haze, pausing to reload and fire again. The volleys raked the stunned Indians to devastating effect. He saw the lieutenant, sword in hand, directing his men and shouting out orders as they fired with rapid and deadly accuracy. Unnerved by the withering fire, the Indians halted in confusion and then abruptly broke off the attack. Leaping onto the backs of ponies or lifted up behind their comrades, they fled the field while uttering cries of rage and disappointment.

The lieutenant's voice rose above the din, shouting for the men to hold fire.

Exhausted, Purchase wrapped an arm around Jubal's shoulder.

'By God, but we are still alive!'

The lieutenant sent out scouts who returned to report that the Indians had indeed fled, leaving behind eighteen killed in the grass—a figure brought up to thirty-one when the ones within the line of wagons were included. 'They've skedaddled back to the hills,' the army scout reported. 'They've lost too many to try again.'

The camp had suffered sixteen casualties—nine dead and seven wounded, the popular Stringer among the fatalities. The troopers had suffered two deaths and four wounded, one of them likely to prove fatal. The shocked survivors wandered around in a daze, hardly able to believe they were still alive. Smoke drifted over the wagons as the blackened grass smouldered under the hot sun. The wounded and dying were tended to, the bodies of the dead Indians dragged out into the scorched grass and left there for the buzzards to feed on. The nervous livestock were calmed and secured. Ludlow went around issuing orders as the chaotic aftermath of the battle was cleared away and the camp slowly restored to something resembling its former self.

Returning to deposit their weapons in the tent, they found it ripped from its tethers and their belongings scattered across the grass. Jubal, his face grimy with sweat and dirt, slumped down into the grass. 'God in heaven! I thought we were doomed certain as all get out.'

'That last Injun almost skewered me clean through.' Purchase sat down alongside, overcome with weariness.

Jubal muttered in disbelief. 'How in Hades did we come through?'

Purchase lay on his back to stare up at the wispy clouds. He was breathing hard, his thoughts in a whirl. If that Injun had gutted me ... He felt something hard poke into his hip. He reached for the object, thinking it was a cartridge. To his surprise, his fingers closed around the sliver of granite he had chiselled from the rock. He fingered the talisman, marvelling at the desperate battle and his narrow escape from harm. *I forgot I put it there. The buffalo got me through it. Maybe it—or old man McLennan was looking down on me. I'll tell pa. He'll think so, too.*

'You boys!' A harried Jesper walked up. 'Grab a spade! There's dead that needs burying.'

THE ELEVEN DEAD—PLUS ONE other who had succumbed to his wounds—were buried in a line, the lieutenant making notes over the graves of each dead trooper. When the bodies were all interred, Ludlow said a few brief words in praise of the men, followed by the lieutenant. Ludlow then recited a psalm—'The only one I could remember,' he later confessed.

Blessed is the man that walketh not in the counsel of the ungodly, nor standeth in the way of sinners, nor sitteth in the seat of the scornful. But his delight is in the law of the Lord; and in his law …

He paused, frowned, and turned to Jesper, who shook his head. With a mutter, the lieutenant stepped up.

… And in his law doth he meditate day and night
    And he shall be like a tree planted by the rivers of water, that bringeth forth his fruit in his season; his leaf also shall not wither; and whatsoever he doeth shall prosper.

A pause followed. Ludlow looked at the lieutenant. 'Amen?' he said. The mourners followed. 'Amen.'

The lieutenant nodded to a young trooper who put a bugle to his lips. As the melancholy, twenty-four-note requiem sounded over the graves, Purchase's thoughts drifted back to the war and the many battlefield burials he had attended. He caught a sombre glance from Jubal and guessed his companion was thinking the same. Long-buried grief for Winslow, Elias, Abe, and other departed comrades surfaced as tears sprang to his eyes.

He helped place simple wooden crosses over each grave, the effort dispelling some of the gloom that had gripped him during the ceremony. But his heart was heavy as he made his way back to the collapsed tent. Jubal walked alongside. Neither man spoke as they sat in the grass, each ruminating on comrades lost, battles survived, and the randomness which had fetched them to this spot—sitting, remembering. Alive.

A meal was served, and the exhausted men ate hungrily. Now that the battle was won, a mood of angry discontent simmered throughout the company as bitter voices demanded revenge. 'Don't forget. They slaughtered Pickler, too—and Tully,' a man remonstrated, urging an attack in reprisal. 'And don't forget poor Strings.'

'Nor what the devils did to Huckstep!'

'We ought wipe out every one of the cussed savages!'

'Kill them all!' someone chorused.

The lieutenant, assisted by Ludlow, attempted to pacify the rising swell of grief and anger—the former with little success as his own, resentful troopers now joined in the growing demands for vengeance.

'They harpooned poor Jed like a fish!' A trooper, his face wrenched with grief, stood up and pointed to the grave of his slaughtered comrade. 'I say we head out and burn up a village or two!'

'Stand down!' The lieutenant glared at the man before bending an ear to Ludlow, who whispered to him. Nodding, the lieutenant faced the mutinous troops again. 'Our job here is done. Finish up. We march back to the fort within the hour.'

The decision—branded as cowardice by the enraged runners and skinners—was greeted with sullen resentment by the troopers, who nevertheless climbed to their feet. 'I'll leave the medic to tend to your wounded,' the lieutenant said to Ludlow. 'Fall in!'

A short time later, the soldiers trudged out of the camp, their departure accompanied by brays and insults. 'Go back to your mammas!'

'We'll fight the Injuns for you!'

In spite of Ludlow's orders that they 'Act right and forget this foolishness,' the inflamed men took a vote and decided there and then to ride out and shoot up the nearest Indian village in reprisal. 'There's one over by Little Creek,' said someone.

'That's Mandan!' Purchase objected, having listened with growing alarm to the calls for vengeance.

'What's the difference! They're Injun, ain't they?'

'They are peaceful Indians. Heck, they hate the Sioux worse than you do.'

'Not hardly! I say we pay 'em a visit! A courtesy call, like.' The bitter jest raised harsh laughter.

'Round up the horses! Let's pay 'em a call!'

'Stop! Those are company horses!' Ludlow's attempts to halt the angry men were brushed aside as they collected their weapons and made toward the corral.

'And what about poor Stringer?' demanded a veteran runner. 'Step out of the way if you don't want to help!'

Alarmed, Purchase took Jubal to one side. 'That's Half Moon's village. I must warn her. See if you can stop them—buy me time.'

'The boss is right!' Jubal stepped forward, arms raised. 'Let's think this thing through. Hell, the Sioux might be on their way back for all we know!'

This gave the mutinous men pause as voices argued in favour of 'whipping the savages' while others urged caution—even demanding to send a rider after the soldiers to bring them back, 'Jest in case.'

As the dispute continued, Purchase stole away to the corral. Picking out a horse, he led it out into the grass. Behind him, the men were still arguing, although with less passion, few having the stomach for more fighting. He glanced back at Jubal, who gave an urgent nod as signal for him to go.

'Skit!' He set off for the Mandan village.

The day was hot and dry, the grass blackened where the wind had flared the fire back toward the bluffs. He rode at a canter while keeping a vigilant eye out for any Sioux who might have remained in hiding, ready to pounce. The warm wind scoured the grass, blowing dust and burned embers against his face. He approached a group of antelope, the creatures bouncing away on stotted legs.

HE FOUND THE VILLAGE scorched and burned, the lodges lying on their sides or standing like skeletal shells, the hide covers burned away. At first, he thought the fire had swept through and caused the inhabitants to flee. But then he saw the bodies lying in the dirt. Some had arrows protruding from their backs. Others bore the bloody marks of war clubs and hatchets. Women and children lay sprawled among the dead, many showing signs of mutilation. A bunch of bodies lying close together showed where the few remaining Mandan warriors had made a desperate stand. Ornamented hides, pottery, woven baskets, hoes, and decorated skulls lay scattered in the dirt. A few dogs wandered among the corpses, too cowed to snarl at him.

He steered the horse toward Half Moon's lodge. Like the others, it was empty, its scorched hide coverings flapping in the breeze. A body lay amid the hides and furs, and he jumped down from the horse to turn the corpse over. It was Eats Much Corn, his brains dashed out by a hatchet. Holding the Sharps at the ready, he searched among the other bodies, finding no trace of Half Moon. *Perhaps she got away—or maybe the Sioux took her.* Sobered at the grim prospect, he remounted the horse and steered it out of the burnt, desolate village.

He encountered no revenge party on the way back and gave silent thanks to Jubal for his assistance. The camp was strangely quiet as he corralled the horse and made his way toward the wagons. A group of men stared at him as he passed and looked away again. Concerned, he hastened his steps toward where Ludlow, Baumann, Halverson, Jesper, and a few others stood speaking quietly outside the bunkhouse. They looked up as he approached.

'Purchase! Where you been?'

'Why? What is it? What's wrong?'

'I'm dreadful sorry, Purchase.' Halverson laid a consoling hand on his shoulder.

'Sorry? What—'

'It's Jubal. He's been mortal shot.'

'Jubal?' He frowned, uncomprehending. 'How could he be? I jest left him.'

'One of the Indians was playing possum. He up and took a shot. Hit poor Jubal right in the lungs.'

'Where is he?' asked Purchase, his voice tight with shock.

'Inside.' His face grave, Ludlow stepped aside and held open the door.

The smell of chloroform hit his nose as he entered. Jubal lay stretched on a table, the army medic bending over him.

'Jubal!' He rushed to his companion's side. Jubal lay naked from the waist up, his white body marred by a suppurating hole just above the ribs.

'The medic grimaced. 'I've tried to make him comfortable,' he said, his voice indicating the limits of his ministrations.

'Jubal!' His comrade's face was deathly pale, his brow damp and shining with a dull sheen. His breath came in long, wheezing gasps. He didn't seem aware of Purchase, a haggard, exhausted look on his face as he gasped for air. Purchase looked at the medic, who shook his head.

Taking Jubal's hand in his own, he sat there, listening to his comrade's agonised, rasping breaths. He spoke at times, reminding Jubal of the great adventures that lay in store for them. 'I reckon we might go to Californy, as you wanted. Heck, it wouldn't surprise to find you swept up by some pretty little gal and hitched like a bound steer. We'll have a grand time, my friend. Ride the railroad all the way east and eat a steak at some fancy New York restaurant. You hear me, Jubal?'

Jubal lingered for most of the night, his breaths becoming more laboured, his face ashen and dewy with sweat. Toward dawn he gave a soft, shuddering groan and lay still.

'Jube!' He felt his companion's hand grow lifeless in his own.

'He's gone, son.' The medic laid a sympathetic hand on his arm. 'It were best this way. He couldn't have survived that wound.'

As news spread, the door opened, and several men came in to express condolences. 'He was a good comrade,' said one.

'A fine shot,' murmured another.

As full morning broke, he took his companion's hand one last time, his eyes glistening with tears. 'Goodbye, Jubal. You were the best and truest companion a man could wish for.'

Going outside, he was met with sympathetic glances from Ludlow and Baumann. 'It was damnable bad luck,' said the former. 'The blamed Injun was …' His voice trailed off and he shook his head.

'Will you notify his parents?' asked Purchase. 'He had a mother in Missouri.'

'I will. It's a sad part of being boss. And I'll see that his mother gets his owed wages. You have my word.'

Purchase nodded, too dazed to think.

An hour later, he watched as the men dug a grave for his departed companion, placing it at one end of the line of fresh mounds. Wrapping the body in a length of wagon canvas, they laid it in the trench. He listened, numb with grief as Ludlow recited part of the same psalm he had uttered the day before. The men stood in sombre silence. *He was standing here beside me, listening to the bugler, just yesterday.* A gust of wind ruffled his hair, and he looked up at the sun-shadowed swells and bluffs. He thought he saw a buffalo feeding in the long grass and strained to see.

'Purchase?' The boss looked at him, inviting him to speak. He shook his head.

Ludlow nodded. 'Fill her in, boys.'

That night, he was unable to sleep for picturing Jubal's body lying white and lifeless on the table. Getting up, he took a blanket and went outside, sleeping beneath a wagon. He saw Jubal's face as his comrade chuckled in anticipation of their plans. 'New York and Boston. And then head out west. The two of us.'

He awoke stiff and cold. Heavy dew was on the grass and the sky was a hazy blue. Crawling out from beneath the wagon, he made his way back to the bunkhouse. A few men were playing cards by the stove. No one had left the camp to hunt, the danger from Indians being judged too great a risk. He collected his bedroll, thrusting his few belongings into the army rucksack he still favoured. One of the men looked up in surprise as he made his way to the door.

'Where in tar are you off to?'

'Home,' he said, and pushed open the door.

12

St Charles

IN THE SUMMER OF 1873, Purchase returned to St Charles flushed with almost ten thousand dollars in credit and a scorecard of over eighteen thousand buffalo hides and tongues to his account. Intending to remain home just for the summer, he stayed into the New Year, helping his mother nurse his ailing father. Horizon McLennan had fallen prey to a wasting illness that stripped the flesh from his bones and drained the vitality from his body. After enduring several months of leeches, compounds, and ill-tasting potions, he angrily refused any more treatments, preferring, as he told his son, 'to die and get it done with.'

Purchase did his best to bring cheer to the old man, regaling him with tales of Missouri steamboats, buffalo running, Indian fighting, and, above all, accounts of his visits to the patriarchal rock. 'I wish you could have seen it, Pa; it was just as you described. Big, fierce, and impressive as I don't know what.'

'Lord, how I wish!' The old man fingered the sliver of granite his son had presented him with, pressing the hard rock with his gnarled thumb. 'To think—that he might have touched this!' He wheezed for breath, his lips frothing a bead of saliva. 'How I wish!' he murmured and closed his eyes.

Purchase and his brother, Samuel, and sister, Lilly, buried their father in a fenced plot several hundred yards from the farmhouse. After the burial, Sam returned to his freight business in Kansas City while Lilly returned to her husband and children in St Louis. At a loss what to do, Purchase took over the running of the farm—a quarter section of grain, chickens, hogs, and a few cows, while casting about for his future. He deliberated taking over the farm on a permanent basis—urged to do so by his mother. But the same restlessness that had propelled him to the territories returned to nag during each idle hour. At night, he dreamt of standing out in the blowing grass to gaze up at the weathered stone while the wind tugged at his shirt and the vast sky whispered in his ear. 'I don't know why it affects me so,' he confessed to his mother during one such bout of introspection.

'It's because you still haven't found your own buffalo,' she said, in words that echoed his father's. The coincidence deepened his indecision while causing him to question what that buffalo might be. Perhaps I am intended to be a mere caretaker, he reflected, custodian of the patriarch's great legacy. The thought occasioned a profound dissatisfaction which only sharpened his doubts as to his future. But the more he avoided thoughts of the carved rock, the more it haunted his dreams until he conceded to himself that his future was somehow irrevocably linked to the granite sentinel. I just like to be near it, he admitted to himself. The why or how don't matter.

The thought was postponed when he drove into St Charles one April morning almost a year after his return to purchase a teapot as a surprise gift for his mother. Reacquainting himself with the familiar streets and sidewalks of the town, he wandered into a general store to pass some time before heading back. The store seemed unattended—the long counter empty—except for a man sitting behind a desk in a back room. He was idly browsing the pots and pans when he heard the man's voice. 'Felice! Who's minding the store?'

'All right, Pa! I've only got the two hands the good Lord gave me.'

He looked up as a young woman emerged from a storeroom, slapping dust from her hands. 'Gingersnaps!' She puckered her brow and frowned at some speck on the wood counter. 'It's come here, go there, stand still! Until a body doesn't know if she is up or down.'

'I heard that, Felice,' the voice came.

'*I heard that Felice!*' she mimicked under her breath, while contorting her face with comical effect. Purchase stared from where he stood behind the single row of shelving, entranced by her animated expression. The blonde-haired young woman wore a simple, homespun dress of gingham with strikingly mismatched sleeves, and over it a calico apron tied at the waist. Her face was sharp featured, her movements quick and energetic. Suddenly realising she was not alone in the store, she glanced in his direction. 'Sweet Moses! Give a body a fright, why don't you!'

'Beg pardon, Ma'am. I was looking at the skillets.'

'And were they looking back?'

'Pardon?'

She said nothing, regarding him with folded arms. 'And did you fall in love with a particular pan?'

'Now, now, Felice.' The man emerged from the back office.

'Don't pay her no never mind, friend. She be a mite eccentric.'

'Eccentric! I ain't the one taking a shine to the pots and pans!'

'Never no mind.' The father leaned his hands on the counter. 'May I help you, sir?'

'I was looking at this.' He picked up an iron skillet.

'See!'

'Hush, Felice. Go help your ma. Go on now!'

With a pert expression, the young woman stepped around her father and vanished into the storeroom. 'Leastways I ain't in love with a skillet!'

The father shook his head. 'Excuse her, friend. She is, as I said, a mite peculiar in her ways. But she means no offence.'

'None taken, I assure you.' He fetched the skillet up to the counter. 'How much is this?'

'Finest cast iron. Just fifty cents.'

'I'll take it.'

As the father wrapped the skillet in brown paper, Purchase perused several barrels of sugar, molasses, and flour, hoping the young woman would reappear. To his disappointment, she did not. He paid for the skillet and went outside to where the wagon was parked. He was about to climb up onto the seat when he was hailed.

'Purchase McLennan! By golly if that ain't you!' A young man in a sack coat and a flat-brimmed hat strode toward him.

'Gordy Jenkins!' He shook the other man's hand.

'Where you been, Purchase? I heard you were in the war.'

'I was.'

'Mother Goose!' The man shook his head. 'And you came through all right?'

'I guess I did.'

'Lord! If that don't beat all!' Gordy gave a broad smile. 'Why don't you come calling? I know my wife Peg—Peggy Northcomb, remember her?'

'I do.'

'Well, she's Peggy Jenkins now!' beamed Gordy. 'She sure would like to see you. Why not come for supper one evening?'

'I will,' he promised. 'But I have to get back to ma now.'

'I heard about your pa.' Gordy, sighed, his face turned sombre. 'He was a good man, Purchase.'

'He was that. Say,' he said as he was about to climb back onto the wagon. 'That's a new store, ain't it?' He motioned toward the store he had just stepped out from.

'It is. Run by the Bell family. New in town. Or were, a few years back.'

'I met the father and his daughter.'

'Felicity?' Jenkins chuckled. 'She's a perk!'

'What do you mean?'

Jenkins tapped his head. 'They say she's touched in the steeple.'

'She is, or they say she is?'

Gordy furrowed his brow. 'I don't rightly know, now that you mention. She seems pleasant enough to me. And Peggy has time for her.'

'She's married, I expect?'

'Why, you son of a gun!' Gordy punched him on the shoulder. 'Nope! Free as a jaybird. That sharp tongue of hers keeps the fa-inthearts at bay. Are you interested?'

'No, just wondering, that's all.'

'Well, if you're wondering, she's the same age as Peggy—twenty-two, as she told Peggy herself. A mite curly in the mane if you ask me—to be so sharp, and all.'

'It was a pleasure seeing you again, Gordy.' He climbed up onto the wagon.

'Supper! Don't forget now. I'll tell Peg.'

'You do that. Har!' He shook the reins.

Back at the farm, he asked his mother about the girl, making his voice as noncommittal as possible.

'I heard of her. Ain't seen her. But heard she's a handful—a mite sassy. Glory be!' His mother's eyes widened as she unwrapped the brown paper. 'A skillet! Why on earth!' She stared at her son. 'We have a perfectly good one on the stovetop!'

HE MADE THREE MORE trips to the store in the following weeks, pestering his mother if she didn't need extra molasses or sugar or salt. 'I suppose I could use a mite of sugar, but it can wait,' she said, checking the pantry.

'No, I'll drive in and fetch some,' he said. 'The mules need some stretching, anyway.'

'Really, Purchase. It can wait. I just baked—'

'They need a run-out. I'll be back afore you know I'm gone.'

To his pleasure, the young girl was behind the counter, still clad in the same parsimonious dress and apron. She appeared not to recognise him when he stepped in from the sunlight and he removed his hat, hoping it might make the difference.

'Yes?' She barely spared a glance from the yarn she was busily snipping with scissors.

'I need some sugar,' he said. 'And maybe salt.'

'Sugar we have. *Maybe salt's* a special order. The same with *p'raps pepper*. Course we have the regular kind. But without that special *maybe* tang, it just don't taste as good. They might have some in New York City, I suppose.'

Just then, a plump woman in a brown apron stepped out from the back room. 'Felice, you finished cutting that—' She broke off when she saw Purchase. 'Good day to you, sir. What would you like? Felice!' She glanced sharply at her daughter. 'Are you assisting the gentleman?'

'He's after some special kind of *maybe* salt. I told him what's in the tub is in the tub.'

'Pardon, sir,' said the mother, with a glare at her daughter. 'But she's been feeling under the weather all week.' She offered a smile to Purchase.

'I have? Well I guess I'd better run fetch Dr Jones. If he ain't out frolicking with that pesky Mrs.—'

'Felice!' The mother fluttered her hands in mortification. 'Salt, you said, why, it's here, in the tub. There's a scoop inside.' She took the lid off the barrel. 'Finish that yarn!' she said, with a stern glance at her daughter.

'Finished anyhow!' The young woman held up the strip of material against herself. 'What do you suppose, Mr Salt?' She crooked her neck and fluttered her eyelids as she pressed the yarn against her throat.

'Heavens to Betsy! Felicity, go inside—at once!'

The young woman gave an arch look at Purchase before disappearing into the back room, much to his disappointment.

Grumbling, the mother replaced the lid on the barrel. 'Excuse the poor girl, sir. She ain't been herself since catching the fever last month.'

'I guess we should introduce, Ma'am. Purchase McLennan. My family farm is just outside of town.'

'Why, the McLennan farm! I guess I know it—or heard of it, leastways. Pa'—she turned her head as the same middle-aged man he had sighted on the previous visit came in through the shop door carrying a sack under one arm—'meet Mr McLennan.'

'How do! Abraham Bell, sir, at your service.' The man put down the sack and reached out his hand.

'We met last week,' said Purchase, shaking hands.

'Why, so we did! These old eyes of mine.'

'And is there a Mrs. McLennan?' asked the mother. 'If you don't mind?'

'No, I don't. And there isn't, not yet.'

The mother flashed a look at the father. 'My, my, handsome as all get out, and still a bachelor.'

'Careful, Mr McLennan. She'll have you married within the week!'

'Felice! Come fetch some sugar—it was sugar?—for Mr McLennan.'

'My hands are full,' came the daughter's voice from the back room.

'Well, unfull 'em!'

'Would you take a dram, sir?' The father stepped behind the counter and leaned down to fetch a bottle from underneath.

'Abe! It's hardly past noon. I'm sure Mr McLennan ain't so disposed as yourself.'

'Come, mother, a harmless drop. Mr McLennan?'

'I guess one drop couldn't hurt.'

'Felice! Ain't you got ears?'

Grumbling, the daughter emerged from out the backroom. 'I got ears. And a neck to hang 'em on, too.'

'Father?' The mother begged, 'Speak to her.'

'Be good, Felice. We've company.'

'Our daughter, Mr McLennan. Free and unattached as yourself.'

'Ma!'

'Have you introduced yourselves? Abe!'

At the mother's sharp look the genial host coughed and gestured to the young woman. 'May I present my daughter, Felicity, Mr McLennan. A fine girl, although a put-upon when she's in the mood.'

Felicity gave a half-curtsy. 'Pleased, I'm fairly certain.'

'Purchase,' he said, bowing slightly. 'Purchase McLennan.'

'My, and fine manners, too!'

'Felicity went to school back in Boston, Mr McLennan,' said Mr Bell, 'where we lived before moving here.'

'She has a beautiful hand!' gushed the mother.

'Two of 'em!' The girl shook both hands in the air.

'Father?' The mother shot the husband a despairing look.

'I can't keep up!' He shook his head. 'Another drop, Mr McLennan?'

All the drive home, the girl played on his mind. He laughed to himself as he pictured her holding up the yarn and fluttering her eyelids. 'Har!'

'I never asked for flour! And molasses!' His mother exclaimed in amazement as she beheld the contents of the wicker basket. 'Biscuits! Heavens above. Since when did you ever buy biscuits?'

He went about his chores, milking the cows and feeding the chickens while seeing the girl's animated face in front of his eyes and hearing her voice in his ears. *A mite sassy*, he reflected, and smiled to himself.

HE ACCEPTED THE SUPPER invitation from Gordy Jenkins and his wife, swapping stories of the past while mining the couple for news of changes in the town. 'Lots of newcomers,' he said. 'I hardly recognise anyone in the street.'

'Let me think.' Peggy put a finger to her chin. 'There's the Bells,' she said, 'in charge of the general store. They purchased it from the Millers some years back. From Boston, I believe.'

'That's where I ran into Purchase. Asked me about Felicity.' Gordy winked.

'Indeed!' Peggy affected a knowing look. 'A pretty thing, in her way. Although …'

'Although what?'

'Nothing, really.' She glanced at her husband. 'Forward, maybe—in her manner that is. I'm sure she don't mean nothing by it.'

'You mean she's a flirt?' asked Purchase.

The question brought a guffaw from Gordy. 'I heard her pa tell her not to keep sparking up the soldiers that went into the store.'

'Flirt?' Peggy mused on the term. No, I wouldn't say that. She's a respectable girl. I mean forward … with her tongue.'

'You mean rude?' asked Purchase, Gordy chuckling at the question.

'No, not rude. Not exactly. More like … forward.'

'Sharpish,' put in Gordy. 'I heard her pa say so himself.'

'Why, I do believe, Purchase, that you are interested?' Peggy regarded Purchase with raised eyebrows.

'Not a bit of it. Well, maybe a bit.'

'More whisky?' Gordy leaned forward, topping up his glass.

'How bittish?' Peggy fixed him the practical glance of the married woman. He mumbled, faintly embarrassed.

'Mind, it's not like the town is stacked with eligible girls. And she has a very neat hand.'

HIS GROWING INTEREST IN Felicity was put on hold when, in June, he travelled by train to Kansas City to attend his brother Samuel's engagement to the daughter of a local magistrate. While on the train he fell into conversation with a bone merchant who informed him of the vast quantities of bison bones being shipped east for conversion into fertiliser and china.

'There can't be much profit in old bones?'

'Eight to ten dollars a ton.'

Purchase whistled. 'That's a lot of buff—bison.'

'And an awful lot of bones!' The man gazed out the window as the train clanked to a halt at a station. 'They say twenty tons were shipped east on the KP alone last year. Heck. Soon there won't be any bison left on the Kansas plains. Nothing but bones for the picking up.'

He didn't hear, his mind once again returning to thoughts of Felicity Bell. These thoughts were strengthened on the return journey when, having met Samuel's fiancée and having observed his brother's happiness at the coming matrimonial, he returned to St Charles determined to court the object of his infatuation.

Accordingly, three days after his return, he presented himself at the Bells' store with a bunch of prairie flowers in one hand and his hat in the other.

'Yes? Mr McLennan!' Mr Bell looked at him, and then the flowers, and then back at Purchase as if stupefied.

'I have come, sir, to call upon your daughter. With your permission, of course.'

'Call who?' The other man's face showed even greater perplexity.

'Abe, what on earth's the—Mrs. Bell stepped out of the back room. Her glance went straight to the flowers. 'Lord above!' she breathed.

'I was hoping, Ma'am, to call upon your daughter.'

'Felice!' The mother clasped her hands. 'Why, Mr Bell. Where's your manners? Pour the gentleman a drink. Felice!'

'Pepper 'n' spice! Is it the Judgement? Are we about to absquatulate?' The young woman stopped short on seeing Purchase, a look of surprise on her face.

'Felice, Mr McLennan has come calling.' The mother beamed at her daughter.

Felicity stared at the flowers and then at Purchase, much as her father had done.

'Felice, say something. It ain't like you to be tongue-tied.'

The young woman took in every inch of his frame as her eyes wandered up and down his person. 'You are calling on me?' she said, her voice doubtful.

'I am.' Suddenly nervous, he stepped forward and thrust the flowers at her. 'For you. I picked 'em myself.'

'He picked them himself!'

Felicity took the flowers. 'You picked them yourself?'

'Goose eggs if there ain't an echo in here! Mr McLennan, a drop?' The father held up the bottle.

'I would, indeed.' He licked his dry lips. Felicity had yet to respond, despite a sharp elbow from her mother.

'Ouch, Ma! You figuring me for a pin cushion?'

'Felicity! The gentle—Mr McLennan is waiting on a reply.' The mother gave an urgent nod in his direction.

'What do you have in mind, Purchase?'

Her mother gasped. 'Felice! Manners!'

The father paused, the bottle suspended in the act of pouring. 'Now, Felice. Ain't no call for such presumption.'

'I don't mind,' he said. 'Purchase is fine. It's my name.'

'See. He does know!' The young woman screwed up her eyes to better observe him. 'I suppose I might be agreeable to a walk about the town,' she said. 'Or did you fix for us to sip tea in the parlour?' She glanced at her mother, who was looking faint.

'I don't … Abe?'

'A walk is fine, Martha. Your health, Mr McLennan.' The father downed the whisky in a gulp.

'Felice, go fetch your shawl. And put on a bonnet!'

Five minutes later, fortified by the glass of whisky, he strode along Main Street with Felicity's hand resting on his arm. He struggled for something to say while hoping he wouldn't run into Gordy Jenkins or anyone else he knew.

Beside him, Felicity seemed quite herself, stopping every so often to admire something in a store window while expressing wonderment at the price. 'I could sew that in a heartbeat! Peppering jackrabbits—look at the cost of those shoes!'

They continued along the brick sidewalk. The day was cool and cloudy with a hint of rain in the air. The Missouri ran to their left through a screen of trees. He glanced at a fishing boat as it cast a net, his thoughts idly returning to his voyage upriver on the steamboat.

Beside him Felicity cleared her throat. 'Are you going to speak or have you taken the vow?'

'Vow?'

'Of silence. Like them dusty old monks?'

'I'm glad you agreed—to come walking.'

'Why did you call?' she asked, turning to gaze at him, her eyes frankly curious.

'Why?' He cleared his throat again. 'Shouldn't I have?'

A wagon drove past, throwing up dust. 'Persimmony!' She coughed and flapped a hand in front of her face.

He took out a handkerchief he had thought to bring and offered it.

'What's that for? Have I a smudge on my cheek?'

'No. I, uh, thought …'

She took the handkerchief and pushed it back in the breast pocket of his father's best coat, a gesture which pleased him immensely. 'What do you do—besides farming?' she asked, switching the subject, 'or is farming the be all and end all?'

'I'm not a farmer. Leastways not always a farmer.'

'Leastways not always,' she repeated. She gave a frowning pout, as if he had spoken in Chinese.

'I was a runner—a buffalo hunter,' he said, entirely smitten by the pout, 'up in Dakota Territory.'

'A buffalo hunter?' She arched her eyebrows in surprise. 'Pa always said they are rough and stink to high heaven! Are you rough, Mr McLennan?'

'Rough? No. I just go my own way.'

'Go your own way? Now ain't that a fine thing.'

He stared, uncertain whether she considered it a good thing or not.

'So why did you come back—and go to farming?'

'My father died. My mother needed the help.'

'Shall we cross here? There's a dress shop on the corner I like to peep into.'

'Yes, of course.' He held up his arm, which she had momentarily dropped.

'And do you plan on staying put—on the farm?' she asked, looking along the street for approaching horses.

He took a breath, set back by her propensity *for shooting straight to the lungs*. 'I guess not. I have hopes.'

'Hopes?' Her eyes widened and she laughed merrily, the sound music to his ears. 'Well, before we step any farther, Mr McLennan, let's hear those hopes!'

THREE MONTHS INTO THEIR courtship, he plucked up the courage to ask for her hand in marriage. It was a warm, blowy evening in fall and they had just completed a walk along the shore of the Missouri. The light was beginning to fail as they headed back toward her parents' house. Her arm was linked with his and he patted her hand as a prelude to speaking.

'Felice ...' He stopped and cleared his throat. 'Felice,' he began again, having taken up the diminutive in imitation of her father.

'Yes, for both of us,' she said, perplexed at his apprehensive, sideways glances.

'What?' He stared at her.

'Oh, go on!'

'Felice—'

'Bell the cat! Yes, for the third time.'

'I was thinking—'

To his surprise, she giggled. 'Pardon.' She composed herself. They cut away from the bank and followed the path back to the main road.

'Fel—Will you marry me?' He halted and faced her, laying his hand over her own, his face solemn in the gathering dusk.

Taken aback, she didn't answer at first, searching his face. *So, this was why all the humming and awing and cat glances.* She let him spin for a moment longer and then tugged at his arm, resuming their walk. 'Yes,' she said.

IN TRUTH, SHE CONFIDED to her diary, the proposal—not unexpected—came as a relief. The notion of stepping outside the constricting confines of her father's store blew over her like a breath of fresh air. '*And besides, he is a good man,*' she wrote, '*a little behind at times, but of sterling character—although, he ain't much of a talker. He is handsome, though, and of a kind heart.*' Her mind circled back to the proposal. '*Doubtless, like most men, he is given to yarning when the mood takes him.*' Yarning being, she considered, the antithesis of her own, quicksilver darts from one notion to the next. '*I guess, he'll just have to learn to keep up.*' She entertained herself by signing off the entry, '*Mrs. Felicity McLennan.*'

To his vexation, his mother was somewhat less than impressed after he brought Felicity, chaperoned by Peggy Jenkins, out to the farm to introduce the two over tea and cakes.

'Well?' he asked, after driving Felicity and Peggy home.

His mother sat by the fire absorbed in her knitting.

'Well, Ma?'

'Wait less'n I drop this stitch!' A moment later she set down the wool on her lap. 'She's a salty one, ain't she? She helped herself to that second biscuit afore I could even ask.'

'Never mind the biscuits if you please. What of her character, her manner, her—'

'Salty, like I said.'

'But do you like her?'

'*Like* ain't a word I'd use to describe my feelings. Now, that Elly Dovecot I'd hoped you'd attach to. Her I like—or did afore that Jeremiah Young stole her out from under your nose.'

'Felicity! Your honest opinion?'

'Honest?' His mother picked up her knitting again. 'Well, honestly, I reckon she wouldn't flinch much, if put to it, I daresay.'

'Is that a favourable opinion?'

'Depends.' The mother set down the sewing again. 'If she could control that whipperty tongue of hers.'

'I'm looking for a wife, not a debating partner.'

'Well, debate is what you're gonna get if you hitch up with her.'

'Felicity, Ma. Her name is Felicity.'

'Nothing Felicity about her. Although, as I say, she's hardly one to flinch. And that counts for something.'

'Then you approve?'

'She's a mite long in the tooth, ain't she?'

'She's barely turned twenty-three!'

'As I said, longish.'

'I'm twenty-nine!'

'It's natural for the man to be older.'

'Are we going to fence all night or are you going to give your blessing?'

His mother clicked the knitting needles. 'If she's who your heart is set on, then who am I to say no?'

He furrowed his brow. 'I'll take that as a yes.'

TWO DAYS LATER, DRESSED again in his father's best coat, he turned up at the general store, again with a bunch of flowers in his hand, accompanied this time by a bottle of whisky. With much bustling back and forth Mrs. Bell locked the shop door and turned the *Closed* notice to face the glass. Then she and Felicity listened through the office door as he asked Mr Bell for his daughter's hand in marriage.

'You sure?' The father poured a second shot of whisky. 'She's a spark at times.'

'Landsakes!' came through the door followed by a hushing noise.

'I'm sure.' He gulped the whisky. 'I'll take real good care of her, sir. I give you my word.'

'Like I said, she's a spark but precious to me, and her mother.' Mr Bell regarded Purchase with a benign yet solemn expression.

'The farm—you'll inherit it?'

'I will.'

'Grain prices are up and down. Who knows what they'll be this time next year?' Mr Bell raised his eyebrows with the question.

'I don't rely on the farm to secure our future. I made a considerable sum hunting buffalo for five years and saved nearly every dime. I've plenty enough to raise a family on, I assure you, even if crop prices fall to a cent a bushel.'

'Are you a gambler, Purchase?'

'No, sir. And I ain't much of a drinker, either.'

Mr Bell lifted one finger to scratch his throat. 'You strike me as a decent fellow, Purchase, upright and straight shooting. And Felice thinks that highly of you, and she's no mean judge of character.' He leaned over to refill the glass. 'Very well, then. My blessings—and her mother's—upon you both. Your health!'

"Bout time!' came from beyond the office door.

SAMUEL AND LILLY BOTH returned for the wedding, Samuel acting as best man while Lilly and Peggy Jenkins served as bridesmaids. Following the ceremony, and a brief reception in the general store, he drove his new wife back to the farm where she stood with gloved hands clasped looking up at the farmhouse while he unloaded her trunk.

'Here we are,' he said, as his mother held open the door for them. 'Home.'

She slapped dust from the new, brocaded jacket her mother had sewn for her. 'I guess,' she said, and turned to look back at the way they had come.

IF HE HAD HARBOURED any preconceptions about married life, they seemed beside the point as his new bride took immediate control of the running of the house, even rearranging the spoons in the kitchen drawer to her liking. Although this presumption earned a swift rebuke from his mother, the old lady nevertheless grudgingly acknowledged that Felicity was an efficient overseer. 'Even though peppery, at times,' she complained.

'Salt, and now pepper.' He smiled. 'Soon you'll have to find another spice, Mother.'

'Not me, son. You.'

To his shock, Felicity proved as forward in lovemaking as she was in conversation, taking up her conjugal duties with an enthusiasm that had him hushing her lest his mother overhear.

'This is a farm, ain't it!' Felicity snuggled up to him. 'What does she think the hogs are doing out in the barn?'

'We are not hog—' He abandoned the protest as Felicity clamped her mouth on his. 'Never mind,' he mumbled, hoping his mother had fallen asleep.

Contented with his new station in life, he went about his farm chores with the air of a man who had accomplished an important milestone in his progression to the grave. He even took to whistling as he went about the yard, an innovation Felicity swiftly put a stop to with her curt observation of 'a dreadful shrillness' arising from a 'rackety blackbird' perched in the elm tree.

The novelty of marriage and connubial responsibilities kept his mind firmly in the present as he milked the cows, fed the chickens, and prepared the land for winter seeding. But sometimes as he went about his chores, he paused to gaze at the nearby Missouri, a pensive expression on his face. This distractedness doubled whenever a steamboat passed by—the blast of a steam whistle causing him to stop what he was doing and look yearningly after the vessel.

Felicity

FELICITY TOOK TO FARM life with a practical industry that surprised and delighted her husband. Unused to outside work—or any physically demanding labour—Felicity nevertheless watched and observed and read the *Farmers' Almanac* with a diligence that drew his admiring compliments. By the start of the following spring, she had assumed sole control of the vegetable garden, planting seasonal peas, beets, onions, broccoli, tomatoes, and sweet corn and watching like a hawk for weeds or pests. Catching the dog poking among the squash, she despatched it with a whack from the hoe that sent it howling back to the barn.

She uprooted his mother's cauliflower, which she detested, and replaced it with lettuce and sweet potato, soothing the old lady's ire by cooking a peach pie which her mother-in-law ate, disdainfully at first, and then mouthful after mouthful until half the pie was gone.

'It's the molasses!' Felicity crowed to Purchase. 'It gets so a body can't help but to gobble!' She made a smacking sound with her lips.

'You were made to be a farmer's wife,' he said, entranced by her lips.

The intended compliment drew a frosty response. 'If I thought I had swapped the store for the farm I'd throw myself in the Missouri!' She frowned at his perplexed look. 'Or have you forgotten your buffaloes?'

SHORTLY BEFORE PROPOSING, PURCHASE had revealed his hope, nay, intention, to return to the territories, greatly concerned lest the notion cause Felicity to reject his suit.

'The territories? You mean Nebraska?' Her eyes widened at the prospect.

'No, farther north. The Dakotas. Not yet,' he hastened to add, 'not until it's safe.'

'Safe?' Her mouth formed an inquisitive echo.

'From Indians. Once they've settled down.'

'Is that where that old buffalo is that you harp on about?'

'The rock? Yes. You should see it, Felice. It's truly grand.'

'Grand?' She seemed amused by the word. 'And you would farm there?'

'The soil is rich as all get-out. Anything would grow there.'

'I shouldn't wonder—with all that fertiliser.'

'It would be lonesome at first. But I hear that new settlers are flocking there every day. There's a town, Fort Buffalo, nearby.'

'The wild frontier? Indians and buffaloes!' She twisted her lip in a frown. 'You expect me to live on a dirt floor in a stinky old hovel?'

'No! I would import lumber for a proper house—by steamboat. A wood floor, a stove, glass windows, and a proper roof.'

'And a porch?'

'A porch also, if that's your wish.' He searched her face for approval.

She looked into his eyes, her manner suddenly serious. 'Where would the money come from to do all you propose? I imagine building a house—not to mention the cost of buying and importing the wood—would be mighty expensive. The stove, the furniture, the cost of passage—'

'I have money saved from buffalo running. More than enough. Plenty more. It would be a great adventure, Felice, what do you say?' He looked at her hopefully.

'Let me think on it.'

And think on it she did, although, as she secretly admitted to herself, some small part of her welcomed the astonishing proposition—the notion of escape from the suffocating confines of the small, censorious town into the wider, freer world long a part of her innermost hopes. The frontier seemed the very embodiment of that enticing wider world—the plentiful newspaper stories of its strangeness, vastness, and distance from civilisation tantalising her with every new account.

Childhood dalliances with the dream of moving back to Boston, or even New York—there to spread her wings as belle of the ball or, better, the mysterious, eye-popping beauty from the exotic Midwest—had latterly been displaced by a fascination with the wild Indian country, a fascination fuelled by lurid reports of the splendours and terrors of the far-distant territories that daily filled the newspapers.

Women were accorded special mention in these accounts as the indispensable progenitors of the new type of individual called forth to settle the vast, northern plains. '*No less a requirement than a trusty gun and a stout mule is a hardy and reliable distaff—one imbued with fortitude and equipped by nature to endure the most trying conditions,*' reported the *St Louis Dispatch*.

Colourful stories—paid for, and largely invented by, the railroads—lauded the adventure and romance of 'the wild, untrodden frontier.' Leaflets and handbills dropped around town claimed to recount genuine testimony, purportedly gleaned from the letters and diaries of actual homesteaders, that extolled the virtues of independence and self-sufficiency—virtues dear to her heart—amid a panorama of breathtaking landscapes.

She read such accounts avidly, her impetuous nature deeply stirred as she daydreamed herself stepping foot in that grassy expanse—her youthful optimism glossing over the horrors of isolation, flies, dust, and murderous savages. '*The fact is,*' she confided to the leather-bound diary—one she kept hidden atop the wardrobe, away from her mother's busybody eyes, '*a girl—woman—ought see the world with her own eyes, not rely on some man or some newspaper to tell her about it.*'

Such a radical notion was arrived at independently of any outside influences—her own, thorny temperament and spirited nature the only stimulus required to give considered, if withheld, assent to her future husband's proposal. In truth, the longer she pondered the notion, the more it made her giddy. '*Better to die out on the frontier than perish from boredom in a one-horse town with preachers suffocating a body on every side!*' The exclamation decided it for her. She would marry this strangely affecting 'Purchaser of her heart,' and move with him to the ends of the earth—well, the frontier anyway, where she would blossom and bloom away from pots and pans and sugar and molasses and pernickety yarns.

And as for the rather starchy Mr McLennan? '*Why, I aim to reform him, straighten him out, turn his mind from those stinking buffaloes—from that buffalo—and turn his wheel so to …*' She left the sentence unfinished, ever mindful of her mother's prying eyes. '*Turn him to a devout Christian!*' she wrote, lips compressed.

The question of religion, or of her intended's religious beliefs, had bothered her as little as his penchant for wearing boots rather than shoes. 'As long as he ain't Hindu and worshipping of cows, I ain't concerned,' she insisted, fending off her mother's anxieties in the matter. The thought that he worshipped a buffalo as a close second caused her to giggle, instantly arousing her mother's suspicions.

'Does he attend church?' she demanded.

'He attends lots of places—the barn, for instance.'

'Don't get flipperty-jack with me, young woman! I asked, does he attend church regular?'

'Why not ask him? I ain't his secretary! 'Sides, Pa ain't none too regular in his attendance.'

'Never mind your father. He has reason.'

'What reason?' she asked, her eyes narrowed.

'His health. He has the cripples in the one leg.'

'Cripples! Then oughtn't we equip the poor man with a pair of crutches? I can ask Purchase to cut down a tree—'

'Felicity Bell! You listen to your mother. If Mr McLennan ain't a proper Christian, then …'

'Then what, Mother dear?'

'Then be it upon your own head!' With a foreboding glare her mother swept away.

'Are you Christian—proper Christian, churchgoing and all?' she asked the next time Purchase came calling.

He grimaced at the question. 'I guess I never was much one for the church,' he conceded.

'The temple, then?' she asked. 'Or the totem pole, maybe?'

'What?'

'No need to strike so bewildered. If you don't favour going to church every Sunday, then so be it.' She sighed and pressed the back of her hand to her forehead. 'I guess I'll go alone—or with that fine-looking Mr Patterson that comes into the store every day to inquire after my health.'

'Never mind no Mr Patterson! Go to church if you want. But go alone— or with your mother.'

'Snakes alive!' She blinked. 'I ain't *that* Christian!'

'*That's the question of religion, settled,*' she wrote in her journal. '*Far as I can tell, my husband-to-be worships at the church of the buffalo, and what's a good wife to do but go along with her intended?*'

'Well?' he asked, the question he had posed on his previous visit having caused him no little anxiety as he pondered her likely response.

'Well what?' she said. 'Water in the well?'

'Have you thought over what I said—about homesteading in the territories?'

She tugged her chin and made various murmuring sounds—just to 'crank his wheel' as her mother described it in imparting conjugal wisdom to her recalcitrant daughter.

'Is that what you do to poor pa?'

'Gracious! His wheel fell off six months after I married him.'

Deciding she had spun Purchase enough, she smiled graciously. 'A parlour would be nice. Perhaps I could entertain some feathered gentlemen for tea.'

'Feathered gentle—?' He stared for a moment and then threw back his head and roared with laughter.

14

The Great Land Rush

THE FANTASY OF 'FLEEING to the far plains', as she described it in her journal, was put on hold when she gave birth to a girl thirteen months into their marriage. 'I already named her Amity,' she told her husband when he was allowed in to behold the newborn. 'You can name the next one.'

He peered at the blanket-wrapped infant, gently touching her cheek with his large, farmer's hand. 'Hello, Amity,' he said, his voice filled with pride—or was it reverence? she wondered.

A contented husband and father, he was also increasingly prosperous. That year, he harvested 175 bushels of wheat and 50 bushels of oats, the bulk of which he sold for $170 to a grain dealer from Chicago. The money was added to the buffalo wealth held on cash deposit at the Boatman's Savings Institution. He produced a slip of paper proudly showing Felicity the sum.

'That much?' Her eyes widened at the figure.

'That much.' He chuckled at her surprise. 'We can afford to build the finest house in the territories—when the time comes.' He kept his voice light while watching, with some anxiety, for her response.

She made a noncommittal sound, excusing herself to tend to the baby. She changed the infant, her mind working furiously. *That was before. Doesn't he understand a baby changes things?*

Her former, as she now saw it, girlish indulgence—encouragement even—of her husband's plans to abandon the familiarity and security of St Charles for the remote and dangerous northern plains vexed her with ever greater … *vexation* each time he cautiously broached the subject. 'There's more folk leaving every day,' he said, glancing over the top of the newspaper, as if to assess her resistance.

'I guess that Jem Wilson and his family are headed north to homestead,' he said a day later on returning from town. 'That boy ain't got two sticks to rub together. They'll end up living like hogs in a wallow. Lucky, we got the means to set up a fine house—finer even than this one. Do you hear me, Felice?'

'There's Injuns,' she said, cooing over the baby. 'We could all lose our scalps. And Amity ain't hardly got one to begin with.'

SHORTLY AFTER THE BIRTH, he drove into St Charles to find the streets filled with people and a buzz of excitement in the air. Several men and women were grouped around Mr Hornchurch from the hardware store as he read aloud from a newspaper.

'What is it?' he asked, spying Gordy Jenkins among the throng.

'It's Custer, ain't you heard?'

'Heard what?'

'He got wiped out, up in Montana Territory. Along with his whole command. They say the slaughter was awful, a massacre!'

'It was the Sioux!' a man standing by put in, his face flushed with the news. 'The heathen devils!'

He bought a newspaper and sat by himself to read the sensational accounts that filled the front page.

'You fought 'em, didn't you?' Gordy sat down beside him.

'Who?'

'The Sioux! You fought 'em. You said at supper that one time.'

He nodded. 'I guess I did.'

'The army has promised to wipe out the fiends. Good riddance!'

He mulled on the news all the way home, seeing in his mind's eye the Sioux riding down upon the wagons or hunting him amid the tall, blowing grass. The whole territory will be in an uproar, he reflected. He pulled the wagon to a halt in front of the farmhouse, and sat there on the seat, still digesting the news.

'You are quiet,' said Felicity when he at last made his way inside after unhitching the wagon. 'You didn't sneak away and get signed up to be one of those Indian missionaries, did you?'

'I guess not,' he mumbled, still preoccupied with Custer.

'Heavens, the enthusiasm! What is it then—did the preacher elope with a cow?'

'General Custer got slaughtered by the Sioux, up on the northern plains.'

She sat down, Amity in her lap and, in another of those frank displays of practical intimacy that left him confounded, opened her blouse to allow the infant to suckle. 'She 'minds me of Pa sucking on the bottle,' she had mused once, a remark that left him temporarily speechless.

'So General Custard got slaughtered by Indians,' she said, adjusting her teat. 'What does that mean for us and our great pilgrimage?'

'It's Custer, Felice, show some respect,' he said, in a rare admonition. 'Him and his whole troop were wiped out.'

'My, but she's greedy today! Try the other one,' she said, shifting the baby. 'This one's plumb dried up.'

After a slice of pie and a cup of coffee, he went outside, taking a second cup with him. He sat on the steps to finish reading the newspaper. He lifted the cup to his lip and halted it there, his hand frozen as his eyes took in a story almost buried under the accounts of the massacre on the wild Montana plains.

SOUTHERN BISON GONE TO ETERNITY
Our correspondent filed this report by telegraph from Fort Riley, Kansas, yesterday.

I travelled this day from Fort Wallace to Fort Riley, a distance of 282 miles across the sunbaked Kansas plains. During that entire seven-hour ride on the Kansas Pacific Railroad, I saw not a single buffalo. This fact will be an astonishment only to those readers who have never made this journey within the past five years or so. During that time, and at all times previously, the grasslands were blackened with the grazing herbivores. Often, entire trains were brought to a halt as immense herds blocked the railroad tracks for hours or days on end. The buffalo were so plentiful that passengers fired from the windows into the teeming ranks without making the slightest impress on their numbers. Now all that remains of that unprecedented abundance is a plethora of bones and skulls which despoil the plain as far as the eye can see. Veteran buffalo 'runners' tell me that there are no more than two or three hundred buffalo left on the Kansas plains—those remnants soon fated to join their deceased brethren in eternity. It might be truly averred that the entire range from Kansas to the Nebraska Territory is now one giant graveyard of the woolly monarchs that once roamed the country in their countless millions. The stink is still there from the mounds of decayed carcasses, but the proud sovereign of these plains is no more—although, reputedly, there are large herds still roaming freely in Texas and parts of Oklahoma. Intelligent minds now ask what will become of the smaller, northern herds as the skinners and tanneries switch their attention to that resource? Reactions to the great southern decimation are mixed. I heard at least one army officer proclaim that the plains were now safe for the raising of domestic cattle. So, one quadruped replaces another. What was once wild and untamed is now domesticated and made safe for civilised society—the warring red man no longer able to roam freely in the absence of the animal which was his larder, provisioner, and houser.

He set down the newspaper, his mind reeling as he pictured the vast sea of buffalo that had rocked the train and threatened to sweep it from the tracks. His nose filled with the remembered stench of decaying carcasses left strewn alongside the track as the carriage clanked past. And still, the entire plain was alive with buffalo! The notion that this cornucopia had now vanished from the earth struck him as so absurd he briefly wondered if the correspondent had not lied about the extent and impact of the slaughter. How is it possible? he wondered.

The door opened behind him, and Felicity stuck out her head. 'Are you fixing to sit there until the Rapture?'

IN MAY 1877, SHORTLY after Amity turned one year old, news came of the surrender of the Sioux war chief Crazy Horse and the final pacification of the plains Indians. Purchase read with incredulity reports of the fearsome Sioux being forced onto reservations where they would learn to clothe and farm 'like white folk.' A celebration was organised in the town and a special commemorative medal struck to mark the occasion. Barely had the celebrations concluded when it was reported that Crazy Horse was dead, killed by the US Army. 'Sioux War Chief Shot Down!' trumpeted the headline in one paper. 'Plains Made Safe for Civilization!' shouted another. One account mentioned a rush of buffalo hunters headed onto the northern plains, where they might shoot, uncontested, the last remaining herds.

The simmering desire to return to the territories occasioned by such reports was brought to a boil by breathless accounts of the number of homesteaders flocking to the newly opened-up Dakotas in pursuit of 'free, Indian land.' The railroad opened an office in St Charles to promote the giveaway, while flyers and specially struck newspapers extolled the virtues of healthy and independent living on the lush frontier. Colourful posters sprung up around town advertising a 'New Eden' or 'Garden of the World' yearning for the plough. 'Land for the taking! Free, virgin soil!' were the catchcries on everybody's lips. Land agents walked the streets thrusting leaflets into eager hands while promising unparalleled prosperity for those brave enough to take advantage of the opportunity.

Emigrants from both the eastern United States and overseas flooded into Kansas and Missouri as word of the great land bonanza spread to Europe and beyond. Families from Russia, Denmark, Sweden, Germany, Italy, and Poland—their passage facilitated by overseas agents of the railroad companies—arrived in their tens of thousands to join the stampede for free land. Each day, hundreds of eager homesteaders crowded the steamboat offices, vying for tickets upriver as the cost of passage leapt threefold. The discovery of gold in the Black Hills heightened the influx by drawing miners and prospectors, hustlers, conmen, gullible tinhorns, gamblers and former slaves, until the overcrowded streets were choked with oxen, horses, mules, and conveyances of every description.

'Why in tomfoolery are they all here—and not in Kansas City, where's there room?' asked the local newspaper, even while adding extra pages to accommodate the surge in advertisements.

Driving into town, Purchase muttered with irritation to find the streets thronged with emigrant families stocking up on goods as they awaited passage upriver. He had just stepped down from the wagon when he heard a familiar voice hail him.

'Purchase!' Gordy Jenkins strode toward him, his face elated as he waved two steamboat tickets in the air. 'I'm off, Purchase! To Nebraska! Peg and I are going to stake our claim. They say the land is rich and just waiting for the plough.'

'But you are a joiner, Gordy, not a farmer.'

'I can learn, can't I? Heck, what is there to do but seed and furrow?' Gordy laughed merrily, his face pink with enthusiasm. 'I might even raise hogs! A quarter section, Purchase. For the asking! Now I gotta go tell Peg about the tickets. Come with us, why don't you—before the best land is all snapped up!' With that, he hurried off down the sidewalk, clutching the prized steamer tickets in his hand.

Felicity shook her head when told of the encounter. 'I can't imagine Peggy Jenkins chasing around after hogs.' The image amused her and she laughed. 'And Gordy? Why, that man has trouble lacing up his shoes. Farming? Lord help us.'

'But you can't blame him for trying,' he said, seeing the opportunity to press his own claim. 'The government is practically giving away land. We can homestead a quarter section for fourteen dollars! Think of it, Felice. Our own piece of the frontier. It's what I want for us. Don't you recall?'

'What's wrong with St Charles?' she asked, setting a pot of water to boil.

'But we agreed to go—when the time was right.'

'Pass me that spoon, please—the large one,' she said to her mother-in-law as the latter came in from outside. She stirred some salt into the pot. 'What do you think, Ma, about all those folks rushing to the territories?'

His mother sat in a chair as Felicity placed a cup of tea in front of her.

'I reckon half of them will be back home ere long.' His mother sipped, eyeing Purchase over the cup. 'Why risk your neck for farmland when you're sitting on some of the best, right here?'

Felicity looked at Purchase, her eyebrows raised in agreement.

'I've decided,' he said, his voice blunt. And with that, he opened the door and went out, leaving the two women to exchange glances and shake heads.

'Try and change his mind, Felicity.'

'Lord knows, I've tried. He's as stubborn as a mule on the subject.'

'It's that buffalo dragging him there. You do realise that? It's got inside his head so he can't think straight.'

Felicity sighed. 'Then I'll just have to find something else to occupy his mind.'

'What?'

'Something,' she said, and stared out the window.

SHE SAW FOR HERSELF the reality of the much talked about land rush when she drove into St Charles to allow her ma and pa a visit with their granddaughter. 'Such a mess of folk I never did see!' she exclaimed on arriving at her parents' house. 'I almost couldn't get through the streets.'

'It's good for business, Felice, that's all I can say,' remarked her father, tamping tobacco into his pipe.

'They stink to high heaven,' her mother said, gushing over Amity.

'Who?'

'Those peasants from all over! Ain't they heard of soap over there?'

'Over where, Martha?' asked her husband.

'Over wherever it is they come from! Cooee!' Her mother buried her nose in Amity's stomach.

'Half of them are from right here in the United States.'

Well, then, they ought to know better. It's downright un-American!'

'BEFORE THE BEST LAND is all snapped up!' The words haunted him. What if some homesteader decided to claim the land around the rock? The alarming thought was a thorn in his side as he pictured the pastures around the giant sentinel dotted with homesteads. Walking the fields, he sighted yet another steamboat—the fifth that morning—packed to the gunnels with emigrants, the children calling out and waving as the pilot tooted the whistle. Brimming with impatience, he stared after it, his mind a whirlwind of envy and frustration. 'Jumping polecats!' He kicked a clod of earth.

Two days later, he drove into town to pick up supplies, his mind still on the northern plains. After purchasing the supplies, he left the wagon unattended while he crossed the road to visit the office of Robert Orland, a local architect. 'I want to build a house up in the territories,' he said without ado. 'A proper house, like the ones here in St Charles.'

Orland, a thoughtful, Harvard-educated man, looked up from his drawings. 'The territories? You'll need lumber, lots of it,' he said. 'And a crew of carpenters—unless you're fixing to build it all by yourself.'

'I can take care of that—the lumber, and the crew,' he said.

'Well, then!' Pulling open a large drawer, Oland showed him several simplified plans, talking up the merits of each.

He settled on one that allowed for two bedrooms, a kitchen and parlour and a porch. The two men shook hands before Purchase carefully tucked the plan into his coat pocket. 'Good luck to you, friend,' said Orland. 'You can check that list of supplies,' he added. 'It itemises everything, including timber, door frames, window glass, and bricks for the chimney.'

Buoyed by this step toward his goal, Purchase walked down the street to the lumber yard to discuss fees and estimates for shipping lumber upriver. Returning home, he withheld these interactions from Felicity, intending to introduce them as trump cards the next time the contentious subject of migration to the territories came up. In his mind, he set an arbitrary date for this to happen, planning a departure day no later than the summer of 1878.

The birth of a son, Jubal, in late 1877 forced him to put his ambitions on hold, his pride at the event tempered by huge frustration at the timing. It will have to wait, at least for now, he conceded, resigning himself to the fact. There's Felice, and the children to think of, not to mention mother. Barely assuaged, he headed to the barn to milk the cows.

But his resolve lasted only until the next sensational newspaper story on the veritable flood of migrants headed west to claim a stake in the great land bonanza. The story breached his dam of self-restraint as he despairingly pictured the rock location overrun with eager homesteaders. On the instant, he made up his mind to travel to the territories in order to stake a claim. 'If I don't, we risk losing out on the best land,' he argued to Felicity. 'This way, we can be sure that the land is waiting for us.'

'What else would it do but wait?' she protested.

15

The Claim

SIX WEEKS LATER, HE stepped off the steamboat in Yankton, Dakota Territory, a wallet containing three hundred dollars tucked inside his shirt. It was shortly after one o'clock in the afternoon and the weather was cool and rainy. The boat had been crowded with eager homesteaders, many of them clutching papers provided by the hordes of unscrupulous 'land agents' working the riverboat towns.

'I guess they'll be disappointed,' one man, a merchant, remarked within his hearing. 'They sold everything and ain't got spit all left to return to. And that land?' He laughed to a companion. 'Ain't worth shit! I know for a fact some of it's been sold three times over!'

Determined to complete his business and start the return journey as soon as possible, he went off in search of the Land Office. Turning the corner to the building, he was dismayed to find a long line of prospective homesteaders waiting to file claim. The line, stretching halfway down the block, was mostly full of single or married men. However, he saw a few women waiting in line together. All wore the same eager yet slightly anxious look, as if the land might run out before their turn came. Stout, plain-clad migrants from Germany and the Nordic countries stood cheek by jowl with small, wiry individuals from Eastern Europe dressed in heavy woollen coats and flat caps. Asians waited alongside Irish, Russians, Greeks, and Italians. Ex-Confederate soldiers stood with Blacks from Chicago and ex-Unionists from New York, all shuffling forward to claim a piece of land that had once belonged to the nomadic Sioux and Cheyenne and, before them, to the lodge-dwelling Mandan and Hidatsa.

He waited in line for three hours before his turn came to enter the office. The premises were stuffy and dimly lit, with large survey maps tacked to the walls. The register and receiver clerks stood behind a wooden counter, the former entering claims, the latter taking the fee payments and issuing receipts. He stood impatiently behind a pair of brothers from Denmark who dithered over the township maps, drawing exasperated glances from the clerk, who exchanged constant head shakes with his co-worker. Finally, the brothers agreed on a tract, and it was his turn to step up to the counter.

'Where'd you wish to stake a claim?' The clerk, a small, harried man darted a glance at the wall clock. 'Sioux Falls is filling up fast.' He placed a territorial map on the counter.

Purchase studied the map, peering at the inked titles. 'There,' he said, and pointed to a place name.

'Where's that?' The clerk squinted. 'Fort Buffalo,' he answered himself. 'Heck, that's up in Monroe County.' He glanced at Purchase, raising an eyebrow. 'That's range country. More suited for cattle. We don't get too many for there. You sure?'

'I am.'

'You planning on running cattle?'

'No.'

The clerk regarded him a moment longer before turning to a pile of maps on the table behind him. 'Hold on,' he said, thumbing through the pile. 'Hey, Whitcomb,' he said to the receiver. 'We got a map on Monroe County?'

'Beats me.'

'Here.' After another search, the clerk took a map to the counter. 'The settlers are outrunning the surveys,' he grumbled. 'Heck. We ain't got half of Monroe surveyed.' He spread the map, titled *Upper Missouri Townships*, on the counter. 'There's Monroe,' he said, pointing to a grid. 'And Franklin, the county seat. Hey,' he said, 'ain't they got a land office there?'

'I don't know. But I'm here now, I don't figure on going all the way upriver just to find out.'

The clerk considered this. 'I guess we could always transfer the papers if you find out they do. He turned his attention back to the map. 'You're in luck,' he said. 'The townships have been surveyed out to ... there' He tapped a blank area of the map. 'Wait on.' He turned back to the table and rummaged through the pile again before producing, another map. 'Here we go.' The map was headed *Plat Map of Monroe County: Containing Seven Ranges*. It showed a number of uniform squares, each one neatly subdivided into numbered grids. 'That's half a dozen townships done, so far.

This here is the Fort Buffalo township. And there's Franklin. And over there—Hey, Jeb! You old coot!' The register interrupted himself to greet a tall, sun-browned man who entered the office. The man nodded curtly in reply and disappeared into a small room. 'That's Jeb, one of the surveyors. Now, where in bejesus was I?' The clerk returned to his perusal of the map. 'There's lots of land, friend, nobody's filing for up there, except for maybe in the Pembina, so choose your poison.'

Purchase studied the grids. 'There.' He pointed to a square. On it was lettered, 'Big Rock.'

The clerk peered doubtfully at his selection. 'You sure?' Just then, the inner room door opened, and the sun-browned man emerged. 'Hey, Jeb. Didn't you survey Monroe County?'

'I did. What of it?'

'Looky here.' The register pointed to the map as the surveyor stepped forward to see. 'It says "Big Rock."'

'I know what it says. I wrote it, didn't I?' The surveyor frowned at the clerk. 'It's a boundary—that's a marker,' he explained, with a glance at Purchase. 'We include them on the map as a reference point. And that rock is about the biggest marker in the whole county. It also happens to be square on the section boundary.'

'This here fella wants to lay claim to it.'

'You sure?' The surveyor gave Purchase a doubtful look. 'It's the durndest thing I ever saw. It takes up a fair chunk of grass. You won't be able to do anything with it except stare at it.'

'Hey, is that the buffalo totem you were on about?' At a nod from the other man, the clerk shook his head. 'Doggone Indians!'

'It's what I choose,' said Purchase.

'How you going to farm a rock?' The clerk pinched his chin. 'I don't know that we're supposed to file claims to land that can't be improved.' He studied the map, a dubious look on his face.

'Were you in the war?' asked the surveyor, scrutinising Purchase.

'I was. Union Army.'

'Where'd you fight?'

'Fredericksburg, Gettysburg ...'

'Gettysburg? Me, too. That was a tough fight.' He turned to the clerk. 'You heard the man,' he said. 'It's what he chooses.' With a nod to Purchase, he walked away.

The clerk glanced up at the clock. 'Hell, what do I care, its your funeral. You ready to file?'

'I am.'

'You got the fee—fourteen dollars?'

'Right here.'

'Then fill out the application.' The clerk pushed a sheet of paper across the desk. He placed a bottle of ink and a pen next to it. 'You understand the legals?'

'I do.'

'You got to break at least ten acres the first year. You gotta occupy the land. You can't be gone more than six months. After five years, the land is yours—the whole hundred and sixty acres, courtesy of the US government. You just got to prove it up and Sam's your uncle.'

Purchase signed and dated the application. 'No one else can claim it?'

'Not once you've paid the fourteen dollars to old Whitcomb over there. Hold fire a minute.' Glancing at the survey map, the register made entry into the tract book murmuring the details as he copied: 'Section 8, Township 145, Range 31W.'

'That's my land?'

'That's your claim.'

'What if I want more land?'

'More?' The register cast a frowning eye. 'You're only entitled to the hundred and sixty acres.'

'To buy, I mean.'

'How much more?'

'Say, another one sixty—on the other side of that rock.'

'That'll cost you a dollar twenty-five an acre. But you got to build a house on the first section and live in it six months first.'

'Can I buy it now?'

The clerk blew on the book to dry the ink. 'Nope. Six months minimum.'

Reaching into his inner pocket, Purchase produced a ten-dollar bill which he laid on the map. 'I'd appreciate to purchase the whole parcel, right now.'

The clerk licked his lips and darted a glance at the receiver, who was busy issuing a receipt. 'I guess six months ain't that long,' he said, laying a hand over the ten-dollar bill and deftly sliding it toward him. 'But Whitcomb's gotta be taken care of, too,' he whispered, nodding toward his companion.

He left the office 214 dollars lighter in pocket, but the owner of 320 acres of Dakota Territory real estate, with title due to him in five years. He hurried back towards the landing, murmuring thanks for the buffalo riches.

HE WAS DELIVERING SOME sacks of harvested grain to the mill when he was astonished to see Gordy Jenkins walking down the street toward him. 'Gordy!' He stopped in surprise, a sack of grain on his shoulder.

'Hi-yup, Purchase.' Gordy stopped to shake hands. He looked older, his face lined, his expression glum.

'What in tarn happened? I imagined you'd be settled by now, up in Nebraska?'

Gordy scratched his nose, hummed, looked about, and pushed the hat back on his head. 'Shucks, the truth is, it didn't work out.' He lifted one boot and used it to rub the back of his leg. 'The land was rough. Peg hated the loneliness, the weather …' Gordy blew out a sigh. 'The gist of it is, I ain't much of a farmer, Purchase.' He gave a nervous laugh and shook his head, staring at his boots. 'I guess I'd have done better sticking to joining. It cost us some. It cost us.' He scratched a boil on his neck, a worried look on his face. 'How about you, Purchase?' The question was listless, Gordy seemingly anxious to continue to wherever he was headed.

'I'm doing well. I have a son now.'

'Yeah. I guess so.' Jubal looked past him at something farther along the street. 'Well, it was nice seeing you again, Purchase. I gotta go.'

'Why not come out for dinner, one day? You and Peggy?'

'Sure. That too.'

He watched the other man trudge down the sidewalk, his head bent as if looking for something on the ground.

'Did you see anyone in town?' asked Felicity when he got home.

'Not enough to mention,' he said, and placed a sack of beans on the table.

One evening, his mother complained of feeling unwell at supper. 'I feel poorly,' she said, her face suddenly pale. She took to her bed soon afterward, complaining of 'chills' in her bones.

She died in her sleep a week later, her fingers clutching her favourite wool shawl. Rocked by the death, he sat by the body, his senses numb with grief. After a while Felicity took him by the hand and gently led him out of the room. 'She's at peace, Purchase, don't begrudge her that. She's with your pa.'

HE BURIED HIS MOTHER next to his father in the family plot, standing over the grave with his head bowed. Toby, her favourite dog, lay stretched on the earth nearby, whimpering and whining.

The burial was attended by his brother and sister and an elderly aunt who made a hasty journey from Lawrence for the occasion. The November day was cold and wintry. Felicity stood to one side, cradling Jubal in her arms. Lilly stood alongside her, holding Amity. The preacher coughed and wiped his runny nose in between reciting, in a frail, windblown voice: 'The Lord is my light and my salvation; whom shall I fear? the Lord is the strength of my life; of whom shall I be afraid?'

Wrapped in his father's old buffalo coat, Purchase turned his gaze to the faded cross above his father's grave. *You never did get to see the buffalo, Pa. And I'm sorry for that. It won't be too long afore I set eyes on it again. I'll see it for you.*

The aunt started to sob, and he looked at Felicity. She stood determinedly erect, her face pale but composed. *You were right, ma. She ain't one for flinching.*

'He maketh me to lie down in green pastures: he leadeth me beside the still waters,' intoned the preacher.

Struck by the words, Purchase glanced up at the Missouri where it flowed past their own green pastures. *Only you are not quiet. You are broad, boisterous, American.*

The epithets mildly confounded him. He took a deep breath, the clear, cold air seeming to make his thoughts transparent to himself—he, who had never been afflicted with self-knowledge or dwelt much on the nature of things—content with the earth and sky and breath and bone. But now, as his mother was laid to rest, the chain of death and loss stretching all the way back to the war tightened—each link a reminder of mortality and the tears that underlay the world. *Even you, the great Missouri, are made up of tears, the flood of grief that started in Eden and rolls on to the end of the world.*

Humbled, he stared at the fresh plot of earth, understanding that he, too, was part of that chain, as was Felice—with all her salt and sass, and, in time, Am and Jubal. *And then there will be the grass, and perhaps the buffalo, and the sound of the wind sweeping over the land.* The thoughts, novel to his mind, weighed on him, offering a bleak awareness that outshone the grey sky, the keen air, and the ragged, sniffling voice of the preacher.

Felicity glanced at her husband, taking in his stoic grief, his head bare to the wind, his face sober with loss. *He is a good man. Decent in his ways.*

The preacher momentarily lost his place and she frowned, an irksome knit upon her brow. *There was that other preacher, the younger one. At least he wasn't coughing up his insides.* Jubal felt warm against her breast, and she hugged him closer. *Will he remember this—or his grandma?* Amity turned to cast a pleading look at her. *Soon!* she mouthed. The preacher had started on another verse, and she muttered under her breath. *What was it his ma had said? 'He needs to find his own buffalo?' Well, ain't this farm a buffalo? Aren't I, and the children, a buffalo—of sorts?*

She heard her mother-in-law's voice intoning in her ear. 'Men are funny creatures, possessed of the oddest notions. They are as restless as all creation, like their pants are on fire. Always wanting to be elsewhere.'

A gust of wind brought moisture to her face, and she glanced up at the grey sky. *Is that snow on the air?* She hugged Jubal tighter. *We have a good life here. Better than Peg Jenkins chasing after her hogs way out in Timbuktu. On the other hand, I did agree—or at least didn't disagree. And*

I did want—goodness, am I forgetting? My pants were once on fire, too! She sighed, her breath frosting on the air. Would it be so bad—the frontier? It ain't London, or Paris, or even New York. But it's something. Something new and different. Her gaze lingered on the fresh grave. In her mind she saw another plot alongside it and shuddered. Otherwise, it's to lie here one day, the world unseen. She glanced again at Purchase where he stood, head bowed. He has a strong neck. Why did I not notice that before?

Hush now! she mouthed as Amity turned again, a tearful look on her face.

The service concluded with a ragged rendition of his mother's favourite hymn: "Swift to its close ebbs out life's little day, earth's joys grow dim, its glories pass away." The preacher sneezed and signed a blessing, and the ceremony was over.

Following the service, he sat down in the parlour with his brother and sister, the union of the three of them strained and awkward minus the distracting presence of their mother. 'Felice and I plan on heading out west, to the territories,' he blurted out, impatient with the sombre silence.

'Out west?' Lilly spoke up in protest. 'What does Felicity say?'

'She agrees.'

'She does?' Lilly glanced to Samuel for support. 'But Jubal, he's still on the teat,' she said.

'Do you want the farm?' He looked at Samuel.

'Is this the time?' Samuel frowned.

'What better time—when we are all here?'

Samuel grimaced. 'I have my own business to attend to.'

'Lilly?'

She shook her head. 'My husband hates farming worse than poison.'

'Then I'll sell it and divide the proceeds three ways. Agreed?'

'But their graves … Who will tend to them?' Lilly wept and blew her nose.

'I GUESS NOW IS a good time—to think about the territories, like we had planned."

The words, coming so soon after his mother's death, surprised and displeased her. Couldn't he have waited?

'Why now? Besides, I like it here. Things are peaceful. We have good neighbours. There's ma and pa.'

'The land's paid for. If we don't occupy it, we breach the conditions. If we sell the farm and leave by early next spring, we can build us a house and settle in before winter,' he said.

'So soon?' She twisted her lip, severely doubtful of the entire reckless enterprise now that it was almost upon them. 'That's less than six months!'

'It were best.'

She sat down, fingers twisting her apron. 'I shall have to tell ma and pa.'

'How will they take it, do you think?'

'Hard, I expect. Ma will likely fall down and screech like she's receiving the Lord.' She gave a deep sigh. 'And poor pa will smoke his pipe 'til he sets himself afire—or grab for the whisky.'

He kissed her brow. 'It will be the start of a new life.'

'The start of a new life.' She deliberated on the phrase, copying it to her diary, where she underlined it, her brow knitted in doubt. Well, it's what I wanted, wasn't it? One time, at least. She held the pen in suspension, gripped anew by the enormity of the decision. Good Lord, the infernal plains! Momentarily at a loss what to write, she capped the ink bottle and closed the journal. 'Til my head sorts, she told herself.

Her mother came to visit, but she couldn't bring herself to break the news. 'By the way,' said her mother as she stood up to leave. 'I saw Peggy Jenkins last week. She's back from Nebraska. She asked about you.'

The news stunned her. 'The Jenkins are back—for good,' she told Purchase at supper. 'Ma says things didn't work out for them in Nebraska. Imagine that?'

He shrugged. 'The plains aren't for everyone.'

A week later, she asked Purchase to drive her and the children into town.

'Are you going to tell your parents?' he asked.

'Soon,' she said.

Finding out from her mother that the Jenkins were staying with Peg's parents until they were back on their feet, she left the children with their grandparents and headed for the house, intensely curious to discover the reason for their return. 'I'll just pay a visit,' she said when questioned by her mother where she was going as she tied on her bonnet. 'To be polite,' she said.

She was not far from the house when, turning from Elm into River Street, she spied Peggy herself walking toward her. Her friend was dressed in a blue cotton dress, a plain grey bonnet and a shawl around her shoulders. She walked with her head down, only raising it as though startled at Felicity's greeting.

'Peg! What a surprise to see you! I was just headed to buy some sugar. I haven't seen you in an age.' Felicity kissed the other woman's cheek.

'Uh huh.' Peggy toyed with the strings of her bonnet, her face lined and distracted.

'How was Nebraska?'

'Oh, Nebraska!' Peggy smoothed down her skirt. 'It wasn't for us. I told Gordy I didn't like it and simply insisted we return. All that grass!' She shuddered. 'Poor Gordy, he—' She broke off and looked at Felicity, her eyes full of misery. 'Well, anyhow. I put my foot down.' She wiped a hand across her cheek. 'There I go again!' She attempted a smile. 'The frontier is no fit place for a woman,' she said, looking past Felicity.

'Is everything all right, Peg?' asked Felicity, concerned at the other woman's state.

'Oh! Everything is fine now we're back.' Peggy smiled again, her eyes brimming. 'I must go. Nice to see you again, Felicity.' And with that, she hurried past.

'Peg, wait!'

But the other woman hurried on as if she had not heard.

Troubled by the encounter, Felicity reported the conversation to Purchase as they rode back to the farm. 'She didn't seem herself. She was off-colour. You remember Peg—how sociable she was?'

'Maybe she was poorly.'

'No. It was Nebraska that changed her.'

'Gordy has no sense when it comes to homesteading.' He glanced at her, concern on his face. 'You won't fret about it, will you? We're in a different way. There's the buffalo money, the sale of the farm. I know the territory. Heck, Gordy had no business going as he did.' He looked at her, waiting for a response. 'Felice?'

'I said I'd go, didn't I?' She clutched the seat as the wagon jolted. *At least Peg didn't have young 'uns to fret about. I have two. Doesn't he see?*

The next morning, she took Amity and Jubal down to the river to watch the boats go by, it being a fine winter's day. A steamer was headed upriver, running a wide ripple in its wake. The pilot caught sight of them watching from the shore and gave a blast on the whistle, causing Amity to shriek with excitement.

She held Jubal up close to her face. 'That's the boat your pa will take us on—all the way to Indian territory! Would you like that?' She gazed at the infant, her thoughts in a whirl. *Lord help me, but I'm in two minds. What if it don't work out—like with Peg?* The baby opened its mouth and gurgled. 'I expect your pa just wants to be by that silly old buffalo,' she said, and sighed, wiping the baby's chin.

With Felicity's reluctant assent, he made plans to advertise the farm in the *St Charles Journal*. In February, barely a month later, a carriage rolled up to the farmhouse with two, dark-suited men aboard. Purchase took them on a tour of the farm, after which Felicity served them coffee and hotcakes in the kitchen. A short time later, the men stood up and shook hands with Purchase before bidding her farewell. She stood with her husband to watch them climb back into the carriage. 'Well?' she asked.

'It's done, Felice.' He turned to her, a pleased look on his face. 'The farm is sold.'

'When?' she asked, hardly knowing what to think.

'They want to take possession by spring. That suits us fine.'

She spent the rest of the day in a semi-daze. *'From a life of gay abandon in a general store to a farm wife to a homesteader in Indian territory!'* she wrote in her journal, struggling to comprehend the speed of the changes in her life.

When next she visited her folks, Purchase insisted she tell them about their plans. 'The longer you put it off, the harder it will be,' he warned. He squeezed her hand. 'Remember to ask your pa to order the woodstove you like. Time is running out.' Depositing her on the sidewalk outside her parents' store, he drove off to inquire about steamship fares and cargo rates.

'Good luck!' he called, turning his head. She watched him go before taking a deep sigh and pushing open the door.

'The plains!' Her mother turned white at the announcement. 'Abe?' She turned to her husband, her face wild with panic.

'That's a crazy notion, Felice.' Her father reached for his pipe.

'Crazier than two cats in a sack!' Her mother clutched Felicity's arm, her voice imploring. 'You'll get scalped by wild Indians! The children! You'll choke to death on dust! Abe!'

'It's a fair ways, Felice. There are no schools—'

'Or churches! Why, there's nothing, save grass and wild beasts! Think of Peg and what happened to her. You'll perish from lonesomeness!'

Her father nodded. 'That, too. There's hardly a body to be found—'cepting Injuns.'

'And stinking buffaloes!' Her mother looked faint with horror at the prospect.

'My husband is very attached to buffaloes. He's thinking of saddling one and riding it around to visit the local Indians.'

'Now, Felice. This is no time for sass. Your poor ma is mortal afeared for you.'

'I ain't sassing! Don't you read the newspapers—or look outside the door? There's a passel of folk leaving for the territories every day. Why, I expect it to be so crowded I might have to poke with my elbows.'

'Lord, make her see sense!' her mother beseeched, raising her eyes to heaven.

'Why, it's a shock.' Her father reached to the cabinet for a bottle. 'I hardly know what to say, Felice. I'll miss you so.'

Her eyes filled with tears. 'I'll miss you, too, Pa. But I'll write—every month.'

'Mercy that I let her marry that man! Now he's stealing her away!' Her mother broke out into sobs.

'He ain't stealing me anywhere. It's as much my idea as his!' She twisted her mouth, concealing the half-truth.

Her mother set her face in her hands, wailing and sobbing. 'I'll never see you again—or the children!'

'Now, Martha.' Her father placed a consoling arm around her shoulders. 'Don't carry on so.'

'Never again!' Her mother let out a prolonged wail and collapsed into a chair.

Her father gulped the contents of his glass. 'I expect she'll come 'round,' he said, and poured himself another. 'Martha. Don't take on so,' he soothed as his wife burst into a fresh fit of sobs and cries. 'When do you plan on leaving, Felice?'

'Purchase figures on spring—now that the farm is sold.'

'Spring? Merciful Jesus!' Overcome, her mother buried her face in her apron.

HOW DID IT GO? He mouthed the words as Felicity came out of the store, escorted by her father. Her mother was nowhere to be seen.

'Trials and tribulations,' she muttered, looking distressed. 'Amity, stay put!' Climbing up onto the seat, she held out her arms as her father deposited Jubal into her embrace. 'You'd better go see to Ma,' she said.

'Purchase, I 'spect your mind is made up?' Her pa looked across Felicity, a hopeful tone in his voice.

'It is.'

'Consarn and all!' Her father heaved a great sigh. His face was grey and grizzled, a drop of moisture on his lips. 'Consarn!' He repeated, looking to Felicity suddenly very old.

'Go see to ma,' she said, her eyes spilling with tears.

16

Dakota Territory

AFTER A WINDY JOURNEY up the Missouri—during which they passed numerous wrecks and narrowly escaped sinking themselves—Felicity McLennan stepped off the steamboat, *General Custer*, to find herself immersed in the stir and bustle that was the Fort Buffalo levee. The date was May 2, 1879—a date she carefully noted in her journal. She followed it with the simple notation, '*Arrived, Fort Buffalo, Dakota Territory.*' With Jubal tightly cradled in her arms, she followed her husband down the stage and onto the busy landing.

'Make way! Make way!' The roustabouts were already depositing the cargo onshore, where it formed a growing pile of crates, hogsheads, lumber, hardware, kegs, and barrels.

'Follow me! Stay tight!' With Amity's arms clutched around his neck, Purchase made his way through the crowd of miners, prospectors, buffalo hunters, soldiers, emigrants, homesteaders, and traders that milled about the levee. A wooden resting station had been built not far from where the boat lay drawn up and he led them there. He deposited Amity on a bench and bid Felicity stay put while he saw to the cargo. He was making his way back toward the boat when he heard his name called. 'Purchase! Purchase McLennan?'

He turned, astonished to see Jeb Halverson hailing him. The former teamster was older and burlier, but as affable as ever as he pumped Purchase's hand. 'Son of a gun! I never expected to see you again!'

'I'm here with my family,' said Purchase, delighted to see a familiar face.

'Family?' Halverson raised an eyebrow. 'I thought mebbe you had come back to run buffalo?'

Purchase grimaced. 'My buffalo days are behind me. What happened to the old outfit?'

Halverson sighed, his sunburned face turning solemn. 'After you left, the Sioux got terrible bad. We lost a half-dozen men over summer and winter. Ludlow figured it wasn't worth the headache and closed down the camp. Charlie—you remember Baumann?—and me took over the wagons and stock and started a freight business. We hired some of the boys—Mace, you recall? —and supply the mining camps and trading posts. But what about you?'

They spent a few more minutes reminiscing before he asked for Halverson's help in managing the freight, to which the other man readily agreed. 'I can store it for you,' he volunteered, 'and ship it to wherever you want, when ready.'

With lightened step Purchase returned to where Felicity waited with the children in the dusty rest station. 'The cargo is taken care of,' he said, his voice cheerful. 'There's a hotel in town where we can rest for the night. Tomorrow I'll arrange for mules and a wagon.'

The crowd around the landing had thinned out. The steamer was already preparing to leave, the embarking passengers bound for Montana Territory farther upriver.

Purchase led the way along the beaten track toward the cluster of buildings that made up the town. The fort looked the same—the Stars and Stripes hanging above the ramparts—and he wondered if the lieutenant who had helped save them from the Sioux was still stationed there. They passed a group of men talking by the side of the track. The men stopped talking to gaze curiously at Felicity. One raised his hat, and she nodded primly in return, recalling her mother's warning about the 'thieves and cutthroats,' that swarmed the frontier. She felt hot and tired under the heavy skirt she had worn for the journey. Jubal was crying and squirming in her arms and she wished for nothing more than to wash the dust from her face, sit down, and drink a cup of tea.

As they entered the town, Purchase looked around in amazement at the changes that had taken place in the six years since his departure. The tents and sod houses had largely disappeared, replaced by a broad and congested thoroughfare lined on both sides with planked sidewalks that boasted an impressive variety of stores, saloons, boarding-houses, a laundry, a bank and a post office. The braying of mules and the noise of men calling and shouting vied with the creak of leather harnesses and the rattle of wheels as drays, carts, wagons, and livestock jostled for space. Several of the buildings were two or even three storeys high and boasted large, painted signs. He searched for the former Doyles and found the establishment—if it was indeed the spot—replaced by a brassy saloon from within which came the sounds of a piano and loud voices.

'Tarn, Felice. I hardly know the place.'

She said nothing, almost overcome by the foul odours wafting up from the piles of festering garbage that littered the street. Flies were everywhere, the insects buzzing her face as she stepped over the fresh mounds of horse-shit. Large puddles had collected in the pits and ruts left by the wagon wheels. Every second person seemed to be a gold miner or prospector, the men guiding mules laden with pickaxes, shovels, pans, and other supplies. Disreputable-looking characters in soiled jackets or shirtsleeves lounged about in front of the boarding-houses. A window opened from a second-storey room and a woman's face stared down at her. The face tightened with disapproval before disappearing back behind the curtain.

'Look out! Step aside!'

Her husband shepherded them to one side as a stagecoach creaked down the middle of the thoroughfare, its wheels splashing up dirty brown water from the puddles. The driver, perched high on his seat, shouted for room as the horses snorted and fussed. A man in a narrow-brimmed hat gazed at her from the stage window, turning his head to stare. She placed a protective hand over Jubal's mouth as the equipage threw up mud and water in its wake.

They passed a hardware store and a telegraph office, Purchase all the while shaking his head and exclaiming to himself. 'There used to be a stable there,' he said, to no one in particular. They stopped before a dilap-idated wood building with a sign painted above the door in faded letters: *The Dakota Hotel and Rooming House*. And, below it, a second line: *A fine establishment*.

The shady interior brought some relief from the noise and mud that choked the street. Purchase booked a room with a seedy looking clerk who kept raising eyes to glance in Felicity's direction. 'Welcome, folks, to Fort Buffalo,' he said, his eyes discreetly devouring her. Doing her best to ignore his impertinent gaze, she followed her husband up a set of narrow stairs to the room.

Exhausted, and coated with mud and dust, she removed her hat and coat and sank into a chair. Apart from the chair, the only items of furniture in the small, stuffy room were two narrow cots and a dresser. A dirty, fly-blown curtain hung over the single window. A jug stood on a shelf above a tiny handbasin. The children were tired and out of sorts, and she laid them down on one of the narrow cots, where they instantly fell asleep.

'Are you feeling all right? You look a mite under the weather.' Purchase looked at her with concern. 'This is only for a few days while I sort out the lumber and buy a wagon. Before you know it, you'll be in your own little house.'

She gave an irritable *tsk* to let him know that lumber and wagons were the last things on her mind.

'Where are you going?' she asked as he put his hand on the door.

'I have to go and make some arrangements.'

'Not now, surely? Rest first.'

'It's best to do it straightaway. I want to hire a wagon so I can visit the claim tomorrow. I'll be back as soon as I can. Lock the door.' And with that, he closed the door behind him.

Feeling faint in the warm, airless room, she loosened the collar of her blouse and poured water into the basin to splash her face. She looked around but could find no hand towel. She dabbed her face with a handkerchief. Not even a looking glass! Hearing a commotion from the street, she held up the tattered curtain to peep out. Two wagons had collided, and the drivers stood nose to nose, loudly cursing each other as a crowd gathered to watch. She peered up and down the muddy thoroughfare. The buildings appeared oddly ramshackle, as if thrown together in a hurry and about to fall down. She felt eyes on her and glanced down to find a man staring up at the window. Stepping back, she drew the curtain and sat down on the bed, overcome with fatigue. The children slept soundly on the other cot. She took in the musty, shabby room, her mind still in a daze at the transition from the windy steamboat to the dirty, noisy town. Exhausted, and slightly nauseous, she sank back onto the hard, lumpy bed.

'FELICE?' HER HUSBAND STOOD over her, shaking her shoulder. The children were up and crying. 'They're hungry. Let's go and get some supper.'

After eating in the empty, dank-smelling dining room, she put the fretful children back to sleep and sat on the other cot. Her husband was pulling off his boots, and she sat in silence waiting for him to notice her.

'What is it?' He sat up, still holding one boot.

She said nothing, only shaking her head. Setting down the boot, he came to sit next to her on the bed.

'Tell me.' He took her hand between both of his.

'Is this it, our new home? It's not exactly St Charles, is it.' She tried to keep her voice light but failed.

'Not here, Felice. Out there—' He gestured to the window. 'Out on the prairie. The town ain't much, I know. But you should have seen it some years back! Mr Halverson, the fellow I mentioned, said it's growing like gangbusters with miners and prospectors and—heck, you saw all the families on the boat. All of them settlers like us, come to start a new life. You'll like it once we are all set up in our own home.'

She nodded, not trusting herself to speak. Standing, she began to unbutton her dress.

'It will look different in the morning,' he promised.

Still awake, in spite of her tiredness, she lay next to her sleeping husband and listened to the noises from the street. The window was half-open to permit air into the room. Profanities floated up to her ears as the saloons emptied and drunks or wastrels staggered down the street to wherever they called home. She heard the sounds of a quarrel and listened intently as furious voices were exchanged. She turned on her side as other voices joined in. *"Where will the children go to school? You'll perish of loneliness!"*

Her shaken equanimity was hardly restored the next morning as they sat again in the hotel restaurant surrounded by rough-looking men who turned to stare rudely as she took a seat. She fussed over the children, ignoring the conversations and the glances cast her way. Amity was teary-eyed and bad-tempered and asking why they couldn't go back to the steamer. 'It smells here!' she whined, drawing a guffaw from a nearby table.

After breakfast, she sat in the shabby room while her husband left to make plans. 'I'll be back afore you know it,' he promised, closing the door behind him.

In his absence, she did her best to settle Jubal, who cried continuously while Amity alternated between grimacing and twisting her hair, and casting moody looks at her mother.

'Good heavens, you're three years old, Amity McClennan! Act like it!' Exasperated, she picked up Jubal as he began to cry again.

Two hours later, her husband returned, his voice confident as he outlined plans for their immediate future. 'I've hired a wagon from Mr Halverson. He's also promised to put a crew together of several trustworthy hands—some of them I know from before. They'll haul the lumber out to the prairie and start building the house and barn. You'll have a new home, Felice, as soon as next week.' He waited for a response. 'With a stove and wooden floor,' he added as no response came.

'Amity! Stop chewing your hair.'

'It will be all right, you'll see,' he said, and lingered uncertainly for a moment before reaching for his hat. 'I need to mark out the spot.' He held up a piece of paper. 'I got the claim marked right here. I'll be back before supper.'

'Wait.' She stood up as he prepared to leave again.

'What is it?'

'We are coming with you.'

'What?' He opened his mouth in protest.

'Or do you intend to abandon your wife and children to this fly-infested hovel while you gallivant about on the prairie?' Her voice was strained, her nerves at breaking point.

'Gallivant? I'll be staking out our new home.'

'Aren't I and the children part of that new home?'

'But there's nothing there to see. It's too hot—'

'I didn't come here to be separated from my husband, nor the children from their father.' She smoothed down her linen skirt. 'Amity. Fetch your bonnet.'

'For God's sake, woman!' Unable to think what to say, he sat back down on the chair.

'We'll need to bring food—and lots of water, for the children.'

'Shucks, Felice, see sense—'

'Amity McLennan. Tie your pinafore properly.' She picked up the wicker basket and handed it to him. 'We'll need chicken—or pork—hard-boiled eggs, and some fresh bread.'

He got to his feet, a frown on his face. 'It ain't right, Felice. It's hot as Hades outside. And it'll be worse out on the grass.'

She said nothing, busying herself with dressing the children. He sighed in defeat. 'Have it your own way, then—just don't complain if the children start to bawl and carry on some.' Shaking his head, he left the room.

'—And some cold pie, if they have any!'

Sitting down with Jubal in her lap, she reached for the wide-brimmed straw hat she had purchased for the journey and put it on her head.

'Are we going for a picnic?' asked Amity, her face brightening at the prospect.

'Yes. A picnic—out among the wild buffaloes.' She adjusted the girl's blue bonnet.

'Ma?' Amity peered at her as she tied the bonnet ribbons beneath Amity's chin.

'Let's go find your pa.'

17

A Crushing Vastness

SHE SAT ALONGSIDE HER husband on the hard wagon seat, with Amity squeezed in between. She held Jubal firmly in one arm while clinging to the seat with the other, worried she might shake clear off as the wagon pitched over yet another rut. Purchase had placed the wicker basket in the wagon box, along with dozens of pointed stakes, nails, patches of torn cotton and a hammer. 'It's a bother!' he complained, climbing back onto the seat. 'I had planned to stake out the house first. Wouldn't you rather wait?'

'I came all the way from St Charles. I guess it won't hurt none to go a little farther.'

Shaking his head, he picked up the reins. 'Har! Git!'

They set off, bouncing and swaying down the main street. The pack mules and wagons that had crowded the street the day before were largely gone. Dogs, and a large pig, scavenged on the mounds of refuse left behind. A few soldiers lounged and smoked on the sidewalks. A man, drunk or unconscious, lay on his back in the street. She averted Amity's eyes from the sight as the girl turned to look. They wheeled past a group of settler families congregated around a line of wagons laden with furniture and provisions. The children waved to Amity, who happily waved back. Felicity was relieved to see the women, reassured by the presence of other proponents of civility and domesticity.

At the edge of town, they passed a row of grimy, weather-stained tents. Between the tents, several women knelt before large tubs, washing and scrubbing clothes. One thin, exhausted-looking woman looked up and stared as though she might have recognised Felicity. She gazed back, trying to decipher the prolonged glance, her emotions all over the place.

The town fell behind them, the rutted dirt track giving way to grass. The wind was hot and gusty, and she released her grip on Jubal to tighten the ties that held her hat in place. The wind blew dust and grass spores into her face, and she covered her mouth. The wagon bonnet gave little relief from the sun, and she covered Jubal's head. *I should have brought a parasol. This sun will burn us alive. Why didn't he say something?* She looked at her husband, resentful of his slow, cogitating mood as he gazed ahead.

In spite of the bone-jarring motion of the wagon, she felt sleepy, the bright sun bothering her eyes. Amity had already fallen asleep, and Jubal, too, his head limp against her shoulder. She laid him across her lap and then picked him up again, suddenly frightened lest an errant bounce snap his neck. The four mules snorted and panted, sweat glistening on their backs in the summer heat. Her head nodded and she hugged Jubal closer.

SHE OPENED HER EYES to find herself surrounded by mountainous swells of grassy bluffs. The only sounds to disturb the silence were the snuffling pants of the mules and the creak of the wagon. On all sides, the empty plains undulated to the horizon under a great, cloud-flecked sky and she wondered at how quickly the town, and civilisation, had given way to wilderness. The immense desolation induced a sense of unreality, as if she might be dreaming this while tucked up safely in her bed back in St Charles. She was briefly overcome by vertigo—a sensation compounded by the impression that they were voyaging into a deep, mutable ocean, the wind gusting and moaning as if it might, at any moment, pick up the impudent cockleshell and blast them all to perdition.

She glanced at Amity. The girl was staring, wide-eyed—hushed into silence at the petrifying nothingness that stretched all around them. *She feels it, too—that the sky might crush us*. Newspaper accounts of women driven to madness by the soul-crushing solitude of the great plains sprang to mind, the lurid tales suddenly frighteningly real. *Will that happen to me? Will I go mad from lonesomeness—as ma warned I would? Isn't that what drove poor Peg to distraction?* She felt a sudden, strong affinity with the latter—the sympathy abruptly replaced by a new and terrifying thought. *What if a wheel should break or my husband meet with an accident?*

'Is it far?' Her voice trembled, the words more an attempt to hear something reassuringly human amid the endless wind-tossed swells than a question.

'Not so far.'

'Not so far! What does that mean?' A shrill note of panic pitched in her voice.

'There are no roads or mileposts, Felice,' he said, his voice remote and strange sounding in the crushing vastness.

She clutched Amity's hand, squeezing it so firmly the child cried out in protest.

Her husband seemed perturbed at something, working his jaw as he searched the horizon.

She gasped as her senses were assaulted by a sudden fetid and over-powering stench. 'Goodness!' She pinched her nose to block out the stink. 'What in ginger—'

'Buffalo.' Her husband pointed to where a mound of decaying flesh lay half-concealed in the tall reeds. 'And there!' He pointed to another, lying not far from the first.

As they continued, it soon became apparent that hundreds, if not thousands, of buffalo carcasses, each in varying stages of decomposition, lay partly hidden in the long grass. Some were barely more than bones. On others, the shaggy heads sat like great black lumps atop the maggot-infested bodies. The stench from the festering remains was so foul on the air she feared she might faint. Amity started to cry, her face wrinkled in protest at the fearsome stench.

'Cover your mouth!' Purchase pulled his neckerchief up over his nose and mouth.

Turning, she rummaged in her bag, pulling out a handkerchief which she gave to Amity, pressing it against the girl's mouth. She took out another for herself, breathing in the faint perfume but unable to block the over-powering smell of putrefying flesh. Jubal woke up and started to wail. She pressed him close to her bosom.

What happened to them?' she asked, her voice faint with revulsion.

'Robe hunters.' Purchase's voice was tight, her husband seemingly as shaken as herself by the grisly jamboree. The rotting carcasses became more numerous, dead and decaying buffalo now despoiling the grass on either side for as far as she could see. Each was stripped of its hide, the white, maggoty flesh or bleaching bones all that remained. It seemed to her as if they were travelling through a vast burial ground that stretched away on all sides. *Excepting they ain't buried.* Scavenging birds feasted on the remains, flapping up as the mules approached.

Amity leaned forward and retched over the wagon tongue. 'Ma!' She was crying, her face wet with tears.

'It's all right, Am. Here—blow your nose.' The distraught girl snuggled into her side, burying her face in her dress. 'Climb into the back. The bonnet will protect you from the sun.'

'No! I want to stay with you. Please, Ma!'

'It's nothing to cry about,' she soothed, feeling light-headed and on the point of being sick herself. 'It's only some dead old buffaloes.'

The carcasses were so abundant that Purchase was forced to steer the spooked mules through the maze of rotting flesh and bones. 'See there!' He pointed at a shape in the grass ahead.

At first she thought it a rock or hump of stones. But as they drew closer she saw that the knoll was made up of bones, the stacked bones resembling a pyramid and piled up to the height of a person. Within a short distance, they passed another, similar mound—this one composed entirely of skulls, many with shreds of flesh attached. The gorge rose in her throat, and she hugged Amity closer to her side, feeling dizzy and nauseous.

'I don't understand—why pile the bones?'

'Easier to gather. The bone collectors come along after the hunters have stripped the hides and the scavengers and maggots have stripped the meat.'

'Why?'

'The bones are valuable. They are sold for fertilizer. Ten dollars a ton, last I heard.'

They passed several more of the bone piles—the silent, bleached mounds giving her a disturbing sense of trespass, as if they intruded upon the aftermath of some great and unspeakable tragedy.

It was another hour before they came upon a stretch of fresh grass and left the acres of rotting carcasses behind. She sucked in a draught of air, suddenly thankful for the blustery wind that scoured the bluffs. The sun was now blazingly hot. She poured some water onto a cloth to moisten her brow. Amity had opened her eyes again and she coaxed the reluctant girl into taking a drink. 'Come on, swallow, or you'll shrivel up in this heat.'

Her husband had cocked his head as if listening. 'Nothing,' he muttered.

'Nothing what?' The dizziness and nausea had returned.

'We ought be seeing buffaloes—live ones.' He flicked the whip.

Jubal had fallen asleep again, his face still wrinkled from the stench of rotting flesh. They continued on, journeying ever deeper into the realms of grass. She was hot and thirsty and bothered by a constant queasiness in her stomach. 'How much farther?' She glanced over her shoulder. Behind them, the monotony of featureless grass rippled into the distance under an endless blue sky. A sensation of immense and suffocating desolation pressed upon her, causing her to stifle a scream.

''Tain't much farther now. I should water the mules, but—look!' He jabbed a finger at the distance.

She shaded her eyes. 'What is it?' Ahead, a tall, solitary rock stood out amid the blowing grass. 'That's it, Felice! That's the buffalo!'

'That?' She stared, unimpressed.

'See—the head! And there, the hump.' He pointed with the whip, urging her to see.

'The children need water,' she said. 'And a bite to eat.'

'You don't see it?'

'See what?'

'The buffalo, woman! Straight in front of you. Surely, you see it?'

'Landsakes! I do see it. What there is to see but a lump of old rock?'

'Git!' He flicked the whip over the sweat-slicked mules. 'Git!'

As they bounced and jolted and the rock loomed larger in the distance, she admitted to herself that it indeed bore a resemblance to a buffalo. Although why in Sam Hill a body would get the notion to make such a thing in all this gosh-forsaken wilderness was an amazement to think on. Her husband was gazing at the rock with a look on his face that upset and annoyed her in her flustered state.

'This is what you've talked about all these years?'

'It don't matter!'

The monolith seemed to swell in size as they drew closer. The plain had flattened out, the bluffs giving way to level terrain.

A SHORT TIME LATER, they drove into the shadow of the towering rock. She felt cooler in the shade and sighed as the wagon drew to a halt. *At least it shuts things out.*

Purchase helped her down and she stretched and stamped her feet, glad to be free of the hard, unyielding seat. While Purchase gave water to the thirsty mules, she spread a blanket in the grass in the lee of the granite shade. Opening the wicker basket, she took out the food and water. 'Amity, look after your brother.'

'I want to go with Pa!'

Her husband was walking up and down the rock, stopping to step back and admire, his hat in his hand. *Goodness if he ain't come to pay devotion— like a heathen!* She stared for a moment, mystified by his seeming reverence toward the object. *What does he see that I don't?*

She turned her attention back to the children. When she looked up again, Purchase had disappeared around the front of the rock and her heart beat faster as the terrifying emptiness was again thrust upon her overwrought nerves. 'Where's pa?' asked Amity, a note of panic in her voice.

'He's gone to worship,' she said, attempting to sound like her old self. 'Now eat something.'

He completed a circuit of the rock, the heat and gnats forgotten as he ran his hand against the hard stone and took in, once more, the granite solidity of the colossal beast. His eye was caught by some marks on the granite and he leaned closer to observe. Someone had etched geographic coordinates into the rock at eye level. The numbers gave the latitude and longitude plus the range and township coordinates. The tall, sun-browned surveyor he had encountered while filing the land claim came to mind, and he muttered at the violation.

'Purchase McLennan! Do not abandon your wife and children to the grass and wind.'

He made his way back to where Felicity sat in the grass with the children. 'I'm here,' he said, angry at her indifference to the singular creation that rose above them.

'I imagined we had come all this way to map out the homestead,' she said, resentful in turn at his perplexing fixation with a misshapen lump of stone. She felt another twinge in her belly and placed a hand there. Her dizziness in the wagon, the seasickness amid the wind-rushed swathes of grass, and the nausea induced by the fetid carcasses all confirmed the messages sent by her body. *Now is not the time to tell him. I'll mention it on the way back. Or maybe tomorrow, when this finnicky old rock has left his senses.*

He tried one more time to alter her opinion, picking up Amity after they had eaten and carrying her out into the grass. 'Your great-great-grandpa carved this buffalo,' he said to his daughter, waiting for Felicity to join them. 'What do you think?'

The girl looked up, squinting in the sunlight. 'It's huge! How long did it take grandpa to make it?'

'Great-great—never mind. A long time. Most of his life, I shouldn't doubt.'

It was on the tip of Felicity's tongue to ask what folly would prompt a sane man to waste his life on such an outlandish pursuit, but she resisted, saying, instead, 'Jubal needs a change.'

He nodded, but lingered, as if unwilling to be drawn away from the creature.

'Are you coming?' *One has to shout out every word. This infernal wind drowns out everything.*

'Look around, Felice. It's all our land—on both sides of the rock. As far as you can see.'

She looked around at the bare, windswept horizon. 'Here?' She could not keep the shock from her voice.

He frowned. 'What did you expect—streets and houses?'

'No. But not this. I thought there would be other homesteads. All those settlers we saw on the boat, and in town …?'

Her husband fanned his face with his hat. 'They are mostly east of here, over toward the Red River.'

'Then why in feathers ain't we over toward there?'

He said nothing, returning to the mules to check the harness.

'It's this gosh-forsaken lump of stone, ain't it?'

'The land here is good, Felice.' He glanced up from what he was doing. 'It's flat and right for farming. We won't be bothered by anyone. We'll be happy here. I just know it.'

She said nothing. The sun burned against her face, the blustery wind roared in her ears. The feeling of unreality she had experienced earlier came over her again.

'It's why we came here,' he said.

She said nothing, her throat constricted. *He really means for us to live out here. With nothing. No neighbours. Not another soul to speak to.*

'Felice?' He helped her up onto the wagon.

She sat in a daze as her husband drove in a direct line outward from the rock. He appeared to be counting, muttering to himself and turning to judge the distance. 'This is it—about a half mile,' he declared, halting the mules.

'A half mile to where?' The rustling bluestem—tall as a person—bent and swayed all around them.

'This is where our house will be.' Climbing down from the wagon, he rummaged among the pickets in the bed.

'Here? But there's not even a creek!' An incipient sense of panic threatened to undo her.

'We passed one on the way. Just over there. That's why we should build here.' Carrying a hammer and stake, he walked a few yards from the wagon. He tied a length of red cotton to the top. Walking along an imaginary line, he pounded another.

She watched, her senses numb, as he pounded the stake into the firm earth. *It doesn't bother him. He doesn't even notice. There's no one to call on. No other women. Who will the children play with?*

Her husband paced off a square, hammering pickets along the way. When he had finished, a section measuring roughly a thousand square feet, an area larger than her parents' house in St Charles, was staked out in the long grass. 'This is it, Felice. Our future home.' He slapped dirt from his hands. 'I promised you a porch, and by jinks, a porch you shall have.'

'And a wood floor,' she reminded, her voice mechanical.

'And a wood floor. Heck, it will be a proper house—you'll see. Nothing like those old claim shacks or dugouts or sod houses, but a proper home, fit to live in.'

Taking more of the stakes, he paced off several hundred yards from the marked square and began hammering again. 'The barn,' he said, his voice cheerful. 'Where would you like the smokehouse?'

THEY WERE HALFWAY BACK toward town when he suddenly flicked the reins. 'Git!' He barked, a note of urgency in his voice. He had taken a different route back to avoid the field of dead buffalo.

'What is it?' Aroused from the torpor that had claimed her, she glanced up. A bolt of sheer terror shot through her as she saw, atop a hummock to their right, a party of three mounted Indians. The Indians were motionless and appeared content to simply sit and observe the wagon.

'Who are they? What do they want?' Her heart pounded fit to bust clear out of her body. She clutched Jubal to her breast.

'It's all right,' he said, his eyes on the Indians. 'They probably mean no harm.'

Probably! Her mind screamed the word.

The Indians prodded their horses and walked them down the slope, clearly intending to intercept the wagon. Amity was staring, wide-eyed, her face white as she caught her mother's fear.

The Indians continued toward the interception at a leisurely walk, their silence unnerving. They were a little over five hundred yards distant and she could see their half-naked bodies, blackened by the sun. They carried bows and lances.

'Whoa!' Drawing the mules to a halt, Purchase jumped down into the grass. Reaching under the seat for the Sharps, he loaded and raised it in one swift movement. The Indians halted at the sight.

The sudden, sharp crack would have made her scream, had she any voice. Smoke issued out from the muzzle as he fed another bullet into the breech. An Indian held up his arm in a conciliatory gesture. After a long moment, the Indians turned their ponies around and began to head away from the wagon, albeit at the same, leisurely pace. Purchase watched for a moment and then clambered back on board. Laying the rifle across his lap he shook the reins. 'Skit!' The wagon lurched forward.

She stared at the retreating Indians, her face pale with anxiety. 'Will they follow?'

'No. That was a warning shot. They understood that and backed off.'

It took another mile—and the assurance that they were not being pursued—before her madly fluttering heart settled again in her chest. Her husband seemed remarkably calm about the entire affair, more concerned about its effects on her. 'They were from the reservation,' he said, attempting to reassure her. 'Probably jumped it in search of buffalo. They won't bother us again. Am?' He patted the girl's hand. 'There's nothing to fear,' he said.

In spite of herself, Felicity began to shake uncontrollably, her mind reeling as she recalled the Indian atrocities reported in the newspapers. She had said nothing since the appearance of the Indians, and he cast several anxious glances in her direction.

'Ma?' Amity looked up, her eyes brimming.

'I'm all right. It's all this grass!' She buried her face in Jubal's blanket.

'Felice?'

'Stop fussing!' It was all she could do to prevent herself from shrieking aloud.

'Pa!' Amity gave a small cry and pointed.

A group of perhaps thirty buffalo grazed the grass on the side of a nearby escarpment. 'Whoa!' Purchase pulled up the mules, grateful for the distraction. He lifted Amity onto his lap. 'At last! See?'

The girl clapped her hands, her earlier fright forgotten. 'Moo!'

'They ain't cows!' He chuckled, hoping to cheer up Felicity, who sat rigidly, her hands clasped around Jubal.

Among the herd, a half-dozen cows with calves in tow browsed the grass, their patchy summer coats light gold in colour. The calves were orange-red, sticking close to their mothers as they nudged the latter for milk. The boss cow raised her head, sniffing the wind.

They watched for five minutes or so as the buffalo continued to feed. She was about to urge him to continue to the safety of the town when the cow gave a bellow and spun around in the grass. The three Indians they had encountered earlier appeared over the ridge, whooping and spurring their mounts as they rode down on the herd. The cow took off at a run, followed by the others. A young bull faced the onrushing Indians, snorting and shaking his head. The Indians fired a volley of arrows and he slumped to his knees with a sneezing grunt. The Indians raced past without a second glance, galloping in pursuit of the fleeing herd. They were intent on the chase, and she wondered whether they had even noticed the wagon. The buffalo fled over a bluff, the Indians in hot pursuit.

In the silence that followed no one spoke. Amity sat silently on her father's lap, her eyes wide at what she had just witnessed.

'We should go.' She felt Amity's brow. 'The children will get feverish in this heat.'

'Those Indians were only interested in buffalo, not us. They are all camped on the reservation now, with the army watching over them. We'll be fine here.'

She didn't respond, fingering a button on her dress.

'Felice?'

'All five of us,' she murmured.

'Five?' He looked puzzled as she waited for him to figure it out. 'Oh!' His eyes widened. 'Oh!'

18

The Homestead

O N ALL SIDES, THE summer grasslands shimmered with a profound and oppressive stillness that both awed and disconcerted her. Shielding her gaze with her hand, she stared at the distance. After a time, she dropped her hand and turned back toward the farmhouse, her shoulders heavy with the burden of grass. Amity was playing in the yard with the new puppies, her face smudged with dirt.

'Ma, look!' She held up a squirming pup.

'Don't let them wander off into the grass. And keep an eye out for snakes.' She paused in the doorway, blinking to adjust to the shade. Jubal was sleeping on the tattered old buffalo robe her husband had insisted on bringing. She stood over the infant, a distracted look on her face. After a few moments, she walked over to the shelf beside the stove and stared at the tins and jars lining the wall. Unable to remember what she wanted, she stood there, her fingers on a tin, a distant look in her eyes.

Two months after moving into her new home, the nervous shock occasioned by the transition from the ordered, domesticated streets of St Charles to the brutal desolation of the prairie grasslands still had not worn off. On certain days, it reignited like a dormant fever, and she wandered around in a daze, reluctant to open the door and be confronted by the tidal grasslands outside—the wind cascading through the cloud-shadowed bluffs in giant, twisting runs that gave her a headache to see. The sprightly energy and waspish tongue that had characterised her in St Charles seemed to have dissipated before the crushing vastness of the plains, leaving her feeling diminished to the point of vanishing.

The plains were, she decided, an entire world of terrifying extremes, each event a grotesque distortion of what she had hitherto considered natural. Her first experience of a prairie thunderstorm was so nerve-racking she had cowered in bed, clutching a fearful Amity as the heavens cracked with ear-shattering booms that seemed prelude to the end of days. Most days, the wind raced through the tall grass with a tremendous *whooshing* roar, bending the stalks hither and thither, like waves on the sea. And in between terrifying storms and crashing gales, the plain sweltered in a stifling, humid heat that made her feel as though she might die from having her insides broiled. At times, she was so driven to distraction by swarms of pestilent, choking gnats that she wished for nothing more than to drown herself in the creek.

The romantic accounts she had consumed so avidly in newspapers and cheap novels now returned to mock her with their wild exaggerations and false promises of adventure amid the 'luxuriant garden' of the western plains. She recalled, with bitter irony, the colourful posters that decorated the St Charles shopfronts with their breathless messages of a fertile, sun-blessed Eden. '*All is parched, drear and bare,*' she confided to her journal. '*There's nothing for the eye to settle on. Just more of the same, which is nothing, everywhere you look. And no sound to disturb the silence save for that horrid, roaring wind forever noising in my ears.*'

On 'grass days,' as she named those periods when she felt the unrelenting silence press in with more than usual force, she sought refuge in writing long letters to her cousin in Boston or, more guardedly, to her mother in St Charles. Loath to admit to fraught sensibilities, she skipped lightly over the details, omitting all mention of the soul-sickness she feared would engulf her the longer she stayed on the wild, lonesome frontier. To her cousin, she wrote:

> *I make clothes for the children and practice Amity on her words and letters. I read to her and she copies it down as best she can. I worry about her schooling—there not being a schoolhouse within two hundred miles— although my husband reckons they'll have to open one up in town once the number of homesteaders increases. I'm that busy churning and salting, mending and baking, and tending to cuts and bruises and a thousand other things that I can hardly think.*'

Considering the list of chores to be overly telling—and recalling her cousin's fondness for balls and Boston fashions, she added a rider: '*If nothing else, all this pioneering builds strength of character.*' Still dissatisfied, she added a postscript. '*The newspapers say the future of this country is in the west. So here I sit, waiting for America to catch up!*'

To her mother she complained of the 'infernal dust, forever snooping into corners,' and the 'horrid wind that blows a body from one place to another.'

> *Tell pa the plains are every bit as windy as he advised. The country is so vast you can see a visitor coming three days away, 'cepting there ain't none. I could use some neighbours, especially female ones. My husband works*

hard clearing and cultivating ground to lay in a wheat crop. Amity is in good spirits and seems not at all disturbed by the wild prairie all around us.

Interrupted by a sudden blast of wind that made the house shake, she got up to look out the door and check that the children were safe. '*Mercy, if this wind ain't a live thing!*' she wrote on her return.

EACH MORNING, SHE GOT up before her husband and children to light the stove, scraping an iron nail across the flint to produce a spark and ignite the tinder. She waited until the combination of dried buffalo dung and corn husks emitted its odorous burn before going outside to the well—blinking, as if surprised anew each morning by the intimidating immensity of grass and sky outside the door.

While Amity fed the chickens and collected eggs from the coop and her husband milked the cow, she made breakfast of cornbread, beans, fried eggs, and potatoes. After breakfast, she watered the livestock and helped Purchase rake out the stalls. She then pumped more water from the well before washing the clothes in a tub and hanging them to dry in the blustery gales.

Aware of the pressing necessity to put in a garden to ensure adequate food for the winter, she marked out a large plot of grass behind the house and set about transforming it into a vegetable patch. In the mornings, before the sun grew too hot, she dug up the ground, perspiring as she turned the hard earth. As Amity played with the puppies and Jubal slept in the shade, she hoed and raked the soil, wearing leather shoes and a large straw hat to protect her fair complexion. Consulting the old *Farmers' Almanac*, one of three books in the house, she planted beans, carrots, summer squash, cucumber, tomatoes, and onions in careful rows a foot apart. In a corner of the plot, she cultivated lavender, marjoram, savory, thyme, sage, and germander from seeds brought with her from St Charles. It's a start, she told herself, surveying the square plot and neat rows, her joints aching from kneeling and digging.

On days when the weather was temperate, she allowed Amity to play by herself in the yard while forbidding her from entering the thick grass for fear she might fall down and never be seen again. She developed a horror of rattlesnakes and was constantly on the lookout for the loathsome creatures, wielding the hoe like a sword whenever any slithered out of the thick reeds. The dogs were a reassurance in this regard, growling and barking madly and bouncing straight legged with alarm at any snake that came near the house. Once, the male dog was bit and spent two days lying on its side and convulsing before finally regaining its feet again, shakily at first, but otherwise none the worse for the ordeal.

'Jubal?' She looked up from the pie she was making but couldn't see her youngest. Suddenly fearful, she hurried to the door, calling his name. She breathed a sigh of relief as she saw him sitting beside the vegetable patch, where Amity had placed him while she played mother.

'Goodness! But these weeds need thinning!' Amity squatted to pluck at a weed while chatting gaily to Jubal who sat open-mouthed, following her every move. 'I reckon if I don't pluck 'em they'll gobble up all the carrots!' Amity clucked crossly at the weed in her fingers, imitating her ma to good effect. 'Ginger if they won't!'

Ordinarily—that is, back in St Charles—the sight would have made Felicity laugh and summon her mother to watch. But now it pierced her. Who knows when ma will get to see her—or Jubal, again? And with that thought weighing on her mind, she went back indoors.

IN THE HEAT OF early summer, the four-man construction crew had dug holes, sunk posts, and raised walls as the four-room house quickly took shape. The methodical Robert Orland back in St Charles had arranged for the house lumber to be bundled in numbered lots, each lot corresponding to a detail on the simplified house plan. As a result, the construction proceeded swiftly in carefully planned stages, the construction crew foreman—an experienced carpenter—and Purchase agreeing on each step before commencing the next. The crew slept in tents on the site until work was completed. Jeb Halverson visited several times to check on progress, staying on afterward to share a glass of whisky before heading back to town.

In addition to the planked floors, the crew insulated the walls with tar paper, which Purchase then whitewashed to give the interior a cheerful, homely feel. He looked on proudly as glass was installed in the windows— leading Halverson to jest that he was building a mansion, not a farmhouse.

'But it's what she deserves—to give up the comforts of St Charles for these plains,' said Purchase.

'As you say,' answered Halverson, repeating his offer for Felicity and the children to stay with his wife and himself in town until the house was completed. 'It would be a sight more comfortable than that tent,' he said. 'Especially with the young 'uns and all.'

Purchase shook his head. 'She won't hear of it,' he said, pride in his voice.

Felicity had insisted on sleeping in the same canvas tent as himself, telling Amity it was an adventure, 'Like Indians living in a tipi.' From the canvas shade, she tended to the children and cooked over an open fire, washing clothes in the creek while Purchase laboured with the crew to lay the foundations.

Orland had cautioned against a shortfall in the building materials, so Purchase had over-ordered, arranging for plenty of lumber in order to accommodate a barn, the smokehouse, a corral and a root cellar with steps leading down below the ground. 'It's jest as well,' remarked Halverson, commending his perspicacity. 'I doubt there's a tree within twenty miles—at least one that hasn't been cut down.' He eyed Purchase curiously. 'It must have cost a deal,' he said, inflecting the remark as a question.

'You think I shot all those buff for nothing?'

Halverson smiled. 'You were always a canny one with the money, Purchase. No wonder I could never get you to join me in Hays.'

'While you were away gambling and whoring, I was shooting more buff.'

'—And salting the cash,' Halverson pondered. 'I wish I'd had your brains.'

The house and outbuildings were completed in five weeks, the crew finishing the porch as a light rain began to fall. The day after completion, his old comrade, Mace the teamster, delivered the stored furniture in a freight wagon and helped him set the cast-iron stove in place. Mace returned a day later, transporting the family plough with its two-bottom gang and the disassembled McCormick reaper. Another former teamster delivered a remuda of four horses and two mules. Mace returned again, hauling thirty sacks of animal feed, dried corn husks for the fireplace, and several cages of chickens. A milk cow was roped behind the wagon. Three hogs and a pair of dogs trotted alongside.

Purchase stood in the doorway, watching as Felicity opened and closed the drawers on the Ohio stove and then wandered around the kitchen, her lips pursed as she pushed a chair into place or ran her hand over the china cabinet transported from the farmhouse in St Charles.

'Jeb Halverson reckons it's the best house in the territory,' he said. 'Did you think we would live in a sod house or claim shack?' he teased, when she made no reply. 'Felice?'

She was peering at the china cabinet. 'My pa made that mark. Ma gave him all kinds of wrath for it.' She rubbed her finger over the polished wood. 'What?' She looked up, distracted, at the sound of her name.

AS A FINAL STEP, he had paid the crew sixty-five dollars to break twenty acres of land and dig a well. Halverson came out one last time to collect outstanding payments for construction and freight costs, the remaining buffalo wealth comfortably accommodating the expense. 'You've done yourself proud, Purchase,' he said, surveying the farmhouse and buildings. 'Hard to believe it was all grass just a while ago.' With a promise to 'come visit, and bring Mrs. Halverson,' he rode off, lifting his hat to Felicity.

'Next spring I'll plant our first crop,' said Purchase the following day, saddling the mare for a hunt. 'In the meantime, there's plenty of deer and turkey to shoot.' About to ride away he stopped and turned in the saddle, his voice jubilant. 'Shucks, Felice. It's ours! All of it.' He waved a hand to encompass the distance. 'Everything you kin see!'

THE ROCK DOMINATED THE landscape, it being the first thing she saw when she opened the door each morning. It was only much later—years after, in fact, that she discovered that her husband had deliberately oriented the house this way. When she did finally realise it her first impulse was amazement, and then anger that he should be so besotted as to wish to gaze upon the object of his infatuation first thing each morning and last thing each night. Unlike her husband, she took no comfort in its proximity, irritated by the way it seemed to rise self-importantly from the grass. 'If it ain't the very definition of an eyesore,' she complained, shaking her head as she swept the porch. She leaned the whisk against the wall, frowning at the buffalo as if vexed by its presence. What in tar hollow does he see in it, she wondered for the hundredth time, that would make him locate his family a thousand miles just to be by it?

As her disenchantment with all things frontier deepened, she came to project her fears and doubts upon the granite colossus, blaming it for her disquiet with the bug-infested, wind-bothered nothingness that bedevilled her senses. One morning, carrying Jubal in her arms, she headed toward it, combining exercise with curiosity as she determined to figure out, once and for all, the source of its perplexing draw upon her husband. The day was fresh and cloudy, a contrary wind shaking the grass. Amity trudged at her heels, querulous and complaining. A flight of grasshopper sparrows rose up at their approach, their screechy song sounding on all sides. The sun emerged from behind a cloud as she neared the object, its brightness bothering her eyes so that she stopped in place, shading her gaze to take in the oddly shaped lump. What is it looking at, anyway? Landsakes—but to spend an entire lifetime carving such a thing!

'Ma? Can we go?' Amity tugged at her skirt.

'Hush now. Be patient.' She felt—or imagined she felt—a movement in her belly. 'There's that big old rock your pa fusses so about. I'm talking to the baby,' she explained as Amity looked up in confusion.

'He can't hear!'

'And how do you reckon that Miss Know-It-All? I talked to you when you were in my belly. Or don't you recall?'

Amity grimaced, a fretful look on her face.

Felicity smoothed her belly. 'I expect you'll be seeing him—or her—with your own eyes soon enough.'

'Jumpy!' Amity gave a shriek as her pet dog came gambolling up through the grass. Throwing her arms around its neck she smooched and hugged it. 'He can have the next one, can't he, Ma?'

'Jubal?'

'The baby!'

'How do you imagine it's a he?'

'It's what pa says.'

'Does he? And suppose he is a she? 'Gracious, close your mouth, you'll catch flies. But no matter. He or she can have a puppy if they like. Heaven knows, but there are enough to pass around.'

Jubal woke up and gurgled, his eyes on her. 'Amity, leave pestering the poor dog and answer me something.'

'What?'

'Suppose we could take a boat back to St Charles tomorrow. Would you wish to?'

'Would pa come, too?'

'Yes.'

'And Jumpy?'

'Corn fries! Jumpy, too.'

The girl gave a suffering sigh. 'I suppose.'

'Suppose what?'

'I suppose I might want to.'

'You suppose or you would?'

'What?'

It was her turn to sigh. 'Never mind.' She turned her attention back to the rock where it glittered in the sunlight. How in hickory could a body bear to waste their life hammering a heap of old rock in the middle of God knows where? Maybe he was touched by the sun. Didn't ma say something about his pa being an odd fish?

'Ma?'

'All right! Goodness, child, where'd you fetch to be so impatient?'

They walked back to the farmhouse, her long skirt brushing the reeds. She saw Purchase raise a hand as they passed by the corral. Jubal squirmed in her grasp, and she stopped to shift him from one arm to the other. 'Amity McLennan—you stay close.' She swatted a fly, turning in a half-circle to take in the shimmering plain and immense, cloud-laden sky. Perish if it don't seem we are the only creatures left on earth. Perturbed by the notion, she continued toward the house.

SHE WAS DARNING BY the fire, a pensive frown on her face. Purchase sat nearby, cleaning the breech block of the disassembled Sharps. After several glances at his wife, he put down the block and moved the chair so that he sat alongside her.

'It's just us, Felice.' Taking her hands, he held them between his two large ones. 'No one to bother us. I wouldn't swap this spot for all of New York City.' He pressed her fingers, as if to will back the lively, opinionated girl he had tumbled head over heels for in St Charles.

'There's no one to bother us 'cos there ain't no one.' She drew back her hands and cut the thread with her teeth.

'Once the first crop is in, things will go easier.' He deliberated for a moment, his eyes on her. 'We can go into town, if you like. I hear there's a new general store. We could shop for things. Some comforts around the house.'

'I doubt I could stand the excitement.' She picked up her sewing basket. He watched for a moment as she busied herself with selecting another garment to mend. With a sigh, he moved back the chair and returned to his task.

'Come outside,' he urged the following day after supper. He took her by the arm. 'Sit with me awhile. It's a fine evening.'

'Talk to Jumpy,' she said, pulling away. 'Even if he has trouble forming words, he listens well enough. I got a heap of mending to get to.'

'Just for a minute or two,' he cajoled, tugging. 'It will do you good—to sit for a while.'

In spite of her protests, he coaxed her outside, hoping the placid dusk and rising stars would impart some of the pleasure he himself took in the dizzying confluence of wind, sky, and grass. 'Look,' he said, gesturing at the full moon. 'Why, it looks so close a body might reach out and touch it.'

Over the next several days, he insisted they 'sit for a spell' to enjoy the prairie twilight, hoping the remission from care would help settle the doubts she felt but did not express, in spite of his attempts to draw her out. At most, she admitted only to 'feelings' for their old life back in St Charles. 'But that's gone,' she said, her voice sounding bleak even to herself.

Occasionally, he took Amity onto his knee during these dusk soirees, encouraging her to chat and laugh in an effort to domesticate the gathering night. 'What do you say, Am, could you outrun the wind?' He smiled, glancing at Felicity as the child prattled on about her ability to 'hop' through the waving grass. 'Hear that, Felice? I reckon we are raising a jackrabbit.'

The air was balmy, the vast night sky glittering with millions of stars. A breeze kept the mosquitoes away. The house door was open, lantern light forming a small yellow pool in the yard.

'Amity, it's past bedtime.' She stood up, taking the girl by the hand.

'Jest another minute, Ma.' The child pulled away.

'Go inside.'

'But Ma!'

'Now!'

She followed the protesting girl indoors.

'Sit with me, Felice,' her husband called after her. 'She can put herself to bed.'

'It's late, and I'm tired.'

'A while, only?'

Pretending not to hear, she went inside. She sat on the bed in the lantern light, listening to see if he'd followed her inside. When she was sure that he hadn't, she sighed and got up to unbutton her dress. I ought be grateful, she told herself. He's doing his best. Guilt at the disappointment in his voice pricked at her as she lay the dress over a chair and smoothed the material. But I'm truly tired. She turned down the bed covers. And all those stars!

SHE WAS ON HER knees, plucking weeds, when Amity gave a cry and pointed to the distance. 'Ma!'

'What is it, child? What do you see?' Getting to her feet, she shaded her eyes. At first, she saw nothing other than the hummocky hills and blowing acres of grass. But then she made out a number of tiny figures slowly making their way through the grass in the distance. Squinting, she determined them to be Indians—men, women, and children. She looked around for her husband but couldn't see him. She returned her gaze to the grass, screwing up her eyes against the glare.

The plodding procession was led by half a dozen men on horseback, each horse dragging a travois. A line of women and children walked behind, some of the women carrying infants on their backs. A number of dogs, pulling packs and mustered by youths, brought up the rear. She stared intently, her initial alarm replaced by curiosity as the tableau slowly progressed through the rippling swathes. Whether they were aware of her or the homestead she was uncertain, but they gave no signs of anxiety at being observed as they trudged onward. In that moment, they struck her as tragic figures inching across the infinite grasslands, more to be pitied than feared.

'Where are they going, Ma?'

'I don't know,' she said, her eyes still on that forlorn caravan. She returned to her weeding, glancing up every now and then at the distant Indians. When she looked up again, they had disappeared, swallowed up by the mutable sea as if they had never existed. She poked at the earth, her brow furrowed as she dwelt on the sight. Over supper she mentioned it to Purchase.

'They were nomads, probably. There are still some of them around. They refuse to go on the reservation and would prefer to live as they have always done.'

Nomads. The word lingered in her mind—conjuring images of Arabian deserts, the dunes replaced by grassy bluffs, the camels by plodding horses. *It is a desert, of sorts,* she reflected. *And just as hard on a body.* She studied her reflection in the small mirror. Her eyes were red-rimmed, her once-pale complexion sun-burned and wind-roughened, her cheeks rouged with dust and soil. She leaned closer, moving the lantern to cast pallid light on her unkempt hair and sun-blistered lips. *I've weathered so. Ma would have a fit.*

Perturbed by the presence of the Indians, she insisted that Purchase teach her to load and fire the forty-calibre Sharps. He considered for a moment before agreeing. 'All right, have it your way. I'll fetch the rifle.'

Standing in the yard, she aimed at a tin can set on a stake, hitting it once out of six tries as Amity watched with wide eyes. Thereafter, whenever Purchase was away hunting, she kept the rifle within reach, only partly reassured by its sturdy feel in his absence.

19

A Stocktaking

THE HEAT OF LATE August was intolerable, the air so stifling she felt it burn her throat. The broiling sun and hot, prairie winds were a constant menace, forcing her to seek refuge indoors whenever she thought she might faint from the suffocating heat. Slumping back in the rocker, she fanned herself while Amity protested and tugged at her linen smock. 'I can hardly breathe!' she whined, and panted with small, rapid breaths to make the point. Jubal cried in the large wicker basket that served as a cot, his tender skin mottled pink by a heat rash. She placed a dampened cloth on his brow, worried the oppressive heat might suck the life from his tiny body.

The heat continued to build, the thunderstorms she had come to dread a frequent occurrence. Their ear-shattering booms were accompanied by brief but intense downpours that turned the yard into a quagmire and brought all outside activity to a halt. 'Some years are worse than others,' was her husband's sanguine comment when she despaired at their frequency.

One impossibly hot day, she was hanging out a line of washing when she saw Purchase hurry back from the barn, gesturing and shouting to attract her attention. Looking around for what might have alarmed him she was startled to see that the sky on the horizon had turned black. A strange, funnel-like mirage twisted and danced in the distance. At the same time, a roaring sound, like nothing she had ever heard before, came rushing to her ears. Grabbing back the washing, she threw it into the basket before running to help her husband as he rounded up the livestock.

'Suffering cats! What is it?'

'It's a windstorm! Git!' Her husband chased a horse into the barn.

The blue sky above turned suddenly dark and a volley of hailstones swept across the yard, drenching her where she stood.

'Hurry!' shouted Purchase and pulled her toward the house as hailstones pelted all around them.

'Ma?' Amity hovered in the doorway, a frightened look on her face.

'Go inside!' She hustled the girl indoors, turning to look for Purchase. He had returned to the barn and now came running back, some lumber under his arm and a hammer in his hand. He began hammering a piece of wood across the window as the intense hail soaked his clothes and hair. Above and all around, the sky was a sinister black as if an unknown hand had tugged a thick woollen blanket across the sun. The hailstones were now pelting down with such force that they bounced high off the ground.

'Get back inside! Close the door!' A drenched Purchase pulled the door shut and put the bar in place. Hail rattled against the roof with a sound like drumsticks furiously tapping.

'Ma!' Amity wailed in fear and clung tightly to Felicity's side.

She put an arm around the girl. 'Hush now! You'll frighten your brother,' she said, hardly able to hear her own voice above the roaring wind.

'It's nothing to fear, just a hailstorm,' said Purchase, his voice tight.

It was now so dark she lit a lantern. A gust of wind shook the walls and rattled the door. She picked up Jubal and held him in a tight embrace, her heart pounding. Purchase mouthed something she couldn't hear. She felt the house sway and exclaimed with fright, fearful lest the wind rip the roof from above their heads.

Purchase was shouting into her ear but, try as she might, she couldn't make out a word. Something struck the side of the house with such tremendous force she feared the wall might cave in. Shocked, she looked at Purchase, whose expression of strained vigilance showed he feared the worst.

The howling winds continued for ten minutes or so and then abruptly subsided, leaving an eerie silence in their wake. The sky cleared and sunshine once again illuminated the house. Amity followed her father with a wide-eyed stare as he opened the door to check for damage.

'It was the outhouse,' he said, his voice sombre. 'The wind picked it up and blew it against the wall.'

She went to see, shaken by the violence of the storm. Smashed pieces of wood lay strewn across the yard. The tall grass had been flattened, and large, glistening hailstones lay amid the debris. Purchase was already pulling and tugging at the shattered planks. 'I can rebuild it,' he said. 'There's some spare lumber in the barn.' He looked at her, shaking his head. 'We're lucky the wind didn't blow the durn roof off.'

'Have you seen this before?' Her voice was strained.

'Once. At the buffalo camp. It blew the tents all to hell.'

'Will there be more?'

'Hard to say. With luck, they'll pass us by.' He wiped an arm against his brow as he surveyed the wreckage. 'It's lucky I hadn't put in a crop. We'd have lost it for certain.'

That night, her sleep was disturbed by a vivid dream in which she wandered the great, tidal grasslands, crying out for her husband and children. All around was the bleak, wind-rushed plain—even the stone buffalo vanished to the limitless grass. She searched and called frantically, consumed by fear at being abandoned to the forsaken wilderness. So powerful was the dream that she woke in fright, her heart pounding. The mournful howl of a wolf came to her ears, and she shivered, picturing the pitch darkness and the wild, savage plain. The howl set up a furious response from the dogs and she listened to hear if the children were awakened by the noise.

Unable to get back to sleep, she got up from the bed, careful not to wake Purchase. Dim light filtered through the window. She unbarred the door to peer outside, tugging the wool shawl around her shoulders. The debris caused by the storm had largely been cleared away, and the yard looked peaceful in the greyish light. The air was cool, the prairie still deep in shadow. To the east, the sky was edged with a thin, red streak. The dogs leapt at her, whining and licking. 'Hush!' she said, afraid they would start barking again.

On impulse, she picked up the wooden pail and stepped outside into the cool dawn. Uncertain why she chose to fetch water at this dismal hour, she made her way slowly across the yard. The dogs followed at her heels, their panting breaths giving some reassurance in the dawn silence. At the well, she heard a shriek and set down the pail, listening. All around, the rustling grass and immense plain lay shrouded in semi-darkness. This was my dream! she realised. For a moment, she fancied she was back in her bed, dreaming this.

Lured—or propelled—by the tall, dewy grass, she ventured out beyond the boundary of the yard, treading cautiously, as if stepping into unsounded depths. The prairie stalks shivered in the breaking light. If she had stopped to ask herself what she was doing, venturing into the whispering grass that swayed and shook and disappeared into the dawn shadows, she might have turned back. But she pressed on, stealing a glance back at the house. *If Purchase gets up, he will wonder where I've gone.* A gust of wind blew up from out the tidal gloom, rushing through the grass with an audible sigh that raised the hairs on her neck. The dogs barked and growled at something in the reeds and suddenly her courage deserted her. Turning, she fled back to the house. Safely back inside, she leaned against the door, her heart thumping. She put a hand to her belly. Did he feel it, too?

THE LONG DAY HAD been especially trying—Amity unhappy at the lack of a playmate, and Jubal crying over nothing until he exhausted himself into sleep, only to wake and start wailing again. Upset by his crying and tired from the long day, she stared at the journal page in front of her, a dull glow on her face from the lantern. Purchase sat by the fire mending a harness laid across his lap. She felt his gaze several times but refused to look up.

'What are you doing?'

'Feathering ducks.' She dipped the pen into the ink bottle.

'I didn't see any buffalo, not even a sign,' he said, referring to the day's unsuccessful hunt. 'I can't think where they've gone. It's a concern. You should have seen them a few years back. It's just as if they suddenly disappeared.'

She gave a distracted 'um' in response.

'Read me something,' he said after a moment. 'I'd be obliged.'

'You ought start your own journal. You could talk pages about your buffaloes.'

'I like hearing yours more.'

Sighing, as if greatly put upon—the way ma sighed!—she moved the lantern closer to the journal. Turning back a page she recited in her firm, dry voice.

We have now been here four months. The house still smells new, of wood and whitewash. But our own smells are taking over and making the place our own. The children continue in good health and play in the yard next to the house. This bracing prairie air seems to agree with their constitution. Jubal is now two years old and totters along after his sister. My new stove is sturdy and reliable and keeps the house warm. I light it up first thing in the morning and place a pot of water on top. I baked a rabbit pie the other day. It came out warm and crusty—

'I remember that pie,' he said. 'Read me some more.'

With an irritable tsk! she acquiesced, turning another page.

I miss the bakery shop on Ann St in St Charles. They had the best bread. I also miss the Italian ice cream parlour over on South Main. Mother and I used to drop by for their lemon ice cream after church on a Sunday.'

'Are you content, Felice?'

The question threw her. 'How in Betsy did you fetch that from lemon ice cream?'

'I know this life is hard on a woman.'

'I agreed to it, didn't I?'

He grimaced. 'Is that all?'

She made no reply, furrowing her brow as she considered the page.

'Do you not take some small pleasure from it—in spite of the hardship?'

'I suppose,' she conceded, wishing he would stop talking.

'Suppose what? Life here is not so bad.' He waited for a response. 'Out with it,' he said, exasperated at her silence. 'You have that look on your face.'

'What look?'

'You're not your usual self. Haven't been since—'

'Since when—the Flood?'

'Something's bothering you. Share with me. I'm your husband.'

Then don't pry! it was on the tip of her tongue to reply. Instead, she put the cap back on the bottle, exclaiming at the ink smudge on her fingers.

'Things will get better. There are more settlers coming into the territory every day. In time, we'll have neighbours we can invite over.'

'When?' She looked at him, her face demanding an answer.

'In time, Felice. In time.'

She felt suddenly close to tears. 'In time we shall all perish, like the buffalo.'

THE ONSET OF WINTER was deceptively mild, and she welcomed the reprieve from the storms and draining heat of summer. A thin layer of snow bathed the landscape in a benign light that soothed her soul and made her long for the streets and meadows of St Charles. She continued to tend the garden and give the cow its afternoon milking as her pregnancy entered its fifth month. Sitting on the stool and watching the milk as it squirted into the bucket, her thoughts roamed to her parents and the store on Main Street. Lord, how Pa loved his pipe—*Loves!* She stood up and lifted the heavy pail. She set it down again as she felt a gripe in her guts. *Who are you?* She placed a hand on her swollen belly. Boy or girl? She stood in the doorway, gazing absently at the house. *Perhaps you will be neither, but a new and special creature, with wings and a kind face.*

As she grew rounder and fuller, she sat in the rocker, indulging her newfound love of needlepoint. Using coloured yarn, she stitched the shape of a house, embroidering the sun above it. Underneath she stitched, 'Our Home'. She fixed the finished canvas to the kitchen wall, standing back to admire the tiny patch of colour on the otherwise monochrome white. She started another—of the barn, eliciting praise from her husband. She added several more to brighten the house and make it feel more like a home.

To bring further order and domesticity, she employed the inventorying skills learned from her father, minutely cataloguing and specifying the contents of the farmhouse—what was missing and what needed to be added when her husband was next in town. Encouraged by the results, she itemised the chores and duties that needed to be performed—and at what point of the day—for the house to remain workable and shipshape. 'Necessities,' she wrote, compiling a pantry list:

flour
sugar
molasses
almonds
ginger spice
baking powder
lemons
oatmeal
pickles

She ticked off each item in the manner of her father checking off the sacks of beans and jars of condiments. 'Lord, but I feel like a sack of beans,' she complained as she felt the baby kick.

She incorporated the lists in the letters to her mother, including them as evidence of domestic diligence while filling the remainder of the letters with snippets from her journal and anecdotes drawn from the busy day.

Make sure you write when you receive this. Tell me all the news. How is pa? And how is that old scold Mrs. Anderson that so fussed over the wrong-coloured yarn? Can you still smell bread from the bakery when the wind is right? Purchase mentions he will be going into town next week, when he will post this.

So, goodbye for now.
Your loving daughter, Felicity.

PS: I guess Purchase didn't go to town after all. Maybe next week, he says. Each passing day he falls more in love with that goshfaluting rock. You should see it, pa—as big as all get out and twice as ugly. I can't think what it is about it that enchants him so. Ma, I might get you to send some of Dr Carrow's cough potion—you know, the pinkish one that tastes like sour cherries? Jubal gets a mite chesty in this dry air. Amity is growing

*up fast as a weed and I must unstitch her dress and add more length.
It's this pesky wind to blame. I swear it stretches a body.*

Letters in reply were a rare and special triumph—the missives read
again and again, the words scoured for any missed meaning or inflec-
tion. The letters, addressed to the freight office in Fort Buffalo, appeared at
two-monthly intervals. She stood in the doorway each time her husband
returned, scanning his face for any indication of mail. Whenever a letter
was produced, she made herself a cup of tea—or, increasingly, the coffee she
had come to prefer—and sat in the rocker to devour every single word of
the precious missive. Once read, she carefully folded each one and placed
it in her linen drawer along with the others—to be taken out at regular
intervals and pored over again until each word and each line was registered
in her mind.

20

A Birth and a Virgin Crop

IN JANUARY 1880, SHE gave birth to her third child, a son. Lodged at the Halversons' in Fort Buffalo for the occasion, she was attended to by the motherly Mrs. Halverson and delivered the baby in the small, wallpapered bedroom while her husband waited anxiously outside. The following day, she returned to the homestead, her newborn swaddled in a buffalo robe and held tightly in her arms as her husband drove the wagon across the frozen grass. 'You are a prairie foundling,' she murmured to the sleeping infant. 'You will grow up with the wind and the grass in your bones.'

She wrote to her mother, describing the infant's feeding and sleeping habits and enclosing a snip of hair.

> *His name is Boundary. My husband named him. He claims it's an old family name from his ancestral Scotland. He has his father's nose, but his eyes 'mind me of pa's. He sleeps soundly for minutes at a time during the day and wakes up at night for a good cry. Amity is all affection and constantly cuddles and fusses over him. Purchase is most attentive and frequently talks to him—mainly about his hairy old buffaloes, I suspect. We will come visit soon. I promise.*

Unable to resist, she set down the pen and crossed to the basket. She lifted the sleeping infant in her arms, marvelling at his placid demeanour as he awoke, eyes fixed on hers. The weather being mild, she took him outdoors, enjoying the feel of his warm body next to her own. The breeze was invigorating in the bright, winter sunshine. She cradled the infant while cooing of grass and sky and his pa's clever way with the mules. 'Who does he 'mind you of?' she asked, bending so that Amity could see.

The girl contorted her mouth to think. 'Pa?'

'Well, I hope it ain't Jumpy!' she said, to the girl's blinked surprise.

IN SPRING, SHE RETURNED to her garden, glad of the warmer, blustery gales that chased away the frost and lingering snow. She planted fresh lettuce and carrots and fussed over the herbs and spices. With Amity by her side, she pickled tomatoes, onions, green beans, and cucumbers, carefully storing them in glass jars. Discovering a patch of chokeberries growing beside the creek, she boiled them into a jam that she spread on home-made cookies—watching as her husband and children made short work of consuming the entire plate. For Jubal's third birthday, she consulted her mother's much-thumbed copy of *Miss Beecher's Domestic Receipt Book* before deciding on a feather cake. She substituted nutmeg for lemons and baked a pile of gingerbread cookies to surround the cake.

'Hands!' She swatted Jubal's hand as he made to steal another cookie. Changing her mind, she gave him one anyway, widening her eyes in pretended horror as he bit off the head. 'I guess I'm raising cannibals! Amity. You take one, too.' She went to the wicker basket and lifted Boundary up into her arms. Sitting back in the rocker, she nursed him while Amity and Jubal played together. 'Mind your brother,' she said as the girl dragged her squirming brother along the floor by both legs. 'He ain't a wheelbarrow.'

The door opened and Purchase stepped inside to fetch a cup of coffee. After a swallow, he set the cup down and came over to where she sat. 'He'll be a farmer, like his pa,' he said, bending to trace a thick finger along the side of his son's face.

'Or a missionary,' she suggested, 'converting the heathen.'

'You're looking ... brighter, Felice,' he said.

'And why wouldn't I?'

'No reason.' He straightened up, anxious lest he spoil the moment. 'I'll be in the barn,' he said.

A WEEK LATER, HE returned from town to report near-neighbours—a Russian family that had claimed a section of land less than four miles from their own. 'I met them, but they can't speak a lick of English,' he said. Not three days later, he returned from a hunt with news that a German family had claimed a section even closer, a mere two miles away. 'And they speak tolerable English,' he said, recounting an exchange of greetings with the husband. 'We should maybe invite them over for supper. What do you think?'

To her surprise, the prospect gave no immediate comfort. *'Sufferation if I ain't fixing to all this solitude like my husband.'* she wrote that evening. She stared at what she had written, pondering the startling notion that there was something in the abundant grasslands that called to her, despite everything.

Purchase went into town and returned with a familiar face seated beside him on the wagon. 'Felice, you remember Elijah?'

'Eli,' the youth corrected.

''Course I do. You helped build the house.'

'Elijah—Eli—is going to help me plant the crop.'

From then until after harvest, the youth, hired at sixty-five cents a day, joined them for meals and slept in the barn while helping her husband about the farm. He proved a willing, albeit taciturn, worker, and ate, she remarked, his own weight in pork and grits.

The April weather was cool and blustery as Purchase planted the land broken the previous summer. He fertilised the seeded furrows with ground buffalo bones purchased in town. Eli worked alongside, stopping every now and then to grimace up at the sky and complain about the 'pernickerty' wind.

As the weeks passed, Purchase kept an anxious eye on the growing plants, patrolling the fields several times each day to look for signs of mildew, rust, or blotch. He inspected the flowering plants for beetles, stem maggots, or sawfly, plucking the shoots to crush between his fingers as he checked the stems. 'I reckon this first crop has caught the bugs by surprise,' he joked to Felicity, pleased that the plants seemed to be developing so well.

Temperate rainfall and long, warm days produced a flourishing crop of green plants which stood waist-high by July. Standing in the fields to survey the grain, he felt a flush of satisfaction at knowing the harvest would feed his family for the coming year. The dogs came to investigate as he stood there, whining and tail-wagging as they looked up at him. Humming, he headed off toward the barn, the dogs following.

A profusion of heads began to appear as a week of mild weather raised his hopes for a bountiful virgin crop. He walked the furrows, scouting for insects. Eli did the same, across the field. Plucking a head, he roughed out the kernels, testing for hardness.

'Pa!' He turned to see Amity walk toward him, munching on a carrot. 'Pa?'

'Come here,' he said, kneeling. He placed some grain kernels in her hand.

'What are they?'

'Those are wheat berries. See how soft they are? Squish them with your finger.' He watched as she did so. 'That's the milk. Soon the seeds will grow hard and dry and be ready for harvesting.' Amity watched, wide-eyed, as he placed a kernel between his teeth. 'When you can crunch them, they are ripe.'

She put one in her mouth and grimaced before spitting it out. 'Ugh!'

He laughed, delighted with the ripening grain, the bright day, and his inquisitive, rosy-cheeked daughter. 'It tastes like that now, but when we grind it into flour, it's different. Your ma will use it to bake the fresh bread you like so much.' He gestured to the flowering acres. 'Look around you, Am. This is our virgin crop, the first of many. And one day your brothers will be out here to help me sow and harvest.'

'I'll help, too!'

'That ain't the way it works.'

'Why ain't it?'

'You'll be busy with other things.'

'What things?' she asked, her eyes narrowed.

'House things. Like your ma.'

'But I want to work with you. Jubal can do the house things!' She stamped her foot in protest.

He laughed. 'You're your mother's child.'

'But I want to!' She stared up at him, tears in her eyes.

'All right, you can help, too,' he said, and kissed her brow. 'I guess you'd have helped carve that old rock, too, if you'd been around back then.'

Mollified, she turned her attention to the object, her eyes curious. 'Why did Grandpa make it?'

'No one knows. I expect he wanted to plant something—just like I'm planting this wheat.' He gazed at the buffalo, conceiting an umbilical cord that stretched from the rock to the fields, the cord binding him to the past even as it bound his patriarchal ancestor to the future. Not given to dwelling on such fanciful notions, he nevertheless hummed an old army song as he led Amity back to the farmhouse, shuffling his feet to her chortled delight.

OVERNIGHT, OR SO IT seemed, the green plants turned to gold and all energies turned to harvesting the crop. While Amity looked after the children, Felicity followed her husband and Eli, tying and bundling the cut stalks as the two men used grain cradles to cut the wheat. The work was exhausting in the prairie heat, and they stopped frequently for rest or water. Her skin was burned where it was exposed to the sun, her face dirty, and her hair tufted with wheat chaff. Her reddened eyes itched and watered from the grain dust, and she washed her upper body in the tub at the end of each long day. Purchase had planned to thresh the grain himself, but finally decided to avail himself of a travelling threshing crew when they stopped by, offering the services of a steam-powered thresher.

The virgin harvest exceeded his expectations, bringing in 181 bushels which he sold for $170. With the proceeds, he purchased three hogs and two additional milk cows. He and Eli broke twenty more acres of land before he discharged the latter for the winter, promising to rehire him the following spring. 'Next year, we'll plant ten acres of oats and another two of potatoes,' he said to Felicity. 'The farm is paying for itself. Grain prices are high.'

To add to his pleasure over the bumper crop, Felicity seemed noticeably more settled. He watched as she fussed over the infant or smiled at Amity and Jubal, the fretful, short-tempered wife replaced by the attentive mother and conscientious, albeit sharpish, helpmate. Buoyed by her raised spirits, he welcomed her stinging reproof as he carelessly dragged mud into the house one rainy afternoon. Winking at Amity, he sat down on the step to tug off his shoes. 'How was your day, Felice?' he asked at supper.

'It began in darkness and then grew light,' she said, refilling the gravy boat. She halted in surprise at his sudden, delighted guffaw. 'Your pa has taken leave of his wits,' she said, even more surprised when Amity joined in the merriment.

HE WAS RETURNING FROM town, pleased with the sale of a bushel of potatoes, when he sighted some activity at the foot of the rock. Driving closer, he saw a wagon and three men moving about.

'Howdy, friend!' A slim, sun-browned man in shirtsleeves hailed him as he drove up. Two other men were laying a long chain along the ground.

'What are you doing? This is my land.' He stepped down from the wagon.

The man held up his palms in a placatory gesture. 'We are just checking survey lines for the county. That's all.'

'By whose authority?' He ignored the proffered hand.

The man nodded, seeming to take no offence. 'By the authority of the US government. But everything seems hunky-dory, so we'll get out of your hair. I see that the rock has already been marked as a boundary.'

'Without permission.'

'Friend, I don't think we need your permission. This is official government business.'

'The government don't own the rock.'

The man laughed. 'Heck, the government owns everything—including you and me! Morgan!' He signalled to one of two men lounging against a wagon to observe the conversation. 'Bring that map over here.'

The man ambled over, followed by his companion. With a nod to Purchase, he handed the map to the surveyor.

'See—here we are, and here's the rock.' The surveyor pointed to an X marked on the grid.

'I know that,' said Purchase, his voice testy. 'I knew it when I paid for the land.'

The surveyor's two companions exchanged looks. 'I ain't a lawyer,' said one. 'But I don't see how you can claim a rock as a part of arable land.'

'I never claimed it as such. I bought it for its own sake.'

The surveyor considered this. 'I guess you can buy whatever land you want,' he said. 'My interest lies only in its function as a natural boundary.'

'Boundary to what?'

'Why, to this section, for one thing. Heck, it's so big, it's the only landmark for miles around.'

'I thought they had already surveyed around here?'

'They did, but only to put in reference points. We're here to join the dots.'

One of his companions squinted. 'That's some rock. I never seed anything like it.'

'My great-grandpa carved that.'

The other man blinked. 'Your grandpa? You've been on the land that long?'

'No. He was here first. I came later.'

'How late?' The other man's tone was curious rather than challenging.

'Later.'

'I never seed such a thing.' The offsider scratched the back of his neck. 'I figured the Injuns made it.'

'No. It was my great-grandpa.'

The man glanced at his boss before replying. 'If you say so.'

'I do.'

'Well, whoever made it—'

'I just told you.' He grunted with annoyance. 'It was my great-grandfather.'

'Yes, you did.' The surveyor rubbed his chin. 'I guess we'll be getting back to work.'

'Just so long as you know you are on my land.' Purchase climbed back onto the wagon.

'Duly noted, friend. We'll be out of your hair in no time.' The surveyor turned to his crew. 'Put the chain back on the wagon.'

'Nosey-poke surveyors!' he grumbled over supper as Felicity dished up some venison steak.

'What are they doing?'

'Measuring, I guess,' he said, cutting some venison and putting it into his mouth.

'Measuring what, Pa?' asked Amity.

'Measuring everything that ain't bolted down. Soon the whole frontier will be measured and sectioned off.'

'Is that bad?'

He put another chunk of meat in his mouth. 'Depends,' he said.

'On what?' asked Amity and her mother both together, Amity giggling at the chorus.

'On whether you like being measured,' he said lamely, unable to think of a better reply.

21

A Great Silence

I N 1881, THE PRICE of wheat reached a dollar a bushel, and he reaped 395 bushels, earning a return of over $400 for a mixed harvest of wheat and oats. This figure was supplemented by the sale of poultry and eggs, increasing his income for the year to $450. 1882 was even better. With increased acreage under cultivation, he reaped 750 bushels of wheat, 90 of oats, and two of potatoes. He sold the harvest for $800, earning an additional $120 from the sale of livestock products. That year he spent $451 on farm equipment and household expenses, spending freely on groceries and dry goods. Felicity listed the outlays in an account book, keeping track of income and expenditure in the manner her father had taught her.

Wheat prices dropped in 1883, but he reaped his largest harvest yet—over 1,200 bushels, for which he received $1,050, plus an additional $150 from the sale of butter, lard, and eggs. His expenses for the year reduced to $279, giving him a net profit of $921. The following year, he planted flax as well as four acres of potatoes, deciding the diversity offered better protection against fluctuations in the price of grain. He spent over $1,100 on new farm machinery and an extension to the barn.

That he had drawn down on his returns did not unduly worry him—the outlay being an investment in the future, and the accumulated surplus offering a protective fence against the vagaries of weather, fire, and grasshopper plagues. Indeed, in the spring of 1884, he might have described himself as a prosperous farmer, with seventy acres under cultivation, money in the bank and plenty of unbroken acreage yet to cultivate. Meanwhile, the remaining 'buffalo swag', as he referred to it, remained on deposit in St Charles, providing the secure bedrock that underlay his optimism for the future.

The single fly in the ointment of his otherwise contented existence was the continuing and alarming disappearance of buffalo from the ranges. The previous fall, he had encountered the occasional fresh trace or sighted small groups in the distance. But weeks now passed before he came across a few, isolated hoofprints alongside a creek. He followed them for a half mile before they vanished in the grass. They should be fattening themselves for winter, he told himself, a puzzled frown on his face as he surveyed the empty bluffs. Returning from another fruitless search, he contemplated the approaching homestead, taking in the house, the barn, the corral, and the livestock. *Buffalo paid for all of this. And now they are nowhere to be seen.*

Even though buffalo were scarce on the ground, there were plenty of deer and antelope with which to fill the smokehouse. On occasion, he came upon wagon tracks or signs that hunters, or perhaps other homesteaders, had passed by. But for the most part, the ranges remained remarkably free of settlers or homesteads. Although it was now rare to encounter Indians, he maintained, out of habit, a sharp-eyed vigilance as he rode through the hills in search of game. On one hunt, he found himself searching for where Pickler and the other skinner—what was his name? —had lain butchered in the grass. He sat the mare, his mind roaming back to the day he discovered the mutilated corpses. Riding a little farther, he recognised the bluffs where he had been hunted by the Sioux on the same fateful day. *They used to own this land. And now they are gone, just like the buffalo.*

Filled with melancholy reflection, he rode on to visit the site of the old buffalo camp, a spot he had previously avoided. The site lay bare and undisturbed save for a few rusting cans and the blackened remnants of the bunkhouse half-buried in the grass. *You'd hardly know we had been here.* He tightened his jaw as he remembered the battle, his mind picturing the burning stalks, the smoke, the shrieking Indians and the desperate volleys of the defenders.

Searching the grass from the back of the horse, he spotted a weathered wooden cross. Climbing down, he peered at the scratched letters but was unable to make out a name in the cracked, peeled wood. He looked around for the familiar earth humps that would indicate a grave site. But all was overgrown grass and featureless earth. *How are you, Jubal, old friend? We never did get to see New York—or any other place, did we?* Despondent, he gazed out over the blowing grass. The afternoon was warm, the sun casting cloud shadows across the bluffs. *I guess I told you I would come back here to farm one day. And here I am. And here you are, too.*

Crouching, he pulled up some grass and held it in his palm, watching as the wind carried it away. *You'd be surprised, Jube. The camp is gone, and so are the Indians, and even the buff. You'd hardly know the place.* He remained crouching for a while, gazing at the blowing grass and trying to summon up the noisy, smelly camp. 'Durn everything!' He stood up, his despairing cry carried off by the wind. With a heavy heart, he climbed back on the mare.

'Skit!' he barked and rode off without looking back.

As spring ripened into summer, he came across plenty of old ruts and wallows but no glimpse of the animal itself. The only evidence of their former omnipresence were skulls and bones bleaching amid the reeds. Climbing down from the mare, he examined some dried scat and stood up, a baffled look on his face. *Their shit is still here, but where are they?*

He came across a wagon deep out in the grasslands, the runner and skinner on board engaged in the same pursuit as himself. 'Ain't seen none since a couple of bulls we shot a week back,' the runner said, motioning to two fresh hides in the back of the wagon.

'Where are they?'

'All shot to hell, I guess,' the runner, a thin, scratch-bearded fellow, said.

He was returning from a hunt, a whitetail draped across the mare, when he heard an almost forgotten drumming sound that echoed among the bluffs and made his heart leap. He pulled up, listening, his senses pricked in anticipation. The sound grew louder and he was unable to restrain from an exuberant whoop as a herd of several hundred buffalo loped across a nearby ridge. The herd made its way to an escarpment and dispersed to feed on the grassy hillside. He rode closer, careful not to spook the nervous beasts. There appeared to be plenty of yearlings among the herd, plus a scattering of reddish-tan calves grazing alongside their mothers. He stayed put for a quarter-hour, drinking in this evidence that the buffalo still roamed the grasslands.

His face lit up as he described the incident to Felicity. 'You should have seen them, Felice. Shucks, I feared they were all gone. It was like the old days had come back again.'

Perceiving her distinct lack of interest, he took Amity up on his lap where he regaled her with tales of the buffalo. 'There must have been four hundred or more. But that ain't much. At one time there were so many you couldn't count.'

She contorted her face. 'I wished I'd seen them, Pa.'

'And maybe you will. Who knows but they've been feeding some-where—up in the Yellowstone, or Canada, maybe, away from the hunters.'

'Why didn't you shoot one?' Felicity asked. 'You were supposed to be hunting.'

He stroked Amity's hair as he mulled a reply. 'I guess I shot enough buff for a lifetime. I used to take up to ninety a day.' He pondered the figure for a moment before smiling again at recollection of the grazing beasts. 'How do you think this house was built?' he said to Amity. 'On buffalo hides.'

The next day he rode out to where he had spotted the herd. Approaching the spot, he noted with alarm the presence of the wagon he had encountered the previous week. A considerable number of stripped carcasses lay in the grass around the wagon, the bodies still glistening with fat. Dozens of hides were staked out to dry.

'Howdy!' The same fellows, now drenched in blood and gore, greeted him as he rode up.

'What in blazes happened to the herd?'

The runner laughed and extended a hand. 'As you can see!'

'All of them?'

The runner peered up at him. 'Don't go to fret, partner. We took less than half. Go find the rest, if you're that keen.'

He glanced at the staked hides. 'Those are calves,' he said, eyeing some small, reddish-brown skins.

'Sure. It's still leather, ain't it?'

'You ain't one of them preservationists?' are you, asked the skinner, his eyes suspicious. "Cos that jest ain't right.'

'No.' His voice tight, he turned the horse. 'But you should leave the calves.'

'Why? Hell, if we don't take 'em, someone else will!'

A WEEK LATER, STILL rankled at the hide hunters, he was in town on business. Passing the newspaper office, he nodded to a man dressed in waistcoat and shirtsleeves and smoking a cigar who stood outside the premises holding a pile of newsprint under his arm.

'Good morning!' The man hailed agreeably and handed him a two-page sheet printed on both sides. 'The *Fort Buffalo Dispatch*,' explained the man. 'Issued every Friday. Cheap rates for advertising. This copy free, friend, to honour the milestone.'

'What milestone?'

'Why, the elections!' The man pointed to the news sheet and read the headers. *Fort Buffalo to Elect Mayor and Council! July 1884 Marks New Date in Town History.*

'I thought we already had a mayor—that Jackson fella?'

'That rogue! Mayor of his own piss pot! We are incorporated now. This one will be a real mayor, under territorial charter.' The man stuck out his hand. 'Quintus Bellow, publisher and editor.'

'Purchase McLennan.'

'You a homesteader, Mr McLennan—if you don't mind me asking?'

'I am.'

'Anything you want to buy or sell ...' Bellow tapped the pile of sheets he carried. 'Best rates, guaranteed.'

'I'll bear it in mind.'

Folding the newspaper and putting it into his pocket to show Felicity, he crossed the street and made for the feed store. The store had a large poster pasted out front proclaiming the elections and announcing council positions to be contested. He passed another poster, showing three like-nesses under a banner heading: *That's the Ticket! Eli Buskins for Mayor! Ben Wilkins for Treasurer! Art Blomquist for Constable! Every vote counts!* A little farther on, he stopped, bemused, at a poster of a large American flag with the centre cut out, replaced by a black-on-white drawing of a stout, bearded man with a cigar in his mouth. *Uncle Eli for Mayor!* read the caption underneath.

Passing the steamship office, he stopped, his eye caught by a printed sheet nailed to a post. He stepped closer to read—his interest sparked by a single word. "Wither the Buffalo? Esteemed explorer and natural historian Mr Thaddeus Walker will speak on the tragic plight of the American bison. Free entry. Saturday, June 30, 10:00 a.m. sharp. Union Street Chapel."

ON THE APPOINTED DAY and hour, he presented himself at the chapel. Inside, approximately two dozen people, men mostly, but four or five women also, were seated on the wood pews. The plain interior was illumi-nated by four windows, bright sunshine filling the room. Bellow stood in the aisle behind a large box camera mounted on a tripod. Purchase took a seat, nodding to the man next to him.

A small upright desk, which served as a pulpit, stood on a raised plat-form at the front of the hall. Amid a shuffle of feet, two men ascended the three steps to the platform. One, a slim, neat man with smooth, composed features, sat down on a chair against the back wall. The other, a robust individual with a woolly beard and open-collared shirt, stood behind the pulpit. Chewing vigorously on a plug of tobacco, he nodded and smiled to acquaintances in the pews while waiting for those still entering to take a seat.

The doors were closed, and the burly man fingered the plug from his mouth, looking around for a spittoon. Finding none, he ejected a stream of yellow tobacco juice into a small collection tin.

Wiping a hand across his mouth, he looked up. 'Gentlemen!' he said, in a booming voice, 'and fairer flowers!' The door opened and a latecomer took his place.

'Remember, folks, elections for mayor and council posts are but two weeks away. You can cast your vote right here. And vote Eli Buskins, friends, if you wish to get things done.'

He worked his mouth for a moment, forgetting he had removed the plug. 'What's that you say?' He cupped an ear—the affected gesture drawing chuckles. 'What will I do as mayor, you ask? Never say Eli Buskins ducked a hotcake! I fully intend to urge the Northern Pacific Railroad to extend the line to Fort Buffalo! It will grow this town as big as Bismarck! What do you think of that? No more reliance on steamboats! We can ship in goods from the great world and export our grain right back again!' He beamed at the audience. 'And the first order of business—from day one—is to get the county seat removed from those thieves up in Franklin and move it to where it properly belongs, right here in Fort Buffalo!' This drew applause, on which Buskins visibly swelled before taking the opportunity to castigate the residents of Franklin Township as 'plate-spinners, dime-lickers, and gen'ral artichokes,' to the enjoyment of the audience. 'What in lambassery has Franklin got that we ain't?' he demanded.

'A gold strike!' came the response, drawing guffaws.

'Gold? Why, look around you! We *grow* gold. Shucks, in Franklin they have to dig for it! And they can't eat it, all they can do is sell it. We can eat or sell ours and then grow some more!' What's that, madam?' He cupped his ear again. 'George Hackensack? Joe Wilson? Why, one's a two-bit drunk, the other a known Romanist! I can hardly tell which is worse! Vote no to Joe!' he boomed, to more laughter.

His oration was interrupted by a discreet cough from the other occupant of the platform. Ignoring the reminder, he was about to continue when a man in the front row objected.

'We ain't here to groan under your windbaggery, Eli Buskins! Give us the speaker!'

As Buskins made to override the objection, several other listeners joined in, demanding he introduce the fellow occupant of the platform.

Affecting a surprised, yet good-humoured look, Buskins held up a hand. 'As you wish, friends. As you wish! Swills and papists aside,' he flapped a hand under his nose, 'it's my considerable pleasure, as your preferred mayoral candidate, to introduce the celebrated natural historian come all the way from Ok—Ohio, to give us a yarn. Mr Thaddeus Walker!'

Wincing at the introduction, the speaker stood up to a polite scattering of applause. He walked to the front of the platform, where Buskins pumped his hand vigorously, looking toward Bellow and the camera. Bellow ducked under the sheet as Buskins held the pose, gripping Walker's hand in his own, to the visible discomfort of the other man.

'Hold still!' Came a muffled voice.

They stood there for some time as Bellow fiddled with the camera. He emerged from the sheet, taking out a fob watch which he held in his hand for some seconds as the figures on the platform stood motionless. 'Thank you, gentlemen!' Bellow put the watch away as the room relaxed. Buskins immediately dropped the speaker's hand and took up the vacant chair against the wall.

Walker tugged at his high collar and cleared his throat as he took up position at the front of the platform. Ignoring the stand-up desk, he faced the audience in a confident, practised manner. 'Good morning, ladies and gentlemen, and welcome to this lecture on the tragic plight of the plains bison, better known, perhaps, as the buffalo. My name, as you just heard me introduced, is Thaddeus Walker. I am by profession a naturalist—that is, one who studies Nature with an eye to understanding her causes and effects.'

The door opened to admit another latecomer. As it closed, Walker gave a quizzical frown. 'I note that, in a town of some six hundred souls, hardly more than a handful attend to learn of the dire plight of the buffalo. Whereas the saloon across the street is reliably filled—even at this early hour.'

'And the sooner you get started the sooner we can join 'em!' A man called out, prompting laughter. From his seat behind the speaker, Buskins raised a jovial thumb.

Walker gave the impression of a smile. 'Very well, let us begin. I travelled here today as part of a speaking tour of the frontier whose purpose it is to alert concerned citizens to the tragic destiny of the last remaining plains bison—that ruminant which once roamed the American continent from northern Mexico to the snows of Canada. The grandest and most numerous quadruped in all the natural world!' Behind him, Buskins fingered a fresh plug into his mouth.

Walker thrust a thumb into his waistcoat pocket and introduced his topic by describing the singular habits and instincts of the plains bison. Speaking in an assured voice, he gave a detailed account of its feeding and migratory habits before landing on its most salient feature, its prodigious numbers—'unprecedented in the whole of natural history.' Pitching his voice in the manner of a professional actor, he digressed to humorously recount his own, often hair-raising encounters with the animal. 'Why, one time, up on the Cheyenne, I was forced to jump clear into that flowing stream to escape the close attentions of an irate cow!' He embellished the anecdote with several others, drawing gasps and chuckles as he described being nearly stomped to death while sleeping in his tent as a herd of stampeding bison appeared from nowhere to rush through his camp. 'I escaped perdition by a hair's breadth, ladies and gentlemen. By a hair's breadth!' He held up a thumb and forefinger to illustrate.

Confident in the attention of the audience, Walker changed tack to praise the 'natural ethos' that had permitted Indian and buffalo to flourish alongside each other—'for eons'—in productive harmony. 'The buffalo provided for all the red man's needs and wants: meat for sustenance, robes for shelter, bones for tools, and horns for headdress and decoration. Little wonder, ladies and gentlemen, that he—the Indian—worshipped the beast as a god.' The remark drew murmurs.

Walker raised a practised eyebrow. 'What? You doubt the sincerity of such reverence? Then consider this. Not twelve—' he glanced at Buskins for confirmation, the latter holding up all ten digits '—not ten miles from this house of worship there stands upon the open plain, for all to see, a wondrous stone carving of the buffalo in all its manifest glory. A marvel of the ages that is hardly known outside of this small town. I myself laid eyes on it for the first time but yesterday on the passage from Bismarck. Think of it, ladies and gentlemen. A buffalo carved out of solid stone—who knows how many ages past? A totem carved by primitive yet worshipful savages now themselves passed into the dust of time.'

His eye alighted on Purchase. Mistaking the latter's agitation for disbelief, he held up a hand, commanding the audience with his voice. 'I ask you, friends: If savage minds, acting out of simple veneration, can honour the buffalo in such original fashion, how then is it possible that we—endowed by the Creator with far superior intelligence—cannot do likewise?'

He let the question hang while sipping water from a glass.

'Far from extending any form of toleration, let alone admiration, toward such an astonishing exemplar of God's bounty, we seem hell-bent on wiping it from the face of the earth. And why? The answer, friends ...' he studied the audience before raising his voice in angry denunciation, 'is greed! Naked and unrestrained greed!' He paused, allowing the sentiment to marinate the pews.

'Several territories, notably Montana, Idaho, Kansas, and Wyoming, have passed laws to regulate the wanton slaughter: regrettably, to little or no effect. Congress, meanwhile, sits on its hands and does even less—captive to business interests while neglecting the public trust. For the buffalo is a public asset, ladies and gentlemen. An asset owned not by the politicians or the railroad companies but by you and me. They squander that which is not theirs to squander!' Taking out a handkerchief to dab his lips, he contemplated the audience with solemn gaze as if pondering whether to impart some withheld pearl.

'People up and down this great country ask me who or what is to blame for the senseless destruction of such a precious national treasure.' He paused, his face grim. 'The answer, friends, is not hard to find. I give you not one but *three* principal causes.' He stabbed three fingers into the air. 'Three causes responsible for the deliberate and sustained extermination of the buffalo from these plains.'

'One!' The sudden bellow caused the ladies in the front pew to jump.

'The rapacious demands of tanneries for bison skin to turn into leather to satisfy the cry from factories and manufacturers.' He let this sink in before grasping the second of the raised fingers.

'Two! The unrestrained and indiscriminate slaughter wreaked by buffalo hunters who wantonly shoot tottering calf and pregnant cow alike in their greed for dollars.' His voice grew animated and scornful. 'Every knucklehead with a gun and a wagon imagines himself a peerless buffalo hunter and is out shooting whatever he can see from dawn until dusk. From dawn until dusk, ladies and gentlemen.' His eyes swept the audience as if seeking out culprits.

'And to this dismal list, we must add a third primary cause.' Pausing, Walker took a sip of water as the listeners hung on the revelation. 'The third of our unholy trinity.' Another sip and a longer pause. '... An agent of destruction so monstrous that it threatens, by itself, to devour the last remaining herds.' Buskins sat forward.

'The *railroads*, ladies and gentlemen!' Walker's voice rose to a shout. 'I speak of the railroads!'

Ignoring a loud snort from the candidate, he continued, his manner agitated. 'The unstinting demands of the railroad companies—for meat, robes, and tongues to carry to distant markets—is the single most pernicious engine that drives the wholesale slaughter of the buffalo.' He raised an accusing hand. 'Like leaves scattered before a storm!'

'Good riddance!' The remark—from the man next to Purchase—drew claps and shouts of agreement as well as several words of protest.

'They feed the murderous savages,' a voice claimed.

'And chew up all the grass,' added another.

'O ye that doubt!' The naysayers fell silent before the speaker's stern, chastising gaze. 'I declare—after travelling these plains for over thirty years as explorer and naturalist—I declare to you that such reckless and malicious slaughter is the greatest mass murder of a species that has ever been witnessed upon this earth!' The utterance brought a shocked hush.

Swelling with tragic authority, Walker prosecuted his case. 'Just a decade ago—a decade! —the buffalo herds were so prodigiously abundant that they blackened the entire plain. Stories abound of their unprecedented fecundity. The greatest assemblage of animals ever to shake the earth with their footsteps. Think of that, ladies and gentlemen. Not even the plains and savannas of Africa could boast the like. And now, to our great and abiding shame, they are all but vanished. On the train to Bismarck, I failed to see a single animal along the entire length of the track. Not one!' He drew a hand across his brow as if wearied by such unutterable foolishness. In the silence, he slowly extended one arm, his features gaunt with sorrow. Then, like a great, tragic actor, his voice dropped to a stage whisper. 'Thus passes into the veil of eternity the greatest herds that ever walked upon the earth. We shall not see the like again, ladies and gentlemen, though we live a thousand years.'

The passionate urgency of the speech, together with the speaker's grieved countenance, visibly affected the listeners. A woman dabbed her eyes with a handkerchief. A few of the men openly expressed dismay.

Two or three in the audience started a tentative clap, only to be forestalled by Walker reaching into his jacket and pulling out a folded newspaper. 'But do not take my word alone, ladies and gentlemen.' With newly established pep, he held up a newspaper. 'The *Bismarck Tribune*. Written but two days ago.' He began to read from the publication, with side glances to the audience. "*A perplexing phenomenon*," it begins.

> *Various reports, gathered in this office, confirm that the great buffalo herds which once populated the northern plains are no more. A scout from Fort Buford reported a group of one hundred or fewer individuals along the Yellowstone, echoing similar accounts from Forts Pembina and Stevenson.*

Walker looked up, his countenance wreathed with dismay. 'Fewer than one hundred, ladies and gentlemen. One hundred from little short of one hundred million!'

With strained voice, he continued reading.

*Several efforts have been made to protect what remains of the buffalo—
thanks mainly to a few concerned ranchers. But we shall never again see
the boundless herds that once roamed this entire continent in biblical profusion. While many mourn their loss, others are openly gleeful, claiming
that the land is now cleared for the raising of crops and the introduction
of domestic cattle—*

'See then! The durned *Tribune* agrees with us.'

'Ain't that exactly what we been saying?'

'Tell him, Eli, why don't you? Set him straight and you'll get my vote!'
The remark brought laughter. The bearded candidate grinned and raised
two thumbs in acknowledgement.

'Join with me!' Ignoring the disruption, Walker cast a beseeching gaze
on the audience. 'Demand that Congress act to preserve this noble creature
before it is too late. Otherwise, I fear that, like the dwindling remnants of the
once-abundant passenger pigeon, it, too, will soon perish from the earth.'

'We can but hope!' A man behind Purchase stood up, kicking back
the pew.

'Where you going, Jethro?' asked someone.

'To shoot me some durn buff!' The reply brought guffaws and a few
boos.

Sensing the moment opportune, Buskins rose to his feet. 'Gentlemen!
I open the floor to questions.' The startled speaker looked on, his face
twitching in dismay, as he was sidelined by the would-be mayor.

A man stood up. 'What are you going to do about that pile of rubbish
outside the old livery stable?'

'It's a disgrace!' a woman piped up. 'A terrible eyesore!'

'The buffalo, Madam! I pray you.' protested Walker.

'And the foul stench from that hog pen down on Cotton Street?'

Buskins launched into a condemnation of the 'pitiful nature' of the
street in question, blaming his 'sot' of a rival for the problem. The meeting
degenerated into a free-for-all as friends of the rival candidates spoke up
in their defence. As the debate grew more heated, the speaker took his seat,
a look of severe disappointment on his face.

Buskins held up his arms as the audience, still arguing over rubbish
collection, began to vacate the hall. 'Don't forget the election for mayor,
July 14th! And council positions to follow! Vote Eli Buskins for a name you
can count on. Honest Eli, for an honest deal!'

THE MEETING FILLED PURCHASE with angry despair all the ride home. He was still despondent after supper, despite Felicity dishing up his favourite apple cinnamon pie for dessert. Sitting in the rocker, he pulled Jubal onto his knee. 'Am, fetch me that robe.'

The girl did so, struggling with both arms to hold it.

Setting down Jubal, he spread the robe in his lap. 'Feel it,' he said. 'This is what folk wanted.'

He watched as the children ran their fingers through the worn robe.

'It stinks!' Amity turned up her nose. 'Can I shoot one?'

'I wish you could. But there may be none left.' The enormity of the statement caused him to emit such a heartfelt groan that Felicity looked up from where she was clearing the dishes. He smoothed his hand over the robe. 'There used to be so many … When I first came here there were thousands—many tens of thousands—just standing around waiting to be shot.'

'Why?' Amity looked baffled.

'Why what?'

'Why were they just standing there? Why didn't they run away?'

'I wish to heaven that they had!'

'How could they all just disappear?' he asked of Felicity after she had put the children to bed. She made no answer, engrossed in embroidering a piece of needlework.

'It don't make sense.' He scratched his head, rueful to the point of distraction. 'This was all buffalo range. You couldn't count 'em.' He spoke to himself, Felicity still preoccupied with sewing.

He sat in the rocker after she went to bed, mulling into the fire as his mind reached back to the vast herds that had first fetched him to the territory sixteen years before. 'I don't understand it,' he murmured. He got up, bewilderment on his face, and added a fresh log, poking the fire. 'You couldn't count 'em,' he repeated, and gave the fire another poke.

To Felicity's exasperation, he insisted on riding out again the next day, the speaker's galling words still echoing in his mind.

'Why in jasperation?' she demanded as he mounted the horse. 'I thought you said but yesterday there were none left?'

'I need to make sure.' He watched her walk back into the house. 'Keep a sharp eye,' he called out, issuing his customary caution before flicking the reins and heading out.

He stayed out for the entire day, making a wide loop of the prairie without success. Toward late afternoon, he reined in on top of the tallest bluff for miles around to survey the plain. A herd of mule deer foraged in the distance. A flock of shrikes flew overhead. A cool, gusty wind rippled the tall grass. He listened, cocking his head to one side and then the other. The only noise was that of the wind in his ears. He sat for long minutes, scanning the distance, his senses attuned for the sudden, thunderous rumble of hooves or the dust cloud that signalled an approaching herd. As the sun sank toward the west, he turned the mare and slowly headed home, slumped in the saddle with feelings he was too heartsick to put into words.

That night he slept badly, tossing and turning, his sleep haunted with images of the iron-browed beast, its black, baleful eye turned on him as he raised the Sharps to fire. He moaned in his sleep, the noise drawing an irritable protest and a poke in the ribs from Felicity. 'Perish if it ain't like sleeping next to a buffalo!'

A Fruitful Tree

FIVE YEARS OF HOMESTEADING had wrought a subtle adjustment in her own 'affective weather', as she characterised the shifts in mood and temperament that afflicted her whenever thunder growled in the sky or a windstorm swept dust and soil into every corner and crevice of the house. Her husband's contentment and the children's strong attachment to the windblown grasslands that surrounded them had tempered her initial dismay—nay, fright—at the terrifying isolation. They have a freedom here, she acknowledged, standing in the doorway, although they may never know the comforts of polite society. 'Amity McLennan! You get up from that dirt. Where'd Jubal run off to?'

Her relations with her husband, too, had taken on a new and altered tone as the years had passed. Exhausted by the arduous necessity of creating and maintaining a household from scratch, as she put it, she found less and less time to indulge the frivolities of speech and manner that, since childhood, had helped her suffer those around her and, indeed, endure the passing of time itself. The wind, the endless grass, her fatigue at the end of the day all imposed a tax upon words that strained her to the utmost.

Expressiveness gave way to economy, sharp observation to practical utterance. The words that had draped the pots and pans of her father's store became tools that pointed, issued, despatched until all was in order and tasks achieved. Observant as she was, she first noticed the change in her journal, the descriptions more caustic, the asides—once amplifying, enlarging, fleshing—sparer, more cognisant of dust, effort, and the thousand and one things vying for her attention. The excess fat of sentimentality—with which she had never been overly burdened—was scraped from her observations as colour and florid declaration gave way to a new particularity and clarity that clung like gristle to the bone. 'I feel like a rabbit stripped of its fur,' she complained to her husband. 'This busybody wind has picked everything clean away.'

Cleaning out her drawer one day, she took out a bunch of unsent letters tied with a red ribbon. Sitting down at the table, she began reading, shaking her head and pausing to wonder at her first impressions of her new home. I don't think that now, she reflected, surprised at what she had written. Or do I? She carefully retied the letters, deciding they might someday make a valuable memoir for her daughter. *Perhaps I might even gather them into a book,* she mused, revisiting a youthful fancy. *'Letters of a Homesteader,'* she speculated, conjuring up possible titles. *'A Young Woman's Account of the Territories.'* She heard Amity's querulous voice calling her from outside. *'The Tribulations of a Prairie Mother'* she sighed and put them back in the drawer.

Each year when winter closed in, she kept herself busy with a variety of household projects. One winter, she quilted bedcovers from matching materials, utilising the task as a practical lesson to the children on the value of harmony. Next winter, tired of the sameness, she unstitched the covers and spoke warmly of the virtues of difference. Indulging her fondness for needlework, she embroidered a cushion cover with an image of her grandmother's house in Boston as she remembered it. *'It being the only place I was truly happy,'* she wrote to her mother.

Summer, with its pestilential flies and mosquitoes and sudden, roaring windstorms, was still a trial, but less of one as she began to 'catch' the rhythms and mutability of the prairie weather. Her only real fears were the spontaneous grass fires that leapt up out of nowhere and constricted her heart as she kept an anxious eye on their progress and direction. Purchase had hatched an escape plan in case of necessity, one which involved collecting her and the children into the wagon to 'fly like the wind' ahead of the flames. She got Purchase to show her how to hitch up the horses, slapping her hands with satisfaction when she accomplished the task.

Delighted at her new skill, she climbed up into the seat, waving off her husband's attempt to assist. 'I can do it!' she said. She bunched the reins in her hand, flicking them in the same manner as her husband. 'Skit!' she sang and steered the horses around the yard and out into the grass with the children hanging on the backboard, gleeful at the adventure. She recalled her success as she prepared for bed. *I can shoot, ride and hitch. Perhaps this homesteading ain't all bad,* she told herself.

Thus, day by day, week by week, month by month, and year by year, she found herself growing into her prairie home and the wild expanse and towering skies that so entranced her strong-necked husband.

WALKING OUT INTO THE yard one morning as winter beckoned, she searched for the children, not seeing them but hearing their cries. Jubal suddenly appeared around the root cellar, running ahead of Amity as she dashed in pursuit, holding up her dress and whooping like a wild Indian.

Cornstarch if she ain't turning antelope! 'Jubal, go fetch your brother.' She shivered at a gust of wind, reminded that the 'song days of autumn', as she poetically termed them in her journal, were rapidly fading. Hugging herself against the cold, she returned inside.

'Amity is eight years old,' she prompted Purchase as she poured him a cup of coffee. 'You need to speak to that good-for-nothing Mayor Buskins about opening a school in town. Lord knows but they have enough saloons—a school wouldn't hurt. And Boundary scarcely knows one end of a pencil from the other.'

'We could send her back to St Charles,' he said, sipping the coffee, 'to attend school.'

The suggestion rocked her. 'St Charles?'

'I hear there's a new school in Bismarck. Or Franklin, maybe.'

'And where would she live—in a tipi?'

Having no option but to continue schooling the children herself, she cast about for a more reliable means of instruction—her own inventiveness having exhausted itself—before deciding on scripture as a recourse. Never overtly religious in spite of regular church attendance—the forms and comforts of belief satisfying her as much as the opaque content— she nevertheless established the habit of reciting a scriptural passage each morning after breakfast, reading aloud from the McLennan family Bible.

'I wanted Purchase to have it,' her mother-in-law had said, bequeathing Felicity the heirloom shortly after taking to bed with the illness that claimed her. 'But he is so neglectful in his ways, he might lose it. My mother handed it down to me. I wish for you to take it when I'm gone.' Pale and exhausted from illness, the old woman clasped Felicity's hand. 'It will comfort,' she said.

Whether her mother-in-law's unusual display of affection was prompted by religion or the hope that Felicity would cherish the gift, she nonetheless faithfully guarded the bequest, wrapping it in layers of protective oilcloth for the journey up-river. Shortly after moving into the homestead, she had unpacked it and placed it on the dresser, where it had sat ever since, the most ornate object in the home. Its black leather cover was embossed with brass clasps at the corners and lock plates to secure the contents. Its gilt-edged pages featured a variety of sepia, colour, and black-and-white chrome lithographs and three register pages to record births, marriages, and deaths.

From time to time—following her mother-in-law's advice—she sat down with it in her lap, reading aloud to the children. The daily readings formed the basis for practical lessons in arithmetic, handwriting, general hygiene, and family lineage. After reading a passage, in her dry, clipped monotone, she questioned the children on matters of understanding. "Oh, that I had the wings of a dove," she declaimed in a precise voice, scanning the children's faces for signs of comprehension. 'A dove is a bird, like a crow,' she explained, 'only pure white.'

The children gazed solemnly while picturing a white crow fluttering above the prairie snow, a palm of Lebanon extended from its beak.

'Pick up your pencils,' she instructed. Sitting down with each in turn, she carefully guided their fingers as they spelled out *dove* and *Lebanon*. 'Shem and Ham were the sons of Noah,' she said, expanding into genealogy. 'And they had a brother called Japheth.' She spelled out the name, leaning over to inspect as the children transcribed. 'You are mentioned in Genesis,' she told a mystified Jubal, showing him the passage. 'The biblical Jubal played the harp and had a brother, named Jabal, just like you have a brother named Boundary.'

She liked Genesis—at least the early bits—and the familiar tales and parables. She largely avoided the histories which, she claimed, lacked credibility. She also skipped all mention of slaughter and conquest, which reminded her too much of accounts of the bloodthirsty Sioux, preferring the psalms and proverbs and discovering new depths in their pithy directness. "Surely in vain the net is spread in the sight of any bird," she read out. 'Jubal. What does that mean?' She waited with growing exasperation as the boy grimaced and scratched and wrinkled his brow. 'The answer ain't in your ear, so quit tugging at it!'

Her husband sometimes interrupted these sessions, coming back to the house for a cup of coffee or to warm himself before the fire. Standing before the flames, hands outstretched, he listened as the children recited a passage after their mother. 'There are other things they could learn from,' he said, his brow furrowed. 'Why not use the *Almanac* instead?'

'I may as well use the cookery book! Besides,' she said, guiding Boundary's hand, 'Ma used read to me every now and then, and it didn't hurt a bit. Or do you wish them to be like the Indians and worship rocks and buffaloes?'

'At least the Indians worship what is around them.'

Unusually for her, a retort failed to leap to her lips. 'Never no mind,' she said, employing her father's favourite phrase. After her husband had returned to his chores, she sat for a moment, a dismayed look on her face. Perish if all this lonesomeness ain't affecting my mind!

One morning, prompted by an innocent question from Boundary, she turned to the family register pages. 'See here—gather round.' She pointed to where the single entry recorded the marriage of Abbie Wheeler to Horizon McLennan in April 1838. 'Abbie and Horizon were your grandparents—on your father's side,' she said. 'Amity, surely you remember your grandmother?'

The girl popped her cheek with her tongue. 'No,' she said.

'You don't? She held you in her arms often enough.'

Amity popped the other cheek. 'I don't remember.'

After determining that the child was being truthful, and not wilful, she decided on an educational project that would combine history with genealogy. 'It's about time you learned your family tree,' she said, resolved to fill in the registry blanks.

Over the next few days, she interrogated her husband, extracting as much information as she could about the family tree, piecing it together with what she had learned from his mother and sister. 'Prospect was the name of your grandfather's brother?' she repeated, a twitch of her lips the only comment on the choice of name.

When she had collected the names all the way back to the rock patriarch—'it don't go back further, that's where it starts,' her husband had insisted—she carefully copied the results onto a sheet of paper. Purchase leaned over her shoulder as she wrote the last entry, murmuring in surprise as he traced the names. 'I've never seen it laid out like this. It seems …' He paused as he searched for the word.

'What?'

'I don't know. Like the plat that surveyor fella showed me.'

'This is your family tree,' she said to the children. She went through the generations, pointing to each name in turn as the children stood around the chair. 'First, there was Boundless McLennan. He was the patriarch, just like Abraham. He begat that rock your father worships. Boundless McLennan and Mrs. McLennan—we don't know her Christian name—had two sons, Claim and Prospect.' She pointed to the names. 'Prospect married a woman named Anabelle. And they had four children. Amity, why don't you read out their names?'

Amity peered at the page. 'Prosper?' She looked at her mother, her face doubtful.

'That was the firstborn, a daughter. Continue.'

'Expan …'

'Expanse. Go on.'

The girl wrinkled her nose. 'That's a silly name!'

'I'm sure Expanse wouldn't think so. Prosper was the eldest,' she said, taking over. 'Just like you are the eldest. See?' She pointed to the sheet of paper where she had diagrammed the McLennan generations. 'You are leaves on the same tree.'

Amity gazed at her name, a doubtful look on her face.

'What's the matter?'

The girl picked at a tooth but said nothing.

'Boundary, Jubal. Do you see your names? Prosper had a sister—Prairie—and two brothers, Expanse being one, and Territory the other. Expanse married Hannah and she gave birth to Horizon who was father to your pa, Purchase. Jubal, what does that make you in relation to Expanse?' She pointed to the family tree.

He bit his lip, glancing at his sister for direction.

'Count the names. Each one is a generation. One: Expanse—the father. Two: Horizon—the son. Three: Purchase, your father, the grandson. And four …?' Her finger hovered over Jubal's name. 'Me?' He grimaced in confusion.

'Yes, you! The great-grandson. Amity, stop grinding your teeth like a hog and pay attention. Now remember her?' She turned to the bible registry page. 'Amity, I've already told you her name. What is it?'

'Ab … Ab … Abe …'

'Mercy! *Abbie*. Abbie Wheeler. Your grandmother, whom Grandpa Horizon married in 1838. Abbie gave birth to your pa and his brother—your uncle, Samuel—as well as his sister—your aunt, Lilly. The one you don't remember from St Charles.'

'What happened to the other one?'

'What other one?' She frowned at Jubal. 'Be precise.'

'The other brother, Clam?'

'*Claim*. We don't know. People just disappear sometimes, like in the Bible.'

She turned the book on the table. 'So, there you have it. Your family tree, just like Abraham's. Boundless McLennan begat Clam—*Claim*, and Prospect McLennan, who begat Expanse McLennan, who begat your grandpa, Horizon McLennan, who begat Purchase—your pa—who married me and begat you!' She tweaked Jubal's nose. 'Counting from Prospect, you are the fifth begat! Now, each of you sit down and copy out the names.'

She moved around the table to sit with each in turn, carefully guiding their fingers. 'Expanse means a broad plain, like the wilderness of

Beersheba,' she instructed Amity, 'or a wide stretch of land like the one around the Tower of Lebanon which looketh upon Damascus. Claim is the legal ownership of the land of Canaan which the Lord promised to the Hebrews,' she explained to Jubal as he lettered his great-great-grand-uncle's name. 'You might say that he gave your pa claim to that rock, except that it would be more truthful to say he gave the rock claim to your pa.'

'Boundary!' With a sigh she shook her head. 'Try and copy in a neat hand.'

She returned to Amity. 'Prospect is generally the view toward the south, except when it lies toward the east,' she said, citing Ezekiel. 'Or the north if you are one of the sons of Zadoc,' she said recalling that morning's reading.

'Who was Zadoc?'

'Just a name,' she said. 'They are all just names.' Later in the day, when she was sweeping the floor, she halted the broom as the remark popped back into her mind. Is that all we are in the end, just names? Disquieted by the notion, she resumed sweeping.

IT WAS LATE MARCH before winter released its grip, and another month before the returning spring warmed the frozen earth and ducks quacked overhead. The interim between spring and summer was her least favourite time of year—the melted snow turning the surrounding prairie into a vast bog of cold, slushy water that seeped into the house. Nevertheless, it was with profound relief that she opened the door to allow in light and air as the children shrieked and raced in the wet yard.

As the warm weather slowly dried the ground, she strolled with the children in the fresh grass around the homestead, supplementing their studies by pointing out wildflowers and teaching them the names of the various birds she recognised. 'Why, Amity McLennan. I do declare you are developing a hand,' she said, hovering over the children as they sat in the grass to write. 'Jubal, you write like a coyote with three legs. The words hop all over the page.' Tutting, she took up his exercise book. 'Never mind,' she said, handing it back. 'Perhaps you will be a farmer, like your pa, and talk to the plants.'

She was tilling the garden in preparation for spring planting when Boundary gave a cry and pointed up at the sky. A flock of birds approached overhead. She shaded her eyes. 'Are they ducks?'

'They're pigeons!' Hearing the commotion, Purchase had emerged from the smokehouse to look.

'There must be a hundred!' shouted Jubal.

'Hundreds,' she corrected, still peering up under her hand. 'Multitudes,' she corrected herself, remembering the bible passage from that morning and feeling a thrill at the resonance.

The flock passed overhead. 'They are good eating,' said Purchase. 'I wish I could shoot a few for supper.' He kept his eye on the flock as the birds dipped and dropped down from the sky.

'They are stopping!' She used both hands to shield her eyes against the glare, screwing up her eyes as the flock settled down on the rock and began congregating in the shaded grass. 'What are they doing?'

'Maybe resting or feeding. By hooky, but I could bag a few!' Her husband disappeared inside the house, returning moments later with the shotgun.

'Pa!' Amity and the boys raced after him as he made toward the rock.

'Amity! Jubal! you come back—' She broke off with a sigh and watched them go.

'Hush now!' Purchase silenced their excited chatter as they neared the rock. Hundreds of birds sat roosting in the sun or walking up and down the head and spine. But his attention was focused on the squally mass hunting for insects in the grass. 'Stay here!' With a stern glance at the children, he crept noiselessly through the tall grass, coming up on the birds as they pecked. Careful not to alarm them, he dropped to his belly and wormed closer. Like hunting buff, he thought. To his chagrin, the flock took sudden fright and rose, fluttering, into the air.

'Tarn!' Leaping to his feet, he raised the shotgun and fired. One bird fell to the ground as the others flew off.

The children ran up as he searched the grass for the shot bird. 'Help me find it,' he said.

'Pa!' shouted Boundary as he stood over the pigeon where it lay in the reeds.

He lifted the bird, laying it in his palm for the children to see. Its pinkish chest was splattered with blood. 'See.' He passed the bird to Amity, laying it in her hands. 'There's not much more than a mouthful. Hardly worth cooking. I'll have to dig the shot out.'

'It's dead!' Amity had tears in her eyes.

Jubal gave a scornful laugh. ''Course its dead! Pa shot it, didn't he?'

'I doubt it felt a thing, Am. When I was buffalo running, we used to see flocks like this all the time.'

He stood up, holding the bird. 'Let's get back to your ma. She'll want to see.'

For days after the incident, Felicity recalled the tremor she felt at the unexpected correspondence between the abundances of the Old Testament and the pigeon flock. The notion that the wild frontier should resonate with the burning deserts of Judah and Canaan struck her as improbable to the point of absurdity. But the conceit nevertheless teased at her as she went about her chores until the notion slipped away, swallowed up in the unfathomable enormity of grass and sky.

23

A Picnic

ON A LATE SPRING day when the sky was a delightful whitish blue and the scents of sage and wildflower a ravishment to the senses, she took the children on a picnic to the rock, insisting that Purchase join them. 'I will,' he promised. 'As soon as I get that hole in the barn roof fixed.'

She strolled the half-mile to the object, a wicker basket in her hand, and the rifle looped across her shoulders. The children ran ahead, whooping and laughing as they raced through the grass. The rock loomed above them, its cool shade striking her, in that moment, as protective. *It knows us. It keeps us safe from harm.* She muttered a reproof at such foolishness, blaming her husband for the contagion. In the shade, she spread the linen tablecloth as the children took turns rushing up to the rock and 'skittering' off it. Opening the basket, she took out cold chicken, bread, jam, pie and milk and set them on the cloth. 'Children, come and eat.'

'Where's pa?' asked Amity, kneeling in the grass.

'He should be here soon 'cepting he fell through the barn roof.'

'He wouldn't let me up the ladder,' Jubal complained between mouthfuls of chicken.

'You can fall off when you get older. Boundary, stop playing with the pie.'

The picnic was a success, the breeze keeping the mites at bay. Her husband made an appearance before they had finished, slumping to the grass, grimy with toil, to chew on a chicken leg. 'Dang, Felice, but this tastes good,' he said, ripping the meat with his teeth. The compliment added to the absurd feelings of contentment which had overtaken her on the walk from the house.

'It sure dang does!' she said, giddy with feeling. Her husband and children stared before Purchase laughed out loud, the children gleefully joining in.

Later, while she gathered up the remnants of the picnic, Purchase took Boundary on his shoulders and walked up to the rock. With Amity and Jubal in tow, he repeated the oft-told tale of the family legacy. 'See the horn—where it juts out?' He set Boundary down and lifted Jubal and Amity in turn so that they could better see. 'Your great-great-grandpappy sat up there and carved it—out of the solid stone. This is McLennan rock. Feel it. Put your hands against it.'

The children did so, Amity rocking back on her heels. 'It's pushing me!'

'Can we climb it?' asked Jubal.

'It's too high. And there are no steps but maybe one day,' he said.

'How did grandpa get up there?'

'Your great-great—never mind. I don't know. There's lots no one knows. But he did, however he managed it.'

'Managed what?' Felicity came up, brushing down the pinafore she wore over her skirt.

'I was telling them how he—the old man—carved the rock.'

'The patriarch? Remember our lessons, children? Amity, explain what a patriarch is.'

'I don't remember!' The child jutted her bottom lip.

'Jubal?'

The boy scrunched up his face. 'A bible fella?'

'Lord, see Thy fruits!'

'I NEED TO MAKE a run into town,' said Purchase over breakfast, 'to pick up some supplies.' She watched as he mentally ticked off twine, nails, grease, rope, and kerosene. *He has the same look on his face as pa when thinking over the stock check.*

'Yep, I reckon I'll go next week,' he said, talking to himself. 'And I'll order some lumber while I'm at it.'

'I'll make up a list,' she said. 'I need some molasses and—'

'Why don't you come, too?' he said, surprising her. 'It will be a change.'

Four days later, she clung to the seat as the wagon lurched toward town. She held Boundary on her lap while Amity and Jubal, full of excitement at the rare outing, sat in the back or leaned over the sides pointing at birds and the occasional coyote. The air was crisp and mild, the sun shining in a clear blue sky.

The town had swelled in size since their arrival over five years earlier. A new tent city, to replace the previous one, had sprung up on the town margins to accommodate the influx of settlers, prospectors, and itinerant labourers. Within the town proper, several blocks had been added, along with commercial establishments. They passed by a hardware store, a new hotel, and the newspaper office. Cross streets bisected the main thorough-fare and Felicity was surprised to glimpse a row of houses, some with porches, like those in St Charles. They joined a line of wagons trundling up and down the broad, rutted Main Street. Groups of women, some clutching infants, strolled the boardwalk. Felicity turned to gaze at them.

'New settlers,' her husband said, guessing her thoughts.

Soldiers in uniform mingled with the pedestrians. A man paused at the entrance to a saloon and raised his hat as the wagon trundled past. The Bismarck stage and several freight wagons were parked along the thoroughfare.

'It's getting big as St Charles,' said Purchase, a note of disapproval in his voice. 'Whoa!' He pulled up the wagon outside the general store. Two men were laying a chain across the mouth of an alley adjoining the store.

'What are they doing, Pa?'

'They are surveyors, Am. I guess they are marking out the streets,' he said, taking the infant and assisting Felicity down from the wagon.

'Why?'

'So everyone knows where their property is.'

One of the men looked in their direction. 'Howdy!' he said. Purchase recognised the man as the same offsider he had encountered years previously at the rock.

Another man looked up from a notebook where he was taking down measurements. 'Why it's the rock fella!' he said.

'What are you doing?' demanded Amity, Jubal giggling at her boldness.

'We are taking measurements, young lady. Platting the town. That means everybody knows where they stand, and who owns what, and where.'

His partner began to loop up the chain. 'Leastways we know who owns that big rock,' he said, and winked at Purchase.

'What did he mean?' Felicity asked, as he held open the door to the store, 'about owning the rock?'

'He was just being smart. I'll meet you back here in a half hour.'

'Where are you going, Pa?' asked Amity. 'Can I come?'

'No. Stay with your mother. She'll maybe buy you a sugar twist,' he added, seeing the disappointment on her face.

He made his way to the Golden Fleece saloon. It was his habit to visit the establishment occasionally to sit over a glass of whisky and yarn with whoever was of a mind. Sometimes Mace, the former wrangler, dropped by to share a glass and a tale of the old days. He had barely taken a chair in the half-empty saloon before he was engaged in conversation by a grizzled cowpoke seated by himself at the next table.

'Good day, pardner. Join me, if you're of a mind to warm the air.' The man obligingly kicked out a chair. Getting up, Purchase swapped tables.

The man pushed over a bottle. 'Help yourself,' he said, his voice amiable.

'Thanks. But I'm tight.' Purchase raised his glass in acknowledgement and sipped the whisky.

'Sam Northcomb.' The other man stuck out a callused hand.

'Purchase McLennan. Pleased to meet you.'

'And you, pardner. I jest drove in two hundred head of cattle from Texas. My throat is that parched I could suck the dew off a frog.'

'From Texas?'

Northcomb laughed. 'Well, from Mandan, anyway. They were rail-roaded from Texas.'

'That's a long way.'

'It sure is.' Northcomb gulped his whisky. He poured another glass, again proffering the bottle to Purchase, who shook his head.

'Where are they—the cattle—now?'

'Over by the Little Missouri River. You know the area?'

Purchase nodded. 'That used to be all buffalo range.'

'Used to be. Or is, mebbe. Won't be much longer. They'll all end up like that fella.' Northcomb gestured to where a large buffalo head was mounted over the bar. His face grew solemn. 'Cattle, Texas cattle, are the future of this territory, Mr McLennan. I say that without a shadow of doubt. Soon, these ranges will be filled with steers. They are crying out for beef back East. And cattle are pure gold. Know why? 'Cos they look after themselves. It don't cost nothing to raise 'em. You brand them, turn them loose for the winter, and then round them up in spring. Each steer that cost but twenty dollars back in Texas doubles and triples its value after a winter grazing in the territory. Cattle are the wealth of this country. A wise man would buy up as many head as he could and watch his investment fatten up on all that free grass.'

'Free grass?'

'Sure. No need to even buy the land. There's millions of acres that used be Indian country. Now it's jest lying there, free for anyone to use. Best cattle country in the world.'

'And the railroad transports them?'

'Sure does. All a man has to do is herd them to the range and then ship them back east when they're fattened up. Mark my words, Mr McLennan, cattle are the future, dollars on legs. There's money pouring into the territories from New York, Pennsylvania, Texas, why, even England and France. All them rich fellas are planning to get even richer on cattle.'

'I thought it was supposed to be wheat—the future,' said Purchase.

'Mebbe, over to the east—where the land ain't so fit for cattle, but every-where else, it's cattle country.'

A youth, no more than fifteen or sixteen, entered the saloon and looked around. Spotting Northcomb he came over to the table. 'Sam, we gotta go. They're waiting on us.'

Northcomb drained his glass. 'Sure, kid. Say howdy to Mr McLennan, Henry. He's been homesteading in these parts for quite some time.'

'That right?' The youth stared at Purchase, a look of curiosity on his face. 'Say, mister, you ever see a real live buffalo?'

24

Jacob Greenbriar

S HE WAS STANDING ON a chair to hang some vegetables above the door to dry in the hot July sun when she glimpsed something moving in the distance. Squinting, she discerned a rider plodding toward the farmhouse. 'Boundary, go fetch your pa,' she said.

By the time Purchase arrived back at the house, the approaching rider was clearly visible as a figure atop a mule. He waved from the distance while hollering in a loud, cracked voice. 'Friends! I bid you fond greetings!'

The dogs barked and growled as the stranger rode into the yard. Felicity put her arms around Amity's shoulders as the girl pressed back against her.

The stranger hauled up the mule, doffing his battered, wide brimmed hat. 'A glorious day, is it not?' He croaked the words, his voice hoarse with trail dust. Sitting there, he cut a faintly ridiculous figure, his long legs sticking out either side of the mule, his long black hair slick with sweat, and his face pale and emaciated beneath the sunburn. 'It's hotter than hellfire!' he complained and wiped a sleeve across his brow. His eyes were bloodshot and red-rimmed with grit and fatigue. His lips were dry and blistered, and the skin beneath the speckled, unshaven cheeks raw from scratching. He had on a patched and tattered frockcoat as dishevelled as himself. A large, square-shaped package was suspended from the back of the mule, which hawed and bared its teeth in distress.

'Who are you, and what is your business here?' demanded Purchase, suspicious of the stranger's eccentric appearance.

'With your permission, friend?' The stranger slipped down from the tired mule. With a flourish of the floppy-brimmed, badly worn hat, he stepped one foot in front of the other and dipped into an elaborate bow, his lank, greasy hair all but touching the dust of the yard. 'Jacob Greenbriar, at your service, sir. Landscape artist and portrait painter.'

Purchase directed a questioning glance at Felicity who stared, as nonplussed as himself, at the grotesque figure. 'And where are you from, Mr Greenbriar?' she asked.

Greenbriar straightened up, his face flushed. 'From, Madam? Why, from the several corners of the earth! From rosy-fingered Greece … From shining Venice … From the imperial city—Rome, friends. And from the cobbled streets of old London Town herself!' Thus acquitted, he bowed again.

Felicity murmured and took a tighter hold on Amity. Boundary and Jubal stared wide-eyed as Greenbriar coughed and spat phlegm into the dirt. 'Pernickety dust!' He wobbled suddenly, looking as if he might topple over with exhaustion. Licking his cracked lips, he pressed both hands together in the fashion of a monk or penitent.

'Water, friend. A drop of water, I beseech thee!'

'Amity, go fetch the gentleman a cup of water.'

Greenbriar struggled out of the dusty coat, contorting his bony body to accomplish the task. 'Such heat would torment the angels!' His complexion turned an even more sickly hue and he held to the sweat-slicked mule for support.

Amity returned bearing the cup of water. Her father took it from her and handed it to the visitor, who gulped its contents in a single swallow. 'A thousand thanks! I foolishly consumed my own shortly after leaving Bismarck. The journey was more arduous than I—' All of a sudden, he turned deathly pale. Amity screeched with alarm as he uttered a moan and collapsed against the mule.

'Jubal, water the mule and put it in the barn. It looks about done in.' Purchase assisted the exhausted Greenbriar inside the house. The visitor looked feverish and woebegone, as if he might faint again. Purchase helped him into a chair as Felicity fetched more water.

'An angel! An angel of succour!' Greenbriar glugged so rapidly that the water splashed down his chin. 'It was the interminable grass and the hot sun!' he panted, accepting another cup, which he drained as rapidly as the first. Felicity handed him a dampened cloth, which he accepted with profuse gratitude, mopping his face and brow.

'Have you eaten?' she asked.

'Air and dust, Madam! Air and dust!'

Amity and Boundary were still standing, mouths agape, in the doorway. 'Run along now,' chided Felicity. 'Don't you have chores to do?' Going to the pantry, she returned with a hard-boiled egg and a leg of chicken which she placed on the table in front of the stranger. 'Eat this, Mr Greenbriar.'

'A thousand thanks, Madam!' Without more ado, the stranger greedily devoured the egg and chicken—all but swallowing the bone as he sucked it free of gristle and skin, his mouth working feverishly to consume the portion.

Purchase, who had observed the foregoing with a perplexed look on his face, spoke up. 'And what is your business in these parts, Mr Greenbriar?'

'Indeed, friend—if I may call you such.' Greenbriar sucked the bone and set it down. 'I came—' Racked by a coughing fit, he reached into his pocket. His long, spidery fingers delicately spotted a frayed lace handkerchief against the grease on his lips. 'Pardon. 'Twas all the dust I ingested. Where was I? Ah! —drawn here to inform the world of the wondrous edifice.'

Purchase frowned with irritation. 'What edifice? What in shakes are you talking about?'

'Pardon, friend, for my opacity!' Greenbriar half-turned and pointed a long finger toward the open door. 'I speak of the marvellous obelisk. The prairie sphinx carved from time itself!'

Felicity followed his finger. 'The rock, Purchase! He means the rock.'

'What in creation …?' Purchase shook his head, his face drawn into a perplexed grimace.

'The very same!' Greenbriar brought up spittle into his handkerchief. 'Pardon, Madam—the dust! I attended a lecture in Kansas City wherein was mentioned this ancient marvel of the plains. On hearing the report, I at once headed for this spot to see for myself whether such a titan really existed. And I see that it is true, friends. As true as God's shining light!'

'You came here—all the way from Kansas—just to look at the rock?'

'I did, sir.'

'Why?'

'To capture it, friend, on canvas, that the entire world might know of its existence.'

'This lecture you mention—do you recall the speaker's name?'

Greenbriar looked suddenly nauseous. 'Indeed, it slips me for the nonce.'

'And how long do you intend on staying, Mr Greenbriar?'

'But a day or two, Madam.' His head began to nod. 'To capture the creature in the light of dawn, noon, and eve.' This last came out in a murmur as his eyes closed with fatigue.

Purchase glanced at Felicity, who gave an urgent nod. Reluctantly, he turned to the visitor. 'I guess you're welcome to stay in the barn if you want.'

'The charity of the Samaritan! With your permission, I shall rest, sir, but a moment, in the shade.' And with that, the exhausted Greenbriar slumped forward in the chair and fell fast asleep with his head on the table.

Later, after the fuss over the stranger's arrival had died down, Felicity noted the incident in her journal, pleased to have something other than the routine day to record.

*Mr Greenbriar snored like a mule for what seemed an age. After which,
he suddenly leapt to his feet, almost causing me to drop my mixing bowl!
He then bobbed and scraped for a good minute before launching out
the door in pursuit of his blessed easel. Later, he was spotted striding
toward the rock, coattails flapping in the wind, the easel under one arm,
a leather satchel in the other. Lord, if I ever before set eyes on such a
gothic creature!*

The following morning, a revitalised Greenbriar readily accepted her
invitation to take breakfast with the family. Dressed in canvas trousers and
a linen shirt with the sleeves rolled up, he perched on the chair, his overlong
legs folded beneath him as he ate. He had shaved to reveal a youthful countenance and fine, expressive features beneath the sunburn and washed-off
trail dirt. He had combed his long hair—pulling it back from the scalp
and tying it into a tail. Fresh and reanimated after a good night's sleep, he
feasted with gusto, regaling the family with lively accounts of his overseas
adventures between ravenous mouthfuls of fried egg and beans.

'I spent every last penny I had on visiting the stupendous galleries—'
he spooned more beans into his mouth, chewing hugely on the portion.
'I was an impoverished student—such beans!' He speared another fried
egg and thrust it into his mouth, the yellow yolk flecking his lips. 'A repast
for the ages!' He tore off a second piece of bread, mopping the bean juice
before cramming the bread into his mouth. The children ogled at his every
gesture, their own meals largely forgotten.

'And you studied there—in the galleries?'

'Indeed, Madam. Long, exacting days copying the masters. The French.
The Italians—the great Michelangelo himself!' Greenbriar hungrily eyed
the pot of beans.

'Please,' she said, wondering just how much food he could gobble into
his bony frame. 'Help yourself.'

She observed him as he ate, intrigued by his coarse and yet somehow
graceful manner and tales of exotic places she had once yearned to visit.
'Amity, drink your milk. Jubal, stop fidgeting. And for how long did you
study there, Mr Greenbriar?'

'For two years, Madam. I had planned to leave after just twelve months
but—friend, have you abandoned the egg?' At Purchase's surprised nod,
Greenbriar leaned over and nimbly speared the remaining half of the egg.
''Twould be a shame to leave any morsel of such a banquet!' He smothered the egg with beans and consigned it to his mouth. 'Ambrosia for the

angels!' Scooping up the mug of milk, he gripped it with both hands and noisily suckled the contents.

'I'm obliged you find the meal so agreeable. But you were telling us—'

'My studies!' Greenbriar took out the lace handkerchief and dabbed at his lips. 'One memorable day, I caught the eye of the great Herr Joseph von Führich as I copied a canvas of his. Such blessing! Such fortune! We fell into conversation, and he, learning of my circumstances, proposed I assist him as an apprentice for which service he would in return accept me as a student.'

'And what drew you to be a painter, Mr Greenbriar?' asked Felicity, determined to take advantage of this rare opportunity to model the social graces.

'No less than a powerful thirst for the sublime, Madam.' Covering his hand with the handkerchief, he picked a tooth.

'The sublime?'

'Indeed. And where art beckoned, I had no recourse but to follow.'

'And God does not come into it?' she asked, enjoying the all too-scarce occasion to make conversation.

'The sublime, good lady, is but a word for God—whose magnificence shines forth in every blade of grass.' His eyes appeared at that moment glazed, whether from conviction or surfeit of eating.

'An original thought,' Felicity conceded. 'You're quite the most civilised visitor we've had by some distance. Amity. Why don't you—'

'Do you intend painting this morning?' The blunt interruption from her husband caught her by surprise.

'For today, sir, sketches and charcoal only.'

'It's mighty hot out there. You'll fry your brains unless you stick to the shade. And there ain't none.'

'I shall observe your advice, friend, and thank you for it. Now, if you will pardon, I must catch the light.' Unfolding his limbs, Greenbriar climbed to his feet, taking the opportunity to thrust one last portion of bread into his mouth. 'A feast for the blessed saints, Madam.'

'You'll want some refreshment for later.' She went to the pantry and retrieved a parcel wrapped in cheesecloth. 'There's some boiled eggs and pork. You can fill your canteen from the well.'

'O daughter of Shunammite! Goodness be thy name!' Greenbriar gave an elaborate bow, eliciting fresh open-mouthed stares from the children.

She stood at the door to watch as the painter set off toward the rock, the easel strapped to his back and a large leather satchel slung over his shoulder. 'Why not take the mule?' she called after him.

He turned, raising his hat. 'The poor creature deserves a rest, good lady. Even as the noble donkey that carried our Saviour into the Holy City!'

Beside her, Purchase snorted. 'If he ain't a donkey himself!'

'Hush now!' She shot an admonitory glance toward the children. 'He's a mite … eccentric,' she agreed. 'But harmless.'

'You are talking about the mule?'

'Why, Purchase McLennan! Children, collect your books—and stop gawking!' Wiping her hands on her apron, she went to fetch the Bible, wondering who exactly was this Shunammite.

HIS THOUGHTS NIGGLED AT him as he went to the barn to fetch the hoe before heading into the fields. The wind was hot and dry and blew soil into his eyes, further souring his mood. Every now and then he looked up from hoeing, squinting at the rock. Who in blazes is the fellow and what gives him leave to paint and sketch as though he owned the thing? His annoyed thoughts returned again and again to Greenbriar as he plucked leaves to look for pests. What did he mean—to show the world? What gives him that right?

His weeding brought him closer to the rock, and he shielded his eyes to stare, thinking he glimpsed where the artist had set up his easel in the shade. The sight rankled, a mix of proprietorship and jealousy galling him as he hacked at a weed. It must be that same fellow I heard speak in town. What the devil was his name? He stabbed the earth between the green shoots. He might have asked permission—not just turn up and help himself. Toward noon, he could contain his pique no longer and set off toward the rock, abandoning the hoe.

He found the artist sitting cross-legged in the grass, a large sketch pad open in his lap. He glanced up at Purchase's approach.

'Welcome, brother, on this bountiful day!'

'As you say. Do you mind if I look?'

'Not at all. Not at all.' Greenbriar handed over the sketchbook.

Purchase peered at the drawings, slowly turning the pages. The buffalo was illustrated from various angles. Some sketches isolated the head or hump, while others captured a detail of the flanks or jaws. He paused at one, his eyes widening. The sketch showed the buffalo in profile with what appeared to be figures skipping up and down its spine. 'What's this?' He leaned down to show Greenbriar.

'Those, friend, are angels.'

'Angels?'

'Indeed.'

'Where in Toledo did the angels come from?'

'I draw what I see, friend. And what I see are angels dancing in delight up and down the creature. Do you not see them?'

He stared at the artist. 'You see angels?' he asked. 'Atop the rock?'

'Indeed I do, friend. They have been dancing and singing all morning.'

'Singing?'

'Can you not hear?' The artist cocked an ear, a beatific smile on his face.

Purchase listened for a moment. 'I hear birds and the wind, and that's about it.'

'Then you hear the angels!' The artist gave a beaming smile. 'Come,' he said as Purchase stared, nonplussed. 'I am about to render the charcoal.'

Shaking his head, Purchase followed as the artist led the way back to the standing easel. A sheet of white paper—shining in the sunlight—was secured to a portable frame that rested on the easel. Beneath the frame was a small shelf containing charcoal sticks and stubs, brushes, a feather, and patches of cloth. To his surprise, he saw the artist take a piece of that morning's bread from his pocket and place it in his mouth, sucking and working it like a tobacco plug before removing it and placing it among the sticks and brushes.

Greenbriar lifted up the easel and moved it back in the grass a few paces. Glancing up, he moved it again. Satisfied, he picked up a stick of charcoal, which he held longwise, scrubbing it from right to left over the white, textured paper. Swapping the stick for another, he began darkening the middle portion of the sheet.

'What are you doing?' asked Purchase, curious in spite of his pique.

'Laying the foundation, friend. The method is to tone the canvas.' Taking another stub, the artist coloured in the top part, sweeping the stick vertically up and down. Swapping the stub for a cloth, he began blending and softening the wash. He stood back to cast a critical eye over the effect. Murmuring to himself, he picked up a pencil-like holder containing a fine charcoal stick. He began to make marks in the powdery mass, revealing the white paper beneath. Intrigued, Purchase watched as Greenbriar swapped between stick and brush, feather and cloth, stepping back every now and then to glance up. And gradually, the rock began to appear on the canvas—a simple shape at first, and then becoming more distinct as Greenbriar worked assiduously to capture the buffalo. At times, he reached for the kneaded bread, using it to erase a line or to create an effect.

The sun crept up to the line of shadow and then beyond, drenching them in bright light. Greenbriar worked tirelessly, absorbed in his vision and seemingly indifferent to the hot sun and whispery breeze. Under his expert fingers, the buffalo mass asserted itself against the charcoal, the head and hump clearly delineated against the darker, surrounding tones. Humming a familiar hymn, and seemingly forgetful of Purchase's presence, the artist highlighted features and details, adding a few clouds for perspective. He worked deftly with feather and brush, his long, delicate fingers pausing to smudge, blend, or subtract as a faithful representation of the buffalo emerged onto the canvas.

'Pa!' Purchase heard a shout and saw the children skipping through the grass toward him. Felicity followed, wearing a sun hat and holding a jug of water or milk.

'Shush!' He held a finger to his lips as Greenbriar worked on, unperturbed. The children stood with bated breath as they gaped at the portrait. Still holding the jug, Felicity followed the artist's every movement as Greenbriar added several fine touches before stepping back to study the effect.

'I would value your opinion, Mr McLennan.'

Surprised at the invitation, Purchase stepped forward to peer at the canvas. 'I ain't much for drawing, but I guess that's it all right,' he conceded, his resistance to sharing the rock giving way to grudging respect for the artist's skill.

'It's the very likeness!' Felicity stepped forward, her voice full of wonder as she digested the sketch. 'Why, Mr Greenbriar, I do believe you have captured the essence of the thing.'

'The essence!' He smiled. 'The very effect I had hoped to achieve.'

'Then I expect you'll be wishing to be on your way back to Bismarck?' suggested Purchase.

Greenbriar laughed, a rich, delighted sound, which came from deep in his chest. 'Not yet, friend! I must capture it from all angles to do it justice.' Removing the frame from the easel, he knelt in the grass and held the canvas upright with one hand. With the other he reached into the satchel, withdrawing a sealed jar and a brush.

'What are you doing?' Amity crouched down beside him.

'Applying resin, dear child. To fix the charcoal. Else would it disappear like dew before the sun. Would you hold it—by the sides?'

As Amity held the canvas he unsealed the jar and applied the liquid to the sketch. 'There!' He held the canvas up for view, drawing gasps from the children. 'It's the buffalo, Pa!'

'Children, you shall draw the rock for your lesson tomorrow. Perhaps Mr Greenbriar might be so kind as to provide some brief instruction?'

''Twould be my pleasure, good lady, in small repayment for your generosity.'

Purchase's sour mood reasserted itself as he watched the painter wrap the canvas in protective linen. 'What will you do with the drawings?'

'Use them to make paintings, brother. And display them so that the world may know of such a marvel.'

'Display them where?'

'In Boston, New York, Philadelphia—wherever I can find a gallery.'

'Then you should at least know the story of how it came to be.'

The painter blinked with surprise. 'It was not the Indians? The speaker said as much.'

'It was not—as I tried to tell him.'

'Indeed? Then I should be most glad to hear the tale. Most glad,' he repeated, his genuine interest mollifying Purchase.

'It's getting fiendishly hot,' said Felicity. 'Why not come back to the house for some refreshment, Mr Greenbriar?'

'Why, Madam, I thank you. But the light is good and I wish to capture the other side.'

'Then at least take some water,' she said, holding out the jug.

'A blessing!' He guzzled the water, emptying the jug. 'A thousand thanks, dear lady!' Wiping his mouth with the back of his hand, he gave back the jug.

He then set off, carrying the easel. As he made to round the rock, a gust of wind almost blew off his hat. 'The angels are singing!' He held the hat to his head with one hand before disappearing from sight.

'Is he crazy, Pa?'

'Amity McLennan, where do you get such notions?'

'Listen to your ma. Let's get back to the house.' They set off through the grass, Amity's hand clutched in his. 'As crazy as a three-eyed mule!' he whispered, setting the girl to giggles.

WATCHING FROM THE HOUSE, she saw the artist return after a long day of sketching. In the fading light, he struck her as a figure from a fairy tale, the easel strapped to his back giving him the appearance of a strange, humpbacked creature. When he did not present for supper, she insisted on going out to the barn with some cold chicken, a slice of bread, and a mug of milk. 'Would you permit the poor man to starve?' she said in response to Purchase's protest. 'Amity, come with me.'

She found Greenbriar kneeling over a canvas, delicately picking at details by the light of a lantern. He had untied his hair, the lustrous locks falling about his face as he worked. A row of drawings and sketches stood against the barn wall.

'I guess you could use some supper,' she said, setting down the food. He murmured appreciation, absorbed in small details. She watched for a moment, admiring the way his hand moved over the canvas with quick, precise strokes, his finely drawn features a study in absorption as he sharpened a detail or highlighted a feature. 'Does it bother you if I look at the sketches?' Amity had wandered off to play with her dog.

'Not at all, Madam.'

She took the lantern and moved along the line of canvases leaned against the wall, her eyes widening at the skilful representations. 'I never did much care for that old rock,' she confessed over her shoulder. 'But it seems …' She shook her head, lost for the word she wanted. She paused before a charcoal rendering approximately a foot square. The buffalo stood majestically proud against a cloud flecked sky amid a wash of brownish grass. She blinked and looked closer at what appeared to be feathered limbs projecting from the side. 'Are those wings, Mr Greenbriar?'

He glanced up. 'Lances, Madam. Feathered lances to recall the suffering Christ—an analogue to be found in all of nature, if we but truly observe.'

'Indeed?' She stared, captivated by the image. The scene conveyed to her an immense loneliness—the winged buffalo suspended between an eternity of grass and sky. *Maybe that's what Purchase sees when he looks at it.* To her surprise, tears came to her eyes.

Greenbriar came up beside her, brushing crumbs from his shirt. 'Do you like it?' His voice was warm and engaging in the lantern light.

'It's very fetching.' She felt herself softening, as if basking in the charcoal sketch. 'I cannot say why, but it seems …' She stumbled for the word. 'Not the rock … but the rock,' she finished, confusing herself.

He smiled. 'Then I have modestly succeeded. My task—the task of every artist—is to improve upon Nature, to capture the ideal residing within the object and thus clothe it in beauty. Life must imitate art, else all is lost.'

'Is it so?' She stammered the words, aware of his warm breath against her cheek.

'Ma!' Jubal called from the doorway. 'Pa said what's taking you so long?'

'I ought to be going,' she said, her voice brisk once more.

'For your great kindness.' Picking up the sketch, Greenbriar presented it to her.

'I couldn't,' she protested. 'It wouldn't be right.'

'But I insist.' He pressed the drawing into her hands, his long fingers briefly covering her own. 'I have applied the varnish and, if you wish, I will construct a frame that you may hang it.'

She flushed. 'No. Thank you. It's just fine as it is. Amity, come along.' She was about to leave when an idea struck her, and she turned. 'Mr Greenbriar. I'd very much like a sketch of my husband, and the children, too, if it ain't too much trouble. I'll make you breakfast in return—tomorrow, before you leave. And I'll make that blueberry pie you hanker to, as well.'

He smiled in gratitude. ''Twould be an honour, Madam,' he said, and smiled warmly, causing her to swallow as she turned and left the barn.

THE FOLLOWING MORNING, SHE put on her best dress and combed the children's hair. Purchase watched, a frown on his face as Greenbriar set up his easel. 'You, too,' she said, brushing a hand across her husband's hair.

He grunted. 'I've chores that won't wait.' He opened the door. 'I'll be nearby, in the barn. Holler if you want anything. Leave the door open.'

Greenbriar arranged her and the children, steering her into a chair with deft hands. He placed the children standing beside her. 'Ready?' He stood, pen in hand, behind the easel.

After a quarter hour of standing in place, the children rebelled. Amity tied and untied her ribboned hair while Boundary and Jubal fidgeted and sulked, driving Felicity to distraction. Purchase popped back several times for water, peering at the canvas before leaving again. 'Pa!' Amity begged as he exited again.

'They may leave, if they wish,' assured Greenbriar. 'I have the shapes and composition I desire.'

A short time later, he invited Felicity to inspect the result. Her eyes widened as she took in the details. The portrait showed her sitting at the kitchen table, eyes looking off to the side, while the children stared solemnly at the artist—the tableau presented against a wash of russet-brown ink. A ray of light from an unseen window shot through the wash, forming a halo of sunlight around her. '*Madonna of the Plains?*' she queried, reading the title he had written below the portrait.

'Modelled after the Italian original at the Uffizi Gallery in Florence—where I copied it with my own hand.'

'Is my face so doleful?' she asked plaintively. 'And where'd my youngest fetch all those curls?'

'They were in the original, madam, I assure you.'

Still pondering the portrait, she went to fetch him pie and milk.

'Ah! The ambrosia!' exclaimed Greenbriar, clapping his hands with delight. He gobbled the large portion in three bites, exclaiming again when she cut him a second slice. 'Such bounty on a plate!' He licked the sticky spoon, his tongue flicking over the blueberry jam.

Purchase entered for more water. 'Husband, look.' She showed him the portrait.

He scratched his jaw. 'It's you, Felice,' he conceded. 'Although Boundary looks a mite curly.'

'You don't think my aspect doleful?'

'Doleful?' He shook his head.

'And now, sir, to complete the tableau.' Greenbriar had set aside the plate and taken out his sketch pad.

'I've chores. No time to sit and idle.'

'Hush now and sit!' Ignoring his protests, Felicity pressed her husband into a chair as he made to leave. 'You ought to be thanking Mr Greenbriar. How often does a person get to sit for a portrait in these wild plains?'

With a grimace, Purchase sat down, stubbornly demanding to drink coffee while sitting. He sat for a quarter hour, and two cups of coffee, as Greenbriar sketched with pen and ink. The children came in to look, peering past Greenbriar as he worked until their mother chased them back out into the yard.

''Tis done, friend!' Greenbriar handed Purchase the sketch pad.

He studied the likeness, a dubious look on his face. 'Is that me? I hardly recognise myself!'

She took the drawing from him. 'Peppering cats! You look like a grizzled old buffalo.'

'Let me see, Ma!' Amity gawked at the sketch. 'Who's that?' Pressing a hand to her mouth, she chortled with laughter.

'Amity McLennan! Apologise to Mr Greenbriar this instant.'

Greenbriar accepted the criticism with unruffled good grace. 'And now, you, Mrs. McLennan, if your husband will permit?'

She sat as he completed another pen and ink portrait, sketching with professional economy as she gazed out the open door, a distant look upon her face that she hoped would draw comparison with a literary heroine.

'For you, Madam!' Greenbriar presented the full-face sketch.

'Gracious! I look like ma.'

Her husband came to look. 'That's you, Felice—to a T!'

'Are my features a mite sharpish?'

'Not so much you'd notice.' The remark drew a sharp look of its own.

'Time flies!' Greenbriar began to pack up the easel.

'But you are leaving—so soon?'

'I must to Bismarck, before the weather turns.'

'It ain't turning nothing but hotter,' said Purchase. 'But you'd best get started. It's a ways.'

'Here, take this.' She presented the artist with the remnants of the pie, wrapped in cloth.

'The very perfection of pies!' Smiling with gratitude, Greenbriar placed it in his coat pocket.

The family stood in the doorway to watch him depart aboard the mule, still burbling in praise of the pie. 'Publius himself was not more charitable!' He lifted his floppy, broad-brimmed hat into the air. 'Farewell, dear friends, and goodbye! Come, brother mule. *Au revoir!*'

'It's fine weather for travelling!' called out Purchase.

'God's blessed day!' Greenbriar called over his shoulder. 'Glory on every leaf!' His voice rose in a hymn as he rode off, his long legs trailing either side of the mule.

'If that ain't the rarest soul,' said Felicity, watching him sway on the mule.

Her husband grunted, whether out of annoyance or relief she could not tell.

Mr Greenbriar departed today—the queerest sketch-a-body I ever did see. I've no doubt but that he is bobbing and scraping all the way back to Bismarck. He left behind several drawings of myself, Purchase, and the children. I have a sharpish nose.

That night she dreamed of the eccentric painter, picturing his long fingers moving skilfully over the bare, white canvas, stroking and cajoling the buffalo into life. She murmured in her sleep, dreaming of a charcoal-rendered house, shaded by tinted trees, and guarded by a slumbering dog that somehow resembled a buffalo. 'Ah!' she murmured, and extended her hand, her fingers reaching for the charcoal door.

THE BAND OF SIOUX had jumped the reservation three days earlier, half-starved on the meagre rations distributed by the agency. Bitter at their treatment, they angrily rejected the pleas of their elders—stealing away early in the morning while the soldiers slept. Avoiding homesteads, they headed for the tribe's traditional hunting grounds bordering the Missouri. They searched the flats and hummocks for two days, increasingly frustrated at their failure to find any trace of buffalo. Tiring of the search, two of the youths returned to the reservation, drawing the scorn of their companions.

Late in the afternoon of the third day, Spotted Tail, the self-appointed leader, revealed his intention to raid a homestead to steal a cow or chickens and whatever else he could find. Bare-legged and wearing a patched army shirt, a bow across his back, he tried to convince his reluctant companions to join the raid. They were camped on a bluff, angry and dejected, their bellies tight with hunger.

'Do you not remember how the bluecoats punished the people last time?' Red Bird, the oldest of the band, objected. 'Five of our brothers were hanged.'

Spotted Tail snorted. 'Do you wish to live like a Mandan squaw? I had rather die like my fathers before me than skulk back like a dog with its tail between its legs!'

Shadows in the Grass muttered in agreement. Seeing this, Red Bird turned to the remaining member of the party, who had kept his own counsel so far. 'What is your opinion on the matter?'

Strong Horse grunted and placed his hands on his crossed knees. When he spoke, his voice was solemn. 'The homes are well defended. If they catch us, we may have to kill a white man. What will happen then?'

The four began to quarrel, arguing points on both sides as the sun sank lower in the sky.

'I am tired of eating the stinking cows they send us! This land once belonged to the Lakota. And now we beg like crows for scraps!'

'The white hunters have killed all the buffalo. Maybe if we kill the settlers they will return.'

'No.' Red Bird shook his head. 'The whites are too many. And if we kill any, the soldiers will surely take revenge. I do not wish to dance on the end of the white man's rope.'

Strong Horse nodded in agreement. 'Nor me. We should go back.'

'I wish us to fight and die like men—not to cower like frightened women in our tents! My hatchet thirsts for the blood of a white devil!'

The other three exchanged looks increasingly perturbed at what their hot-headed companion was suggesting.

'What is that?' Shadows in the Grass climbed to his feet. 'I see something.'

The others joined him, peering into the dusk.

'It is an elk!'

'No. It is a man. See how he walks.'

'Where is his horse?'

'I do not see one.'

'He is by himself!'

'What fool walks alone through Lakota land.'

'Maybe he has food.'

'Or fire water!' Spotted Tail leapt onto his pony.

'Where are you going?'

'Go back if you wish! As for me, I will fight this white devil!'

'He will shoot you!'

'Not if I kill him first!' With a whoop, Spotted Tail started the pony down the slope. His startled companions glanced at each other before leaping onto their horses to follow.

HALFWAY TO BISMARCK, THE mule gave a loud bray and pulled up short. Dismounting, Greenbriar discovered a swelling on the soft tissue above the rear hock. He attempted to lead the animal, but it refused to move, hawing loudly. Not having a gun, he comforted the stricken animal as best he could, praising its character and faithful service. After a few minutes, he unloaded the easel, the leather satchel, and the almost empty canteen, anxious to reach Bismarck before nightfall.

Farewelling the mule, and carrying the easel on his back, he set off through the long grass. Braying in distress, the mule hobbled after him for a few minutes before giving up to stand forlornly in place. The sun was scorching. A warm wind blew across the grass. Greenbriar rested wherever he found a semblance of shade, resisting the impulse to drink from the canteen, despite his thirst.

After walking a mile in the heat, he took off the frock coat and looped it around the easel. The sun beat down and he slaked his parched throat with the last few drops of the precious water. 'By God's grace I may yet encounter a creek or stream,' he told himself, licking his cracked lips. The satchel was heavy in his hand, and he transferred it to his back, looping the handle over the leg of the easel. Bowed beneath the weight, he continued, desperate for water. The bare, empty plain lay all around, the cloudless sky a blue radiance above. After walking for two hours, he sat down, exhausted, and fell asleep while still sitting up.

He awoke with a start, staring around at the rustling grass. Nothing stirred. A bird flew high overhead and he followed enviously its passage.

The sun was cruel, the heat unrelenting. Panting, he got to his feet, feeling himself adrift amid the immense, grassy sea. As he continued, his thoughts strayed back to Florence and the richly oiled canvases adorning the walls of his favourite gallery. He imagined his own work displayed there—the buffalo canvas that would make his name hanging between the oiled portraits. He felt a burst of pride at the image—the symbol of a new, American school that would draw enthusiastic crowds to gaze admiringly at this colossus of the far western plains. *The Stone Buffalo Pictured At Sunrise*, he ruminated, conjuring titles.

With the sun setting, he spied some riders approaching through the dusk. 'Hail, friends!' he croaked, his throat cracked and dry. He raised his hat and waved it in the air.

The Indians reined their ponies to study the strange creature.

'He is not a man but a grasshopper!'

'He has no gun. The fool is unarmed.'

'Perhaps he is a ghost-spirit. Look how he welcomes us like brothers!'

The suggestion made the others nervous. Red Bird patted his snorting horse. 'I say we let him pass and return to our lodges. The bluecoats will be searching for us.'

Spotted Tail shook his lance in disdain, his eyes fixed on the intruder. 'You gossip like frightened children! He is not a ghost, but a man, like us. With an ululating cry, he kicked the pony forward. The others followed, curious to inspect this strange looking creature. They walked around him in a circle, taking in his drawn appearance and the strange apparatus tied to his back.

'What is that he carries, like a mule? It must be worth something.'

'How do you know?'

'Why else would he carry it—on a hot day!'

'Power and resplendence, brothers!' Greenbriar swept off his hat and bowed.

The Indian ponies neighed with alarm at the sudden gesture, the warriors cursing as they struggled to control the spooked animals.

'Go away, demon!' one of them shouted, shaking his lance at the stranger.

'Do you have water?' Greenbriar made a drinking motion with his hand.

'What is he saying?'

'The fool wishes us to part with our water!' Spotted Tail leaned down from the pony. 'Who are you to ask for water, white devil!'

'He does not understand. Speak the white tongue!'

'You speak it! It chokes my mouth like buffalo shit!'

'What is he doing?'

Greenbriar had set down the easel to rummage in the leather satchel.

'He is looking for a gun!'

'No, wait! That is no gun.'

Retrieving the sketch pad, the artist found a stub of charcoal and held it up. 'A sketch, brothers! In exchange for water, and perhaps guidance? I fear I may have lost the path.' Folding open the sketch book he began to draw with swift strokes of the charcoal, capturing Spotted Tail, who had reined his pony to a halt directly in front of him.

They sat their ponies, baffled at the strange behaviour. 'What is the wolf's turd doing?'

'I have seen it before. He is making marks on paper. They are harmless.'

'Do you see?' Greenbriar held up the drawing in the fading light. 'For you, friend,' he said. 'In exchange for water.' He lifted the canteen slung over his shoulder and rattled it to show that it was empty.

'What sorcery is this?' Spotted Tail snatched the sketchbook. '*Ai!* The white devil seeks to capture my courage!' His companions nudged their horses forward to see.

'It is as Red Bird says,' said Shadows in the Grass. 'The marks are harmless.'

'No, it is his likeness,' said Strong Horse. 'Perhaps the white ghost is a thief of spirits.'

'What is it you do?' Spotted Tail glared at Greenbriar, his outrage growing as the other man smiled and repeated the drinking motion.

'He is thirsty,' said Red Bird. 'Give him some water.'

'He is a crazy man,' speculated Shadows in the Grass. 'See, he does not fear us. It would be bad medicine to harm him.'

'White dog!' Without warning, Spotted Tail lunged with his lance, spearing the unsuspecting Greenbriar in the ribs.

With a look of astonishment on his face, the artist staggered back a few steps. 'Brother, you have wounded me!' Pressing a hand to his side, Greenbriar sank to his knees, blood issuing between his fingers. He looked at the blood as if greatly surprised to find it there. 'Vermilion!' He looked up at his attacker, his face pale. 'A thousand pardons, friend, but I must to Bismarck.' He moaned and tried to regain his feet.

'*Aiiii!*' Grabbing his hatchet, Spotted Tail kicked the pony forward. Uttering a wild cry he brought the hatchet down on the painter's head, splitting the skull beneath the thick hair and cleaving the brain. 'Die, white ghost!'

Greenbriar slumped instantly to the grass and lay still.

Spotted Tail was already off his pony. Lifting the dead man by the hair he draggged his knife across the fractured scalp. Yelling in triumph, he held up the grisly trophy. 'It shall hang from my lodgepole this night!' Uttering wild cries, his companions shook their lances in the air.

Dismounting, they emptied the satchel of its contents, disgusted to find more paper with marks. 'It is the rock-totem!' exclaimed Shadows in the Grass, holding up a sketch. 'I have seen it many times. It is not far from here.'

'It is worthless. Like his worthless hide!'

They threw the sketches aside while rummaging through the dead man's pockets. Strong Horse gave a gleeful shout as he pulled out the pie wrapped in cloth. He shoved it into his mouth, gorging on it while grinning at his companions through the mashed pieces.

'Is there more?' They searched the other pockets, disappointed at not finding more food.

'We should hide the body,' suggested Red Bird as they made ready to leave, 'lest the bluecoats find it.'

'Leave the fool!' Spotted Tail tucked the bloody scalp into his deerskin tunic before climbing back onto the horse. 'The wolves will feast on his bones.'

With triumphant whoops and yells, the hunting party rode off, leaving the broken easel lying in the grass along with the dead Greenbriar. The artist lay on his back, his head and bloody scalp—shorn of hair—turned to one side. His eyes, still open, stared lifelessly into the thunderous red sunset. A scrap of paper had lodged in his shirt, the charcoal sketch smudged with blood.

The full moon rose, casting a silvery light over the gruesome scene. Wolves crept up out of the shadows. Discovering the dead body sprawled in the grass they circled it, sniffing the air but reluctant to touch the strange-smelling animal. One wolf raised his head and let out a plaintive howl, his companions quickly joining in. The long, mournful wails sounded through the prairie night. The torn and scattered sketchbook lay not far from the body, the ripped pages lifted by the breeze and floating like white ghosts over the rustling grass.

25

A Chance Discovery

IN THE FIRST SNOW of winter, he was tracking a small herd of ante-lope when he spotted buzzards rising from a kill in the distance. As he drew closer, he saw four carcasses lying close together in the grass. He muttered with surprise. 'Buffalo!' The buffalo—all cows—had been skinned and the tongues removed. The rich white fat of the exposed flesh gleamed with blood where the buzzards had torn at the meat. He studied the scene for a few moments as the buzzards circled overhead. He was about to ride away when he noticed tracks leading away from the kill. The cloven, half-moon prints were distinctive and unmistakable in the fresh snow. 'Skit!' He nudged the mare in pursuit.

He followed the tracks across the snow to where they led to a brushy ravine. He rode carefully down the slope, halting as his ears registered a series of familiar, snorting grunts. The noise came from a stand of brush at the bottom of the draw. He listened intently, laying hold of the horse's muzzle to quieten it. Absurdly, he felt his heart begin to race—the killer of 10,000 buff thrilled to hear once more the sneezing, snuffling song that he had feared forever silenced. He strained to see through the brush. *One,* he thought, *maybe two.*

Dismounting, he trod cautiously down the draw for a better view. The grunts grew louder, and moments later, first one, and then a second buffalo appeared through the brush. The buffalo were mere calves—less than a quarter the size of an adult, their coats a black-brown colour. Both specimens had rounded backs rather than humps, and stubs for horns. He remained motionless, watching as they brushed aside the light snow cover to get at the grass beneath. As he watched, an idea formed. He made his way back to the horse, careful not to spook the calves.

He waited patiently out in the open grass for the calves to emerge from the draw. The sky was a slate grey with a light westerly breeze. Snowflakes drifted on the cold air. He warmed his hands in his armpits as he waited, his eyes dwelling on the skinned buffalo carcasses. After several minutes, the two calves appeared out of the gorge. He took the rope hanging from the saddle and made one end into a loop, tying the other end to the saddle horn. The calves were intent on feeding, seemingly unaware of his presence.

Their steps took them back to the dead buffalo. They stopped, nosing the carcasses. The smaller calf nudged one of the fatty mounds.

Several more minutes passed before their foraging took them into the open grass. As soon as he judged them sufficiently clear, he kicked the horse forward. The smaller calf turned and trotted back toward the draw as it saw him, the other following. 'Har!' He headed them off, driving them back out to the grass. They broke into a run, and he chased after them, snow spraying up from the mare's hooves. The larger calf suddenly stopped running and stood as if confused, breath steaming from its nostrils. Riding alongside, he jumped off the horse and wrestled the calf to the ground. As it snorted and thrashed, he looped the rope over its head before leaping clear of the lashing hooves. The calf got to its feet and promptly ran underneath the mare, which pitched in alarm.

Seizing the bridle, he stepped the mare clear of the rope. The calf bellowed and attempted to flee. He clung onto the rope, hauling it to a stop. He climbed back into the saddle and wound the rope around the horn before kicking the mare. 'Skit!'

To his surprise, the calf accepted the rope and followed the mare without resistance. He glanced back, pleased to see the other calf trotting along behind. They proceeded in this fashion for three miles until the rock came into view and, beyond it, the homestead. Smoke rose up from the roof in a thin column. The wind had grown colder, and snowflakes drifted in the air.

He headed for the corral, checking to make sure the second calf still followed. The door to the farmhouse opened and he saw Felicity look out as he pulled open the gate. The two calves had wandered off to feed, pushing the snow aside in search of grass. Waving his hat, he hazed them back toward the corral. 'Har! Git!'

'Pa!' The children came racing out of the house to investigate as he shut the gate behind the calves. Felicity followed, a wool shawl around her shoulders.

'Pa's found some cows, Ma!' The children clambered up onto the rails, gawking at the calves.

'They ain't cows.' Felicity stared, open-mouthed, at the calves, her cheeks pink in the cold air. 'Where did you find them?'

'Out on the range. Their mothers were dead. Robe hunters. They are buffalo, not cows,' he said to the children. The news sent them into spasms of excitement.

'Jubal. Take the mare up to the barn. Make sure you give her plenty of water.'

'Do you intend to butcher them?' Felicity drew the shawl around her shoulders.

'These ain't for eating.'

'Then what?'

'I don't rightly know. It was something that fellow said in town. You remember—that meeting I went to a few years back? He mentioned something about ranchers saving a few specimens to breed.'

'Breed?' Her eyes widened at the notion.

'It can't be that much different from raising cows. Amity! Boundary! Get those dogs away afore they get stomped!' The dogs were growling and barking, hair erect and tails stiff as they confronted the strange-smelling creatures.

'Jumpy!' Amity caught her pet by the ruff, pulling him back as the calves uttered snorts and trotted to the rear of the enclosure.

'How old are they? They look like babies.'

'Five or six months, I'd guess, maybe a little more. I'm hoping that smaller one turns out female. They may be the only buffalo left on the range—at least around here.'

Felicity stared at the calves, her imagination caught by the remark. To her eyes, both had the general shape of a buffalo without the distinctive features that informed adults of the species. Their black-tufted tails swished the air as they dropped their heads to nuzzle for grass.

'It seems a shame to shoot them,' he said. 'And if I left them, wolves would have got them for sure.'

'Amity, I thought I told you to leash that dog.' The dog was growling and snapping and trying to squirm under the bottom rail as she laid hold of him.

'I'm trying, Pa! Boundary, grab his tail!' Together, the two children wrestled the growling dog away from the corral.

'How will you feed them?'

He scratched behind his neck. 'I guess I'll have to figure out a way.' To forestall further questions he couldn't answer, he went up behind Amity where she peered through the rails, entranced by the calves as they snorted gouts of steam into the air.

'Can we keep them?'

'Sure. They are ours. I found them. Boundary, come here.' He lifted the boy up and set him down on the top rail. 'These are buffalo, son. I doubted you'd ever get to see one.'

Amity hung over the rail, her eyes following every step the calves made.

'Can I name them?'

'I'm not sure you name buffalo. They are not like cows.'

'Are they both boys?'

'I don't know. One, I think. I'm hoping the other's a cow.'

'Blackie!' She pointed to the larger one. 'And Mary!' Pointing to the other.

'Mary!' Boundary hooted with derision. 'You don't call a buff Mary!'

'Children, get down from that fence and come inside from the cold.' With a clap of her hands, Felicity herded the children back toward the house. With a last, lingering glance at the buffalo calves, Purchase followed.

THE NEXT FEW WEEKS were a time of constant experiment as he struggled with how best to care for and contain the calves. They refused to eat the feed he left out for them, and constantly butted the fence in their desire to escape back to the grass. He released them, sitting the mare to watch over them as they fed on the snow-covered sedge. They wandered as the grass took them and he was forced to chase several times to turn them back.

They had formed an attachment to the mare and followed without protest as he led them back toward the corral. But once inside the fence, they immediately grew agitated, charging the gate to get loose. He brought down the milk cow and sent her inside to try to settle them down, but she bellowed with fright as the calves jostled and butted her. He quickly took her out and replaced her with the mare.

'You spend all your time nursemaiding those two,' said Felicity when he went inside to warm up. I caught Amity the other day trying to hand-feed them grass.'

'I'll talk to her.'

'I don't want you climbing on that fence,' he told Amity the next morning before releasing the buffalo to feed.

'Can I sit on one?' asked Boundary, sticking his head through the rails despite his father's warning.

'Sit on one? They are wild animals, son. You don't ride them, like horses.'

'Look at Blackie!' Amity pointed. The larger calf was clumsily trying to mount the other, who trotted off.

'It's what they do,' he said. 'It's how they make more buffaloes.'

'Like the cows?' She squinted up at him.

'Yes. And like the dogs and hens, too.'

'Here, Mary!' She poked a handful of grass through the rail.

'I thought your ma told you not to do that.'

'She likes me!'

Worried that the buffalo were losing fat, he turned them loose for the entire day as more snow fell. I don't see how I can manage them, he confessed to himself, racking his brains for a way to feed and house the animals through the long winter. If the snow freezes over, they'll likely starve. He was still wrestling with the problem a few weeks later as the temperature dropped overnight to ten below zero. 'Perhaps I could get some advice from that lecture fellow,' he said to Felicity over coffee. 'I guess I'll head into town and send him a telegraph.'

'You could sell them. They must be worth something.'

'Do you not understand—they may be the last of their kind?' The exasperation cut through his voice.

'Then they'll be worth more.'

He tried again. 'Felice. This whole range was once—'

'Landsakes, I know! Blackened with buffalo.' She broke an egg into the mixing bowl. 'Maybe you could tame them and offer 50-cent rides at the town market.' She beat the egg and added flour.

'That artist fellow—Greenbriar—would understand.' He studied her with the remark.

'Well, he ain't here, is he? So, I guess we'll never know.' She stirred briskly.

'I guess he must be back in Kansas by now,' he said, his gaze curious.

'I guess. 'Do what you want with the calves,' she said, wiping her hands on a damp cloth. 'I just worry that the children—Amity in particular—will get stomped if she ain't careful.'

'I'll see that she is.'

He went back outside to the corral. Amity and Jubal were already there, hanging over the rail to gawk at the calves. 'Take a good look.' He stroked Jubal's neck. 'I don't know when you'll see another one.'

'Will they freeze in the snow?'

'No. They are made to survive weather far worse than this. See their coats? They are thick, to keep out the cold.'

The larger calf trotted up to the gate, butting it and uttering pig-like grunts.

Amity turned, her eyes bright. 'He wants out, Pa!'

'I reckon he does.'

'I like to watch them,' she said.

'So do I, Am. So do I.'

Felicity appeared in the doorway to summon the children. He watched them go and then leaned on the rail to gaze at the calves, idle thoughts running through his head. The farm was in good shape, he told himself. His family were well-fed and happy and he still had a small surplus in the bank, not even counting the buffalo wealth. 'I owe it all to you fellows,' he acknowledged, eyeing the calves. 'You fed and clothed the Indians and did the same for me. Now I guess I can pay something back.'

THE WEATHER TURNED WORSE, a freezing gale dumping fresh snow over the grass. The calves seemed equal to the challenge, brushing aside the snow with their heads, their steam-breath pouring into the air. The smaller one even led the way back to the corral as he hazed them back late in the afternoon. 'Why not put them in the barn?' suggested Felicity when he expressed concern at the weather.

'Maybe I will,' he said, 'although the cows may have a fit.'

The next morning, he caught Amity inside the corral, standing next to the smaller calf and stroking it.

'Am!' Jumping the rails in his haste, he led the protesting girl out. 'Do you want to get stomped?' He crouched down, a stern expression on his face. 'That buff is wild. There's no telling what it might take into its head.'

She started to cry, the tears glistening on her pale cheeks.

'What is it?' He wiped away a tear with his gloved hand.

'I don't want you to eat her!'

'What in Sam Hill makes you think I'm fixing to eat her?'

'Jubal said you're jest waiting for the hump to grow.' Her tears became sobs.

'Hush now. I've no intention of eating her—Jubal, maybe! but not the calves.'

'Promise?' She regarded him with large, tear-stained eyes.

'I promise! Now come inside afore you freeze.'

A WEEK LATER, HE was sitting at breakfast when the door flew open. 'Pa! Pa!' Jubal rushed in, his face flushed with excitement.

'Jumping cats!' exclaimed Felicity. 'Close that door afore we freeze.'

'They're gone, Pa!' Jubal was breathless with the news.

Purchase frowned. 'Calm down. Who's gone?'

'The buffalo! They are gone!'

'Gone where?'

'The gate was open!'

Perturbed at the detail, he got to his feet. 'I'd better go see,' he said to Felicity.

'It wouldn't surprise me if they tore it up,' she said. 'Jubal, go stand over by the stove. You'll catch your death.'

A short time later her husband returned, a furious look on his face. 'What is it?'

'They didn't escape, they were taken!' He took down his coat and tugged it on, his voice grim. 'I found tracks—unshod ponies.'

She put a hand to her mouth and stared, not wishing to say the word and frighten the children.

'During the night sometime, I heard the dogs bark, but thought it was that coyote that's been hanging around.' He took down the Sharps and checked the breech.

'What are you doing?' She couldn't keep the alarm from her voice.

'I'm going after them. Bar the door and stay sharp. Keep the children inside.'

'Can I come, Pa?'

'No. Stay with your ma.'

'Pa?' Amity and Boundary came in, eyes wide with apprehension.

'I'm going out for a while. Stay inside with your ma.'

'Why go?' She tugged his arm, her voice frightened. 'It could be dangerous. Wait, and send to the fort for help.'

'Whoever took them will be long gone by the time the soldiers arrive—if they can be bothered in this cold. I'll be all right. Stay inside.' He kissed her forehead. And with that, he was gone.

HE FOLLOWED THE TRACKS all morning, his anger mounting as he considered how the Indians might have slipped past the dogs to get to the calves. *I haven't seen the dogs. They probably killed them.* He clenched his jaw at the thought. On two or three occasions in the recent past he had observed an Indian, mostly solitary or with a single companion, ride past the homestead, giving it a wide berth. But since a fracas a year or so back when some young bucks from the reservation had allegedly killed a family, there had been no incidents he was aware of.

'Some wild bloods jumped the reservation, but their whooping and scalping days are over and done with.' The colonel, summoned from the fort by the mayor, sought to reassure the anxious audience of townsfolk and settlers as rumours and alarm swept the township in the wake of the killing.

'And what about this family they slaughtered?' a man demanded, standing to his feet inside the crowded saloon where the meeting was held. The question was greeted with a chorus of approval.

'Not a family!' The colonel held up his hand as others took up the cry. 'A single traveller. Hell, we ain't even sure he wasn't a fellow Injun they fell out with.'

'You could hardly blame them—for jumping the reservation,' a brave soul objected. 'Seems to me the army is starving them to death.'

'Then starve them and be done with the murdering hell-devils once and for all!'

For several nights after the meeting, he had maintained a discreet but cautious vigilance, sometimes getting up from bed in the pre-dawn darkness to survey the shadowy plain as Felicity and the children slept.

And now this! Cursing, he kicked the horse, the tracks easy to follow in the snow. They haven't killed them—not yet, he told himself, picking out buffalo prints among the tracks. Hopeful that he might yet recover the calves, he urged the horse into a canter, eyes scouring the snowy plain ahead.

Late in the morning, he observed smoke rising on the air. The sky was keen and blue, a stiff breeze spinning snow flurries. 'Skit!' A cold anger driving him, he headed toward the smoke.

THE INDIANS WERE HUDDLED around a fire, cramming portions of hot meat into their mouths. So intent were they on devouring the meal that they were unaware of his approach. Suddenly one of the women glanced up and uttered a screech of alarm. He had taken the Sharps out of its leather scabbard, his finger resting on the trigger as he took in the scene.

The calves had been split open and gutted, their bloody entrails a bright red smear against the snow. One was already half-eaten. The tongue had been cut from the other and the nascent hump removed. Chunks of meat sizzled on sticks over the fire, the smell of burning flesh causing his blood to boil.

'They were my buffalo!' His voice was harsh in the cold air. 'Mine!' He pointed to himself.

One of the Indians, an old man with long grey hair, stood up, his hands held out. '*Oh-tah'-koh-tah,*' he said, in a pleading voice. He wore a thin blanket around his shoulders. '*Oh-tah'-koh-tah.*' In the bright, winter sunshine, his face was haggard and drawn.

Apart from two youths, the others were women and small children, their faces pale and pinched with hunger. The children's clothes looked patched and worn—scant protection against the freezing cold. The women were wrapped in tattered blankets. Three small ponies nuzzled the snow to try and reach the grass. The women stopped eating—fearful of the rifle. Their mouths were shiny with grease. He could see no weapons, apart from the knives they ate with.

'*Yúta!*' One of the women picked up a spear of meat and offered it to him. '*Yúta!*' she urged.

He ignored the offer, his anger at the slaughtered calves burning hot inside him.

The old man fell to his knees in the snow and started to chant, his hands spread out from his sides. The wailing chant rose eerily on the air, the man closing his eyes as his voice wavered in trembling staves.

He saw a sudden movement from one of the youths and, without thinking, fired. The noise sounded like a whip crack in the freezing air. The youth uttered an agonised cry and slumped to the snow. Yells of anguish rose from the women as they rushed to attend the stricken youth. He glimpsed a brown hand outstretched in the snow, fingers closed reflexively around a chunk of buffalo meat.

The women wailed, beating their breasts in grief. The children stared with frightened eyes. The youth had stopped moaning and lay still, a pool of blood seeping from beneath his body. The old man had suspended his chant, a look of horror on his face.

Purchase lowered the smoking Sharps, drained of anger. 'I'm sorry,' he muttered, but 'they were my buffalo.' He stared at the scene a moment longer and then turned the mare toward home.

26

A Visit Home

I N THE SPRING OF 1886, Felicity and the children took the train all the way back to Missouri. The previous year, the Northern Pacific Railroad had at last laid in a spur track to Fort Buffalo, the event eliciting a noisy celebration that featured a military band and fireworks. To mark the occasion, the railroad had gifted the town a lot on the corner of Second Avenue and Third to build a schoolhouse. 'A school and a railroad!' Mayor Buskins shifted the plug of tobacco from one side to the other as he weighed the prospect. 'Hell, why not! It will bring in settlers.' He glanced at his fellow council officers.

'It will cost money—to build and to hire a schoolteacher,' one pointed out.

Coolly measuring the distance, the mayor ejected a stream of tobacco juice into a spittoon. 'Have we issued the licence for that new saloon?' he asked.

'No, what's your point, Eli?' asked the treasurer, Ben Wilkins.

'My point is that one licence ought equal one new schoolhouse.'

'You mean …'

'I mean, we kill two buzzards with the one stone.'

'That's a mighty big stone, Eli', pointed out Art Blomquist, the town constable. 'It could put noses out of joint.'

'Then you push 'em back again. But that's the price.'

THE TRAIN JOURNEY BACK east took three days, the hard wood seats a trial as the endless prairie rolled past the windows. 'Amity. Stop playing with your bonnet,' rebuked Felicity. 'Are you pleased to be seeing grandma and grandpa?'

The girl fiddled with her bonnet strings before answering. 'I miss pa,' she said.

'Do you remember St Charles at all?'

The girl shook her head.

'You'll like it there. They have a school with lots of young girls your age. Boundary, quit scratching the window.'

Her parents were waiting on the platform as she stepped down from the train. 'My, but you look just like your ma!' A beaming Mrs. Bell embraced

Amity. 'The last time I saw you, you were no higher than my knee!' She turned to Felicity with tearful eyes. 'She's grown so!'

'Now, now, Martha. Don't fret yourself.' Her husband laid a consoling hand on her shoulder.

'And you!' Martha enfolded a squirming Jubal in her arms as Boundary took refuge behind his mother.

'Don't crush him, Martha! We sure missed you, Felice,' said her pa, his voice gruff with emotion.

'And I you, Pa!' She kissed his lined face, her heart pained at how tired and old he had become in her absence.

'Let's get them home, Martha. They must be tired after such a long journey. My, my,' he shook his head at Felicity. 'You go up by boat and come back by train. The world sure is changing.'

As the hired carryall drove through the streets of St Charles, Felicity looked about her in anticipation. The familiar thoroughfares looked much the same but different somehow. Or is it me that is different? she wondered as she darted looks on every side. Her mother had Boundary on her lap, plying the child with questions, while Amity hung onto the side of the carriage, eyes wide at the broad, tree-lined streets. 'There are folks everywhere!'

''Course there are. This is the city, not the prairie.' She stroked the girl's hair. 'Look!' She pointed at a store with a yellow-painted front. 'There's the ice cream store I told you about. We can try some later.'

Boundary wriggled out of his grandma's lap to join Jubal and Amity in expressing wonder at the sight.

The house, like everything else, seemed smaller than she remembered. She stood in her old bedroom, her heart heavy with nostalgia as she pictured her younger self brushing her hair before the mirror or writing in her journal.

'We kept it like it is, Felice,' her pa said beside her, 'in case you took it into your head to come back.'

'Who wants tea and cake?' Her mother clapped her hands.

On the second day, she slipped out by herself to walk the familiar streets, stopping to exchange pleasantries with acquaintances. She visited shop after shop to peek at dresses and fine condiments, all the while wishing she could transport the entire street back to Fort Buffalo. The children seemed generally delighted with their new surroundings, begging to be taken back to the ice cream parlour again and again, and quickly making friends with neighbouring children of their own age. Amity, though, remained aloof, grimacing at suggestions she should consort with the two daughters of the local pastor. 'They are too uppity!' she protested. 'They don't like to run. And they're scared of horses! When are we going home?' she asked, her voice plaintive.

'She's headstrong—like you,' Felicity's mother remarked to her daughter. 'And what about her schooling? I fear she's growing up wild out there on the prairies. A young girl needs to be with other girls her age.' She directed a hopeful look at Felicity. 'The seminary is just six blocks away. They say it's a fine school. Mildred Horton's youngest goes there.' Encouraged by her daughter's silence, she pressed on. 'You could leave her here, with us. We'd take good care of her. It's no less than she deserves.'

'We'll see,' said Felicity, her mind flashing back to the conversations with Purchase on the issue.

She had planned to stay the entire summer. But as June drew to a close, she started to find the stores and houses and busy sidewalks oppressive in a vague, unsettling way that she couldn't quite put her finger on. The daily greetings and pleasantries became a chore—her mother's well-meaning 'socials' something to be endured. In between sips of tea from cups of fine china—'made from buffalo, I shouldn't wonder,' she remarked aloud to one such gathering—she found her mind turning to the windblown parlour outside the farmhouse door, and the boundless, cloud-shadowed pastures that greeted her each morning. Why, even that big old rock, she admitted, was a comforting reminder of home. The sentiment surprised her even as she declined a slice of fruitcake from her mother.

'Felice.' Her mother gave her a poke. 'Mrs. Greer asked you a question.'

'Oh?' She raised eyes to her interrogator—a frumpish woman from the linens shop.

'What's it like, Felicity, to be living out on the wild frontier?'

'Like?' She put a finger to her lips. 'It's like nothing at all. It's like being free and oneself.'

'Felice!' Her mother frowned at her. 'I'm sure Mrs. Greer wasn't asking after such … fancies.'

Mrs. Greer set down her cup. 'It's quite all right, Mrs. Bell. I'm interested in Felicity's true feelings. Free?' she asked. 'In what way? Are you not free here, in St Charles, for example?'

'It's different.' Felicity pursed her lips as the ladies from her mother's tea circle regarded her, faces expectant, as if waiting for some revelation—something to titillate or scandalise perhaps.

'I mean a body is free to run wild through the grass or shout out her feelings to the sky with nobody around to say boo!'

'Well, I never!' Her mother leaned over to cut more cake. 'I'm sure a body has other things to do than run around and holler.' This drew a titter of approval, the ladies glancing at each other with knowing looks.

'Of course, there's always the savages.'

'Savages!' Mrs. Hardwick, wife to the butcher, gave a gasp and spilled her tea.

'Wild Sioux, you mean?' Mrs. Greer leaned forward, one hand to her throat.

'I mean the townsfolk in Fort Buffalo. They can be a put-upon at times—their manners leave something to be desired.'

'Felice!'

ONE EVENING IN MID-JULY, six weeks after their arrival, she sent Jubal and Boundary to bed, asking Amity to sit with her on the porch awhile. Delighted at such grown-up privilege, Amity sat sipping a glass of milk, trying to look adult as a few strollers passed by the house. Gaslights, another novelty, illuminated the street as dusk began to fall.

'Did you like our walk along the river today?' Felicity began, hoping her mother would not insist on joining them.

Amity nodded. 'I wish we could take another ride on a steamboat!'

'Do you like it here, in St Charles? There's so much to see and do.'

'I reckon.' The girl looked wistful.

'What do you reckon?'

'It's noisy. And there are folk everywhere! And there are no chickens or hogs to play with.'

'Your pa and I talked before we left. He's worried, like I am, that you're missing out on school and other things. Here, you'll have the opportunity to learn to dance and perhaps attend parties when you're older. Wouldn't you like that?'

'I wouldn't want to dance!'

'You don't wish to spend your life milking cows, do you?'

'I like cows!'

'It's important that you learn to socialize with other young girls your age.'

Amity furrowed her brow and sipped her milk.

'What your pa and I decided is that you should stay here—with grandma and grandpa—and go to school.'

'Stay here?' Amity shot her mother an anguished look. 'I don't want to stay here! I want to go home!'

'And you will. After proper schooling.'

'I want to go back with you!' Amity burst into tears as she pleaded with her mother. 'Please, Ma. I don't want to be here. I want to go home.'

'I know you do.' Felicity felt her heart wrench. 'But its best you stay here. It's for your own good. Tomorrow, we'll see about enrolling you at the seminary.'

BY THE END OF the two-month stay, Felicity found herself, much to her surprise, anticipating, rather than dreading, her return. 'It's a hard life—but so wild and free you couldn't imagine,' she remarked to her father. 'You can look almost to the ends of the earth in every direction.' They were sitting on the porch, nursing coffee following breakfast.

'So, I guess you'll be going back soon? Your mother will miss you.' Her father's voice was soft with regret.

'It's where my husband is.' She wanted to cry, her usual sass deserting her.

'You're doing right—by leaving Amity here. We'll take good care of her.'

On impulse, she got up and kissed him on his wrinkled brow.

'I know you will, pa,' she said, her voice breaking.

'Ah, Felice.' He heaved a sigh.

To prepare for her departure, and soften the blow of leaving Amity behind, she took the entire family to a photographic studio on Sherman Street. Amity resisted going, complaining mightily as her ma dressed her in her best wear and brushed her hair flat to her head. 'Why ain't pa included?' she demanded, wincing at the firm brush strokes.

''Cos he ain't here. Look around. Do you see him? Stand still while I brush.'

The photographer, a middle-aged, fastidious fellow named Mr Lipscomb, began by taking a number of family portraits. Felicity and her parents posed stiffly and self-consciously on stuffed chairs as the children sat at their feet. Following the group pictures, Felicity and the children sat for individual portraits. The children's initial interest quickly turned to boredom with the lengthy process, and they fidgeted throughout in spite of Lipscomb's repeated and exasperated pleas to 'remain still as angels.'

While he exchanged plates, Felicity sat Amity by herself in the chair, the girl moody and resistant as her mother smoothed her hair with wetted fingers. 'Sit still! You wriggle like a gopher.' Amity grimaced and set her teeth as the photographer bent beneath the camera.

'Goodness, child! Is that how you wish your pa to see you? Do at least try to look pleasant.'

A few days later the prints were delivered to the house and the family sat down to view the results. The images drew exclamations as the grown ups marvelled at the way they were captured in light. The sepia tints gave a dull glow to the photographs that seemed to Felicity to preserve the family in an air of stiff, straight-laced propriety which she contrasted with the vivid immediacy of the charcoal and ink drawings by Greenbriar. *We were more alive in his sketches*, it occurred to her.

Around her, the children admired their likenesses while poking fun at each other. 'Am, you look like you're sucking on a lemon!' hooted Jubal, drawing chuckles from his grandparents.

Before supper, Felicity spread the prints on the table, carefully fixing each one on cream-coloured mounts between the pages of an album brought for the purpose. 'Your pa will want to see these,' she said to Amity.

She hesitated before closing the album, studying her portrait one last time before glancing at her mother. 'Does my nose look a mite sharpish?'

A WEEK LATER AMITY was all tears at the railroad station, protesting to the last moment. 'Ma!' she wailed, wriggling free from her grandmother as the porter shut the door behind Felicity.

'Hush now! I'll write as soon as I get back!' The whistle blew and the train wheels clanked as the train eased into motion.

'Ma!' Amity ran alongside as the train moved along the platform.

'Goodness! You'll slip and fall!' Felicity stuck her head out the window as the train gathered speed and the girl kept pace as though racing through prairie grass.

'I want to come with you! I don't want to stay here! Please, Ma!' The girl stopped at the end of the platform, an anguished expression on her face as the train pulled away.

Felicity steadied herself against the carriage as the whistle blew again and the train cleared the station. 'It's for her own good,' she told herself, tears flowing down her cheeks.

PURCHASE WAS THERE TO greet her at the station, a bunch of wild-flowers in his hand and a relieved smile on his face.

'What! Did you think I was not coming back?' She pecked him on the cheek, pleased at his obvious relief.

'I thought you might stay on a bit longer,' he said, helping her up onto the wagon.

'It occurred to me, but I resisted.'

'It did?'

His disappointment was so plain she pecked him again. 'How on earth would you get along without us!'

'Am?' he asked.

'She knows it's best for her,' she said, closing the subject.

On the wagon ride back out to the farm, she held on to her new purple bonnet, drinking in the grassy bluffs, the wide sky, and the miles of trackless grass. She glanced back at the children, who were laughing and teasing with delight as the wagon jolted along the trail. *This is home to them. The emptiness doesn't frighten them—as it once did me.* She took in a deep breath. 'Lord, but how I missed these pastures!'

'You did?' Purchase shot her a surprised look.

'Why wouldn't I? It's home, ain't it?' She clutched the bonnet to her head at a gust of wind.

The children vied with each other to be the first to spot the homestead. Jubal stood behind her, clinging to the seat and swaying with the motion of the wheels. 'The buffalo!' He cried out with glee as the rock rose up into view. *He's like his pa, half in love with that silly old rock. Am and Boundary, too.*

She settled back, trying to spot familiar landmarks in the undulating bluffs. The path to Fort Buffalo was more travelled now as other settlers moved into the area, the wagon wheels leaving a discernible track through the grass, linking the homestead to the town. As they went farther, they passed several herds of longhorn cattle freely wandering the range. When she expressed amazement at the sight, her husband's response was a mysterious smile.

A mile from the farm Purchase pulled on the reins and brought the wagon to a halt. 'Guess what?' He fixed her an anticipatory smile. Look!'

'What?' She looked around, puzzled.

'Don't you see?' He pointed the whip to where a herd of longhorn steers grazed in the dry grass.

'Yes?' She wrinkled her brow.

'They are ours, Felice.'

'Ours?'

He nodded, pleased at her surprise. 'I bought them from a dealer in Kansas. They came up here on the railroad.'

She stared, nonplussed, at the cattle. 'How many?'

'A hundred. They'll feed themselves. They'll run loose on the range and I'll round them up next spring.'

'A hundred? We can afford so many?'

'We can't afford not to. Everyone's buying them.' Her husband's voice was jovial, urging her to share his enthusiasm. 'This is natural cattle range Felice, the best in the world. There's more profit in cattle than anything else. Why, each one is as good as a gold brick. Cattle are the future.'

'How much did they cost?'

'Why worry about the cost? We'll sell each one for three times what we paid for it. Three times!'

'But they must be expensive—to ship from Kansas, as well? How much did—'

'Expensive—for the dealers who will snap them up come next spring!'

'They're ours, Pa?'

'They sure are, Jube. They have our brand on them.'

'Brand?' she asked.

He nodded, a pleased smile on his face. 'The buffalo rock brand. Tomorrow I'll rope one and show you.'

Taken aback by this development, she was further surprised to learn that she had acquired some new neighbours, in her absence. 'The Hartmanns,' her husband explained as they continued. 'They've claimed a section not a mile from ours. A fine family. You'll like the wife. She's a very pleasant woman. They have four children about the same age as our own. Oh! And something else.'

'What now? I can hardly bear all the excitement.'

'The new school. It's opening for classes next month.' He turned his head. 'Boys, you'll both be going.'

She stared ahead, her heart suddenly heavy for Amity's chatter.

27

Something in the Wind

SHE HAD BEEN BACK home a month before she was aware of a subtle change in her outlook. *The solitude no longer unnerves me.* At times, going about her chores outside the house, she felt the sky shimmer and would straighten up to dart wondering glances at the horizon. At first, it was the shimmer of emptiness that she felt, like a mirage in the desert. But over time, it occurred to her that perhaps she was wrong, that the shimmer reflected something distant and unseen, something that whispered in the bluestem or sparkled in the early dew, something even in the dirt that dyed her face and hands. She mentioned the feeling to her husband, keenly observing his response.

'Well, Felice.' He pushed up the brim of his hat to think. 'I reckon all this grass plays tricks on the mind.'

She said something vague in reply and locked away the sensation while at the same time maintaining a private communion with what she was suddenly certain was something grand in the grass and sky, something even her strong-necked, sunburned husband with his buffalo obsession was not privy to. *I was wrong to suppose it all hard, unforgiving masculinity,* she acknowledged to herself. The notion that there was something womanly about the open, wind-scorched grasslands—something that whispered to her in ancient, crooning murmurs—seemed to her the most astonishing of discoveries. Standing outside the door at dusk, or early in the morning, she experienced, in the vast and profound stillness, a connectedness—one that swept all the way up to the glowing stars. *There is a birthing, here—in the growing wheat, in the fresh spring grass, in the wind itself. A too-and-froing that impregnates and renews. Why did I not see it before?*

'Do you miss Am?'

The question caught her by surprise. 'Amity? More than I can bear.'

He nodded. 'I sometimes think I hear her and whip around, only she's not there.' He looked at her, tugging his lip—a sure sign, she told herself.

'You seem … contented, Felice. Ever since you got back. I feared that perhaps St Charles might unsettle you. But it seems to be the opposite.'

'I missed our home. I'm glad to be back.' She saw how much the words meant to him but perhaps not in a way he understood. The thought briefly discouraged her. 'I even missed that old rock,' she said, to make up for it.

He smiled. 'And it missed you, too!'

One afternoon, she took out the drawings left by Greenbriar, spreading them on the table to ponder. Her husband found her there when he returned from the fields.

'He was an odd duck,' he said, looking over her shoulder. He pointed at the buffalo sketch. 'See the lances sticking out from the side? He told me he saw angels dancing up and down the rock. Imagine!' He snorted at the notion.

She said nothing, collecting the sketches to put away.

'Don't you think so?'

'That he was odd?'

He nodded, peering at her, an intent look in his eyes. 'What does it mean to you?'

'What?' She held the charcoal sketch in her hand.

'The buffalo.'

'Mean?' She laughed. 'What should it mean? It's just a lump of old rock!'

'That sketcher fella acted like he understood something about it. And you do, too. What?'

'Purchase McLennan! You say the strangest things.'

'Maybe.' His eyes lingered on the drawing. 'I knowed it longer than either of you.' He couldn't keep the resentment—or was it jealousy? —from his voice. He turned away. 'I got to wash up.'

She picked up the drawings, her mind busily working. Greenbriar saw it, too—something grand that does not jump out at a body, but must be felt. She carefully pressed the drawings between the pages of the photograph album, feeling as if she had stumbled upon something perhaps important. Is that what he—the old man—saw?

ONE AFTERNOON, PURCHASE RETURNED from town with the news that he had bumped into Lewis Hartmann at the feed store. 'I invited him and his family for dinner next Sunday. What do you think?'

That the thought of company disconcerted her she ascribed to her new fondness for the 'prairie parlour,' with its hills and breaks and whispering grass.

'You'll like them. They're decent, down-to-earth folk,' Purchase said, misunderstanding her hesitation.

Emily Hartmann was a plain, no-nonsense woman of Dutch descent and strong Baptist faith. She arrived wearing an apron, her short black hair encased in a sensible bonnet, and bearing three large pies for dessert. She immediately set to helping Felicity glaze the roasted ham and vegetables, chatting merrily as she did so while confiding an 'awful weakness' for sugared apples. The family proved smiling and obliging guests and the dinner was a success, the neighbours departing after eliciting promises from Felicity and Purchase that they would return the 'social' in a month's time.

She recorded her impressions of Emily in her journal after the event.

She is a large, somewhat imposing woman with fair, freckled skin. Her appearance is belied by her manner—which is pleasant and cheerful. Her conversation was particular and attentive and boded well for a friendship. Her husband is plain of speech and manner, economical with his words and a mite fastidious in his way with a knife and fork. The children are well-mannered and played happily with my own. My only wish is that Amity was here to share the meal. I miss her and wonder how she is faring. I have not heard since her letter last month.

IN LATE AUGUST, SHE and her husband drove into town with Jubal and Boundary. They stopped at Second Street, where a retired Jeb Halverson and his wife, Mabel, had opened a rooming house not far from the new school. The couple readily agreed to board the boys for the two school terms, winter and summer, for a fee of ten dollars. The Halversons also boarded the new schoolteacher, a fact which caused both boys to grimace at each other.

'We'll take good care of them,' promised Mrs. Halverson, pouring tea as they sat in the parlour. 'Where's your girl—sorry, I forget her name.'

'Amity. She's attending school back in St Charles.' Felicity sighed as she stirred her tea.

'Well, I'm sure it's a very good school.'

'Who's the new teacher?' asked Purchase.

'Miss Purlow? She comes recommended from Minneapolis.'

A short time later, they bid the boys farewell, promising to be back on the last day of term. At the door, Purchase shook hands with Halverson. 'Do you remember that day the Sioux jumped us?' he asked.

'I still feel the itch in my scalp!'

'What was that—about the Sioux?' Felicity asked as they drove home. The afternoon sky was pale blue, threaded with wisps of cloud.

'Oh, a fierce scrap we had with them, way back.' The memory set him to musing as he flicked the reins. 'It was different not so long ago. The Indians were in charge, and there were buff everywhere. It all changed so quickly,' he said, speaking to himself as much as to her. 'Sometimes, I wonder …' He trailed off, a note of bewilderment in his voice. 'It just changed,' he said.

They passed a homestead, causing the dogs to bark. The wagon bounced over a rut, and she held on to the side, her thoughts roaming ahead to the empty house. 'I miss the boys already,' she said, a catch in her voice.

'What?' He stared ahead, still pondering the changes.

'I said I miss the boys. And Amity.'

'You'd scarcely believe it,' he said softly, 'as it was.'

28

The Bounded Plain

T HE SUMMER HAD BEEN scorching hot. Several fires had ravaged the grasslands, stripping the ranges of pasture. The drought had dried up the streams and creeks and produced very short grass, denting his buoyant confidence in the recent cattle investment. The *Fort Buffalo Dispatch* remarked on the unprecedented heat and the dire consequences if rain did not fall before the winter.

Several large ranches in the western portion of the territory stand to lose significant numbers of cattle if the drought persists through the fall.

He rode out daily to check on the cattle, concerned at their ability to draw sufficient nutrition from the short, withered grass. The steers struck him as thin and unprepared to face the winter. He drove them a mile to where grass grew along a turgid creek and sat there, watching as they fed, doubt creeping into his mind as to the wisdom of the investment. Newspaper reports that the price of cattle had peaked and was on the decline further stoked his unease. The $750, including the cost of transportation, he had spent on the cattle played on his mind as he rode back to the homestead.

In preparation for winter, he made several repairs to the barn, replacing cracked planks and sealing holes. He did the same for the house, replacing the door with one that fit so snugly to the frame that Felicity complained she could barely push it open. In September, he drove into Fort Buffalo to stock up on feed, concerned that the stockpile of hay would not last the winter. After filling the wagon with sacks, he drove to Jeb Halverson's place to visit the boys. They greeted him with enthusiasm, only falling silent when he questioned them about school.

'It's all right, I guess,' said Jubal, grimacing.

'And how is the teacher? Your ma will want to know.'

Jubal rubbed his nose. 'She's all right, I guess.'

'That's a lot of guessing to pass on.'

'Huh?'

'Never mind. Boundary, what about you?'

'I miss my dog.'

'You'll see him again, soon enough—I guess,' he added. He waited for the boys to smile and shook his head when they did not. 'I'm going to visit with Mr Halverson for a while. I'll say goodbye before I go.'

He sat in Halverson's parlour for an hour, yarning over the old days while sipping on coffee and a glass of whisky. 'You sure were handy with a gun,' said Halverson, admiringly. 'You must have kilt—how many? Ten thousand buff?'

'More.' He sipped the whisky, sober at the thought.

Halverson scratched his jaw. 'And now there are none left, go figure.'

'They say some ranchers have saved a few.'

'Say, did you read this?' Halverson passed him a copy of the *Bismarck Daily Tribune*. 'Look at that.' Leaning over, he tapped a paragraph at the bottom of the page.

While on a tour of the reservation arranged by the Indian agent, Mr Hannity, our reporter was introduced to Hunts for Ponies, a Sioux medicine or 'holy' man. When questioned on the coming winter, the old chief picked up a handful of grass and soil and crumbled it in his hand before scattering it to the wind. 'Bad,' he said. His companions nodded in solemn agreement. Several claimed to have sighted rare artic owls, birds associated with only the severest winters. Others claimed flocks of ducks and geese were seen flying south in late August. Mr Hannity scoffed when told of the conversation. 'They say the same every year,' he said. 'If I were to believe all such reports, I would put on my hat and flee back to Texas.

Putting down the paper, Purchase looked questioningly at Halverson.

'I knew the old buzzard—Hunts for Ponies.' Halverson chuckled. 'He was one of those stirring up trouble back in the buffalo days. Holy man! The only interest he had back in those days was putting a hole in any runner he could find.'

Purchase made one more trip into town, to stock up on coal for the winter. Again, he stopped at Halverson's, this time with specific questions for the boys, dictated by Felicity—who had been exasperated by his previous report. When it was time to leave, the sky was a slate grey and the air so gloomy he could barely make out the end of the street. 'Maybe that old buzzard of an Injun was right,' said Halverson, standing in the doorway with the boys to watch him leave. 'Remember the winter of '72? I reckon we are in for another—or worse.'

By the time he reached the farmhouse, snow was falling. He stood out in the yard as the flakes danced around him, his thoughts on the cattle. 'Come on in. You'll catch your death.' Felicity lifted a lantern in the open doorway, the wool shawl around her shoulders. '*Brrr!*' she exclaimed, shivering as a gust of wind blew past her and into the house.

THE SNOW KEPT FALLING for the entire month, covering the prairie grass with a fine, white powder that glowed in the rare patches of sunlight. Although unusual, the persistent snow gave no indication of what was to come. Thus, the ferocious blizzard which swept in at the end of November caught Purchase—and the rest of the territory—off-guard. Blinding snow, driven by fierce, shrieking winds, made all outside work impossible. Deep drifts laid up against the house and barn and buried the yard and fields under a foot of powder. It grew colder, the daytime temperature dropping to −10°. The cattle will have a hard time of it, he worried, high stepping through the drifted snow to the barn. Even buffalo would have a job to cope with this weather.

In mid-December, a surprise thaw raised the temperature to well above freezing and left him shaking his head. 'Did you ever see such contrary weather?' he asked Felicity. He took advantage of the lull to ride out and check on the cattle. They had scattered across the snowy range and it took him several hours to find and count them all. To his concern, he found that half a dozen were missing. The others were noticeably thinner. He sat the mare for a while, watching as they pushed aside the melting snow to get at the grass. I'm a farmer, not a rancher, he berated himself. Why in God's name did I invest in cattle?

The milder air gave him optimism once again that the worst was over as he made his way home. To lose six, or even a dozen, isn't so bad, he told himself, to ease the growing alarm he felt about the wisdom of his investment. He sighted other cattle in the distance, their hardy stubbornness filling him with renewed optimism. *Once the snow melts they'll start to fatten up.*

His hopes for a continued run of mild weather into spring were dashed when the mercury fell precipitously, plummeting to −44°. It grew so cold he lit a fire in the barn to keep the livestock from freezing to death. Out on the open range, the frigid air hardened the melting snow into a thick, icy layer that sealed off the grass. The starving cattle tried frantically to break through the crust, their noses and mouths bleeding from the hard ice. Battered by gale-force winds and subzero temperatures, many died where they stood, too weak and malnourished to withstand the brutal cold.

At the end of January, a blizzard of unprecedented ferocity struck the entire territory. Razor-sharp winds whipped up clouds of dense, blinding snow that made it dangerous to step more than a yard away from the house. The perilous whiteouts forced Purchase to string a rope between the house and the barn. He clung to the rope, groping blindly, hand over hand, as the wind threatened to blow him clear across the yard. On his return, the gale was so strong he was forced to halt and brace himself as the merciless wind pelted snow against his body.

'Hell and tarnation!' He stumbled inside the house, his eyelashes and beard laced with frozen droplets that gave him a wild-eyed appearance. He sat before the fire, his feet in a tub of hot water Felice had prepared in readiness. 'I've never seen anything like it. There's a foot of snow inside the barn.'

During the day, neither of them ventured far from the stove or fireplace. Icy draughts crept into the house despite Felicity's best efforts to keep them out. 'We're growing cracks!' she exclaimed as she plugged yet another gap. *'The air is so frigid I worry each time Purchase sets foot outside lest he slip and fall and freeze to death,'* she confided to her journal. Setting it down she thought for a moment before picking it up again. *'The nights are long, dark and cold—the days hardly better. It wears at a body.'*

One morning, a disconsolate Purchase returned to report that the calf born in spring had perished during the night.

Another time, he found the body of a steer frozen to death in a drift against the side of the barn. That night, and for several nights after, they heard the growling of wolves as they hungrily consumed every bit of the carcass.

And yet there were days when the air was so rare and still it was possible to go outside without a coat and she could swear that spring had returned.

> *I walked outside today with just a shawl and bonnet. The air was so marvellously transparent—with hardly a whisper of breeze—that I could see in clear detail the features of the rock buffalo. I long to see the green grass again and blue, expansive skies.*

During one such lull, Purchase led the mare out of the barn, anxious to check on the health of the herd. He searched the ranges for half a day before coming upon the bodies of five steers lying frozen in the snow. Dismounting, he examined the brand, brushing aside the snow with his gloved hand. His heart sank as he recognised his own mark burned into the hide. He continued the search for the remaining animals only to be forced to turn back, the mare's feet cut and bleeding from the icy crust.

That evening, he sat silently in front of the fire, his thoughts gloomy as he reflected on the heavy blow to their savings should the entire herd be lost.

'What are you thinking?' Felicity sat down beside him, a shirt and darning patch in hand.

'This cold has to break soon.'

She opened her sewing box and took out a needle and thread. 'The summer was so hot, and winter so cold …' She shuddered and shook her head.

'What? It ain't like you, Felice, not to finish.'

'I wish to Betsy the children were here with us, that's all.' She took up the shirt. 'I can't wait to see them again.'

In March, a warm chinook blew for three days, melting the snow with surprising rapidity and allowing him to go in search of the remaining cattle. He found their carcasses half-rotting in a draw where they had attempted to seek refuge. Aghast at the knowledge he had lost the entire investment, he stood in the wet grass contemplating the ruination of his cattle hopes. The dead steers lay close together as if to draw communal warmth in a desperate attempt to survive the knifing winds. Most of the carcasses had been chewed on by wolves or coyotes—the scene so dismal he turned away.

Felicity's face paled when he gave her the bad news. 'All of them?'

'It's not just us. I came across hundreds of dead steers. It minded me of the old buffalo slaughter, dead critters whichever way you looked.'

She sat down at the table, her eyes fixed on him, a tremble in her voice as she spoke. 'What does it mean—will we lose the farm?'

'Shucks no!' He tried, and failed, to make his voice sound buoyant. 'It just means I go back to cropping. And we have the hogs, the chickens, the milk cows.' He stroked her arm. 'We'll be back on our feet in no time.'

'Back on our feet. Back?' She stared at him, wide-eyed.

'Just a figure of speech. I mean that I go back to what I do best, raising crops. Now, how about some dinner for a starving man.'

On his next trip into town, he picked up the latest copy of the *Bismarck Daily Tribune* and stood in the general store to read the front page.

The winter of '86/'87 will surely go down in memory as the worst that anyone could recall. It, together with the plunge in beef prices, may well prove the ruination of the cattle ranching industry in North Dakota. Tens of thousands of cattle have been observed rotting on the ranges. Many of the large outfits have lost 90 percent or more of their stock. Several have been forced into bankruptcy. Others have simply abandoned their claims and ranches and returned from whence they came. It is doubtful that ranching on the northern plains will ever recover.

The shock of losing the entire cattle herd affected Felicity's spirits as she slowly digested the calamity. Three times she questioned her husband on the details, drawing only muttered replies, until she gave up asking, concerned at its effects on him. '*I don't doubt but that my husband's diligence and hard work will repair the loss,*' she wrote in her journal, narrating an optimism she did not feel.

To preserve money, she scrimped on her shopping list and doubled the time she spent making butter and cheese to sell in town. Her husband, meanwhile, threw himself into raising the next crop, working so many hours in the fields that Henry, the farmhand he had hired, up and quit, professing he'd rather die of starvation than being worked to death.

Her worries over the disastrous investment failed to diminish her late-found appreciation for prairie homesteading. Indeed, the glorious spring which followed the cruel winter served only to mirror her own, blossoming delight in the restless, wind-tossed swells and bluffs. As soon as the wet grass permitted, she collected wildflowers, which she tied in bunches and hung to dry, the fragrance investing the house with the welcome scents of spring. She pressed others into wreathes and hung them until they withered—replacing them with summer flowers as the weather warmed. To celebrate the return of Jubal and Boundary from town, she baked their favourite pies and remarked, over and over, how tall they had grown in their five-month absence.

The boys had no sooner returned than she sat them at the table, interrogating them about every aspect of the school term and their time at the Halversons'. She marvelled at Jubal's much-improved handwriting and shook her head at Boundary's scrawl. She made both recite the tables they had learned and questioned them closely on Miss Purlow and her methodology. 'How many children in the school?' she asked, learning there were twenty-four, of all ages, all grouped into the one class. 'What does Miss Purlow sound like,' she queried, 'when she reads aloud?' After much prodding, Jubal attempted an imitation, the effect causing Boundary to shake with mirth. 'Never mind,' she admonished. 'What is her hand like—when she writes on the board? Are her letters properly rounded?'

'Gracious!' She tutted in dismay at their clumsy efforts to answer. 'Do you pay attention at all? Boundary, do you listen, or do you stare out the window all day long?'

That evening, she wrote to Amity, describing her brothers' educational progress.

> *They aren't scholars, exactly, not yet, and Boundary prefers to take the pen apart rather than write with it. I hope you and grandma are getting along, and that she isn't overbothering you to attend church every day of the week. Give grandpa a kiss from me. Jumpy is as spry as ever.*

Feeling in the mood, she started a letter to her cousin in Boston, ending with a wish to visit her one day.

> *We just got out of the orneriest winter you ever did see. If the rain don't drown us, the snow petrify, or the wind sweep us back to St Charles, you may hope to hear from me again next month.*

WHENEVER SHE FOUND A precious hour to spare, she made it a habit to walk the half-mile to the rock accompanied by her favourite dog, Blackie. Sometimes the boys tagged along—out of curiosity as much as anything else. But she preferred to indulge in the solitude by herself. Occasionally, she was aware of Purchase gazing after her as she walked past the fields, an expression on his face she wasn't sure of. 'Would you like me to walk with you?' he called out once.

'I'll just be a quarter hour or so!' she hollered back, feeling guilty in her pleasure.

Once at the rock, she completed a circuit of the object, walking in shadow on the one side, in sunshine the other. The part of the walk that thrilled her the most was when she stepped behind its imposing bulk and lost sight of the farm and her husband working in the fields. In fancy, she stepped not only into sunlight—or shadow, depending on the time of day—but into another world, one comprised entirely of grass and sky. In those moments, she imagined herself freed from butter-making, laundry, darning, baking, and the thousand and one other chores that occupied her day. It was, she realised, the freedom she had daydreamed about as a young girl in St Charles. Only, in those dreams, she had pictured herself as an independent young woman moving freely within society—in New York or Boston perhaps, or even in London or Paris. That the realisation of those youthful fancies should occur here, in a primitive wilderness once inhabited only by Indians and buffaloes, struck her as extraordinary beyond imagining.

She took off her straw hat, allowing the warm breeze to ruffle her hair. The painter, Greenbriar, came to mind, as he sometimes did. Taking a deep breath, she pressed her front against the cool granite and closed her eyes, fancying she felt the rock tremble against her as though pulsing with a life force of its own. *Is this what the old man felt? Do passions persist through time—like vibrations in the air?* In a moment of giddying clarity, she felt privy to the buffalo's innermost secret, a secret even her rock-besotted husband did not possess. *It's alive!* She felt a rushing in her ears and spread her hands, pressing her palms against the stone while trembling with the imagined sensation.

'Ma! What are you doing?' Boundary gazed at her, his father's curiosity written on his face. Jubal, equally perplexed, stood beside him.

'I'm talking to the buffalo!' She laughed, barely able to contain a feeling of rapturous delight that filled her like a dizzying draught of air. 'Here.' She took Boundary's hand. 'Do you feel it?' She pressed his hand against the stone.

'Feel what?' He grimaced.

'Everything!' She laughed again, causing the boys to stare at her with wide eyes.

'Pa said we should go find you!'

'Well, you have. Shoo!' The skinny-ribbed mongrel—the one Purchase had found out on the prairie and which she had never liked—was growling and jumping up at her. She grabbed it by the ear and yanked until it yelped and leapt away. 'That dog is pure wolf! Come on, let's get back before your pa sends out the US Cavalry.'

THE SUMMER TURNED HOT and 'blowy', as she described it, and she shared her husband's worry about the crop as the drought persisted. One day, shortly before harvest, she heard a shout and rushed to the door. A silvery-dark cloud hovered in the distance. At first she was dumbfounded, wondering how a cloud could appear out of a clear blue sky. And then she saw her husband point, a distraught expression on his face. *Grasshoppers!*

She called in the boys as Purchase hurried back to the house. She shut the door and plugged the gaps with cloth, despair in her heart, as she heard the buzzing rush of millions of wings.

In a matter of minutes, the crop was destroyed, the insects leaving little behind except ravaged, chewed stalks. She joined Purchase and the boys in surveying the devastation, exclaiming with shock as she contemplated the acres of ruined plants, hardly able to comprehend that they were blooming in full flower that very morning. The glittering bodies of grasshoppers still crawled amid the stalks. Her husband was asking her something, but she didn't answer, too numbed at the destruction to speak.

'Felice? Are you all right?'

She looked at him, the despair on his face mirroring her own. 'What will we do?' she asked, dazed at the enormity of the loss.

He took off his hat and wiped an arm across his forehead. 'Plough up the field,' he said, his voice heavy. 'What else is to be done?'

THE LOSS OF THE '87 harvest, coming so soon upon the cattle disaster, hit him hard. For years, what remained of the buffalo wealth had underpinned his every decision, providing comfort and security in spite of poor crops or unforeseen expenses. The knowledge that that security was now gone, entirely through his own reckless ambition, ran like acid through his veins. Spurred on by a sense of failure, he redoubled his efforts to make the farm productive. In the spring of 1888, he planted one hundred acres of mixed wheat and oats, drawing on the help of his neighbours to harvest the crop. But the continuing drought resulted in a harvest of less than 300 bushels. His income for the year was a little over $200.

To make ends meet, he spent as little as possible on farm machinery, deferring the need for a new reaper. But despite such economies, what little money remained on deposit continued to shrink until they had scarcely enough to pay the grocery bill. He planted potatoes, which he sold for less than fifteen dollars for four bushels, and relied on the sale of eggs, cream, and butter to break even. He broke more ground and watched anxiously the price of wheat—which continued to fall. He contemplated withdrawing the boys from school, the ten dollars Halverson charged for their board becoming too heavy an expense. However, he relented, in part due to Felicity's adamant opposition and, in part, to Halverson accepting a slaughtered hog in lieu of cash.

He wasn't the only one feeling the financial strain. He learned that several of his neighbours, including the Hartmanns, had taken out loans from the new savings bank in order to survive the drought. The *Fort Buffalo Dispatch* carried stories of bankruptcies and foreclosures as farmers struggled to survive poor yields and months without rain. Purchase stubbornly resisted approaching the bank for assistance, preferring to depend on his own efforts while continuing to excoriate himself for the reckless gamble in ploughing their savings into cattle. He spent long days toiling in the fields, breaking still more ground to increase the acreage. Exhausted, he grew morose and said hardly a word after supper, falling asleep in the rocking chair and protesting when Felicity woke him to insist he sleep in their bed.

On a blazingly hot summer day, he paused from examining the withered plants, anxious and dejected at the prospect of yet another failed harvest. As he wiped the sweat from his brow, his eye alighted on the buffalo where it rose against the blue prairie sky. It was the first thing he saw each morning, and the last thing at night, its totemic presence a constant reassurance that this was McLennan land, that its soil had been trodden by a McLennan long before the first white settlement in the territory. Now, as clouds layered the sky and a stray sunbeam struck the precipice, he fancied he saw the patriarch himself standing on the horned brow to survey his kingdom—the two exchanging a steady, ancestral glance across the years. 'I endured,' the figure seemed to say, 'and so shall you.'

To his irritation, he occasionally pictured the buffalo as it had been rendered by the eccentric artist—what was his name? —years before, imagining one sunbaked afternoon that he saw wings reflecting from out the granite sides. He mentioned it to Felicity, complaining that the rendition intruded upon his perception of the object. 'He got it inside my head, somehow,' he said, frowning.

'I sometimes see it that way, too,' she admitted.

'You do? What in cornswill was the fellow's name?'

'Mr Greenbriar. Jacob Greenbriar.'

'Greenbriar! What became of him, I wonder? I imagined he'd be displaying his pictures up and down the country by now.'

'Eat your onions,' she admonished Boundary. 'And stop herding them around the plate like they were hogs.'

'What do you reckon became of him?'

'How on earth should I know? Boundary!'

'Do we still have those pictures he made?'

'Somewhere, I imagine. Jubal, get up and clear the dishes if you won't eat.'

BOTH BOYS WORKED FULL-TIME on the farm when not in school, easing the workload on Felicity by churning butter, milking the cows, and assisting Purchase with the crop. They seemed contented with the work, Jubal in particular. Boundary preferred to spend time on the farm machinery, watching closely as his father tinkered with the reaper or made repairs to the threshing machine.

'Go help your brother,' Purchase said on several occasions as the boy abandoned the butter churn to assist him with the machinery. 'Do you hear? Skit now.'

He frowned as he watched the boy trudge off. He ain't the farmer his brother is. Wiping his hands on a rag he mulled the future, picturing Jubal running the farm and Boundary …? He shook his head. And then there's Am. Missing his daughter, he walked back toward the house for coffee. He heard a faint holler and looked up to see Lewis Hartmann passing in the distance, his eldest son sitting alongside him on the wagon seat. He raised a hand in return.

'The Hartmanns have taken out a bank loan,' he remembered to tell Felicity as she poured the coffee. 'He hated like blazes to do it, but that last crop …' He didn't finish the sentence, staring into the coffee.

She sat across from him. Her face, he noticed with surprise, was lined, her hair tinted with grey. She caught him noticing.

'What?' she asked.

'You don't regret it, do you Felice?'

'Regret what? Growing wings?'

'Moving all the way out here—from St Charles?'

'Sufferation, that again?'

'I know it was hard on you.' He gazed at her, feeling responsible for the lines etched on her face and the way her hand tremored as she raised the coffee cup.

'The truth is there's no place else I'd rather be.'

He stared in surprised gratitude. 'You're sure?'

'Sure as raisins.' She stood up and advanced to the open door, summoning Jubal and Boundary for something to eat. 'If Jubal ain't shooting up to be a pole,' she said, watching from the door. 'And Boundary?' She scratched her cheek.

'They'll be off to school soon, 'said Purchase. 'Jubal doesn't care to go. He'd rather stay and help me on the farm. He can read and write now and do arithmetic,' he added when she made no reply. 'There's no point in him staying in school any longer.'

To his surprise, she nodded. 'Maybe one more winter term,' she said. 'I know he'd rather be here with you.'

She served up eggs, pork, and beans, watching as they gobbled them down. Like roosters, she thought, dishing up some fried bread. Jubal hooted with laughter at something Boundary had said, his mouth smeared with bean sauce. He's like his father, a smaller version. Did he spring from me? And Purchase, why was he looking at me like that? She smoothed her hair. It's true what I said, about being here. I do prefer it. I'll go for a walk after, when its cooler, to think on things. Having decided this, she sat down to eat some pie, looking up every now and then to observe her husband and sons, her brow crinkling with bemusement.

THE HARVEST, BADLY AFFECTED by the drought, yielded less than three hundred bushels, his lowest return in six years. His neighbours were equally beset, many going deeper into debt to retain their farms. Driving into town to drop off the boys for winter term, he observed a commotion outside the savings bank.

'Ain't that Mr Hartmann?' asked Jubal.

A small mob had collected outside the bank, arguing with a man in a derby hat he didn't recognise. Mayor Buskins was present, alongside the constable, both men trying to calm the riled-up crowd. He saw Hartmann confront the derby-hatted man, protesting angrily as the latter tried to push past him and enter the bank.

'What's going on, Pa?'

'Some foolery,' he said. 'Skit!' He shook the reins.

After dropping off the boys, he stopped by the Golden Fleece, lingering by the door to watch the scene outside the bank. The angry crowd had largely dispersed, although Lewis Hartmann remained, looking dejected, his shoulders slumped.

'Lewis!' He crossed the street.

Hartmann looked up. 'Oh, Purchase. How are you?'

'How are *you*?'

Hartmann shook his head, a defeated look on his face. 'I guess I lost the farm to the durn bank.'

Shocked, he regarded the other man. 'It's that bad?'

'The drought. The goddamn drought.'

It was the first time he had heard the other man curse.

'I don't know how I'm going to break it to Emily.' Hartmann looked distraught.

'She doesn't know?'

Hartmann mumbled something. 'I barely took in one hundred bushels. It wasn't enough to pay back the bank.'

'They won't extend?'

'They won't nothing!' Hartmann looked suddenly fierce. He took off his hat and pushed a hand through his hair. 'I gotta tell Emily,' he said, deflated again.

'Is there something I can do to help?'

'There ain't no help.' And with that, Hartmann walked off.

The following day, Purchase was working near the boundary line when he heard several shots. He listened for a while before going to investigate. 'The Hartmanns have shot their dogs,' he told Felicity on his return.

The next day, he watched with Felicity as a wagon piled high with furniture and goods trundled down the track that ran past their property. The children sat in the back, squeezed in among the household goods. Lewis Hartmann stared straight ahead, his face a blank mask. Emily Hartmann turned and smiled sadly at Felicity's tentative greeting, before looking ahead again, her face ghostly pale under the cotton bonnet.

DEEPLY AFFECTED BY THE fate of his neighbours, and acutely conscious of his own straitened circumstances, he drove into town, looking for work over the winter. He hired on as a railroad labourer, joining the crew that kept the tracks in repair. His companions were a rough bunch and he endured, rather than tolerated, their company. The lead ganger, an ex-soldier named Lucas, boasted loudly of his exploits in the Indian wars, intimidating some of the younger men with tales of butchery and slaughter. 'You ever kill Indians?' he demanded of Purchase one cold day as they rested from repairing a section of track.

'Some,' he said, annoyed at the man's overbearing manner.

'I bet you shot some Johnny Rebs, too?' goaded Lucas.

'You was in that war, too, Lucas?' asked one of the crew, an impressionable youth who had joined after Purchase.

'Hell, I been in shootin' wars all my life!'

'What about you, Purchase?' asked the youth.

The ganger snorted. 'He done jest told you he was in the Union army. Ain't you got ears?' He spat in the dirt, eyeing Purchase. 'Where'd you fight—in the war?'

He felt the eyes of the four-man crew turn to him. 'Here and there,' he said.

'Here and there!' Lucas bellowed the words. 'Where in hellfire would that be, exactly?'

'Where exactly ain't none of your business.'

The others stared, eyes turning to the ganger for his response. He glared at Purchase before making a sound of disgust and hawking into the dirt. 'Hell if I care!'

'How was work?' asked Felicity.

'I may have to kill the foreman,' he said, only half joking.

ON A RARE REST day in October, he went deer-hunting, intending to ride for miles into the rolling bluffs and leave his festering worries and doubts behind. The day was crisp and clear, and he felt his heart swell as he followed a deer trace through the hills. A nostalgia for the old buffalo days swept over him as the freshening wind brought the scent of sage and dropseed to his nose. For the moment, his worries over farm finances, crop failures, and drought fell away as he took his former delight in the windswept bluffs. The mood lasted only until he sighted what seemed to be a wire fence stretched along the top of an escarpment. Riding over to investigate, he found several strands of barbed wire tightly strung between a line of fenceposts. Angered at the sight, he turned the mare.

Riding in the opposite direction the following day, he came across several more fenced areas. Some fenced in cattle; others seemed designed to keep cattle out—the barbed wire protecting cultivated acres. He came across one section of fence that had been cut, the severed wires lying in the grass. As he sat there, pondering the sight, he heard the sound of hooves. He glanced up to see three men riding toward him.

'Whoa!' The horsemen—ranch hands, he supposed—reined to a halt in front of him. 'What in blazes have you done?' demanded one, a scowl on his face as he gestured to the broken wire. The other two regarded him with hostile expressions. All three carried pistols around their waists.

'I haven't done anything but sit here.'

'Then who cut the durned wire?' The man nudged his horse forward so that he sat directly in front of Purchase. His face was unshaven and limned with dust, his eyes angry under the hat brim.

'Hell if I know. I just rode up here before you came.'

'Then you must have seen who cut the wire,' said one of the other men.

'No, I didn't.'

The men glanced at each other. 'How do we know you ain't lying?' The third man demanded.

'Mind your manners, that's how,' he said, his voice tight.

The first man looked him over. 'I don't see any wire cutters,' he said. 'Who are you?'

'The name's McLennan. I homestead over by the rock.'

'That big rock to the east of here—the one like a buffalo?'

At his nod the other man sat for a moment. 'Well, we've had some trouble with damned cowhands cutting the wire, as you can see.'

'There's folk that object,' one of the others put in.

'I thought this was all open range,' said Puchase.

'It was, but it ain't. Leastways, not anymore.' The first man turned his horse. 'Let's fetch the wagon, boys. We got some mending to do.' He touched the brim of his hat. 'We won't hold you up no more, Mr McLennan.'

He pondered the incident as he rode home, the hunt abandoned. A herd of buff would stomp that miserable fence to the dust, he told himself. He looked around at the bare, sweeping grass, forgetting for a moment, and then remembering.

A State Like No Other

I N THE FALL OF '89, the town was abuzz with talk of the imminent admission of the territory to the Union. A mood of excitement and optimism greeted Purchase whenever he drove in to pick up supplies or sell eggs, cream, and butter at the weekly market. The *Fort Buffalo Dispatch* ran headlines proclaiming the date of admission to be historical and announcing unprecedented advertising rates to celebrate. Stopping off at the saloon for a drink, he listened to the gossip as the patrons argued over what statehood would mean for business.

'Shucks. It jest means more homesteaders and sheep herders and more fences,' argued one man, a prospector. 'I'm heartily sick of tripping over wire everywhere I go.' He turned to Purchase. 'What's your opinion, friend?' The others at the nearby table cast expectant looks in his direction.

'Buffalo, cattle, sheep,' said Purchase. 'Soon we'll be farming rabbits.'

The man gawked a moment before bursting into laughter—joined in by his companions. 'Rabbits! They ought put that in the *Dispatch!*'

'Are you a newcomer?' one of the other men asked. 'I haven't seen you around before.'

'No. I was here when this saloon was a dirt lot.'

'Then you've waited a long time for a drink!' The table laughed.

'You ought to hear it, Felice,' he said on his return home. 'It's all anyone talks about.'

'What is?'

'Statehood. Ain't you been following?'

'Oh, that. I imagined you might be talking about the new pineapple plantation on Fourth Street.'

'What in hick—'

'Is it true they're splitting the territory?'

He nodded. 'North and south. We ought go see it—the celebrations. We can visit with the boys at the same time.'

On the morning of November 2, she put on her best dress and wrapped herself in her wool cape and bonnet to witness the historic occasion. The main street was lined with flags and hung with red, white, and blue bunting in preparation for the street festival. Large posters blazoned the date with the words *North Dakota!* standing out in giant letters. Mayor Buskins declared the day a public holiday, reputedly issuing orders that everyone 'dance 'til they drop, eat 'til they bust, and drink 'til they puke,' in celebration. A brass band had been arranged—playing at the station to welcome the county commissioner and assorted dignitaries from Bismarck, on hand to witness the event.

They collected the boys from the Halversons' and wandered up and down Main Street to take in the festive store windows—'Christmas come early!' declared a passer-by. The street had been cleared of wagons and horse manure to allow dancing. A large wooden podium had been erected for speeches to mark the eventful occasion. By midafternoon, a sizeable crowd had gathered, the brass band playing patriotic airs and rousing marches as the air of anticipation heightened.

'Stay close,' Purchase advised Felicity as the crowd began to swell—every sharecropper and homesteader for miles around crowded into town for the grand occasion. Hoisting Boundary up on his shoulders, he stood against a store front as shouts and hollers greeted the arrival of Mayor Buskins, members of the town council, and the visiting dignitaries. The mayor glad-handed his way through the jubilant crowd, the dignitaries in tow. At 3:30 pm, Buskins stood up on the stage. The throng fell silent as he held up his hand, beaming at one and all, a large, unlit cigar between his fingers.

'Friends! Good people of Fort Buffalo,' he began in his booming voice. His glance swept the crowd. 'Townsfolk. Homesteaders. Miners. Herders. Ranchers.' He paused. 'Ne'erdo-wells!' The crowd laughed. 'Today is the day we pass from no-account territory folk into statehood! Citizens of North Dakota! Newest and grandest state of the good old USA!' The crowd hooted in approval. One of the dignitaries seated on the platform, the county commissioner, made as if to get up and speak, only to be motioned back into his chair by the mayor, now in full oratorical bloom. 'As mayor—the town's first and only! —I welcome this day, one I personally fought for, just as I did the introduction of the railroad to our town!' He paused, grinning at the good-humoured laughs and cheers the words drew. 'We now have a school, council offices, a brand-new hall for entertainments, and several fine wining and dining establishments! What's that, madam?' He drew further laughs as he cupped an ear in his now trademark fashion. 'A helluva fine town? Why, I heartily thank you, madam! I think so, too!' After several more minutes of praising the territory, the new state legislature, and promoting his own ambitions as to the latter, he changed tack in response to shouts and groans of protest.

'Hurry up fer God's sake! We ain't here to watch you lick yerself!' The bawdy comment drew boisterous guffaws.

Unfazed, Buskins good-naturedly joined in the laughter. An aide tapped him on the shoulder and his face grew solemn. Drawing out a fob watch, he studied it with ostentatious deliberation as the crowd fell silent in anticipation. The commissioner made to get up again, only to be firmly motioned back in place. At length, the mayor raised a finger. 'Ladies and gentlemen! I now proclaim we are officially a state of the Union! Hail to North Dakota—the thirty-ninth state!'

The crowd roared in appreciation. The disgruntled commissioner again attempted to speak, pushing his way to the front of the stage. As he opened his mouth, the mayor gave a signal and the waiting band struck up a rousing march. 'To statehood!' The mayor lit the cigar, holding it up in the air as the crowd whooped and hollered. 'Hallelujah!' he yelled, and swigged from a bottle someone handed him. The commissioner, his face thunderous, strode from the platform.

No sooner had the band played its last note than a fiddler took over, striking up a jaunty air. People stamped and clapped in time as another fiddler joined in and then a man with a squeeze box. First one, and then another couple began to dance in the street, quickly joined by several more, as onlookers whistled and cheered. Purchase set down Boundary and looked around for his wife. 'Felice?'

'Landsakes!' She pulled back her hand as he attempted to take it. 'Purchase have you lost your wits? Not for love nor money!'

'Come on' he coaxed, tugging her through the onlookers.

'Boys, stay there.'

Jubal and Boundary looked on, wide-eyed, as their reluctant mother allowed her husband to swing her into a polka, the dancers forming two lines as they stomped and turned up and down the dirt street. The fiddlers then lilted into a spacious waltz as more and more couples joined in the dance.

'Purchase McLennan!' In spite of Felicity's protests, he energetically whirled her to the music. She glimpsed a smiling Mrs. Bellow among the spectators, and Mr and Mrs. Halverson, the latter humming and shaking her head in time to the fiddle. With a sigh, she relaxed against her husband. 'Perish if you ain't stepping all over my feet,' she complained.

Moments later, gasps sounded as a single rocket burst into the air, trailing sparks. The rocket signalled the start of a noisy fireworks display. Flashes, bangs, and sparks filled the wintry dusk as the crowd oohed and aahed. Seizing Boundary, Purchase held him up to watch. 'You're a North Dakotan now, son.'

'Ma?' Jubal tugged at her hand. She pulled him beside her. 'It's like your pa said. You're a North Dakotan now. Didn't Miss Purlow explain?' she asked at his stumped look.

A firework exploded overhead, showering a glittering burst of golden sparks as the crowd hollered and cheered. The fiddlers struck up again as people yelled out 'Statehood!' and waved flags. Whoops went up as a bunch of young men, cowpunchers from the ranches, stomped and tripped on the street. She called out to Purchase. 'It's getting late—and noisy.'

They dropped the boys back at the Halversons'—hushing their pleas to be taken back to the homestead. Mrs. Halverson introduced Felicity to Miss Purlow, a thin lady in her thirties with hair tied back in a tight bun. The schoolteacher surprised her by taking her hand in a firm shake.

'You weren't at the celebrations, Miss Purlow?'

'I had preparation to do. Besides, fireworks give me a headache.'

'It's a new time, though, isn't it? The twentieth century is just eleven years away,' said Mrs. Halverson. 'Imagine!'

'I hadn't thought of it that way,' said Purchase, taken by the fact.

'Are you enjoying your time in Fort Buffalo?' Felicity asked of the teacher.

'Ah! Fort Buffalo.' Miss Purlow sighed. 'I had hoped there might be more to do, here. I miss the playhouses and diversions of Minneapolis. Life on the frontier is hard for a single woman.'

'I'm sure it is. Perhaps you'd like to come out to the farm one day, for lunch?'

'Thank you, I'm sure,' said Miss Purlow, smiling to compensate for the lack of enthusiasm in her voice.

'I keep telling her. She ought go out and meet some eligible bachelors,' said Mrs. Halverson.

'There are none—only dusty old cowboys!' Miss Purlow gave a high-pitched, skittering laugh that prompted an exchange of looks between Felicity and Mrs. Halverson.

'What do you think?' asked Purchase, as they set off through the dusk for home.

'About the price of eggs?'

He chuckled, his amusement pleasing her. A full moon hung low in the starry sky, giving an excellent view of the way ahead. She held on to the seat with one gloved hand as the wagon rocked and bounced along the beaten trail.

'I reckon that Miss Purlow could keep a passel of cowboys in line,' he said.

'I love the grass in the full moon.'

'You do?' He glanced at her.

'Everything is soft, like charcoal.'

'I can't believe it.' He shook his head, bemusement in his voice.

'Believe what?'

'This country. This state. It wasn't so long ago that it was nothing but wild Sioux and buffalo.'

'That's the price,' she said, 'of civilising ourselves.'

'I guess it is. Skit!' He shook the reins.

At home, she peered in the mirror, brushing the dust from her face. She reminded herself to say something to Purchase about the schoolteacher. What was it? She frowned at herself in the mirror. It was on the tip of my tongue, she told herself. And what was her name, anyhow?

30

Ghost Dance

H E WAS IN THE barn, milking the cows, when he heard Felicity call out. Stepping outside, he saw her point to the rock. The fall day was fine and clear. Shielding his eyes, he stared at where she pointed. At first, he could see nothing against the bright sunlight. And then he heard a faint drumming sound and saw dust rise up from beneath the rock. Perplexed, he listened for a few minutes. What in hop-hollow is going on? he wondered as the drums kept up their repetitive beat. After listening for a few more minutes, he saddled the mare to investigate.

'Where are you going?' Felicity intercepted him, a worried note to her voice.

'I'm just going to take a look. I'll be right back.'

As he approached the rock, he was confounded to see a large number of Indians gathered beneath the object. Dozens of tipis were set up behind it. A line of Indians shuffled in a dance while others stood or sat in the grass to watch. The dancers measured their steps to keep pace with the pounding drums while wailing a repetitive chant. Some wore feathered bonnets. Others wore leggings and beaded shirts. The watching women and children swayed and sang along with the dancers. The hypnotic drumbeats and fervent chants seemed to mesmerise both dancers and spectators. Several persons writhed on the ground, apparently in a delirious fit, as the dancers shuffled and gyrated to the chorus of drums and chants.

'What in ginger are they doing?'

He turned in surprise, alarmed to see his wife. 'Felice! What in tarnation are you doing here? Get back to the house.' He jumped down from the mare and caught her by the arm. But she pulled away to stare at the dancers, still breathless from her walk across the fields.

Suddenly, the drums ceased. The prone figures slowly climbed to their feet as if reanimated. Some called out in ecstasy, pointing to the sky as people flocked around to listen. Others wandered purposelessly, seemingly in a daze, their arms outspread and calling out in loud, beseeching voices. A few men and women scratched furiously at the earth, as though digging, before suddenly leaping up and crying out, only to collapse again, whether from hunger or exhaustion Purchase could not hazard a guess.

The drums started up again, and they watched for a further quarter hour before Purchase tugged Felicity away from the scene, mystified as to its import. The dance continued as they left, the Indians as oblivious to their departure as they had been to their arrival.

The dancing continued at intervals throughout the evening, and all the next day—a repeated pattern of drums and chanting followed by periods of silence. Felicity attempted to go back again and it took all of his insistence to persuade her not to.

'They get all worked up,' he cautioned. 'Who knows what they intend?'

On the third day, the soldiers came. He was working in the barn when he heard the blast of a bugle. Hastily saddling the mare, he yelled at Felicity to stay put while he hurried to the scene. He arrived to witness a troop of cavalry advance from north of the rock. Wheeling in line in a cloud of dust, they faced the Indians, carbines at the ready. The Indians had stopped dancing and were bunched together, tense and nervous of the soldiers.

As he galloped toward the soldiers, a scout called out a warning and several carbines were pointed in his direction. 'Don't shoot!' He shouted, raising his hands.

An officer, sitting a dun horse and surrounded by several troopers, called out a command and the carbines were lowered. 'Who in blazes are you?' he demanded as Purchase rode up to where he sat.

'Purchase McLennan. I own this land. That's my farm, over there.' He pointed behind him.

The information appeared to soften the officer's suspicion. 'Captain Whitman,' he said, introducing himself. His face was unshaven and streaked with dust. 'What do you know of this … baloney?' He motioned to the frightened Indians.

'Beats me. It just happened a few days ago.'

'It's a Ghost Dance.' The captain's voice was surly.

'Ghost Dance?'

'Intended to bring back the buffalo, if you can believe such foolishness. What?' The captain gave ear as an Indian scout rode up and leaned toward him. 'You sure?' he asked. The scout nodded.

'Goddamn!' the captain looked at where a young woman suddenly slumped to the grass. 'She just claimed to have visited heaven and to have spoken to Jesus Christ!' He shook his head in disgust. 'They get intoxicated on mumbo jumbo and claim these durnfool notions.' He turned to an officer. 'Lieutenant, search the tipis for weapons. Confiscate any you find. Sergeant, take a dozen men and search and disarm the Indians. Stay alert!' he warned as troopers climbed down from the horses. 'The dance is illegal,' he said, turning his attention back to Purchase. 'It gets them all fired-up for war.'

'They are Sioux?'

'Sioux, Cheyenne, Kiowa. Who the blamed hell knows? They come from all over—Pine Ridge, Rosebud, Standing Rock, and God knows where else.'

'To dance?'

The captain gave a snort. 'Indians! Who can figure?'

'But why here?'

'At a guess, I'd say that rock attracts them. It must be some heathen totem or such. Sergeant! Clear them the hell out of here! Tell them anyone who fails to leave will be shot!'

The dismounted troopers formed a line and advanced on the Indians, pushing and shoving the resistant men and women. The Indians shouted and shook fists, defiant even under the carbines pointed in their direction. The captain turned to the Indian scout. 'Tell them!' The latter at once rode forward and called out in a loud voice. The words incited a hostile response, the Indians surrounding the scout to protest.

'Ready the line!' The captain turned and gave a command to the mounted troopers. 'Give them a volley, boys—in the air!' He raised an arm and swept it downward. In response, the soldiers discharged their carbines into the air. 'Advance in line!' At the order the troopers advanced on the crowd, backing up the line of dismounted soldiers as the Indians reluctantly fell back, the men forming a screen to protect the women and children.

'Keep moving! Drive them back!' The captain kicked his horse forward, following his men. 'If they want ghosts, then by God we'll give 'em ghosts!'

Despite the army's intervention, small groups of Indians returned over the next few days. Purchase heard the drums during the day and saw their campfires at night. 'I hope the soldiers don't come back,' he said to Felicity. 'That captain was spoiling for a fight.'

THE DANCES WERE THE talk of Fort Buffalo, seemingly everyone in town having an opinion on their purpose. Finishing work, Purchase stopped by the newspaper office to pick up the latest issue of the *Dispatch*, taking a minute to chat with the proprietor about the strange gatherings.

'Beats me.' Bellow looked up from the printing press, his hands dyed with ink. 'The paper is full of reports, with more coming over the wire every minute. The Bureau's anxious as hell. They reckon the Sioux are stirring themselves up for trouble. They are mortal scared Sitting Bull is going to join up with the militants.'

'Sitting Bull? He's still alive?'

'He sure as heck is. Down in South Dakota. It's all in there.' Bellow motioned to the newspaper in Purchase's hands.

Following supper, he sat down in front of the fire to read. The front page was full of stories on the Ghost Dance phenomenon. Felicity sat in her chair, darning a pair of wool socks. '*Ghost Dance Raises Trouble on Reservation*,' he read aloud. 'Latest wire story from Pine Ridge, South Dakota.'

'Read to me,' said Felicity.

He obliged, clearing his throat.

Alarm over the so-called Ghost Dance has now reached as far as Washington. The dance, purportedly to bring back the buffalo and roll back white settlement on the frontier, has raised the hackles of Indian agents responsible for supervising the Lakota tribes. According to observers, the Indians dance for days on end, working themselves into a trance as they chant and whirl. Officials fear the ritual dance is arousing a fervour among the Indians that may tempt them back onto the war path. The agitated Indian Agencies are scrambling for ways to stop or prevent the dance.

'Those soldiers sure as heck stopped it,' he said, looking up. 'That captain almost started a massacre.'

Several more articles, reprinted from eastern newspapers, continued on the next page. One, in particular caught his eye: '*Indian Messiah Speaks. Exclusive Interview with the Times. Oct 1890*,' he read out.

'Messiah?' Felicity stopped her needle.

'That's what it says.' He held the paper closer to his eyes.

This day, Oct 14th, I was granted an interview with the Paiute religious leader known as Wovoka.

'Wo-what?'

Wovoka. Considered a prophet by many of his followers both among the Paiute and the plains Indian tribes, he is said to be able to control the weather and to light his pipe with the rays of the sun.

'Imagine!' She shook her head, bemused and entranced at the notion as her husband continued reading.

Whatever the reader wishes to make of such beliefs, there is no doubt that the man himself cuts an impressive figure, speaking calmly and with great conviction of his message. That message is, in many respects, strikingly similar to messianic Christianity. It calls for a "new earth" refreshed by divine influence. All sins, Wovoka believes, will be swept away in this renewal, which will remake the earth as it was in the days of his ancestors. Buffalo will be fat and plentiful, the grass will be renewed, and the rivers and creeks will sparkle with the dew of creation. In this paradisal vision, Indians will walk with their ancestors and white settlers will be swept from Indian lands, which will be restored to their former pristine glory.

Felicity put down her darning to better listen.

And how will this miracle come about? Through dance, Wovoka insists. A great, ceremonial dance that will prepare the way for the divine transformation. That evening he invited me to witness such a spirit or "ghost" dance, a rare privilege, intended to trigger the millennial event. For hours this reporter watched in fascination as hundreds of Indians, including representatives from all the southwest tribes as well as those of the plains, joined in a strenuous dance that went on for days and during which the participants whirled and stepped themselves into a frenzy. Many collapsed from hunger or hysteria and lay senseless on the grass. Afterward, they wandered around in a daze, talking incoherently and claiming, according to my translator, to have visited heaven and to have spoken with the Great Creator.

Purchase glanced up from the page. 'That's what we saw—the Ghost Dance.'

'I declare.' Felicity shook her head, marvelling at the account. 'What else does it say?'

It is this dance, sweeping the Indian tribes from east to west, north to south, which has so alarmed the Bureau of Indian Affairs. In this report-er's opinion, the dance is a harmless manifestation of Indian beliefs and no more threatening than a tent meeting of revivalist Baptists. Indeed, the latter may strike a neutral observer as just as ecstatic and delirious as their Indian counterparts. Wovoka is mild and friendly in manner and seems to lack the requisite prophetic fire. But for all that, he is stead-fast in his message and convinced that this miraculous transfiguration is but a matter of time. One is reminded of the religious certitude of those awaiting the Rapture. The BIA in South Dakota, however, takes an alarmist view of the entire Ghost Dance phenomenon that no amount of contrary argument seems able to dispel. They are deathly afraid that the famous Sioux chief, Sitting Bull, has become infected with the prophetic movement and that his followers are using the dance to whip up warlike aspirations among the Lakota. Indeed, it is alleged that the Indian agent at Pine Ridge Reservation in South Dakota, fearful of an imminent insurrection, has requested, and received, troops to combat such an eventuality.

Purchase laid the newspaper on his knees to stare into the fire. 'Shucks, if dancing could bring back the buffalo, I'd be out there jigging along with the Indians.'

'The remade earth?' mused Felicity. 'It's from Isaiah, surely. How would this fellow, Wovoka, know that? And how does he propose it will come about?'

He picked up the paper. 'It says here only that the earth will shake and roll up like a carpet. And underneath there will be a new—old, that is—world, full of buffaloes and spirit ancestors.'

He was about to put aside the newspaper when a small subhead caught his eye. 'Well, blow me down!'

'What?'

'It says here that the frontier is closed.'

'Closed? How in lickerty can it be closed?'

'Closed, meaning there is no more frontier—leastways according to the Census Office. It's all been settled by homesteaders and such,' he added, seeing her confused frown.

'My, my.' She returned to her darning, shaking her head.

The next morning, after her husband had left for his town job, she went to the photo album and turned the pages. She pulled out a series of sketches carefully tucked between the leaves and laid them on the table. In the light from the window, she considered her favourite: the charcoal sketch. But it was another, similar drawing, this one in ink, which had prompted her to open the album. The drawing showed the buffalo from the front, the figure rising up against a wash of cloud and grass. Feathered lances protruded from its sides like outspread wings. Underneath, in the showy, yet scrupulous, hand she remembered, was an inscription written in black ink: *'For, behold, I create new heavens and a new earth.'*

IN MID-DECEMBER, PURCHASE REPORTED for work on a bleak morning of falling snow. His workmates were gathered around the woodstove, drinking coffee and warming their hands while talking loudly across each other. 'Hey, Purchase!' The youngest member, Drinkwater, turned to acknowledge him. 'You heard?'

'Heard what?'

'Sitting Bull, that Sioux chief. The army shot him dead.'

'Sure did!' The listening Lucas gave a jeering laugh. 'Shot the old buzzard clean through the guts!'

'According to the *Dispatch,* they went to arrest him,' said Drinkwater, 'and I guess his tribe didn't take kindly to that.'

'I guess not!' Lucas gave a snort. 'The devils slaughtered a dozen soldiers during the fracas. Decent Christians slaughtered by filthy heathen devils!'

'The *Dispatch* said a half-dozen,' demurred Drinkwater.

'A dozen, a half-dozen! What in blazes does it matter?' Lucas gave the youth a contemptuous stare. 'They are still dead, ain't they?'

'I reckon,' said the youth, and fell silent.

Purchase mulled the news all morning, the blowing snow keeping them confined to the hut. While the others played poker or yarned over coffee, he sat by himself, recalling the time when the name Sitting Bull had evoked fear and dread across the entire territory. *And now he's gone. Just like Crazy Horse. Just like the buffalo.*

'Hey, McLennan. You ain't mourning for that stinking old Injun are you?' The question was accompanied by a belligerent stare.

'I reckon he was worth two of you.'

The noisy hut fell silent. The men stared at him and then at Lucas and then at each other in the fraught hush.

'What's that, old-timer? You care to repeat those words?' Lucas rose to his feet, a dangerous glower on his face.

'I said,' Purchase repeated, 'that I reckon he was worth two of you.'

Eyes turned to Lucas. The ganger wiped his mouth, glaring at Purchase as if daring him to move. One of the men rose as if to intervene but was pulled back to his seat by another. In the tense silence, a shadow of uncertainty flickered over the ganger's face. He licked his lips at Purchase's unblinking stare.

'Hell-fire!' he said, with a forced laugh. 'I reckon I could care less what you think about some stinking dead Injun!' With another lick of his dry lips, he looked away.

IN LATE JANUARY 1891, on a freezing day of bright sunshine, Purchase stopped in at the Golden Fleece after picking up some supplies. 'Purchase!' A voice summoned him in the crowded saloon. Mace and Halverson were seated at a table along with another man. He made his way through the busy room as Mace kicked out a chair for him.

'Purchase, this is Festus Tilbury. He worked with us a few years back afore enlisting as a soldier boy. Festus, meet Purchase McLennan, peerless buffalo runner.'

Tilbury stood up and extended a hand. 'Pleased to meet you, Mr McLennan.' His thick black hair was slicked back with grease. He wore a full moustache that drooped down the sides of his chin.

'Likewise.'

'Sit down, Purchase, take a load off.'

'I can't stay long.'

'Long enough for a whisky.' Mace pushed a bottle and glass across the table.

'Tell him,' prompted Halverson, speaking to Tilbury. 'Tell Purchase what you jest told us.'

The other man glanced around the crowded saloon.

'It's okay, Festus.' Halverson leaned forward. 'You can trust Purchase. He was with us when the Sioux durn near lifted all of our scalps.'

Tilbury nodded and began to speak in a low voice. 'I was enlisted in the Seventh Cavalry under the command of Colonel James Forsyth. We were sent to track a bunch of Sioux led by Big Foot, on their way to the Pine Ridge Reservation. The rumour was that they figured to join up with Kicking Bear and Short Bull and raise holy hell after what happened to Sitting Bull.' He glanced around the noisy saloon. 'We caught up with the Indians where they were camped in the snow at Wounded Knee Creek. The colonel ordered the Indians to give up their arms. He set up cannon around the village in case they refused and tried to make a fight of it. At daybreak he sent in soldiers to search the tipis for weapons. The Sioux were defiant, but what could they do? The village was full of women and children. Everything was going to plan when suddenly there was an almighty ruckus. A medicine man began that crazy dance, hopping and whooping and trying to whip up the others. See, they wore special shirts that were supposed to protect them from bullets. Then everything went all to hell.'

Tilbury took a gulp of whisky. Mace obligingly leaned over and refilled his glass. Tilbury drained that, too, his voice trembling as he continued. 'The slaughter was awful!' His voice dropped so that Purchase had to lean in to hear. 'Both sides were blazing away at each other. I was sat at the rear, near the colonel. Seeing the firefight, he raised a hand and gave the order for the cannon to open up on the Indians. It was carnage! The Indians—men, women, and children—were cut down where they stood.' Tilbury shook his head as if to rid himself of the images. 'The soldiers kept firing—even after the Indians were out of ammunition and couldn't fire back. There were bodies strewn everywhere. The children were the worst. Half of them had been ripped to pieces by the cannon fire. The troopers were half-crazy, riding down and shooting anything that moved. Heck, I reckon they just about shot each other in the confusion, they were so bound on killing all the Sioux.' He licked his lips, his voice tragic. 'God in heaven if I ever saw such a slaughter.' He fell silent, his face troubled.

'How many?' prodded Halverson, his voice sombre.

'Indians?' Tilbury sighed. 'The official count, after the firing stopped, was a hundred fifty, including the women and children. But I reckon it was at least twice that. Christ, it was half the village! Those that weren't kilt outright were dead or dying. Others were injured or with limbs blown clean off. There was hardly any noise. You know how Indians love to wail and carry on over their dead? There was none of that. Only silence. So hushed you could almost hear the grass grow.'

Halverson shook his head. 'God Almighty. What do you reckon, Purchase?'

'It was butchery!' Tilbury blurted before Purchase could speak. 'There ain't too much in the papers, yet. But when it all spills out, remember— whatever the army says different—it was a goddamn slaughter!'

'Tell him,' prompted Mace, pouring more whisky.

Tilbury swallowed the glass at a gulp. Wiping his mouth with his sleeve, he looked around at the other tables. 'I couldn't sleep after. I guess I jest climbed on my horse and rode out of there. I didn't want any more truck with killing women and children.'

'You'll be all right,' said Halverson. 'The army probably figures you for dead.'

A short time later, Purchase took his leave. Cold sunlight flooded the snow-covered bluffs as he drove the wagon homewards. He heard a coyote yelp, the sound carrying across the desolate landscape. 'Har!' He flicked the whip, ears half-primed for the frosty echoes of ululating whoops and thundering hooves.

31

A Plum Opportunity Lies Waiting

THREE GOOD HARVESTS IN succession had done much to alleviate this financial woes since the disastrous winter of '86/'87. Crop yields in '90 and '91 had been bountiful, in spite of drought affecting parts of the state. In particular, '91 was a godsend, the crop yielding a record harvest of over a thousand bushels of wheat and one hundred fifty of oats. The grain sales, together with the income from eggs, butter, and potatoes, had allowed him to replace some farm machinery and quit his winter job in town. The next year was almost as good—the income from grain and the sale of three hogs and a cow, plus a wagonload of potatoes, fetching a return of over seven hundred dollars. Although still stung by the loss of his buffalo savings, he took comfort in the fact that he had secured a slim financial buffer against future vagaries of weather and grain prices. He was walking through the summer fields, reflecting on the upturn in his fortunes, when he heard a holler.

'Hey! Fella!'

Looking up, he saw a one-horse gig pulled up on the road that ran alongside the fields. The driver, dressed in a green plaid wool suit, orange knot tie, and derby hat, hailed him from the seat. 'I'm looking for a Pur— Whoa, you durned bone bag!' Controlling the skittish horse with curses and sharp jerks of the rein, the man turned his attention back to Purchase. '—Purchase McLennan. Would you be him, by any chance?'

'Depends. What do you want with him?'

'I'm a reporter. For the *Chicago Tribune*.'

'Yes?'

'What do you say, fella? You McLennan?'

Purchase tucked his thumbs into his denim overalls. 'You still haven't told me who you are.'

The man took an exasperated breath. 'Thomas Gilmore is the name. I'm a reporter—a jour-*na*-list'—he dragged out the word, 'for the *Tribune*. That's in Chicago. I'm here to do a story on that there rock.' He indicated with the whip. 'Well?' Confronted with Purchase's continuing silence, the man muttered under his breath. 'I'm told I need to speak to a Purchase McLennan. You him?'

'Why do you want to write about the rock?'

'Mother O'Leary!' The reporter shook his head in frustration. 'It's a new state, ain't it?' He cocked an eyebrow as if anticipating a rebuttal. 'Well, that's settled, then. No need to repeal the amendment! Folks back East are interested. They want to know facts about the place, especially that big ole rock.'

'It's on my land. You can look from the road but stay off my property.'

'Then you must be Purchase McLennan—all this time!' Gilmore used a finger to tilt the derby back on his head. 'Durn hayseed!' he muttered, the insult clearly audible. 'Nobody mentioned private property. I understood the rock stood on public land.'

'It don't.' Purchase turned to go. 'You'd best be on your way.'

'Guess I'll have to rely on that other fella!'

Purchase turned. 'What in blazes are you yawping about?'

'That fella whose grandpop carved the thing! He's meeting me here. Supposed to be here already.' The reporter twisted his head to glance back down the road. 'I reckon he's got the whole scoop on that ugly pile.' He grinned at the scowl on Purchase's face. 'Told me his grandpop carved it! Him and a bunch of Injuns—as a totem pole.'

'Who told you?'

'This fella.'

'It weren't Indians. And it ain't a totem.'

'*Carved by a White Man! Worshipped by Injuns!*' Ignoring the protest, Gilmore extended a hand, as if gazing at the printed headline.

'Go hang!' Purchase started to walk away.

'Hell's bells if that ain't him coming now!' Gilmore shaded his eyes to where a horseman approached from the direction of town. 'It's about time! Guess I'll learn the facts about that misshapen eyesore one way or another.'

Purchase stopped to look, curious in spite of his annoyance at the reporter's manner.

A youth plodded up on a grey mare, both horse and rider sweating in the sun. The rider was dressed in patched dungarees, a flannel shirt, and a hat with a large, floppy brim and leather strings that tied around his chin. 'Are you Mr Gilmore?' He asked, stopping before the gig.

'I sure am!' The reporter climbed down from the seat. 'I'm looking forward to learning all about your wondrous edifice!' He flashed a glance at Purchase as the youth leaned down to shake his hand.

'Axel Bjornson. Sorry I'm late. The train got held up, and then I couldn't find a horse to hire. Finally, a man directed me to some stables where this old—'

'Mighty glad to meet you, Axel.' Gilmore gurgled noisily and hawked in the grass. 'Blamed, shit-eating dust!' He took out a handkerchief to mop his brow. 'Axel, this here is Mr Purchase McLennan—although he'll deny it under oath!' He winked at Purchase.

'Pleased to meet you, Mr McLennan.' The youth leaned on the saddle horn, grimacing as he stretched his back.

'Bjornson?' challenged Purchase. 'I never heard that name before. No one in by family's ever mentioned it.'

'Nor I, McLennan.' The youth's voice was amiable in spite of the retort.

'What's this blather about your grandpop carving that rock?'

''Tain't no blather! My kinfolk carved that rock—all by hisself, except for a few Indians, probably, that helped.'

'That's a lie!'

'I guess it ain't!' The youth stared hotly with the words.

'Now, gentlemen, allow me to referee afore this dispute turns to fisticuffs.' Gilmore ran a finger around the damp collar of his shirt. 'What say we go out to the consarned heap and hash this out in the shade?'

'Suits me,' said the youth, his voice defiant. 'I ain't got nothing to hide.' Both men turned eyes on Purchase.

'I ain't got the time for this balderdash.'

'Too bad.' Gilmore shook his head in sorrow. 'Then I've no choice other than to declare Mr Bjornson's kinsman the sole author of yonder brickwork.'

Purchase glared, furious at the threat. 'And suppose I can prove my great-grandfather carved it?'

'Then let's hear it! What do you say—shall we put this to rest, one way or the other?' Gilmore made as if to climb back aboard the gig.

'I guess I can spare a half minute to clear up a bunch of lies!' Seething at all hucksters and toad-faced liars, Purchase cut across the fields. Behind him, he heard Gilmore start the rig. 'Git! Move those durn bones!'

Reaching the rock, Purchase stood in its shade, asserting possession with folded arms. The other two followed the road, turning off to head through the grass toward him.

'Dang, but it's awful big.' Gilmore pulled up the runabout, looking up from under the canopy.

Bjornson seemed equally impressed, sitting the horse to stare, his eyes wide as he traced the outline of the buffalo. 'Jessy!' he exclaimed, his mouth hanging open.

'If you know so much, how come it's the first time you've seen it?'

'I seed it before, once, when my pappy brung me here as a boy.' Bjornson slipped down from the horse, his eyes still on the rock.

'Anyone could say that!'

'Gentlemen!' Gilmore removed his jacket, folding it and laying it along the seat. Behind the seat was stowed a large camera and tripod. 'We've three claimants,' he announced, taking out a notebook and pen from the jacket pocket. Unscrewing the pen, he licked the nib.

'Three claimants? Where in tar did you fetch three?'

'You. The Swede—beg pardon, Bjornson—and the Injuns.'

'Injuns?' It was Bjornson's turn to look baffled.

'You ain't heard? They claim their ancestors carved the rock into that shape more'n a thousand years ago.'

'Well, I never!' Bjornson gaped at the claim.

'More bull!'

'Now don't go getting riled up. If you can show me the proof that your grandpappy carved the article then we can put the riddle to bed.'

'Him first!' Purchase scowled at Bjornson.

The youth moved a few steps so that he was in the shade. 'My pap told me,' he said. 'And his pap told him.'

'Ha! Call that proof?'

'My pap was no liar! And come to that, where's your proof?' At the question, the reporter glanced at Purchase, pen poised above the notebook.

'I don't need no proof. I *know*.'

'Ha!'

'So you got no proof—either of you?' The reporter grumbled to the notebook. 'No letters, deeds, bits of paper. Anything? Hell, I may as well credit the durn Injuns.' He eyed the youth. 'You say you heard it from your pa? What was his name at least?'

'Lars. Lars Bjornson.'

Gilmore wrote it down. 'And you've no written record—nothing at all—to prove his claim?'

'I guess my pap wasn't one for writing. Hell, why would he need to? I was standing right there!'

'And you?' Gilmore glanced at Purchase.

'I told you, I don't need proof. Everybody knows.'

'Everybody who?'

'Folk. Townsfolk. Runners—buffalo hunters—who were here long afore you.'

'How'd they know? Cos you told 'em!' the youth hooted.

'We ain't settled nothing so far. By purgatory, but it's dry!' Walking back to the gig, Gilmore rummaged beneath the tripod and fished out a flask of whisky. Unscrewing the top, he took a long swallow. 'God's own water!' He took up the notebook. 'Let's see if we can't get a hook on this. Axel, why don't you begin by giving your side of the claim. Then Mr McLennan can fire off a retort. Any objections?' He looked from one to the other. 'No? Then blaze away!'

Bjornson took off his hat and twisted it in his hands. 'I guess it's always been known, in the family, that our kinfolk carved it.'

'So—word of mouth, then?' the reporter hazarded. Bjornson grimaced. 'More than that,' he protested.

'What then?'

'They was honest folk. All of 'em.'

'I see.' The reporter made a pretence of scribbling. 'Honest … folk. And you, Purchase?'

'The hell with your fool questions! I done already told you it was my great-grandpa that carved it.'

'Word … of … mouth,' the reporter wrote. With an exaggerated sigh he pocketed the notebook. 'That's all squared away then. On to the Resurrection!' He squinted up at the rock, as if just remembering the object of contention. 'Mary Jane, it's big! How high would you say?'

Purchase cocked a glance at Bjornson, inviting an answer. 'Don't know?' he mocked as the youth shrugged. 'Or did your pa forget to tell you.'

'How about you, then?' asked the reporter. 'You got a figure?'

'Sixty feet or thereabouts.'

'That's about right,' said Bjornson as Gilmore scribbled down the figure.

'Now he speaks!'

'I got eyes, ain't I? Any fool can see its more than fifty feet and less than a hundred!'

The reporter elicited a few more details concerning length and width, both claimants putting forward rival estimates. 'Two hundred yards!' Purchase blinked in astonishment at Bjornson's assertion of the latter measurement. 'How in the name of perdition is it two hundred yards?'

Bjornson sniffed. 'I was never much good at figurin''

'Never mind. How old?' asked Gilmore, licking the nib.

'The rock or the carving?'

'Is there a difference?

'Heck, do you think it was born that way?' Bjornson shot a scornful look at the reporter, who turned a bland gaze on Purchase.

'Around a hundred years and more,' he offered.

'A hundred years?' The reporter raised eyebrows. Even Bjornson looked nonplussed.

'You just figure the generations. Father, son, grandson, great-grandson ...' Purchase ticked off the generations on his fingers. 'How many years is that?'

Gilmore knotted his brow. 'It ain't a whole lot,' he confessed.

'Two hundred years, by my reckoning,' speculated Bjornson. 'It was my great-great ... something,' he finished sheepishly at Purchase's fierce stare.

'And what's the dogie made of anyhow?' The reporter kicked the stone, wincing at the hardness.

'Well?' Purchase demanded.

'Pa never said. Or if he did, I don't remember.'

'If that don't prove all!'

'Hey fellows, hold fire!' Gilmore walked to the gig and returned toting the camera and tripod. As they watched him set up the equipment, Purchase turned grudging eyes on Bjornson, who seemed fascinated by the process.

'So, where did your kinfolk live when he was supposedly carving my buffalo?'

'Around here, I guess.' Bjornson's eyes followed Gilmore as he moved the tripod around in the grass.

'By himself?'

'Probably with Injuns, or something.'

'And what was his trade?'

'Huh?' Bjornson tore his gaze away from the reporter.

'You claim he was supposed to have carved this rock? If so, how the devil did he do it? And where did he get the tools?'

'Where'd *your* grandpa fetch 'em?'

'How in tarnation did he get up there?' Purchase swept a hand up at the rock.

'How'd *yourn* get up there?'

'Hey, could one of you ladies lend me a hand?' Gilmore took off his hat and mopped his brow. Bjornson sprang to assist.

Torn with resentment, Purchase watched the two men move and set down the tripod, chatting amiably as they discussed angles and shadows. At one point, Gilmore went up and stamped his foot against the rock to illustrate a point. Finally satisfied, he ducked under the black sheet.

'Strike one!' he called after a minute, emerging from under the sheet. Changing the plates, he took another picture.

'Now, how about the front?' Gilmore and the willing Bjornson transported the equipment to the front of the rock, setting it back so as to hold the entire head in view.

'Hey, Purchase! Stand over here.' Gilmore beckoned with a wave of his arm. Bjornson had already positioned himself beneath the granite face, arms folded in a solemn pose.

'To blazes with all this horseshit!' Purchase turned on his heel.

'Where you going?'

'Anyplace that ain't here! You got five minutes to clear off my land.'

'What about the *Tribune*?'

'The hell with the *Tribune*! Print that!'

GILMORE RETURNED TO HIS home in Bismarck on the following day's train, carefully boxing the photographic plates for transport. When he reached Bismarck, the stringer wired the *Chicago Tribune* with the story, notifying the paper that the photographic plates were on the way. He received a reply from an editor two days later advising that the plates had arrived safely and were being processed. As for the story, it had been 'touched up', remarked the same editor, to 'give it some wire.'

Three days after that communication, the story appeared on the front page of the Chicago Tribune under the header "An American Sphinx!" The article featured a grainy photograph of Bjornson standing under the rock and staring gravely at the camera. Beneath the photograph ran the caption "Eighth Wonder of the World!"

One's first sight of the magnificent rock buffalo is on a stretch of flat prairie framed by majestic snow-covered peaks. The enormous creature, carved from sheer granite, stands a hundred feet high and, like the famed Egyptian Sphinx upon which it is modelled, stares blindly and enigmatically at the horizon. Different authors lay claim to the imposing edifice. The strongest claim is that of the local Indians, the fierce Sioux, who consider the buffalo to be a gigantic totem, carved by their remote ancestors. A more recent claim asserts that the carving is the handiwork of one Lars Bjornson, a master stone mason from the Nordic sounds who fashioned it out of admiration for the woolly creatures that once populated the plains in their countless millions. Lars, or Axel, Bjornson—he went by both names—likely came to America as part of the early wave of Danish immigrants who settled around the Chesapeake in the late seventeenth century. How he ventured out into the unknown to create his masterpiece is a secret lost to the mists of time. Needless to say, his claimed authorship is vehemently contested by the Sioux, who insist that their ancestors have worshipped at the rock for a thousand years or more. But these differing claims fade away into insignificance as the spectator stands in awe of the giant figure that dominates the lonesome landscape. Standing two hundred yards wide at the base, the monstrous likeness commands silent awe and admiration. The gigantic head is carefully detailed—the jaws curtained by a great, hanging beard, and the cranium anointed with two giant horns. The forelegs, flanks, and tail are also complete. The buffalo seems to rise up out of the entombing rock to utterly confound the spectator by its presence. It is a great and tragic irony that the massed bison herds that the figure symbolises have now vanished from the plains, and only it remains to remind us of their once miraculous profusion. The fact that the mighty monument is all but unknown outside a radius of perhaps twenty miles—stretching from the local town that bears its name, to the state capital, less than an hour's train ride away—is a mystery second only to the rock colossus itself. With the twin achievements of statehood and the pacification of the Sioux hordes who formerly ruled these plains and kept civilisation at bay, North Dakota has, as it were, thrown itself open for inspection. Surely, inevitably, the monument's fame will spread, and people will one day troop to marvel at it from all corners of these United States and, indeed, the great world itself. Standing in its mighty shadow, one is humbled by the knowledge that a proud, unknown race laboured in the dim and dusty past to give birth to this glorious totem. Truly, a sight for the ages! England has its Stonehenge. Egypt has its Sphinx and pyramids. And now, America has its buffalo!

The story aroused considerable interest and was reprinted in newspapers across the country. Among the curious readers was a Chicago speculator, Edison Lomax, who read it while smoking a cigar, feet up on the polished walnut desk in his tenth-floor office overlooking downtown. Setting the newspaper down on his lap, he stared out the window while puffing on the cigar. 'Willy!' he called out.

'Yeah, boss?' A small, slick-haired man in rolled shirtsleeves stuck his head in the doorway.

'You ever heard of a burg called Fort Buffalo, up in North Dakota?'

'Dakota? Beats me.'
'Call Butch and Leo. And check train schedules to the northern plains.'
'The northern plains? What in bejesus is up there 'cepting grass?'
'Suppose I told you a plum opportunity lies waiting?'
'If you say so, boss.'
'I do. Now go fetch the boys.'

32

A Homecoming

IN 1893, SEVEN YEARS after leaving home, 17-year-old Amity McLennan took the long train journey from St Charles back to Fort Buffalo. Her grandparents had insisted she travel first class, putting her into a Pullman sleeper car as far as Bismarck. There, the dozen or so passengers left onboard were herded onto a single, third-class passenger car. Soon after leaving the station, the train embarked on the long railroad bridge across the Missouri River. Amity pressed her face against the window to see the broad river where it flowed far beneath the tracks. Boats plied the flat, grey tide. She closed her eyes, trying to recall the long steamboat ride up the Missouri when she was a child. She imagined she remembered the steam whistle and the sight of buffalo running over the bluffs that flanked the river, and her father holding her up so she could better see their bobbing heads.

At Mandan, they switched trains again. An elderly man occupied the seat across from her, nodding by way of introduction before opening a paper he had purchased on the platform. He read the first page before dozing off, his head slumped back against the seat. She herself was tired from the long journey, but too full of nervous anticipation to sleep. *Will they recognize me? How will I seem to them. How will they seem to me?*

They passed a series of farmhouses set amid acres of blooming wheat. *Soon, pa will be taking in the harvest.* The train slowed as they clanked by a gristmill, a grain elevator, and a lumber yard stacked high with timber, none of which she remembered. Across from her, the elderly man had awakened and was bent forward in his seat to observe the scenery. The track skirted a road and they passed by several carts hauling farm produce. She gazed at a large factory with several freight wagons parked out front. The driver sounded the whistle, and a work crew standing outside a three-storey flour mill waved. A short time later, the train abruptly slowed as the brakes were applied. Then, with clanging bells and a long blast of the steam whistle, they chugged into Fort Buffalo station. She was home.

She stepped down to the platform, taking a porter's hand as he held it up to assist. She felt suddenly self-conscious in the fashionable coat and summer straw hat with its silk chiffon bow and trailing ribbons her grandmother had insisted she wear for the journey. 'So that everyone will know you are a respectable young lady.' Setting down the leather valise, she searched the faces of people waiting to meet the train. A cloud of steam erupted from the valves as a whistle sounded and labourers began to unload the baggage car. An elderly Black porter pushed a four-wheel trolley toward the mail car, tipping his hat as he passed by.

'Amity!' She heard a scream of excitement as her mother, flanked by her pa and brothers, hurried along the platform to greet her. 'Amity!' Felicity crushed her daughter in a tight embrace before holding her at arm's length to admire. 'You look a picture! And so tall—taller than me! Overcome with happiness at her daughter's return Felicity hugged her again and kissed her on the cheek.

'Am!' Her father embraced her, and she smelt the familiar odours of sweat, dung, and earth that always clung to him. 'Welcome home!' He held her tight, his eyes moist in his delight at her safe return. 'I've missed you, Am!' he said.

The childhood name sounded strange in her ears. *Nobody calls me that in St. Charles.*

Her brothers hung back, shy, and wary of this strange, fashionably clothed young lady they dimly recalled racing through the grass and playing fetch-stick with the dogs.

'Jubal! Boundary! Don't stand there like frogs on mud. Say hello to your sister!'

They half-embraced her, timid and clumsy. A moment passed as she took in her parents, saddened to see the lines on her mother's face and the grey hairs peeping from beneath her now faded purple bonnet. Her father, too, looked older, his face heavier and careworn.

'My Am. But you look different,' he said, taking her arm on one side while her ma took the other.

'Do I?'

'Of course you do, we haven't seen you in so long,' said her mother, squeezing her arm. They proceeded down the platform, the boys following behind carrying her valise between them.

They left the station and walked to where the wagon was parked, her mother chatting ten to the dozen and plying her with questions. 'How is grandma? And grandpa—does he still smoke that old pipe? And tell me all about the seminary and your lessons there. Did you know Boundary goes to school—or did I already tell you that?'

The summer day was hot and breezy. Her father helped her up onto the wagon, decorously tucking her coat around her as she sat. Her mother sat beside her, a proud look on her face. Her brothers sat in the back, staring at this exotic, perfumed creature that claimed to be their sister.

They drove slowly through the town, her eyes darting everywhere as she attempted to answer her mother's interminable questions. The town was larger than she remembered—more shops, more streets and houses, and certainly more people on the sidewalks.

'It's different,' she said, slightly dazed by it all, as she tried and failed to find the old general goods store.

'It's grown some.' Her father pointed to a fancy-looking hotel. 'That wasn't there last year. There's the new town hall.' He pointed to a three-storey brick building with a giant Stars and Stripes hanging from a pole out front. 'Of course, we're a state now,' he added.

Amity stared, overwhelmed by feelings of both familiarity and strangeness. A pedestrian waved as they wheeled past. Her pa raised the whip in acknowledgement. 'That was old Doc Henderson,' said her mother. 'You remember him? He treated you for that ear infection one time. You don't? I'm sure he remembers you.' They passed a storefront office and were hailed by a man just leaving the premises.

'Who's that?' she asked, half-turning.

'That's Mr Bellow. He runs the newspaper. Surely you remember the Dispatch?'

Leaving the town behind, they followed a beaten dirt road, passing several farms along the way. Where did they all come from? she wondered, trying to match the surroundings to her memory. She stared at a sturdy, whitewashed farmhouse set back from the road behind a wood fence.

'There's lots more folk moved here since you left,' said her father. 'I guess Eli Buskins was right about the railroad.'

'Eli Buskins?'

'The mayor. You remember him, surely?'

She nodded. 'He had a loud voice.'

Her pa chuckled. 'You do remember!'

The road threaded between fields planted with wheat and oats. In the distance, where the fields stopped, the prairie grass rose in swells to the horizon. The sky seemed bigger and bluer than she recalled. She felt suddenly unsettled and hankered to be back in her room in St Charles, far away from curious eyes and this wide, disconcerting openness.

'What is it, Amity? Are you not well?' Her ma placed a hand on her forehead.

'She's homesick,' said her father. 'That's all.'

'How can she be homesick when she's home?' piped up Boundary from the back.

The prairie vastness exercised its familiar spell as they continued and the conversation fell away, the horses snuffling and the wheels bumping over ruts. She looked around at the fields of grain, perturbed at her contrary emotions. The bouncing motion of the wagon gave her a vague headache as the tiredness she had felt on the train returned, making her long to close her eyes and sleep. The familiar shape of the rock rose up in the distance and she blinked, as if seeing it for the first time.

'It's still there,' her father joked, following her gaze.

Dust and wisps of grass had settled on her new coat, and she brushed them away. Something lodged in her throat, and she coughed to clear it, putting a gloved hand to her mouth. The wagon hit a rut and she slid in the seat, bumping up against her mother. She turned to check that her valise was safely stowed, and her eyes met her two brothers, staring as if she were some sort of strange sea creature, their mouths agape.

Her pa was talking, ruminating aloud as if she were still the child who loved to ride with him in the wagon all those years ago. He turned to look at her and she managed a smile. By the time they turned off the road and followed the track leading to the farm, she felt as if she simply must sleep. The dogs rushed up to bark and furiously wag their tails as she stepped down from the wagon. And, suddenly, she really was home again.

Emotion swept through her as she took in the house, the barn, and the corral. They were older, weathered, not the new-sprung buildings of memory. A dizziness swept over her, and she reached out to the wagon seat to steady herself. An old black dog hobbled up, whining with excitement. 'Jumpy!' She knelt and flung her arms around his neck. The dog squirmed in her embrace, twisting frantically to lick her face with his tongue. 'I missed you!' she cried, bathed in his warm, panting breath and pink tongue. And then she burst into tears.

OVER THE COURSE OF the next few days, she slowly reacquainted herself with the yard, the farm, and the familiar haunts of childhood. Wearing a straw, wide-brimmed hat against the sun, she purred to the horses, stroking their necks while resisting the impulse to climb and sit on the corral fence as she was wont to do as a child. She inspected the barn, wrinkling her nose in disgust at the powerful, almost-forgotten stench.

Accompanied by Jumpy, she made her way out to the blossoming fields where her pa and Jubal worked side by side. Her pa straightened up at her approach. 'Have you come to join us?' he called jovially, while Jubal simply stared. Plucking a wheat head, she rubbed it between her palms for the remembered feel of the grain. Her father wiped his hands on his dungarees. 'Are you glad to be back, Am?'

She slapped the grain from her hands. 'I think I'll go pay my respects to the buffalo,' she said.

'Be careful of the sun,' he warned. 'You'll need to get used to it again.'

The dog panted behind as she walked through the dry grass beyond the crop fields. The sky was blue and cloudless. A warm breeze chased through the reeds. She stopped to look around her. *This is what I dreamt of for so long.* She closed her eyes and tilted her face to the breeze, willing it to caress her, to sooth and rejuvenate as when she was a child. She breathed in the musty odour of shrubs and soil, the flowery scents of bluestem, dropseed, milkweed, and sweetgrass—even, she imagined, the moist, bracing smell of the wind itself as it swept over the grass, whipping up seeds and insects and blowing the clouds about the sky. *I belong here* she insisted to herself, and continued toward the buffalo, refusing to acknowledge the small yet insistent voice which whispered the attractions of St. Charles and all the clever diversions of the city.

SHE WAS SURPRISED TO observe a knot of people gathered beneath the rock. An omnibus stood in the grass, the two horses grazing and flicking their tails. Perturbed at this intrusion into what she considered a private retreat, she nevertheless smiled politely as a large, florid-faced man looked up and hailed her. 'Howdy there, missy! You all by yourself?' he asked, a surprised look on his face.

'I live just there.' She indicated the farmhouse.

'Oh, my! Well then, you must be well acquainted with the monument?' A woman carrying a parasol addressed her.

'Monument?'

The woman laughed. 'This astonishing creation! What else would you call it?'

'Be careful,' she said. 'There are snakes in the grass.'

The woman gave a tiny shriek and stepped back, tugging at her skirt. The other woman in the party followed suit.

The florid-faced man gave an affronted stare. 'No need for that,' he said, his voice testy. 'We're just here to admire the carving.'

'You say you live here?' a second man asked, his voice curious.

'I do.'

'Then you may know something about the history of this rock?' She felt the expectant gaze of the party.

'My great-grandfather carved it,' she said, pride investing her voice.

The man gave a shocked look. 'Your grandpa?'

'Surely it was the Indians, long ago?' one of the women protested. 'That's what the hotel clerk told us, in town.'

'He was wrong. It wasn't the Indians.'

The group exchanged looks. 'If you say so,' said the woman, disbelief in her voice.

'We came all the way from Bismarck just to see it,' said the florid-faced man, reasserting his importance as spokesman for the group.

'We didn't realise it was your rock,' the first woman said, her arch tone eliciting a titter from her companion.

'Not mine. My pa's. He owns this land.'

'Owns it?' The spokesman looked confused. 'No one said anything about that.'

'Those are our fields.' She indicated the flowering wheat, now encroaching to within a few hundred yards of the rock.

'We didn't mean to trespass,' said a third man, his voice expressing concern.

'It's all right. I'm sure pa won't mind. Come on, Jumps.'

She took her leave, feeling their eyes on her as she walked away.

'There are folk down at the rock,' she told her father on her return.

He made a grumbling sound. 'I can't keep them away ever since that fool reporter wrote about it.'

'Is it still on our land?'

Her pa looked surprised at the question. 'Where else would it be?'

33

Quintus Bellow

WHEN QUINTUS BELLOW, PROPRIETOR and editor of the *Fort Buffalo Dispatch*, decided to hire an apprentice, he remembered the boy who had run an errand for him some weeks previously. Accordingly, he invited Boundary McLennan to the newspaper office and watched approvingly as the candidate for the position exclaimed at the sight of the Washington handpress, running his hands over the iron frame and barely listening as Bellow explained what was required.

'You'll deliver newspapers, sweep up, fetch things, get wood for the stove and light it up in winter. What do you say, son? Would you be interested in working in a newspaper office?'

'Yes, sir!' The boy caressed the platen. 'And would I get to operate this?'

'As part of your duties, you'll help me run the press.' Bellow saw the boy's face light up at the reply.

'I'd say he's a natural, Beth,' he told his wife that evening, recounting the tale. 'Salt me if he didn't fall in love with the press soon as he laid eyes on it.'

Beth set down her sewing to think. 'McLennan? Isn't he the son of that crazy homesteader—the one that claims his daddy carved the buffalo?'

'One and the same—although I beg to differ. Purchase ain't crazy. He's a respectable citizen. Why, he's one of the town's oldest residents. He told me he was here back in the late sixties, when buffalo were still over-running the range.'

'Isn't the boy in school?'

'Sure, for now. He'll help out in the afternoons and on Saturdays for the time being.'

Beth resumed sewing. 'Did you speak to his pa?'

'No, but the boy will be going home this weekend. He's promised to ask permission and to get his pa to call in next time he's in town. Is that coffee I smell?'

SEVERAL TIMES THROUGHOUT THAT afternoon, Boundary—his head puffed with notions of operating the hand press—was reprimanded by an exasperated Miss Purlow. 'Boundary McLennan! Is the prospect outside the window so enticing that you neglect your lesson?'

'No, Ma'am.'

'Then kindly hold up your slate.' Switch in hand, she marched down to his stool. 'Let me see.' She peered at what he had written. 'What in gingham is that supposed to be?'

'That, I guess.' He looked at the blackboard and the list of words written there. His reply drew titters from the class, which in turn drew a sharp glance from Miss Purlow.

'Hush! You guess?' she said, turning back to Boundary. 'Well, I'd guess it looks like a poor attempt at copying the words. Hand out!'

The cane swished through the air, stinging his palm. 'And again!'

Wincing, he held out his hand again.

'And the other one!' The cane swished twice in succession. 'Now maybe you'll learn to pay attention and copy what's written—not to practise Arapahoe!'

Blowing on his sore and reddened palms, he glared at Silas Emerick, who sniggered into his hand.

Miss Purlow returned to the front of the room. 'Children! Sponge your slates. Let us turn our attention to arithmetic.' She wiped the blackboard with a damp cloth.

'Here is a sum for Group One.' She wrote two numbers on the board followed by a plus symbol. 'For Group Two.' She placed a minus symbol beneath the plus one. 'Group Three.' She added the multiplication symbol. 'And Group Four.' She added the division symbol to the list. 'Commence!'

The children perched on stools and boxes as they deliberated over possible answers, the older children in each age group taking the lead. 'Abigail Moore!' Miss Purlow pounced on a small girl with blond ringlets tumbling from beneath her plain white cap. 'Is this addition or subtraction—or something in between?'

'Please, Miss!' The girl burst into tears.

'Don't blubber. Take your slate and go sit in the corner until you've composed yourself.'

An interminable hour later, Miss Purlow clapped her hands. 'School is over for the day! Proceed quietly to the door.'

In the yard, Boundary shoved Silas Emerick, sticking his leg out and causing the other boy to fall over. 'Turkey face!'

'Turkey yerself!' The other boy sprang up and leapt for Boundary. Their schoolmates gathered around, chanting and clapping as the two rolled in the dust, kicking and punching as the spectators urged them on.

'Good gracious!' Miss Purlow appeared, scattering the watchers. 'You and you!' She gripped each combatant by the ear, tugging so hard the boys yelped. 'Inside! The rest of you go home.' She marched the boys back inside the schoolroom as the other children flocked around the single window to watch.

Five minutes later, both warriors emerged, painful looks on their faces as they rubbed their sore hinds to the merriment of their classmates. With dire glances in each other's direction, they went their separate ways.

SATURDAY AFTERNOON SEEMED AN age away, busting as he was to tell his ma and pa of Mr Bellow's offer. Twice, he had been back to the newspaper office, making himself useful by fetching copies and running errands, anxious to impress upon the publisher his eagerness to make the position his own.

As soon as school was dismissed, he set off for home, unwilling to risk his pa encountering Miss Purlow. He was two miles down the road before he saw the wagon trundling toward him, raising up dust in its wake.

'Whoa!' His pa drew up the wagon as Boundary scrambled aboard. 'I thought I told you to wait until I came and fetched you?'

'I reckon I was in a hurry,' he said.

'In a hurry for what?'

Unable to keep the excitement from his voice he blurted out his news. 'Mr Bellow offered me a job at the newspaper! Can I take it, Pa?'

'He did?' His father gave a look of surprise. 'If that don't beat all.'

'The newspaper office?' Felicity slapped the flour from her hands when told of the news. 'What would you do, exactly?'

'Sweep up. Fetch stuff. Operate the press. Please, Pa, it's what I want to do.'

'What about the farm? I figured you'd help out, along with your brother.'

He furrowed his brow, his face sullen. 'I don't care for farming.'

'And it don't care for you!' Jubal jutted his chin.

'Please, Ma?'

'How much will he pay you?'

'Nothing at first—until I learn—and then twenty-five cents a day.'

'That ain't much to live off.'

'At first. More later—when I quit school. He said so.'

'He'd be learning a trade, Felice.' His pa considered for a moment, noticing for the first time the ink stain on his son's shirt. 'I'll speak to Mr Bellow next time I'm in town.'

HOME BUT A MONTH, she felt itchy in her own skin. Her ma was a daily irritant, her pa was absorbed in his fields, and Jubal scraped on her last nerve. She wrote long passages in her journal bemoaning her exile from the diversions of St Charles. Shortly after her return, she had swapped the St Charles finery for a dress that had belonged to her mother, hoping the change of habit would help reclaim the ease and comfort in her surroundings she remembered from as a child.

She examined the result in the mirror, running a critical eye over the blue-floral cotton dress with its simple lace filigree neckline. The dress struck her as plain and sensible and … homespun. 'And I am homespun in it,' she opined, pondering her reflection.

Following a leisurely stroll, she made her way back to the house, Jumpy following. Her mother stood in the doorway, a cross look on her face. 'Where have you been, child? You'll catch fever in this sun if you ain't careful.'

'I'm sorry, Ma. I just needed to get me some fresh air.' She sat down in the rocker, fanning herself with her hat. 'Everything's different,' she complained, fanning.

''Course it is. Did you expect it to be the same?'

'No, I guess not.'

Her mother sat down holding a flannel shirt. 'Now that you're home, you can help out with the chores. What do you have in mind, anyhow? We haven't had a chance to talk.' She opened the sewing box.

'In mind?'

'Unless you plan to occupy that rocker for the rest of your days. What are you going to do with yourself?' Felicity took out some thread and a darning needle. 'You'll be eighteen come next birthday.'

'You make it sound so old!'

'Well, it is and it isn't, depending on what you plan to do.' Her mother sucked the end of the darning thread. 'If you're set on marrying, its young. If you're set on doing something else …' She didn't finish the thought.

'Marriage! Who'd I marry in this one-horse town?'

'There's dozens of young men around, I daresay.'

'Hayseeds and clodhoppers, every one of them!'

It was on the tip of Felicity's tongue to warn her daughter against sassiness, until she thought of her own mother. *Oh my!* She threaded the needle.

'I'll maybe get a job in town.'

'Doing what? They already got a schoolteacher.' Her mother pushed the needle through the fabric. 'I expect Jubal will be stringing next.'

'Jubal! He's but fifteen.'

'I didn't say tomorrow, did I? But he has his eye on that young Schamber gal.'

'Schamber?'

'The family that moved into the Hartmanns' old place, year afore last.'

'I don't know what I'll do.' She gave an exaggerated sigh, weary of everything.

'There ain't but two choices—seeing that teaching ain't open: a private tutor or to work in a shop—which would be a waste of all that education.'

'Maybe I could find work as a lady's companion or a governess—back in St Charles.' She glanced at her mother.

'You'd like that?'

'No.'

Unexpectedly, her mother laughed, a throaty sound that shook her chest as she sewed. 'You mind me of myself. I used drive Ma half crazy.' She chuckled at the memory.

'I'd like to visit town. Take a proper look around to see all the changes.'

'Ask your pa; he'll take you. Or maybe Jubal.'

'You wouldn't mind?'

Her mother put down the shirt. 'It ain't like there's so much to do around here—unless you plan to feeding the hogs.'

'I don't know what I want!' She moaned, miserable with the stultifying boredom.

'Give it time. You've only been back five minutes.'

'Did you know what you wanted?'

'Only to skedaddle away from pots and pans and such.'

'And then pa came along?'

'There were others interested, afore your pa.'

'Really? Who?' She looked at her mother, enjoying this rare intimacy.

'There was Teddy Wilson, for one.'

'Who was he?'

'The local butcher's boy. I never did care for him. One eye had a squint—like this.' Her mother contorted her face into a grotesque mask, causing Amity to giggle. 'I 'spect he's chopping and filleting right now, just like his pa.' She sewed for a minute. 'You've got to find your buffalo.'

'Pardon?'

'It's something Purchase's pa said to him after the war. It applies to men, mainly. Although I don't see why women shouldn't pursue a buffalo, too, if it takes them.' She closed her sewing box. 'It means finding something you'd like to do—that you couldn't imagine not doing.'

'Like that painter that visited us once?'

'Goodness. What made you bring him up?'

'I just thought of him—when you said that about the buffalo. Do we still have his drawings around?'

'I 'spect so. Somewhere.'

'I think I'd quite like to be a painter.'

'You would? Do you have any talent?'

'Miss Fitzgibbon, the art teacher, thought so.'

'And you enjoy it?'

'As much as anything.'

'Do you keep a journal?'

The question caught her by surprise. 'Yes. All the girls did—do.'

'Would you read it to me sometime?'

'Ma! Some things are private!'

'What's so private you can't tell your mother?'

'Did you show your journal to your ma?'

'Lord, no!' Felicity chuckled. 'But I suspected she read it anyway.' She set down the shirt. 'I still keep it most days—'cepting when I'm too tired, or I plain forget.'

'What do you write about?' asked Amity, curious.

'Things. The farm, your pa. Your brothers.'

'And me?'

''Course about you.'

'What sort of things?'

'It's just like writing a letter—only it's to yourself.'

'I'd like to read the parts—the early parts, when you were my age.'

'Maybe you will, one day. I'll leave them to you when I die.'

'All of them?'

'Mostly.'

'Mostly?'

'There are some things that ought to remain private.'

'What things!' Her eyes widened.

'Silly things, that's all.'

'Such as?'

'Such as why don't you fetch the broom and sweep before your pa and brother come back?'

'CHILDREN, WE HAVE A special treat today.' Her arms crossed in front of her, Miss Purlow surveyed the class. Beside her stood a burly man in a checked suit. A beige stretched waistcoat showed through the unbuttoned jacket. 'Do you know who this is?' Miss Purlow indicated the figure beside her.

'That's Charlie's pa!'

Laughter broke out as eyes turned to where Charlie Buskins squirmed with mortification.

'Hush now! That's right. This is Charlie's father. But do you know who he is in his official capacity? That means in his job of running the town?'

'The constable?' someone guessed.

'No, not the constable, although you're close. Anyone? Charlie, what's your father's job?'

'I reckon he's the mayor,' came the answer as the burly man beamed with satisfaction.

'That's right. And Mayor Buskins has taken the time out of his busy duties to speak to you today about the importance of a sound education. Mayor?' She stepped back.

'Thank you, Miss Purlow!' The mayor's stentorian voice caused the children to sit up. 'Miss Purlow is right, boys and girls. An education is the handiest thing you can ever have. It will stand beside you like a faithful comrade, helpful and forever willing to assist, wherever you go in the world.' He hooked both thumbs in the pockets of his waistcoat while gazing at each child in turn, a benevolent expression on his face.

'Whatever you want to be, three loyal companions—reading, writing, and 'rithmetic—will help you be it. I remember my own school days, when I was sitting where you are now—'cepting not here, but in Yankton—the only place with a school in those days. Did you think it ever crossed my mind to be mayor? Not likely!' He paused for chuckles. None being forthcoming, he continued. 'Why, you could even run for mayor yourselves, one day. You girls, too. I hear there's a town in Kansas that has already elected a woman to the post. What do you make of that? Charlie, sit up straight. The town's growing by leaps and bounds, and it will need folks who know how to read and write and gen'rally carry on. And you boys, you'll be expected to vote when you come of age. How will you know who to vote for if you can't read the papers or make up your mind if somebody's speaking guff?'

After a short oration on the wonders of the democratic ballot, the mayor finished by bidding the class, 'Tell your folks what you learned today, and who from,' and stood aside for Miss Purlow.

'Children, let us thank the mayor for his valuable words,' she said, and led the tentative claps.

'Pity they can't vote already!' Buskins joked before exiting the room. 'Bye, Charlie!'

Boundary watched through the window as the mayor hailed an acquaintance, ostentatiously raising his hat in the air to hold up a wagon as he crossed the street.

'What did you learn at school today?' Quintus Bellow asked his usual question as Boundary entered the office and tied an apron around his waist.

'The usual guff.'

'Guff?' Bellow uttered an exclamation and shook his head. 'Don't you know it's a privilege to attend school?'

'The mayor came.'

'He did? What did that two-dollar suit have to say?'

'Something about 'rithmatic.'

'Deuce and double deuce! I'd sharpen your ears with this pencil knife if I could. Do you want to be a newspaperman one day? Well?' He demanded as Boundary took a broom and began sweeping the floor.

'Do you mean a printer?'

'No, tarn! Set down that broom a moment and listen.' He waited until Boundary perched on a stool.

'Printing is only part of it—the mechanical part. There's also reporting—'

'And taking pictures? You promised you'd show me how the camera works.'

'Heavens to a crow! Yes, picture-taking, too. But that's more mechanics. If you want to be a proper reporter you must learn to look, observe, and, above all, listen! You've got to be able to sift—do you know what that means? It means you have to be able to pick through things, decide what's important and what's not. It's like a miner, panning for gold. He must be able to pick out the nugget from the twigs, dirt, and sand. Do you follow?' At the boy's grimace, he sighed and shook his head. 'Never mind—stop with the durn broom for a moment!' He pulled out a notebook. 'Tell me, what did the mayor say, exactly?'

'I can't work out whether the boy's an imbecile—in which case I shouldn't have hired him—or merely dull,' he complained to his wife over supper.

'I'm sure you're being too hard on him, dear. Boys are … *impenetrable*, sometimes. Things don't seem to stick with them as they do with girls.'

'Then maybe I should have hired his sister. She's back home, he tells me.'

'A girl? In a newspaper office?'

'Why not? The world is changing, Beth. According to Mayor Buskins, there's a female mayor somewhere up in Kansas.'

'Where'd you hear that?'

'From young Boundary—after I dragged it out of him.'

'Well, I never. Soup?'

34

Harvest Dance

'A MITY! QUIT MOPING AND go feed the chickens.'

'Yes, Mam.' She put away the journal, tucking it among her undergarments in the drawer.

'Gracious, girl. You look half-asleep. Your pa will nail that bedroom door shut one of these days and then where will you be?'

'Here,' she muttered, drawing a sharp glance from her mother.

The day was hot and sunny. A long trestle table had been set up in the yard. The table was already laden with bread and fruit and platters of ham and pork, the food covered with dampened cloths. Jubal, his face smudged with grime, was dragging wood benches into place. 'You still here?' He feigned astonishment. 'I figured you'd run off—hightailed it clear back to Missouri.'

She stuck out her tongue and picked up the scraps bucket.

Standing in front of the chickens, she scattered the feed, watching dispassionately as the hens clucked and bobbed—squawking and flapping wings as they came up against each other. Her thoughts drifted to the letter she had received the previous day announcing the betrothal of her best friend in St Charles. A hen pecked at her shoe, and she brushed it away. The late August day was stifling. She set down the bucket, shading her eyes to search the horizon. Nothing! She turned to look as a wagon drove into the yard. Her mother came out to greet it, calling out a welcome as several women aboard climbed down, cooing in acknowledgement. *Since when did Ma get to be so sociable?*

She watched as the women began transferring baskets of food. Her mother turned in her direction and called out.

'Amity! Fetch some water!'

'Yes, Mam.'

She made her way across to the well. Her father and brother, assisted by several neighbours, were harvesting the last of the winter wheat. Men were gathered around the steam thresher, the rhythmic thrum of its engine beating like the pulse of her own heart.

'Amity! Where's that water?'

She returned to the house to find the women busily preparing food. Her entrance caused a stir as the women clustered around to greet her.

'Goodness, Amity, you've shot up.' A plump, merry-faced woman pecked her on the cheek, reminding her of the hen pecking at her shoe.

'Thank you, Mrs. Gershon.'

'Isn't she a dish!' The women fussed over her for a moment, touching her hair and exclaiming at her smooth cheeks.

'My, but you've become a young woman!' A silver-haired woman familiarly known as Grandma Peters, kissed her on the cheek. 'How long has it been, dear, since you were home?'

'Seven years,' she said, trying her best to smile.

'Seven years! Imagine.'

'Are you coming to the dance next Saturday?' asked a young woman.

'Amity. This is Polly Emerick. Sally's oldest. She's but a year apart from you.' Her mother made the introduction as Polly smiled and touched her hand.

'What dance?'

'The harvest dance, silly! You *have* been away.'

This drew skitters of laughter even as Grandma Peters clapped her hands and summoned everyone back to work. 'The men will be here in a trice.'

She endured the communal feast, running to fetch more water or milk as dictated by the women while the men gobbled down the food—just like the chickens! She felt the eyes of several men on her as she served, and self-consciously flicked at her hair or smoothed her cotton dress. After the meal, as the men were preparing to leave, an older man winked at her, a leer on his face, while ostentatiously licking the corner of his mouth with his tongue.

'*Men are such frightful creatures.*' she wrote in her journal. '*I intend never to marry.*' The thought of what she *would* do returned to plague her as she suspended the pen over the page. '*Perhaps I shall be a governess to a wealthy family in New York,*' she mused, '*or a painter, living by my brush.*' The latter notion greatly appealed to her with its connotations of independence and possible celebrity. That afternoon, she requested her pa buy her an easel and art supplies on his next visit to town.

'An easel I can make,' he said. 'Just tell me how you'd like it.'

As Saturday approached, the family prepared for the harvest celebration to be held at the Zeller farm, three miles distant. Her mother baked all morning while Jubal washed in the tub outside in the yard and put on his best shirt.

'Am, ain't you getting ready?' her father asked, surprised at her lack of preparation.

In spite of her protestations that she had 'no use' for a dance, her parents insisted, her mother chiding her lack of sociability. 'We sent you to the seminary to learn some social charms, young lady,' she said. 'It's about time you used 'em.'

An hour later, she sat miserably in the back of the wagon as her father drove to the harvest dinner. Her mother sat up front, twisting to inspect Amity's bonnet. 'You can take it off after the first dance,' she said. 'And smile, if you want to find a partner. Jubal, I don't expect to see you fawning over that Susie Schamber. Allow the poor girl to breathe.'

THE DANCE WAS HELD in a clearing alongside the farmhouse. Several tables had been set up with food and drink. Boards had been laid down to form a dance floor along with some chairs for the musicians. Lanterns had been hung and colourful bunting draped from a beam. Gigs, carts, and wagons were parked in the grass, the unhitched teams grazing alongside. An air of festivity emanated from the dozens of neighbouring families and invited guests gathered for the event. Young men and women, dressed in their finest, stood in segregated groups, eyeing one another and gossiping as introductions were made and courtesies observed. A tall, rangy youth in a cloth cap was treading the boards as if practising his steps. 'That's Joe Buskins, the mayor's oldest,' said Polly Emerick, coming up to take her arm. 'He's as handsome as all get out!'

'But he gasses on like his pa!' Another young woman joined them, giggling at her own description.

'Amity, this is Elspeth Moore. Elspeth, this is Amity McLennan, just home from the seminary in St Charles—that's in Missouri.'

'St Charles!' The young woman gasped, putting a hand to her mouth. 'Why in pork fry did you come back here?' She wore a pink-and-white-checked gingham dress. She wore her blond hair swept up on her head in a fashion she had copied from a magazine.

'I ask myself!' The response drew laughter.

Two other girls came up to join them as Polly demanded to know all about distant St Charles. 'What fashions do the women wear?'

'And what was it like travelling all that way by yourself?' asked one of the other girls.

'And what are Missouri fellas like?' asked another.

She answered as best she could, embellishing where required for effect and drawing admiring gasps as she described the shops of St Charles and the gas lighting in the paved streets and the latest trend in women's hats— only partly inventing the latter.

Having exhausted her with questions, Polly linked an arm with Amity as Elspeth took the other. 'The three musketeers!'

'Look!' Elspeth leaned in. 'There's Ira Morgan.'

Amity gazed at where a tall, skinny youth stood with hands hanging by his sides. The youth looked uncomfortable in a white shirt festooned with a fulsome black cravat, brown linen waistcoat, and more or less matching pants. 'He's just turned twenty and looking to marry,' Polly whispered. 'He lives with his widowed ma not far from town. What do you think?'

'He resembles a scarecrow!'

Polly burst into laughter.

'True. All that's missing is a stick up the fundament!'

'Elspeth Moore!' Polly attempted to reprove her friend before collapsing into a fit of giggles.

'They're starting!'

To a ripple of anticipation, four men took up position on the chairs. One carried a fiddle, another a guitar, a third a banjo, and the fourth a concertina. The guests clustered around the improvised dance floor as the musicians struck up an opening jig. An older man in a stovepipe hat ventured onto the plank floor. 'Come on, ladies and gents. Don't be shy! Give it a whirl!' The worse for drink, he attempted a spin, propelling out his arms and tripping over himself in the process, evoking laughter and applause. Undeterred, he climbed back to his feet and proceeded to clog-dance in place, whooping and raising his hat.

'Old man Whitcomb,' Polly mouthed in Amity's ear. 'He ain't never nothing but lit.'

The band glided into a waltz, and one or two married couples clutched each other as they trod the plank boards to the music.

'Come on, folks! It's free as blazes!' Whitcomb staggered toward the crowd, drawing shrieks and laughter as several of the women evaded his attempts to haul them onto the dance floor.

'That's Jenny Parsons. Bold as I don't know what!' Elspeth nudged Amity as a young woman in a matching calico blouse and skirt stepped out with a young man dressed in a shiny brown suit. 'Where does she get the brass?'

The band struck up a polka, and Amity watched the young woman hop and skip to the lively air, seemingly oblivious to the crowd's admiring gaze. The dance floor began to fill up as more men and women took courage and joined the dance. To her surprise, she saw her own mother and father join in, her pa dragging her protesting mother onto the floor. She watched as her mother turned, rather stiffly, in her pa's embrace as the music played.

'Oh my!' Elspeth gave a gasp as Ira Morgan made his way over to where they stood.

'Would you like to dance?' The young man stood in front of Amity, his face serious in the lantern light. Up close, he struck her as bony and ill-formed in his tight-fitting waistcoat. Beside her, Elspeth and Polly waited with bated breath for her answer.

She was about to decline, graciously, as taught at the seminary, when Elspeth answered on her behalf. 'She'd be enchanted!' She accompanied the remark with an elbow in the back that drove Amity forward, almost into the embrace of the startled suitor. Biting her lip, she allowed the nervous young man to clasp her hand and lay his other hand on her waist.

Confident in her dancing skills, she did her best to appear poised and feminine as her partner stomped clumsily, trying his best to avoid stepping on her feet. She saw Jenny Parsons glance in her direction and inclined her head as though swept up in the music. Polly and Elspeth watched avidly as she passed in and out of the dancing couples.

Her partner was gawking at her, and she avoided his gaze, looking over his shoulder at where Jubal was laughing and sweeping Susie Schamber around the boards. *When did he get to be so free with the girls?* She saw her pa standing to one side, watching with a proud look on his face. She smiled and lifted her fingers in a wave. The music stopped and she found the young man staring at her, sweat gleaming on his brow, and an eager look on his face. Before she could disengage the band started up again, swinging into 'Camptown Races'. Whoops went up as couples swapped and linked arms to twirl and step to the rhythm. She found herself on the arm of a large, beefy man who reeked of sweat and drink. He spun her so hard she almost went flying back into the watching faces. Another man gripped her arm, vigorously pounding and swinging until she was dizzy. He breathed all over her, the smell of moonshine causing her to wrinkle her nose in distaste.

As soon as a break came in the music, she pulled away, avoiding Ira Morgan as she left the boards. Her companions were dancing. Polly waved an arm to urge her to join in, but she shook her head and made her way to a table where a group of women sat gossiping and eyeing the dancers.

'Amity. Why ain't you dancing?' Her mother sat down beside her. 'I saw you waltzing with that Ira Morgan?' The remark was a question rather than a statement.

'He's as clumsy as a three-legged cow.'

'He has an eye for you.'

'Tell him I have the whooping cough.'

'Here he comes. Tell him yourself.'

She looked up to see the young man advancing toward her.

'Good evening to you, Ma'am.' The youth bent his head politely to her mother. 'Amity, may I fetch you a libation?'

'No, thank you. I'm just taking a spell.'

'Then do you mind if I join you?'

She had a headache, she was quite sure. She felt her mother poke her to reply. 'Why not?' she said, feigning a brightness she did not feel. 'Oh, there's Poll!' She jumped to her feet. 'Why not sit with Ma for a while? She loves company. Polly!'

EACH DAY, AS SOON as school was dismissed, Boundary raced to the newspaper office, watching with keen interest as his employer inked the forms or 'cooked up' a fresh batch of ink over the stove in the back of the shop. His duties included running around town to deliver flyers or advertisements created on the press. He picked up notices for inclusion and dropped off print sheets in between sweeping, cleaning, and fetching coffee.

He quickly became acquainted with every establishment in town, running from the hardware store to the freight yard and from there back to the hotel or over to the telegraph office to pick up the daily wire from the Associated Press. To his delight, he became a focus of interest both at school and in his own home as he recounted tales of the personalities and types encountered during his busy afternoons.

'Mr Cornwallis at the stables has a shiner on account of a quarrel with Mr Svenson,' he bragged to a wide-eyed audience of his peers at recess. 'Mrs. Wilson is worried that her youngest has droop-eye,' he recounted to his family at the supper table. 'And I reckon she's right! I took a squint in the cot while she wasn't looking and heavens to a crow if it didn't squint back up at me!' he said, employing one of Mr Bellow's favourite expressions.

But his most intense gratification came upon those afternoons when he assisted his employer to set type, ink the forms, place the paper on the tympans, and roll the form under the platen. The glow on his face as he watched Mr Bellow hold up the freshly inked sheet for inspection was a source of considerable satisfaction to his employer. 'I don't believe the boy knows, or cares, what's printed on the sheet,' the latter remarked to his wife. 'All he judges on is the crispness of the print and the look of the whole. Hang what the thing actually says.'

'You must bring him for tea,' said his wife, her maternal curiosity aroused. 'What is it?' she asked as her husband gave a chuckle.

'His face and hands are generally so smudged with ink you'd mistake him for a blackamoor!'

Intensely bored with school, Boundary fidgeted throughout the day, drawing the ire of Miss Purlow. 'You loaf about like a wounded hog and then—miraculously! —dash like a jackrabbit at dismissal,' she remonstrated. 'You'll be of no use to Mr Bellow if you can't read the print blocks, will you?' From the look on his face, she correctly judged that was the way to motivate him. From then on she linked his handwriting to blocks of type, nodding as she noticed an improvement in the way he rounded his capitals and elongated his *gs*. 'Maybe the *Dispatch* won't read like a Chinese puzzle, after all,' she commented, holding up his slate for inspection.

His aptitude for mechanics saw him called upon to fix broken chairs, refasten the blackboard, and tighten the hinges on the schoolroom door. 'That is where your abilities lie,' Miss Purlow remarked as she watched him kneel to do the latter. 'But remember, young man, strong hands are only useful when governed by a sound brain. Do you understand?'

'Yes, Ma'am.'

'And do you enjoy working for Mr Bellow?'

'I guess so.'

'Tell me, does that gentleman from the bank—what is his name? —ah! Mr Erickson, I believe. Does he ever have occasion to visit Mr Bellow?'

'Sometimes.'

'What for?'

Boundary shrugged, intent on the hinge. 'Business, I guess.' He knelt back, surveying the mended hinge. 'That should hold it.'

'And do you intend to be a newspaper man, like Mr Bellow?'

'I guess so. I like to print stuff. And maybe take pictures.'

She sighed. 'Such a scholar! All right, run along.'

AMITY HAD NO SOONER come into possession of the homemade easel and a supply of paints and brushes than her ma received word, courtesy of Mrs. Emerick, that the new haberdashery and dress shop in town was looking for an assistant.

'A shop assistant?' She felt faint at the prospect.

Her mother regarded her, a slightly shrewish look on her face. 'Why not? I worked in my pa's hardware store for years.'

'But my painting?' She gave an anguished glance at the easel—already stretched with a sheet of gleaming white paper.

'It ain't going nowhere. You can paint in the evenings or on your days off.'

'Ma!'

'It ain't no use wailing, neither. You've got two hands and legs, put them to use. We ain't so rich you can afford to lie about like a skinned snake. Jubal will drive you into town tomorrow. Her name's Mrs. Hedgepeth. She's a widow, by all accounts.'

'I'll die in a musty old shop!'

Her ma tutted with impatience. 'You can stay in town during the week—with Mrs. Halverson, where your brother lives when he's at school.'

'I'll perish from boredom!' She burst into tears. 'I hate that dusty old town! There's nothing to do or see.'

'Jubal will drive you in after breakfast. Put on that blue cotton dress with the bow, and the blue bonnet. And do something with your hair—it looks a fright.'

Next morning, pale and miserable, she sat alongside Jubal as he drove the wagon into town, each passing mile seeming to seal her doom. Jubal was chatty and good-humoured as he drove. 'You'll like Mrs. Halverson. She's easy-going—easier than ma—and her husband's tolerable, too.'

She gripped the seat as the wagon bounced over a rut. *I'll be horrid to this old Hedgepeth, whoever she is. So horrid she'll chase me out of the shop.*

'I guess you gotta do something.' Jubal was looking at her. 'Cain't jest lie around like a stick all day long.'

'Maybe I'll leave, next week. Go back to St Charles! Did you ever think of that?'

'Ha! And do what, work in Grandpa's store?'

'Maybe I will!'

'Maybe you won't!'

They entered onto the main street of town, the horses raising dust in the fall air. They drove slowly along the street, looking for the shop. 'Whoa!' Jubal drew rein outside a small store with a tailor's dummy in the bay window. Over the window was written, in fresh paint, *Women's Finery and Haberdashery.*

'I'll wait for you here,' he said. 'Or if I ain't here, just wait by the wagon.'

'Where will you be?'

'Shucks, here and there.'

He held out his hand to help her down from the wagon seat. 'Ma says to be sure that you ain't rude. I told her that was just nature.' He laughed at the joke.

'Go find that cross-eyed Susie Schamber—if she'll have you.'

'I reckon she will, just fine!'

'Well, fine then!'

She opened the door to the shop, hearing a bell ring as she did so. A plain-looking woman sitting behind a wood counter got to her feet. 'Yes?'

'I'm here about the assistant position, Ma'am.'

'Indeed?' The woman approached and looked her up and down. 'Your name, young lady?'

'Amity McLennan, Ma'am,' she said, and curtsied.

Widow Hedgepeth was a slim woman in her fifties. Her grey hair was pulled back into a tight bun and fastened by an elaborate clip. She wore a long, black apron over her woollen dress, and a shawl around her shoulders. She wore small readers perched on her nose and used mainly, as far as Amity could tell, for peering over. Her eyes were bright and inquisitive behind the lenses. 'And how old are you, Amity McLennan?' Her voice was dry and abrupt.

'I'll turn eighteen in a few months, Ma'am.'

'And have you ever worked in a shop before?'

'In my grandpa's hardware store in St Charles, Missouri. I helped out on weekends.'

Mrs. Hedgepeth peered over the readers. 'Hardware? That's a long ways off hats and notions.'

Amity said nothing, raising her gaze to glimpse the shelves—stocked with rolls of fabric and buttons and gewgaws. The shop smelt stuffy and close. A large, walnut clock hung on the wall, its ticking clearly audible.

'You can sew, I expect?'

'Yes, Ma'am. I can.'

Mrs. Hedgepeth sniffed. 'So many girls nowadays can't.' She resumed her visual inspection, taking in Amity's leather shoes beneath the ankle-length dress. 'And are you of good character, Amity McLennan? Do you have folk that can vouch for you?'

'I do, Ma'am.'

'And where did you attend school?'

'The Ladies Seminary in St Charles, Missouri.'

'Indeed?' Mrs. Hedgepeth raised her eyebrows. 'Well, that counts for something. Let's find out some more about you. Follow me.' The widow led the way to the back of the small shop, where a sewing machine and two chairs were positioned. 'Sit down. Tell me more about yourself.'

'Yes, Ma'am.' She took a chair, feeling she might die. *It's just temporary, 'til I find a position as a tutor or governess. And if not, I'll suffocate myself in a roll of muslin.*

35

A Bower in the Heart

THE 12:10 PM FROM Bismarck pulled into the station five minutes ahead of schedule. A party of four men stepped onto the platform and stood for a moment, conferring. A porter pushing a two-wheel trolley approached the group to ask about baggage. A man dressed in a suit and a homburg turned to a companion wearing a flat cap. 'Willy. Follow him to the baggage car. Make sure he gets all our bags.'

'Sure thing, boss.'

'And the guns!' another man, a tall, broad-shouldered individual wearing a Stetson and carrying a cloth valise called out.

Ten minutes later, the group emerged from the station, blinking as they took in the dusty main street and plank sidewalks. 'What kind of a shit burg is this?' The broad-shouldered man curled his lip in disdain as he surveyed the street.

'What it is, Butch, is a gold mine, if we play our cards right.'

'If you say so.' The other man's voice was sour.

'Pardon!' A breathless man hurrying to the depot narrowly avoided colliding with the party.

'Durn knucklehead!' The big man gave the pedestrian a menacing stare. 'Watch your step or I'll bang your brains!'

'Now, now, Butch. Apologies, sir.' Edison Lomax flashed a smile at the shaken pedestrian. 'My companion just arrived and is a mite testy on account of the heat and such.' The pedestrian swallowed nervously and hastened off.

'We're here to make friends, Butch. Keep yourself in check.'

'These one-horse towns get my goat.' Butch turned to look behind him. 'Where's that damn Willy?'

'Leo. Go check if the numbskull ain't got himself lost. We'll wait for you at the hotel.'

'Be right behind you, boss.' The fourth member of the party, Leo, a stout individual sporting a bushy moustache, a brown suit, and a derby hat, took his leave.

Lomax and Butch, the latter holding tightly to the valise, made their down the sidewalk. 'Hey, kid!' Lomax accosted a boy in a cloth cap carrying a box in his hands. Can you direct us to the hotel?'

'Which one?'

Butch hawked in the dust. 'More than one? Marvels never cease.'

'The Dakotan,' said Lomax.

The boy turned, clutching the box. 'Straight down the street, on your right.' He nodded to indicate the location.

'Thanks, kid. Here.' Lomax pushed a nickel into the boy's shirt pocket.

'Gee. Thanks, mister!'

'See, Butch. Sweet, not sour.'

'There's always sour.'

'You may be right about that.' Lomax tapped the valise the other man carried. 'But let's try the honey first.'

'Hey, here come the fellas,' said Butch as Willy and Leo appeared, pushing a baggage cart.

'Where'd you get the durned trolley?' asked Butch.

Willy beamed. 'Lifted it while the porter wasn't looking.'

Lomax laughed. 'That's the ticket!'

After checking in at the hotel, Lomax sent Willy off on an errand to locate the telegraph office.

'Right now, boss? I could use a drink.' Willy slicked a hand through his hair, a grimace on his face. 'There's so much dust in this shithole I could pass on dinner.'

'No time like the present. Leo, wire Jay that we're here. And line up a ride for tomorrow morning. Say, nine a.m. sharp.'

'A ride? What for?'

'Ain't you keen to lay eyes on what fetched us here? Sweet Jesus!' Lomax shook his head at the mystified look on the other man's face.

'Oh! Sure thing. Nine a.m.'

'Butch, let's look around. See what's what.'

'And who's who?'

Lomax nodded. 'That, too.'

ALREADY SICK TO DEATH of the stuffy little shop and the smell of linens, yarns, and threads, Amity compressed her lips into what she hoped was a sympathetic look as she listened to Mrs. Hedgepeth complain yet again about the rowdy saloon up the way, and the dung—'droppings,' the widow decorously termed it—dropped by the horses to fester in the thoroughfare. 'Close the door against the stink!' she shrilled each time Amity entered the shop. 'Lord knows but the malodorous air will contage us all!'

On finishing work each day, Amity walked straight back to the Halversons' for supper—shared with Boundary—helped clear away the dishes afterwards.

She then retired to her room, where she read a novel or flipped through a book of poems while lying miserably on the bed and imagining herself elsewhere—living, not perishing. She reflected enviously on Boundary's job at the newspaper office, bemoaning his engagement, however indirect, with the affairs of the world, while she smothered to death amid rolls of yarn and whatnots. *Why should only men lead interesting lives? Here I am, choking for air while Boundary gets to see and hear the comings and goings of the world. And he don't give a straw hat for either! It just ain't fair.*

She earned three dollars a week, half of which went to Mrs. Halverson to pay for her room and board. The remainder she carefully wrapped in brown paper and tucked underneath her mattress. On Sundays, she returned home, sometimes visiting with Polly Emerick or Elspeth Moore.

One balmy summer's day, the three friends enjoyed a picnic down by the creek. Peppering a hard-boiled egg, Amity listened with an impatient air while her companions gossiped of potential suitors or the prospect of fleeing Fort Buffalo for Bismarck, or maybe even Kansas City.

'What do you think, Am?' Polly was looking at her, a cream bun suspended in her hand.

'I think I'd like to be able to fly.' Finishing the egg, Amity lay on her back looking up at the sky.

'I hear your brother's landed himself a job at the newspaper office.'

'For all the good it will do the world!'

'How old is he?' asked Elspeth with a mischievous glance at Polly.

'He ain't but thirteen.'

'And still in school?'

'Ma reckons if he stays on long enough, something might stick.'

Polly lay down beside her, gazing up at the clouds. 'I wish I could fly, too. See that cloud—the one shaped like a face?'

'Where?' Amity shaded her eyes.

'There! I reckon it's Doc Henderson. I swear if that ain't his nose.'

'Or something!' They giggled.

Polly sighed. 'I sure wish I could work for money, like you, Am.'

'Slavery, more like!' She put on a high, fluting voice. "Girl, close that door—it ain't a barn! Don't just stand there, fetch the lady a chair!'

Polly laughed. 'Is she that tiresome?'

'Only between the hours of nine and six. But I'm fairly certain she dances at the saloon of an evening—in feathers.'

They lay looking up at the cloud-flecked sky.

'I wandered lonely as a cloud.' Polly spoke the line with a dramatic flourish.

'Oh, my favourite! Do recite it, Poll.'

Polly obliged, pausing theatrically before the final line, *'And dances with the daffodils!'*

Elspeth clapped. 'Your turn, Am,' she said.

Amity thought for a moment, and then wet her lips.

'Because I could not stop for Death —
He kindly stopped for me —
The carriage held but just ourselves —
And Immortality.

'We slowly drove —He knew no haste,
And I had put away
My labor, and my leisure too,
For his civility —

'We passed the school, where children strove
At recess —in the ring —
We passed the fields of grazing grain —
We passed the setting sun —

'Or rather —he passed us —
The dews drew quivering and chill —
For only gossamer, my gown —
My tippet only tulle —

'We paused before a house that seemed
A swelling of the ground—
The roof was scarcely visible—
The cornice —in the ground—

'Since then —'tis centuries—and yet
Feels shorter than the day
I first surmised the horses' heads
Were toward eternity—'

Elspeth pushed up on one elbow. 'I don't understand. Who's the author?'

'Tennyson?' guessed Polly.

'Uh-uh,' Amity shook her head.

'Browning?'

'Nope.'

'Who, then?'

'Emily Dickinson.'

Elspeth frowned. 'Never heard of her. Have you, Poll?'

'She's American. We studied her works in the seminary. She was a favourite of our arts teacher, Miss Fitzgibbon.'

'Imagine. To be a poetess!' Elspeth let out a sigh.

'Or to be married to a poet!'

'I hear Ira Morgan pines for you, Am.'

Elspeth giggled. 'The poor boy is said to be at death's door. One dance and he was stricken.'

Amity sat up, flicking grass from her hair. 'He can pine until he turns to wood! I have no interest in marrying—Ira Morgan or anyone else.'

'Then how will you live? With your ma and pa all your life?'

'I intend to make my own way in the world. As a private tutor, per-haps—or a journalist.'

'Let's run away together.' Polly smoothed her linen dress.

'We could be cowboys.'

'Or missionaries in the South Pacific.'

'Anyplace but here!'

'I wish to find a kindred soul.' Polly drew a theatrical hand across her forehead. 'Why is that so hard?'

'It's this starchy old town. How is a girl to find a man to admire in such a one-horse burg?' Elspeth pouted her lips in determined fashion. 'What do you say, Amity? Shall we abscond this dreary backwater? We could pan for gold and live as rich, independent women.'

'Independence is in the heart,' said Amity, echoing Miss Fitzgibbon.

'It is?' Polly looked disappointed. 'Drat!'

POLLY'S ELDEST BROTHER, TOM, drove Amity back to town, constantly eyeing her in a manner she found vexing. 'Aren't you scared your eyeballs will pop out?' she said when finally exasperated by his sidelong glances.

'My eyeballs ain't going nowhere!' he said angrily, the response so absurd she giggled, and giggled again each time she thought of it, all the way back to Mrs. Halverson's.

'Here we are,' he said, pulling up the horse, his voice and manner stiff.

'Thank you, Tom, for the ride,' she said, suddenly contrite.

'I guess it was jest a ride! Git!' He shook the reins. She watched him go, flicking and snapping the reins.

That evening she put out the lantern and climbed into bed, gloom descending upon her as she weighed her prospects for happiness. *If I was a painter, I at least could maybe travel, like that queer poke of a creature that turned up on our doorstep all those years ago. What happened to him, I wonder? Is he back in London, or Paris, or somewhere else entirely?*

She sighed into the pillow, recalling his ridiculous appearance and obsessive desire to paint the rock. *He was free, at any rate. There's much to be said for that, no matter his ghoulish air.* She thought about the rock for a while, picturing where it rose up into the sky. *It will stand there forever. Long after ma and pa and me and Jube and Boundary are gone.* The thought saddened her.

"Time is short, girls, shorter than you can imagine. Do something with your lives." Miss Fitzgibbon paused, a faraway look in her eyes. "No matter your circumstances, think of all the things you can do to be free. Write, paint, compose—only create some small bower in your heart. A place to repose amid the cares of the day." Her voice took on a fervent, haunted quality as she surveyed her charges. "As women, we must create such a refuge, even though burdened with toil. Fashion a bower and festoon it with your favourite colours and flowers. Do this for yourselves. Find that garden within and you shall be free in spite of all."

A deep sigh escaped Amity, and she lamented into the pillow. 'Where in lickety-split is *my* buffalo?'

36

'No Free Gawks!'

QUINTUS BELLOW PUFFED ON a Spanish cigar and congratulated himself on his present good fortune. His wife, Beth, nodded approvingly as he read aloud from his latest front-page philippic on the licentiousness of modern literature, the missive warning parents against permitting daughters to read novels unsupervised for fear of improper incitement and the inculcation of indecorous feelings.

He followed this opinion with a letter, purporting to come from a concerned citizen, but penned by himself, decrying the lax licensing regulations which permitted yet another tavern to open. The letter quoted freely from an adjoining jeremiad against Sunday trading, and yet another which urged the removal of all limits on tavern hours, the juxtaposition concerning the proprietor not a whit. 'It simply adds gravitas to the argument,' he explained to his wife.

To stir up readership and improve circulation, he planned to pen a bristling reply to the aforesaid letter and was engaged in a search for suitable passages of scripture to buttress the response. 'A judicious quotation saves a fair amount of thinking,' he advised Beth as she helpfully thumbed through the Bible in search of Hebrew prohibitions against taverns.

Circulation was up to three hundred copies a week, a high-water mark for the paper and a source of immense gratification to the proprietor. The miscellany of wire stories, moral essays, articles on husbandry, jokes, songs, poems, court trials, Indian customs, medical advice, farming tips, and predictions as to the weather had firmly cemented the weekly in the affections of the town and surrounds, and even brought it to the attention of the *Bismarck Tribune* which, twice in the past month, had quoted from its pages.

To his delight, the paper was now a recognised and respected authority in local affairs, the organ of first resort when opinions were sought as to the rightness or wrongness of council decisions. The editor's sharp cynicism regarding politicians was taken as a sign of the paper's robust and independent voice. As sole publisher within the town, he was regularly courted by the mayor and various councillors who vied for his backing whenever factionalism within the council threatened to boil over into lawsuits and public brawls.

'The reputation and integrity of this publication are not for sale!' he blasted on one occasion, roundly condemning the state commissioners when they sought his backing for a contentious new bill which threatened the livelihood of several small business holders by proposing a revaluation of property taxes. The editorial won much favour with the townsfolk while earning him the enmity of the town constable, who stood to benefit handsomely from the bill through a tax reduction on several properties he had recently acquired in a less desirable part of town.

'There's shady business in the poorer parts of town,' Bellow had written in a thinly disguised attack on the constable, drawing on information supplied by the town treasurer, who had bid for the same properties himself, acting on the same inside information about plans by the railroad to build a new hotel in the area. A visit from the constable, a grim, overbearing figure, had failed to deter him from attacking the bill—his only precaution being to hire a night watchman to stand guard over the premises in the face of veiled threats by the elected official.

'That fool is all puff and bluster,' he reassured his anxious wife when rumours of the threats reached her ears. 'He's so corrupt it's a wonder he doesn't stew in his own juices.'

'But he has friends, dear; important people.'

'More important than the press? I'd back my lead soldiers against his drunken cronies any day of the week, and you can throw in public holidays as well!'

To add to his satisfaction, the young apprentice, McLennan, was proving commendably industrious. The boy had already become an expert in operating the handpress and mixing up and applying ink. Indeed, so taken was he by the boy's enthusiasm for every task that he had begun to introduce him to the commercial side of the business, instructing Boundary in the principles of charges and accounting.

'Classify all commercial notices into vice and virtue,' he tutored. 'Generally, add five percent to the former as they pay handsomely and on time whereas honest folk tend to be tightfisted. Taverns come under vice as do 'baccy notices and anything pertaining to entertainments. Baptists and Bible sellers, on the other hand, fall under virtue—excepting for travelling preachers, who are gen'rally no better than snake-oil salesmen.'

The boy learned quickly, rarely having to be told anything twice. And except for the incident where he mistook the founder of the Temperance Society for a dancehall girl, acquitted himself tolerably well with the public. The impulsive streak evident in his nature had been kept under restraint largely, Bellow congratulated himself, on account of his own manly stewardship and wise counsel.

These feelings of fatherly interest were only somewhat modified by the boy's continuing and baffling disinclination to take any interest in the journalistic part of the enterprise. He tested this resolve by offering to allow Boundary to pen an anonymous letter protesting the town treasurer's latest antic—being discovered in a drunken fit in the middle of Main Street. But after several drafts, he was forced to conclude that oratory of any sort was beyond the boy's capabilities. 'The words are there, sure enough,' he admitted to Beth, 'but the feeling for the felicitous adjective, the sentiment to grow and nurture a fetching turn of phrase, are all lamentably deficient. The boy is as he is,' he concluded. 'Manifestly plain and blunt in all his ways.' He sighed and drew on the cigar.

'He's but thirteen!' his wife protested.

'Old enough to learn. I spoke to his teacher, Miss Purlow, last week, inquiring about his schoolwork.'

'And?' she prompted as he reflected on the cigar.

'She rolled her eyes.'

'She never did!'

'Metaphorically. She allowed how he preferred scratching and itching and peering out the window to anything that smacked of learning.'

'I'm sure he'll improve, from your example, dear.'

'You've met him; what's your opinion? Should I keep him on?'

Beth put down the cushion she was needleworking and adjusted her reading glasses. 'I must say, he struck me as somewhat … ' She searched for the adjective, her husband gazing at her, keen to contribute should the *mot juste* escape her. 'Buffaloish!' She exclaimed.

Her husband blinked at the descriptor, preferring instead his own candidate, which he now trotted forth for consideration. 'I know what you mean, dear,' he said sympathetically. 'I myself have often had occasion to refer to his …'—he paused—'intemperateness.' His wife smilingly acknowledged his mastery and picked up the cushion again.

He eased his belly and flicked ash off the cigar, mentally adding the phrase to his epistle against the council's closed-door decision to transfer ownership of several downtown lots back to the railroad free of charge save for a mysterious 'transfer fee' proposed by the treasurer and seconded by the constable. '*Cui Bono?*' he captioned the story, mentally spiking it until such time as his informant inside the council provided more details.

'All in all, things are progressing as they should,' he congratulated himself over a glass of brandy after supper. 'And as for that bonehead of a constable …' Rankled at the memory of the latter striding into his store and brandishing the offending, rolled-up newspaper, he blew out an indignant stream of smoke.

'WHAT DO YOU SEE, boys?'

'A mighty big lump of rock!'

'And what else?'

Willy looked around the bare pastures. It was midmorning and nothing moved except the wind in the grass. The rock loomed above them. The surrey was parked by the road, the driver watering the horses. 'What do you see, boss?'

Lomax grinned. 'I see money!'

''Course you do!' Leo whistled as he stared up. 'Holy Hannah! Would you jest look at it.'

'Even Butch is impressed.'

The latter spat tobacco juice into the grass. 'You telling me some Injun made that?'

'Injun!' Willy hooted. 'Can you see a no 'count redskin coming up with that?'

'There ain't no way,' agreed Leo. 'How in moonshine would he have got up there for starters? It would take a tribe—hell, a thousand Injuns—to carve such a thing. What do you reckon, boss?'

'I see a rest station there, for the ladies.' Lomax pointed to the grass. 'And there, a bar where the men can slake the dust from their throats.' He turned to survey the way they had come. 'And a tarred road, all the way back to town.'

'And guides?' said Leo. 'Someone to show the suckers—beg pardon, visitors—around.'

'Fill 'em up with whackadoo,' grunted Butch.

'And souvenirs,' continued Lomax. 'We can knock off chips and sell 'em for fifty cents each.'

'Stands to reason. Who wouldn't want a piece of the buffalo?' said Leo.

'We need to fence it off, charge admission. Say, two bits a head. No free gawks!' Lomax raised a hand to block the sunlight as he looked up. 'Ain't it grand, though, boys? The marvel is it's stood here so long, and no one's thought to cash in.'

'Someone's coming, boss.'

A figure approached through the bordering fields. 'That's my rock!' he called out as he drew near. 'And this is my land!'

'His land?' Leo glanced at Lomax in confusion. 'Did he say his land?'

Lomax frowned as the man approached. 'I thought this was public land?'

'Well, it ain't.' Purchase stopped, catching his breath. 'It's my land. And I'll thank you to stay off it.'

'And if we don't care to?' Butch squirted tobacco juice into the grass, a menacing look on his face.

'Hold up.' Lomax raised a hand. 'You claim this is your land—not public freeway?'

'That's what I said.'

Lomax appeared dumbfounded by the news. 'And this?' He gestured to the rock.

'That's mine, too.'

'How in hickory can you lay claim to a durn rock?' demanded Leo.

'It's on my land. Therefore, I own it.'

'Like I own the shit under my feet,' said Butch. He chewed the tobacco plug, moving it slowly and deliberately around his mouth as he regarded Purchase with a truculent stare.

Lomax plucked at his chin, frowning as he considered the information. 'How much of the land around here do you own?'

'Just about all you can see.'

'And that's your farm?'

'It is.'

Lomax flapped at a buzzing fly. 'And suppose I offered to buy it—this portion right here, where the rock is?'

'It ain't for sale.'

'You a homesteader? You filed claim on it?' demanded Leo, a belligerent tone to his voice.

'I did, if it's any of your business.'

Lomax extended his hand. 'Edison Lomax, friend, Chicago. With whom do I have the pleasure of speaking?'

'Me.' Purchase refused the proffered hand, earning a slit-eyed stare from Butch.

'And you are—for reference?' Lomax dropped his hand, apparently unfazed by the slight.

'McLennan. Purchase McLennan.'

'Well, Mr McLennan, you haven't heard my offer.'

'And I don't care to. The land ain't for sale.'

'At any price?'

'That's right.'

'It don't look much of a farm. More like a stinking compost heap!'

'Now, Leo, don't insult Mr McLennan. He looks a reasonable man, open to negotiation.'

'I ain't.' Purchase turned to go. 'I'll thank you to clear off my land as soon as possible.'

Lomax watched Purchase walk off. 'Jesus H. Christ!' He thrust his hands into his pockets, greatly put out. 'Nowhere did it say it was on private property!' He kicked at a root, his face tight with frustration.

'He's just a no-account shit-heel! Want me to handle him?' Butch stared venomously at the departing Purchase.

Lomax took a deep breath, controlling himself. 'No, not yet. Willy—' He turned to his offsider. 'When we get back to town, wire Chicago. Tell Jay to get himself up here double-quick.' He thought for a moment. 'Tell him look into this clodhopper. What was his name?'

'McLennan. Purchase McLennan.'

The name drew a hoot from Willy.

Lomax stared at the rock, his brow furrowed. 'Tell Jay to stop off at the Land Office in Bismarck on the way.

'Bismarck?'

'You heard him. He said homesteader. He must have filed a claim somewhere. Likely they have a record in Bismarck.'

'You think there may be something there—at the Land Office?' Leo raised an eyebrow.

Lomax nodded, a thoughtful look on his face. 'There's always something. You just gotta find out what it is—and where it's hid.'

'And if there's nothing?'

'Then you plant something,' snarled Butch. 'After all, he's a farmer, ain't he?'

37

Eli Buskins

'Boys, this is mayor Buskins.' Lomax made the introduction as they sat in the conference room in the council building on Main Street. On the table stood two whisky bottles and several glasses. The air was thick with cigar smoke. In front of Lomax sat a pile of newspapers.

'Howdy, gentlemen,' responded the mayor. 'Allow me to introduce Ben Wilkins, Town Treasurer.' Buskins waved his cigar at a man sat to his right. 'And Art Blomquist, Constable.' The latter, a hard-faced, bewhiskered individual wearing a string necktie and red waistcoat with a gold fob chain attached, gave a nod, his eyes roaming over each of the four men seated across the table.

'I guess these are the fellas that run the town,' said Lomax, by way of explanation to his confederates.

'Duly elected,' said the mayor.

'Willy, fill the glasses.'

'You have a proposition?' Blomquist pushed forward his glass.

'That's what I like—straight to business!' Lomax grinned. 'A proposition? I sure do. One that will make us all rich.' He sat back in the chair, surveying those across the table. 'What do you think of that, gentlemen?'

'Think of what? You ain't said nothing yet.' The constable downed the whisky at a gulp and held out the glass for a refill.

'True enough. Boys, he caught me baiting the hook.' Lomax winked at his confederates. 'All righty then, let's skip the soup and head straight to the steak.' He tapped the stack of newspapers. 'You know all about that big old rock just outside of town? 'Course you do! What you may not know is that it's now famous, trumpeted all across America.'

'You getting to the point?'

'Almost there.' Breezily indifferent to the constable's truculence, Lomax picked up a newspaper from the pile. 'The *Chicago Tribune*, gentlemen. From last month. Guess what's on the front page?' He held up the newspaper for view.

The treasurer, a small, inquisitive man whose face displayed a range of fleeting expressions, each one more furtive than the last, leaned forward.

The front page showed a photo of the rock with a man posed before it, staring at the camera. 'Well, I'll be,' he said. He sat back, looking at the mayor who sat to his left. 'What do you make of that, Eli? The *Chicago Tribune.*'

'Who's that?' Buskins squinted. 'Standing in front of it?'

'Some cornsod.' Lomax picked up another paper. 'The *Kansas City Dispatch.*' The paper ran the same photo on the front page.

'Who took the photo?' asked the mayor, visibly miffed.

'That gasbag of a reporter in town a while back,' said the constable.

'And this, and this …' Lomax held up the *Boston Daily Globe*, the *Pittsburgh Dispatch* and the *New York Tribune* in succession. All ran the same photo—whether on the front page or featured prominently inside.

'The *New York Tribune!*' The treasurer glanced at the mayor, whose features had soured further at each sight of the much-reprinted photo.

Lomax picked up the *Omaha Daily Bee*. "A sight for the ages!" He quoted, reading from the bold print. "Mysterious Indian Carving Discovered," he said, referring back to the *Tribune*. "Giant Bison Sculpture Revealed!" he said, reading aloud from the Boston Daily Globe.

'Why in flapdoodle wasn't I made aware of all this?' The mayor shot an irritable glance at the treasurer.

'Who cares about the durn newspapers! What's your point?' The constable glowered at Lomax.

'I reckon that's plain,' put in Leo, before falling silent at a glance from his boss.

'And in case it ain't …' Lomax picked up the *Boston Globe*. "The small, unknown town of Fort Buffalo is expected to be besieged with visitors, all anxious to set eyes on the latest sensation to emerge from the northern plains." He raised an interrogative eyebrow at those seated across the table.

'You ain't telling us anything we don't already know. There's folk arriving every day.'

Buskins blew out a cloud of cigar smoke. 'Art said it. The town's full of outsiders come to pencil-neck the rock.'

'And who benefits?' asked Lomax. The question hung in the air.

The constable gave a grunt. 'Here comes the sauce.'

'This is a new age, gentlemen.' Lomax took out a fresh cigar. 'Folk have money and leisure. They want to travel, see the world—leastways if it ain't too much trouble. They want novelty and adventure. And they're willing to pay for it. Think of it, thousands of folk—from Chicago, Kansas, New York even. All eager to take a gawk at the rock—and willing to pay handsomely for the privilege. Truth is, gentlemen, your little town is sitting on a gold mine.'

'Go on,' said Buskins.

'Visitors have to stay somewhere. Ergo, full hotels. They have to eat and drink, don't they? Ergo, saloons and steak houses. They have to travel out to the rock to see it, don't they? They can't walk, it's too far. Ergo, demand for horses, stables, carriages. They have to—'

'Hold your ergos!' The mayor blew out a cloud of smoke. 'That rock is on private land. And the owner don't take kindly to trespassers.'

'Fact is,' said the constable, 'he's already chased off a few with a shotgun.'

'And you think it's right—that one contrary old farmer should claim what belongs to the entire town?'

'What exactly is your proposition, Mr Lomax? I assume you have one?'

'Indeed I do, Mr Mayor. It's why me and my companions travelled all the way from Chicago. Let me ask you this.' Lomax leaned forward. 'How'd you like to see Main Street tarred over? What about gas lighting for the town, like in Bismarck? How about getting the county seat moved from Franklin to here?' He paused, measuring the effect of his words, before continuing. 'You've already got the railroad. Throw a world-famous rock into the mix and soon the town will be as big as Bismarck—bigger. And that's just the start. And what do you have to do to gain all these things? Nothing!' He halted, letting the silence take effect. 'Nothing except sit back and let someone organise things for the benefit of the town. Hell, you'd be so popular you could cancel the elections.'

'You just need someone to run things,' confirmed Leo.

'Properly,' added Butch.

Lomax nodded approvingly. 'You heard it, Mr Mayor. Someone to mollycoddle folk. Show them the rock. See that they have a good time while in town. Pamper them so that they go back home and tell all their friends and neighbours about the swell time they had up here. Do you see what I'm getting at, gentleman?'

'And that someone would be you?' said the constable.

'It has to be someone. But you still ain't heard my offer.'

'That's 'cos you still ain't made it.' The constable made a show of taking up the fob watch to check the time against the wall clock.

'In return for exclusive organising rights, I'd pay a handsome fee.'

'At last!'

'You talking about a flat fee or a percentage?' asked the treasurer, drawing a sharp glance from Buskins.

'You figure.' Lomax ticked off his fingers. 'There'd be accommodation to arrange. Special railroad cars to lay on—to bring in folk from St Paul, Des

Moines, Jefferson, Charleston, and Washington. Hotels to build, to house 'em all. Carriages for transport. Dining rooms—you already have half a dozen saloons,' he said, to a grin from Willy. 'And then there's guided tours out to the rock. A paved road, to smooth the way. A rest station against the weather. Maybe a beer garden. Entrance fees, souvenirs—'

'Entrance fees! Preposterous! The rock stands out in the open. How you going to charge folk to view what's as big as all get-out right in front of their eyes?' The mayor snorted, not hiding his distaste for the entire conversation.

'There'd be a fence. Heck, folk would be glad to pay for the privilege of going right up to the rock and touching it.'

'You're forgetting something,' pointed out the constable. 'The rock ain't ours. It belongs to Purchase McLennan.'

'We'll make him an offer.' Lomax's voice was bland. 'Buy the land and the rock.'

'He won't sell.'

'He ain't heard the offer.'

The mayor eyed Butch as the latter uttered the words, the concern on his face spreading to his voice. 'I don't like where this is going.' He turned to his fellow councillors. 'I don't aim to turn this town into a carnival freak show. And I won't have any threats made against McLennan or anybody else.'

'Nobody said anything about threats,' the constable objected.

'Far as I can see, we're just talking about buying land,' agreed the treasurer. 'Normal, legal doings.'

'I know what we're talking about!' The mayor's voice was sharp. 'And I won't stand for it. I didn't bring in the railroad and run this town just to turn it over to a bunch of carpetbaggers.' He glanced at Lomax. 'No offence intended.'

'And none taken, friend.' Lomax picked up his hat and sat back in the chair, running his fingers across the nap on the velvet hatband. 'Boys, looks like we wasted our time.'

'I guess these gentlemen are rich enough already,' agreed Leo.

'We should at least hear him out.' The constable turned to the mayor.

'For the good of the town,' added the treasurer. 'Think of what we could do with all that revenue. We'd put the town on the map.'

Buskins stubbed out his cigar. 'It's our buffalo, our town, why do we need outsiders to do what we can do for ourselves—with no commission fees?'

''Course, you could do it yourselves.' Lomax fingered the hat, his voice mild.

'But that ain't right, boss! We brung the idea.' Leo raised his voice in protest. 'No piss-pot council can steal what we own by right.'

'What do you say, Butch?'

Butch shrugged, his voice as bland as his boss's. 'Sure, they can,' he said. ''Cepting they're forgetting one thing.'

'And what's that?' asked the constable.

'Management. Ain't that right, boss?'

'You called it, Butch. Management.'

'What in Fanny Jezebel does that mean?' Buskins frowned, alert for some trickery.

'It means that you have to manage things. For example, acquiring the rock for the town.'

'Manage this McLennan fella,' added Butch.

'Manage the payment of fees—to all parties,' continued Lomax. He ignored the mayor, addressing his remarks directly to the treasurer and constable. 'Making sure that those that stand behind the venture benefit the most.'

'Things they'd rather someone else take care of,' said Butch.

'Clean hands, so to speak,' put in Leo.

'Nothing to enter or put on the record,' added Lomax, his eyes fixed on the constable. 'And there's one other thing—afore you think of going ahead on your own. Something I bring.'

'What's that?' asked the treasurer, risking the ire of the mayor.

'Capital, gentlemen. Capital to tar the roads, build the hotels, light the streets. Capital to hire the trains, print the posters, buy up space in newspapers—right across the country. All this takes money, friends. Do you have that much spare cash lying around? And even if you did, would you know how to spend it? I bring not just capital but know-how. The know-how to open an office, hire staff, drivers, tour guides, organise schedules and bookings. And to manage the whole operation for maximum return.'

'We ain't as green as you think. This town don't need no Chicago managers coming in. We can look after our own affairs.' Pushing back the chair Buskins got to his feet. 'Sorry you folks wasted a journey.'

'Hold fire, Eli. That old rock could be a boon for this town! Biggest thing since the railroad. And as Mr Lomax says, it's a gold mine just sitting there. Why should old man McLennan get all the profits?'

'He don't make no profit 'cos he don't charge.'

'Art just said he runs folk off with a shotgun. How does that make sense?'

'The matter is closed.' The mayor put on his firmest voice. 'Now, gentlemen, if you'll excuse me, I have another appointment.'

'You don't speak for the entire town,' argued Blomquist.

'We need to put it to the full council,' agreed the treasurer. 'Heck, maybe even a town vote.'

'That's your prerogative. As is mine to speak against it.' The mayor gestured to the door. 'Gentlemen!'

Lomax got slowly to his feet. 'Sorry I couldn't persuade you, gentlemen. I'll be at the Dakota for a few days, should you change your mind.' He put on his hat, sanguine in spite of the rebuff. Squaring his hat, he glanced at the constable. 'I hope to hear from you.'

AS SOON AS THE door closed and he heard the footsteps retreat, Buskins rounded furiously on his fellow councillors. 'Are you numbskulls! Do you know what it is he's really fixing at? Do you have the faintest clue?'

'We got ears, Eli, same as you.'

'Well use 'em! Of all the oily snakes …!'

'You're getting worked up over nothing,' soothed Wilkins. 'From what I heard, it sounds like a pretty good deal for the town. You do want to get re-elected, don't you? Well, here's your ticket.'

'I don't aim to turn this town over to no two-bit Chicago speculators. And I won't put up with threats.' Buskins stared pointedly at Blomquist.

'I ain't threatened nobody—no matter what you heard.' The constable's voice was surly.

'Nobody's talking about threats, Eli. Be reasonable. Think of what we could do with all that revenue. We'd put the town on the map.'

'Durn and blast it! The matter is closed. I have no wish to ever hear another word from that greaseball peddler or his schemes to milk this town.'

'You're just one voice, Eli. You don't speak for the entire council, much less the town.'

'So, you said. But you'll have to fight me.' Buskins eyed the constable. 'Remember the property tax? That didn't go so well, did it?'

'I remember everything. Including who to thank for it.'

'What does that mean?'

'It means what it means. And if I have to fight you on this, so be it. Ben, you with me?'

'Sorry, Eli. But we gotta act for the good of the town.'

'Ha! The good of your own pockets, more like.'

'You weren't always so scrupulous, Eli, I remember—'

'A little election chicanery is one thing—that's natural. Outright threats and corruption another. And make no mistake that's what we're talking about. You crawl into bed with snakes and sooner or later you'll get bit. I won't have it. Damned if I will! Not so long as I am mayor of this town. And since when did you get so all-fired friendly with carpetbaggers?' He shot an accusing glance at the constable.

'Businessmen, Eli. Speculators. Nothing wrong with that. It's how the world works.'

'He has a point, Eli. You should listen.'

'I'm telling you, open the door to his kind and this town is finished.'

'Like Lomax said,' argued Wilkins. 'He's got the capital and the know-how. Heck, even if we ran with your suggestion and organised things ourselves, we'd still have to hire people to run it. Not to mention all the other things Lomax mentioned—the special trains, the hotels, the restaurants, the carriages and drivers and guides and so forth. How are we going to pay for all those things? Raise taxes?'

'Not likely,' said the constable, his voice showing what he thought of the suggestion.

'Let the town decide, Eli.'

Buskins reached for the door, a scowl on his face. 'Long as I'm mayor, I'll decide!'

EDISON LOMAX RETURNED TO his room, the fanciest one in the rather dingy hotel. Stepping inside, he tossed his hat onto the bed and sat down, propping his feet up on a footstool topped with a cushion stuffed with straw and covered with burlap. 'Want some company, boss?' Leo hesitated in the doorway.

'No. You and the boys go have yourselves a drink. But stay close. And send up some fresh coffee. And watch Butch!' he added as the door closed.

Unbuttoning his shirt collar, he stared at the picture on the wall, his mind going back over the meeting. That starched-guts mayor is a problem. The constable though … And that weasel of a treasurer? Skunks, both— dependable skunks. His eyes gleamed at the thought. A knock came on the door.

'Yes?'

'It's me, boss.' The door opened. 'With the coffee.' He watched Leo put the cup down on the table.

'When does Jay arrive?'

'Tomorrow, noon.'

'You booked him a room?'

'Across the hallway.'

'What do you make of our illustrious mayor?'

'Trouble.' Leo frowned. 'But that big lunk of a sheriff—'

'Constable.'

'—constable. I reckon he's a placer.'

'And Wilkins?'

'Who?'

'The treasurer.'

'Oh.' Leo thought for a moment. 'Weaselly-faced little snout. A bet each way.'

'Worth a dime?'

'I reckon. Him and the big fella's worth a double.'

'That's what I thought.'

Leo went to leave but hesitated at the door. 'Remember that time in Kansas?'

'The railroad fella?'

Leo nodded. 'It sort of minds me of that.'

'That didn't work out as we hoped.'

'No. Sorry to raise it. It's just that that ornery bull of a sher—constable—'minded me of him, that's all. See you later, boss. We'll be in the saloon across the street.'

After the door closed Lomax sipped the coffee, his face thoughtful. A good reminder—not to repeat the mistakes of Kansas. Setting down the cup, he twisted the class ring on his finger. That was a blunder—to let Butch off the leash so early. His eyes drifted to a small photograph, set in a silver frame on the bedside table. That cost me you, Lilly. I won't forget.

Leaning back his head, he closed his eyes, imagining he could smell her perfume.

A knock came on the door, and he opened his eyes. 'Yes?'

The door opened to reveal the surly figure of the constable. Blomquist looked cautiously about the room before stepping in. 'You alone?'

'Uh-huh. Sit down and pour yourself a drink.'

'I won't stay.' The constable inserted a finger in his collar and tugged it loose. 'Me and Ben, we got to thinking.'

'Yes?'

'Why should Eli dictate everything? The fellow's as stubborn as a three-legged mule.'

'And?' Lomax raised an eyebrow.

'And we reckoned we should meet. Jest us, to talk.'

'I have a man coming in on tomorrow's train. How about we meet downstairs, around two o'clock?'

'And Buskins?'

'He needn't hear of it. Why don't you stay? We could talk—ahead of the meeting.' Lomax gestured to a chair.

'No, tomorrow's fine.' And with that the constable withdrew, closing the door behind him.

Lomax reached for the cup and finished his coffee. What did I tell you, Lilly? Dangle a coin and count the fingers reaching for it.

"I hear you made a fortune on land speculation and lost it all on railway stocks?" The reporter sat forward, pen poised above his notebook. Lomax glanced at Lilly, sitting pale and composed in the leather armchair.

"Wealth is like a carousel," answered Lomax, summoning up a smile for her benefit. "Check back with me in a year when the horses come round again."

Getting up, he walked to the window to stare down at the street. A few wagons creaked by. A boy delivered a crate of apples, whistling as he wheeled a handcart. A group of men stood gossiping on the sidewalk. His ears pricked at a faint train whistle, and he glanced at his watch.

An omnibus drew up in the street outside the hotel and he watched the passengers alight. A youth hawked tobacco from a tray suspended around his neck, calling out to passersby. He stiffened as he saw the constable and treasurer emerge from the shadows cast by the building, both men busily engaged in conversation. The constable glanced up at the window and he stood there in plain view, looking back. A rag, popular in Chicago, popped into his head. *"Kansas City ain't so much, it stinks and it huffs. But its where my purty little gal lives—she's so fine. And that ain't no guff!"*

His eyes followed a woman hurrying across the street, holding the hand of a small boy. If I can't squeeze this burg for thirty grand a year, every year, then I ain't the man I thought I was. He turned away, humming.

FOR YEARS, HE HAD resisted the farmerish impulse to enclose the land by erecting fences. But now, fed up with the increasing traffic to the rock, he seriously contemplated erecting a fence along the road that led past the object. Instead, he put up a large, painted sign: *Private Property. Trespassers May Be Shot!* But the sign did little to deter the sightseers, who travelled from as far away as Pierre and St Paul to see the rock marvel for themselves. The local omnibus drivers hired a boy to stand atop a vehicle and yell out whenever Purchase was spotted striding toward the site, shotgun in hand. At the boy's cry, the visitors simply retreated to where the omnibuses waited on the road and sat inside while Purchase expostulated with the drivers before striding off again with backward glances and threats of dire consequences should the trespass be repeated.

The omnibus drivers protested to the mayor that the 'crazy old coot' was ruining their trade and threatened to vent their ire at the next council meeting. A worried Buskins complained to a trusted confederate. 'Something's coming, Sam. I can smell it. Those Chicago snakes ain't going to fold tents and leave jest 'cos I say so.' He sighed, a concerned look on his face. As his foreboding grew, he made a visit to the McLennan homestead to argue for tolerance.

'You can't keep shooing folks off like they had the pox,' he said, sitting across from a truculent Purchase. 'Drivers claim you're ruining their livelihood and, well, they won't stand for it. Fine coffee, thank you, Ma'am,' he said to Felicity, sipping from the cup.

'I'd be within my rights to shoot them all. It's what the law says, and it's my land, ain't it?'

'No one's disputing that fact. But you got to see the other side as well.'

'What other side?'

Buskins gave an exasperated sigh. 'The side of trade, commerce, business. Like it or not, that rock is now a public attraction. Folk won't stop coming to see it. In fact, you can expect more, with all the publicity it's received.'

'Then I'll build a fence, and man it with a shotgun if I must.'

'There's another way.'

'What way?'

'Sell the rock—to the town. Shucks, you've plenty of land—you don't even cultivate most of it. You won't notice a missing acre or two. The town will pay you a handsome price.'

'And what would you do with it?'

'We'd protect it, as a valuable asset. Maybe charge folk to see it and use the proceeds to help the town.'

'No.' The answer was blunt.

'No what?'

'No, I ain't selling. And you ain't the first that's come along asking, neither.'

'Oh? And who was the other, pray tell?'

'Some huckster from back East. Just a few days ago.'

'A glad-hander in a three-piece and a homburg?'

'You know the fella?'

'I do. Listen, Purchase. Do the smart thing and sell the rock to the town before it's too late.'

'Too late?' Purchase frowned. 'Too late for what? That rock has belonged to my family for over a hundred years. You think I'd sell?'

Buskins gave a vexed sigh. 'No, I guess not.' He stared at the coffee as if mulling what to say next. 'There's people,' he said. 'Serious people, not to be messed with. And they have a hankering for your rock.'

'That Chicago dandy? He ain't worth spit!'

'Don't underestimate them, Purchase. That would be a mistake. I'll fight them, of course, in council. But the fact is money talks. And when money talks, folk listen.'

'What in are you getting at, Mr Buskins?' asked Felicity, alarm in her voice.

'Nothing, Mrs. McLennan.' Buskins looked at Purchase. 'Jest be careful, that's all. These people don't like to hear the word *no*.' He stood up, reaching for his hat. 'We'll leave it at that. Thank you for the coffee, Ma'am. And look to yourself and your family, Purchase. These are fraught times. Oh! And try not to shoot anybody!'

'What did he mean by that—fraught times?' asked Felicity as the mayor drove off.

'Nothing, I expect. I blame that fool reporter for stirring up things. Where's Jubal?'

She laid a hand on his arm. 'You heard Buskins. He said these men are dangerous. They may mean you harm if they don't get what they want.'

He frowned. 'Are you suggesting I should listen—sell up?'

'No.' She sat down in the chair, a worried look on her face. 'Just be careful, that's all. Eli Buskins didn't come all the way out here just for my coffee.'

'I will.' He laid a hand on her shoulder. 'Don't worry. The law's on our side. I'll be in the barn if you need me.'

She cleared away the table, pondering the conversation with the mayor. Since when did Eli Buskins make house calls—excepting when to wheedle a vote? She picked up the cups, forgetful that she had already washed them.

AMITY HAD AN IDEA—SPARKED by something Boundary had said in passing. She'd advertise! The notion thrilled her. Why not take charge of her destiny? She had a brother who worked in the newspaper office, didn't she? Then why not take advantage of that—advertise her services as a private tutor to the entire county! The more she thought on the matter, the more excited she got. That musty old store was suffocating her by degrees—not to mention the insufferable old widow who owned it. But here was a way out, a chance to take her livelihood into her own hands—through the power of advertising!

Sitting down straight after supper, she opened her notebook and began writing. After several false starts, she smiled, satisfied with what she had written. Now to persuade Boundary to coax his employer into giving her a discount, she told herself. After all, I'm his sister.

Accordingly, the very next issue of the *Dispatch* included a small two-by-two-inch advertisement on the front page:

Private tutor for hire. Respectable young lady, schooled at the famous Ladies' Seminary in St Charles, Missouri. Available to teach language, arithmetic, etiquette, and the domestic arts to young women of good family in their own homes. Reasonable rates that can be negotiated. Interested parties reply to the Dispatch office in town.

'I set it myself,' said Boundary as his sister avidly perused the notice. 'It reads as clear as anything.'

'My, my, Amity,' murmured an impressed Mrs. Halverson when she proudly showed the notice. 'How will you get around to visit the farms?'

'I'll hire a horse and buggy from Mr Cornwallis. And I can drive myself.'

'Gracious!' Mrs. Halverson blinked at the notion. 'All by yourself?'

'Why not? The roads are safe, ain't they?'

'Your ma may not think so, not to mention your pa.'

'They'll come round—especially when the offers come flooding in!'

After three days, a reply came from a family farm nearer Bismarck than the town. Regretfully, she declined it. Another response came two days later, from a German family two miles east of the town. The same afternoon, another letter arrived, this time from a family within the town itself. She recognised the name, Mortimer, and wrote back at once, proposing a visit to settle a fee and make arrangements. Two days later, Boundary turned up at supper bearing a fourth letter, this one from a farm a half-mile outside the town limits.

Brimming with enthusiasm, she returned home to discuss the proposed venture with her parents. 'That's three families,' she said. 'I'll charge them a dollar fifty cents each. That's more than old Hedgepeth pays me—and for half the hours!'

Her pa was dubious, especially over her plans to hire a horse and buggy to drive out to the two families outside of town. 'A woman shouldn't be travelling out alone,' he said. 'It's dangerous.'

'It will be in broad daylight, Pa, on the main road,' she argued. 'Ma?'

'I don't see the harm, Purchase. Lots of the farm women drive themselves around these days.'

'And I could leave that stuffy old shop. I'll die if I have to stay there one day longer.'

'She's eighteen now,' Felicity pointed out.

'Where will you live—will you move back home?'

'No. I'll stay at the Halversons'. It's handy to the stables, and to the families.'

'It won't waste that education,' said Felicity, 'and she'd be working less hours.'

'And once I get established other families will get to hear of me.'

Purchase rubbed his jaw, taking in the eager look on her face. 'Alright, Am, if that's what you want. I'll come into town next Saturday and practise you on the horse and buggy.'

'Pa!' She threw her arms around his neck and kissed him.

The next day, he drove her back into town, dropping her off at the Halversons' and promising to return on Saturday to make arrangements with Mr Cornwallis. She's a grown woman, he reflected, watching as she turned in the doorway to wave goodbye. He shook the reins, ruminating on time and the passage of years as he drove slowly down Elm St before taking the turn that would lead him back to Main. I never expected things, he acknowledged, touching his hat to a woman on the sidewalk. I never expected to outlast the war. Or for the buffalo to run out. I never expected Felicity or the children.

What did I expect? he wondered as the wagon proceeded up Main toward the high road. Nothing, he realised. I just followed where the road took me. Were there other roads? he pondered. And if so, where might they have led? He frowned. There were no signposts—at least none that I was aware of. I just supposed there was but the one road, the one underfoot.

He contemplated the notion as he drove, perturbed at the idea that he might have missed something in his blinkered adherence to the road he found himself on. Would I be the same man on any other road? He dismissed the thought, irritable at such foolish fancies. The road I'm on led me here, to Felicity and the buffalo. That's good enough for me. Eli

Buskin's warning came to mind, and he mulled on it. What did he mean by serious people? Who in their right mind would try to steal a rock? His jaw tightened at the prospect. Let them try!

38

Pro Bono Publico

'GOOD AFTERNOON, GENTLEMEN. MAY I introduce Mr Jay Malting, my lawyer, just arrived from Chicago. Jay, this is Constable Art Blomquist and Treasurer Ben Wilkins. We'll get to Jay later, gentlemen,' he said, signalling his offsider. 'Willy, fetch some more of those peppered eggs and another bottle of whisky. Shall we begin?' he asked of the men seated around the table in the hotel dining room.

'You couldn't find a more public place?' The constable scowled as he glanced around the empty room.

'Don't worry. The room's closed until we're finished.'

'Let's get down to business.' The treasurer flexed his fingers as though prepared to count. 'You said a commission?'

'An administrative fee,' said Lomax, 'for the books.'

'You mentioned a hotel?' interrupted the constable, his voice blunt.

'I did,' said Lomax, 'for housing all the gawkers—sorry, guests.' He smiled.

'The railroad was planning to build one—they've set property aside, said Blomquist, 'but they could be persuaded to hand it over to us, for a price.'

'Here it comes,' grunted Butch, drawing a stifled guffaw from Willy.

'What kind of a price?' asked Lomax.

'I'd want twenty percent. And that's not counting the profits from everything else.'

'And another twenty for me,' said the treasurer. 'Same deal.'

'Hellfire!' Leo glanced at Lomax. 'That's almost half!'

'Ten percent each,' said Lomax. 'And that's generous.'

The constable glanced at the treasurer, who gave a shrug.

'And what about the rest of it—the earnings from the rock, the tours, the rail tickets and other stuff?' demanded Blomquist.

'How about fifty dollars a week each, guaranteed?'

Blomquist gave a snort. 'How about one hundred!'

'How about you pull your blamed horns in?' Butch gave a menacing look at the constable, who stared back, unperturbed.

'And there's others—whose support we'll need,' inserted the treasurer, 'to get everything through council.'

'This whole thing is looking like a bad investment, Ed.' The lawyer, a slim man with a finely adjudicated moustache, made a tent of his fingers as he leaned elbows on the table. 'There's too many minstrels, for one thing,' he said, with a pointed glance at the treasurer and constable.

'You could be right, Jay. Spread the manure too thin and the crop fails,' agreed Lomax.

'We could be back in Chicago by the day after tomorrow,' said Leo. 'Want me to book the tickets, boss?'

'Hold on now,' said Wilkins. 'We can work out the details, ain't that right, Art?'

The constable nodded. 'Enough shit to go round so that everyone gets a crop.'

'There's still that turtleneck of a farmer,' said Leo.

'Jay, tell 'em what you found,' said Lomax.

'I stopped off in Bismarck to check the county land claim records,' said the lawyer. 'It appears this McLennan fella purchased the land legitimately back in the late '70s.'

The treasurer muttered, disappointment showing on his face. 'It figures as much.'

'But there's a crack?' Blomquist aimed the question at the lawyer.

Malting gave a thin smile. 'There's always a crack. It appears McLennan then let things slide while he went back to St Charles, where he had a family.'

'So?' The question came from Wilkins.

'He didn't work the land for at least a year. One might argue he was in breach.'

'In breach of what?' asked Wilkins.

'The act—the Homestead Act—specifies a claimant must reside on the claim, and nowhere else, for six months of the year.' Malting quoted from a sheet of paper in front of him. "And no legal residence elsewhere." He looked up. 'This McLennan had a farm in St Charles at the time, where he resided with his family.'

The constable grunted. 'That's a mighty thin crack.'

'He's proved up the land,' said the treasurer. 'Who the devil cares what happened back then? Challenge him on those grounds and the town will side with McLennan. And so will any judge worth his salt.'

'There's also a question over his claim to a rock, given that you can't prove up a stone.'

'It ain't enough,' argued Wilkins. 'Hell, you start digging into land claims and you'll find cracks in every single one.'

'Agreed.' The lawyer sat back, an expressionless look on his face.

The concession drew surprised glances from others around the table. Lomax, however, appeared unfazed. 'But …?' he prompted.

'But what?' demanded Wilkins as Malting hung fire.

'Eminent domain.' The words were pronounced softly and deliberately.

'Eminent who?' Willy brokered the question, looking perplexed.

'Tell 'em, Jay. Don't hold the boys in suspense.'

The lawyer set his gaze on the two men opposite—both sitting with puzzled frowns.

'There's an act, in law, which gives the federal government and/or the states the power to appropriate private property for public use if that appropriation can be justified and provided adequate compensation is paid.'

'The who what?' Willy looked from one face to the other.

Malting used a finger to smooth his moustache. 'What it means is that a state government can declare a piece of land is of historic significance such that it requires legal protection and public ownership. It would require the requisite authorities, in this case the North Dakota legislature, acting in the public interest, to petition the courts to assign ownership of the property, in this case, the rock, to the state, *pro bono publico*—for the public good.' He held up a palm as the treasurer made to interrupt. 'The town council, being the local authority within whose purview the rock lies, would then petition the governor to exercise trusteeship on the state's behalf. And in the exercise of that trust, the council would be within its rights to award a lease to a reputable company to maintain the rock and its facilities on its behalf—provided that the public, in this case the township, was the clear and essential beneficiary of any monies generated by said trust.'

'Sweet Jesus!' Leo whistled in admiration.

'McLennan will never agree,' objected Wilkins.

'He don't have to agree,' said Blomquist. 'Right?' He addressed the question to the lawyer.

Malting nodded. 'The law will decide.'

'Meaning the district court?'

The lawyer nodded. 'All the way up to the court of appeals and the Supreme Court if necessary. This McLennan won't stand a chance. The cost to fight it would bankrupt him anyway.'

'Maybe he'll see sense and take an offer?' said Leo.

Willy snorted. 'Doubt it! Old buzzard's like a dog with a bone.'

'So, gentlemen?' asked Lomax, looking at Wilkins and Blomquist.

'You're forgetting Buskins,' pointed out Wilkins. 'He's got influence, and friends in Bismarck, too. He could stir up the town. Heck, the blowhard could even force an election on the issue. And he'd fight us on the hotel and just about every other goddamn thing he could. He don't like losing. And he 'specially don't like losing to you, Art,' he said, turning to the constable.

'He can't object if he ain't here.' Butch held up his whisky glass, studying the contents by the light. The comment reduced the table to silence.

'What are we saying here?' asked the treasurer, suddenly nervous. 'Art?'

'You heard the man,' answered the constable. 'Hell, I still owe the bastard for the property tax. *Pro bono publico*,' he said, and took out his watch to wind.

PURCHASE STARED AT THE document in his hand. 'Thieves!'

Felicity exclaimed in dismay as she took the letter to read for herself. 'What can we do?' she asked, looking up from the document. 'It's the government.'

'It's those consarned carpetbaggers!'

'But if Buskins is right, they now have the law on their side. We can't fight the government. Be reasonable, Purchase.'

'It's my rock, my land. I'll hire a lawyer.'

'Can we afford that?'

'I've half a mind …' He didn't finish the sentence.

'Now don't you be doing anything silly, Purchase. it ain't the old days.'

'The worse for it!' He stood up, a furious look on his face.

'Where are you going?' she asked as he reached for his hat.

'Into town. To talk to the mayor.'

'For all you know, he's in on it.'

'I doubt it. He may be bent as a mishit nail, but he wouldn't be part of this. Else why warn us?'

'Take Jubal,' she said, suddenly fearful, and jumping up as he made to open the door. 'Don't go now! Wait a day or two.'

'Why?'

'Just allow things to simmer down. Please, Purchase.'

He stared at her for a long moment. 'All right,' he said. 'I'll give it a day or two.' He cast an angry look at the court notice lying on the table. 'Durn crooks!'

HE WALKED TO THE rock to cool off, his mind a whirl of emotions. It's that Chicago gangster behind it. I know it! He derived a grim pleasure from picturing the fellow blanch in the face of a levelled shotgun. His mood was not improved by the sight of a knot of people standing under the rock, posing or sketching or, his especial hate, chipping off flakes with a hammer. 'Hey!' He shouted, shaking his fist. The visitors stared for a moment before a man quickly rounded them up and shepherded them back to where two buggies stood in the grass. As he approached, the buggies started off back toward the road.

'Hey yourself, you durn hayseed!'

The yelled insult reached his ears as he stood glowering after the intruders. Walking up to the rock, he looked for signs of damage. Spotting a scratch, he examined where the hammer had barely made an impression on the hard granite. Angered, he stared at where the buggies were disappearing down the road. The thought that such intrusions would not only be legally sanctioned but actively sponsored if the court case was successful caused him to stiffen with outrage. *Eminent domain.* The phrase stuck in his mind as he paced beside the rock. Who came up with that crazy notion? Crooks! he answered himself. He leaned a hand against the stone. How could the government take what was rightfully his—what had been legally claimed and possessed? Surely, that made the government no better than thieves or claim jumpers themselves?

And what would he, the old man, make of it? He pictured the patriarch standing atop the rock, a stony defiance written on his face as he stared down at the avaricious mob of lawyers, hucksters, shysters, and crooked politicians clustered at the foot of his great, immovable masterpiece. Pygmies! How he would have despised them. He closed his eyes as if to draw upon the great man's strength of will. The hell with them all! Cussing all such weaselly snake bellies, he headed back to the house.

BELLOW LOOKED UP FROM the wire he was reading, a contemplative look on his face. 'Say, Boundary?'

'Yes, sir?'

'Your pa fought in the war, didn't he?'

'I guess. For the Union.'

'It says here'—Bellow flicked the cable—'that the federal government plans on opening a military park at Gettysburg. Did your pa fight there?'

'He never talks about it.'

'Could you ask him? Maybe we could fill a few inches. We're a bit short for Friday.' He tapped a finger while glancing at the wire. 'Eighteen sixty-three. That's thirty-two years ago. Heck, we could even run a commemorative edition. There'd be special rates. Will you ask your pa?'

'Gettysburg?'

'Sure. You've heard of it, haven't you? Or don't your Miss Purlow teach you anything?'

Boundary mentioned it in school the next day, the question drawing raised eyebrows from the schoolteacher. 'Why, Boundary McLennan. I declare that is the first time I ever heard you ask a question! What is it, exactly, that you wish to know? How about we start with its whereabouts?' she suggested at his grimace.

'Gettysburg,' she said, writing the name on the board in block capitals, 'is, I believe, in the state of Pennsylvania. What makes you ask about it?'

Boundary scratched his ear, a habit he had picked up from his employer. 'There was some fighting or stuff that happened there.'

'There was?' She looked out of the window, frowning to recall. 'It must have been to do with the War Between the States,' she said. 'But nothing special comes to mind.'

TRUE TO HIS PLEDGE to Felicity, he drove into town to speak with the mayor, determined to hash out some strategy to foil the government. Jubal sat beside him, his mother having impressed upon her son the necessity of keeping his father out of trouble. 'Keep watch on him,' she said while out of earshot of Purchase. 'See that he don't go flying off the handle.'

The town seemed unusually busy. A group of people were congregated outside the newspaper office.

'Whoa!' Purchase pulled up the horses just as the door to the office opened and Bellow emerged to speak to the crowd, who seemed agitated.

'What's going on?' Purchase asked a man standing nearby.

'Ain't you heard? It's the mayor.'

'What about him?'

'Someone blew his durn brains out!'

39

A Great Attraction

IN JULY 1895, THE Sixth Judicial District Court in Bismarck found for the state in the case of the *Government of North Dakota v. Purchase McLennan*. The presiding judge sanctioned the state's request to 'condemn' or appropriate fifty acres around the buffalo rock monument, which the court—after hearing from a string of expert witnesses hired by Lomax—declared 'a landmark of compelling historic significance to the nation.' Purchase's bid to overturn the verdict went to the Eighth Circuit Court of Appeals in St Paul, Minnesota, which upheld the original decision despite his vehement objections. The legal costs forced him to sell one hundred acres of prime farmland to avoid bankruptcy, the combined effects of the sale and appropriation reducing his holdings to 170 acres. Embittered by the 'legal theft,' he looked on with increasing anguish as the rock buffalo quickly became a celebrated attraction, drawing visitors from near and far to behold its solitary grandeur.

Shortly after winning the court case, the state delegated administration of the monument to the Fort Buffalo town council. The council, in turn and on behalf of the state, delegated management and administration of the landmark to the newly formed Buffalo Monument Trust. The trust, jointly chaired by the mayor and a 'sterling' businessman from Chicago, energetically promoted the rock as the 'American Sphinx,' laying on special trains from as far away as the nation's capital. Upon arrival at the distant prairie town, visitors were housed in a newly built hotel before being ferried out to the monument in a fleet of omnibuses owned by the trust. To celebrate the amazing success of the attraction, which rapidly became the town's single most important source of income, Edison Lomax urged the council to petition the state governor to change the town name from Fort Buffalo to Buffalo Rock, thus stamping both the monument and the local stakeholders with the same 'brand', as he termed it.

Lured by colourful posters and positive newspaper stories paid for by Lomax, visitors poured into the town—it being not uncommon for a casual observer to note twenty or thirty enlarged omnibuses at a time lined up in the road alongside the site. Once at the rock—or monument as Lomax insisted on referring to it in all publications—the eager pilgrims were escorted around the edifice by knowledgeable local guides who eloquently explained its creation as the result of a concerted effort by a little-known group of early inhabitants, labelled *Dakota Man*. The invented tribe purportedly inhabited the area in the distant past—variously conjectured at between nine hundred to one thousand years ago—and were reputed to have carved the totemic buffalo and worshipped it as a god. Evidence for the existence of such a population was provided by an archaeologist hired by the trust, who claimed that bone fragments and sophisticated stone tools found in the vicinity of the rock attested to both the tribe's existence and their extraordinary ability to work even the hardest stone.

The claims were scoffed at by neutral observers who dismissed them as outrageous concoctions and called for independent scientific investigation of the rock's origin. But such was the power of the trust, and so influential was Edison Lomax as a political donor and fundraiser, that the calls were ignored. And meanwhile, in spite of, or perhaps because of, the contentious claims surrounding its creation, the rock continued to draw sightseers in ever greater numbers. On weekends and public holidays, it was not unusual for the number of visitors to exceed four hundred or more on any given day. They were wined and dined at a beer garden and restaurant set up in a giant 'refreshment pavilion' designed to block view of the monument from outside the gates. Inside the canvas pavilion, paid visitors were entertained by a band of musicians featuring 'genuine' Indian dancers. Visitors had their photographs taken by trust-appointed photographers, paying handsomely for the privilege, and purchased slivers of rock from the souvenir gift shop to take back home.

Ever on the lookout to 'milk the cow,' as he derisively referred to the rock in private, Lomax hit upon the idea of positioning a large winch on top to lift paying guests up on to the summit. The brave and exhilarated men and women who took up the 'adventure of a lifetime' then proceeded up and down the monument, clinging to ropes and stanchions as they gasped at the wild, windy prospect and peered down at the upturned faces below. The innovation proved inspired, with eager tourists lining up to boast of 'riding the buffalo' and clutching the embossed certificate to hang on the wall back home.

Income from the attraction paid for paved streets and gas lighting for the town as well as generating a plethora of new businesses calculated to cash in on the swarms of visitors. In spite of demands from various parties, including the *Dispatch*, the trust accounts were never made public, the management committee claiming charitable privilege. Eventually, the trust won legal exemption from the requirement at the urging of the governor, now a close friend and confidant of Edison Lomax, who was rumoured to have invested generously in the governor's re-election campaign.

PURCHASE WATCHED WITH MOUNTING despair the desecration of his rock, fulminating with rage at the constant passage of omnibuses along the newly tarred road that ran by his farm. The trust had erected gas lamps to entertain visitors long into the summer evenings, the noise of music and merriment sounding to his ears like dirge bells. At times, he felt a murderous itch to take his Sharps and blast away at all the 'consarned rubbernecks' as he called them, defiling his patrimony. At other times, he sat on the porch sipping on a bottle of whisky while bemoaning the days. 'Even the pestiferous Sioux have been turned into minstrels,' he complained, savagely critical of Lomax's latest scheme—to recreate the 'birth' of the monument through pageantry and dance.

'The suckers will pay through the nose for it,' the businessman assured his cronies.

To further induce a sense of drama, Lomax scoured the state for ranchers willing to sell the few dozen buffalo remaining in private ownership. 'They could graze or shit or whatever the hell it is they do while folk pay to have photographs taken,' he speculated. 'Maybe they could be tamed and saddled to permit riders to parade up and down in the grass. Imagine the dough that would bring in!' To his great annoyance, he was unsuccessful in securing the animals, despite offering a king's ransom for the beasts. 'They'd foul up the grass anyway,' he complained, souring on the venture.

He partly compensated for the loss by commissioning the publication of a book, handsomely illustrated with photographs, purporting to tell the true history of the rock, and tracing its origin back to the mythical Dakota Man while throwing in a chapter on 'Buffalo Bill Bjornson' at the behest, and generous financial contribution, of the State Nordic Society. The society had taken a vital interest in the monument and pushed tirelessly to champion the authorship of Bjornson whose 'possible' likeness they featured on posters and flyers boasting of his Scandinavian birthplace and credentials as the state's—and possibly America's—first conservationist. They hosted a series of events featuring Axel Bjornson and other descendants who spoke glowingly of their countryman and of his love and admiration for the buffalo and proud attachment to his Swedish roots.

Quick to seize upon the immense public fascination with all things monument related, Lomax ordered a series of lavishly coloured posters featuring Bjornson astride a buffalo or gazing far-sightedly from the top of the rock. The posters and accompanying leaflets sat unashamedly side by side with other posters illustrating feather-bonneted Indian chiefs paying homage to the 'imperishable buffalo totem.'

'Hell, I'd advertise a Scotsman in a kilt if that would sell tickets,' declared Lomax, brushing aside criticism of the contesting claims to authorship. 'Folk don't care about history,' he asserted on more than one occasion. 'What they care about is full bellies and something novel to gawk at.' This view was anointed the Lomax Doctrine in a sceptical account published in a Kansas City newspaper, which questioned the entire foundations of the venture as well as the bona fides of the trust and the town council itself. An enraged Lomax sent emissaries to purchase and burn every available copy while threatening the reporter with serious and irreparable harm if he ever again stepped foot in North Dakota. And so, the years passed and the buffalo riches rolled in while Lomax and his fellow runners grew fat on the profits.

ON THE SECOND ANNIVERSARY of the mysterious slaying of the town mayor, Quintus Bellow printed an investigative article—or 'public autopsy', as he referred to it—that resurrected suspicions about the circumstances surrounding the assassination. The *Dispatch* was promptly subjected to a defamation suit after airing 'unanswered questions of conspiracy and complicity on behalf of unknown persons who probably still inhabit the town.' The plaintiff, Art Blomquist, demanded a retraction and public apology for a paragraph in which Bellow recounted the constable's claim that he had no choice but to shoot the presumed killer—a no-account drifter named Orly Merlson—'clean through the heart,' when the latter allegedly resisted apprehension.

On Bellow's refusal to retract the controversial article, Blomquist sued for libel. Bellow's use of the word 'allegedly' in relation to the unfortunate Merlson's resistance was the instigation for the tort. Bellow escaped censure, however, by insisting he had followed both legal and journalistic protocol in his account. The district court agreed, asserting that, the use of 'allegedly' notwithstanding, the article as a whole failed to rise to the level of prima facie proof of defamation. The article did much to revive the widespread rumours that had followed the murder, in particular the scapegoating of Merlson, a harmless drunk, and the suspiciously coincidental arrival of the constable on the murder scene even as it unfolded.

Buskin's successor as mayor—interim at the time but subsequently confirmed by ballot—the former treasurer, Ben Wilkins, poured scorn on the *Dispatch* account, lambasting its veracity and the reputation of its publisher at every opportunity, even while leaking information to the same despised organ in an attempt to damage political opponents. But the revived suspicions persisted, shadowing the constable and prompting his reluctant withdrawal from candidacy as county commissioner a few weeks later.

Several anonymous death threats followed the failed libel action, prompting Bellow to start carrying a pistol and making certain everyone knew of the fact. At Mrs. Bellow's insistence, Boundary accompanied his employer to his residence each day after work. 'Heck, if they wanted, they could just as well shoot me on the way to work,' scoffed Bellow to his anxious wife. 'The main thing is that everyone will know it was Blomquist's hand behind the act. That's why he can't risk it.' Patting Boundary on the shoulder as he bade him goodbye, he whispered in his ear, 'Only thing keeping me alive!'

40

A Heart That Feels

IN THE PERIOD FOLLOWING her escape from the stuffy embrace of Widow Hedgepeth and her rolls of silk and muslin, Amity tried valiantly to assert her independence. Proudly driving the hired horse and buggy, she rode out into the countryside to tutor at first two and then three farmhouses, spending the morning at one and the afternoon at another on successive days. She became a familiar sight to houses along the road, gaily returning the greetings of children who stood on the fence rails to watch her wheel pass.

Once with her charges, she adopted what she considered a professional but nurturing air, instructing the farm daughters in matters of deportment, etiquette, dancing, and conversation. To her disappointment, her skills in arithmetic and penmanship were rarely, if ever, called upon, the families more intent on marrying off their daughters than educating them. 'We have Miss Purlow for that' they answered whenever she brought up the matter. 'Teach them to talk right and not trip over themselves when they dance, and we'll be satisfied.'

Her 'project', as she termed it, went well for the first two years, the number of families willing to pay for her services stretching at one point to six. She briefly moved out of the Halversons' and returned home to save money, but soon moved back out again, frustrated at her mother's nosy intrusion into her affairs. 'A woman can't be self-sufficient lessen she supports herself,' she declared to the now-married Polly Buskins, wife of Joe, the dead mayor's eldest son. 'The essence of independence is financial self-sufficiency.'

The brave words belied a growing disenchantment with her life as the gnawing doubts which had accompanied her return to the homestead from her sojourn in St Charles revisited to tease and perplex her with notions of an unfulfilled destiny. She had taken up painting again and did several drawings and watercolours from the window of her room in the Halversons' residence, rendering the street, with its vehicular traffic and Dutch elms and weathered house fronts, in both charcoal and paint. The canvases won the praise of Mrs. Halverson, who insisted on framing her favourite, a flowering elm, and hanging it on the parlour wall. 'Amity, you are so accomplished!' she gushed, admiring the hung canvas.

On weekends and public holidays, Amity drove herself out to the farm to visit with her parents, taking along the easel and paints. She did several views of the rock—sketching from a distance to avoid the crowds of tourists. She entertained notions of putting some of the canvases on display in the trust gift shop, but in the face of her pa's vehement objections, she abandoned the idea. 'Perhaps you can sell them in town,' her mother suggested. Desirous of securing an additional source of income, she approached the Widow Hedgepeth, hoping to convince her former employer that a few tasteful canvases hung in the shop would enhance the store and lead to a sale, of which the widow would receive a guaranteed 15 percent commission.

'No and no again!' The widow objected, flatly refusing the proposal. 'This is a drapery, not a fancy art gallery.' Disappointed, she tried several other shops with the same result. Mr Jervis, the owner of the local general goods store did, however, purchase a watercolour of a stretch of wild prairie for his own pleasure, declaring that the canvas would cheer his sickly wife. 'It will 'mind her of what waits for her when she recovers from the pleurisy,' he announced with great satisfaction, briefly indenting painting and illness in Amity's thoughts.

In despair at her inability to supplement, or entirely replace, her tutoring duties with the profession of artist, she grew increasingly dissatisfied with her efforts, bemoaning deficiencies of form and colour. 'You're too hard on yourself,' her mother commented during one such bout of critical introspection. 'Folk look past what they don't like until they find something they do.'

Unconvinced by the advice, she suddenly remembered something. 'What happened to the sketches made by that odd creature—I don't recall the name—when I was a child? I should like to see them to compare them with my own.'

In spite of her mother's protestations that she couldn't remember the last time she set eyes on the sketches, she searched the house, eventually coming across them tucked into the pages of the photograph album. Thrilled at the discovery, she carefully unfolded the heavy, creased paper and stared at the almost forgotten renderings. 'Oh my!' she exclaimed, as the ink and charcoal images leapt to vivid life under her gaze. The sketches struck her as bold and original as the day they were drawn, rendering her own attempts pallid by comparison.

'Pippikins!' she muttered, poring over the quick, inventive lines and varnished tints, which impressed her as only enhanced by the patina of years. A tear came to her eye as she dwelt on the image of her mother and siblings bathed in a ray of light. She recalled the deft, spidery fingers and flowery oration which produced the images, seeing again the lanky, lustrously haired artist as he bent over his work, humming and murmuring to himself. She gasped in astonishment as she turned to the sketch of her father, the lined face and unkempt hair a faithful replica. 'This is pa!' she exclaimed to her mother. 'He's grown into his own likeness!'

'It's the light,' her mother demurred, taking the sketch from Amity and holding it at an angle.

'It's still pa!' she insisted, to which her ma grudgingly agreed. 'Look, Pa, it's you!' she declared before supper, holding up the sketch in front of his eyes.

He took it from her, holding it carefully in his large hands, which now trembled from age and toil. 'Blow me down,' he said, his eyes widening at the likeness. He handed it back. 'Show me the buffalo,' he said. 'Ah!' He studied the windy rendering for some minutes. 'Those are wings,' he said, indicating the feathered lances protruding from the side of the creature. 'I thought them crazy at first, but now they don't seem so queer.' He set down the sketch, a doleful look on his face. 'I wish they were real and that the rock could jest lift up and fly away from those durned rubbernecks!'

Amity carefully put away the sketches, her own attempts striking her as pitiful by comparison. The truth of her own limitations was like gall to her soul as she decided there and then to abandon the foolish notion of living by the brush. She wandered outside to nurse her disappointment. The autumn day was cool and breezy and she wrapped her arms around herself as she pondered the rock, recalling that hot, summer day when the artist stood patiently in its shade, capturing the creature with his long, nimble fingers in a way that she never could. The unfairness of frustrated hopes hung over her like a dark cloud as she put away her brushes and sticks for the last time.

The next day, still feeling out of sorts, she asked her father to harness the buggy. 'Mrs. Haussauer has invited me to stop by for coffee,' she told him as he helped her climb up onto the seat. 'I suspect she wants me to instruct her girls.' She wore her large straw hat against the bright sun.

'I thought you didn't care for her?'

'On certain days,' she said and shook the reins, leaving Purchase to scratch his head as he stared after her.

THE MORNING WAS FINE and blowy, the wind pushing clouds across the sky. The horse trotted down the tarred road that led past the rock—already busy with sightseeing vehicles. Eyes turned to look, surprised to see a woman out driving alone. She held her head high as she passed the slower conveyances, flicking the reins as though expert and long used to such independence.

A short way past the rock, a wagon came toward her, slowing as the equipages converged. 'Miss McLennan! Howdy!' The driver, a pock-faced, bearded man wearing a soiled, floppy hat, hauled up the team. His wife gazed curiously at her.

'Mr Witherspoon, Mrs. Witherspoon,' she said, her voice prim-sounding to her ears.

'You are alone, Miss McLennan?' The wife peered at her from beneath a white sunbonnet.

'I am on my way to visit with Emily Haussauer.'

'You must visit us one day—for coffee and fixings.'

She smiled, hoping it wouldn't present as a grimace. The three sat and looked at each other for a minute. 'I won't detain you,' she said.

The other woman poked her husband. 'Oh!' he said. 'Good day to you, Miss McLennan!' He shook the reins and the wagon lurched past. She continued her journey as the tar gave way to dirt, resisting the impulse to look back. *I feel her eyes on me!* The Haussauer farm appeared just ahead. She could see Mr Haussauer and his two grown sons working in the fields. A line of laundry flapped in the wind behind the farmhouse. She continued along the dirt road before they saw her.

Hers was the only conveyance on the road as it wound into the distance. A stretch of cultivated land lay to her left. On the right, the wild, open prairie stretched to the horizon. On impulse, she steered off the road and into the grass. The mare resisted at first, neighing and trying to regain the track. 'Skit!' she said, employing her pa's command. 'Git, for goodness' sake!'

She drove for a quarter hour into the bluffs, leaving both the Haussauer farm and the rock far behind. Thrilled, and a little abashed at her own daring, she continued, the buggy lurching and rocking over the uneven ground. She was surrounded by hummocks and swelling grasslands on all sides. A buzzard whistled overhead. She pulled down the brim of her hat against the sun. Where in flapjacks am I? she wondered but pressed on as if helpless to turn back against the claim of the wild, unfolding savanna. I could go on forever, she imagined, the wind gusting in her ears and the boundless sky overhead.

Concerned lest she break a wheel, she reined the panting horse to a stop. The mare was snorting, unused to such exertion. Heat rose in waves from her crest and withers. Amity looked around, momentarily frightened at the desolate, cloud-shadowed swells and the deafening silence. She was suffering dreadfully from thirst and reprimanded herself for not bringing water. The mare whinnied, the noise startling in the silence. She wanted to climb down but was afraid the mare might wander off in search of water and leave her stranded. She sat there, trying to control her nerves as she took in the enormous, windblown prospect. She was utterly alone—a brief, fragile creature suspended amid the vaulting cradle of grass and sky. Is this freedom? she wondered. She imagined herself cast back a hundred years or so, sat in the same, untamed wilderness, its only inhabitants buffalo and Indians.

She removed her hat, closing her eyes as the wind lifted her hair. Opening them again, she spotted something shining in the grass. After a puzzled stare she realised it was a bleached buffalo skull lying amid the reeds. Her gaze lingered on it, a sense of despondency stealing over her. The old man, the rock-patriarch, made something out of nothing. He left evidence. Evidence of what, she was uncertain, but it felt, she told herself, the right word. And that painter-body—what in Heaven was his name? —was another. They expressed their longings and made them flesh. Anguish seized her. I have no hand to carve with or paint. A heart that feels but cannot express. A soul that hungers, but with no object to fix upon. She turned her eyes on the vast acres of cloud-rippled grass, a sense of despair piercing her soul. 'Where is the buffalo to succour me?' The cry leapt from deep inside her, the wind sweeping away the words even as they left her mouth.

JUBAL MCLENNAN HAD JUST turned nineteen years of age and was planning to pledge himself to Susie Schamber when he was murdered in a saloon fight. He had gone into town planning to buy Susie a betrothal gift when a friend invited him to the newly opened Silver Spur saloon for a drink. Shortly after sitting down, he became involved in a dispute with a disgruntled cowpoke at the next table. The cowboy, angry at losing at cards, swore at Jubal and cursed again when challenged over the remark. The cross words quickly escalated into a physical brawl, other patrons scattering as chairs were overturned. Jubal was getting the better of the encounter when the cowpoke suddenly yanked out a knife and thrust it deep in the young man's ribs. Jubal hung on to life for a few, tortured minutes as his friend frantically tried to staunch the blood discolouring his shirt. Doc Henderson was sent for, but Jubal had already expired, breathing in tortured gasps and calling for his mother. The cowpoke, meanwhile, had beaten a hasty retreat, mounting his horse and whipping him out of town before the law could intervene.

His parents took the news hard, Felicity trembling so violently she would have fallen but for her husband's arm around her waist.

THEY BURIED THEIR SON in a grave Purchase dug behind the house, his mind numb as he spaded the earth. At the service, Amity cried and cried, while Boundary stood alongside her, a dazed, uncomprehending look on his face. Purchase stood straight and stiff, his thoughts alternating between grief and a desire for revenge against the unknown cowpoke. Felicity leaned against her husband, her face ravaged with sorrow. She barely heard the voice of the elderly preacher, Pastor Jacobson, as he intoned the words of woe and parting. The service was briefly interrupted when Susie Schamber gave a loud cry and collapsed in her mother's arms.

Afterwards, all Amity remembered was Boundary escorting her back to the house and sitting her down in a chair where she sat in a daze until her pa gently chided her into retiring. 'Come on, Am. You need to sleep. You'll feel better in the morning.'

The words, although suffused with sorrow and kindly meant, pricked her. 'I never shall again!' she said and burst into fresh tears.

Bellow printed news of the incident himself, sparing Boundary the task. 'It's the least I could do,' he told his wife. 'He shouldn't have to live it over.'

FELICITY AGED OVERNIGHT, HER already frail condition worsening with grief. Each day in the week following the funeral, she set a place for Jubal at the breakfast table, her husband merely nodding, with sorrowful face, at the sight. 'Where's Jubal?' she asked one morning, confusion on her face. 'I don't remember seeing him all yesterday.'

'He's out back,' answered Purchase, not knowing what else to say. She accepted this, pouring coffee into her son's cup. 'He'd better hurry before the food's cold,' she said. It was only later, when she sat darning his shirt, that the realisation seemed to strike her. 'Oh!' she cried and wept, freshly heartbroken, pressing her face into the flannel.

Burdened by the loss and driven to near madness by the daily festivities at the rock, Purchase abandoned the fields, retreating to feed the livestock and dig the vegetable patch. He kept his hands as busy as possible, shutting out the noise from the rock and his own thoughts as he mended a fence or tended the cows, moving from task to task with mechanical purpose.

Amity reduced her work week to two days and moved back from the Halversons' to help look after her parents. They were old now, and in need of assistance, she realised, the knowledge surprising and saddening her. '*Pa was always so strong and busting with energy,*' she wrote in her journal. '*It grieves me to see his slow steps and his breath so short. And ma seems lost to the world. Yesterday, she forgot my name and seemed confused when I reminded her. Her hair is entirely grey.*'

Her own sorrow at the loss of her brother ate away at her, compounding the uncertainty and unhappiness she felt with her own life. She briefly considered moving back to St Charles but just as quickly abandoned the notion. My place is here, for better or worse, she decided. And as for happiness, I'll just have to figure that out. It was this fatalism with regard to her future that prompted her, to her own surprise, to accept the offer of marriage proposed by Ira Morgan on a condolence visit to the farm.

'*Ma is feeling better now and pa urges me to accept out of concern for my future,*' she wrote. '*And to tell the truth, Ira has grown on me with his kind words over Jube. He is steady and dependable, like pa, and will make a good husband.*' And, with these words, she consigned her own destiny to wedlock and a small, tidy farm one mile the other side of town. '*The Soul has bandaged moments,*' she quoted enigmatically in her journal, uncertain what she meant, her eyes glistening with tears.

41

Artefacts of Love

THE UNBEARABLE LOSS OF her eldest son had reshaped Felicity's frail body, rendering it bent and crooked so that she no longer resembled, nor remembered, the lively quickness of her former self. When asked a question by her husband or visiting daughter, she mused on the answer, sometimes dwelling on it to her private satisfaction until reminded of the question. 'Never no mind,' she would answer and giggle to herself at the bemused look on the face of the questioner.

A doctor came one day to examine her—Henderson, he called himself—claiming she knew him. And she did, in some part of her, recollecting a man with bushy eyebrows and bright eyes who told her to pour medicine into her daughter's ear. 'Why?' she asked him now, her voice sharp with distrust.

'Why what, Mrs. McLennan?' he answered, peering into her eyes in a manner she found rudely impertinent.

'Never no mind,' she said, averting her eyes.

He asked her a series of questions, further annoying her before peering into her eyes again. Finally, he turned and looked at her husband. 'It's as you say,' he said, straightening up.

'What is?' she wanted to ask, but didn't, shy of those bushy eyebrows.

As winter passed into spring and the weather grew warmer, she felt better, suddenly recollecting things and enjoying the sunshine. 'Crocus!' She raised the cane her husband had carved for her on the advice of the doctor and pointed and jabbed in triumphant recall. 'Crocus! Yellow violet! Forget-me-not!'

She glanced at her husband as if he might disagree. But he nodded, smiling. 'You used to love the first wild violets,' he said.

'Still do!'

'Would you like to pick some—put them in a vase?' he asked.

'They are better off in the grass, where they belong. They ain't harming none,' she said.

Her daughter and her other son, Boundary—where did he fetch that name? —visited often, the latter insisting on walking her around the yard whether she felt like it or not. 'I ain't an invalid!' she protested, although secretly pleased at the way he took her arm, guiding her as if she had forgotten her own way around. Her daughter sometimes read to her from a journal, glancing up between sentences. 'Do you remember, Ma? You wrote that when you were just sixteen.'

She pretended to remember, nodding, and humming. 'Read me some more,' she said, liking the story.

Amity picked up another journal. 'Your first impressions of the prairie,' she said. She read a half-page, surprised to jog her own memories of thunderstorms and wildfires. 'Do you recall?' she asked, annoying her mother, who grumbled and stared off into the distance in protest.

'Jumpy.' Amity pointed to the page. 'Do you remember him?'

''Course I remember! I used feed him scraps. Or was it Jubal?'

'You remember Jubal?'

'Where's your mind at?' Felicity said, her voice sharp. 'Wasn't he standing here but one moment ago?'

Her husband was attentive, out of habit as much as anything, she supposed, when she still supposed things. One evening he took out a scrapbook she had kept years before, while still in St Charles. 'Look, dear.' He drew up a chair to sit beside her and set the book in her lap. He turned the pages, showing variously a picture, a pressed flower, the words of a favourite poem. 'Do you recall?' he asked several times, studying her face for signs of recognition. He turned another page, puzzled to see a strip of cloth pinned to the stiff paper. 'What's this?' he asked.

'Let me see.' She lifted the book close to her face. 'Beats me!'

He turned the page, exclaiming with pleasure at a small, glued card dated from their first days of courtship and written in her distinctive hand. '*To my dearest heart. With all my affection.*'

They pondered the item for a moment, like two archaeologists who'd stumbled upon lost artefacts of love.

'You must have given me something,' he guessed. 'A gift, perhaps.'

'Maybe it weren't for you,' she said. 'Maybe it was for someone else!' She cackled at the notion, and he joined in, both of them smiling and chuckling at the memory of love.

'You 'mind me of someone,' she said another time.

'Who?'

'Someone. Are you my pa?'

His face saddened. 'I'm Purchase, Felice. I'm your husband.'

She looked confused for a moment, and then frowned, her voice peevish. 'Gingersnaps! I knew that!'

'I WANT YOU TO try your hand at reporting.' Bellow had been idly watching his charge sweep the floor while mulling over the young man's future.

'Reporting?' Boundary looked baffled. 'On what?'

'Fandango! Is there nothing in this entire town that moves you to want to investigate, to examine, to know more about?'

'I guess not.' Boundary resumed sweeping.

'You don't care, for example, to know who it was fired a shot at Mortimer Gully the other night?'

'Long as it wasn't at me!'

Bellow watched Boundary put away the broom and pick up the ink balls in preparation for printing a poster. Taking out a cigar, he wet the end with his lips, his eyes still on Boundary. 'Son,' he said as he fished for a match. 'You ever wonder why I started a newspaper?'

Well versed by now in his employer's verbal ruminations, Boundary shook his head and said nothing.

Bellow struck the match and lit the cigar, leaning farther back in the chair to lift his feet up onto the desk. 'I did it because I was curious about things.' He examined the cigar, reflecting on the notion. 'It's a privilege to work as a newspaperman, for then you get to witness—at second hand, admittedly, but witness nonetheless—the workings of the world. But to get a notion of how the world works—its operations and all the oiling that goes to grease the wheels—you must first of all figure out why things are the way they are. Did you ever think of that?'

He watched for a moment as Boundary tested the chase for firmness. 'Take, for example,' he continued, 'this great country of ours. What makes it flourish? What makes it thrive?' He spat out a grain of tobacco. 'The answer'—he pointed with the cigar—'is consumptibles!' He smoked on the word, savouring it's satisfying roundness. 'The wealth of a nation is in the production of consumptibles. Read Mr Smith—every man his own merchant. And my own production? Why, I be a purveyor—a purveyor of words. Words are my capital. As they increase so, too, does my influence over those who consume them. The return, you might say, for my labour. And you, young man, what is your production? Nay,' he said, holding up a hand at Boundary's confused expression. 'I shall answer for you. Machines, sir. Is that press not a machine? And you, son, you keep it working. Your labour smooths the parts, engages the gears, and turns the screw that produces the page that carries forth my poor words into the world. Our labour, joined together, produces this newspaper. A thing, friend, a consumptible!' He puffed on the cigar. 'Do you follow?'

'No.'

'Gadzooks!' Swinging his feet down, Bellow sat up in the chair, an impatient frown on his face. 'Do you wish only to operate that press for the rest of your life? No! Don't answer! Well, if you can't see the benefit in rising up in your occupation, in embracing the entirety of the newspaper business, then I must be your mentor and inspiration in that regard.' He eyed Boundary, who was setting type in the compositing stick. 'I want you to stop that and to go down to the railroad station.'

'The station? Why? You need something picked up?'

'I want—I wish—for you to observe, and to bring me back word of what you see. You will then write it up to my satisfaction and we shall include it in Saturday's edition. Maybe even on the front page. How does that please you?' He sat forward, tipping cigar ash into the cup on his desk.

'You want me to see what?'

'Heavens to a crow! Do I need to spell out everything? Bring me back what you see with your own two eyes. You decide what's worthy of observation and reporting. Use your brain, your judgement, your discernment, as to the answer. There are folk flocking in every day, for example, to view that dang buffalo. Report what they have to say—about the journey, their expectations, and so forth. Do you follow? Think of it as an exercise, if you will. A valuable opportunity to develop your journalistic skills.'

Thus, a quarter hour later, a discomfited and thoroughly puzzled Boundary stood, notebook and pen in hand, on the platform of the railroad station, awaiting the next train. As he waited, he noticed an Indian family, a father, mother, and two children, standing a short distance away. The father wore a round, narrow-brimmed hat decorated with a blue ribbon. He was clad in a waistcoat and striped trousers tucked into moccasin boots. The mother was bareheaded and wore a long, cotton dress down to her ankles. The dress had a line of bone buttons down the front. The two children wore smocks and moccasins, their dark hair hanging freely. The family appeared to be waiting for the train to appear, possibly as passengers, he figured, but more likely out of curiosity to see the iron horse for themselves. One or two inquisitive bystanders, and then a small crowd, soon gathered around the family, it being unusual to see Indians on the platform.

'Which tribe are you?' a young man asked, hands on his hips as he confronted the father.

'Mandan?' the youth shrieked with derision at the answer. 'I thought the Mandan were all massacred—the Sioux put paid to 'em!'

Others in the small crowd offered comments, some curious, some amused, and some hostile. More people gathered as the children looked nervously from their father to their mother. Both parents maintained a silent, stoic air as the crowd, emboldened by their passivity, began to taunt the family. 'What in bob-snake are you doing here?' a man demanded.

'Durn Injuns!' offered another. 'They don't belong with decent white folk.'

'This is a Christian country,' contributed another. 'We don't need no godforsaken savages fouling it up!'

'Heck, yeah. Get out of here!' a youth, scarcely older than the Indian boy, shouted. 'Dirty savages!'

The crowd grew more hostile in the face of the family's impassive silence. 'This is a civilised town,' a man jeered, his face sharp with indignation. 'Why are you stinking up the place? You should be out on the prairie living in a wigwam!'

A man Boundary recognised as Jasper Lehmans, a newly arrived homesteader from Germany, rudely bumped the Indian, thrusting his face into the latter's. 'Go away! And take your heathenish ways with you!'

Just then, a whistle sounded, and a train entered the station, steam hissing from its pistons and smoke pouring from the stack. The mob surrounding the family dissipated as the participants went off to meet passengers. The train doors opened, and people stepped down, some obviously emigrants with their quaint costumes and foreign words. Others, just as clearly, were visitors, bound to see the buffalo. A half-dozen men walked up and down the platform, some holding placards, calling out the name of the Buffalo Trust and steering visitors in the direction of a large counter set up to one side. The counter was emblazoned with the name of the Trust and decorated with posters and photographs of the rock.

'Come see Bjornson's marvel!' a man shouted, cupping his hands to his mouth.

'Get your buffalo tickets here!' trumpeted another.

'The buffalo? This way,' another man called out, attempting to shepherd a group of visitors in the direction of a waiting omnibus.

'Git, you son of a bitch!' A tall, broad-shouldered man in a Stetson rudely accosted the tout. Grasping him by the collar, he roughly propelled him along the platform before flinging him to the floor. 'I warned you!' he threatened. The man's two companions were dealt with just as violently, along with a half-dozen other, unlicensed drivers.

'Ladies, gentlemen!' Another man appeared on the scene, soothing the alarmed visitors. 'They ain't Buffalo Trust employees, but thieves and charlatans here to take your honest money. You can count yourselves lucky we were here to protect you! This way, ladies and gentlemen, to see the buffalo. Ride in an honest, approved Trust omnibus and you can be assured of a safe and comfortable ride. This way to the buffalo!'

The platform was now crowded as more and more people stepped down from the carriages. One party, wearing badges proclaiming they were from Oak Bluffs, Iowa, gathered around a man in a brown suit with a Buffalo Trust ribbon draped over his shoulder. 'First the hotel—first class—to refresh yourselves and get something to eat. And then meet your personal guide, who'll tell you everything you need to know about the eighth marvel of the world. Step this way, ladies and gents! Follow me.'

'Well? What did you see?' asked Bellow on his return.

'A bunch of visitors, I guess, come to see the buffalo.'

'And?'

'Some emigrants. Leastways they looked like emigrants.'

'Heavens to a crow! Anything else? No angels descending, no miracles taking place?'

'Huh?'

Bellow sank his head in his hands. 'I may as well have sent my shoes!'

'Oh, and there was a ruckus.'

'A ruckus?' Bellow looked up, his eyes bright. 'Pray describe.'

'Some big old fella in a Stetson put the rush on another fella.'

Bellow gave a shuddering sigh. 'Run next door,' he said, his voice bleak. 'Fetch me coffee.'

THE COMMUNION HE HAD once imagined he felt with the buffalo was broken, burst apart under the weight of sightseers, touts, hucksters, and souvenir hunters who each left an imprint on the granite skin, their unwelcome presence threatening to obliterate his own ancestral connection with the towering beast. The bitterness he had felt ever since the condemnation surged up anew at the sight of each crowded omnibus arrived to disgorge yet more guests eager to clamber on and defile his rock. The sounds of music and merrymaking in the long summer evenings, when Lomax organised dances and carnivals to squeeze more money from the excited revellers, made him itch to turn a cannon on the carousers and blow them all to kingdom come.

His anger only slightly abated in winter when the rock lay desolate and abandoned in the freezing cold. At such time, he had it largely to himself, apart from the few, hardy enthusiasts who paid a Trust photographer extra to pose beneath the monument wrapped in coats, scarves, and hats. Strapping on snowshoes, he made a daily circuit of the object, stopping to mutter and scowl whenever he came across a discarded tobacco pouch, candy wrapper, or even a glove, left lying in the snow.

'It ain't yourn anymore—if it ever was,' a Trust employee had once observed after Purchase complained at finding evidence of another sliver of granite chipped from the base of the rock. 'It belongs to the Trust, now,' the man taunted, shooing him away. 'You gotta buy a ticket, jest like everybody else.'

'I was here when there was nothing but Indians and buffaloes in these parts!' protested Purchase, outraged at the man's insolent manner.

'Well, there ain't no more Injuns, and this is about the only buffalo left, so git along!' The man laughed at his own joke. 'Git, little dogie!'

For a moment, he seriously contemplated going back to the house and fetching the Sharps. *A bullet through the gut would settle his hash!* But now, with the last snow of winter draining from the grass, his chief preoccupation was not the buffalo, but Felicity. He had watched over her during the winter, fearing he detected a further decline in her health in the severe cold. He hovered and fussed, insisting she wear the warm buffalo robe across her shoulders, despite her complaints that she felt she was burning up under it. He insisted she take the medicine prescribed by Doc Henderson for her condition, although privately wondering if it did any good. 'It's just coloured water,' he complained to Amity when she visited. 'What your ma needs is her mind back.'

'Something that can't ever be given,' murmured Amity. She sat in silent commiseration, noting the lines and crags on her father's face. 'How are you holding up, pa?' she asked, breaking the silence.

'I miss your mother,' he said. 'Even though she's here.'

'I'll try and come by more often. Sometimes, though, it's hard to get away.'

'Don't over-trouble yourself.' He patted her hand. 'We manage just fine.'

If Felicity was even aware of the conversations occurring around her, she gave no sign, insisting, whenever asked, that she was 'hanging on' for spring. 'It's getting warmer,' she said. 'I feel it in my bones.'

And indeed, her condition improved with the return of the warm weather. She felt livelier, more remembering of things, and more alert to what was going on around her. 'I ain't ready for the shoebox yet,' she joked, puzzling at the wince this brought to her husband's face.

EDISON LOMAX WAS INORDINATELY pleased with himself. The 'cash cow' was raking in money as its celebrity spread and sightseers from as far away as the southern states and even Europe flocked to lay eyes on it. A compliant council, dazzled by the continuing flow of riches, acceded to his every wish, even holding special 'buffalo days' when townsfolk, dressed up as runners, pretended to hunt the animal. They did so to the accompaniment of whoops and yells from Indians hired from the nearby Mandan reservation to the delight of the crowd. The fact that there were no actual buffalo was a minor inconvenience, as domestic cattle draped in buffalo robes served the purpose just as well.

The year before, he had finally managed to secure two mature bulls from a breeding ranch in Kansas, importing them into town with great fanfare. The beasts were paraded up and down Main Street to cheers and gasps from the crowd of spectators. The nervous animals were showered with applause as they were led by experienced handlers via stout leather collars around their necks. Horsemen rode alongside to ensure the spooked beasts didn't charge into the crowd.

Following the parade, the buffalo were penned in an enclosure set up near the rock. Eager easterners were charged two bits a head to pose in front of the animals as they grazed behind the fence. Lomax had the animals photographed beneath the rock itself, the result printed on postcards and sold in the gift shop at a dime each. The shop also boasted a range of buffalo earrings, necklaces, bracelets, and even chocolates, all stamped with a facsimile of the rock monument that was the patented brand of the Buffalo Trust.

Ever restless for new sources of income, Lomax hit upon the idea of selling buffalo bones. Inspired by stories in the national press, he sent out carts to pick up every bone they could find, buffalo or not, which were then stacked into a wall six feet high and thirty feet long. An exclusive 'package tour' offered visitors the opportunity to explore the rock and then ride in special carriages to view the wall and pick a bone, paying extra for photographic mementoes of the excursion.

Gratified by the excitement aroused by this reminder of the perished abundance, he despatched teams of gatherers to scour the prairie in further search of skulls. And such was the plenitude of skeletons still littering the plains that the teams managed to gather sufficient skulls, cracked and weathered, to form a single giant pyramid, fifty feet high and three hundred fifty square feet at the base, made up entirely of thousands upon thousands of bleached skulls.

Guides led sightseers around the immense bone pile, drawing murmurs as they described the extent of the uncountable herds that once made the plains tremble with their passing. 'Biggest herds in all the world, even bigger than those in Africa,' they expounded, spreading out arms in an attempt to convey the magnitude of the great bison treks. Visitors flocked on horseback and in wagons and carriages to view the spectacle, the more adventurous lining up to scale the bone mound and have themselves pictured sitting or standing on top of the pyramid in a vindication of American enterprise.

Lomax himself sometimes accompanied the tours, travelling incognito, as he listened to comments or complaints and made note of further ways to skin money from the flow of visitors. He also kept a sharp eye out for instances of staff skimming profits by offering 'special' opportunities to take home a dried bone or a cutting of 'live' buffalo wool from the captive animals. Indeed, observing one enterprising young staffer offer the latter, he promptly included the token as part of the special tour package, offering 'a clip' of buffalo wool for an extra ten cents, while firing the offending employee.

'How much this week?' he asked Charles Tewksbury, the accountant he had brought in from Chicago to keep track of income and expenses.

Tewksbury, an unsmiling, diminutive man with an obsession for numbers, looked up from the ledger open on the table before him. 'We pulled in 1,749 dollars, fifty-five cents,' he answered. 'Just forty-eight dollars down on last week.'

'That everything? Hotels, meals, drinks, transport, buffalo fees?'

'Everything, including souvenirs.'

'Anybody ask about the figures?'

'The mayor dropped by, asked to look at the books.'

'And?'

'And he asked to see you. Reckons he's getting hornswoggled.'

'Which books did you show him?'

'Those ones, of course.' The accountant gestured at two ledgers that sat in a tray.

'Then how did he figure he's getting steamed?'

The accountant tipped his visor back on his head. 'Ask me, he's got someone inside.'

''Course he does.' Lomax tightened his lips, an angry glint in his eye.

An hour later, he sat in the Silver Spur saloon nursing whisky and a cigar. Butch, Leo, and Willy sat at the table with him. 'What's the name of the mayor's inside man?' he asked.

'That would be Billy Montague, the bus driver.'

'You handling him?' he asked Leo.

'Sure, boss. He tells the mayor what we tell him to say.'

'There's someone else.'

'Who?'

'I don't know. Someone close to the money.'

'Tewksbury? I never did trust that pan-faced—'

'Not that close!' He puffed on the cigar. 'Any new hires lately?'

'The beer tent. We're always taking on help to set things up.'

'Anyone else? Butch?'

The other man frowned, knitting his brow to think. 'That slippery little runt we hired to sell tickets at the gate. What's his name?' He turned to Leo.

'Rosen? The Dutchie?' Leo shook his head in bemusement. 'He seems fair and square.'

'Hey!' Willy wiped beer from his lips. 'I saw the spitball gagging with the mayor last week. They were off beside the tent, parleying.'

'Then there's your snake.'

Butch lifted his eyebrows. 'Want me to handle it?'

Lomax took the cigar from his mouth and pursed his lips, blowing out a thin stream of smoke. 'Sooner rather than later,' he said, surveying the smoke. 'But first, find out what he told the goddamn mayor. Willy, fetch us another bottle.'

42

A Surprise Return

FELICITY WOKE WITH A fright, uncertain where she was. The room was illuminated with the cavernous light of a winter morning. A sense of panic swept over her, and she breathed in short, quick pants. Slowly, the panic subsided as she recollected who and where she was. She stared at the man next to her, gasping and muttering in sleep. *Purchase. Purchase McLennan. My husband.* Angry and frightened at her own forgetfulness, she snuggled back beneath the warm buffalo robe, shivering as she pictured the snow outside and the bleak, frozen prairie. Cradled under the covers, her fright subsided as her breathing grew deeper. Murmuring, she enumerated thanks for her three children—mistaking the count in the early light—and the summer wildflowers she loved and even the household items in the manner drilled by her father. 'But that's not all,' she muttered in protest, adding to the tally a stockholding of abundant plains, diaphanous skies, and the long, liquid light of buffalo grass.

And soon she melted away from her sleeping husband back to the foothills of her childhood and long days spent laughing and gossiping with school friends at Miss Gibbon's Academy for Young Ladies back in Boston. 'Felicity Bell! Hush or I'll sew up your mouth; see if I don't!' Faces whose names she no longer recalled stood alongside her in the choir, singing—and sticking out tongues the moment the choirmaster's back was turned. One face was that of her mother, and another of Amity, both smiling sweetly and puzzling her with their presence. She hummed softly, enjoying the hymn, but forgetful of the words.

When she awoke again, her husband was still asleep, snoring and grumbling to himself in the uncertain light. Slowly she got out of bed, thrusting her feet—how gnarled they looked! —into the woollen slippers before making her way to the kitchen. The stove was still warm, and she blew on the embers, inciting a small flame which she fed with scraps of paper and shreds of wool. She made her way to the door, stopping with her hand on the bar, trying to remember what she wanted.

Removing the bar, she opened the door to peep outside. It was past dawn and fresh snow had fallen in the yard. Shivering in the wintry air, she closed the door again. She picked up a pot and dipped it in a pail of water before setting it on the stove. She sat down at the table, pulling the wool shawl around her.

Her husband found her there, dozing, when he got up. 'Felice?' He bent over her, anxious until she responded, blinking as if surprised by his presence. 'Stay there,' he said. 'I'll make us breakfast.'

She watched him move about the room, her brow knitted, as if trying to think of something important that needed to be said. They ate a silent breakfast of cold pork and reheated beans. Then, astonishingly, and without a word being said, they climbed back into the still-warm bed and fell upon each other with all the passion formerly reserved for flowers and buffaloes, engulfing each other in a silent yet urgent sucking of tongues and desperate yearning for flesh and warmth. And afterwards, they lay in each other's arms, frightened yet reassured by the other's need and reluctant to get up again and face the cold winter's day.

'I bet you never reckoned on that,' she teased, having recovered sufficiently to tease her husband's flowing beard. To her gratitude, he kissed her and stroked her hair. The taste of pork and beans was still on his mouth as she rather shyly returned the kiss and shifted to her side.

That was the last time she ever kissed her husband. When they got up for a second time following a passionless post-coital nap, each returned to the grassy solitude which stamped their days. He went out to the barn to shovel dung and wonder at what had just happened, while she sat at the fireside with her needlework, staring into the flames, swathed in an inconsolable sadness at the passing of days.

THE EVER-INCREASING FLOW OF visitors and dollars into the town had not escaped the attention of Quintus Bellow. The publisher of the *Dispatch* publicly called on the council to reveal the income from the monument and the disbursement of funds. The reply came in the form of an itemised list, detailing the number of new gas lamps to light the streets, the newly resurfaced downtown area, donations to the Women's League and the Temperance Society, and funds set aside for the construction of a modern brick hall suitable for concerts and other public entertainments. The list was delivered by the trust's lawyer, Jay Malting, who hinted, none too subtly, at the inconveniences involved with public discussion of such matters.

'Why get folk riled up over nothing?' he asked as he handed over the requested list inside a brown envelope. 'You'll find all the answers to your questions in there,' he said, watching as Bellow pulled out the list.

Bellow ran his eye up and down the items. 'There's nothing about salaries. Nor percentages, nor how much the trust costs to operate.'

'Folks don't care about that stuff. They care about lighting in the streets.'

'And what do you care about, Mr Malting—in your three-piece suit?'

'Me? I care about peace and safety, Mr Bellow. Peace and safety.'

'Meaning?'

'Meaning public order, the safety of businessmen to go about their dealings and earn a fair return for their efforts. You're a businessman, ain't you, Mr Bellow?'

'I hear they found a trust employee in a ditch with his throat cut. Know anything about his safety?'

'Unfortunate. But nothing to do with me. Guess he trod on somebody's tail.'

'Some no-account maybe? Like the one that did for Mayor Buskins?'

Malting's face wrinkled with exaggerated interest. 'You reckon they're connected?'

'Boundary! Get the door for Mr Malting. He's just leaving.'

'Don't forget, Mr Bellow. It's all there, in that list. Everything you need to know. Anything else, come see me. I'm sure we can work something out.'

Bellow watched as the other man stepped out onto the sidewalk. 'That perfumed dandy is a bigger thief than the mayor!' He drummed his fingers and stared at the door, a pensive frown on his face. 'What do you hear?'

'About what?'

'Jumping Jeremiah! The price of eggs! Are you a newspaperman or not? Do you even care about what goes into those sheets you love so much?' He sighed, exasperated at the sullen look that came over Boundary's face. 'Never mind! I guess I'll write, and you print.' He scratched an ear, thinking ahead to the next editorial, 'Like a preacher mulling his Sunday sermon,' his wife had teased, the analogy pleasing him.

'The press is like a church, a secular church,' he'd replied, expounding on the comparison, 'calling elected officials and big business to order.' He was so inspired by the phrase that he considered using it as a masthead for the *Dispatch*, until someone pointed out that potential advertisers might be unimpressed. Instead, he settled for *Voice of the Public,* later refining that to *Voice of the Common Man.*

'There's something or someone rotten in Denmark,' he mused aloud. 'And it ain't Hamlet.'

FELICITY WAS SITTING IN the rocker Purchase had placed outside for her, a blanket across her knees. She saw him straighten up and put his hand over his eyes to peer into the distance. 'Is it that old rock again?' she grumbled. 'It ain't going nowhere, so quit gawking!'

'It ain't the rock.' A rider on a grey mare plodded through the grass toward them.

'Who is it?' she prompted, peevish at the day.

'I ain't a fortune teller.' He strained to see as the rider drew closer. 'Maybe a neighbour come to call.'

The rider entered the yard and pulled rein. To his surprise, the stranger was an elderly Indian woman. She was dressed in worn clothes made from animal hides and decorated with beads and coloured threads. Her head was bare, her face lined and blackened by the sun. Her hair was gathered into thick grey plaits, twined with ribbons that hung down her back. She regarded him for a moment before sliding down from the unsaddled mare, the horse almost as old and weather-beaten as herself.

'Who are you?' he asked. 'And what do you want here?'

'I'm Half Moon,' she said. 'Your wife. I've come home to die.'

He stared, dumbstruck, as the woman regarded Felicity.

'Who are you?' Felicity's voice was sharp.

The woman walked over to where she sat. 'I am your sister,' she said.

'You are?' Felicity stared in wonderment. 'I've never had a sister before.'

'Then we shall be good friends.' The woman turned to Purchase, who stood rooted to the spot, his mouth open in shock. 'Husband,' she said. 'My horse is thirsty.'

43

A Confederacy of Hearts

PEERING INTO THE MIRROR, Amity hardly recognised the self—fretful and petulant—that peered back. What in molasses was I thinking? she asked the self in the mirror. *You weren't*, came the blunt reply.

'Amity! Are you there?'

She turned away, her lips tightening at the sound of her mother-in-law's voice.

'There you are!' Fleur Morgan grimaced, rubbing her shoulder as Amity stepped out of the bedroom. 'I need you to rub some of that ointment in,' she said. 'And I could use a spoonful of medicine.'

'I thought Doc Henderson told you to ease up on that stuff?'

'I need it for my shoulder.'

Amity fetched the bottle, noticing it was a quarter drained. 'Here.'

She watched the old woman pour a large spoonful and slurp it down. With a grimace, Fleur poured more of the reddish-brown liquid onto the spoon. 'It helps me settle,' she said.

'She's a thorn—a large, pointy one, in my side,' Amity wrote to Polly Buskins—now moved with her husband to Bismarck. As always, she was careful to edit her emotions with respect to her marriage lest she confirm Polly's surprised misgivings at her impulsive decision.

'Ain't it a mite reckless?' Polly had ventured when told of her acceptance of Ira's proposal. She glanced at Elspeth for support. 'I mean, Ira's a decent fella and all, but why so sudden?'

'It ain't what you think,' she'd replied. 'I guess it's just that Ira's the right fella for me.'

'I might as well be on the moon,' she complained in the same letter to Polly. *'There ain't another body—leastways one worth bothering with—within miles!'* The surrounding range had been largely abandoned by ranchers—the industry having never recovered from the disastrous winter of '86–'87, so that the homestead was, she confided to Polly, 'cocooned in its own little turtle shell of hermitude.' *'I could bear it if were just me and Ira,'* she moaned, *'but his ma flaps around like a one-eyed bat.'*

The farmhouse was small—smaller than her parents'—with just four rooms: a kitchen-parlour and two bedrooms, a tiny one for her mother-in-law, and another, barely larger, for herself and Ira. A small storeroom completed the layout. Feeling suffocated by her mother-in-law's tetchy presence, she'd persuaded her husband to convert an unused cart shed near the house into a small study. In it, she kept her sketchbooks and a hope chest containing a trousseau of linens and sentimental knick-knacks. She had moved in a small table, which served as a desk, and a lantern for the purpose, she told Polly, of 'lightin' out' whenever her mother-in-law grew too unbearable. The friendship-by-post had created a voluminous correspondence, which she kept neatly tied with red ribbons in the hope chest along with the dozen or so notebooks preserved from her time at the St Charles seminary.

In the twelve months since the wedding ceremony—conducted at her folks' place by Pastor Jacobson—she had come to think of the study as her private retreat, a sequestered cell from within whose confines she pondered her unsettled emotions while at the same time finding relief from the hourly vexations of her mother-in-law. '*How shall I best describe her?*' she wrote to Polly in a moment of candour. '*Grim-faced, sourish of disposition and resentful that her husband 'fetched off' (her words) so many years before. A prairie Miss Havisham, jilted by life.*'

In response to a request for advice from the still unmarried Elspeth, she replied by counselling patience and restraint—qualities, she ruefully reflected, she lacked in herself. '*It is most important that you and your future husband share similar interests. Ideally, the intended will possess a lively, passionate mind equal to your own, and be full-busting with curiosity about the world. It don't matter if suitors ain't lining up at the door. At the right time, the right fella will show up.*' Distrustful of her mother-in-law's snooping, she hid the letter until she was able to go into town, unescorted, and post it.

The weeks and months of her first year of marriage passed slowly, the isolation adding to the strain on her overstretched nerves. She did her best to keep her mind off her misgivings by rereading her seminary journals or confiding in Polly and Elspeth. '*There's plenty to occupy the hands,*' she observed dryly, '*no doubt about that! It's the mind—or is it the heart? —that thirsts for novelty and finer things.*'

She made efforts to be the dutiful, loving wife she knew her husband craved. She helped milk the cows and feed the chickens, and churned butter and cream as her mother had done before her. She kept the house and cared for her irascible mother-in-law with teeth-clenched forbearance. At night, she accommodated her husband's affections with awkward complaisance even as her mind roamed to her next letter or unfinished tasks. And when it all got to be too much, she escaped for long walks in the prairie grass, where she held manic 'busting fits' under the cloud-racked sky or took soul-saving buggy trips into town to visit Boundary.

'*I'm fairly positive my husband doesn't mean to be such a trial,*' she wrote on a scrap of paper. '*But he makes a body to spin sometimes! And I could swear his shrew of a mother has horns hidden under her lace cap.*' She studied the paper for a moment, feeling she could breathe again, before carefully tearing it up into tiny bits.

The following day she woke up to a rainstorm, the weather matching her mood as she made breakfast. She begged off attempts by her husband and mother-in-law to join them as they played the Vice and Virtue board game while waiting for the weather to clear. 'Off to that dusty old shed again?' Fleur gave a sour look over her glasses as Amity adjusted her shawl.

'Stay, take a turn,' her husband urged, but she shook her head. 'I'm afraid I find it dreadfully dull.'

The admission drew raised eyebrows and a pursing of the lips from Fleur. 'And what is in the cart shed, pray, that is so much more interesting than spending time with your husband?'

'I wish to write in my journal.' It was an excuse her mother had often used, the memory suddenly coming to her.

'Why don't you read it to us?' said Fleur, a glint in her eye. 'It would divert us from the rain.'

'It's of no consequence, and of no interest to anyone except to myself.'

'And yet, you abandon your husband to commit to it.' Fleur turned gimlet eyes on her. 'There must be something of interest to warrant such devotion?'

'Nothing. I assure you. Have you taken your medicine today, Mother?'

Covering her head with a coat, she dashed through the rain to the shed. Once inside, she opened the hope chest, brushing dust from the lid. Untying the bundled letters, she took out the most recent one, from Polly, to re-read:

Dearest Am, I have the fetchingest news! I'm with child! So far, only you and Elspeth know. And my folks. And Joe's ma. If the child is a girl, we'll call her after ma. If a boy, Eli, after Joe's pa. I had a letter from dear old Elspeth last week. She lamented the fact that she is still unmarried, and with no prospect in sight. Penny to a pancake she gets hooked by the end of this year! Bismarck is such a city! Full of wide streets and grand boulevards, with shops on every corner. And department stores, too. Proper ones, running to three storeys, with every bauble and gewgaw you'd ever think to see. Joe is interested in politics, like his pa, and is considering a run for mayor, once we've established ourselves. We get on so well. The other day he told an amusing story that had me in stitches until suppertime. That's him now whistling in the door! Must dash!

Fondest affections, Polly.

She sat holding the letter for a few moments before retying it and placing the bundle back in the chest. She took out the journal given to her by her mother shortly before her wedding. 'Jot down whatever peeves you,' her mother had said at the time. 'It will keep you from pulling your hair out or slaughtering the carrots.'

And so, she took up daily journaling again, having set aside the practice shortly after her return from St. Charles, half-convinced that her imaginative life was over.

The tidy, leather-stitched volume had started life as a series of random jottings on the unpredictability of the weather, recipes she had tried, and selected quotes from the *Farmers' Almanac* or the 'Ponderings' section of the *Dispatch*. But over time—and influenced by the memory of her mother's example—it had evolved into a daybook of her deeper thoughts and feelings, so much so that she now considered it an indispensable release valve for the inchoate 'steam' of suppressed feelings she felt pressuring for release within her.

'*I despise my mother-in-law*' she had confessed in a moment of pique. '*I wish she would climb on her broomstick and fly away!*' She tore out the page and then tore it into little strips of paper, which she placed in her apron pocket for disposal in the wood stove. Stirred by something in Polly's letter, she turned the pages until she found the quote she was looking for, copied from the *Dispatch*: '*Companionship, true companionship—a confederacy of hearts and minds—is the essence of a loving marriage.*' She set down the journal to think.

'YOU SURE DO FIX a good breakfast, Am,' Ira praised one morning, complimenting her flour cakes. She smiled, feeling a little distracted after a broken sleep during which she awoke several times in an incipient panic while listening to his snores. 'You seem a mite pale,' he continued. 'Maybe try some of Doc Henderson's potion? Ma swears by it.'

'It's nothing. More coffee?'

'I'll save it for later,' he said, pushing back the chair.

She observed from the doorway as he made his way across the yard to the barn, trudging with slow, farmerish steps, a milk pail in each hand. She watched as he put down the pails to pull back the barn door, frowning at his slow, deliberate movements. *If only he would astonish me one morning.*

'I could eat a soft-boiled egg and a slice of bread. Nothing else. My insides are in a spat.' Fleur, wrapped in a heavy wool shawl over her nightgown, sat down at the table, complaining of a 'bother' in her wrist. 'I must have slept on it,' she grumbled, rubbing the bone.

Amity put the egg in the pot and set the latter on the stove to boil, preoccupied with the form such an astonishment might take.

'This coffee's cold. And the cup looks dirty.'

'I'll fetch another.'

The answer eluded her as she poured fresh coffee into the cup, murmuring absently in response to the old woman's complaints. That's up to him, she decided, checking on the egg. Else it wouldn't be a surprise. She rolled the egg with a spoon, lost in gazing at the water as it bubbled up. She scooped the egg up out of the water, herself bubbling for colour, tone, or unexpected light to break upon her marriage. 'Here, Mother. Try this.' She set the egg in the cup and watched as Fleur cracked the shell to reveal the soft, yellow yolk. Such a thing, she imagined, might save her.

44

Half Moon

H ALF MOON TOOK OVER Amity's old bedroom, moving in her sparse possessions—a bedroll mostly and a few items of clothing—and settling in as if it were the most natural thing in the world. She slept on the floor on top of an old robe, disdaining the bed, and lit a bundle of sweet grass whose smell, much to Purchase's irritation, permeated the house.

Bewildered at her return, he took her aside more than once, questioning her, his voice suspicious at times and regretful at others as he tried to make sense of her answers. 'I haven't seen you since the Indian wars,' he said, peering into her eyes. 'The camp was attacked. Afterward, I rode out to your village. Everyone had been killed by the Sioux. And I couldn't find you. What happened to you?'

In spite of his avid curiosity, her answers were vague and disconnected, as if the past no longer interested her. 'I hid when the Sioux came,' she said. 'But they found me and took me away with them. I lived with a man who beat me. But after a time, he became my husband, and then he was not so bad. He was killed by the soldiers, at the buffalo dance.'

'And what happened to you?' he repeated.

'I went to live in the white man's mission.'

He pondered this, observing her wrinkled face and grey hair and trying to reconcile both with the smooth-skinned young girl he had known.

'Did you come to see me?' he persisted. 'Is that why you came back?'

'The buffalo told me it was time,' she said.

He frowned. 'The buffalo?'

She didn't reply, rolling up her blanket and leaving him confounded and full of questions he didn't know how to ask.

To his surprise, Amity and Boundary seemed to accept Half Moon's presence with minimal fuss, their questions easily satisfied by the few answers he could give.

'She and ma have taken a shine to each other,' Amity remarked as if that were all that mattered. Boundary was his usual uncurious self, merely noting that Half Moon 'sure looks Injun,' before wandering off to inspect the rusting harvester.

'I will go and pray at your buffalo,' said Half Moon one day. 'Does your other wife pray there?'

'My other wife?' He scratched his head. 'No, I guess not,' was all he could think of to say.

AS SPRING TURNED TO summer, he continued to be confounded by Half Moon's return, only slowly and grudgingly accepting the fact—in contrast to Felicity who seemed reinvigorated at Half Moon's presence. Purchase watched their relationship blossom, both relieved and jealous at the tonic effect on his wife—his other wife! —he corrected himself, shaking his head at the notion.

The two women quickly became inseparable, calling each other 'sister' and walking up and down the yard arm-in-arm while Felicity prattled on about this or that and Half Moon listened with a solemn expression on her face.

'Ma seems almost like her old self,' remarked Amity on a visit. She sat at the kitchen table, watching as the two women paused to examine a wildflower poking through the yard. 'Whoever this Half Moon is she provides a companion for ma, don't you think, so, Pa?'

'Whoever she is?' He was about to repeat the words but held back, unwilling to open up that chapter of his life for examination. 'I guess,' was all he said in response.

Several times it was on the tip of his tongue to demand Half Moon leave—even while impressed at her ability to make herself instantly at home. It's like she belongs here, he reflected, and perhaps she does. The notion that time ran in circles diverted him as he sat with his daughter and watched his two wives circumnavigate the yard. Briefly he yearned for the old days, for the war and Elias and Winslow and Jubal. The memories brought on a shuddering sigh. Amity, mistaking its import, stroked his hand.

'Ma still depends on you,' she said.

ONE MORNING, HE AWOKE to find Felicity missing from the bed and the house empty. Alarmed, he hurried outside, calling out her name. Unable to find her or Half Moon, he stood confounded for a moment, anxiously scanning the outbuildings. *Where in thunder*—he began before his eye fell on the rock. Acting on instinct, he hastened toward it, increasingly worried at the women's absence.

At this early hour, the monument site was deserted save for a few employees setting up a second beer tent. They paid him no notice as he hurried around the rock, relieved to see the two women standing in its shadow side. He was about to call out, cross at their unannounced absence from the house, when he stopped, curious as to what he was seeing. Half Moon stood facing the buffalo with both arms raised while chanting in a tongue he half-recognised as her tribal speech. Felicity tried to imitate her, abandoning her cane to spread her frail arms and turn her face upward to the rock. Half Moon supported her while continuing her chant. Felicity recited a biblical verse in a trembling, disconnected voice, the two women chanting side by side in the grass.

He waited until the women had finished, irritable, curious, and jealous all at once. 'What in blazes was that about?' he demanded. 'What were you singing?'

'Things,' answered Felicity, brushing aside the question.

'What things?'

She didn't answer but clutched at Half Moon's arm. 'Come, sister,' she said, her voice tremulous. She started off back toward the house, walking with her now-native stooped stance. He followed alongside, attempting to take her other arm. 'I have my cane,' she complained, and pushed his hand away.

A dozen or more times over the course of the summer, he observed Half Moon, either by herself, or accompanied by Felicity, visit the rock to raise her arms and chant. He mentioned the phenomenon to Amity, who was sufficiently curious to wish to observe it for herself. 'But I can't come that early,' she said. 'Ira would wonder and want to come along.'

'Then why not bring him?'

'Maybe,' she said, her tone indicating that this was not a possibility.

IRA WAS IN THE barn, and she took him out a glass of milk. She studied his face as he drank, observing his fluxing throat, the flush under his stubbled cheeks, his large farmer's hand as it grasped the glass. He's dependable, reliable. A hard worker, and a good husband, she told herself, her mind casting back to Polly's letter. But he doesn't see me.

'Much obliged, dear.' Wiping his mouth, he handed back the glass.

She put the glass back on the shelf and looked out the door at the cloudy blue sky. A gusty wind shook the grass and a large black crow *kraa'd* on a fence post. She listened, suddenly fearful lest the yearnings she felt bubbling deep inside her would one day dry up like a sun-scorched spring. '*What torture,*' she scribbled in the journal, '*to feel, and be unable to express.*'

'I wish I had musical gifts,' she remarked the next day when she sat next to Ira in the barn, milking.

He laughed. 'The things you say!' Seeing the hurt look on her face, he quickly commiserated. 'I hear you singing, sometimes. I like the sound of your voice. There must be some milking songs,' he reflected, peering into the milk pail.

'Why does it have to be about milking. Why can't it be about love or death or something equally grand?'

'I guess it could be,' he grunted, pulling down on the udder. Then, to her surprise, he began to sing himself, a tuneless warble about a cuckoo bird. He swung his head and raised his voice, inviting her to join in with the chorus.

'You're missing the pail.'

'Consarn!'

Sometimes, in her desperation for intimacy, she imagined she detected a note of sympathy in her mother-in-law's voice and hovered on the brink of confiding in her, of seeking her counsel, if not comfort. But invariably the old woman would dash these hopes, turning cranky over the weather or the 'picklish' taste of the pork at dinner. 'It's high time you had young 'uns,' she remarked one day. 'By your age, I was with child twice.'

The thought brought about a panic in her. *What sort of a mother would I be?* Unconsciously she rested a hand on her stomach. Her husband, too, raised the subject, at the behest, she had no doubt, of his mother. 'I figure it's about time, Am,' he probed. 'Don't you reckon?'

'It ain't for your lack of trying!' she retorted.

'It's your wifely duty,' her mother said when she complained of Fleur's now constant harping on the subject. 'It's why you got married, ain't it?' Felicity added, before drifting off into one of her prairie silences.

'You'll dry up afore you know it,' said Fleur that same day, unconsciously tapping into Amity's deepest fears.

Returning from the well, she lingered at the open door, watching dust blow across the yard.

'Amity! For heaven's sake, close the door. Do you intend us all to catch a fever?'

'What's for supper?' called out Ira.

And so, the dreary days passed by, unbroken by novelty or the surprises of love her soul craved.

45

Those Are Good Things

BOUNDARY CAME BY ON a rare visit, bringing with him the latest copy of the *Dispatch*. He pointed to a small column at the foot of the front page. 'I wrote that,' he said, a bashful look on his face. '*Stable Catches Fire*,' ran the header. Amity peered at the copy.

> *Mortimer Gulley's large stable at the corner of Fourth Street and Bismarck caught flames last night, threatening the attached premises until it was brought under control by the volunteer fire brigade. Arson is suspected, as a lock was found broken on the rear door. A witness claimed he saw two men running away from the fire. The stables housed three omnibuses belonging to Mr Gulley, and he cogitated if they, not the stable itself, were the true target of the suspected arsonists.*

'Cogitated?' Amity laughed.

Boundary flushed. 'Mr Bellow polished it up.'

'And how is old Bellow?'

'Fine. And he ain't so old!'

Amused, she returned to the page. 'What's this?' she murmured, her eye caught by another item.

VENERATED SCHOOL MARM LEAVES FOR MINNEAPOLIS.

> *Miss Purlow, redoubtable mentor to many of Buffalo Rock's finest young scholars, has announced her intention to quit the school and move back to Minnesota to be with her family.*
>
> *Miss Purlow was the first appointed teacher at the opening of the school, eleven years ago, and has guided and nursed it ever since. She will be missed by many in the community. Commenting on her imminent departure, Mr Groves, the school superintendent for the township, praised her commitment to her young charges as well as her unflagging devotion to duty. 'We would do well to find a like replacement,' he said. He assured the town that the school board would find a suitable candidate as quickly as possible to ensure that any interruption to lessons is kept to a minimum.*

'You never told me!' She looked crossly at her brother.

Boundary frowned in puzzlement. 'What's it to you? She never taught you.'

'Not her—the position.'

'What?' He gaped at her. 'You're a married woman.'

'Married ain't dead!'

'But I need you here to help run things,' Ira objected when she sought his permission to apply for the post. 'Besides, ma needs your help.'

'We can hire someone. My wages will pay for it.' She looked him square in the eye, her voice determined. 'Ira, I need this. I'm going crazy trapped in this house.' *With her!* she almost blurted out. 'Don't deny me this.' She laid her hand on his arm. 'It will make me happy.'

He sighed, giving in, as she knew he would. 'If ma agrees—she's feeling poorly,' he said.

Certain that her mother-in-law's latest ailment was a strategic one, aimed at preventing her from applying for the position, she drove straight to the schoolhouse when next in town, hoping to find out more about the vacancy. To her great disappointment, she was informed that the position had already been filled by a Miss Ida Martins, from Bismarck.

'If we had known of your interest earlier, we would have gladly considered you,' explained Mrs. Elizabeth Chestnut, president of the school board, 'even though you're married. The fact is it would have saved us considerable trouble. Why, speaking of which …' A pretty, fresh-faced young woman with shoulder length brown hair entered the room.

'Miss Martins, I'd like you to meet Mrs. Morgan,' said the older woman, her eyes sweeping up and down the young woman's boldly coloured dress.

'Pleased to meet you, Ma'am.' Miss Martins smiled and offered a simple curtsy, the appellation and gesture disconcerting Amity.

'How old are you?' she asked, uttering the question before she could think.

'Old?' Miss Martins' eyes widened in surprise. 'Eighteen, Ma'am. This month. Excuse me, but I must run. I have an appointment with my dressmaker.'

'Do you mean Mrs. Hedgepeth?' she asked, wondering at the 'my.'

'One and the same!' With a gracious smile, the young woman withdrew.

Mrs. Chestnut harrumphed in the wake of her departure. 'Far too pretty for my liking! But the superintendent was so besotted he about fell over himself. She's overly familiar with the pupils and mollycoddles them at every turn. I have no doubt but that she thinks herself modern.'

She pronounced the word with distaste as if discovering lemon in a mouthful of jam.

The meeting with Miss Martins stayed on Amity's mind, her heart envious each time she dwelt on the young woman's air of breezy optimism. *That was me, once.*

ONE MORNING, SHE TOOK out her sketch pad and brought it into the kitchen, deliberating whether she should take up drawing again.

'What are those?' Ira looked over her shoulder.

'These? Some sketches I took from the window of Mrs. Halverson's when I lived there, and of pa's farm. What do you think?' She waited as he studied the illustrations.

'They are pretty,' he decided. 'But why not draw faces or people rather than trees or that old rock?'

'I guess I could,' she replied, stung by the remark.

Looking back, she recognised the trivial conversation as the moment a gulf opened between them. A gulf not of distance, but of feeling, she pondered to herself. He has his feelings, too—toward me, to the farm, to the cows, to his shrew of a mother—she acknowledged. But her own feelings, she now knew for certain, were of a different consistency, like lumps in oatmeal. '*Ira likes things to be such and such a way,*' she wrote, accounting to herself for the differences between them. '*I like surprises and odd things. They appeal to me. I don't know, or care, why. Perhaps it's ma's influence.*'

One afternoon, she was riding in the wagon with her husband and mother-in-law, returning from one of their rare trips into town together. The old woman had fallen asleep, her head slumped on Amity's shoulder. A flock of corncrakes flew overhead, and she followed them with her gaze as they flew toward the horizon.

'What are you thinking?' probed Ira.

'I was wondering what it would be like to fly, like those birds.'

'Fly? Where to?'

'Somewhere. Anywhere.' The old woman stirred and mumbled against her shoulder.

'I guess we don't need wings. That's why the good Lord gave us legs.'

'Maybe one day we could go somewhere—to Chicago or New York even,' she suggested.

'New York! Why ever?' He gaped in amazement.

'Just to see.'

'I guess there's plenty to see here—without going to New York.'

'Have you ever wished to do something else, other than farming?'

He frowned. 'What's wrong with farming?'

'Nothing. My pa's a farmer. But did you ever wonder if you might have gifts elsewhere?'

'Gifts?' He grimaced. 'I got two hands and a strong back. I guess they're good enough for me.' He shook the reins, his eyes narrowing into the distance as he looked for the homestead.

She glanced at him—stolid, steady, and reliable. And felt that gulf again.

A SUCCESSION OF VERY warm days put her further out of sorts, the sultry weather baking the small house in a stuffy, airless inertia. Her aggrieved mother-in-law rolled up her sleeve to show where scratched mosquito bites pinked the thin, white flesh. 'They're gnawing away at me,' she whined. 'Where's that paste you made up?'

She fetched the paste of baking soda and witch-hazel—her mother's remedy—and applied it to the old woman's arm.

'Ouch! Your nails are digging in!' Fleur shot an irritable look. 'Where's your mind at, girl?'

'Would you prefer to do it yourself?' She wiped an arm across her brow, exasperated by the heat, her mother-in-law, and Miss Martins.

'My, such temper.' Fleur dipped a trembling finger in the bowl of paste. 'I guess I never knowed it was such a hardship to rub some paste on a body.'

The heat broke a week later in a tremendous thunderstorm that confined all three occupants to the house. She took up a half-finished needlepoint and continued the embroidery her mother had taught her while listening to the rain as it lashed down. 'At least it will cool things off some,' Ira said. 'I hope the barn roof don't leak.'

The rain stopped and dried up in the yard as the sun came out again. She tended to the vegetable patch, rooting out weeds and scooping a furrow for the carrots she planned on planting. She cooked supper and, afterward, assisted her mother-in-law to bed. She then sat in the rocker to darn a pair of dungarees. Ira pecked her on the cheek.

'That meat loaf sure tasted good, Am.'

She smiled over her mending.

After a while he got up. 'Are you coming to bed?'

'In a minute,' she said. 'You go ahead. I just want to finish this.' She waited until she heard him snore before putting aside the garment and getting up from the chair.

THE SHARP, EARLY FALL presaged another cold winter. Snow began to fall midway through October, whitening the grass and drifting across the yard to settle against the barn. Despite the cold, Felicity insisted on sitting outside for an hour each day, sitting in the rocker alongside her sister, both cocooned in old buffalo robes. Activity at the rock monument had largely drawn to a close, although a few curious visitors, some of them returnees, still turned up for the picturesque sight of the buffalo dusted with snow. Lomax sent out a photographer to capture the scene, planning to use the pictures in a calendar. He also insisted on sending the photographer to the top of the rock to take, as he instructed, 'a grand panorama of Indian country.'

'It ain't Indian country, not no more,' the photographer objected, doubtful of the wisdom of standing atop a rock slippery with snow and ice.

'Then call it buffalo country. What the hell do I care as long as folk will pay to see it?'

It was on the tip of the photographer's mind to point out that the buffalo were gone, too, but an aggressive stare from a big man in a Stetson discouraged him from doing so. 'It's your dime,' he said.

'It sure is. And don't you ever forget it.'

'There's a crazy old Injun woman that carries on at the rock sometimes. How about I include her?'

'What do you mean, "carries on"?'

'I dunno. Something heathenish.'

'Really?' Lomax stroked his chin. 'Then get one of her standing beneath the rock. Stick a feather or two in her hair.'

'She might not care to.'

'Give her a trinket or something from the gift shop, but nothing worth anything.'

The following day the photographer, a dour, cynical individual named George Friesen, walked to the farmhouse. As he approached, he hailed two old women sitting side by side on the porch. 'Howdy, ladies,' he said and removed his hat for good effect.

The door opened and a man stepped out, a suspicious look on his face. 'What do you want?' he demanded.

'Howdy, Mr …?' With no answer forthcoming, Friesen volunteered his own name. 'I work for Mr Lomax. He runs that rock,' he said, turning to point. 'Mr Lomax wants—'

'Get off my land!'

'Now, friend, there's no need to carry on so. I just want to ask this woman'—Friesen nodded toward Half Moon—'to come and stand beneath the rock. For a picture. I'll give her a copy in payment.'

'Get off my land, now!' The irate farmer produced a shotgun from inside the door.

'Jesus Christ, hold on! No need for that.' Friesen beat a hasty retreat, walking backward through the grass, his eyes never leaving the shotgun. 'I was only being polite!'

'Git!' Purchase advanced on the porch, the gun pointed threateningly.

'You crazy old coot!' Friesen turned on his heels and ran.

Purchase heard a shriek of laughter and turned to see Felicity shaking beneath the robe. 'I guess he flew like a jackrabbit!' she chortled, her face crinkled with glee.

She was still chuckling when Purchase turned and went back inside. After a while, the chuckles subsided and she gazed at the rock, a troubled look on her face. 'I never did much care for it at first,' she said, 'but it grew on me. I guess I'll miss it.' Turning to Half Moon, she laid an arthritic, bony hand on the other woman's arm. 'Who are you?' she asked.

'I am Half Moon, your sister.'

'Really?' The reply pleased her. 'I had a friend once, lived in ...' She thought for a moment, tutting when memory failed her. '... somewhere not here. Pa owned a store. He smoked a pipe every day. Ma liked to bake things.' Thick flakes of snow began drifting across the yard. 'I forget things,' she confessed. 'But I liked to laugh and tease.' She gazed at the distance, which was already beginning to blur. 'I wish things would last forever,' she said.

'Nothing lasts forever, sister.'

'Not even the rock?' Felicity stared, fright in her voice.

'Nothing. Even stories die where there is no one to tell them or no one to listen.'

'I remember the stories they told us at school. And the songs my ma liked to sing.' Felicity started to hum and then stopped, a forlorn look on her face. 'I remember the air, but not the words. I'm afraid,' she said, a tremor in her voice.

'There is no need to be afraid. I shall be with you.'

'You will?' She looked gratefully at her sister. 'What will it be like?'

'There will be lots of buffaloes and fresh, spring grass that stretches as far as the eye can see.'

'Will I see ma and pa and ...' Her thoughts were frail now. 'Jumpy! I remember!' Tears came to her eyes.

'What else do you remember?'

'I remember the purple sky at dusk and the fresh wind in the mornings. I like the way it feels now, on my cheek.' She gave a deep, exhausted sigh.

'Those are good things, sister. Remember them.'

HE AWOKE WITH A start, forgetting for a moment where he was. He must have napped in the chair. He looked around for Felicity, muttering as he realised she was still outside. 'Felice?' Calling, he opened the door. The two women sat with eyes open, and hands joined. Half Moon's head rested against the chairback. Felicity had a faraway look on her face. She had taken off her bonnet, her bare, grey head flecked with snow. The old buffalo robe was pulled up to her throat.

'Felice?' Tenderly, he touched his wife's cheek, as though she slept. Her face had regained some of the smoothness of youth that he remembered from St Charles. After a long moment, he gave a heavy sigh and sat down on the steps. Snow drifted over the porch and the wind ruffled his hair as he sat there. 'I don't understand,' he muttered, suddenly conscious of the cold, stark weight of the world. *I've never understood,* he realised, the truth troubling and humbling him. In the distance, the rock stood firm and implacable in the wintry light. He stared for a while and then turned, his face strained, to where the women sat, motionless. 'Felice?'

46

A Visit

Following the death of her mother, Amity made it a point to drive out to the homestead at least once a week to check on the welfare of her pa. Sometimes Boundary accompanied her, she taking the buggy into town to pick him up at the newspaper office. Her husband was sanguine about the weekly visits, occasionally asking if his mother might accompany her on fine days, 'for the air.' But she demurred, citing the dust and bumps along the road and the vagaries of prairie weather. The irascible old lady herself helped in this regard by waving her walking cane and complaining of a stiffness in her joints. 'Why would I wish to bounce about all over the road like a rag doll?' she demanded of her son. 'My bones would likely crack.'

'Git, little Sugar!' Amity sang as she drove out to the homestead, enjoying the illusion of independence created by the open road. She passed several Trust omnibuses along the way, all packed with spring tourists eager to view the rock. They hailed her as she passed, entertained to see this evidence of self-reliant prairie womanhood. She played up to their expectations, aware of the figure she cut, geeing the mare as she rolled by in the light buggy, holding the whip and calling out 'Har!' or 'Skit!' The women seemed especially surprised at the sight, holding on to their bonnets and hats and staring, wide-eyed, as she passed by. 'Hi-yup!' she sang, flicking the reins.

The rock came into sight, squat and massive in the sunlight. She glimpsed tiny figures moving along the top. Someone stood atop the head, peering at the distance with a telescope. For a moment, she conceited it was the patriarch himself, surveying his domain. The thought of their blood relationship pleased her. *He was a smiter of rock, perhaps I shall be, too.* An omnibus passed by in the opposite direction, and she veered slightly to one side. *Or am I destined to be smitten?* The notion beguiled her as she ruminated on the ways that might be possible. It intrigued her so much that on returning home later that afternoon she copied it into her journal.

Her pa stepped outside at the noise of the rig. His head was now entirely grey, although he still carried himself with the same, uncomplicated purpose she remembered from growing up. He helped her down from the buggy. 'No Boundary?' he asked.

She shook her head. 'Not today. Old Bellow has him taking apart the press or something.'

He unhitched the mare while she stepped inside the house. As always, it struck her as silent and forlorn absent her mother's touch and presence. She looked around the room, half-expecting to hear her mother's voice.

'How can you stand it, Pa?' she asked when he joined her after watering the mare. 'Why not move into town to live with Boundary? I wish you could live with me, except …'

'This is my home,' he said. 'Your ma would expect no different.' He sat down in his chair—always pulled out. 'There's fresh coffee in the pot.'

She poured them both a cup and joined him at the table. The touch and feel of the wood brought a flood of emotions as she imagined her mother's quick, economical presence.

'You mind me of her, Am,' he said, guessing her thoughts. 'She's still here, long as you are.' He had taken up pipe-smoking since his wife's death and he took out the briarwood pipe, thumbing tobacco into the bowl. 'What does the *Dispatch* have to say?'

She had brought the latest copy with her to read aloud, in spite of her pa's excellent eyesight. 'The council's up for election,' she said. 'It's reckoned that Ben Wilkins is a shoo-in on account of all of the improvements to the town.'

Her pa grunted. 'Not to mention his bank account.'

'And it says here that the rock received over nine hundred visitors last week, including a record three hundred ninety on a single day.' She put down the paper at the frown on his face. 'Now don't go to fretting, Pa. What's done is done. And folk, townsfolk at least, will always know it was your great grandpa that carved it.'

He took the pipe from his mouth. 'I wish that were so. But the truth is that durn Lomax has spread so many lies it may as well have been carved by the man in the moon.'

'Then I'll write a letter to the *Dispatch*.' She brightened at the thought. 'Set folks straight. Mr Bellow will publish it—Boundary will see to that.'

'No.' He shook his head, his voice firm. 'Lomax is dangerous. Don't cross him or give him cause to come after you.'

'Me? A woman?'

'Times have changed.' He grimaced with disgust. 'Remember what happened to Buskins.'

'You still think that was Lomax?'

'Ha! I know it was. Now that your ma's gone, I've a mind to fetch my gun and put paid to that crook once and for all.' His eyes narrowed at the thought.

'Pa, don't even think such a thing! Why, they'd string you up—if they didn't shoot you first. Promise me you'll do no such thing.'

He made a grumbling sound. 'What else do they say in the paper?'

'Oh, I forgot to tell you. The cow birthed last night. But the calf died. Ira said he near pulled its legs off to get it out. When he finally dragged it out it was sucking air to beat the band. It just licked his hand and died. He was that upset.'

Purchase nodded. 'Same thing happened to me once, back in St Charles.'

She started to read again when he interrupted her. 'When I go, Am, make sure you bury me under the rock, alongside your ma. You remember where I put the mark?'

'Pa, don't go getting maudlin' on me.'

'I ain't.' He held up a hand in placation. 'Just being particular. But it must be done in secret, like I did with your ma and Half Moon. Do you understand? Else that scoundrel Lomax will have me dug up. Don't fret, now. It's the natural way of things.' He gave a rueful smile. 'Think of it as filing our claim—an eternal one. Who knows, but that some day—long after that blackhearted thief Lomax has gone on his way—some government surveyor may chance along and find my bones.'

'Pa, such talk!'

'Promise me, Am.' His face was solemn.

'But what about Jube? He'll be all by himself.' She started to cry.

'I mean to move him one day—when no one's around. Promise me.'

'Of course, if that's what you want, Pa.' She dabbed her eyes. 'Although, heaven knows, I'll miss you to pieces.'

'You'll always know where I am, and your ma, too, no matter what happens to this old place.'

'What will happen to it?'

'That's up to you, and your brother. Sell it if you like. Don't be sentimental. Just make sure you fetch what it's worth. Oh!' he remembered. 'Your ma gave the Bible to Boundary—God knows why, but she wanted him to have it. She wanted you to have these.' Getting up, he took some sheets of paper down from the china shelf.

'Drawings?' She leafed through them, pausing at one of her sitting on a chair, a petulant look on her face that made her smile with remembrance.

A full-face sketch of her mother made her want to cry, the drawing so painfully evocative of the vanished face. She brushed the lines with her fingers before turning to another. 'Oh, *Madonna of the Plains*. I remember the day he drew it. I was such a fusspot! Poor ma. I wouldn't stay still. I kept wriggling about like a fish on a hook. I'll have it framed and hung in the house,' she decided. 'Where is the buffalo sketch?' she asked, coming to the last of the drawings. 'You know, the charcoal that ma liked so much.'

He furrowed his brow. 'I don't rightly know. Perhaps your ma threw it out.'

'No, she wouldn't. Last I saw it was tucked between the pages of the Bible.'

He raised an eyebrow in surprise. 'It was? So, she did keep it after all.'

'She treasured it.' Amity puffed her lips in an expression of pique. 'I wonder why she didn't wish for me to have it. It's wasted on Boundary.'

'Maybe she just forgot. Or wanted you both to have some. Why don't you ask him the next time you see him?' He nodded to indicate a brown paper parcel sitting on the cabinet. 'She didn't say anything about her journals. But some time back, she remarked that you might want to read them someday. They're all there.'

Tears filled her eyes. 'Have you read them?'

He sighed. 'I didn't have the heart. You read them and tell me what they say, if you like.'

She was melancholy all the ride home, sighing each time she thought of her ma's journals and her pa sitting alone in the empty house. A sob escaped her as she pictured the rock, the scratches in the stone, and the bodies interred in its shade. I won't be able to place flowers. It was our land, our rock. It ain't fair. Even as she thought the words she heard her mother's snorted rejoinder. "*You want fair, buy a ticket to the carnival! Life is what it is. We don't order it around. If we're lucky, it lets us be.*"

HER MOTHER-IN-LAW WAS A special trial that night, complaining about the soup and the buttered biscuits, tugging her shawl tightly around her and hogging the fire in spite of the summer warmth. Amity was relieved when the old woman finally took a spoonful of medicine and shuffled off to bed, still grumbling about things.

'She gets testy, Am, I know,' her husband said, his voice apologetic as they lay in bed. 'But I think she missed you, today. As did I.'

He leaned over her, kissing her neck and throat in a manner that made her think of the abortive calf. Despite her passivity, he continued, murmuring endearments and tugging up her nightdress. He thrust into her, causing her to wince. *I'm not one of your old cows!* But when he had finished, she relented, a feeling of guilt replacing annoyance as she heard him snore. Why can't I be the loving wife he requires, and deserves? What is wrong with me that I take no pleasure in his arms? She thought of her pa and his worn, lined face and started to cry.

She woke up before dawn, her mind churning. Unable to get back to sleep, or shut off her thoughts, she got out of bed, wriggling out of her husband's arms. She took the key from its hiding place between the bed and the wall and unlocked the hope chest—which she'd had her husband carry into the house. With a glance at the snoring Ira, she took out her journal. Sitting down at the kitchen table, she turned the pages, peering at the contents in the lantern light. It was cool and she got back up to wrap herself in her shawl before returning to the table. She heard her husband mutter in his sleep and raised her head to listen. He started snoring again and she returned to the journal. Near the middle, she found the lines that had woken her—running through her head as she blinked in the gloomy darkness. *'What is it you fear most? asked the owl to the dove. Is it that someday you may no longer fly or that you may no longer sing? The dove wept in reply. The thing I fear most is the loss of myself.'*

She was rereading the almost forgotten words, copied from a book of fables back at the seminary, when she was interrupted by her mother-in-law calling from the bedroom. 'Amity? Are you up? Is there tea?'

'WHAT WORD ON THE school teach?'

Boundary picked up a rag to wipe ink from his hands. 'I heard she ran off.'

'Heavens to a crow! The whole town heard that!'

After less than six months in the position, Miss Ida Martins had eloped with Eustache Johnson, school superintendent and father of four young children, to the great scandal of the Buffalo Rock community. 'Last observed hightailing it to Chicago,' Bellow had dryly noted in his reporting of the scandal. The abandoned wife continued to live in the town with the children before moving back to Franklin, where her parents lived, unable to bear the gossip and pitying glances.

'No word on her replacement?'

'I guess not.'

'You guess not.' Bellow heaved a great sigh. 'Didn't you say your sister was interested in the position?'

'She was.'

'And?'

'And what?'

'Give me strength! Is she still interested? Does she intend to apply?'

'I reckon not. Her husband's against it.'

'Get along to the school—or wherever that polecat Elizabeth Chestnut has her lair. Find out what the school board thinks.'

'Thinks of what?'

'The price of rice in China! Never mind. I'm passing that way.' Bellow stood up and reached to the hat stand for his coat. 'Norm Fenton should be along with information on that poster he wants. Can you handle that?'

'Sure.'

'Sure, he says! Anyone asks for me, tell 'em I've gone fishing.'

'That boy is a trial,' he grumbled to his wife over dinner. 'I try to bring him along, but all he cares about is that press and operating the camera. I swear he polishes it six times a day.'

'The camera?'

'The press.'

'Then oughtn't you be pleased, dear? I mean, you never did care overmuch for that side of things.'

'True.' He speared a pea. 'But I have hopes for him—in the business.'

'I'm sure you do. How's he doing since his ma passed?'

IN THE AFTERNOON, SHE helped Ira milk the cows, stopping to take in the early, purple dusk on the horizon as they finished and stepped outside. 'Ma loved this time most,' she said, setting down the pail. She inhaled the smell of sage and bluestem, transported back to childhood. Ira put down his pail to close the heavy barn door.

'That cow still looks greenish.' He picked up the pail again. 'What about ma? She seemed a mite grumpy this morning.'

'When ain't she? She took a few spoonfuls of medicine and calmed right down.'

Following supper, she went into her mother-in-law's room to check if she needed anything. Fleur was snoring in the rocker, the Morgan family Bible open on her lap. She picked it up, careful not to disturb the old woman.

'What?' Fleur woke suddenly, clutching Amity's wrist in her tight, clawlike grasp.

'I'm sorry. I thought you were asleep.' She let go of the Bible.

'You look pale—are you coming down with something?' Her mother-in-law gave a sharp, distrustful glance. 'Cos if you are, don't share it around.'

'No, I'm just preoccupied.'

'Preoccupied? That means you ain't busy enough!' Fleur compressed her lips as she studied Amity, a spiteful look on her face. 'I know what ails you, girl, and it ain't the weather.'

'I ain't ailing. And I'm plenty busy, thank you.' She turned to go.

'You're waiting.'

'What now?' She turned, frowning. 'Waiting for what?'

'To be smitten!' Her mother-in-law gave a small shriek of triumph as Amity froze in the doorway.

'What in cornstarch are you talking about?'

The old woman gave her a glimmerish look. 'Don't none of us get what we want, girl, only what we deserve.' Her face took on its usual dour countenance. 'Put up with it!' she snapped, and took up the Bible, signalling that the conversation was over.

AT HER HUSBAND'S URGING, she accompanied her mother-in-law on a visit to Bismarck where the latter's married sister resided. After an overnight visit, which she described in her journal as 'excruciatingly dull,' they boarded the morning train for the short journey back to Buffalo Rock. Minutes before they were scheduled to leave, a young man hurried aboard. After pausing to catch his breath, he approached where they sat and politely asked permission to occupy the opposite bench. 'Pardon, ladies, he said, raising his brown derby and speaking in accented, but not unpleasantly so, English, 'but this side is in the shade.'

Mistaking her mother-in-law's raised eyebrows as a sign of approval, he sank into the seat with a gratified sigh.

Amity gave a polite smile as he placed a new, leather valise on the seat next to him.

'Herr Hans Rumbald, he said, encouraged by the smile. He was young—no more than a few years older than herself, she guessed—dressed in a brown wool morning suit and a white shirt with a high, starched collar. He sported a neatly groomed moustache. 'I beg pardon—*Mr* Hans Rumbald, he said, correcting himself as the train departed the station in a cloud of steam.

The wheels clanked rhythmically as the train crossed the trestle bridge across the Missouri, the iron spans giving glimpses of the river below. Her mother-in-law had fallen asleep, and Amity felt the man's gaze on her as she observed his reflection in the window.

'You are going to Mandan, Madam?' The question was asked *sotto voce* as her mother-in-law began to snore.

'Buffalo Rock,' she said.

'I also! I am the new schoolmaster.'

'You are?' She gave him a sharp look.

'You live in the town?' he asked, his voice curious.

'On a farm, outside of town.' She glanced at her mother-in-law to ascertain whether she still slept.

Rumbald took out a handkerchief and blew into it. His quick, intelligent features studied her for a moment over the handkerchief as if he were deliberating whether to risk speaking again. Decorum was preserved by the shuddering arousal of her mother-in-law. 'Are we there?' she demanded, her voice testy from sleep.

'Soon,' Amity answered.

Ira was waiting at the platform to greet them. She took her mother-in-law's arm while glancing around for Rumbald. 'A pleasant good day to you, ladies!' He passed by with a doff of his hat.

'Who was that?' Ira glanced after the man.

'That was the new schoolteacher.'

'To replace the tramp that ran off,' added her mother-in-law.

She was mostly silent as they rode home, listening to her mother-in-law expound on the buildings in Bismarck while expressing distaste at her sister's husband, 'a born idler, if you ask me,' she said. 'Don't you think so—Amity?'

'Pardon. Who?'

'My dolt of a brother-in-law. Who do you suppose I meant?'

47

Hans Rumbald

H ANS RUMBALD LUXURIATED IN his good fortune, the young man exceedingly pleased with himself at having landed his first employment in America, even if it was in a godforsaken town on the wild frontier—of which he had heard so much in his native Bohemia. A former student at the University of Prague he, like his philosophy professor father, had become embroiled in radical politics and the intense debates that pitted German-speaking liberal reformists against the conservative Czech majority. Following a violent riot during which unknown antagonists had fired on protestors, killing several, the family had been forced to flee, barely escaping ahead of the secret police.

They had arrived in Chicago just two months previously, destitute and facing an uncertain future in their new country. Unable to find work as a professor, his father had taken a job at a factory which barely provided for their minimum needs. Anxious to help support the family, Hans had spotted the advertisement for a schoolteacher in a distant prairie town while thumbing through the *Chicago Tribune*. He straightaway applied for the position despite the opposition of his mother and sister.

'It may as well be on the moon!' exclaimed his mother on being informed of its distant location.

'You will be murdered by wild Indians,' worried his sister, Maria.

'There are no more wild Indians,' he soothed.

'Bandits, then,' protested his mother, turning to appeal to her husband.

'If it pays well, then why not?' said his father.

A few days later, he accepted the wired invitation of the Buffalo Rock school board offering him the position contingent upon an interview to ratify his suitability and qualifications. The very next day, he boarded the train for Bismarck armed only with a copy of the essays of Heine—a parting gift from his father—and a burning desire to restore the family fortunes. 'In America, more than anywhere else, achievement counts above birth,' he reminded his sister. 'Has not Mr Emerson said as much? And what is better to achieve than a name—a name that is synonymous with some great thought or invention? Is that not the very essence of this America?'

Flushed with this ambition, he endured the long journey to the frontier, marvelling at the wealth of farmland along the way. 'The country is so large it could swallow Bohemia along with the entire empire and not even notice,' he observed, gazing in silent wonder as the interminable miles rolled by and the limitless American prairies unfolded outside the carriage window.

Excitement and anticipation quickly turned to fatigue as the train toiled to cross the four hundred miles between Chicago and Minneapolis–St Paul. The crowded car, packed with emigrants, stank of sweat and other body odours. He had travelled third class to save money and regretted that decision as the noise and smells conspired to give him a headache. The carriage clanked noisily and swayed from side to side, adding to his discomfort. The train made frequent stops at hamlets, most of them without railway platforms, the passengers scrambling down from the high cars. At times, they stopped seemingly in the middle of nowhere to pick up or drop off passengers, the driver hailed by people waiting alongside the tracks.

He slept as best he could on the hard, unforgiving seats and purchased food from railroad platforms along the way. Unexplained and interminable delays during which the train simply sat on the track for hours at a time added to his frustration. Several times the passengers were forced to change trains and railway companies, each transfer occasioning a mad scramble for available seats.

Two hundred miles from Chicago, they halted in the middle of a meadow for the entire day, the conductor passing through to explain that a wooden truss bridge ahead of them had partly collapsed into a ravine and needed to be repaired. While they waited, the passengers climbed down all along the train to sit or walk in the grass, miles from the nearest settlement. Toward evening, it started to rain, causing a rush to climb back on board.

They finally started moving again in pitch blackness, the train whistle sounding with an eerie shriek in the darkness. As the train crept across the repaired bridge, those emigrants who understood what was going on explained the situation to their fellow passengers, causing much alarm and provoking a round of hymns and prayers.

Finally, four days after leaving Chicago, the train steamed into Minneapolis–St Paul. Here, he purchased a ticket on the Northern Pacific Railroad that would take him west across North Dakota to Bismarck. He took his place on board among the swarms of emigrants. The journey was again subject to delays, this time due to a wreck farther along the line. At one point, they stopped to take on board dozens of passengers from a stranded locomotive, the newcomers filling every available space.

Close to Bismarck, he was congratulating himself on the rare pleasure of having an empty seat beside him when a cheerful Russian, much gone with drink, claimed the space and, despite Hans closing his eyes and pretending to sleep, kept up a nonstop chatter all the way to the terminus. The immense, rolling landscape did little to allay his tired frustration. By the time he reached Bismarck and changed trains for the last section to Buffalo Rock, he was sore and bruised and heartily sick of both trains and the endless prairie.

HE HAD INTENDED TO arrive two days before his appointment with the school board but, owing to the disrupted journey, arrived the same day, barely one hour ahead of his scheduled interview. After hastily combing his hair and wetting a finger and brushing it over his moustache, he hurried off to find the school building on Elm Street.

He arrived ten minutes early but was kept waiting for a quarter hour before being invited into a small room where a table had been set up with six chairs—five for the elected board members and one for himself. The meeting was presided over by Warren Cotton, the newly appointed superintendent of schools for the township. But the panel, including Cotton, appeared to defer to a Mrs. Elizabeth Chestnut, a woman of formidable demeanour, who chaired the meeting. She gave Rumbald a searching look as he entered the room.

'Mr Rumbald?' she inquired—nay, demanded—in a no-nonsense voice. At his polite murmur, she motioned to the empty chair. 'Sit down, if you please.'

No sooner had he taken a seat than she fired off a second question. 'I understand you are German?'

'Yes, Madam, from Bohemia,' he answered.

Her eyebrows arched at the reply. 'I've never heard of such a place. Where is it?'

'It is part of the Austro-Hungarian Empire,' he explained. 'The largest city is—'

'And yet you speak English?' The question sounded much like an accusation.

'From a young age,' he answered. 'My father is an ardent admirer of your great American philosophers, in particular Mr Emerson and the transcendentalist school.'

The board looked doubtful at the reply, and he hastened to amend it. 'I myself hold a particular admiration for Mr Alcott and his novel theories on pedagogy, which I find both refreshing and deeply humane.' He glanced at the school superintendent for approval, only to receive a blank look in reply.

'As to the position,' interrupted Mrs. Chestnut, steering the discussion back to native waters, 'we would normally expect a young woman to apply, but—'

'Miss Martins!' Another woman interjected.

'Indeed, Miss Martins.'

The school superintendent coughed and took out his watch. 'I was against her from the start. Those impertinent eyes—'

'No matter!' Mrs. Chestnut frowned at her fellow members. 'The point is, Mr Rumbald, *the point is*,' she said with a glare at another attempted interruption, 'that it is essential the board have full confidence that whoever we appoint is of the highest—the very highest—moral character.'

The other three ladies murmured in agreement. Superintendent Cotton seemed more interested in his fob watch, winding the stem and holding it up to his ear.

'We have the care of innocent souls,' said Mrs. Chestnut. 'Isn't that right, superintendent?'

'Indubitably, Mrs. Chestnut. Indubitably.' The superintendent put away the watch under the chairwoman's raised eyebrows.

'It says, in your application, that you are unmarried, Mr Rumbald?' The questioner, a pale-faced woman in a blue bonnet, peered over the tops of her pulpit eyeglasses for the response.

'I am, Madam.'

'And do you have plans—for the future?'

'For the time being, I assure you that I am, as the saying has it, a confirmed bachelor.' He hesitated. 'I am not in a position to support a wife, much less a family.'

This drew nods of approval, the spectre of Miss Martins evidently weighing heavily on the minds of the board.

The board questioned him for a further hour, satisfying themselves on matters of religion, morals, and disciplinary methods. 'I prefer to reason, rather than punish,' he volunteered in response to a question on the latter. 'It has been my experience that it is better to impress the mind rather than the body.' The reply drew an exchange of looks.

'Laudable, I am sure, Mr Rumbald, but a firm hand is often necessary to impose order, do you not agree?' Mrs. Chestnut inclined her head for an answer.

'A good thrashing,' added the superintendent, 'works wonders—depending on the circumstance, of course,' he conceded.

Rumbald murmured in reply, bowing his head in deference to superior wisdom.

He was asked to leave the room while the board considered his application. He was soon summoned back and hired at a salary of thirty dollars per month plus a housing allowance of two dollars a week. At the recommendation of the committee, he secured room and board at the home of Mary Russell, a widow and devout Christian, at her modest but tidy home on Lincoln Street. After concluding the interview and making his way to the residence, he was shown to a pleasant upstairs bedroom, complete with a small table and a polished walnut bureau for his belongings. 'Enchanting,' he praised as the widow showed him the room and then the parlour where he would take breakfast and supper.

'There is one other lodger,' she said. 'Mr Carswell, a grain dealer from Kansas.'

It was still early afternoon, and he felt immensely gratified at having secured, within three short hours of his arrival, both confirmed employment and lodgings. He toyed with the idea of sending a telegram to his, no doubt anxious, parents but baulked at the cost. He would write a letter instead, but not before taking a stroll around the town—*his* town, now that he was about to become a productive part of it. With a light heart, he stepped out the door, eager to immerse himself in the frontier settlement.

HE WALKED PAST SOME stores, stopping to admire the contents of the window displays. They have the same sort of goods I might see in Chicago, he noted, impressed at the variety on offer. Wagons and horses passed up and down the wide street and pedestrians strolled the sidewalks. Some of the passing men, he observed, had gun belts strapped to their waists. The sight, although unnerving, reminded him anew that this was frontier America—the subject of endless romantic speculation in his homeland. The men seemed polite, if curious, lifting a finger to their hats while scrutinising his wool suit and leather shoes. The women were dressed in capes and bonnets and mostly averted their eyes as they passed, although one or two looked him boldly in the eye and said hello. The forwardness both charmed and slightly shocked him and he made note to mention it in his letter home.

The wide main street was reasonably clean, although he came across two pigs rooting amid garbage while being harried by a pack of mongrels.

Passing the Golden Fleece hotel and saloon, he stopped to observe the arrival of the afternoon stage from Mandan. Three men and a woman stepped down, pausing to arrange themselves as they took in the street.

'More gawkers come to gape at the rock, no doubt,' said a voice behind him. Rumbald turned to see a middle-aged man with a cigar in his mouth, leaning against a post to observe the arrivals.

'Pardon, sir?'

'The rock, the famous buffalo outside of town. Surely, you've heard of it?'

'I have, sir. Although I have not yet seen it. An oversight I am anxious to correct as soon as possible. I myself am a newcomer.'

'Are you now?' The man summed him up before extending his hand. 'Quintus Bellow, owner and editor of the town's finest, and only, newspaper, the *Buffalo Rock Dispatch*.'

'Hans Rumbald, sir. Honoured to meet you.'

'What brings you to our fair town, Mr Rumbald, if it ain't that rock?'

'I am the new schoolmaster, sir, just arrived from Chicago.'

'Well, well!' Bellow chuckled. 'You didn't happen to pass a Miss Martins on your way in, did you?'

'Pardon?'

Bellow shook his head. 'No matter. Welcome to our town.' He blew out a cloud of smoke as the stagecoach passengers took their luggage and headed into the hotel. 'Rumbald?' he asked, turning his attention back to Hans. 'From your accent, I'd hazard you're German, ain't you?'

'I am—although from Bohemia.'

'A fine people. Honest and hardworking.' Bellow studied him. 'Folk will be interested to know all about you, Mr Rumbald. Maybe once you're settled in you might visit my office—right there.' He pointed across the street at a storefront office. 'I'll write up a little welcome in the *Dispatch*. What do you say?'

'It would be my pleasure, sir.'

Delighted at the invitation, he continued his tour of the town, nodding and tipping the brim of his hat to people he passed in the street. They struck him as plain, honest folk, enrobed in that wonderful, unselfconscious *Americanness* described so eloquently in the pages of Hawthorne and Twain. He hummed to himself as he strolled, his mind turning to the charges he would meet for the first time on the morrow. A woman clutching a young boy by the hand passed by, and he raised his derby, smiling at the boy. I am presently a stranger, but in a few short weeks the entire town will know who I am! The thought gratified him as he retraced his steps to his lodgings.

Following a supper of cold ham and boiled eggs served with biscuits and followed by apple pie—how enchanting! How American! —he returned to his room. Taking off his suit jacket, he sat down to convey news of his triumph. '*Dear mother and father*,' he wrote, writing in the English his father insisted upon since their arrival in the New World.

I arrived in Buffalo Rock late this morning after a somewhat tiring train journey. I met with the school board, including the superintendent himself and, after a thorough interrogation, was duly hired. I must say, the manner of engaging teachers in America is somewhat quaint. Questions of pedagogy or method are brushed aside in favour of a 'hog swill' (a phrase I have but recently learned) discussion of manners, morals, and discipline. I am expected to fill the woodstove each day and sweep out the classroom following school. The school itself is a sturdy brick building situated in the 'downtown.' It has two large windows, a board, and an assortment of stools, chairs, and benches for the children. It has a desk and a high stool for my use—the desk replacing the former hogshead, as proudly pointed out by the board. Pupil attendance, I am informed, revolves around crop planting and harvesting and other family duties. Tomorrow, I will teach my first class. It appears much study time was lost owing to the abrupt and somewhat mysterious departure of my predecessor in the post. Some scandal attached to the circumstances, which still seems to 'rile' the members of the board whenever they are reminded of it. I must find out more. The pay is $30 per month, at least half of which I expect to be able to wire back to you in Chicago. I have arranged lodgings at the house of a respectable widow recommended by the board. I have yet to fully explore the town, much less view the celebrated buffalo monument, which is situated nine or ten miles outside the town limits. I am most eager to see it and will convey my impressions as soon as I do so.

Buffalo Rock itself is a pleasant little settlement with broad streets, many commercial establishments, and friendly inhabitants. The town exists to serve the many farms in the surrounding area, with plenty of hardware stores, blacksmiths, stables, etc. But even on cursory examination, it is evident that the famous buffalo is the major reason for such prestige as the town enjoys. I witnessed a stagecoach delivering sightseers and am informed that this is a twice-daily occurrence—with far more people coming in by train.

This afternoon, the publisher of the local newspaper, the Dispatch, introduced himself to me in the street in that wondrously informal manner unique to Americans. He wishes to announce my appointment in the newspaper. You see, dear mama and papa, your son is already on his way to being that distinguished figure that will make the name Rumbald known far and wide! I plan to re-read Goethe and Schiller in my spare time and to continue studying the essays of Heine that you, Papa, gave me as a parting gift. And finally, dear Maria, a fond kiss for you! I shall write again tomorrow with news of my first foray into the school room.

Your loving son, Hans.

He sat for a while before retiring to bed, his thoughts drifting back to the fetching young woman he had encountered on the train. She had a captivating smile. Was that her mother or her chaperone accompanying her? Perhaps I shall meet her again. I earnestly hope so.

THE NEXT MORNING, HE rose early, eager to meet his pupils and give his first lesson as schoolmaster. Unlocking the door to the schoolroom, he swept the floor and rearranged the stools and chairs. Glancing at his watch, he then took up position at the door, hands loosely crossed in front of him, a benevolent expression on his face, as recommended by Mr Alcott.

Shortly before nine o'clock, a straggle of children made their way across the small yard toward the school. 'Good morning, children!' he called out merrily as they blinked up at him and filed past into the schoolroom. The girls wore smocks, the smaller boys knee pants. All carried wooden pails containing their lunch. To his surprise, no fewer than twenty-two pupils of varying ages and sizes filed into the room.

When all were assembled, he introduced himself, smiling with pride as he spelled out his name on the board. 'Mr Rumbald,' he said, tapping each letter with a pointer bequeathed by his predecessor. 'R-U-M-B-A-L-D!' He then went around the room eliciting the name and age of each pupil. The youngest was five years old, the eldest fifteen. 'Temperance, did you say?' he said, stopping at one name. 'Wilhelm?' he said, stopping at another. 'Your family is German?' He stroked his moustache at the bony youth who stood before him.

'I guess.'

'You guess?'

'I reckon.'

He cocked an eyebrow, bemused at the oddities of frontier speech, so different from the eloquence of Emerson or James. Returning to the front of the room, he surveyed his charges, his fingers tented thoughtfully against his lips in a manner that betokened the great and sacred enterprise on which they were about to embark.

'What do you know of history?' he began, seeking to ignite the spark of interest that would, in time, he fervently hoped, burst into flame. 'It was my favourite subject, at school,' he prompted, searching the faces looking back at him. They struck him as pinched and sullen, not at all like the those of his schoolmates at the *Primarschule* of his own boyhood. 'Do you know who is the president of the United States?'

An uncertain hand went up. 'Yes?' he asked, his face brightening.

'Sir! Tommy's pissed hisself!'

48

An American Sphinx

THE DAY WAS WET and dreary, and only a few passersby were on hand to witness the arrival of the morning stage from Bismarck. Four passengers stepped out, enthusiastic to be in the 'Home of the Buffalo' in spite of the weather. While they looked about and waited for their baggage to be handed down, a fifth passenger emerged, stooping to survey the street before stepping down. He was tall, dressed in a black coat and waistcoat over a white shirt with a high buttoned collar and no tie. He wore a black, Amish hat which framed a gaunt, severe-looking face with thin, compressed lips. He was clean-shaven apart from a tuft of beard beneath his jaw. In one hand, he clutched a Bible. His fellow passengers shot looks of dislike as he waited for his single trunk to be handed down. He had said little or nothing on the journey from Bismarck, instead studying the Bible or giving occasional ear to the conversations of the other passengers as they enthused about the buffalo monument.

'You!' His firm voice caused the other passengers to startle as he pointed a bony finger at two boys lounging on the sidewalk. 'A dime if you carry my trunk.'

'Where to?' asked one.

'To the Miller boarding house.' He reached into his pocket and pulled out a dime, which he flicked in the air, catching it again.

'A dime each,' said the second boy.

The stranger grimaced, his skull-like face pulling tightly over high cheekbones. 'A dime,' he said, 'and the blessings of the Lord.' He held up the Bible in his other hand. The boys glanced at one another.

'Carry it yerself!' said the first, drawing a gasp from a female passenger.

'Then tell me the way to the Miller house,' the man said, seemingly unperturbed by the answer.

'That way!' One of the boys pointed down the street.

Without more ado, the stranger grasped the trunk by the handle and began to drag it down the street in the pointed direction. His fellow passengers swapped glances as they watched him go, bent over as he dragged the trunk. 'Leastways he ain't staying in the hotel,' said one, a relieved look on his face.

He was perspiring by the time he reached the boarding house. He looked about the quiet street before knocking. A carriage was parked across the way and a man on horseback rode slowly up the centre of the road, his head nodding as if asleep.

The door opened and an elderly woman peered out. 'Yes?' she said, her eyes noting the Amish hat.

'I made a reservation, Madam. From Kansas.'

'Preacher?' she said, her eyes widening. 'Come on in.' She held open the door. 'We've been expecting you!'

RUMBALD HAD GROUPED THE pupils by age, appointing the eldest as group monitor in the manner advocated by Horace Mann and other reformers. He went from group to group, teaching spelling to one, arithmetic to another, and grammar to a third. He was tolerant and forbearing, encouraging the children and only rarely giving vent to irritation. He supplemented the homely injunctions of the McGuffey Readers by sprinkling in references to the wider world and slipping in generous draughts of history and poetry that, to his dismay, left his charges grimacing or mumbling in confusion.

Miss Purlow, whose formidable reputation still hovered over the school more than two years after her departure, had been liberal with the stick, sometimes lining up the children in threes and fours for a thrashing. This struck him as an evasion of the teacher's responsibility to teach civilised, enlightened behaviour along with the 'three Rs' beloved of the school board. As a result, he dispensed with this punishment, relying instead upon encouragement, praise, and the occasional frowning glance to maintain order.

The superintendent himself came in to observe, the tall, black-clad figure drawing apprehensive looks from the children. The superintendent positioned himself at the side of the class, where he proceeded to shine his shoes with a rag, lifting one foot onto a chair shared by a pupil. This done, he observed the class for a quarter-hour before consulting his watch and excusing himself, his duty done. Mrs. Chestnut also attended, tightening her mouth as she watched, and afterward taking Rumbald aside to advise he make free use of the switch. 'Miss Purlow was a strict disciplinarian. She knew how to pop their sass!' But the other members of the board approved of his methods, one even praising his 'patient approach' and 'air of learning.'

Frustrated by the slow pace and basic nature of the classes, he toyed with the idea of opening the school to adults who wished to learn something of history or philosophy, only for Mrs. Chestnut to veto the notion.

'The farm folk have got all their heads will carry,' she said firmly. 'And as for the others, they are too busy ferryin' and fetchin'.' What the words implied, he never found out, letting the idea rest.

School was over by 4 pm, after which he swept out the schoolroom, washed down the blackboard, and brought in wood for the stove. Before returning to his lodgings, he took a half-hour of exercise by strolling up one side of Main Street and down the other. He then retreated to the boarding house for a simple supper of cold chicken and soup before retiring to his room. There, he read, penned a few lines of poetry for his own edification, and caught up on his correspondence. *Life is generally pleasant but dull,* he wrote to his sister. *The children are about as dutiful as could be expected and respond 'gamely' to instruction. The school board, on the other hand, is undisciplined and at times badly in want of correction.*

He got to know several of the parents and accepted dinner invitations to local homes. Despite his lowly status as a schoolteacher, one or two mothers fancied him an acceptable 'catch' for their unmarried daughters until it became obvious that his passion lay in books rather than potential sweethearts. He remained eager to learn more about the town and its history, and particularly the celebrated buffalo, which he still hadn't made time to see.

When questioning the children as to their knowledge of the object, he was surprised to find they treated it as of little more interest than a barn or grain silo. 'You have all seen it?' he asked.

'About every day, I reckon,' said one.

'Twice a day!' said another, to laughter.

'And what do you know of it—its history, its composition, its significance?' he asked.

The questions drew blank looks. 'Gertrude?' he asked, addressing one of the brighter pupils.

The girl blew out her cheeks. 'My pa says it was Injuns that built it.'

'And for what purpose?'

She frowned at such obtuseness. 'To look at, I guess.'

'It must have some significance,' he tried again, 'Some meaning beyond being looked at. What do you think that might be? Chesney?'

'What?'

He drew a breath. 'The buffalo has some meaning. Yes? What do you suppose that meaning might be?'

'Beats me.' The boy was sullen. 'I didn't chip it.' This drew laughter, which in turn drew an even more sullen scowl from the boy.

Returning to his lodgings that afternoon, he questioned his landlady as to her knowledge of the object.

'That old buffalo?' Mrs. Russell set a hand to her cheek to think. 'They say the Indians built it, a long time ago, as a sort of heathen altar.' She knitted her brow at the notion.

'But they have no proof—no archaeological studies, no scientific investigations, as evidence?'

'That Mr Lomax is mighty particular whom he lets near it. A government fella came up one time, all the way from Washington, to study the rock. Mr Lomax had him near whipped off the property.'

'He can do that—defy the government?'

'Folks reckon he *is* the government, leastways around here.'

'So, there is no scientific literature on the rock?'

'Scientific? No. Only what Mr Lomax—the Trust—puts out. There're some leaflets lying over there if you'd like to see.' She pointed to the sideboard.

Curious, he picked up a leaflet. '*Come See the Great Marvel of the Northern Plains!*' it was headed in large print.

Only two bits a head, half price for children under 12. Stand in awe of the buffalo monument, a world-famous totem carved by mysterious, unknown hands thousands of years in the past. Get your picture taken for posterity for just 5 cents each! Reasonably priced refreshments available on-site.

A second leaflet depicted an engraving of a man astride a bucking buffalo.

Come ride the buffalo! Unique opportunity to scale Bjornson's marvel! Take the adventure of a lifetime and ride, in complete safety, to the top of the tallest edifice in the state of North Dakota! Just 50 cents per adult. Must be 16 years or older. Discount tickets available for parties of 10 or more. Boast to your friends! Spectacular views from the top. An experience not to be missed!

He set down the leaflets. 'These say nothing about the history or origin of the monument. And who is this Bjornson fellow?'

'Some folk, Swedes mostly, claim that he made the rock, not the Indians. Mr Lomax generally plays it both ways, lessen he lose some money, I reckon.'

'I intend to view it for myself this Saturday.'

'Then best go early, afore there are sightseers climbing all over it like flies.'

AFTER A PLAIN BREAKFAST of two boiled eggs and a slice of buttered toast, the guest sat in a fireside chair for a half hour, reading the Bible while Mrs. Miller cleared the table, murmuring an apology at the noise. He appeared to take no notice, crossing his legs and turning the page while reciting to himself under his breath. As the clock chimed, he stood up, fixing her a glance that made her nervous. 'I understand there is a disused chapel on Union Street?'

'There is, Preach—sir. It used to belong to Pastor Jacobson. But since he died, it's stood empty.'

'Direct me there,' he said, with what might have been a smile touching the corner of his mouth.

A quarter hour later, he stood in front of the vacated building. A sign above the door read *Haven of Peace Chapel.* He looked up, pondering this for a moment. He then tried the door. It was locked. Looking around, he spied a man crossing the street toward him. 'Mister …?' The man held out his hand.

'Preacher,' he said, ignoring the outstretched hand.

'Mr Preacher, I got your message. I'd be glad to show you—'

'Just Preacher.'

'Huh? Oh!' The other man removed his hat. 'Pleased to meet you, Preach.' The preacher stood immobile 'Right!' The agent fished in his pocket for a key. 'Let's take a look!'

The inside was dusty and smelled of mildew. The potential client looked around—at the benches, the windows, the raised platform at the front of the hall. ''Course, it ain't been used in a few months, since the pastor died.' The agent straightened a few benches. 'It's pretty plain, but a lick of paint—'

'I'll take it.' The preacher tugged at the tuft of beard beneath his lip. 'On a monthly rent, unless you object?'

The agent frowned. 'Renting is fine, although I expected you to buy it outright.'

'In time. Within six months, perhaps?'

'In that case, we have a deal!' The agent stuck out his hand again, only to withdraw it a moment later, a perplexed look on his face. 'What church are you?' he asked, suddenly suspicious. 'You Methodist, for instance, like Pastor Jacobson?'

The preacher walked up and down the aisle between the two rows of benches. 'I'll want a new sign painted above the door.'

'What did you have in mind?'

The preacher turned, a triumphant certitude in his manner. '"Temple of the Heavenly Kingdom." Is there a broom handy?'

'I rented out the chapel,' the agent said on returning to the office.

'That fella from Kansas?' His partner sat with his feet up on the oak desk as he scanned the newspaper.

'A strange bird. Looks like he eats brimstone and shits fire.'

'Long as he pays on time. What you doing?'

'I promised him a mop and bucket.' He looked around. 'Where in tar is that no-hoper Lester when you need him?'

'I sent him for coffee. What did you say the fella's name was?'

'He ain't got one, far as I can tell. Calls himself Preacher, like he was something.'

'Preacher?' The other man shook his head. 'Jest so long as he ain't peddling snake oil.'

ON SATURDAY, TWO WEEKS after arriving in the town, Rumbald rented a buggy, the stable hand grumbling at the early hour. 'The rock ain't even open yet,' he complained. 'Make sure you give her plenty of water,' he said, leading out the mare.

The streets were deserted as he headed out of town. The buggy wheels turned smoothly on the tarred surface, and he wished some of his pupils were around to observe. Scholarly and bookish by nature, he yet felt a burst of satisfaction as he left the buildings behind and was greeted by the freedom of the open road. The morning was fine and sunny, with the promise of a warm summer day. He flicked the reins, enjoying the motion of the gig and the snuffling of the horse. He passed a farmhouse, and then another, a dog dashing out to investigate his passage. The road was bordered on both sides by fields of wheat, the bending, rippling motion of the crops creating the illusion of waves on the sea.

'Good day, sir!' He raised the whip in acknowledgement as he passed a wagon loaded with farm produce headed toward town.

'Morning, schoolteach.'

The unexpected salutation delighted him. *Well, and so I am!* He shook the reins, already mentioning the sobriquet in his next letter home. 'Hey up, Nelly!'

After travelling for a quarter hour, his early exuberance began to wane. He stretched his back against the hard seat, certain he had a bruise, and wishing he had thought to bring a cushion. *That stable hand might have thought to mention it. I shall tell him on my return, remind him of his responsibilities.* He stared ahead, eager to catch his first sight of the celebrated rock. He passed a large wooden sign by the side of the road. 'The

World-Famous Buffalo Straight Ahead!' And, underneath, 'Just Two Bits to Enter!' A mile later, he passed another sign, this one dominated by a huge, coloured illustration of the rock. 'Ride the Buffalo! Just 50 Cents for the Thrill of a Lifetime!' He had just passed it when he glimpsed the object itself, stark and dominating, in the distance. His heart beat faster at the sight. *It's bigger than I imagined!* The nearer he drew, the more it resembled the fabled creature that had inspired it, the massive head seeming to defy the prairie vastness.

The tarred road ended at yet another sign, one proclaiming the proximity of 'The Marvel of the Ages!' A track ran over the grass to a high fence which, from this vantage, blocked a view of the carving. He drove up to a large double gate, over which stood a wrought iron arch spelling the words 'The Buffalo Trust Monument.' Two flagpoles flanked the sign. A poster tacked to the gate announced that the monument would be open for viewing from 10 am until sunset. Climbing down, he peered through the gate. He glimpsed a ticket office and, beyond it, several tents, the largest of which resembled a pavilion. Behind it stood the rock, its bulk dwarfing the pavilion tent. The day was growing warmer, and the area appeared deserted.

An iron trough near the gate was full of water, and he led the thirsty mare to it. While she drank, he looked around, wondering how best to get past the gate. Deciding there was no easy ingress, he climbed back aboard the buggy and retraced his route for a quarter mile until the fence ended and a stretch of fallow pasture, overgrown by weeds, began. A dirt track led from the road past the field. He followed it, guessing others had chosen the same route to avoid paying the entrance fee.

Arriving at the end fence post, he climbed down from the buggy. Leaving the horse to graze, he proceeded past the fence and onto the site. A large sign warned that trespassers would be prosecuted 'to the fullest extent of the law.' Wary of a watchman, he proceeded past a broad enclosure which, he guessed, was reserved for horses and the carriages they pulled. The great rock now loomed before him in all its impregnable splendour.

The excitement he had felt earlier returned as he ventured into its shadow. The colossal stone beast soared high above his head, the early-morning solitude lending it an air of gravitas and ancient mystery. He reached out to touch the cool granite, marvelling that such a thing should exist. A sensation of sacrilege evoked an apologetic murmur, as though he trespassed on some sacred, forbidden shrine. He walked alongside, trailing his hand over the stone while fancying himself in the shade of some solemn deity, as old as time itself. Reaching the front, he looked up at the immense head, marvelling at its particularity of detail. This was no happy accident of time and erosion, he told himself, thinking back to one of the leaflets he had read, but a meticulously planned and executed likeness.

He walked around the rock to the other side. Once there, the gaudy pavilion and posters left behind, he was confronted by the vast, unbounded prairie and experienced the full grandeur of the great buffalo sentinel as it gazed out over its domain. He had once visited Stonehenge, entering that stone circle with an awe that amounted to veneration as the air of centuries past enveloped his impressionable senses. He now felt the same, rarefied transport—the vast, overarching sky, the sibilant breeze, and the trembling, obeisant grass all conspiring to induce a heady sense of the numinous that rocked him to the core. Who created this? How? Why? Questions whirled through his head as he attempted to comprehend the imposing presence of the monumental beast.

He walked slowly alongside the rock, his mind buzzing with conjecture. Could the popular belief be true—that some unknown civilisation, now lost to history, had laboured to create the giant likeness? The scholar in him reasoned that the impenetrably hard stone would require sophisticated iron tools and knowledge of line and perspective to produce the spectacular resemblance. Nevertheless, the local legends of immemorial workmanship seemed suited to the air of profound mystery evoked by the colossal, enigmatic beast. He rounded the object, taking in the etched hindquarters and tufted tail. Completing the circuit, he stood once more beneath the massive head, perspiring in the early warmth, an overpowering sense of solemnity and awe rendering him speechless.

He took off his hat to wipe his brow, certain he stood in the presence of something no less ancient and sacrosanct than the groves of Delphi or the Temple of Apollo. Surely, it was created for religious purposes—for worship? His thoughts raced from one possibility to another. Was it modelled on the desert Sphinx of antiquity? Or was this indeed the model for the Sphinx? He gasped at the startling notion. The fanciful conjectures he had heard voiced in town—of an unknown tribe from remote antiquity, of a master Swedish, or was it Danish? stone mason devoting his life to completion of the creature—even the oft-repeated claim that the likeness was begun by wind and erosion and 'finished' by human hand of unknown provenance, raced through his thoughts, the possibilities bubbling over, one into another.

Overwhelmed, he sat down in the grass, struggling to grasp the implications. There is a great mystery here to unravel, he pondered. A magnum opus of unknown origin—a monumental artwork situated in an obscure corner of the northern plains, far from the great centres of learning and civilisation—how was such a thing possible? The enduring enigma of Stonehenge came back to mind as he speculated on the rewards of being the first to unravel the buffalo's secrets. The definitive answer would surely establish the discoverer's reputation, win him national—nay, worldwide—renown.

The tantalising prospect thrilled him to the core as his mind blazed with possibilities. No more toiling in backwoods obscurity, but universal celebrity as the unraveller of the riddle of the American Sphinx! The feat would be rewarded with invitations to learned conferences, perhaps the offer of a prestigious post at an eastern university! Dazzled by the prospect of scholarly riches, he picked himself up from the grass and, with a last, marvelling glance back at the colossus, made his way back to the gig. He stepped aboard, picturing his name in large print, perhaps with a photograph of himself—posed like an adventurer or discoverer—beneath the towering beast, like the illustrations of Egyptologists he had admired in books. Barely able to contain his excitement, he shook the reins. 'Home, Nelly! Ride like the wind!'

49

A Neighbourly Hand

AMITY HEARD A HOLLER from outside and went to look. Norm Ketchfield, their neighbour from a mile down the road, drove into the yard, raising dust with the wagon wheels. Perched on the seat beside him was a small girl and an even smaller boy. Puzzled as to the reason for the rare visit, she waited on the porch while Ira approached the wagon. After a few moments, he turned and beckoned her to join him. 'Amity, you know Mr Ketchfield?'

'Of course. How do you do, Mr Ketchfield?'

'Middling well, thank you, Mrs. Morgan.' Ketchfield tilted his hat. 'These are my young 'uns, Temperance and Harry.' The two children stared at her, wide-eyed.

'Seems Mrs. Ketchfield has taken poorly,' said Ira, 'and needs to go to the hospital, in Bismarck. Mr Ketchfield needs someone to look after the children.'

'For about a month—two at the most.' Ketchfield licked his lips, his eyes fastened on her.

'Me?' She blinked in the sunlight.

'It would be mighty neighbourly of you.'

'What do you say, Am?'

She noticed the distraught look on the face of the little girl. 'Yes,' she said. 'Of course.'

Ketchfield uttered a huge sigh of relief. 'Mighty appreciate it, Mrs. Morgan. Between Mary in the hospital and running the farm … I don't know what.' He shook his head. Climbing down from the seat, he held out his arms. 'Come on, Harry, step down.' He lifted down first the boy and then the girl. 'I'll come for them soon as Mary's fit enough to manage. Children, be good for Mrs. Morgan. Don't go giving her any trouble. And don't fret, your ma will be all right.' He climbed back on the wagon. 'Greatly obliged,' he said, his voice strained. Taking up the reins, he glanced at the children. 'Remember, be good now! Har!'

The wagon rumbled out of the yard, raising more dust. 'Pa?' The young boy ran after the wagon. The young girl burst into tears.

Fleur appeared on the porch, a cross look on her face. 'What in beeswax is going on?'

EVER SINCE HIS ENCOUNTER with the rock, its image had haunted him, the great beast rising spectre-like in his dreams and intruding on his thoughts during the day. Consumed with a sense of the importance of the task, he sought avenues to begin his research into the object. Locals he spoke to on the matter were exasperatingly at odds in their accounts. 'It was the Sioux, fer sure, I had it from an old medicine man,' said one informant. 'It was the Mandan—they were here afore the Sioux. Or, if not them, then some other Injuns we don't even know about,' conjectured the clerk at the telegraph office.

'Why don't you ask Purchase McLennan,' suggested his landlady. 'He supposedly knows more about it than anyone else. He even claims his granddaddy carved the thing, if you can believe such starch.'

'Who is he?'

'A homesteader. Been around these parts longer than most. His son, Boundary, works down at the *Dispatch*.'

He made a note of the information in the new journal he had purchased for the research. To bring order to his somewhat feverish speculations, he jotted them down in a letter to his sister.

My dear Maria,

I hope you are feeling better and not so much "under the weather" (an American expression) as expressed in your last letter. (And do try to write in English. It is hard, sometimes, I know, but you will be the better for it, I assure you.) Do you remember my previous letter, when I described my pilgrimage to view the stone buffalo the entire country is talking about? I have since been inspired to write a monograph on the astonishing figure. No one, as far as I know, has attempted such a thing—little wonder when you consider the prairie wasteland it inhabits and the lack of any nearby centres of learning. But that is good news, for it means I shall be the first to acknowledge its singular magnificence and the purpose behind its creation! Such an undertaking, if successful, would make my reputation and establish me as the foremost—indeed, the only—authority on the object. But the research into its origins is proving frustratingly difficult. It seems that every single man or woman in the town has a different theory regarding its creation. There is much to investigate. I must first determine if there is any truth to the alleged connection between the rock and the homesteader whose land it once occupied. I must also investigate how such a thing came to be: the tools and methods used to fashion it; the models, if any, upon which it is based;

the techniques of scaling and hammering such a very hard stone. In short, my darling sister, I must discover everything there is to know about the creature. As I am the first to attempt such exhaustive research (so far as I am aware), I have an obligation to be thorough and methodological in case a later scholar may attempt to steal my thunder. Please excuse my dwelling so long on the subject, which quite possibly you find foreign and boring to your ears. But were you to see it you would gasp and almost faint! It is the largest sculpture of its kind that I have ever encountered. It rises up over the prairie like the great Sphinx of Egypt itself—the only rival to which it may be compared, in terms of size if not antiquity. I shall leave off, for now, and retire to ponder the way ahead.

Your loving brother, Hans.

Setting the letter aside, he opened the thick, leather-bound journal and turned to the first page. In his neat, careful hand, he wrote across the top: 'An Inquiry into the Origins and Significance of the Buffalo Rock Monument in North Dakota.' Beneath the title he jotted some ideas: 'Composition and age of the stone. Theories as to origin and purpose. Carving techniques and methods of working. Required masonry skills. Possible models? Date of creation? Competing claimants: Indian, Lars(?) Axel(?) Bjornson. "Many hands" theory?' He glanced at the list, more ideas running through his head. A considerable project, he told himself, the prospect filling him with anticipation. He undressed and climbed into the narrow bed, his head buzzing with notions. Boundary? Did that not refer to a point of land? Such strange names these Americans have!

THE CHILDREN WERE QUIET and well-behaved, although frightened and confused over the illness of their mother and the absence of their father. Amity did her best to comfort them, answering their questions and reassuring them that their mother would recover and be back to fetch them in no time.

'You oughtn't feed 'em candy when it's doubtful their ma will ever get well,' admonished her mother-in-law. 'They won't thank you for it.'

'And how do you know. You a doctor now?'

Fleur let the impertinence pass. 'I hear she has a weak heart—same as that which killed Mrs. Jimerson some years back. She won't be walking around long.'

'People do recover. Besides, there's no need to upset the children any more than they already are.'

'Have it your way—you usually do!' Her mother-in-law sniffed. 'But you'll have no one to blame but yourself if she passes.' A thought occurred to her. 'Why, you may be stuck raising two that ain't yourn!'

The notion alarmed Amity so much that she sought reassurance from her husband.

'If anything happens to their ma, Mr Ketchfield has already told me he plans to sell up and move back to Iowa, where his family lives. He can't stay and farm with two children to raise.'

'They need to go back to school. They've already missed half a term.'

He nodded. 'It ain't far. They can walk.'

'Ira Morgan! The boy's no more than five years old. I'll drive them in the buggy.'

'Why? It's no more than a mile or so.'

'They were left in our care! Or do you wish them to get caught in the rain and get sick, like their ma?'

He frowned. 'Heck, I guess I—' He abandoned the protest on seeing the look on her face. 'Have it your way,' he sighed, echoing his ma.

Concerned at the children's doleful air, she decided to take them with her when next she went to visit Boundary, promising to stop afterwards for ice cream. 'Any flavour you like,' she said.

Thus, on a fine but cool October day, she wrapped them in hats and scarves and lifted them up into the buggy. Her mother-in-law stepped out onto the porch to watch alongside Ira as she picked up the whip. 'We'll be home before supper!' she called out, ignoring the beadish look on her mother-in-law's face.

'It's time you had one of your own,' Fleur had sniped, disapproval in her voice as she watched Amity dress the two.

She pondered the thought as she drove into town. Beside her, the children stared silently at the passing fields, their faces anxious. 'Who can spot a three-legged cow?' she said, playing a game her pa used play with her. 'What! Who said there ain't such a thing?' The children exchanged looks but said nothing. *I guess their pa ain't one for games.* Harry snuggled up against her for warmth. She adjusted her pa's old buffalo robe so that it covered his knees. 'Skit!' She shook the reins.

They entered the town outskirts, the ride growing smoother as they made the transition from dirt road to sealed tar. They drove past the post office and the bank, the sidewalks noticeably emptier now that the buffalo monument had closed for the season. A man lounged outside the new hotel, watching as they passed.

Boundary was sweeping the sidewalk outside the newspaper office. 'Where's Mr Bellow?' she asked as he set down the whisk and opened the door to allow them in.

'He ain't here,' he said, following them inside.

'Jumping feathers, I can see that! Where is he?'

'He's gone home to eat dinner with Mrs. Bellow.'

'Harry, Temperance, take off your hats and scarves,' she said, feeling motherly. She took off her own coat and sat down near the woodstove. 'I told the children you'd explain how the press works.'

She was reading through the sheets of the next issue of the *Dispatch* when the door opened. To her surprise, Mr Rumbald, the schoolteacher, stepped inside. He seemed equally surprised to see her.

'Mr Bellow ain't here,' said Boundary.

Rumbald smiled—at her, not Boundary—and raised his hat.

'Indeed, I came to see you, Mr McLennan.'

'Me? Why? You need something printed?'

'No, quite another errand. May I?' He indicated a chair.

'Help yourself.'

'Thank you.' Rumbald sank into the chair. His eyes returned to Amity again, bright with pleasure at finding her there. She felt herself blush under his gaze, the warm blood rushing to her cheeks. 'Good day to you, Mrs. Morgan. And Temperance, and Harry,' he added, recognising his pupils. 'You are looking after them for their mother?' he asked. 'I heard about her illness,' he said, his voice sympathetic. 'Do you have children at the school?'

'Me? No.'

He nodded and smiled. Was that a pleased look on his face? 'I'm in town visiting,' she said, 'and thought I'd bring the children along. Boundary is my brother.'

'He is?' Rumbald brightened. 'Then I come to see you, as well, Mrs. Morgan.'

'Your business?' asked Boundary, his manner striking her as rather blunt.

'My business, sir, is the buffalo.' Rumbald fiddled with his hat brim at Boundary's look of confusion. 'I am writing a short monograph—a scholarly article—on the origins and significance of the object. My landlady, Mrs. Russell, remarked that your family has some … familial connection to the object. Am I correct in this assumption?' He glanced at Amity, including her in the question.

'My pa's grandpa carved it.'

Rumbald, who had taken out a notebook, raised his eyebrows at the reply. 'His grandfather? But I was given to believe that it was fashioned by wild Indians—long in the past.'

'Nope. It was my pa's pa. Or maybe his pa,' said Boundary.

Rumbald squinted in confusion. 'You mean your great grandfather?'

Boundary grimaced. 'I get a headache with all those greats!'

'Our great-great-grandfather,' Amity corrected remembering her childhood lessons.

'Oh!' Rumbald's look of puzzlement deepened. 'Then that would mean the object—the artwork—is only …' He made a quick calculation. '… Somewhere between a hundred and ten and a hundred and twenty years old?' He looked to Amity for confirmation.

'That sounds about right,' she said. 'Harry, mind that ink! You'll stain your clothes.'

Rumbald fingered his moustache to think. 'I was under the impression it was considerably more ancient,' he said, his voice betraying his disappointment.

'Well, I guess it ain't,' said Boundary.

'Forgive me the impertinence, but do you have any proof of your claim?'

'We don't need no proof.'

Rumbald wrinkled his brow in confusion. 'Not for yourselves, but for the public—who may be interested in the matter?'

Just then, the door opened, and Mr Bellow pushed in. He stopped short on seeing Rumbald, a surprised look on his face. 'Mr Rumbald? You've come by on business?'

'Indeed, sir.' Rumbald stood and gave a brief bow. 'But buffalo business, not the print kind. And now I must hasten back to the school.' He turned to Amity. 'Mrs. Morgan, I greatly desire to pursue this matter further. Is it possible that we may meet again to discuss it at a time of your convenience?'

She felt herself colour again. 'Perhaps. Come children, time for ice cream!'

Bellow took off his coat as the door closed behind them. Hanging it up, he took a sheet of paper from the pocket. Going to his desk, he put up his feet and read the wire again. '*Preacher full name Silas Leaf. Expelled church Cincinnati for zealotry. Suspect in arson and incitement to murder.*'

FOR HIS FIRST SERMON, he had thrown open the doors, pontificating to an empty chapel. After a time, a curious passer-by, attracted by the oration, stuck his head in. He ignored the man, demanding of the empty benches that they repent and prepare for the glorious coming of His Kingdom. 'For the Heavens shall part and He shall descend in clouds of glory!' After a time, the male spectator was joined by a woman, who listened at the door for some minutes and then entered to timorously sit down on a bench in the last row. It was only then that he interrupted his sermon. 'Welcome, sister! The Lord gladdens to see you!'

The first spectator wandered off, deciding he had heard enough. But before the end of the sermon, the woman had been joined by three more congregants, two other women and a man the worst for liquor and looking for a warm place to sleep it off. The preacher stood with raised arms, despite the small audience, his voice dominating the quiet chapel. 'Gather me the people together, and I will make them hear my words!' He looked upward, beseeching the heavens. 'Gather them that they may learn to fear me all the days that they shall live upon the earth!'

Afterwards, he stood, sere and unbending, in the doorway, nodding with solemn gravity in response to praise for the sermon. 'Tell your friends,' Was all he said. 'Tell them to come and worship in the house of God.'

One of the women offered to bring flowers, 'to brighten up the place,' and he accepted, laying a hand over hers in a manner that caused her heart to flutter. 'Flowers are the symbol of He who sits and watches from above,' he said.

WORD SPREAD QUICKLY ABOUT the new preacher—his oddity of name, or title, seeming only to enhance his mysterious presence in the town. The next sermon was attended by a dozen people, most of them curiosity-seekers rather than worshippers. It mattered little to him, his fiery denunciations echoing from the roof and bouncing off the walls. Abandoning the pulpit at strategic moments, he strode up and down between the pews like a general exhorting his troops to battle. And, indeed, he projected the enemy, Satan, to the congregation, describing, evoking almost, the archfiend himself with dramatic words and gestures that drew gasps from the worshippers. 'He stands outside these doors, waiting to ensnare!' he thundered. 'In here is sanctuary. Out there is danger and wickedness!' He pointed at the doors, now closed. 'I see him without, with eyes like glowing coals!' The declaration drew a shriek from one congregant and nervous glances from the others. 'Get thee gone, arch tempter!'

Throughout the fall, the congregation remained at a dozen or so regulars, his severe manner and brimstone sermons frightening off others— most of whom yearned for the days of the peaceable, pipe-smoking and ale-drinking Pastor Jacobson. A curious Quintus Bellow himself attended one sermon, afterward writing an editorial in the *Dispatch* in which he questioned 'religious performances that smacked of the hot desert and Old Jerusalem.' '*Religion oughtn't frighten folk to death,*' he sermonised. '*The twentieth century is but two short years away. We ought be celebrating progress, not scaring the children with boils and hair-raising pulpitry.*'

The editorial drew a thundering condemnation in response, the preacher devoting the following week's sermon to a scathing denunciation of 'agents of Satan, masquerading as neutral observers to entice the innocent by wicked words and evil purposes.' Bellow responded with a jeremiad of his own, accusing the preacher of deliberately riling up folk through fear and punishment. '*This is a peaceful town, full of decent citizens going about their business. What need have we of unholy fulminations that disturb the horses and keep the nervous awake at night?*'

'There's but one established religion in this town,' he remarked to Boundary. 'Worship of the dollar. And that durn buffalo is the altar.'

The editorial drew praise and censure in equal measure, the congregants emboldened by the conscription of Thurston Wake, a wealthy local rancher with messianic tendencies of his own who championed the new preacher and increased enrolment at the Sunday sermons by his presence. 'The town's gone all to hell,' he declared. 'And the Lord sent along the preacher to straighten us out!' Recognising a valuable ally when he saw one, the preacher took Wake into his confidence, wooing the rancher with extravagant ardour while the latter sang his praises in return. 'I feel reborn!' he announced to acquaintances and strangers alike. 'I tell you, the Lord speaks through that man.'

But in spite of such enthusiastic endorsement, the congregation remained small, scarcely rising to two dozen at a time, their contributions barely enough to pay the rent. The preacher mulled on this throughout the cold winter, convinced the hand of Satan was at work. The Lord sent me here for a purpose, he brooded, setting down the ever-present Bible. He will provide. He will show me the way. He thought more about it, pondering in front of the woodstove as the harsh, prairie wind howled outside. He had moved out from the boarding house, equipping a small room at the back of the chapel with a narrow bed and woodstove—upon which he prepared his meals or reheated the pots of food provided by parishioners. His needs were few, the furnishings as meagre as his own gaunt appearance as a warrior of God. It was spring, and visitors were flocking in again to view the buffalo, before he stumbled upon the revelation that would trumpet his mission.

SHE WAS NERVOUS, FUSSING over the children and avoiding Ira as he hitched the buggy. 'I won't be long,' she said, for the second time. 'I'll just drop off the children and maybe see if Boundary is free for a visit.' She watched as he swung Temperance up onto the seat, followed by Harry.

'Be careful. The road will be slippery after that rain.' He helped her up. 'Did you ask Ma if she wanted to go—for the ride?'

She shook her head. 'She ain't up to it. It's her joints. Gee-up!'

The sun broke through the clouds as she drove into town. The children stared straight ahead, gripping the lunch pails Ira had made for them. The town was slowly stirring into life, the morning train from Bismarck just a few minutes away. They passed the hotel and the new steak house, the manager hanging out a sign to proclaim they were open for business. He looked up as she passed and called out a cheerful 'Good morning, Ma'am!' She nodded in reply, pointing out to the children the expanded hardware store, still closed at this early hour. The saloon was open, a man sweeping up outside. The freight office was also open, Billy—the Halversons' boy—leaning in the doorway. 'Mrs. Morgan!' He raised a hand in greeting as she passed.

She pulled up outside the school. He was there, standing in the yard, a stricken look on his face as he saw her. 'I'll be back this afternoon to collect you,' she told the children. 'Be good you hear?' She shook the reins, pretending she hadn't seen him. 'Home!' she called out, louder than was necessary, her mouth dry with nerves.

The bright morning had given way to a grey, cloudy afternoon when she asked Ira to hitch up the buggy again. 'It ain't far,' he said, frowning. 'A walk would do them good. Any word on how Mrs. Ketchfield is doing?' he asked, when she insisted on going anyway.

'I'll see if I can't fetch some news,' she answered. Her mother-in-law sat in the rocker, eyeing her, she felt, with suspicion.

'It's about time he took them back. We ain't a boarding house,' he grumbled.

'That ain't Christian, Ira.'

He wiped a hand under his chin. 'I guess not. Don't it make you hanker, though, for your own?' He gazed at her, a hopeful look in his eyes.

'They're good practice,' she said. 'For when I do.'

He smiled, pleased with the answer. 'I reckon so.'

Rumbald was there again on her return, standing outside as though awaiting her. 'Mrs. Morgan!' He advanced to meet her, his face flushed—with nerves or excitement, she couldn't tell which. 'Do you have time to discuss the stone monument?'

'I have but a few minutes,' she answered, her voice prim as Harry and Temperance ran up to her. 'Children, I need to speak to Mr Rumbald. Run and play. I shan't be long.'

He assisted her down, his warm hand grasping hers, his eyes darting over her face. She avoided his ardent gaze as he led her inside the schoolroom, his manner as skittish as a youth seeking to impress a sweetheart. He sat her down inside the empty classroom and sat across from her, a notebook in his hand. He made extravagant reference to it, opening and smoothing the pages as if it were of primary importance to the matter at hand. He spoke to her, asking questions, his voice grave and soothing, not probing as the voices of men so often were when addressing her. She answered as best she could, forgetting the replies as she watched him note the information, his smooth fingers gripping the pen and moving it with quick, deft strokes.

'It is remarkable, is it not?' he said—his voice startling her.

'What is?' She blushed.

'That the buffalo'—he had taken to calling it that in imitation of her—'is so new, so young. I had imagined it many hundreds, if not thousands, of years old.'

'I must be going.' She stood up.

'Of course, Madam!' He leapt to his feet, extending a hand as if to assist. She felt his breath, warm on her cheek, together with the smell of chalk. 'Perhaps we might speak again?' he asked. 'To clarify certain points?'

'Perhaps. I must go. I am late for my husband.'

He offered his arm as she climbed up onto the buggy alongside the children. She felt the soft wool of his suit sleeve. 'Skit now!' She flicked the whip. 'Skit!'

SHE SPOKE WITH HIM several more times over the next few weeks, the conversation gradually shifting to her life and experiences as a farm wife. He was a skilled and delicate interrogator, gently questioning, murmuring in commiseration, once touching her arm in sympathy. The conversation shifted—how subtly! —to her hopes while still a pupil at the seminary in St Charles. He was an excellent listener, nodding, making soft noises in his throat, his eyes on her as though entranced. As she became more at ease, she was gratified to note her effect on him—the hitch in his breath when she raised her eyes to meet his, the rush of emotion to his animated features when she let slip a small confidence, the look in his eyes when she insisted she must go or 'be missed.' The latter phrase—slipping unmindfully from her lips—frightened and alarmed her.

For the next week, she avoided encountering him, letting the children down a half block from the schoolhouse and arranging to pick them up at the same spot after school. One warm day, she even permitted them to walk by themselves into town, relenting at the last moment and driving in to fetch them when school was finished, her mother-in-law seated beside her. She pretended not to see as he came out to observe, unnecessarily shepherding the children to the buggy and darting imploring glances at her in spite of the old woman's presence.

'Mrs. Morgan!' he said. 'And your mother?' He smiled at Fleur, who corrected him in a cross voice.

'No I ain't! And I ain't a grandmother, neither. Leastways not yet. Foster ma is the best I kin do right now.' She flashed a resentful glance at Amity.

'Nice to see you, Mr Rumbald. The children were good, I take it?' She risked a glance into his eyes.

He nodded, a tragic expression on his face. 'Of course. Temperance has the makings of a scholar.'

She smiled, pleased for the child. 'I'll be sure to let her pa know. Good morrow, sir. Sit down, Harry,' she said, taking up the reins. 'Skit!'

At night, she dreamed of his moustache and his warm, intelligent eyes that seemed to look into her and proclaim, 'I see you!' Ira was fast asleep, and she luxuriated in thinking back on Rumbald, dreaming of him as sleep overtook her.

Mr Ketchfield returned with the news that his wife was still poorly. 'I'd be mighty obliged if you'd hang on to the children for another few days,' he said, his face strained.

'She ain't got long,' Fleur said, watching him whip the wagon away from the yard. 'What will you do with the children then? Give 'em back, I guess, if he still wants them,' she sniffed, answering herself before Amity could reply.

Later that afternoon, Amity left to collect the children, telling Ira that she would take them for ice cream afterward as a treat, 'to take their minds off their ma. I may be a little late,' she said, her heart, if not yet her mind, set.

At the school, Rumbald led her inside, taking her hand, his eyes never leaving hers. He didn't sit her down, as customary; instead, taking her other hand also, so that he held both, trapping her in a willing snare. 'Amity,' he murmured, using her given name for the first time. She looked up into his eyes, her entire body trembling.

'*Liebste!*' The word was whispered, causing her a sharp intake of breath. His brown eyes were soft, imploring, his hands warm upon her own as he leaned in so close that their lips touched. '*Liebste!*'

50

A Schoolroom Tryst

HANS RUMBALD WAS A man transformed. His naturally romantic cast of mind, harshly suppressed in the suffocating cocoon of deprivation and anxiety enforced upon it by circumstance since leaving his native Bohemia, now emerged, full-blown, from its quarantine. Amity Morgan, *mirabile dictu,* had been blown to him like a wounded bird from out of the wild grasslands. Her grave, circumspect nature, stricken yearning for love, and pent-up suffering called out to him like a wood dove cooing to its mate. How she came alive in his arms! How tender were her kisses, how affectionate her lingering embrace! It was almost too much for this combustible man of intense yet nervously repressed feelings. He was like a fine spring—tightly coiled and taut for release. Teaching was one freely spinning rotor for this pent-up energy; his determination to 'unriddle' the colossal buffalo monument another; and now, to the intermeshing gears of humiliation and ambition was added the balance wheel—love. But love, the regulator, was foreign to the deeper workings of his temperament. A cool, analytical mind, praised by his professors for its grasp and acuity, was overlaid on a bed of igneous rock—shifting, liquid, answerable to still deeper fires, causing an inexorable pressure to build beneath the detached temperament of the gentleman, scholar, and philosopher. His instinctive, passionate nature—that dynamic flux of boiling magma—yearned for his beloved's presence nay, *demanded* it. The detached scholar weighed and observed, the man himself slanted and flowed like burning lava in a tilted glass. Amity Morgan, fluttering helplessly against the shutters of her dovecote in the very midst of the prairie wilderness, was at once the inspiration and the mainspring of his hopes. Thus, consumed with desire and ambition, he paced restlessly in the empty schoolroom, counting the hours until his beloved was in his arms again.

Meanwhile, the object of his intense devotion had flung open the windows to the cleansing breath of spring—incurring the wrath of her mother-in-law, who grumbled endlessly of the cold. In the bright blue dawns, she rose before her husband, stepping outside into the yard to enjoy a few minutes of birdsong and cooing blissfulness before the chores of the day. Drawing in deep breaths, her face turned to the sun, she felt the light leach into her bones, dissolving the winter hardness and the calcified deposits of interminable snowy days and long, freezing nights. Her face had regained its natural colour—a pink rosiness and fresh bloom that shone back at her from the mirror and reflected in the faces of her two young charges as she laughed and played hoop and stick or ring toss in the yard.

Fleur observed this newfound happiness with suspicion, standing inside the doorway, a frown upon her face as she watched her daughter-in-law whirl a gleeful Harry by the arms or challenge Temperance to a footrace. The two giggled and laughed as they held up their long skirts while breathlessly racing toward a stick planted in the yard. 'Something's amiss,' she remarked to her son, eyes narrowing at a fresh outburst of gaiety.

'She's taking their minds off their ma,' he said, pleased by her new-found joy—reminiscent once more of the cheerful, independent girl he had courted.

'It's about time their pa fetched them back. This ain't a nursery.'

'Charity, Ma, charity. The poor man's got enough on his plate.'

Fleur harrumphed, retiring to her room where she pondered her daughter-in-law's transformation. Has she been smitten? she wondered.

SWEPT UP IN HER feelings for the enigmatic, haunted figure of the schoolteacher, Amity was grateful for her husband's stolid immersion in the daily routine of plants and livestock. If, at times, he felt the impulse to comment on her newly found vigour and energetic attention to the children or to household duties, he was easily enough led off into questions of barn repair and fence mending. She could, she felt, safely assign one quarter of her mental and emotional energies to easing her husband and maintaining the house. Of the remaining three quarters, she expended one in her garden, working the hoe with a quick competence that bespoke her flushing vitality—routing with ease the errant weeds that sprouted between the plants. Another was spent in entertaining the children, immersing them in the tomboyish sports and antics that had delighted her as a child. The remaining quarter she idled away in luxuriant sojourns on the porch rocker, imagining the feel of *his* careful husbandry, the strong yet tender fingers which probed and opened her yielding face and lips, the light touch of hand against her cheek which produced a deep thrill in her receptive nerves—his accented mouth kissing and murmuring in her ear, his brown eyes warm and keenly observant.

And whenever she could steal away—using the children as cover—they would sit and hold each other, her head resting on his shoulder while he whispered of foreign lands or enchanted her with tales of sorrowful flight and soulful homecomings. She felt wrapped in a warm blanket as she lay nestled in his arms and listened to his heartbeat—the small sanctuary behind the classroom protecting and sanctifying their embrace. She could breathe, she felt, draw in air and love without restriction, as if a tight corset had been unlaced and her organs suddenly freed to rise and fall in accordance with their own natural needs and volition.

But beyond the allotted quarters, she felt a terrible darkness pressing in upon her. She awoke at night from dreams of burial, her chest constricted, her heart pounding as she listened to her husband snore. Sometime during each night, she wriggled away from his grasp, retreating to the edge of the bed and shivering at his touch as if seared with fire. In the mornings following such nights, she felt hardly able to cope. She fed the children, passed the ham to her husband, and searched his face for signs she might have said or done something during the night to give herself away. Sometimes, in the false light of dawn, he reached for her, and she quickly climbed out of bed, pleading the need to pass water. Although he lay waiting in the greyish light, she avoided returning to bed, slipping on her coat and wandering out into the yard to watch the sun mount the horizon. At times, she felt the weight of her two lives crushing her, depriving her of breath, and she ached to be alone, far out on the plains, each mental journey taking her out to the deep, shadowy grass or back to the town and the intimate haven behind the classroom.

'You saw your brother just three days ago,' Ira complained as she climbed up onto the buggy.

'I promised Harry he could watch Boundary print the newspaper,' she said. She laced her bonnet and kissed his cheek. 'We'll be back before you are done milking.' To her surprise, he gripped her arms and drew her into an embrace, kissing her awkwardly on the mouth.

'I must go,' she murmured, eluding his further embrace. 'Boundary said they start printing at noon.'

HER BROTHER WAS ABSORBED in setting type in the composing stick, glancing up to offer a distracted greeting as she bade hello to himself and Bellow, seated behind his desk. 'I have a few supplies to pick up,' she said. 'Can I leave Temperance and Harry with you for an hour or so?'

He nodded, absorbed in the type. 'I guess so.'

She stepped back out into the bright sunlight, feeling the same mixture of relief and shame she had felt the last time she had lied to her brother. She headed to the general store, where the stratagem continued. 'Please fill this list,' she said to the storekeep. 'I shall return in one hour. I am going to visit with my brother at the newspaper office.' She gave the air of being busy, of being occupied by important matters as the man took the list and checked it over.

By the time she set out for the deserted schoolroom, she felt the eyes of the town fastened upon her. Along the way, she stopped to peek into the basket she carried as if the task of bringing lunch and necessary supplies to the school was an exacting and onerous one. One or two women passing her on the street nodded familiarly, although she discouraged such courtesies through elaborate preoccupation with her basket. A sense of shame and guilt engulfing her, she walked straight past the schoolroom to the end of the street, where she examined a bulletin posted on a wall, her eyes seeing only a mass of print. Turning around again, she proceeded slowly back up the street toward the schoolroom, her eyes cast down, her ears alert for cries of 'Shame!' or that other, awful word—her sins exposed in the bright sunlight of the dusty street, her charges forced to watch as she endured the public humiliation of being named and driven through the streets in disgrace.

Rumbald was pacing up and down inside the schoolroom, his face taut with anxiety. As soon as the door opened, he rushed up and gripped her in a fervent embrace. '*Liebste!*'

He kissed her furiously yet tenderly, pulling her tight to him. As always, she feebly resisted this first embrace, pulling back, trying to assert some polite normality on their encounter—his feverish embrace a shock to her marriage vows. And then she was returning his kisses, unable to bear the disappointment on his face; and worse, wantonly pushing herself into him, reaching her arms around his neck, pulling his face down to her own. *O Lord*, she cried out to herself. *Cause thy face to shine, and I shall be saved!*

Lying naked on his bed, she felt no shame. Listening to his calm, accented voice, she felt transported—away and over the plains, looking down from a great height as the farm receded below her and she swooped above the great rock sentinel, following the sight of its westward gaze into the setting sun. The warm breeze uplifted and suspended her so that, wings outstretched, she glided on the wind, rapturously dipping and soaring far above the grassy plains. He was murmuring in her ear, bringing her back to earth, stroking her face and urging, for the hundredth time, that she come away with him.

'*Sie selber, aller Liebe Wonne,/Ist Rose und Lilie und Taube und Sonne.*'

The words tickled her ear, his breath soft and warm like a caress. She blinked at the dust motes dancing in the sunlight shafting through the small window. 'The children!' she remembered. 'I must be getting back to the store.' She tried to get up, but he pulled her back.

'We must do something,' he said, his voice filled with despair. He took her cheeks between his two hands—oh, the fire of his touch! —and turned her face to his. 'We could leave here,' he begged. 'Together or separately. Start a new life where no one would ever find us.'

She shook her head, clasping his hands with her own. 'I cannot,' she said, her heart tormented. 'I have a husband.'

He remonstrated, promising Europe, the cities of the East, a small house in a respectable town, his voice desperate to make her glimpse the splendid future he saw lying in wait for them. His body pressed against her as she drew away. 'Then what is to be?' he agonised. 'Are we to continue like this?'

As always, the question reduced her to despair. A moan escaped her, and she put a hand up to her mouth as if she might ward off the unbearable truth. 'It cannot be,' she said, the sense of suffocation returning.

'You do not love me.' He lay on his back, his voice despondent.

'No, I—' She turned and reached for him. 'It cannot be,' she repeated, her voice choked with tears.

Rumbel let out a heartfelt groan. 'This is cruellest torture!' His smooth, scholar's face was creased in misery. The fine moustache under his nose trembled as he contemplated the dreary days ahead until he would see her again.

She exclaimed in wonder as she saw the tears stream unashamedly down his cheek. She had never seen a man cry, she realised, and the sight both astonished and moved her. If only Ira had tears for things! Tenderly, she pressed her fingertips into the glistening tears on her lover's face. *Lover!* The word both shamed and thrilled her. His candid emotion, his delight in their nakedness together, his frank and frequent declarations of love were like water to her thirst. His amusing disquisitions on the members of the school board, on the obtuse superintendent, or the odd way Mrs. Chestnut's nose twitched when he objected to one of her proposals, drew laughter from deep inside her. The memory of their trysts shimmered in her mind on the lonely nights she lay in bed listening to her husband sleep and the doleful yelp of coyotes out on the dark grasslands.

'This is what you have released in me,' she said, and experienced a deep gratification when he nodded gravely in response, his face shining as he gazed on her.

THE HURRIED WALK BACK to the general store was an agony of suspense. Her hand went to her throat a thousand times to check that the clasp of her blouse was secure, that her hair was tucked neatly into her bonnet, that her skirts flowed smoothly and discreetly around her. Then the unbearable torture of the clerk's friendly greeting, the trip back to the newspaper office, where she declined to get down from the buggy, pleading lateness and urging the children to climb up on board; the hurried farewell kiss to her brother, shrinking back lest he detect a whiff of chalk or schoolroom dust— until she was headed back again over the open prairie, her heart gradually settling back into its cage, her breath becoming regular and uniform once more as she stared ahead, searching for the first glimpse of the farm.

Her husband stood expectantly in the yard, his honest hands soiled from labour, his face searching hers, reaching up to assist her down from the rig, asking about Boundary and the supplies and the road. And at night, she climbed into bed, holding herself stiffly as his arms enclosed her and drew her to him, his face nuzzling her neck as she pictured the full prairie moon and wondered if her heart would burst from shame.

She lay awake listening as the dogs barked, her mind a maelstrom of emotions. Her husband snored beside her. The weight of the yellow moon pressed through the curtain as she roamed out with it, flying swiftly over the billowing waves, directed like an arrow at the rock buffalo rising up out of the earth, before crashing into the great shoulder hump and fluttering helplessly from the dark sky.

51

Preacher

Tourists milled around the pavilion, indulging in beer and refreshments, and lolling at the shaded tables as a ranger gathered a group together for the two o'clock guided tour. Children laughed and raced up and down in the warm, spring sunshine. A line of eager 'riders' stood under the rock, waiting their turn to be winched to the top. Families wandered around the tents, stopping to pose for the Trust photographer or headed to the gift shop to purchase from the abundant selection of memorabilia. Another omnibus arrived from town depositing yet more eager sightseers, each clutching the souvenir program issued as part of the ticket price. Scarcely a cloud disturbed the blue sky as a young woman held up her 'bison broach' to the admiring eyes of her companions.

'Beware ye the ways of the idol worshippers!' A man dressed entirely in black and holding a Bible aloft, strode through the cheerful crowd. His powerful voice cut through the gossip and merriment as people turned to stare. Holding the raised Bible in one hand, he pointed an accusing finger at the stone buffalo with the other. 'Hear ye the words of the Lord! Ye shall make ye no idols nor graven image, neither rear you up a standing image, neither shall ye set up any image of stone in your land, to bow down unto it: for I am the Lord thy God!'

The chatter and laughter fell away as more spectators flocked to see the cause of the disturbance. The speaker, a grim, forbidding figure in his dark vestments, observed all and sundry with fire in his eyes. 'Confounded be all they that serve graven images, that boast themselves of idols!' He turned and strode directly up to the rock, scattering onlookers before him as he went. Stopping in the very shadow of the idol, he turned a fierce eye on the sightseers while loudly denouncing 'all blasphemers and sinners.' As if in defiance of naysayers, he thrust the Bible toward the crowd. 'Thou shalt not worship a graven image! Repent before the eyes of the Lord!'

A small child started to cry as several among the onlookers called out in protest. 'We ain't worshipping nothing! Go bother somewheres else!'

'It's that crazy fool from the temple!' another voice called out.

Two men hurried out of the crowd and grabbed the resistant preacher by the arms. Still shouting out dire warnings, he was propelled away from the scene and toward a small tent. 'Apologies, good folk!' A man sporting a bushy moustache stepped forward to reassure the alarmed spectators. 'Some half-wit escaped from the asylum, no doubt!' The remark drew uncertain laughter. 'No need for concern! We'll see he gets the treatment he deserves. Enjoy yourselves! Cheap ices over at the refreshment tent!'

'Son of a bitch!' Inside the tent, Butch stood over the preacher, a snarl on his face. 'You think we give a buffalo fart for your bible-gabbing horseshit!' In a fury, he struck the preacher, knocking him to the dirt. 'I'll rip your guts out, you fish-eyed snake!' He kicked the dazed preacher in the ribs, delivering several more forceful kicks before stomping on the preacher's bloodied face.

'Hold off, Butch, you'll kill him. Ed will want to see him.' Leo restrained his enraged companion while shouting for their offsider. 'Willy! Willy!'

Willy hurried into the tent to be met by a barrage of curses. 'Don't stand there like shit on a stick! Fetch the goddamn rig! Butch, hold off!'

LOMAX LOOKED UP IN surprise as the preacher was dragged into the room—his face swollen and bruised, his shirt collar ripped and bloody. More blood leaked from a fresh cut on his lips. Groaning, he hung suspended between Butch and Leo, looking as if he were about to be sick.

'What in hog grit do we have here? Butch?'

'This durn cockle mouth was sulphurating out at the rock. Lathering on about idols and blasphemers and frightening folks half to death.' With a ferocious snarl, Butch tightened his grip, causing the preacher to wince and moan.

Lomax scratched his neck, studying the dishevelled figure. 'So, you're this preacher I been hearing about?'

The preacher made a gasping noise, his breath issuing in laboured pants. Lomax signalled to his confederates, who released the captive. He fell to his knees choking for breath, his face white with shock.

'Well, padre? What do you have to say for yourself?'

'You busted my durn ribs!' Grimacing with pain, the preacher pressed a hand to his side. He attempted to stand but collapsed to his knees again, supporting himself with his arms on the floor.

'I guess you ain't so all-fired preachy now!' taunted Butch.

'Hold fire, Butch. Well, padre?'

'I speak—' the preacher coughed up a mouthful of blood. 'I speak as the Lord directs.' He drew a rasping breath as he sat slumped on the floor, his face ashen.

'Willy!' Lomax bellowed out the name. 'Willy! Where in Hades are you?'

'Sorry, boss.' Willy hurried in from the outer office.

'Where in Sam Hill did you get that god-awful coat?' Lomax's eyes widened at sight of the brushed cotton sack coat. Leo gave a guffaw.

Willy beamed and stretched out one side of the coat. 'Picked it up this morning, from the store down on Main.'

'Must have been the feed store,' chuckled Leo.

Lomax shook his head. 'Never mind. Pour our guest a glass of water.'

The preacher coughed up more blood and shook his head, rejecting the proffered glass.

'Your funeral.' Lomax reached into the desk drawer for a cigar. Sitting back in the chair, he clipped off the end while eyeing the preacher. 'So, what's your beef, Padre? Why get so het up about a lump of rock?'

The preacher said nothing, wheezing as he sat, slumped and bloodied, his face pale with distress.

'Do you want Butch to ask the questions?'

'Durn shit-talking gobble-mouth!' Butch struck the preacher in the face, the force of the blow knocking the preacher against the wall where he sat in a sitting position, holding his hand against his ribs.

'Now, Butch. Show some respect for a man of the cloth. We are reasonable folk around here, padre, despite what you may have heard. Ain't that right, Leo?'

'Civil to beat the band.'

'I ask again. Why get so het up about an old rock?'

'It's a blasphemy! And those that attend it are idol worshippers!' The preacher exhausted himself with the pronouncement, moaning afresh at the pain in his busted ribs.

'Hear that boys? The man says we are idol worshippers.' Lomax drew on the lit cigar, blowing out a stream of smoke. 'There's no need for us to quarrel, Padre. Hell, I was raised in the church. How about you, Butch?'

'Can't say I had the pleasure.'

'Leo?'

'Every day. Twice on Sundays.'

'See? Christian folk, like yourself.'

'You bow before an idol!' The preacher spat out the words, his eyes filled with scorn.

'What's that the Bible says? *Give to Caesar the things that are Caesar's?* How about we say no harm done, and I make a donation to your collection plate?'

'Keep your cursed silver!'

Lomax shook his head in professed amazement. 'When did showing folk a good time—and bringing money into the town—turn into blasphemy?'

'When you abase yourself before a heathen idol!'

'He's a lost cause, boss. Want me to take care of him?'

Lomax shifted in the chair. 'Preacher? What the hell kind of a name is that? Or *is* it your name? What do your folks call you?'

The preacher muttered through clenched teeth, spitting up more blood as he did so.

Lomax twisted the wedding band on his finger, his eyes weighing the other man. 'Almost,' he said, 'Thou persuadest me to be a Christian.' The words drew a startled glance in response. 'Almost,' said Lomax. 'But not quite.'

'Leo. Make a note,' he said. 'Tell Jay to check this bird's credentials. Find out who he is and where he comes from.' He considered the preacher. 'In my experience, snakes like you don't just crawl out from under any old rock. You get me?'

'Do your worst! You do not frighten me!' The preacher panted with the words.

'Listen to me carefully.' Lomax sat forward, his voice full of menace. 'You pull a stunt like that one more time, and you'll be digging yourself a hole in the grass. Do you understand?'

'You are a flea! A worm! God shall strike you!'

'Shut your pan!' Butch went to hit the man again only to be forestalled by a raised hand from Lomax.

'So that's how it is.' He poured himself a whisky. 'I see it now. You're quite the martyr, ain't you? Is that what you aim for? Or are you saving up that pleasure for others?' He gulped the whisky. 'Your game ain't so hard to figure. Just remember what I said.' He nodded to Butch who dragged the moaning and bloodied preacher from the room by his shirt collar.

'WHAT'S THAT TUNE YOU'RE humming?' Ira paused as he walked by with the feed bucket.

'Oh!' Amity gave a little jump. 'I thought you were in the barn,' she said.

'It's like something I heard somewhere before,' he said, his brow furrowed. 'But I can't remember where or when.'

'It's an Indian hymn,' she explained, dusting off the front of her dress and wondering how long he had been standing there. The children were off playing in the grass, shouting and laughing as they chased after the dogs. She watched them, envious of their carefree laughter.

'I didn't know Indians had hymns.' Ira frowned, trying to comprehend this detail.

'Sometimes they did,' she answered, her gaze on the children.

'Where'd you learn it?'

'From Half Moon.'

'And what was it about?'

'About the weather, or some such, I expect,' she said, wondering why he didn't go away.

But he stayed rooted to the spot, troubled by a familiar despondency he heard creeping into her voice.

'Would you like to take the children and visit Boundary?' he asked, knowing how those visits brought cheer to her heart. 'Or maybe your pa. You haven't visited him in a while, have you?'

Although he meant the words kindly, they nevertheless struck turmoil in her heart. Part of her longed to flee to the schoolroom and the eager embrace of the importunate Rumbald, but another part of her rose up in horror at the impulse, smothering her with unbearable shame and despair at her own licentiousness. The conflict in her breast was so intense she started to cry silent tears, facing away from her husband and desperately hoping he would resume his duties.

He moved toward her and placed a hand on her shoulder. 'I'm sure he misses you, too,' he said his voice gruff.

She whirled around to face him. 'Who?'

'Why, your pa, of course.' He touched her gently on the cheek. 'I know he must miss your ma something awful. Maybe we could go together? It's been a sight since I saw him last.'

She smiled through her tears. 'Maybe,' she said. 'That would be nice.'

'What's got her all wrung up?' his mother asked as Ira returned to the house for his work gloves.

'She misses her pa.'

'Her pa?' Fleur made a huffing sound. 'Is that what you think?'

'Why else?' He frowned at his mother. 'What are you trying to say?'

'Me? I ain't saying nothing. 'Cept it's a wonder she ain't pining to visit the town.'

'To visit her brother, you mean?'

He was about to enquire more when he heard horses and the creak of a wagon. 'It's Mr Ketchfield,' he said, surprised. He went outside to meet the wagon, still wondering over his mother's remark.

'Pa!' The children raced to greet their father. 'Pa!' Temperance threw herself into her father's embrace as he climbed down from the wagon.

Amity watched as her neighbour knelt in the dust to hug the children in an unusual display of affection. 'Mr Ketchfield?' She studied his face, noting with alarm the misery written there. *Mrs. Ketchfield?* She mouthed the words above the joyful exclamations of the children. He glanced up and shook his head.

'Oh!' She put a hand to her mouth.

Still kneeling, Ketchfield embraced Temperance and Harry, kissing both and looking as if he were about to cry.

'What is it, pa?' Temperance looked at her father, a worried look on her face.

'Nothing. Nothing, dear. I'm just that glad to see you, is all.' He tried to smile, wiping a hand across his eyes. 'Now git along and play while I speak to Mr and Mrs. Morgan.' He watched them run off. 'I don't know how to tell them.' He said, his voice breaking.

Amity and Ira commiserated, murmuring condolences as he stared glumly at the children. 'I'll come by tomorrow and collect them,' he said, as if he hadn't heard. 'I've arranged to sell the farm. I guess we'll head on back to Iowa. My folks are there. They'll help raise—' The sentence was choked off. 'I gotta go,' he said. Turning, he climbed aboard the wagon. 'Mighty obliged,' he mumbled. 'Right neighbourly of you.'

'Pa!' The children came running over. 'Ain't we going with you?'

'Tomorrow!' He wiped a sleeve across his eyes. 'Git!' He shook the reins, urging the horses forward.

'Pa!' Temperance stood looking after him, tears streaming down her face.

'It's all right. Your pa will be back tomorrow to take you with him.' She hugged the girl, barely suppressing her own tears. 'Now, take Harry and wash up for supper.'

Her sadness for the happy, unsuspecting children tore at her heart as she ladled the soup and passed around the bread, coaxing the bubbling Temperance to finish her meal. 'Tomorrow, we get to see ma!' The girl chortled with glee, crumbs spitting from her mouth.

Her brother was just as giddy at the prospect, peppering his sister with questions. 'Will she come fetch us? Will we still have to go to school?'

'Hush now and eat.' Amity glanced at Ira, her heart breaking.

Later, as the children prepared for bed, she sat down in the chair. 'I'll miss them awfully,' she said, her eyes welling with tears.

Ira leaned down to place a log on the fire. 'Me, too. I got used to having them around.' He placed a comforting hand on her knee.

'You know the cure for that.' Fleur tugged a handkerchief from her sleeve and put it to her nose.

'Ma! Now's not the time.' Ira's voice was sharp.

'Then when is? It seems it ain't never the time.' She sniffled and dabbed at her nose.

'We're trying. These things take their own course,' he said.

'Perhaps you should try in town,' she said, with a vindictive glance at Amity.

'What do you mean?' Ira's voice was perplexed rather than accusatory.

'Talk to Doc Henderson. Why, what do you think I meant?'

Amity got up, suddenly frightened. 'I'll see if the children are asleep,' she said.

She sat on the side of the girl's bed to wish her good night, reluctant to leave the room. Harry slept soundly, clutching his wool rabbit. She kept the girl awake by asking if she missed her lessons in the schoolroom, who was her best friend, and which subject she liked best and why. And what did she think of the schoolteacher, Mr Rumbald? Finally, taking pity on the girl's yawns, she leaned forward and pressed her lips to the girl's forehead. 'Would you like me to read to you from the Bible?' she asked.

Temperance opened her eyes wide. 'Oh, yes, please!' she said. 'Then I could sleep.'

Amity approached Fleur in the other room, requesting the bible which the old lady held in her lap. 'May I?' she asked. 'For the child,' she explained.

It took a sharp word from Ira before his mother reluctantly surrendered the book, her bony hand resistant as Amity pried it from her grasp. 'Now you won't be able to take 'em to that school every day,' she said, her voice spiteful.

Back in the bedroom, she found Temperance still awake. Sitting down on the bed she opened the cover. 'Look,' she pointed to the inside page. 'Those are the names of my husband's grandmother and grandfather. Do you recognise them?'

The child peered at the carefully inked names in the lantern light. 'Hope,' she read slowly. 'And Ethan.'

Something in the way the girl mouthed the words caused Amity to cry, prompting Temperance to give her a childish hug. Amity held her tight, tears flowing down her face.

'Why are you sad, Mrs. Morgan? Is it because you'll miss us?' Temperance reached up to touch her face.

She took the girl's small fingers and kissed them. 'Yes. I'll miss you and Harry very much.'

'But you'll still see us. You can come visit, for dinner. You'll see ma and pa.'

'Of course. I'm just being silly.' She pulled a handkerchief from her sleeve to dry her eyes. 'Now close your eyes while I read to you.'

She opened the Bible, and turned the pages to Ruth, her mother's favourite book. She ran her finger down the verses. *Intreat me not to leave thee. Or to return from following after thee.* Copious tears fell from her eyes as she read. She glanced at Temperance. The girl was already sound asleep, a smile upon her face. Closing the Bible, she set it on the bed. Her husband had gone out to the barn. She pulled the shawl around her shoulders as her gaze drifted to the window. Night had fallen and an owl hooted out in the grass. She sat there unmoving until her husband came back from the barn. He went into the bedroom, softly calling her name. Still, she sat, the lantern flickering, the moon lancing through the glass. Only when she heard snores from the bedroom did she at last get to her feet, tired and despairing, and blow out the lantern.

THE TEMPLE WAS FULL, word having spread of the confrontation at the rock. Horrified gasps sounded as the preacher emerged from the back room. His gaunt face was marred by large, purpling bruises and an engorged lip. One eye was swollen almost shut. 'Oh my Lord!' A woman screamed.

Pale, and walking slowly with the aid of a cane, the preacher breathed heavily as he made his way to the upright desk that served as a pulpit. Once there, he set aside the cane and gripped the desk for support, looking as though he might collapse at any moment.

A tide of outrage swept the packed benches as the preacher turned so that the full effects of the beating were evident. He said not a word, standing silently amid the cries of protest to display the marks of the assault.

'This is downright shameful!' A man jumped to his feet, his face suffused with wrath. 'Who would assault a man of God!'

A second man stood up, 'We know who did this! Edison Lomax!'

The words brought shouts of anger and exhortations to the Lord. The preacher gripped the pulpit, his eyes glinting as he took in the response. And still he refused to speak.

A man turned to the packed room, his face livid. 'We ought teach that no-good skunk a lesson!' The words were greeted with cries and furious denunciations. Threats were shouted against the Trust, Lomax, the mayor, and anyone else connected to the rock.

'Brothers and sisters in Christ!' The angry voices hushed as the preacher at last broke silence, his voice hoarse and forceful. 'Such marks as ye see I bear willingly, as witness to God's command!'

'Praise Jesus!' a woman called out, the exhortation repeated by several others.

'I have seen with my own eyes the evil that besmirches this town.' The preacher's words were laboured, but his eyes blazed with fervour as he gripped the pulpit. 'Brothers and sisters, I have stood before the pagan idol and condemned it in all of its false glory!'

The declaration brought forth shouts and hollers. The preacher leaned forward, his normally thunderous voice muted by the pain in his ribs. 'Will ye permit this blasphemy to bring down God's wrath upon the town, or will you stand with me and shout, "There is but one God and thou shalt not permit graven idols to stand in His place!"'

'Hallelujah!' a voice shouted, the cry taken up and echoed throughout the packed benches.

'Praise be His name!'

'Blessed are the righteous!'

'We stand with you, Preacher!' A man leapt to his feet, a wild look on his face. Others followed his example until the entire congregation was on its feet, hollering and beseeching, their faces lit with ecstasy.

'Lead us, brother, and we will follow!'

'Show us the way!'

The preacher's eyes swept the congregation. 'Let His will be done!' His voice broke out in a harsh, ragged hymn:

Fully persuaded, Lord, I believe!
Fully persuaded, Thy Spirit give;
I will obey Thy call; low at Thy feet I fall;
Now I surrender all, Christ to receive!

As voices swelled in fervent response, a small, dapper man, dressed in an incongruously fashionable coat, slipped out of his seat and made for the door.

SHE WATCHED WITH HEAVY heart as the wagon creaked out of the yard. The children waved and called out cheerily as the conveyance, loaded with furniture and supplies, rumbled off on the start of the long journey back to Iowa. She smiled and waved through tears as Temperance shrieked and blew kisses. 'Goodbye, Mrs. Morgan!'

'I don't understand why he ain't mentioned their ma.' Ira stood alongside, watching as the wagon bumped and lurched down the road.

'He hasn't the heart. Maybe when they get home to Iowa.'

'Amity!' Fleur stood in the doorway, wrapped in her shawl and nightcap. 'Ain't it time for breakfast?'

'She's coming, Ma!' Ira took her arm. 'Things will be quiet around here, I guess.' They started walking back toward the house. When she reached the door and glanced back again, the wagon had disappeared in a cloud of dust.

OVER THE NEXT FEW weeks, she walked around as if in a daze, her thoughts alternating between the children and Rumbald as she tried desperately to bring some semblance of order to her roiling emotions. Torn by guilt and shame even as she yearned to be in his arms, she avoided the town, avoiding Rumbald even as she imagined him looking out eagerly as the children arrived each morning. He must know I cannot see him with the children gone. Surely, he won't do anything foolish. The thought alarmed her even as she longed to flee to his embrace and listen to his soothing murmurs as her head rested on his chest. Her mother-in-law, meanwhile, sipped coffee and followed her around the kitchen with narrowed, probing eyes.

'I reckon you're practised enough to have your own,' she said.

Amity whipped eggs in a bowl. 'We're trying. These things happen in their own time.'

''Course, it helps if your heart's in it.' The old woman's voice held a spiteful edge.

She ignored the remark, busying herself with cutting the fried ham into chunks.

'I guess he's mighty eager, ain't he?' Fleur added.

'Ira, you mean?' She looked directly at her mother-in-law, raising her eyebrows in challenge.

''Course. Who else would I mean?' The old woman sneezed and cast a baleful look at the dog as it cocked its head. 'I don't know what's happened to the weather,' she complained. 'I reckon on Sunday you and Ira can drive me to temple. I want to hear the preacher.'

The old lady had become a fervent follower of the preacher, quoting his sermons at the supper table and provoking Amity with her references to the 'great blasphemy' outside of town.

'It ain't blasphemous and it ain't his business to say so!' she said, her voice sharp.

'My! Such passion.'

'Ma, you know it ain't right to repeat such guff.'

'I'm only repeating what the preacher said.' The old lady sulked under the reproof, mumbling to herself and wondering aloud what the world was coming to that a body couldn't speak her mind without giving offence. 'Anyway,' she said, her voice raised in defiance, 'Preacher says it won't be there to offend much longer.'

'What do you mean?' Amity looked up at the remark.

'It ain't what I mean, it's what he means.' Fleur bit into her bread, chewing greedily.

'And what does he mean?' asked Ira, exasperated with the conversation.

'I couldn't say, I'm sure,' said Fleur, a catlike smile upon her lips.

52

A House Divided

THE ANGRY CROWD MARCHED from the temple to the three-storey building that housed both the council chambers and the office of the Buffalo Trust. Singing hymns and chanting, the noisy throng brought people out onto the sidewalk to watch as it proceeded down Main Street, whipped on by the preacher's more zealous adherents. 'Satan has set up his foul pigsty in our town!' went the cry, the crowd urging the onlookers to join them. 'Forsake the idol! Reject the corrupter!'

Several onlookers stepped down from the sidewalk, slapping shoulders and shaking hands as they joined the aroused mob.

The owner of the Golden Fleece saloon stepped out to view the commotion, his face rigid with disdain as the shouting congregants filed past. 'You durn fools! That buffalo saved this town!' Others joined him, whistling and hooting with scorn as the mob passed by.

'Tell that fool preacher he ain't needed here!'

'Get back to praying and leave honest folk to drink in peace!'

The crowd returned jeer for jeer, shouting insults at those who refused to join in the march and threatening a 'new day,' when scores would be settled, and 'palaces of infamy' closed down.

As the singing and chanting procession neared the council chambers, a man lounging on the sidewalk straightened up and rushed inside to raise the alarm. 'Ben! Where's Ben?' He threw open a door, interrupting a meeting in progress. 'Ben! There's an all-fired mob on the way!'

Uttering an imprecation, the mayor jumped to his feet. Hurrying from the chambers, he stepped out onto the sidewalk, where he took in the advancing mob, now swollen in size. 'Jesus H. Christ!' He turned to the man who had delivered the warning, his voice frantic. 'Run and find Lomax! Tell him to get over here as fast as he can!' He turned to another man. 'Where the hell is Art? Never mind! Go find him. Tell him we have a goddamn riot on our hands!' With that, he hastened back inside, locking the door behind him.

The worked-up crowd came to a halt in front of the building. Blocking the wide street with their numbers, they angrily demanded the mayor emerge. One bold fellow stepped nimbly onto the sidewalk and shook the door handle before stepping back to kick the door. 'Come on out, Wilkins! And bring that toad-face Lomax with you!' The crowd roared in approval.

'Come out, you fiend!'

'Show yourself, you durn lickspittle!'

'This is our town, not Lomax's!'

'Watch out!' An alarmed voice cried out above the ruckus.

A number of men armed with rifles were seen hurrying down the side-walk toward the protestors. Butch was at their head, his face furious as he made his way down the sidewalk, pedestrians scattering to give him path. The crowd drew back as the men formed an armed line in front of the building.

'Get back, you sons of bitches!' Butch pulled out a revolver and flour-ished it in the air. 'Get back or I'll blow your goddam brains out!' He pointed the revolver at the man who had tried the door, the latter hastily retreating into the crowd.

But others were not so daunted. 'Send out the mayor!' one demanded, shaking his fist. This gave courage to the rest as the crowd once again edged forward, demanding the mayor show himself.

'There's the weaselly bastard!' A man pointed up to a second-floor win-dow where the face of the mayor could be seen peering out from behind the curtain. The face abruptly disappeared as the protestors erupted into taunts and name-calling.

'Where's Lomax?' shouted a man in a brown canvas duster. 'He's sucked this town dry!' The accusation incited yells and threats as the mood of the crowd grew more volatile. Emboldened by their numbers, the mob pressed forward, causing the defenders to retreat until they were backed up on the sidewalk. Butch stood in front, brandishing the pistol, and threatening, with violent oaths, to step down into the street and 'knock the brains' of anyone foolish enough to try him.

Leo stepped forward, holding up his arms to placate the baying mob. 'What happened to the preacher was a misunderstanding! Nobody meant him any harm!'

'Harm? You durn near beat him to death!' an incredulous voice shouted. The reminder of the outrage, if reminder were needed, provoked a fresh outburst of threats and insults as the crowd advanced onto the sidewalk, hemming in the nervous defenders as they were pressed back against the building.

'Get out of our town, you no 'count thieves!' A retired gold miner, his face contorted with anger, stepped forward to deliver the insult.

The taunt was at once taken up by the baying mob. 'Thieves! Get out of our town!'

Butch stepped toward the miner, a bloodcurdling oath on his lips. Before the man could react, he was knocked senseless by a sweeping blow from the pistol. He dropped where he stood, blood streaming from his scalp. The suddenness and ferocity of the attack momentarily stunned the protestors into silence. Butch stood over the insensible man, his eyes flashing fire as he dared any to step forward and challenge him. 'Who's next?' he roared, cocking the pistol.

Instead of retreating, the enraged mob surged forward, shouting for revenge. A mass brawl ensued as protestors and guards fought wildly in the street. In the melee, Leo was sent flying, rolling desperately to one side to avoid the stomps aimed at his head. Butch had a man by the jacket collar, holding him upright while dishing out a savage beating with the pistol. Curses and screams rang out as the guards struck out with rifle butts, doing their best to protect themselves from the infuriated mob.

A sudden volley of gunfire brought an abrupt halt to the fighting. Heads turned to where the constable, flanked by three shotgun-toting deputies, fired a pistol into the air. 'Go back to your homes, you damn fools, or by God I swear you'll regret it!' He signalled to his deputies, who levelled the shotguns directly at the crowd. 'Back off or be blasted!'

The mood of the crowd changed in face of the threat. Picking up several injured comrades, they slowly retreated from the raised weapons. Butch, and a dazed and bloodied Leo, joined with the constable, the trust employees forming up to stand alongside the deputies. The stricken miner lay senseless in the street, a pool of blood beneath his head. The constable turned to a deputy. 'Pick that shit-heel up! Get him out of here.'

"THE TOWN IS SPLIT in two," declared Bellow in a front-page editorial following the riot.

"One man is dead and another severely wounded as a result of the lamentable fracas on Main Street; three others are confined to their beds with serious injuries. The situation is fraught, with the potential to turn even deadlier. If the town council and the Buffalo Trust between them cannot defuse tensions, then the governor ought be petitioned to send in the militia."

He read the editorial aloud to his employee, humming with satisfaction. 'That ought poke a stick up the mayor's fundament.' He glanced at Boundary. 'You'd better get your head around this, young fella. There ain't no other news but this in town—heck, in the whole state. So, take your mind off that press and get a handle on what's going on. Do you hear?'

'I hear.'

'How old are you now?'

The change in tack surprised Boundary. 'Nineteen. I'll be twenty come the new year.'

'And how long you worked here?'

'Seven years, I guess.'

'Seven years,' repeated Bellow. 'That's an apprenticeship.' He tapped his fingers on the desk, ruminating on the fact.

'You want me to set up the press?'

'I want you to walk around the town and find out what in tar folk are thinking. And if you ask me what about I'll crank your witless head through the press.'

The sullen demeanour on Boundary's face as he opened the door gave Bellow no confidence that his employee and charge appreciated the gravity of the situation. 'With that so-called preacher and Thurston Wake stirring up things on one side and Lomax and his cronies conspiring and thieving on the other, the whole town's a powder keg. One that could blow up at any minute,' he worried to his wife.

'Perhaps they ought do as you say and call on the governor to intervene,' she suggested, setting down her knitting needles.

'Ha! Lomax, you can be sure, has already thought of that. The governor owes him his election and Lomax will demand repayment in full when the time is right.'

'What will he do?'

'The governor?'

'Mr Lomax.'

'That's just it.' Bellow sighed, a concerned look on his face. 'There's no telling what he *won't* do—to preserve all he's got riding on that rock. I fear he may even attempt to snuff out the preacher.'

'Snuff out? Oh! He wouldn't dare.'

'It would be a risk, but one he probably figures worth taking if those zealots down at the temple carry out their threat to protest at the rock. They'll frighten all the tourists away—if they haven't already.'

'Is the preacher right—about the corruption?'

'Without a doubt. Wherever he's getting his information from— Thurston Wake, I suspect—he's right about that. The whole town's corrupted by buffalo money. Heck, things would stop working if it ever dried up.'

'Do you plan to write about it?' Her voice was anxious.

'There's knowing and there's proving. Lomax and that puke of a lawyer make sure of that. There's something else,' he said, after a moment's reflection.

'What?'

'Young Boundary. He's going on twenty.'

'And?' His wife peered with raised eyebrows.

'I'm thinking of bringing him in, as a junior partner.'

She said nothing, surprise written on her face as her husband continued. 'He's been with us for seven years. He lives and breathes the place—well, the press, anyhow.' He gazed at her. 'What do you think?'

'Is he ready—for the responsibility?'

'Probably not, but he's trustworthy and willing. And I won't be around forever.'

'Hush!' She frowned. 'You could always sell up,' she said, after returning to her knitting and thinking on the matter. 'We could go back East—to New York, or Boston.'

'Maybe.' He rubbed his face. 'Maybe.'

THE MILD SPRING TURNED into an uneasy summer. The preacher thundered from the pulpit three times a week as followers from as far away as Franklin, Fargo, and Bismarck flocked to join the crusade against the 'Babylonian calf,' which was now held to blame for drought, floods, dust storms and crop failures.

'Drunkenness, every night! Debauchery every day!' railed the preacher, his language growing ever more violent as the numbers jostling to enter the crowded temple increased. 'O good folk of Buffalo Rock, for how long will you endure this wickedness?' The constantly reiterated demand stirred up outrage among the faithful while drawing fierce denunciation from opponents as the town split into two dangerously opposed factions just as Bellow had feared.

In response to the growing outcry against the trust, Lomax spread around more money, hosting a gala dinner for widows and orphans, and paying for a free concert with artists imported from Chicago and Kansas City to entertain the crowds. He toyed with the idea of opening a chapel and bringing in a preacher—'a sensible fella'—from elsewhere who might provide an antidote to the venomous imprecations heaped upon the Trust by the preacher. He only decided against the move out of concern it might inflame matters further. 'That lunatic has half the town eating from the same rabid bowl as himself,' he said in anger.

'There's but one way to deal with his kind,' said Butch. 'Ain't I been telling you all along?'

One night, as he went for a walk, the preacher was fired upon, the unknown assailant getting off three shots before slipping away into the night. The shaken preacher escaped with a slug to the shoulder. The displayed wound was hailed as stigmata by his infuriated flock, who demanded vengeance as tensions threatened to boil over.

In an attempt to police the situation, the constable patrolled the streets with half a dozen armed men as the saloons were forced to close early by mayoral decree. The situation grew dire enough that Bellow put out a special edition urging tolerance and patience and reminding people of the special event looming on the horizon:

"In a few short months, the whole world will welcome in the new century. We ought to put all of our energies into celebrating this signal event in the history of the town, not tearing ourselves apart. The future is here, good citizens, and we should usher it in like we did the last one. In eighteen hundred, this town was just an army outpost, surrounded by buffaloes and Indians. In nineteen hundred, we are a modern metropolis with gas lighting, stores full of goods, and a railway that connects us to the greater world. Let us set aside our differences and celebrate our progress!"

The plea fell largely on deaf ears as the warring sides continued to spar and snipe at one another throughout the late summer and early fall, each incident threatening to erupt into open warfare. The unseasonably warm weather helped keep passions high, the mild gales seeming to fan the flames on either side. Whipped up by the preacher's increasingly strident sermons, people flocked from far and wide to applaud his furious condemnations of the 'great blasphemy.' He presided over a memorial for the dead miner, a large crowd turning out for the event, singing hymns and marching down Main Street to the cemetery. Standing over the grave, the preacher publicly anointed the dead man 'a martyr of God,' while promising that 'All shall rise, cometh the day.'

On Sundays, the temple was full to bursting with people eager to be electrified by the rolling oratory of the ''buked and scorned' preacher. Those worshippers unable to squeeze inside congregated on the sidewalk, ears pricked to hear the voice thundering within. Concerned for the preacher's safety following the assassination attempt, Thurston Wake had assigned two of his cowhands to act as bodyguards. The armed men escorted him everywhere, guns at the ready, watching protectively from the rear of the

Temple as the preacher fulminated against the buffalo wealth corrupting the town, while violently condemning the 'mangy Judases with their hands outstretched for silver.'

And amid all the strife, the committee charged with preparing the town for the centennial celebrations went about their mandate: hanging banners, planning events, hiring bands, and organising food and drink for the public festivities.

The irony was not lost on Bellow, who hired an artist to draw a picture of two fiercely opposed factions separated by a line of cloth-covered tables brimming with food and drink and presided over by a gracious hostess wearing a sash inscribed with the words *Good Will!*

The cartoon won much favourable comment, the praise causing the beaming proprietor to consider taking on the artist full-time. 'People need pictures as well as words,' he remarked cheerfully. 'Circulation is up. If nothing else, this buffalo brouhaha is good for business.'

So pleased was he with the artist's work he hired him to draw pictures of the proprietor at his desk and of Boundary standing beside the Washington hand-press. 'Can you work a camera?' he asked. Assured by the artist that he could, Bellow got him to take several photos of the office, including the latest run of newsprint. 'Now me and Boundary together,' he said, placing a proprietorial hand on Boundary's shoulder.

'I should have done this long ago,' he said, admiring the results with his wife. 'Something for the town records. After all, we are a big part of its history.'

THE PRETERNATURALLY WARM WEATHER continued into November, the cheery blue skies interpreted by the preacher's followers as a sign of God's grace since his arrival to the town. Never one to miss a favourable omen, the Preacher incorporated the beneficent weather into his sermons, orating that the mild blue skies were a presage, a portent of some great awakening that would bring the whole state back to His fold, 'From whence it has been led astray by false prophets and moneychangers who deceive as they corrupt, and sow evil even as they spout virtue. Awake, good people! Awake ye who would embrace righteousness!' The preacher shook with zeal, his eyes flashing fire as the congregation rose as one to its feet, greeting each new jeremiad with hollers and rapturous acclaim.

'A great day is coming!' the preacher cried out above the jubilant *hallelujahs*. 'A glorious day when God's will shall be revealed!'

WHAT THE PREACHER MEANT by the words was the source of much speculation. The more fanatical of his followers hailed it as a literal and divinely inspired prophecy, which foretold a Great Awakening. Naysayers denounced it as self-serving bunkum designed to impress the gullible. 'The Rapture is coming!' was the cry in the town streets, delirious believers buttonholing passers-by with wild-eyed fervour.

'The Rupture, more like!' came the dismissive reply as the mood within the town grew ever more volatile.

'The damn fool is planning something, mark my words.' The mayor wrung his hands in frustration at a crisis meeting called to discuss the situation.

Lomax sucked on a cigar, his expression ill-humoured as he listened.

'Maybe it's time we called on your friend the governor,' the mayor suggested. 'A word from you and he'll have a whole troop of soldiers here by morning.'

'You're forgetting something,' the constable objected. 'That fork-tongued son of a bitch has friends in Bismarck, too. Powerful friends. You've seen for yourself the suckers flocking in by stage and train to catch his ballyhoo. And he's not the only one we got to worry about. That rancher, Wake, too, is well-connected. I know for a fact that he has friends in the governor's mansion.'

The mayor put his head in his hands and groaned. 'It's too bad your man missed the bastard.'

The constable cast a sour look at Butch. 'Where'd you find that no-hoper, anyhow? He couldn't hit a cow's ass with a banjo!'

'The fool got himself drunk while waiting his chance.' Butch grimaced at Leo. 'I told you we ought do it ourselves.'

'No matter.' Lomax stubbed out the cigar, his voice crisp with anger. 'The aim now is to find out what he's—' He stopped and looked around the table. 'Where in tarnation is Willy?'

'He was here five minutes ago,' said Butch. 'He probably went off to buy another jacket.'

'He reckons the preacher is planning another ruckus at the rock,' offered Leo. 'Only this time with half the durn town in attendance.'

'When?'

Leo shrugged. 'He didn't say.'

'I could issue a proclamation—forbid it?' The mayor flashed a hopeful glance at Lomax.

'And you think that would help?' Lomax's voice was acid.

'Then what the hell do you suggest?' snapped the constable. 'I vote we run the four-flusher out of town. Tar and feather the lunatic while we're at it.'

Conversation stopped abruptly as the door opened and Willy stuck his head in. 'Boss, you gotta see this.' Entering, he handed over a copy of the *Dispatch*, sneaking a glance at Leo, who gave a minute shake of the head.

The others waited as Lomax scanned the front page. 'What? This bull about the riot? Old news.'

'No, boss. The other story. Under it.'

Lomax went back to the newspaper. As he read, he muttered in amazement. 'Does every son of a bitch in this shit burg have a bugle to blow?'

'What is it?' asked Malting, who had yet to offer advice.

Lomax cleared his throat, his features sharp with displeasure. 'This knucklehead, whoever he is, claims that the rock is no more than a hundred and some years old. Claims he can prove it, too.' He glanced at the name above the story. 'Who in jasper is this Rumbald?' He turned to the others with the question.

'He's the new schoolteach,' answered the mayor. 'He replaced that flossy that ran—'

'Where in hog swill did he crawl out from?' In a temper, Lomax balled up the newspaper and flung it to the floor.

'I don't get it.' The constable looked bewildered. 'Who cares what some no-account schoolteach thinks!'

Malting grimaced. 'We trade on mystery, Art. Folk pay to see something they believe was created a thousand years ago by unknown hands. Who's going to hand over coin to see something that's barely older than their granddaddy?' He glanced at Lomax. 'We got to do something, Ed. Preferably before the nationals pick up on it. Or else there go our marks—from Washington to Chicago.'

'If it ain't one thing ...' Lomax muttered with anger. 'Butch—no, Leo, pay a visit to this damn schoolteach. Have a word. See if you can't make him see reason.'

'Consider it done.'

'He claims to have research to back up his story ...' Lomax raised eyebrows at the other man, the implication clear.

'That, too,' assured Leo.

'Meanwhile,' said the mayor, 'what to do about that firecrack of a preacher?'

Lomax drummed his fingers. 'What do you think, Jay?'

'We got to keep on the side of the law. Anything blows up there'll be an inquest, and Bismarck will get involved. Wake will see to that. But the preacher ain't the whole problem. He's got the town that riled up that the wrong move could blow everything all to hell.'

Lomax took out a cigar and rolled it on the table as he considered the advice. 'We wait and watch,' he said finally, 'for the moment. Willy, keep eyes on him. Find out when he plans this ruckus.'

'Sure thing, boss.'

The mayor heaved a sigh of relief. 'Wise words, Ed. Best to keep our heads. What do you reckon, Art?'

The constable growled, his displeasure evident. 'Sure. Let the lunatic twist the rope around his own neck. Then we kick the chair out from under the black-eyed son of a bitch!'

53

A Proposition

HALFWAY THROUGH PENNING A fresh editorial on the 'buffalo strife' threatening to rip the town apart, Quintus Bellow collapsed at his desk and died of a stroke, the pen still clutched in his hand. Boundary, busily mixing up a fresh batch of ink, remained so absorbed in the task that it wasn't until late morning that he turned to find his employer slumped at his desk, his head blotting the copy he was working on. He stood for a few moments, gazing at the proprietor's balding crown, uncertain whether he was sleeping, as sometimes happened. At length, he gently shook his employer by the shoulder, causing the pen to drop from his grasp and dig its point into the floor.

'Mr Bellow? Sir?'

Had he been there to witness, Mr Bellow might have been gratified at the calm and orderly manner with which his apprentice picked up the pen and gently removed the half-finished epistle from beneath his cheek. He would have been even more gratified to observe how the young man wiped the ink smudge from his ear and composed both hands on the desk before locking up the office and going to break the news to Mrs. Bellow.

The funeral was held two days later, attracting a large crowd of town dignitaries, rivalries being set aside for the occasion. The constable—flushed and uncomfortable in a stiff collar—stood among the mourners at the graveside, 'To make sure the ornery bastard was properly dead,' he declared in the saloon afterwards. A visiting pastor conducted the service, the preacher refusing to bury someone he denounced as a notorious and unrepentant blasphemer. 'God's judgement is sure and swift,' he remarked from the pulpit, drawing upon the event to fortify the resolve of his flock.

The pastor read the eulogy: "Never has the written word contributed so decisively to the growth and moral character of the town and district," he declared, quoting from the deceased's own editorials, provided by the widow. Boundary supported the widow at the graveside, his mind still stunned at the loss. He had developed a trust and dependence on his employer and mentor and felt a mix of resentment and despair at his sudden death.

Escorting Mrs. Bellow back to her house, he stood uncomfortably in the parlour as she wept. At length, mumbling an excuse, he let himself out, returning to the newspaper office to finish printing the latest issue.

A week later, he found himself summoned back to the old lady's presence. Dressed entirely in black, with a pendant locket containing a coil of her husband's hair around her neck, she motioned the apprehensive young man to sit on the upholstered chair and join her in a pot of tea. 'What will you do now?' she asked, filling his cup.

Boundary stared glumly at the tea, having pushed the thought from his mind. 'I don't know,' he confessed. He studied his hands, indelibly stained with ink, and picked at a scab. He had come to define himself by his trade, the title 'printer' pleasingly solid and active to his imagination. It bespoke iron, moving parts, and a reassuring firmness as the plate pressed against the bed. It denoted progress and mechanical things as opposed to the organic dreariness of his father's occupation. It spoke of cities and important institutions rather than empty grasslands and the endless buzz of summer flies around the barn.

His employer's legacy to his young apprentice had been to impart a sense of the solemnity of the printed word—not the idea, therein, but the inked word itself, shining from newness, needing oxygen and careful handling to settle on the crisp, white sheet. And from the printing press it went out into the wide world of commerce and affairs, where men of importance held the pliable sheet, folded it, and thrust it into their pockets for further debate or passed it around and uncreased it for reading at the kitchen table or over a glass of whiskey. Above all, the physicality of the word—its creation from roller and block—seemed to him to guarantee its vitality, its reputation for thrusting itself into the minds and mouths of politicians, debaters, and dissenters, as well as the ordinary man in the street. And now the originator of those words, in their mental dimension at least, was dead.

'My husband thought a great deal of you, Boundary,' the widow said, by way of introduction.

He stared at the pot standing on the small, varnished table and mumbled something which she did not catch.

'Have you made any plans as to your future?' she asked.

He shook his head in reply and scratched his ear in a manner reminiscent of her husband, the similarity catching her heart. 'Then I have a proposition for you, young man,' she said.

He gave no indication of having heard, his attention now switched from his ear to his foot, which he tapped nervously on the floor.

'Boundary!' she said sharply. 'Do stop with that foot!'

He glanced down at the errant appendage as if surprised to find it attached to his leg. Mrs. Bellow gathered her breath. 'I have a proposition for you,' she repeated. 'How would you like to manage the paper until I find a buyer?'

She realised she might as well have spoken in Chinese judging by the look of bewilderment that crossed his face.

'What?' he said, as he tried to unpuzzle the question.

With a sigh, she repeated the offer. 'I need to find a buyer. It will take some time, and the paper cannot sit idle until I do. Well?' She paused, the fine china teacup at her lips.

Boundary fiddled with his hands, flexing and unflexing his fingers, his face wrinkled into a perplexed frown.

Mrs Bellow gave an exasperated sigh. 'Do stop pulling faces!' She added more sugar and stirred the tea. 'The good Lord knows, it's just sitting there,' she continued. 'I need someone I trust to manage it for the time being. What is your opinion?' To her irritation, his attention now seemed fixated on the milk jug. 'I know my husband would approve,' she prompted. 'He was most fond of you.'

'I don't care to write. I'm a printer.' The words burst out of him.

'Sweet heaven! Then *find* someone! Do what my husband did: reprint stories from the wire, re-run old articles and such. Do this for me; my husband would want it,' she said, tears again filling her eyes.

'Don't worry, Mrs. Bellow,' he said, contrite despite his misgivings. 'You can count on me.'

'Thank you, young man. I knew I could. Here,' she passed a sheet of paper to him. 'These are—were—my husband's thoughts for his next editorial. See what you can do with them.'

'Yes Mam,' he said, carefully folding the page into his pocket.

SHE TOOK THE RIG out to the homestead to see her pa, resolutely avoiding the turnoff that led to town. Nevertheless, her eyes, and her heart, turned that way as she passed the tarred road and fought the desire to whip the horses straight to the schoolhouse. Have I no shame? she whipped herself. Is there no boundary I will not cross? Tears stung her eyes as she gripped the reins.

When she arrived at the farm, she was surprised to find her brother there, emerging from the doorway to greet her alongside her pa.

'Hello, Am.' Her pa helped her down. 'Your brother was just telling me about the hullaballoo in town.'

'Why? Has something else happened?' she asked, reading her brother's face.

'What ain't!' Boundary looked glum as she removed her bonnet and sat down at the table. 'A bunch of drunken jarheads tried to burn down the temple. There was a shoot-out and Nelson Butland—you know him, the stable hand? —anyway, he took a bullet in the chest and died an hour later. The constable is investigating, but …' He sighed and rubbed his face. 'I guess I gotta say something about it in the paper.'

'Just write the facts,' she advised.

He turned the cup, his face miserable. 'Mr Bellow would take those facts and stretch them every which way. Heck, he might even put out a special issue and charge extra for advertising. I sure do miss him. Say!' He stared at her. 'You could write it! You're good with words.'

'Me?'

'Why not? We don't need to use a name. Shucks, Mr Bellow used to make up half a dozen names a week and put 'em to letters and such.'

'Why not ask Mr Rumbald, the schoolteacher?' The words came to her mouth before she had time to think.

'Rumbald?' He frowned. 'Why him?'

'He's good with words too, ain't he?'

WORDS WERE THE LAST thing on the mind of the subject of the conversation as he stood in the doorway of the schoolhouse, eyes anxiously searching the few adult faces escorting their children to school.

'I guess you heard about Mrs. Ketchfield?' said one, ushering her daughter in the door.

'Mrs. Ketchfield?' He stared blankly for a moment, his eyes looking distractedly past her at the road. 'Oh! Yes, of course. A tragic business.'

'To go like that!' The woman shook her head. 'He works in mysterious ways.'

'Who does?' Was that her—driving the wagon? He stood on tiptoe to see.

'Why, Mr Rumbald!' The woman stared.

He paced constantly, his nerves stretched to the breaking point, his mind ablaze with fears. She has abandoned me! She has changed her mind. Perhaps she has confessed all to her husband! On Saturday, unable to bear the suspense any longer, he visited the newspaper office, ostensibly to check some minor family detail.

'Did you say his name was Boundless or Bounded?' he asked, now convinced of the veracity of Amity's account.

'Who?'

'Your great-great—the ancestor who carved the buffalo.'

'Boundless. —Say, perhaps you could write something for the paper?' Boundary looked hopeful as he asked the question.

'No, I am still collecting facts.' Rumbald looked fretfully at the door, willing the beloved to walk through and, careless of all restraint, fling herself into his yearning embrace.

'Then write about anything.' Boundary scratched his neck. 'Heck, write about Germany, for all I care.'

'Germany?' His distracted mind focused on the question. 'Why Germany?'

'You're from there, ain't you?'

Rumbald clicked his tongue in exasperation. 'Bohemia.'

'Then Bo-he-mi-a or wherever. I gotta fill the pages.' Boundary stared glumly. 'Mrs. Bellow is counting on me. And Amity said you might.'

'She did?' Rumbald's mind seized on the comment, hope and gratitude flaring in his breast. 'I could write a few words, I suppose. Perhaps I might discuss with your sister her opinion of the present animus against the monument?'

'Anything!'

'When is she due to visit you next? Perhaps I might meet with her here?'

'She comes by when she wants to.'

Then summon her! He wanted to roar out the words. But instead, he put on his hat, restraining his emotions. 'Perhaps you could ask her to stop by the school next time she visits? Good day, Mr McLennan.' He opened the door and stepped out onto the street, torn between misery and hope. *Where is she? How can she torture me like this?*

HE HAD SOLD OFF most of the livestock, keeping just two horses, a few hogs, and the chickens. The fields lay untilled, the furrows grown over with weeds. He ate little, in spite of his daughter's protests, having lost interest in food. He drank more whisky and smoked the pipe endlessly. 'I miss you, Felice,' he mumbled, having fallen into the habit of talking to his dead wife while he went about his few remaining chores. The house had grown shabby through neglect, the furniture covered with dust. Amity cleaned up whenever she visited, scolding and making him promise to take care of himself. 'I will,' he said, and went straightaway back to his old ways.

'You'd frown on this coffee, I expect,' he said at the breakfast table. He pulled a sour face as he sipped. 'Heck, even I kin barely stand to drink it. How's Half Moon?' he asked. 'Does she miss her old rocking chair?' Sometimes he answered himself, carrying on a conversation with the empty room. 'I know you ain't here, Felice, but I miss your voice. And yes—I did wipe my shoes.'

Each morning, before the omnibuses arrived, he was in the habit of walking out to the rock, approaching it from the grass side to pay his respects. Standing before the two small crosses scratched in the granite, he took off his hat, mulling on the grass, the rock, and the surrounding plain. 'Standing this side, it's like nothing has changed much,' he said. 'The ground's a bit scuffed up. But you can't see the tents or hear the durn city folk come to gawk. Sometimes I wish it would all just roll back to the old days,' he said, ruminating into the distance. 'Do you remember, Felice? When we first got here? You thought you wouldn't hold out. But you did. And you came to love it, even this rock.'

A sound distracted him, and he listened for a moment before continuing. 'I guess you don't hear what's going on with that preacher fella? He's whipping up the townsfolk something awful.' He made a rasping sound in his throat, suddenly angry. 'Claims this buffalo is some sort of pagan altar. An idol! Durn fool. What does he know about anything?' He simmered on this for a while before turning his attention back to the grass which concealed the graves. 'There's that schoolteach, you remember him? He's writing a book of some sort. He says it will tell folk that our kin carved the stone, just like we always said. Maybe it will settle the hash of that thief, Lomax.'

He pondered for a while, his mind roaming in different directions. 'I gave Boundary the Bible, like you said I should. Am has got your writings and those old sketches. Do you remember, Felice, that painter fella?' He chuckled. 'The queerest bird I ever did see.' He scratched his chin, frowning. 'I wonder whatever happened to him?'

He heard noises, and the next moment three or four people rounded the rock, stopping in surprise upon discovering him. He tipped his hat, pretending he was a visitor himself. 'Well, Felice. I gotta go now. I wish I could lay Jubal here, as well. Maybe I'll get the chance when all this tom-foolery is put to rest. It won't be too long, I guess, afore I'm lying alongside you. The children will see to that.' The sightseers were approaching. He rubbed his thumb across the first cross scratched into the stone. 'I hope to see you again, dearest. Soon.'

IN PART TO TAKE advantage of the unprecedented good weather, and in part to spite the preacher, Lomax had extended the visitor season, intending to run it into December, when he had planned a huge New Year's celebration to rival, and compete with, the one in town. He had stockpiled fireworks and commissioned banners and posters proclaiming the *1,000 Year Era* of the buffalo, not a whit concerned at the rival hundred-year estimate being promulgated by the pestiferous schoolteacher. He had also booked a brass band, a huge dance tent, and several photographers, determined to make the event a success. He sent out invitations to a variety of important newspapers, promising spectacular scenes and historic celebrations that would, he hoped, propel the 'nation's monument' to even greater prominence across the entire country. 'I'd like to see us on every front page from here to New York,' he declared at a meeting of the Trust board to discuss the event.

The grit in his stew remained the ominous rumours of some spectacular event—entirely different to the one he had in mind—being planned by the preacher. He hired extra guards and redoubled his attempts to isolate his antagonist, paying considerable sums to spread rumours of madness, illegitimacy, corruption, and moral baseness against this festering thorn in his side. His investigations into the preacher's background had yielded nothing substantial beyond unproven allegations of involvement in arson and murder. He nevertheless blew these up to maximum effect, planting newspaper stories in the *Dispatch* and *Bismarck Tribune* hinting at all kinds of nefarious behaviour and quoting an unnamed source who suggested the preacher was a paid government informant.

The stories planted in the *Dispatch*—coming on top of a new article penned by Rumbald dismissing allegations that the buffalo was a pagan idol as 'superstitious nonsense'—caused much offence, the accusations arousing intense anger among the preacher's supporters. One morning, Boundary arrived at the newspaper office to be surprised by a dozen men gathered outside the door.

'There he is!' a man shouted. 'There's the printer!' The others turned to stare as a finger was pointed in Boundary's direction.

'What in nation did you mean by printing this?' The local hardware store proprietor, a man he recognised as Walt Pence—a fervid adherent of the preacher—thrust the latest edition of the paper under his nose.

'What?' Bewildered, he scanned the front page. *Much Ado About Nothing* read the headline. *Notion of Pagan Idol Entirely Unfounded*, ran the subhead.

'I don't understand,' he said, genuinely puzzled. 'Are there mistakes in the type?'

'Mistakes, he says!' Pence thrust his face into Boundary's. 'Do you even read what goes into your rag?'

'I don't—'

'He says he don't!' Pence roared out the words, drawing exclamations of scorn from his companions.

'No, I meant—'

'We know what you meant!' Pence thrust his face even farther into Boundary's. 'You calling the preacher a liar, boy?'

'What in smoke are you talking about!' In a temper, he shoved the other man.

Taken aback by the shove, Pence regrouped. 'If the preacher—a man of God—declares that durn buffalo a pagan idol, then that's the end of it! You hear me?'

'Not to be questioned,' added another man standing just behind Pence.

'But it ain't an idol. I know that for a fact! My great grandfather—'

'Oh! He knows it for a fact!' Pence turned to his followers. 'What do you reckon, boys? This pup claims to know things for a fact!'

'I reckon he could use a history lesson,' suggested another, a snarl in his voice.

'Or mebbe we ought fire his office,' menaced another. 'That would learn him.'

'What's going on here?' The men turned as a deputy approached along the sidewalk.

'Nothing, Jim. We're just conversating with Mr McLennan here over those lies he prints in the paper.'

'They ain't lies!'

The deputy, a thin, saturnine man with long sideburns nodded, his face sour as he glanced at Boundary. 'I hear you, Walt. But I gotta keep the peace, Blomquist's orders.'

'Maybe we ought go pay a visit to the schoolteach?' a man suggested. 'Seeing as how he's the fool that wrote the bull dung.'

'Maybe you orter leave off for the day!' said the deputy, his voice short. 'Mr McLennan, go about your business.' He watched Boundary enter the office and close the door behind him. 'And you men do likewise. I know!' He held up a hand as Pence opened his mouth to protest. 'It may be bull dung, as you say. But I got my job to do. Now move along!'

Others, however, welcomed the article, reading it as a vindication of the buffalo and the good the monument did for the town. Complete strangers approached Rumbald in the street to shake his hand and congratulate him for having the 'sand' to show up the shortcomings on both sides. 'All of that to-do over a rock that ain't even a … thing!' A woman trilled, boldly stopping him to praise the article. 'When will your book come out?' she asked. 'I'd sure like to buy it!'

'A monograph, Madam, a scholarly work. I intend to publish—'

'An autograph? Well, I reckon it's deserved!' she said, and walked off, leaving the baffled Rumbald in her wake.

The unaccustomed celebrity helped leaven the anguish he felt at his beloved's continuing absence, and he basked in the attention. Inspired, he promptly penned another essay, this one lamenting the pernicious influence of religion and 'sundry diseases of the mind.' *In the dawning light of the new century, it is high time we put aside childish fancies and recognise the wholesome and unbigoted truth of science,*" he wrote, giving unbridled license to the liberal theories imbibed from his professors at the University of Prague.

The essay, published in the *Dispatch*, was reprinted as far away as Kansas City and Chicago. It caused outrage in the town and drew rare, united condemnation from the various pulpits—both the Methodist and Baptist ministries decrying this attack on the 'glue that binds the nation.'

Delighted by the controversy and the unaccustomed platform for his progressive views, Rumbald boasted to his parents that he was finally embarked on the epic voyage that would see the family name in the mouths of citizens 'the length and breadth of the country.' He listed the several newspapers that had reprinted the article, voicing the hope that it might make its way overseas, perhaps even to Bohemia itself! 'The name Rumbald will be read by princes and prelates alike!' he trumpeted, giddy with his success. For the first time, he considered publishing his detailed investigations of the stone buffalo in the newspapers rather than through the onerous and time-consuming academic journals. 'Soon,' he murmured, mentally rubbing his hands at the prospect.

The unanticipated backlash, however, served as a sober reminder that celebrity was a two-faced beast. Indeed, the rancour aroused by the article was such that he felt nervous when walking the streets, the angry glances cast his way a splash of cold water on his fond hopes that the beloved might be irresistibly compelled to fly to his side in joyous admiration. Angry parents questioned his influence over their offspring, some refusing to speak or even look at him when they escorted their children to school in the morning. One mother, much to his embarrassment, publicly removed her child from the classroom while loudly proclaiming her disgust. 'I'll not have my Tommy exposed to sinful notions!' she objected and marched the delighted boy out of class.

The open displeasure of the school board obligated him to issue a clarification in a letter prominently published on the front page of the *Dispatch*. In the letter, he affirmed his respect for the sensibility of the town generally regarding religion, and confirmed his own neutrality, nay, silence even, on the question when it came to his young charges.

The public mea culpa did little to allay the outrage of those most offended by the essay, some of whom, to his alarm, loudly demanded his removal from the post of schoolteacher. Aghast at the scandal, coming so soon upon the heels of the 'prior matter,' Elizabeth Chestnut called an emergency meeting of the school board to argue for his immediate dismissal. 'We have hired a heretic!' she wailed, her chins wobbling at the thought.

'Not a heretic, Mrs. Chestnut,' pointed out a new member of the board, Mrs. Elsie Perez, a member of the nondenominational church. In spite of such allegiance, she found herself not unsympathetic to the schoolteacher's views. 'Mr Rumbald might properly be described as atheist, inasmuch as he dismisses, equally, all religions.'

Shocked at this challenge to both her authority and sense of propriety, Mrs. Chestnut opened her mouth to roundly condemn the sentiment. Apoplectic with rage, she attempted to speak, but nothing emerged save a strangled gasp.

'Mrs. Chestnut?' The other members of the board exchanged glances at her florid countenance.

'Better he had eloped with the superintendent!' she gasped, finding her voice.

The motion to fire the schoolteacher was defeated by one vote, Mrs. Perez convincing the other members that to do so would engulf the board in further controversy. 'Best lie low and hope it blows over,' she counselled, the homely advice finding a receptive ear among those members tired of Mrs. Chestnut's hectoring ways.

MYSTIFIED BY THE STORM of public outrage provoked by the article, the publisher of the offending essay shut himself up in his office to reread the piece. Interested only in smudged letters, dropped capitals, and unsightly line breaks—and well-versed in his former employer's more outrageous concoctions—he could find nothing untoward or exceptional in the writing, and set the newspaper aside to plan for the next edition.

That same afternoon, he received an urgent summons from Mrs. Bellow. Guessing the reason, and fearing the worst, he combed his hair and put on the tweed jacket Mr Bellow had insisted on gifting him 'so as to look like a newspaper man at least.' He turned up at the appointed time, knocking just once on the door before Mrs Bellow answered.

'Boundary!' The frosty reception confirmed his fears. His heart sinking, and heartily regretting ever soliciting, much less printing, the bothersome piece, he stepped into the parlour.

'Sit down!' She motioned to a chair. Sitting opposite, she immediately gave vent to her irritation, ignoring the usual formalities of tea and polite conversation. 'When I made you manager of the newspaper, I hardly expected you to turn it into a scandal sheet!' She peered accusingly over the rim of her glasses.

He stuttered to defend himself only to be silenced by an upraised hand. 'No doubt my husband, were he here, would excuse you on the grounds of mental impairment!' The words were accompanied by a severe glance that drew an inward groan as he foresaw his instant dismissal and the loss of his beloved press. 'We are not in the business of making ourselves into a public talking point!'

It was on his lips to protest that such was precisely her husband's intention, but he held his tongue in the face of her stern displeasure.

After a prolonged and severe telling-off, her tone, and her expression, softened, restoring some faint hope that he might yet keep his job. 'As it happens,' she conceded, her rigid posture slackening, 'The attention was not entirely negative. In fact, I received several offers from persons interested in acquiring the newspaper, presumably as a result of the ...' She searched for the word, 'notoriety!' She allowed this to sink in, her eyes piercing into his own. 'It would be a crime, Boundary, a crime, were this interest to be dispelled by any further scandals of this nature.' With the warning, she concluded her peroration, having established her thorough misunderstanding of a situation that would have delighted her late husband. 'Do I make myself clear, young man?'

He swallowed with relief. 'You do, Ma'am. And I am heartily sorry for the distress you have been subjected to on my account.'

She nodded, her features softening further. 'Good. And no more stories from this Mr Rumbald, are we agreed?'

'Yes, Ma'am.'

'Good. Then the matter is closed.'

And closed it might have been had not the preacher carried the offending newspaper into the pulpit the very next day and raised it in the air to prove—if proof were needed! —that Satan and his cohorts in the press had been given full rein to corrupt not only the good folk of Buffalo Rock, but their innocent children as well! For the best part of an hour, he railed against godless schoolteachers and the debasement of impressionable minds. Gasps were heard as he reached into his pocket and produced a box of matches. Holding them aloft as instruments of God's justice, he set light to the newspaper. Flames consumed the pages as he cast it aside to burn—to shouts of hallelujahs! and amens! from the congregation. The smell of burning smoke drifted through the chapel as his voice thundered with prophetic power, the aroused worshippers hanging on every word.

'Good people of Buffalo Rock! I promise you a bright new day is coming. A day when the Lord shall deliver us from the great blasphemy that besmirches our town! And ye shall witness His judgement with your own eyes.' The congregation drew a collective breath as he gripped the stand, a violent cast to his face, a fanatical glint in his eye. 'O men of Levi, your day is nigh!'

THE NOVEMBER MORNING WAS calm and bright, the sky a blue veneer that promised greatness in the coming day. Marvelling at the unprecedented weather, Purchase stood on the porch breathing in the smells and breezes of the sparkling plain. I don't remember it ever being this mild and becoming, he told himself. That was Felice's word, he mused, lingering on the thought. He brought a cup of coffee onto the porch and sat for a while, taking in the wide blue sky and the bright, transparent air. Memories trooped across his mind as he saw Felicity and Am, and Jubal and Boundary consorting in the yard. He willed them to turn and smilingly acknowledge him, their faces shining and fresh in the morning light. He mentally raised a hand in return, his eyes glistening. If I had it to do all again!

After a half-hour of sitting, he felt restless and a little cold. He rose stiffly to his feet and stood for a while, drinking in the distance and the shimmering bluffs. Making his way to the corral, he saddled his favourite horse and tied his bedroll behind the saddle. Oats, his one remaining dog, whined and rubbed against his leg, as frizzled and woebegone as himself. 'You stay here,' he said. 'Your old bones need the rest.'

He headed for his favourite spot, a trail which led between the bluffs toward his old buffalo haunts. On reaching the head of the trail, he pulled rein and sat upon the rise. He took off his hat to wipe his brow as he surveyed the homestead and the overgrown acres of grass surrounding it.

His eyes came to rest on the buffalo where it rose distinct and implacable above the grassy plain, its brooding stare an acknowledgement, perhaps, of the familial bond which bound him to itself. You fetched me here, all those years ago—as maybe you fetched him also.

He pondered the distance, yearning for the aloof beast to at last reveal itself and impart the secrets of its mysterious gaze. A sense of greatness in the day swept over him, the exhilarating transport drawing a hopeful gasp. He leaned forward in the saddle, eyes fixed on the buffalo, his heart pounding, his senses keenly alert for the illumination he so yearningly sought. But all he felt was the prairie wind teasing in his ears and the trembling portent of the wintry blue sky.

He gave out a deep sigh and sat back, shoulders slumped, the expectancy seeping out of his bones. You never did speak to me, he accused. Not as you did to Felice. She knew something—something given to her, but not to me. Even that queer painter fella—he felt something, too. I know he did. He sat for long minutes, anger and jealousy clawing away at him as he ruminated on the stony distance. Finally, he turned the mare and kicked her forward, envy and resentment clouding the gift of the shining day—that he, no less than his illustrious forebear, was both subject and object of that sightless gaze.

He rode far out into the ranges as a flight of late ducks flew overhead, lured to stay by the clement weather. If he rode far enough, he fooled himself, he might come upon fresh, untrodden country where the buffalo still roamed and where there were no farms or towns or houses. He rode on for hours, with no thought of turning back, rode until the bright autumnal light began to fade and stars twinkled in the dusk.

Unsaddling the mare, he built a small fire from some sticks he carried with him. Venturing out into the gloom, he shot a jackrabbit, humming at the sure crack of the Sharps. He skinned and roasted the rabbit, reminded of his early days as a peerless hunter of buffalo. Wishing he had some coffee, he laid out the bedroll and looked up at the stars blazing brightly overhead. A cool wind scudded the grass as he lay there, vexed by memories and regrets. There was Jubal and Elias and … He struggled to name others whose faces he no longer recalled. Winslow! Good old Winslow! He chuckled up at the stars.

He reached out a hand and plucked a tuft of grass, holding it up before his eyes. He released it, watching the breeze carry it back to the ground. 'I don't understand,' he confessed aloud. 'None of it. It don't make no sense. Why were those boys killed, and not me? What was the point of it all?'

The old man, at least, he reflected, had left something behind. Something hard and strong. But that, too, would one day crumble, just like the grass. And what would be left? The songs of the prairie night wind carried far-distant yelps and cries to his ears. There were the Sioux, and before them the Mandan. And before them, the buffalo. But where are they now?

Anguish surged up inside him as he contemplated the fiery cosmos. If I could dance the days back again like that crazy old Indian, I would! For a moment, he felt like leaping to his feet and whooping around the fire. The notion struck him as so foolish it tired him to think on it. 'You're an old man,' he grumbled to himself, 'and prone to such fancies.' He felt sleep coming on, the vast prairie night cool and insistent against his face. He stared up at the countless stars, tears wetting his eyes. But there was gladness, too, and gratitude. 'I would!' he vowed, before pulling the hat down over his eyes, blocking out the night, the stars, and the endless, whispering grass.

54

O Men of Levi!

ALL WEEK, THE TOWN had been buzzing with rumours of some spectacular event to take place at the rock. Despite numerous enquiries, Boundary was unable to ascertain the nature or even the time of the supposedly imminent event. 'You'll see!' one worshipper declared when he accosted the man on the latter's way back from the temple. The man was about to say more when he was ushered away by a fellow congregationalist.

'A miracle!' his companion declared, a gloating look on his face as he glanced back at Boundary.

'The whole town's gone crazy,' he complained to Marshall Watkins when the chief agent for the freight company stopped by to inquire about printing an advertisement.

'It's that fool preacher. He's got folk so riled up they don't know if its Saturday or Sunday. But he's planning something, that's for sure.'

'What?'

Watkins shrugged. 'Beats me. Ain't you the newspaper man?'

Stepping out to fetch coffee later that day, he happened to see Thurston Wake ride into town accompanied by one of his cowhands. Mindful of Mr Bellow's dictum to 'chase the smoke to find the fire,' he followed to observe as they dismounted outside the temple. The cowhand remained outside to watch the horses.

He approached the man as he rolled a cigarette.

'Good morning, friend. May I ask what brings you into town?'

The man paused from rolling the cigarette. 'You that reporter fella?'

'I am. Boundary McLennan, the *Dispatch*,' he introduced himself.

The man slowly licked the cigarette to seal it, his eyes on Boundary. 'Figures!' he said and spat into the street.

'What figures?'

'You printed them lies about the preacher.'

'I printed a story. It had nothing to do with the preacher.'

'Lies!' The man's expression was aggressive as he fished for a match in his shirt pocket.

'Have it your way.' He was about to leave when the man spoke again.

'Guess you'll find out soon enough.'

'Find out what?'

The man was about to say more when the temple door opened and the preacher and Wake emerged, deep in conversation. Wake's eyes narrowed as he caught sight of Boundary. 'What have we here? He turned to the cowpoke, his voice suspicious. 'You been gassing, Jed?'

'Me? I ain't said a word!' The man put on an expression of injured innocence.

'Mr McLennan.' The preacher's mouth tightened into a grimace. 'What gives us the honour?'

'They say some sort of service is planned out at the rock. Is that right?'

'Now look here, McLennan.' Before the preacher could answer, Wake bunched a fist and raised it under Boundary's nose. 'You go printing any more bull about the preacher and you'll answer to me!'

He felt the rancher's angry breath on his face.

'It's all right, Thurston. No need for threats.' The preacher laid a restraining hand on the rancher's arm. 'Mr McLennan's just doing his job.'

'You've been told!' Wake and his companion mounted their horses. 'Remember.' The rancher flashed a warning look from the saddle. 'No more lies!' Kicking the horse, he rode off.

'Are you a churchgoer, Mr McLennan?'

'What?' Sore at the threat, he turned to find the preacher eyeing him.

'I asked if you were a churchgoer. Are you?'

'I guess I manage to get along without it.'

'You do! My, my. This town is full of "get along" folk. Maybe you'll "get along" cometh the Judgement?' The preacher's eyes glinted with the question.

'I guess I will,' he said,

'It's never too late to repent—Madam!' The preacher stood aside to allow a woman to pass. A flash of something unreadable crossed his face as his eyes followed after her. 'Well?' he said, turning his attention back to Boundary.

'I got nothing to repent for.'

'Ain't you the lucky one!' The preacher stepped closer, his eyes burning with zeal. 'I suppose you're a freethinker'—he spat out the term as if it was bitter salt in his mouth—'like your friend the schoolteacher?'

Boundary took an involuntary step back. 'It ain't your business what I am.'

'No.' The preacher's voice was grim. 'But the Lord watches. I guess it's *His* business, ain't it?' He stared at Boundary, as if inviting a reply. When none was forthcoming, he turned away, his lips curled with contempt.

'What's all this guff about some doings planned at the rock?'

'You tell me.' The preacher looked back, his hand on the temple door. 'Ain't you the newspaper man?'

BOUNDARY WAS NOT THE only one concerned about the swelling rumours of some great spectacle planned to take place at the monument. At a trust meeting held in the mayor's office, Lomax ordered a doubling of the watch, his mood foul as he berated his subordinates for their lack of information.

'Now Ed,' be reasonable, the mayor protested. 'It's almost the New Year. Now's not the time to stir up trouble. Even that bonehead of a preacher knows that. Folk are looking forward to a party. Why, the whole town's dressed up—'

'Are you blind as well as dumb?' snapped Lomax. 'That's exactly why that crazy son of a bitch would choose this time. What better way to bring in the new century than with some sort of lunatic stunt?'

'Him and that damn rancher have gotten awfully tight,' affirmed Butch.

'Willy. Hang out at the saloon. Buy the drinks. See if you can't get some of those stinking cowpokes to talk. Find out if they know anything. And you,' he considered Leo, his mood sour. 'Start attending temple.'

SHE HAD COME TO regard her husband's silences and slow, ruminative habits of thought as indicative of the land itself. A notion plants itself in spring and ripens in the fall, she told herself, contrasting his practical, rural sobriety with Rumbald's mercurial wit that found consuming interest in every detail of the passing day. 'Mrs. Schaefer walks like a goose!' he said, imitating the woman by walking across the floor and squawking, his head bobbing back and forth in a manner that provoked her to helpless laughter.

'The light! How it glitters!' he exclaimed another time as he peered out the window following one of their increasingly rare trysts.

'Do you think so?' She came up beside him, keeping out of sight as he bent to better observe the light reflecting on a barrel of water standing in the yard.

'If I were an artist, I should paint that rain barrel, with you standing beside it, a bouquet of lilacs in your hand!'

'You would?' She laughed. 'Why lilacs?'

'Why not? Perhaps you would be naked, with only the flowers to preserve your modesty.' He raised his eyebrows, his eyes alight with mischief.

She smiled to herself as she recalled such moments, clinging to them even as she longed desperately to fly to his embrace. Goodness, what would

Ira make of such talk! The thought sobered her, brought her back to the dull house with its dull surrounds and the aching, shimmering sky.

'Am?'

She turned, startled at the sound of his voice.

'Didn't you hear me calling?'

'No. I was … thinking.'

'Thinking about what?'

She sighed, irritated with the question. Why must he always want to know? 'About nothing. Just passing thoughts.'

'I need a hand with this hog. Can you hold it down while I trim it?'

She knelt in the cold, hard mud, holding down the squealing piglet as Ira shaved the dew claw with a sharp knife. I wish he *would* paint me. Naked!

'Am!'

'Sorry.' She pushed down on the piglet.

'This weather is something, isn't it? I don't remember it being so fine so late in the year.'

'I wish it would just snow!'

'You do? Why?'

'I don't know. For the change, I guess.' She released the piglet and stood up. 'I should prepare supper.'

'How are you and ma getting along?'

'Okay, I guess.' She dusted her hands and smoothed her hair. 'I should go to town before the snow gets in. There's a list of things I need to get.'

'I'll go, too. I need some wire and nails.'

'I can fetch them, if you want.'

'Suit yourself. Take ma, too. She likes to buy things.'

'You don't think it's a mite cold for her?'

He looked at her in surprise. 'You're thinking of going this minute?'

'No. Tomorrow, maybe. I was just thinking she was a little chesty this morning.'

'Then the fresh air will do her good.' He paused, thinking. 'Maybe I should go, too. There's talk about that preacher and some goings-on.'

'What talk?'

'I don't know. It was something Ben Lucas said last week when he stopped by. I 'spect it's nothing.'

'Do you know anything about some supposed goings-on in town?' she asked her mother-in-law at supper.

Fleur paused from slurping the soup. 'Why would I know?'

'You attend temple, don't you? Supposedly the preacher—'

'He's a good man! 'Spite what certain folk say.'

'I didn't say he wasn't, did I?'

'I saw some fella today.' Fleur wiped her mouth with a cloth napkin while giving Amity a sly glance.

'What fella?' asked Ira.

'Some fella. Watching.'

Ira made a grumbling noise. 'What fella? Watching what?'

'Just some fella. Watching from the road.' She blew her nose into the napkin. 'Reckon he looked like that schoolteach—from the distance.' She raised her eyebrows at Amity.

'More soup?' said Amity, refusing the bait.

'So, what's the preacher up to?' asked Ira.

Fleur bit smugly into a slice of bread. 'I guess we'll see,' she said.

WITH SCHOOL SUSPENDED FOR Christmas, he was fretful and desperate. Twice, he dropped in at the newspaper office, making up a vague excuse each time while fishing for news of the beloved. 'And you will be spending Christmas with your family, of course?' he remarked to Boundary.

'I guess so.' Boundary peered into the ink mix, dipping his finger in to test the colour. 'I'm sorry you can't write for the paper no more, Mr Rumbald. It's just that folk are just plain ornery sometimes.'

'No matter. Perhaps it is for the best, at least for the present.'

'I hear the school board came down on you. It's that Mrs. Chestnut, ain't it? Mr Bellow had no time for her.'

'Then you will be spending the holiday out at your brother-in-law's farm?'

'I reckon.'

You reckon! Seething, Rumbald took his leave and walked down the street. The dolt would drink that ink if he could! He pulled his coat tighter, reprimanding himself for not bringing the warm wool scarf his mother had knitted for him. The sky was bright but cold, his breath curling in the late December air.

The stores were decorated with wreathes and festive bunting for Christmas and the New Year, the latter event described as the biggest in the town's history. '*One Hundred Years of Steady Progress!*' read one giant banner hung across Main Street. Although no one was certain of the exact date of the town's founding, 1800 had been chosen, the arbitrary date the cause of much dissension. A lively dispute had broken out in the letters pages of the *Dispatch*, some claiming the town's birth coexistent with its founding as a buffalo camp, others with the establishment of a trading post, and still others with the building of a military fort. 'Centennial has a nice ring to it,' decided Edison Lomax, and the matter was settled.

With Christmas Eve less than two days away, Rumbald felt dejected and homesick. He wandered the decorated streets, stopping to examine the store windows as if in pursuit of some gift. Not for the first time, he wondered if he shouldn't have taken the train home to Chicago to be with his family. But the thought of being away from the object of his consuming passion was too much to bear, the prospect of seeing her an opportunity too great to pass up. In a moment of wild inspiration, he pondered tricking the brother into inviting him to join the family for the celebration. But a moment's sober reflection dashed the thought. It would be the sheerest torture! For her and for me.

He had received two or three invitations, his current pariah status notwithstanding, and toyed with the notion of accepting the one extended by the Perez family if only to spite the crassly offensive Elizabeth Chestnut. But the misery of deprivation together with a penchant for solitude decided him on the baked goose and rhubarb pie being offered by his landlady. Returning to his lodgings, cold and dejected amid the festive streets, he poured his discontent into a letter to his sister, careful to conceal the real cause of his angst.

I confess I am at a loose end as Christmas and the New Year fast approach. The town is festooned with banners and flags in preparation to welcome in the new century. But I am like the empty shop front that sits forlorn and desolate betwixt its gaudy neighbours. I miss you, and, of course, mamma and papa. Someday, I hope to have a family of my own, to make the passing hours and days less burdensome. It would be nice to sit by the fire with a pretty wife and two or three darling children to hug and console one and on which to rain countless kisses!

In your last letter, you enquired as to the progress on my buffalo monograph. I am pleased to report it is almost complete. It lacks but one or two geological details concerning the probable age of the rock and its unusual occurrence on an otherwise flat plain. I am pursuing these questions through written enquiries and hope to have the answers soon. I plan to release the finished draft to a newspaper rather than a scientific journal. This is an unusual step, but I think the dividend, in terms of public acknowledgement and swift recognition, will more than justify it. After all, were not the newspapers the first to make widely known such achievements as Schliemann's discovery of Troy, or the equally remarkable discoveries of the celebrated Spanish cave paintings?

Later, lying in bed, the comparisons returned to upset and deject him, their importance shining inadvertent light on his own, rather commonplace discovery. His early, fantastical optimism about 'unriddling the buffalo' had given way to a more sober assessment of the value and worth of his achievement. *In the end, I have just an interesting newspaper story,* he acknowledged, doleful at the paucity of his conclusions. The vapours of a thousand-year-old mystery had vanished with the increasing probability that the famed carving was almost certainly little more than a hundred or so years old. The evidence provided by Amity and her family, even if unsupported by actual proof, had convinced him of the monument's age and provenance. *Why, it can hardly be much older than the town itself! Who would care whether it was McLennan or Bjornson or some unknown tribe of Indians that carved it?*

Sobered by the admission, he moped and dithered on completing his findings, the grand project consuming no more than two dozen pages of the journal. Frustrated, and yearning for the presence of the beloved, he hired a buggy on Christmas Eve and drove out to the Morgan farm in the hope of catching a glimpse of Amity. He turned the buggy and drove slowly past three times, on each occasion straining to see. On the third go-round, he pulled up on the side of the road and sat there, staring at the farmhouse, willing his beloved to step forth. In his yearning thoughts, she did so. Startled to see him, she dropped whatever she was carrying and ran across the field between them, crying out his name, unable to resist her desires any longer.

He stared hopefully as a woman emerged from the house. She stood on the porch, shading her hand over her eyes. Suddenly it dawned on him that the woman—stooped and frail-looking—was peering at him. Taking fright, he shook the reins and drove off. Glancing back, he saw the woman still outside, still peering.

Cold and bereft, he drove back to town, a sense of fatalism engulfing his hopes for the future. *She will never leave her husband. She does not love me enough!* Burdened with misery, he drove beneath the colourful banners overhanging Main Street. He wheeled slowly past a group of carollers holding a sidewalk concert, a brass band accompanying their efforts. A girl he recognised as one of his pupils waved to him, mouthing the words 'Merry Christmas!' He returned his gaze to the street, staring bleakly at the festive banners and the gaslights installed by the Buffalo Trust. Once back in his room, he threw himself on his bed, lovesick to the point of despair. *'Geliebte'*, he groaned over and over. *'Beloved!'*

55

A Graven Idol

Two days before the end of the year, Boundary got wind of a service of some kind planned at the rock for that morning. 'The preacher's gonna preach!' said his informant. 'It's hush-hush!'

'Does Lomax know?'

'Sure—for the day after!' The man grinned and tapped his nose.

He had barely finished breakfast when he was disturbed by the noise of activity in the street. Holding his coffee, he stood in the doorway with his landlady—the widow Halverson—as several wagons, horses, and buggies made their way up the quiet street. A farm cart creaked past, a man and woman sitting alongside each other on the seat. Two children sat in the back, their eyes turning to him as the cart rolled past.

'What's happening?' Mrs. Halverson looked at him, bewilderment in her voice.

'Nothing to worry about. They're headed out to the rock.'

'But it's Sunday morning!' she protested as he handed her the cup and reached for his coat.

Hurrying down to the newspaper office, he encountered a man, still wearing nightclothes under his coat, stepping outside his house to discover the cause of the unusual traffic disturbing the post-Christmas hush. 'What's going on, Mr McLennan?' the man asked, recognising him.

'I don't know.' He quickened his steps.

Turning into Main Street, he saw a rider, dressed in a suit, pass by, headed out of town. The man touched his hat and he recognised him as a shopkeeper who regularly advertised in the *Dispatch*. He was about to cross the street when he saw Marshall Watkins approach in a buggy.

Stepping into the street, he held up his arms to stop the rig. 'Where in tar is everyone headed?'

'Whoa!' Watkins pulled up the horses. 'Something big! Half the durn town is headed out to the rock.'

'Why?'

''Cos the preacher told 'em to!' Marshall patted the seat beside him. 'Climb aboard if you want to join the fun.'

'Har!' Before he was even properly seated, Marshall had shaken the reins again. The morning was cold, and Boundary wished he had had time to fetch a warmer coat. Grey clouds obscured the sun, and the surety of snow was carried on the chill breeze. 'About time,' said Marshall, glancing up at the sky. 'I never knowed the snow so late.'

BOUNDARY WAS NOT THE only one perturbed by the unprecedented activity disturbing the peace on a sleepy Sunday morning. Just a few minutes earlier, an aide had interrupted the mayor at breakfast at his favourite restaurant. Whatever he whispered into His Worship's ear had provoked a look of alarm and a voluble curse.

'Should I fetch the buggy?' asked the aide.

The mayor stared in amazement. 'Have you lost your wits?' He returned to his eggs, a woeful look on his face. 'So it begins,' he was heard to mutter.

On the way to the rock, they passed a procession of wagons and carts headed the same way as themselves. The occupants seemed in high spirits, hollering out greetings. One man, recognising him, called out, 'There goes the *Dispatch*!' The remark drew a guffaw from his companion.

'Well, lookee here!' said Marshall.

Ahead, a large group of men, women, and children walked on foot toward the rock. Surprised at the unusual sight, he studied their expressions as the buggy wheeled past, perturbed to note the same look of joyous anticipation on each face. 'Something ain't right,' he said, above the clop of hooves.

'You figure!'

SCORES OF ABANDONED WAGONS, buggies, and omnibuses were lined up by the side of the road. Marshall drove past the conveyances, turning the horses onto the tarred side road that led directly to the rock. To Boundary's alarm, the entrance gates had been torn down along with several Trust signs.

Marshall halted the buggy and climbed down, his face alive with excitement. 'The horses will be fine. Come on!' Urging Boundary to follow, he joined the mob of gleeful pilgrims trampling over the wrecked gates.

The sound of singing reached his ears as he followed his companion. Huge tents had been erected for the New Year celebrations in two days' time. Someone had cut the ropes of one tent, and it sagged in the breeze. A large banner proclaiming the new century had been torn down. A growing sense of unease gripped him at the sight.

As he passed beyond the tents and came into full view of the rock, he heard voices raised in a stirring hymn. A sizeable crowd was already gathered, singing lustily in the cold air. If he had been prone to irony, like his late employer, he might have speculated if they were not engaged in worship of the stone beast. 'You're right. Half the town must be here,' he said, catching up to his companion.

'More than half, I reckon!'

'What's going on?' he asked a man singing and carrying a stick on which fluttered a homemade flag emblazoned with a cross.

'Ain't you heard? The preacher's gonna lay it out!' The man resumed singing, his face glowing with anticipation in the morning light.

Boundary moved among the worshippers, noting the same expression of smiling expectancy on every face. The men and women seemed unfazed by the wintry air, their faces flushed pink as they raised their voices in song. He saw a dozen or so men armed with rifles forming a line at the base of the rock, and the unease he had felt earlier returned. He was further alarmed to observe four individuals, presumably the guards stationed by Lomax, sitting in the grass, their arms tightly bound. Thurston Wake, recognisable in the high Stetson he habitually wore, was engaged in animated conversation with several cowhands. A farm cart stood in the grass, the horses grazing in harness. A canvas sheet was stretched across the box, concealing the cargo from view. One of the men talking to Wake returned to the cart and climbed up on to the seat. 'Git!' he called and flicked the whip. The horses set off, towing the wagon beneath the head of the buffalo, where they pulled up.

Increasingly perturbed, Boundary tugged Watkins by the sleeve. 'What does he intend?'

'Who knows?' Marshall barely listened, his attention on the jubilant worshippers.

The crowd grew as more conveyances arrived from town. The new arrivals were greeted with hearty handshakes and loud exclamations of 'brother!' and 'sister!' from those already present. 'The train jest got in.' one man explained. 'There's lots more waiting for transport in the town.'

Thoughts of his former employer came to mind as Boundary gazed about in amazement, wondering if the long-rumoured spectacle was nothing more than a revivalist meeting inspired by the preacher. *But why then the armed guards?* prompted an exasperated Bellow. At the latter's instigation, he took out his notebook and jotted an estimate of the crowd, guessing their number at better than a thousand. The men and women were dressed up in their Sunday best, behaving as if the fields were a giant, open-air camp meeting. Dozens of people knelt in the grass, offering up prayers together. Those standing nearby contributed encouraging calls of 'Praise Jesus!' and 'Amen!' To his surprise, he glimpsed Elspeth Moore and the newly wed Susie Schamber among the throng, their faces lit up with ecstasy as they sang and raised arms along with the exultant worshippers.

The crowd seemed to be waiting on someone or something, the mood of restive excitement growing by the minute. Suddenly, shouts and hollers broke out as people pointed up at the rock. Following their gaze, he was shocked to see the preacher standing atop the monument, a speaking trumpet in hand. The sight of the charismatic figure provoked the crowd of jubilant worshippers to a frenzy of praise and exhortations. 'Hallelujah! Praise the Lord! Sing out His name!'

The clamour continued for some minutes as the preacher stared down, his expression unreadable from the distance. Thurston Wake was doing his part to whip the jubilant flock into ever greater raptures, striding up and down and urging them to raise their voices in praise.

'O people of Zion! The hour is at hand!'

The whoops and chants fell away as the preacher pressed the trumpet to his mouth. 'Prepare ye, for the judgement of the Lord!'

The voice, distorted by the trumpet, incited a frenzied and tearful response. Women clasped hands and men lifted infants up on their shoulders to watch as religious mania swept the crowd.

The preacher stepped forward to the very edge of the buffalo, his amplified voice hoarse with evangelical fire. "Ye shall make you no idols nor graven image, neither rear you up a standing image, neither shall ye set up any image of stone in your land, to bow down unto it: for I am the Lord your God!"

The words drew delirious cries of 'Amen!' and 'Blessed be His name!'

The distorted voice boomed from on high. "Thou shalt have no other gods before me! Thou shalt not make unto thee any graven image, or any likeness of anything that is in heaven above, or that is in the earth beneath, or that is in the water under the earth!"

The preacher paused for a moment, taking in the worshippers, before raising the trumpet to his lips. 'Brothers and sisters in Christ! I promised you that the day would come when Jehovah, in all his righteousness, would smite the heathen idol. That day has now come!'

A woman standing nearby raised her arms and shrieked in ecstasy before falling to the grass in a dead faint. Boundary stared in astonishment, shocked at the fervour of the crowd. Those around him began clapping their hands in rhythm as their voices lifted in a joyous hymn of praise.

'Where in heck is Lomax! Surely, he can't be good with this?' Watkins was beside him, searching above the heads of the rapturous worshippers. 'They say there are folk from Bismarck and Fargo and all over!'

Above the noise of singing, the preacher's voice rang out in exhortation as he returned to scriptural injunction. "Thou shalt not bow down thyself to them, nor serve them: for I the Lord thy God am a jealous God, visiting the iniquity of the fathers upon the children unto the third and fourth generation of them that hate me!"

The words drew a tumultuous response, men and women wailing and waving their arms and crying out in rapture, their faces shining with faith.

Boundary heard a commotion and turned to see, standing on tiptoe as cries of alarm interrupted the worship. At first, he could see nothing above the heads of the crowd. And then he glimpsed several armed men shoving and barging through the worshippers. Edison Lomax was at their head, a furious look on his face as he led the way through the press of bodies.

Marshall turned, his face pale with alarm. 'This ain't good! Better get the hell out of here!' With the words, he pushed off through the crowd. Boundary was about to follow when Bellow kept him there, reaching out from the grave to admonish his spooked employee. *Observe! Listen! Note everything!*

The preacher, from his vantage, had also spotted the incursion. Immediately, he abandoned the sermon, leaning down to shout urgent instructions to Wake at the foot of the rock. In response, Wake signalled the men waiting around the cart. They scrambled into action, pulling back the canvas cover to reveal that the box was packed with barrels of gunpowder.

'Fear not, brothers and sisters!' The preacher's voice boomed through the trumpet. 'Behold how Jehovah stretches out his hand to smite the ungodly and tear down the idolatrous calf!'

The admonition was lost as panic swept the worshippers. The barrels were being passed hand to hand from the wagon and piled up against the rock. One of the men began unwinding a long fuse. 'Jesus Christ!' a voice shouted. 'He's going to blow the durn rock!'

The cry incited further panic as people turned to flee. But so great was the press and confusion that the crowd milled in place. Frightened cries rose above the noise as women tried to carry the children to safety.

Wake was in a state of great agitation, his eyes alternating between the approaching threat from Lomax and his confederates, and his own men as they hastened to unload all the powder barrels. Finally, Lomax broke through the crowd, stopping in alarm at sight of the attempted sabotage. 'Stop that you goddam fools! Get those barrels away!' He pointed an accusing finger at Wake. 'It ain't right! It ain't lawful!'

As if summoned, the constable stepped forward, holding up his badge of office. 'I order you to drop arms! Any man who does not is in defiance of the law!'

Seeing the words had no effect and that the men were continuing to stack the barrels against the rock, Lomax turned to his men. 'Fire if they don't stop!'

The men hesitated, wary of the threat from the cowhands as the latter raised rifles in response to a shout from Wake. 'Ready, boys!'

'Hold fire for God's sake! There are women and children here!' A man in a fedora and duster stepped out from the worshippers, his voice frantic as he held up his arms to beseech calm. 'Back off! Back off!' he cried, directing his plea to Lomax.

He was cut off by a loud, bloodcurdling scream. The crowd gasped in horror. Boundary looked up to see where the preacher, in his agitation, had overstepped the edge of the rock. He gave out a despairing cry as he toppled to the grass below, spreading out his arms as though to halt the momentum of the fall. A stunned silence swept the scene, the spectators raising their hands to their mouths in fearful dismay. Wake rushed up to where the body lay prone at the base of the rock. The suspenseful silence held as he bent over the preacher and then stood up. Turning to the assembled worshippers, he shook his head.

Cries of shock and lamentation went up as the crowd took in the import of the headshake. Ignoring the threat of an explosion, several men and women rushed forward to where the body lay. 'Get back, you fools!' Wake interposed himself to prevent them from reaching the body. 'You are in grave danger! Go back!'

'He's firing the powder!' A man pointed to where a kneeling cowhand had struck a match. The cowhand applied the match to the fuse. It started to burn rapidly, heading for the piled powder kegs. 'Run for your lives!'

'Son of a bitch!' Butch, standing alongside Lomax, raised his revolver and fired several rapid shots at the cowhand as he retreated from the lit fuse. The shots incited an immediate response from the man's edgy comrades as they unleashed a volley of rifle fire, shooting wildly across the narrow space that separated the two sides. The air crackled with gunfire as the Trust employees returned fire. Gunsmoke drifted into the air as men and women screamed in panic, trampling each other in their desperation to escape the flying bullets. Boundary threw himself to the grass, raising his arms to protect his head as feet rushed past him. The shooters on either side were attempting to find cover while still pouring fire at one another. Shrieks of terror mingled with the sharp crack of rifles as the battle continued.

He was weighing up whether to crawl away or make a dash for safety when a tremendous explosion rent the air. To his horror, he saw a plume of thick, black smoke rise up from beneath the head of the buffalo. The explosion was so loud it momentarily stilled the crack of rifle fire.

'He's blown it up!' a voice shouted in disbelief. 'He's blown up the god-damn buffalo!'

56

Bounty

PEOPLE WERE FLEEING BACK to town as the plume of smoke curled into the sky. Boundary scrambled aboard a passing wagon, drawing a startled curse from the driver, whose terrified wife and child sat next to him. He refused the man's threats to 'Get the hell off!' as the latter whipped the startled horses through the throng of people and vehicles congesting the road. Wails of fear rose on the wintry air as the panicked worshippers mobbed the parked carriages, desperate to get a ride. Clinging to the backboard, he looked back to where smoke wreathed the face of the buffalo. He exclaimed in shock, thankful his pa wasn't there to witness the desecration. Dejected, he sat back against the side, ignoring the alarmed glances from the man's wife as she held tightly to her child.

They reached the cutoff to the town, the agitated driver whipping the horses straight past the turn. 'Let me down!' He crawled to the front, taking the driver by the shoulder. 'Let me down!' he shouted again. With a curse and a wild look, the driver barely slowed the horses as Boundary jumped over the side, rolling in the grass alongside the road. Battered and sore, he picked himself up as the wagon lurched and bounced down the road.

The sidewalks were eerily quiet as he limped down the street toward the newspaper office. He saw frightened faces peeping from behind windows, eyes following him as he made his way down the street. He heard a rumble of wheels and turned to see an omnibus rush past, the vehicle going pell-mell down the street as the driver cracked the whip. He saw the shocked faces of passengers huddled inside. Reaching the Dispatch office, he unlocked the door and then locked it behind him, his hands trembling. With a profound sigh of relief, he sank into Bellow's chair, his mind barely able to comprehend what had happened.

He had sat there barely five minutes, still trying to digest what he had witnessed, when he heard a frantic pounding on the door. He looked up to see the face of Marshall Watkins peering in at him. The other man gesticulated wildly for him to unlock the door. As soon as he opened it, Watkins pushed inside. 'You gotta hide!'

'Hide? Why?'

'The preacher's followers! They've gone plumb crazy!' Watkins heaved for breath. 'They've formed a mob and are hunting anyone connected with the Trust.'

'But I ain't connected! I just run the newspaper—'

'But you printed the stories!' Watkins stared as if Boundary were a lunatic he was trying to reason with. 'Heck, they blame everyone!' He shot a glance out at the street as gunfire erupted in the distance. 'Go! Hide yourself!' With the warning, he hurried back out the door.

The enraged mob found the newspaper office empty when they arrived. Breaking down the door, they proceeded to smash the printing press and whatever else they could find before setting fire to the place. 'Where the hell is he?' a man demanded. 'Where's that goddamn snake of a printer hiding?'

'We'll find the lying son of a bitch!' swore another.

'The schoolteacher!' Yet another speaker rallied the men as they stood, frustrated and angry, on the sidewalk outside the burning office. The words were met with a roar of approval. 'Let's go find the godless bastard!'

THE FIRED-UP MOB HUNTED throughout the day, scouring the town for enemies, real or perceived, beneath banners proclaiming the new century and the iconic date, 1900, in large, gold-coloured letters. Furious at being unable to find their quarry, they overturned the bandstand set up for the celebrations and ripped down and set fire to a banner. They stopped the few, frightened pedestrians still on the street to demand the whereabouts of 'the consarned printer,' and the equally dastardly schoolteacher.

Gunfights broke out as the authorities, aided by supporters, tried to regain control amid the chaos. Toward dusk, troopers from the capital rode into town to restore order. The colonel in charge, acting under direct orders from the governor, declared martial law and ordered the streets cleared under threat of shooting any who defied the curfew.

But still the hunt went on, small groups of men keeping to the shadows to avoid the troops as they searched high and low for those they blamed for the preacher's death. They dragged out several 'sinners' and lynched them even as their helpless victims wept and pleaded their innocence. Still not satisfied, they left the dangling bodies for the soldiers to find while they continued their hunt for the printer and schoolteacher, bursting into homes and terrifying the occupants before leaving to continue the search. Lomax and his confederates had retreated to the council building along with a dozen heavily armed Trust employees. They fortified the building against attack by dragging desks and shelves against the door.

They then took to the upper floors, shooting from the windows as a party of the preacher's militant followers attempted to break in.

HE HAD TAKEN REFUGE in the widow's house, assuring her he would leave as soon as it was safe to do so. 'I can light out for my sister's place, just outside of town,' he promised. He crouched by the window, scanning the darkened street. Flames could be seen leaping up into the night sky from buildings set alight in the downtown area. Isolated shots could be heard as men on both sides defied the curfew to settle scores.

'You stay right where you are, young man. I ain't afraid of a bunch of fools taking the law into their own hands.' Mrs. Bellow was pale faced but calm as she boiled water for tea. 'Goodness knows, if Quinton were here he would no doubt be frightening me to death by roaming out with his blessed notebook for quotes.'

He sat down, his face distraught. 'I hope Mr Rumbald's all right. They have it in for him, too.'

'They have it in for about everybody, from the sounds of it. Sit down. Drink some tea.'

He did so, his ears pricked for gunshots or sounds of rioting.

'The soldiers will quieten things down,' said Mrs Bellow, pouring tea into a bone china cup.

'I hope the office is all right,' he said, too agitated to drink the tea.

She sighed. 'If it ain't, it ain't. Now, take a cookie.'

'I'm real sorry, Ma'am,' he said, suddenly contrite.

'And what are you sorry for?' She peered at him over her glasses.

'Everything, I guess.'

'Nonsense. You'll be blaming yourself for the weather, next.'

'But if I hadn't printed those stories …'

She harrumphed in reply. 'What happened today had precious little to do with any stories and everything to do with that durn preacher!'

He glanced up, surprised at the cuss word.

'My husband's word.' She smiled. 'Now don't you go to fretting. You're safe here. By morning, those lunatics will have come to their senses. More tea?'

He stiffened at the sound of a commotion in the street. Hurrying to the window, he peered through the curtains at where a party of men holding lanterns and carrying rifles had gathered outside.

'McLennan, you in there?' a voice yelled. 'Come on out, you yellow-livered dog!'

He reacted in alarm as Mrs. Bellow got to her feet. 'Where are you going?'

'I must answer, Boundary. If I don't, the scoundrels are liable to break down the door.' And with that she stepped outside, pulling the door closed behind her. He froze as he listened from behind the door.

'Do you dare disturb an old lady? I'm the only one here. Now go away before I summon the soldiers!'

'You sure you ain't got that printer in there? He works for you!'

'No one works for me as the newspaper office is closed and presumably burned down. Now go away! If my husband were here, you wouldn't dare intrude like this. Jeb Colson, is that you? It's no use stepping back, I recognise you. Does your wife know you're out and about threatening defenceless old ladies?'

Straining to listen, he heard a muttered colloquy from outside as the men argued among themselves.

'Sorry to bother you, Mrs. Bellow,' a voice said at length. 'I guess the man we're looking for ain't here, like you say. Good night, Ma'am.'

And with that, the voices moved off down the street.

Mrs. Bellow bolted the door behind her and returned to the parlour.

Boundless sank back into the chair. 'Heavens to a crow!' he said, his voice shaking.

'Witless fools! They're more likely to shoot each other.' Mrs. Bellow picked up her cup and made a grimace. 'The tea is cold.'

He sat in a daze as she boiled fresh water, his shocked mind trying not to picture what the men might have done had they broken in and dragged him out into the street.

'Here.' Mrs. Bellow returned with the refilled teapot and poured fresh tea. As he picked up the cup, she studied him, a frowning look on her face. 'You said you'll go to your sister's?' He nodded, scorching his lips on the tea.

'And that's at your brother-in-law's place, just outside of town?'

'It is.'

She made an umming sound as she sipped her tea. 'That may not be far enough,' she declared, setting down the cup.

'What do you mean?'

'I mean that it might be wise for you to leave town for a while, until these hotheads are brought to heel.'

'To Bismarck, you mean?'

'Or farther.' She considered for a moment, her mind working as she stirred the tea. 'I have a cousin, in Plattsburg. You could go there for a while if you wished. He would give you shelter.'

'Plattsburg? Where's that?'

'It's a small town in upper New York State, toward Canada. God knows it's far enough away that nobody could find you if they tried.'

He drummed his fingers nervously. 'I don't know, Ma'am. I guess I'd as soon take my chances at my brother-in-law's place.'

'Have it your way. But remember my offer if things go from bad to worse, as I suspect they will.'

'I will. And thank you, Mrs. Bellow. I'll be out of your hair as soon as things settle down.'

'That, as my dear Quinton would have said, may be a hope too far.'

AS FRANTIC REPORTS CAME in from townsfolk fleeing along the road of some 'awful goings-on' at the rock, Amity became petrified for Rumbald's safety. Her fears increased as the early reports of dead bodies gave way to dire claims of 'a slaughter,' and then 'a massacre.' Beside herself with panic, she busied her trembling hands with household chores. Ira went outside several times to listen, satisfying himself before returning inside and barring the door.

'No one will bother us. It's all right, Ma, don't be feared,' he said, reassuring his frightened mother. 'We have nothing to do with this,' he said. 'Am. Why don't you put on some fresh coffee? It will blow over by morning,' he said, rubbing his mother's arm. 'You'll see.'

She was unable to sleep that night, moaning out loud in her concern for Rumbald. 'Don't be afraid, Am.' Ira pulled her closer as they lay in bed. 'I expect Boundary is safe and sound. No one has cause to wish him harm.'

Later, as he slept beside her, she stared into the darkness, her thoughts frantic. *I should have listened to him. We could have gone away together and avoided all this. We would be happy, I know it!* As the night wore on, her desperation grew until she thought she might burst into uncontrollable tears. *I'll do it! I'll ride into town tomorrow. I'll find him and we'll run away together. Take the train to Bismarck and then just keep on going 'til we get where nobody knows us.* Her continuing grief for her pa intensified her fears as her thoughts turned to her brother. *He's got sense. He'll keep his head down.* She turned restlessly, projecting her worst fears onto the darkened room. *He's a schoolteacher, a man of learning. They'll respect that.*

After a sleepless night, she was even more tightly wound, pestering Ira to ride with her into town.

'Have you lost your senses?' He stared in amazement. 'The whole town's under martial law. Why in hickory would I want to go there? Why would *you* want to go there?'

'My brother! He got caught up in it all. I'm fearful for his safety.'

His expression changed and he took her in his arms. 'I'm sure he's all right. The soldiers will keep the peace. Tomorrow, or the next day, I'll ride in and check on him.'

Later that morning, a horse galloped into the yard. Ira took down his rifle, peering through the door as the horse came to a stop and a rider, heavily muffled, climbed down.

'Don't shoot! It's Boundary!' Amity flew out the door to embrace her brother. 'What happened? I thought you were wounded or worse!' She fired questions at him as she escorted him into the house. *And where is Hans?* a voice inside her screamed.

She helped him struggle out of the coat before he sat down, pale and exhausted. 'The whole town's gone mad! The soldiers are trying to keep the peace, but they can't control the mobs. The preacher's followers and Lomax's party are taking turns to snipe at one another. It's a risk to be out on the streets!'

'And the school—I mean the schoolchildren, they are safe?' She couldn't prevent the words from tumbling out of her mouth.

He turned a puzzled look on her. 'The school? There ain't no school!'

Ira sat down opposite. 'Tell us what happened.'

Boundary recounted the few details known to him as best he could, his voice shaking. 'A soldier stopped by Mrs. Bellow's house. He said there was awful carnage out at the rock, bodies everywhere! He warned her to stay inside—that a mob was searching for me and Rumbald.'

'The schoolteacher? Why were they looking for him?' Her face was white, her voice strained as she gripped her brother's arm.

'I ain't sure!' He was trembling, unable to keep the agitation from his voice. 'I ain't sure if he's alive or dead. It was awful! There were women and children, too. And bullets flying everywhere! And then that durn—sorry, Ma'am.' He glanced at Ira's mother, who listened, ashen faced, a hand to her mouth. 'That rancher fella, Wake, tried to blow up the rock—.'

'Blow it up?' Ira interrupted in amazement.

They stopped talking and stared at each other in alarm at the sound of hooves clattering to a stop outside.

'Stay here!' Grabbing his rifle, Ira positioned himself at the door as someone knocked frantically from without.

'Open up!' a voice demanded. Fleur gave a scream and looked as if she might faint.

'Who's there?' Ira pulled back the hammer on the rifle.

'A message! A message for Boundary McLennan! Mrs. Bellow sent me!'

Ira glanced at Boundary who nodded, licking his dry lips. Opening the door a crack, rifle at the ready, Ira allowed a youth to stumble into the house, a wild look on his face. 'Mr McLennan!' he cried as his gaze lit on Boundary.

Boundary stood up, recognising the youth as someone who helped out occasionally at the newspaper. 'Thomas, is that you?' The youth nodded, wide-eyed, his face flushed from the ride. 'For you!' He thrust a haversack and a folded up note at Boundary. 'I gotta be getting back!'

'Wait!' Ira forestalled him as he went to open the door. 'What in blazes is going on in town?'

'It's bad!' The youth's voice shook with the telling. 'They reckon the constable's shot dead and the mayor's hightailed it for Bismarck. The town's shut down and there are soldiers everywhere. I guess there are plenty of folk kilt.'

'How many?' Amity's eyes were wide with alarm.

'Heaps, they reckon. I gotta go! Ma will be worried! Read the note, Mr McLennan.' The youth pulled open the door and rushed out. They watched him scramble aboard the tired horse and urge it out of the yard. 'Git, Smoky. Git!'

Boundary sat down at the table and unfolded the note as the others gathered around.

Dear Boundary, I hope you made it safely to your sister's place. You should know that things here are going from bad to worse. Lomax has pressured the authorities to arrest a bunch of people he blames for the fracas at the rock. Your name is included, along with that of John Spencer, Charles Duckett, and several others, including the schoolteacher, Mr Rumbald. As if that ain't bad enough, a Mr Marshall Watkins (who claims to be a friend of yours) came by with a warning. He claims to have heard a rumour that Thurston Wake and his confederates have drawn up a 'death list,' to avenge the preacher. He fears that your name is most certainly on it. He says you should lie low or pay for it with your life. The soldiers struggle to control the situation and have sent to Bismarck for reinforcements. There have been several incidents of shocking violence, including lynchings. I fear it's only a matter of time before either Lomax or Wake and his confederates figure out you've taken shelter at your sister's place and search for you there. I strongly urge you to leave town until this foolishness is sorted out and the law takes back control. Remember my cousin in Plattsburg? I advise you to go there. Bismarck, or Chicago even, may not be far enough. My cousin *is a good man and will, I'm certain, be willing to put you up until it is safe for you to return again. I urge you to head there without a moment's delay. I'll wire my cousin and tell him to expect you. When you get to Plattsburg, check in at the local telegraph office and you'll find instructions from me together with his address. I sent to your lodgings to pack a few clothes and things. They are in the sack. If you check between the pages of the bible you'll find the $300 I've placed there. The money is in part payment for the last month's employment, and in part a loan against future earnings until this sorry business tides over. At such a time we can review the prospects for restarting or selling the newspaper. Godspeed, Boundary. Do not be downhearted, but do not linger!*

    Mrs. Beth Bellow.

WITHIN AN HOUR OF receiving the note, he had left town, riding one of his brother-in-law's fresh horses and leaving his own in its place. Uncertain of the danger he was in, but fearful of being recognised, he had largely avoided the main road to Bismarck, riding instead a circuitous route that took him to the capital in the late afternoon. The delayed winter had arrived with a vengeance, and thick snow was falling as he rode into the city. He sold the horse, together with the bridle and saddle, for seventy dollars and used the money to purchase a warm buffalo coat that hung down to his ankles, a new hat, and leather gloves lined with wool.

'A prosperous New Year to you, friend,' the shopkeeper said, handing him the change.

'What?'

The shopkeeper blinked. 'Why, it's New Year's Eve!'

'Of course! I had quite forgot.'

Tired and miserable, he made his way to the railway depot, where he booked a ticket for Minneapolis–St Paul. With time to spare, he purchased the *Tribune*. To his alarm, the newspaper blazed news of the incident in sensational, twenty-four-point typeface: "Massacre of Innocents!" Several subheads spelled out the dire details: "Dozens Slain in Murderous Crossfire and Explosion; Hunt for Instigators Continues; Beloved Preacher Among the Dead; Monument Closed Under Governor's Orders; New Century Rings in Tragedy."

Shaken, he took it into the waiting room to read. The room was warm and stuffy, a woodstove blazing in the corner. A few other passengers sat huddled on the benches and he joined them, removing the heavy coat to lay it across his lap. He then returned to the newspaper. The several stories gave graphic, and sometimes conflicting, accounts of the incident, which the newspaper persisted in labelling a 'massacre.' Scanning the accounts, he was shocked to note his own name listed as 'one of several progenitors of the tragic event.'

> The editor of the local newspaper, the Fort Buffalo Dispatch, is accused of printing various inflammatory articles prior to the incident. These are said to have enraged local worshippers by casting grave aspersions on the preacher and calling into question the utility of religion generally. A warrant has been issued for his arrest on grounds of sedition, but he has of yet escaped detection. He is believed to have fled, perhaps with several confederates, east toward Fargo or north to seek refuge in Canada. A bounty has been placed on his head, and local authorities are urged to watch out for him.

A bounty! Shocked, he reread the paragraph several times, his heart pounding faster each time. He glanced up to observe a man studying him.

'Such goings on!' the man, a fellow passenger, said, nodding to indicate the newspaper headline.

'Oh! Yes. Terrible news.'

'Where you headed?' the other man asked, his interest apparently genial.

'To Kansas City,' he lied, his heart thumping.

'Kansas City!' The other man's eyes widened. 'I'll be!'

He waited anxiously for the train to arrive, fearful that at any moment armed men would storm the waiting room and haul him outside to his doom.

ONCE ABOARD THE TRAIN, he pulled his hat down and pretended to be asleep, at times casting covert glances at his fellow passengers. Snow on the tracks and strong winds forced the train to proceed at a snail's pace, the two-hundred-mile distance to Fargo taking an agonising twelve hours. The miles, and the stops, rolled by, the journey seemingly interminable as the train stopped to take on fuel, freight, or to allow another train passage. He dozed intermittently, seeing again the preacher fall, arms flailing, or hearing the cries of the wounded as lead hummed through the air with a sound like angry bees.

'Wake up, friend.' The conductor was shaking his shoulder. 'You're bound for Minneapolis, ain't you?'

'Yes.' He mumbled, collecting his wits after the nap.

'Well, this is Staples. You change here. Take the branch line south to Little Falls.'

'What time is it?'

'Just past two o'clock in the morning.' The conductor grinned. 'Welcome to the twentieth century!'

'What time is the train?'

'Depends. Ought be nine o'clock. But this weather …?' The conductor shrugged.

He passed a cold and miserable night in the waiting room along with five or six other passengers. Using the haversack for a pillow, he lay down on a hard wooden bench and tried to sleep. Around 4 am, the fuel in the woodstove gave out and he sat hunched in the buffalo coat to keep warm. The other passengers either slept or sat up, trying their best to keep from freezing. Finally, exasperated and shivering with cold, one of the passengers broke up a chair and put the pieces in the woodstove. 'Help me light it,' he said, looking to Boundary.

The fire brought some warmth back to the room. They broke up another chair and fed it to the flames. 'Best be on the train afore the stationmaster finds this,' the other man said through clenched teeth.

It began to get light around 8:30 am, the tired and dispirited passengers rubbing their hands and waiting anxiously for the sound of the train. Finally, it arrived, huffing and puffing into the platform as they trooped outside to board. He took a seat by the window, stiff and cold and longing for a coffee and some breakfast. They sat in place for a half-hour, the conductor coming through to mention that they were waiting on some mail bags. Shortly after, another man passed through the car with newspapers for sale. He purchased one, asking the man when the train would get to Minneapolis.

'Any day now,' the man said and winked.

A glance at the newspaper was sufficient to show that the news was all about the incident at the rock and the continuing strife in the town:

The army is now firmly in control and law and order reestablished following the lawless few days of shootings and lynchings. Edison Lomax, president of the Buffalo Monument Trust, assured reporters that the monument would reopen sometime in the New Year. He added that it was 'most unfortunate' that the tragic events had caused the cancellation of the planned celebrations. Several arrests have been made, the most notable being that of Thurston Wake, a local rancher accused of helping orchestrate the massacre that killed at least thirty of his fellow citizens. He maintains his innocence and points the finger directly at the Buffalo Trust employees, blaming them for starting the gunfight. Critics have maintained that the investigators heavily favour the Trust, with all of the arrests coming from those associated with the late preacher. A Mr Jay Malting, spokesman for the Trust, denies this and says simply that those arrested were criminals whatever their association. The town flags were lowered as a mark of respect for those killed during the fracas. Several more interments took place today as the last of the victims were laid to rest. Meanwhile, the hunt continues for several wanted men who escaped arrest by fleeing the town. The new town constable, Butch Reynolds, promises that no stone will be left unturned in the effort to apprehend the fugitives.

Several more stories painted lurid details, one suggesting that the preacher was shot before falling from the rock. Another story listed the names of the dead. He scanned the list, recognising many of the names, including that of Art Blomquist, Joe Gershon, and Susie Olson, née Schamber.

He looked up as a whistle sounded on the platform. A bell rang and the car shuddered as the train lurched forward. 'Fix yer durn stove,' a passenger muttered as the car passed the stationmaster standing on the platform holding a flag.

'Minnie–St Paul the last stop,' said the conductor, moving through the car. 'All tickets, please!'

57

Plattsburg

LITTLE FALLS, SAUK RAPIDS, Clear Lake, and Anoka rolled by as the monotonous journey continued, the train stopping at each station to take on or discharge passengers. At Coon Creek, the train halted for some unspecified reason and the passengers were able to get off and obtain food at a nearby diner. 'The train won't leave without you,' assured the conductor.

They reached Minneapolis–St Paul as darkness fell. Boundary secured a bed for the night at a local hotel, reading more accounts of the incident, which continued to be the main news story across the country. One piece in particular caught his eye:

FAMED MONUMENT SURVIVES ATTEMPT AT DEMOLITION

The renowned stone buffalo came through its attempted destruction largely unscathed, according to accounts. Although still closed to the public as authorities continue their investigations at the site, this reporter can confirm that the monument survived the attempt to blow it to kingdom come due to the haste, or inexperience, of the saboteurs. The explosion, although sizeable in nature, was deflected outward from the granite mass, taking the path of least resistance. As a result, the giant figure sustained only minor damage to its frontispiece, shards of granite being blown away from the stone. The lasting legacy is a large black powder stain covering a considerable portion of the granite. But this, too, is likely to fade in time as a result of wind, rain, and ice. Mr Lomax is reportedly urging the authorities to reopen the site as soon as possible so that visitors can once again partake of the wonders of the stone colossus.

Greatly relieved at the news, he blew out the lantern and slept soundly until morning.

NEXT DAY, HE DECIDED to send a wire to Mrs. Bellow informing her of his progress. He changed his mind when, approaching the station, he spotted a police constable eyeing him with what he deemed a suspicious stare. Turning down a side alley, he pretended to walk away from the train depot, only to turn back again and approach it from the rear.

At 8 a.m., he boarded the Chicago and Northwestern express, guaranteed to be in Chicago in less than fourteen hours. The journey passed without incident, although, in his fraught state, he suspected the conductor did a double take on checking his ticket. 'How long to go?' he asked, searching the man's face.

'Not long.' The conductor moved along the car, calling for tickets.

He arrived in Chicago just before 10 pm on a freezing cold night and checked into a hotel in the downtown area. The following morning, he rose early to return to the station, marvelling, in spite of his anxiety, at the many tall buildings, wide, snow-covered streets, and the numerous carriages, carts, omnibuses, and pedestrians out and about despite the severe weather. Crossing a street, he stopped in astonishment at seeing his first horseless carriage pass by. The four-wheeled vehicle was open to the elements, the exposed driver heavily muffled against the cold as he gripped the wheel. A cloud of exhaust smoke followed the carriage down the street. He stood looking after it, mentally scratching his head at the sight. *What would Mr Bellow think?*

He saw several similar vehicles as he continued toward the train depot, gawking at each one as it passed. He paused to appreciate one building that soared twelve stories above the pavement. A passerby grinned at the look on his face. 'It ain't going nowheres but up!' the man joked.

He paused at the entrance to Grand Central Station, admiring its imposing clock tower. Despite the early hour, the terminal was bustling with people: passengers, porters, rail workers, shop clerks, and uniformed officials in blue jackets and peaked caps crowded the busy concourse. Walking past a row of shops, he noticed a telegraph office next to a diner. He walked inside, determined to risk sending a telegram to Mrs. Bellow: '*In Chicago. Will proceed as planned. Please advise Amity.*'

He paid the telegraph officer, an amiable man with time on his hands. 'Did you say Buffalo Rock?' The man asked, glancing at the form.

'I did. I have relatives there.'

'Wasn't that where they had that massacre?' The officer eyed him curiously. 'It's all over the papers,' he said, pointing to an open newspaper on the desk. 'They say scores of folk were all shot to bits while on their knees praying.' The man shook his head in disgust. 'Who knows what this world is coming to?'

'It was a great tragedy.' Boundary opened the door to leave.

'A great tragedy,' the man echoed behind him.

He walked up to one of several open wickets situated beneath a giant board showing train times and destinations.

'Yes?' The ticket agent was gruff and impatient.

'I need to get to Plattsburg, New York,' he said.

'Plattsburg?' The agent scratched his bewhiskered jaw. 'Hold on.' He consulted a schedule, grimacing as he traced the details with a tobacco-stained finger. 'You go from here to Schenectady—I can sell you a ticket all the way. From there you switch railroads. Take the Delaware–Hudson. That will get you up to Plattsburg.'

'How long before we get there—Schenectady?'

'How long?' The agent consulted the schedule again. 'Twenty hours to Schenectady. Train departs at midday. Platform five. There's a dining car on the train.' He peered at Boundary. 'Coach will cost you sixteen dollars. There's a Pullman car if you want to pay extra?'

He shook his head. 'No, just a regular seat.'

With a few hours to spare, he explored the large concourse, stopping to pick up both the *Times-Herald* and the *Chronicle*. He was making his way toward a row of seats when he was given a rude shock. Passing by a large notice board, he saw a number of "Wanted" posters. And, pinned to the centre of the board, was a "Reward" poster with his name prominently displayed together with a promised reward of two thousand dollars for his apprehension. Faint with horror, he scanned the print: "Fugitive from Justice. Wanted for Sedition and Incitement to Riot." The poster gave his name, age, height, hair and eye colour, and occupation.

His senses reeling, he walked away, certain that all eyes in the busy concourse were upon him. Where could they have obtained my description? Almost at once, the name and face of the illustrator Bellow had commissioned leapt to his mind. Nervous as a cat, he found a seat and sat down, burying his face in the newspaper.

HE HAD SAT THERE for a little over an hour, impatient for the train to arrive. Scanning the area, he noticed a man in a flat wool cap and a bushy moustache looking in his direction. The man looked away as soon as they locked eyes across the concourse. Shuffling the newspaper, he watched covertly as the man walked up to the wicket and spoke to the gruff agent who had sold him the ticket. With growing concern, he watched as both men conferred, once glancing in his direction. He saw something pass between the two—payment, his overwrought imagination suspected. With another glance his way, the man walked to the telegraph office and entered.

Now thoroughly alarmed, he got up and hurried to the departure platforms, noting from the several clocks that it was but a quarter hour to noon. The guard checked his ticket and allowed him through the gate. Several other passengers were waiting on the platform. Standing in a recess, he looked back at the concourse but could not see the man—whom he now suspected of being a detective or bounty hunter.

Amid clouds of steam and a squeal of brakes, a locomotive reversed up to the platform, pushing a caboose, a mail car, and a half-dozen carriages, including a dining carriage and the Pullman sleeping car. With a last, searching look around, he mounted the steps and was directed to his seat. Walking through the dining car, he lowered his head to scan the platform. The man was nowhere to be seen.

'Ticket, suh!' A young Negro, dressed in railway livery and wearing a brown flat cap with a tarnished brass plate inscribed with the words *Pullman Porter,* approached. He handed the ticket over. As he took it back, he snatched a last quick look at the platform. To his horror, he saw the man hurrying through the gate, reaching the train just as the bell clanged and a whistle blasted. He summoned back the porter. 'My name's Mr McLennan,' he said. Taking out some bills, he thrust two dollars into the pocket of the youth's wool jacket. 'Let me know if anyone asks after me, and I'll give you another two.'

'Sure 'nuff, mister.' The Negro patted his pocket. 'Sure 'nuff,' he repeated, walking off down the car.

Greatly perturbed by the other man's presence on the train, he took off his coat and sat by the window, his mind racing with possibilities. It could all be coincidental, he told himself, the words ringing hollow in his ears. The whistle shrieked and the train began to pull out of the station. He resumed reading the newspaper but was too nervous to take in the contents.

Following a quarter hour of steady travel, he got up from the seat and walked down the centre aisle, his eyes dwelling suspiciously on each passenger. Making his way to the next car, he stiffened as he caught sight of the man, seated by himself and still wearing his flat cap. The man glanced up at him but showed no sign of recognition. His heart pounding, he walked past to the next car. Collecting his breath, he walked back again a few minutes later. The man had not moved.

He took his seat again, chewing on an apple he had purchased at the station. The conductor walked up and down the aisle, announcing each stop in a sonorous voice. 'South Bend! Elkhart! Butler!' He fell asleep to the rocking motion of the carriage. He awakened hours later to the same voice calling out 'Sandusky, Ohio!' The fields and towns outside the window had been replaced by the flat waters of Lake Erie. He was sitting there, preoccupied with thoughts of home, when the Negro porter approached.

'Mr McLennan, suh?' The youth's face was conspiratorial beneath the peaked cap as he leaned down. 'A fella's been askin',' he said, glancing down the car.

'Which fellow? Can you describe him?'

'Shifty looking macaroon, 'bout yay high'—the youth held up a hand to illustrate—'and a raggedy moustache looked like it was growed at his ma's teat.'

'Was he wearing a hat?'

'Sure 'nuff. A flat cap. Too small for his head, I'd say.'

'Do you know his name?'

'Angus Thornburg.'

'What did he want to know?' He took another two bills from his pocket.

'Asked where you is bound. And your name and everything. Asked if you was heading for Plattsburg.'

'What did you tell him?'

'I said you was a fishmonger named Knickerbocker, headed for Tuckahoe.'

Boundary smiled in spite of his anxiety, and added another dollar to the bills in his hand. 'And did he buy it?'

The porter gave a toothsome grin. 'Shucks, I seen his kind afore. Ain't hard to fool 'em!' He tapped the bills where he had placed them in his pocket. 'You want anything else, boss, jest ask for Festus.'

He stared out the window, now fully convinced that his mystery pursuer was indeed either a private detective or a bounty hunter. Feeling hungry, he got up and made his way to the dining car. He sat down and ordered eggs, toast, and coffee. The waiter brought him a copy of the *Sandusky Register* and he flipped through the pages. He found two reports on page three, thankful that the story appeared to have lost its prominence.

The reports indicated that calm had returned to Buffalo Rock, although the hunt was still on for the alleged perpetrators of the 'outrage,' as the reports termed it. The longer account gave the final death toll as thirty-five, most perishing from rifle fire, although a half-dozen or so were fatally injured in the explosion. Turning the page, he found an artist's rendition of a pensive Edison Lomax, captioned, 'Guardian of the Rock.'

Something made him look up and he caught Thornburg staring at him from two tables away. The latter quickly averted his gaze and pretended to read the newspaper while stroking his bushy moustache. In spite of his unease at the other's presence, he sat at the table following breakfast, drinking more coffee as he gazed out at the expanse of lake and sky. The train hummed along the tracks, passing Elyria and Ashtabula before crossing into Pennsylvania, where it made a brief stop at Erie. Shortly before the train reached Buffalo, New York, he got up and returned to his seat. Thornburg was nowhere in sight.

He half-dozed as more towns passed by in rapid succession. 'Rochester, Lake Ontario,' the conductor announced, passing through the car. 'Not far to Schenectady,' he said in response to a passenger.

Shortly before 8 am, the train pulled into Schenectady station. He stood by the door as the conductor squeezed past, calling to a companion. 'Hey, Tuck! Where's Festus at?'

'Beats me. I ain't seen him for a while.'

'Well, he'd better get found afore we stop.'

The train squealed to a halt, and he got off. He stood on the platform looking around at the other disembarking passengers. His heart sank as he spied Thornburg advancing along the platform. The two made brief eye contact as the latter walked past. He waited on the platform as it cleared of passengers, hoping against hope that he might give his pursuer the slip. After ten minutes, he made his way to the concourse, constantly glancing around for the other man. He lingered at a newspaper stand, covertly scanning the busy forecourt. Unable to catch sight of his pursuer, he made his way to the ticket agent for the Delaware Hudson Railroad and purchased a ticket for Plattsburg. 'Platform eighteen,' said the agent, handing over the ticket. 'Train leaves at nine o'clock.'

'How long to Plattsburg?'

'No more than five hours.'

The open platform was deserted save for a woman and child standing next to the station sign. Sprays of snow blew across the tracks. He made his way to a bench and brushed off the snow before sitting down. He kept an eye on the platform entrance, willing the train to arrive. A porter appeared, pushing a trolley. He heard a distant whistle and saw the woman step up to the edge of the platform and peer down the tracks.

Suddenly Thornburg appeared. Boundary's heart pounded as the other man paused to kick something from his boot, stamping vigorously on the platform. Next moment, his pursuer headed directly toward where Boundary was sitting.

'Morning, pardner. Mind if I sit?' Thornburg was strongly built, his square features accentuated by the bristling, sandy moustache. His face was ruddy, his breath pearling in the cold air as he gazed at Boundary with an amiable yet unblinking stare.

'Please yourself.'

'Why, I guess I will!' Thornburg sat down, stretching out his legs. 'Durn snow!' Leaning forward, he slapped powder from his trouser legs where they were tucked into a pair of brown leather boots. 'Where you headed to, pardner?' he asked. 'If'n you don't object to me asking?' His breath smelt of whisky.

'Plattsburg.'

'Me, too!' Thornburg affected a look of surprise. 'You have some business there, I 'spect?'

He made a murmuring sound. 'And you?' he asked.

Thornburg grinned. 'I guess you could say that.'

'You couldn't do it—the business—here?'

Thornburg's grin grew wider. 'I could! But I gotta meet a fella.'

A whistle blasted as the train made its appearance, clouds of smoke issuing from its stack. Thornburg stood up and glanced down at Boundary, his expression hardening beneath the mask of amiability. 'You ride well, now.'

'I guess I'll see you in Plattsburg?'

Thornburg made a chewing motion with his jaw. 'I guess you will,' he said.

HE WAITED TO SEE which of the five cars Thornburg stepped into before choosing another. As he waited, he saw Thornburg lean back from the step, watching for a moment before mounting into the car. That pause convinced him that remaining on the semi-deserted platform would be to no avail—that his pursuer would do the same. Who knows what he might do then? With a fatalistic air, he mounted the steps and took a seat next to the window. What did he mean by meeting a fella? If he intends me harm, why wait until Plattsburg? Surely, I am safe while I am on the train? The reassurance rang hollow as he pictured again the affable grin, the smile belied by the cold blue eyes above the bristling moustache. Who knows what such men are capable of?

With mounting dread, he stared out the window as the wintry landscape rolled by, his mind conjuring up horrors as it leapt ahead to whatever fate awaited him at Plattsburg.

'Ticonderoga next,' said the conductor, passing through.

'How long before Plattsburg?'

'A shade under three hours.'

'Is that the end of the line?'

'No, sirree. We go all the way to Rouses Point on the border.'

'What happens then?'

'What happens? You get off, I guess.'

'I mean, what's after the point?'

'Canada.' The conductor peered at him. 'You're headed to Plattsburg and you don't know that?'

'Can I buy a ticket—to the end of the line?'

'Sure you can. Want to?'

'I'll let you know.'

'Suit yourself.' The conductor moved off. 'Ticonderoga coming up!'

As the train steamed into the station, he stood up, his mind a ferment of panic and desperation. Glancing around to check that Thornburg was nowhere in sight, he hurried to a door at the end of the car. He gripped the handle as the train slowed, determined to take the opportunity to flee his tormentor. The presence of uniformed officials and dozens of people on the platform gave him hope as he braced himself to jump.

'This ain't your stop.'

Startled, he turned to find Thornburg standing close behind him, a menacing look in his eyes. His pursuer swayed forward with the motion of the train as it braked to a stop. The motion pulled open his unbuttoned coat to reveal a pistol holstered around his waist.

'What do you want?' he snapped, casting aside all pretence in his fright.

'What do I want?' Thornburg leaned back against the partition. 'Gee, I guess I want lots of things.'

'Are you a bounty hunter?' He tried to make his voice strong with the question.

'Bounty hunter?' Thornburg appeared to consider the possibility. 'I wouldn't say that, exactly,' he said.

'Then who, or what, the devil are you?'

'Why, I guess you could call me an agent.' Thornburg pondered the word. 'Yep, agent is about right.'

'Agent for who?'

'Ah!' Thornburg shook his head. 'Now that's the question, ain't it?' He leaned his face in closer. 'Mr Newspaper man!'

The conductor appeared, ushering a departing passenger. 'Stand aside if you ain't getting off!'

He took his seat again as the train huffed out of the station. Sensing that Thornburg had taken a seat in the same car, he turned to look, receiving a cold stare in return.

Now in absolutely no doubt of the peril he was in, he sought furiously for a way out as the train whistle blew and they left the station behind. The prospect of being dragged back to Fort Buffalo in chains filled him with horror as he imagined the shocked looks on the faces of his friends and neighbours. The thought had no sooner entered his mind than it was displaced by another. He didn't follow me this far simply to drag me all the way back again. He means to murder me! The stark truth induced a moment of blind panic. He felt dizzy, his insides seeming to rush up into his mouth. For a wild instant he thought of running up to the conductor to plead for help only to dismiss the notion. After all, what proof do I have?

He watched helplessly as the miles rolled by, the train hugging the shores of Lake Champlain. The grey waters stretched into the distance, the white-capped wavelets whipped up by a stiff breeze. They passed a series of small hamlets as the train steamed ever closer to his destination. 'Port Henry!' The conductor boomed. 'Mineville! Westport, coming up!'

The train slowed, coming to a halt next to an open platform on which waited a solitary passenger. It clanked forward again as the man nodded pleasantly and took a seat across the aisle. The conductor passed through, checking the overhead luggage rack. 'Next stop, Plattsburg!'

A short time later, the car swayed around a bend and slowed as the brakes were applied. The whistle hooted. The conductor held onto the back of a seat, lurching with the motion of the train. 'All passengers for Plattsburg!'

He turned in his seat. Thornburg stared back at him, an expression of cold ferocity on his face.

The whistle gave a long, high-pitched blast as they pulled into the station. Steam hissed up in a vaporous cloud as the brakes brought the train to a squealing halt. He saw a hard-faced man in a Derby hat walk alongside the train, peering into each car as it passed. The station was deserted apart from a knot of people waiting to greet the incoming passengers. A man and a woman, the latter carrying a small child, walked down the aisle as he remained glued to the seat, fearful to leave the safety of the car.

'Your stop, Mr McLennan.' Thornburg stood over him, a menacing look on his face. Leaning down, he tapped the window, drawing the attention of the man on the platform. The man nodded in response and pressed his face to the glass, his eyes narrowing as they locked on Boundary.

'Git!' Thornburg hissed. He laid a hand on the holstered pistol to underline the command.

A RUSH OF FREEZING air greeted him as he stepped down from the train. The other man stood waiting, his face a stiff mask as he eyed Boundary. He was clean-shaven, a faded scar running from his eyebrow to his jaw. Nearby, the disembarking couple were greeted by friends and relatives with joyous hugs and endearments. The station consisted of a solitary wood building housing a ticket office and waiting room.

'How are you, Frank?' Thornburg and the other man shook hands.

'I been freezing my goddamn balls off, waiting for this slick!' The man glowered at Boundary.

Thornburg laughed. 'We'll go for some whisky, soon as!'

The other group passed by, smiling and gossiping as they headed for the exit. The stationmaster blew a whistle. 'Stand clear! Train's leaving!'

'Git moving!' The man called Frank shoved him as the train shuddered into motion amid a cloud of steam.

He resisted, clutching the haversack. 'Where are we going?' he demanded.

'For a New York steak! Where'd you think!' The snarled reply drew a laugh from Thornburgh.

'I'm not going anywhere!' He looked around to summon help, but the platform was empty.

'The hell you ain't!' The man pulled out a gun and jabbed it into his belly. 'Move or I'll splatter your guts all over the goddamn platform!' The threat was delivered with such ferocity that he turned and began walking. The departing train clanked slowly alongside.

'It snowed again last night,' said Frank, conversing with Thornburg.

'Sure did. Held up the train a ways back.'

'You see that gal of yours in Chicago?'

'Hell, yeah!'

The exit lay just ahead. He walked toward it with the despairing air of a condemned man. His two executioners followed closely behind, engaged in bantering conversation. The caboose rattled by and he stared after it as a man about to be hanged might yearn after a passing wagon. Seized by desperation, he whirled suddenly and shoved the surprised Thornburg as hard as he could. With an exclamation, the latter fell against his companion, sending both of them sprawling to the icy platform. As furious curses rang out behind him, Boundary rushed after the caboose.

Reaching out his hand, he gripped the end rail and scrambled up onto the small platform.

He glanced back, his heart hammering against his ribs. Thornburg was running in pursuit, an enraged look on his face. The train gathered speed but Thornburg was quick, his breath coming in rapid pants as he lunged for the rail. He watched in horror as his pursuer's hand closed on the bar. Next moment Thornburg slipped, tumbling to the platform and rolling with the impetus, his coat flying open. His confederate had picked himself up and hurried forward to join the chase. Pulling out a pistol, he fired wildly as the train steamed out of the station. Boundary ducked as the bullet struck the wood above his head. The man fired again, the bullet whizzing past the car. Behind the men he saw the stationmaster emerge from his office to investigate and then hurry back inside. He watched, still gasping for breath, as Thornburg limped forward to stand alongside his companion. And then both men were left behind, raging and cursing as they glared after him.

58

End of the Line

'YOU AGAIN!' THE CONDUCTOR blinked in surprise as Boundary made his way back to his seat.

He held out some money. 'How much to the Point?'

Seated once again, he heaved for air, his body trembling from the shock of his narrow escape. The conductor passed by, and he accosted the man. 'When's the next train?' His voice shook with the question.

'Next train's a freight. Due in two hours.' The conductor shook his head in bemusement. 'The line ain't been nearly so popular!'

A little under an hour later, they arrived at Rouses Point. From the train window, the village looked no different from the dozens of other hamlets they had passed along the way. Houses and stores lined the main thorough-fare, and a variety of wagons, horses, and carts occupied the main street. A small number of pedestrians, wrapped against the sharp wind blowing off the lake, hurried along the sidewalk.

'Is there a place where I can buy a horse?' he asked.

'Sure. Bob Dory has a stable just down the street.' The conductor eyed him curiously. 'How come you changed your mind, anyway? I thought you wanted Plattsburg?'

'I did,' he answered, anxious to be on his way.

He walked along the street as directed, halting at a building with a large sign attached to the front proclaiming "Dory Stables" in faded, hand-painted letters. To his intense frustration, the stable was locked, a sign pinned to the door announcing that the owner had 'gone home for grits.' He thought of knocking on doors to search for the man before resigning himself to the fact and taking a seat on a small bench. He slumped back against the seat, his mind still reeling from his ordeal. He pictured the furious look on his pursuer's face as he abandoned the chase to draw his pistol and fire off several shots.

After what seemed an eternity, a man wearing a wool cap and mufflers approached along the street.

'Are you the owner?' He got to his feet.

'I sure am.' The man unlocked a door. 'You looking for a horse?' His breath smelled of liquor.

After examining the half-dozen animals for sale, he decided on a grey mare, wincing at the asking price. 'One hundred dollars!'

'Where else you gonna buy?' The man studied him. 'For an extra twenty, I'll throw in a saddle as well.' He nodded at the haversack. 'Unless you've got one in that gunnysack.'

Purchase tsked with irritation, apprehensive lest the freight train arrive early. 'Is there a place in town where I can buy a gun?'

'A gun?' The owner gave him a longer look. 'There used be a gunsmith, but he closed down last winter. You could probably fetch one at the hardware store.'

'Never mind.' He paid the asking price, buying a bag of oats as well, the man insisting he pay an extra dollar and fifty cents for the feed.

'It don't come for free,' Dory grunted in response to Boundary's annoyed protest.

'How far to the border?' he asked, ears pricked for the sound of a train whistle.

'The border? Less than a mile, that way.' The man pointed.

'And what's over there?'

The man blinked. 'What's over there?' He frowned, itching his neck. 'Depends. What you looking for?'

'A town, or village. Somewhere to stay.'

'Well, you'll find those. Montreal, too, if you care to ride that far.'

'How far is it—to Montreal?'

'About two- or three-days' ride.'

He hesitated. 'And the horse is reliable?'

'Twice over. Wait and I'll throw the saddle on.'

'What time is it?'

The man glanced at a pocket watch. 'Past two o'clock.'

A short time later, he led the horse out from the stable yard and onto the main street. The sky was slate grey, a cold, blustery gale blowing in from the lake. In the dullish light, the hamlet appeared the picture of dreary desolation. He shivered before remembering the wool scarf in the haversack. He tied it around his neck, grateful for Mrs. Bellow's thoughtfulness.

He climbed up on the horse and sat there for a moment to survey the open road, apprehensive of what lay ahead. The single road out of town was bordered by the lake on one side, and flat, wintry fields on the other. To his alarm, he thought he heard a train whistle sound in the distance. He listened intently but could not be certain. 'Skit!' He kicked the horse into motion.

Proceeding at a walk he soon came upon a milestone announcing, 'Quebec, Canada.' A milepost stood alongside, with the inscription 'Montreal, Forty-Nine Miles.' He continued, the wind blowing spirals of snow across the road. The fields were stark and barren under the grey sky. He shivered, glad of the warm buffalo coat. He thought of Mrs. Bellow and imagined the promised telegram with her cousin's address sitting in the telegraph office back in Plattsburg. Am will be worried, he thought. I'll telegraph once I reach safety. 'Durn everything!' He shouted out the words, giving vent to his frustration. He kicked the horse, furious at the way things had turned out. It was that pokehead Rumbald to blame! If I hadn't printed his hogwash then none of this would have happened!

A cart approached in the distance. The driver hailed him, screwing up his eyes to see if Purchase might be someone he recognised. A mile past the border, he turned idly in the saddle to check the road behind him. An exclamation leapt from his lips as he caught sight of two horsemen, barely a mile to his rear. Against the snowy background, the dark-clad figures stood out in clear relief as they proceeded at a fast trot along the road. Greatly alarmed, he kicked the mare into a trot, in no doubt that the two riders were the same assassins he had so recently escaped.

He bounced in the saddle, berating himself for his foolishness in not taking the time to buy a weapon. He thought of his father's cherished Sharps and groaned to have it in his hands. He glanced over his shoulder again. To his fright, his pursuers appeared to have narrowed the gap. The road ahead stretched flat and desolate into the distance before disappearing into a dense wood. He spurred the horse into a canter, anxious to reach the trees with their promise of concealment.

A quarter hour later, he had almost reached the woods. The wind was stronger, blowing loose snow into his eyes. He glanced back, panicked to note that his pursuers were now much closer, whipping their horses in an effort to intercept before he gained the cover of the trees. He urged the tired horse into a gallop, fearful it might lose its footing in the snow. *They would gun me down without mercy.* He drove the thought from his head, feeling a palpable relief as the road entered the trees. He was surrounded by thick stands of maple, oak, and elm, their branches stark and bare in the wintry light. He slowed to a walk. concerned lest he over-tire the horse. The fresh, untrodden road was easy to follow and he looked for a path diverging into the woods, hoping to shake his pursuers. He soon came upon a trail veering off from the road and into the trees. He took it, looking back to see if his tracks were visible.

He followed the path, walking the horse. After a while, he risked pulling up to listen. He could hear nothing save the sound of some birdsong and the wind gusting through the trees. Suddenly, a shot rang out, the sharp crack shattering the deep stillness of the woods. He glanced back but could see nothing through the trees. A second shot sounded, and the mare screamed and bucked, almost flinging him off. He had barely time to pull his feet from the stirrups before it keeled onto its side, snorting and trembling. Blood pumped from its intestines where the bullet had ripped through the gut. More shots whistled above his head, and he fled into the trees, the haversack slapping against his body. He hurried on, hampered by the heavy coat, his mind blank of everything save the urgent need to escape. Behind him, he heard a faint shout followed by the angry crack of a rifle.

He hurried through the woods for what seemed hours, panting and sweating inside the heavy coat. As the light failed, he stopped, listening keenly for sounds of pursuit. Too tired to take another step, he slumped down in the snow, his breath issuing like steam in the chill air. He sat there for several minutes, his back against a maple, concerned that he could easily be tracked through the snow. Despite this fear, he fell asleep, his head lolling onto his chest.

It was pitch-dark when he awoke. He sat in place for several minutes, straining to listen, before falling back into an exhausted sleep. He woke up again as dim light filtered through the trees. In spite of the danger, he lingered there, cold and tired and wishing only to sleep again.

Forcing himself to his feet, he looked around, hoping to get some idea of his whereabouts. But he was deep in the pathless woods, lost and disoriented and with no idea in which direction the road lay. He started off, trudging aimlessly and following the path of least resistance—if path it could be called, it being a mere space between the numerous trunks. He walked until nightfall, eyes probing for any sign of a trail or opening in the trees that might promise to lead somewhere. A light snow began to drift down through the branches, and he sought shelter under an elm, his belly rumbling with hunger.

He walked again the next day, tired and despairing and now seriously alarmed for his survival in the trackless woods. He followed a moose trace for most of the day, stopping in frustration at where it forked in the trees. He took the split trail to his right, his mind dulled by starvation and fatigue. By late afternoon, he was ravenous once more and light-headed. He fell asleep in a patch of dry ferns under an oak tree.

It was broad daylight when he awoke. He heard a sound and froze in alarm. A deer stepped from between the trees. It caught sight of him and stared for a moment before bounding back into the woods. He swallowed a mouthful of snow, feeling desperately thirsty despite the cold. Shouldering the haversack, he followed the trace through the trees, a fatalistic gloom enveloping him as he became more and more disoriented. In the late afternoon, he slipped on a root and dropped the haversack in a snowbank. He shouldered it again, grumbling at the weight. Soon after, he came across fresh deer tracks and followed these for a mile before giving up and spending a cold and miserable night huddled under a tree. He continued in this manner for what seemed an eternity, walking and stumbling by day, and sinking into exhausted sleep by night.

On a day of falling snow, he leaned against a tree, barely able to stand from hunger and exhaustion. He started forward again and struck his head against a low-hanging branch. He moaned and touched his scalp, expecting to see his fingers covered with blood. Next moment, he heard a sharp crack, and experienced a blinding pain in his head. He gave an agonized cry as the ground suddenly gave way beneath his feet. He tumbled down a steep slope, rolling over and over before coming to rest amid a dense patch of maidenhair fern where he lay senseless as if struck dead.

59

Amity

FOLLOWING HER BROTHER'S HASTY departure, Amity sought anxiously for any scrap of news about events unfolding in town. In the afternoon, a passing rider told Ira of more shooting between the rival factions as the army struggled to impose order. 'Folk are mad that that rancher fella—Wake—got arrested, and blame Lomax and his gang,' the rider said. 'I'd advise you to stay clear of town for a few days until this ruckus blows over.'

When told of the conversation, Amity put a hand to her mouth, her heart constricting with fear. 'Did he say anything else—about Mrs. Bellow or Mrs. Hedgepeth or anyone?' she questioned her husband.

Ira shook his head. 'I ain't going to waste another minute thinking on it,' he grumbled. 'I got chores to do.'

The next morning, he ate breakfast and set off for the edge of the property to mend a fence. She stood at the doorway watching him leave. When he was out of sight, she went out to the barn and hitched a horse to the buggy. Fleur came out of the bedroom to watch as she returned inside to fetch her bonnet and cape.

'Where are you going?' Her mother-in-law's voice was anxious, her face pale with apprehension.

'I'm going to town, to check on Mrs. Bellow. Boundary would want that.'

'Don't go!' Fleur clutched at her sleeve. 'Not yet, while there's still rioting and things going on.'

'I'm going anyway,' she said, her voice preternaturally calm.

'It's dangerous!'

'I'll be all right.' To make sure, she took down her father's old Sharps rifle. Taking a box of cartridges, she loaded the rifle.

'Don't go! I'll tell Ira!' Fleur's voice was shrill with repressed hysteria.

'Then you'd better start. 'Tain't more than a half mile to the fence.' She opened the door, letting in a blast of cold air.

'Amity, please, don't go.' The old woman's voice trembled.

'I have to.' She placed the Sharps in the rig and climbed up onto the seat. 'Tell Ira not to follow. I'll be back by afternoon.' She shook the reins. 'Hup!'

APPROACHING TOWN, SHE EXCLAIMED at the sight of black smoke curling up into the air, her sense of alarm increasing. Entering main street, she passed a half-dozen troopers carrying rifles. They stared but made no move to stop her. There were more troopers patrolling the sidewalks as she drove down Main. The town seemed gripped by tension. Only a few pedestrians were about, proceeding under the watchful eye of the soldiers. Most of the stores were closed, their windows boarded up. The shops and buildings were still arrayed with flags and bunting in celebration of the new year. She blinked at the sight, the gaudy decorations strangely forlorn amid the silent stores and empty streets. She sucked in a breath as she passed by a burned building, the charred timbers poking into the air. That was the freight office, she realised with shock.

Frightened at what she was seeing, she passed the Golden Fleece hotel, her eyes seeking the *Dispatch* office. She slowed the buggy as she passed the premises. The front window was shattered, and the door broken in. The press was visible, its lever badly bent, and the platen twisted back at an angle. From the blackened interior, it was evident that a fire had been lit inside. Profoundly relieved that her brother had escaped the chaos unharmed, she urged the horse forward, increasingly fearful for Rumbald's safety. She turned off Main and drove down Second toward the school-house, her eyes scanning ahead. She passed by a man she recognised, and he turned and stared after her, a worried look on his face.

'Whoa!' Pulling up in the schoolyard, she was horrified to see that the school door had been torn from its hinges. She hurried inside, cold fear overtaking her at the wreckage she found there. Chairs had been broken or overturned. The grandfather clock, a legacy of Miss Purlow, was toppled on its side, the door open and the pendulum lying on the floor.

'Hans!' She called out. 'Hans!'

The classroom was in disarray, stools and benches overturned and a window broken. Rumbald's desk lay on its side, its contents scattered on the floor.

'Hans!' Faint with dread, she hurried to the small back room where they had spent so many stolen hours together. The door was wide open. Terrified at what she might find, she stepped inside. The room had been ransacked, the contents strewn across the floor. A pair of legs poked out from beneath the overturned bed, and she screamed in horror. 'Hans!'

Rumbald was lying on his back, his eyes closed, a livid wound in his throat. His face was barely recognisable, his hair matted with blood. One ear hung from the side of his head, partly severed by a knife. His tongue had been cut out, the organ lying on the floor beside his body. The gorge rose in her throat, and she struggled not to vomit. Uttering a moan of despair, she sank to the floor. 'What have they done to you, my love?' Lifting up his head, she cradled it in her lap, her face wan and drained. She brushed her fingers through his hair and caressed his shocked and bloodless face, murmuring to him as when they shared the overturned bed. She kissed his cold forehead, crooning and gently rocking as she held him like a babe in arms.

The wind blew in through the smashed window, picking over the papers scattered on the floor. A burned leather journal, its pages charred and scorched, lay in a pool of ink. A pen, broken in half, lay beside it.

'Hello! Is anyone here?'

She looked up as a soldier came into the room, his carbine raised in caution.

'Ma'am?' He blinked in surprise as he caught sight of her. 'Oh!' He said as he saw the body. 'You can't be here, Ma'am. It's dangerous. Go home,' he said. He stood uncertainly for a few minutes. 'I'll tell the lieutenant you're here,' he said, and left.

SHE DIDN'T REMEMBER LEAVING the schoolroom and getting back onto the rig—hardly recalled driving out from the town, her distraught expression and dazed air drawing glances from the few people on the street. It was only when the rock came into sight that she recovered some semblance of awareness. As she drew closer, she saw a group of soldiers guarding the turnoff. She steered the team off the road and into the grass toward the homestead. The farmhouse looked weathered but otherwise the same—as if waiting for the occupants to return. The rig lurched as it hit a rut. The buffalo rose up before her, remote and inscrutable in its eternal watch. Why didn't you protect us? she accused. Pa always said that you would.

She drove to the grass side, safely hidden from the sight of the soldiers. She stepped down from the rig, her eyes as unseeing as those of the beast that loomed above her. She had driven down toward the tail, away from the graves farther up near the head. She stood for a moment, feeling the wind sigh against her cheek. She raised her hands and removed her bonnet, folding it and laying it on the seat. She retrieved the Sharps and the buggy whip and walked to the rock, her movements slow yet sure, as if she sleep-walked.

Tucking her dress beneath her, she sat with her back against the hard stone. The granite was cold as was the ground beneath her. The wind rose and she exclaimed in surprise as snowflakes swirled through the air. She sat for some time, her back pressed against the hard rock, her eyes fixed on the distance. Whether she took in the horizon, streaked with washes of pearly light, or the withered yet boundless grass as it wecomed the late winter snow she couldn't have said her eyes, like her thoughts, turned inwards.

A crow cawed loudly overhead and she started as if from a dream. She looked down at her dress and smoothed the bloodstain impressed there. Her hand reached for the Sharps and she propped the muzzle beneath her breast, the hard iron nuzzling into the soft flesh. A gust of wind blew snow against her face and she shivered. She felt for the buggy whip and slid the handle down the rifle barrel until it rested against the trigger. She raised her eyes to the cold, barren grass, now disappearing beneath a veil of snow. 'Hans,' she whispered, and thrust the whip down.

The Claim concludes the third part of *Monuments of Grass*, a five-book series charting the creation story of one man's epic vision and its unfolding over time. The five books in the series are *Exile*, *The Fur Post*, *The Claim*, *New France*, and *Voyages of Discovery*. Print copies can be ordered online through bookstores, libraries, and online retailers such as Amazon. The series is also available in eBook format.